ALLERTON AND DREUX

Jean Ingelow

Two volumes in one

Garland Publishing, Inc., New York & London

1975

Bibliographical note:

this facsimile has been made from a copy in the
Princeton University Library
(3795.8.311)

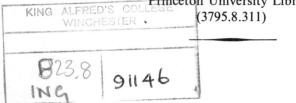
Library of Congress Cataloging in Publication Data

Ingelow, Jean, 1820-1897.
    Allerton and Dreux.

    (Victorian fiction : Novels of faith and doubt ;
v. 29)
    Reprint of the 1851 ed. published by Wertheim and
Macintosh, London, under title: Allerton and Dreux;
or, The war of opinion.
    I. Title. II. Series.
PZ3.I46Al10   [PR4819]   823'.8   75-475
ISBN 0-8240-1553-3

ALLERTON AND DREUX;

OR,

The War of Opinion.

BY

THE AUTHOR OF " A RHYMING CHRONICLE."

IN TWO VOLUMES.

VOL. I.

LONDON:

WERTHEIM AND MACINTOSH,
24, PATERNOSTER ROW.

IPSWICH: HUNT AND SON. DUBLIN: CURRY AND CO.

1851.

MACINTOSH, PRINTER,
GREAT NEW-STREET, LONDON.

CONTENTS.

CHAPTER I.

ASLEEP BENEATH THE CEDARS.

THERE was a quiet chamber in an old country-house, where, once in the depth of winter, sat an old nurse, with a young infant on her knee.

The red curtains were let down before the windows, the floor was covered with a thick carpet, and a large fire blazed upon the hearth; the nurse glanced towards the bed where her lady was sleeping, and then drew her knees still nearer to the flame, and began to moralize. What a strange thing it was, she thought, that the Rector and his wife, whose wish for children had been well known in the parish, should have had none for so many years; while in many a cottage, where they met with but a poor welcome and scanty fare, they came regularly once a-year, though the fathers grumbled at the creaking of the cradle-rockers, and the mothers declared, with tears in their eyes, that they did not know where the crust and the clothes were to come from.

She heard the church clock strike twelve, and thought, with a shiver, how her poor grandchildren were shaking in their beds ;—the snow lay five feet deep in the fields, and was falling still ; a flock of sheep had been dug out in the morning ; such a hard winter had not been known for years. Well, God help all poor folks ! if she had not had such a good supper she might have considered their case with keener consideration ; but as it was, she rocked the sleeping infant softly, and fell into a light doze.

A cautious footstep without presently aroused her. She lifted up her head : " Bless the man, if he isn't here again," she thought, with a slight chuckle of amusement, " and afraid to come in for fear of disturbing 'em." She coughed slightly, to show that she was awake, and the door thereupon was softly opened, and a stout, cheerful-looking gentleman came in with elaborate caution.

" And how are they by this time, Mrs. Keane ? "

" They 're as well as can be, bless you, Sir," answered Mrs. Keane, for at least the twentieth time during the last afternoon.

" I hope this cold night is not against the infant."

" Bless you, no, Sir ; don't be afraid ; they live fast enough when they 're not wanted ; you shouldn't be in such a mighty fuss about it. If you don't think no more about it than other folks, the child will live like other folks' children."

Perhaps the Rector might have thought there was something in this reasoning, or perhaps he thought the old Nurse was tired of his questions. Certain it is that he did not come again till six o'clock in the morning, when he was rewarded by hearing his wife declare herself very comfortable, and also by hearing his child cry with all the strength of her baby lungs.

In time he got accustomed to the honour of possessing a daughter, though he firmly believed that so sweet a child had never existed before, and wondered how he had contrived to pass so many years in tolerable happiness without her.

That very day next year, and Mrs. Keane always said ever after that it was (next to the circumstance of Mrs. Maidley's eldest being born on a Lady-day and her second on a Christmas-day) the oddest thing that had happened to any of her ladies,—the Rector's wife gave birth to a son. It was the same day, and the same time of day, as she always said when she told the story; and what made it more particular was, that whereas the first was the coldest winter ever known, so that the pretty dear never breathed the fresh air (excepting when they took her to be baptized) till she was nearly three months old, the second was, on the contrary, one of the mildest ever known, so that the last china rose had not faded before the earliest primrose came out. Little Marion was a fine child, with light hair and dimpled cheeks; her face almost always expressed the serene happiness which is the natural dower of infant humanity. Her brother was an active, mischievous boy, round-faced, noisy, and good-humoured. Their parents, whose love increased with their growth, began early

to make them the companions of their country walks;
and many a time, when the lanes were too heavy
for his wife to walk in, the Rector would carry his
little daughter with him on his errands of mercy,
that he might listen to her pretty prattle by the
way.

In after-years, when Marion, sitting by the fire
on a winter evening, would try to remember these
days of her childhood, and to recal the image of her
father, there were only a few scattered words that
he had said, and expressions of endearment used
towards herself and her brother, which seemed to
survive of him in her memory : he was confused
and blended with the many baby fancies and wonders which beset a childish reason. She could not
separate him from them ; he had become like a
companion in a dream, an actor in some previous
existence ; and withdrawn into the background of
her thoughts, though often present with them, however vaguely, he still exercised a real dominion over
her : his words were forgotten, but a certain consciousness of the meaning that they were intended
to convey was left : the tones of his voice, before
their meaning could be fully understood, had influenced the first dawn of her feelings ; and early as
he left her, that influence could never be set aside.

But there was one day in Marion's childhood that
she did remember distinctly, and well. It was a
beautiful afternoon in the beginning of August,
perfectly clear and cloudless ; there had been rain

in the night, but not more than enough to lay the dust in the quiet country lanes through which she and her father walked.

It was the first day of wheat harvest, and Marion remembered how she-had listened to the voices of the reapers through the hedge, and how her father had lifted her up that she might gather a long tendril of the wild vine for herself, and had cut her some briar roses with his knife.

She then remembered how they had entered the partially-cut corn-field, and how her father had sat down beside the reapers, who were collected together under the shade of the hedge, eating their afternoon meal.

It might be from having heard some of those who listened then speak of it afterwards and repeat his words, or it might be that her childish mind was more open and alive than usual ; but Marion remembered distinctly some of his remarks as he sat and talked with the reapers.   She thought, too, that she could recal the persuasive tones of his voice, when he said, "Let us now fear the Lord our God, that giveth us rain, the former and the latter in his season ; He reserveth to us the appointed weeks of the harvest." (Jer. v. 24.)

Walking through the corn-field home, Marion had gathered some blue corn-flowers, and picked up a few ears of wheat : these she recollected giving to him to carry for her, and that was the last walk she took with him, and the very last thing she remembered of her father.

On that day, which was the 1st of August, the harvest began in the parish ; that day three weeks the last load was led from the fields.   Some of the same labourers who sat to rest with him under the trees, were with the heavy waggon as it wound slowly through the narrow lanes, past the Rectory-house, and along by the side of the churchyard wall.   They turned their heads that way as they went, and looked towards two cedar-trees that stood in one corner: the long shadow of the steeple seemed to be pointing to a new grave that was beneath them, and to a strange gentleman who stood beside it.   The labourers went on ; they knew who the stranger was, though he had been but three days in the parish.   The dead and the living, the new Rector and the old, had met together ; the old Rector was gone to his account, and another was already appointed in his room.

The new Rector leaned against the trunk of the great cedar-tree, with his arms folded and his eyes fixed upon the grave ; he watched the long shadow of the church steeple, stealing gradually over the tomb of his predecessor—he saw beyond the boundary walls of the churchyard, orchards and corn-fields, scattered cottages and homesteads, peering out from among the thick trees ; blue smoke was curling up from them, and within were people to whose necessities *he* had ministered, and whose spiritual wants he had striven to supply. The scene of his labours was spread out before the eyes of his successor, as well as the place of his rest. Doubtless he had often stood in that self-same place and looked upon that self-same scene. Perhaps the same thoughts and the same perplexities had suggested themselves to his mind, and some warm thoughts of household love besides; for between the green ash-trees that grew by the lane side, might be seen the sloping lawn and the white gables of his earthly home.

The turf had been broken in two or three places not far off: it could not be long since he had stood there. Had he any rejoicing now, any " profit of all his labour that he had taken under the sun ?" Had God acknowledged and blessed it ? Had he entered upon his rest with those so lately committed to the dust, saying of them, "Behold, here am I, and the children that thou hast given me !"

For himself there could not be a doubt that he had died the death of the righteous; but the flock that he had left behind, had they been willing and obedient, would they bear his words in mind now that he was gone ? If so, there was the more hope for his successor. Or would they suffer them lightly to be effaced, like his footsteps in the path that were already obliterated, and the sounds of his voice, the last echo of which had utterly died away ?

The new Rector roused himself at last from his

long reverie, and walked slowly towards the church. The clerk had brought him the key that morning, he had read himself in the day before, and with a vague, uneasy sense of possession and responsibility, he turned it in the rusty lock and entered. The great door creaked heavily behind, and closed with a hollow looming sound, that was repeated in the roof and among the pillars as he advanced towards the chancel.

The church was a fine structure, plain but ancient and substantial; there was room for nearly 800 people within its walls, but the population did not amount to more than two-thirds of that number, and of these a considerable proportion always stayed away.

As he walked up the centre aisle, and turned his eyes first to one side and then to the other, he became conscious in a painful degree of the oppressive stillness of the place, and looking upon it as the scene in which he expected to pass the most momentous hours of his future life—a place which was familiar with the tones of departed voices, which had repeated and echoed the warnings of many a now silenced pastor, and been filled with the psalmody of fore-gone generations,—he felt like one in the presence of many witnesses, brought into unwonted nearness with the past, such contact as almost to make him look upon himself as an intruder, one that had come to the dwelling of beings unseen, the fall of whose foot was strange to their ears, as he moved beneath the high stone arches, observed but not perceiving.

"Work while it is day; the night cometh when no man can work"—this seemed to be their injunction. "O Lord, I am oppressed; undertake for me," was the substance of his answer.

Some time passed while he was examining the church, vestry, and vaults; at length he came back to the door, and turned his eyes again towards the grave. The long shadow of the church had completely covered it now, and two little children in deep mourning were sitting at its head.

The Rector who had died in the evening of that same day that he took the last walk with his little child, had now been buried more than a fortnight, and his tomb, which was a large flat stone not raised more than a foot and a-half from the ground, had been completed only two days. The inscription was simple and short:—

"SACRED TO THE MEMORY
OF THE REV. WALTER GREYSON,
FOR TWELVE YEARS RECTOR OF THIS PARISH.
DIED AUGUST 1ST, 18—,
IN THE 41ST YEAR OF HIS AGE.
'The dead in Christ shall rise.'"

Two little children, perfectly silent, sat together by the stone, as if waiting for some absent person, the one watching him as he came towards them, the other playing with a few daisies that he held in his pinafore. They did not move when he came up to them and looked at their blooming faces, with the full consciousness of whose children they must be; and there was an intentional quietness about them that showed plainly to one so well acquainted as himself with the workings of infant minds, that they imagined themselves in the presence of their father, and had a vague impression that they must not make a noise lest they should disturb him.

" Why do you come here, little Marion ?" said he, stooping down and addressing the elder child by the name he knew she bore.

" To see papa," replied the child in a low, cautious voice.

Humouring her fancy, he sat down beside her, and placing her gently on his knee, parted back her soft hair, and wondered whether her father might have resembled her; then sinking his voice almost to a whisper, he laid his hand on the stone and said, "But is papa here ?"

" Papa's gone to heaven," said the younger child, looking up for a moment from his daisies.

But little Marion, who had gazed at him with a perplexed and dubious expression, now slipped off his knee, and swept softly away with her hand two or three yellow leaves that had fallen from a young lime-tree upon the tomb, and then came back with childlike simplicity, and let him take her in his arms again.

This little action, so full of affection, her evident

though unexpressed belief that her father was there, that he could not leave the place, but yet that it was unkind to leave him there alone, together with the tender and cautious manner with which she swept them away from the face of the cold stone, as if even her father's tomb was already becoming confused in her mind into a part of himself,—these things touched him with a strong feeling of tenderness for her, and little Marion, as the strange gentleman drew her closer towards him, was surprised to see that his eyes were filled with tears.

"Where is your mamma," said he after a long silence.

"Mamma's very ill now," said little Marion, "she can't come and see poor papa."

God comfort her, thought the new Rector, hers is a bitter trial indeed !

Sitting on the tomb of their father with the two children in his arms, he felt that in their desolate state, they were as much given over to him as if he could have heard a voice from the tomb commending them to his care; while they were well content to receive his caresses, quite unconscious that his future affection was to be one of the best blessings of their lives, quite careless as to why he bestowed it, or who he might be.

He was still talking to them when a young servant in deep mourning advanced towards him, and seemed relieved at sight of the children. She accounted for their having strayed into the church-yard by saying, that owing to the dangerous illness of her mistress the house was in great confusion, and they had been sent to play alone in the garden that they might be out of the way.

The children lifted up their faces to kiss their new friend, and obtained from him a promise that he would come again the next day; then turning away with their maid, began to skip about and laugh as soon as they had got a little distance from their father's grave.

There was no rectory in the parish, though the house where Mr. Greyson had lived had naturally gone by that name; there was, therefore, no need for the poor widow to think of moving, or for others to think of it for her; while day after day, and week after week she lay almost unconscious of the lapse of time, and passed through the wearisome stages of a severe illness occasioned by the overwhelming shock of her husband's sudden death, watched over with the utmost tenderness by her two sisters through sufferings that at one time left but little hope either for her life or her reason. However, with the passing away of the old year, which seemed to take all the severity of the winter with it, she suddenly began to revive, and, once able to rise from her bed, her recovery was as rapid as her prostration had been complete.

In the meanwhile the new Rector had been labouring among the poor, and carrying out to the utmost the plans of his predecessor. He, however,

failed at first to make himself acceptable to the
people, and for three or four months had the pain of
seeing the attendance at the church get gradually
less and less. The people complained that they did
not hear him well, that his voice was thick and
indistinct; others declared that though he read the
prayers very well, he mumbled his sermons, so that
they did not understand them. All agreed that he
was a good gentleman, and had a very kind way
with him, but still he was not like Mr. Greyson,
and they did not think they could ever take to any
one else as they had done to him.

So the verdict was given against him in many of
the cottages, and though they bestowed a great
many curtseys upon him, they gave him very few
smiles. There was a certain reserve and silence
about him which the poor mistook for pride, and
not conceiving it possible that a gentleman like him
could be conscious of any such feeling as shyness
or awkwardness in talking to them, drew back
themselves, and increased his uneasiness by their
distant coldness and respect. So the new Rector
lived till Christmas, personally, as well as mentally,
alone. He had very few acquaintances in the
neighbourhood, and the few country families whom
he visited were as much influenced as the poor
themselves by the sensitive reserve of his manners.
He did not seem at ease in society, and as to his
own people he evidently felt that, at least at present,
they had few sympathies in common. But he was

always happy and at his ease with children; it was part of the singularity of his character to understand their motives and enter into their affections without an effort. The expression of his countenance, the tone of his voice, the very touch of his hand seemed to undergo a change when he took a child upon his knee and smoothed down its soft hair with his open palm.

He was a tall man, with a powerful frame, a light complexion, and a slight stoop in his shoulders; his features were rather heavy, and when he was at all agitated he had a slight hesitation in his speech, or rather a difficulty in expressing himself, that gave him an appearance of indecision and vacillation quite foreign to his real character.

At length, though his conscientious care for them in public, and his visits to the sick could not win the hearts of the people, a circumstance very slight in itself, and arising naturally out of his love for children, caused the feeling towards him to undergo a sudden change; he rose at once to the height of popularity, and the reason was no other than this:—

There was a new school-room in the parish, very near the church; it was finished soon after Mr. Greyson's death, and opened for use in the middle of November. The village, which was a scattered one, was situate partly above and partly below the site of the school-room, and those children who had to come down the hill to it were obliged to cross a

little brook that ran over the road, or rather lane,
not far from the house where the new Rector lived.
Now this little brook, as the autumn happened to be
a remarkably dry one, was so slight an impediment
that any child could step across it without wetting
its feet, and this state of things continued for some
weeks after the new room was opened.

One morning, however, when the Rector went to
visit it, he was surprised to see the floor covered
with little wet footmarks, and on asking the reason
of this, as the road was quite dry, the mistress told
him that the rains of the past week had so swollen
the brook, that almost all the children had wetted
their feet in springing over it.

"Indeed, Mr. Raeburn, I don't believe there's a
single dry foot in the school," she said, drawing off
the shoes of a tiny child, and letting the water drop
down from them.

"That's bad," said Mr. Raeburn; "we must
make a little bridge over the stream. Now, children, when you come in the afternoon, mind, you're
not to cross the brook till I come to you."

Accordingly, in the afternoon he went down to
the brook, which, though only three or four inches
deep, was as wide as a man could stride over; here
he found a large attendance waiting for him in a
smiling row, with little ticket bags in their hands,
and, planting one foot firmly on each side, he took
up each little creature in turn, and set her down on
the other side. The children were delighted with

the bustle and importance of being carried, and, above all, with the idea of having a bridge made on purpose for them ; but Mr. Raeburn found to his disappointment, when he examined the place next day, that the lane was so narrow that every waggon which went down it would demolish his bridge with its heavy wheels ; he was, therefore, obliged to repeat the experiment of transporting them himself all through the winter ; their pleasure in the short trip seeming to compensate him for the trouble, and he not being at all conscious that he was winning for himself " golden opinions from all sorts of people," filling his church by this indirect means, and laying the foundation of a popularity that was to last till his dying day ; but such proved to be the case. Every mother's heart is accessible through her child ; her feelings are touched by kindness shown to it, and her pride is flattered by notice taken of it. It is quite true that some of these poor women did not mind particularly whether their children got their feet wet or not, but still it was gratifying to think that the Rector cared, that he did not mind leaving his breakfast to come out and carry them over. It was their children who were of so much consequence, therefore their own importance was increased, and their husbands, fathers, and brothers heard so much henceforward of Mr. Raeburn's marvellous and varied good qualities, that even if they had been disposed to deny them, they must soon have given in for the sake of peace and

quietness. He was pronounced from that time to
be one of the pleasantest gentlemen that ever lived
—a little distant like, but then he could not possibly
be proud, or he would never have demeaned himself to wait upon *their* children. It was also discovered that if his voice was not quite " so clear as
a bell," it was a very pleasant voice, and any one
could hear every word he said that would take the
trouble of listening. Also woe betide the rash
individual who dared after that to say he or she
could not make out the meaning of his sermons.
" Some folks," it would be remarked in reply,
" never knew when they were well off ; but if some
folks would attend to the discourse as other folks
did, instead of going to sleep, looking out of window,
or staring about them, perhaps they would learn the
value of a good plain sermon that had no fine words
in it, and not go to try to make other folks believe
they couldn't make out the meaning of it."

The subject of this wonderful revolution of
opinion, though far from divining the cause, soon
began to rejoice in the effects of it. He found that
wherever he went he was greeted with smiles ; the
best chair was brought near the fire for him and
dusted with the good wife's apron. He wondered at
first, but soon learnt to refer it to the force of habit,
arguing to himself that the people from being used
to him had come to like him.

It was a very pleasant change to him, and one
that soon wrought a corresponding change in his

own manner. As for the children they had no opinion to alter; from the first they had been on his side, for, unlike other gentlemen of his age and gravity, he had a curious habit of carrying apples, cakes, peppermint, &c., in his coat pockets, not apparently for his own eating, for when he met a few small parishioners he used to throw down some of these delicacies in the road, and walk on, without saying a word or turning round to see whether they picked them up.

He had also a singular habit of muttering to himself, as he walked down the lanes, with his eyes on the ground and his hands in his pockets. When first the people saw him thus engaged, and so deep in thought as to be unconscious of the presence of any one whom he might chance to meet, they said he was reckoning over his tithes; but afterwards it was reported that he was repeating prayers,— perhaps for them. Thus it soon became true of him, as of King David of old, " The people took notice of it, and it pleased them; as whatsoever the king did pleased all the people."

So passed the time till the end of January, the two fatherless children of the late Rector becoming daily more endeared to his eccentric successor. He used constantly, when he saw them playing in the garden with their nurse, to call them to the little low hedge, and lift them over to take a walk with him. Many a long mile he carried them, first one and then the other, when the distance wearied them; and they soon learned to substitute him for their father, and gradually began to look to him for their little pleasures, following him about in his garden, and into the church and church-yard, where, with a sweet childish superstition, they always lowered their voices when they passed their father's grave.

Thus he had become a most familiar friend to the children before their mother had seen his face. For the first five months of her widowhood she had not been able to bear an interview with him; but, with her sudden restoration to some measure of health, the natural strength and self-possession of her character returned, and she sent a message to request that he would come and see her.

After the affecting accounts that he had heard of her sufferings, both of body and mind, he was surprised at the perfect calmness with which she received him. She even evinced a desire to speak on the subject of her loss, and turned from more general topics to thank him for his kindness to her children; alluding to their fatherless condition without outward emotion, but with that quiet sorrow that leaves little for a sympathizing friend to say. Mr. Raeburn had not uttered many words before she perceived that he possessed in no ordinary degree the power of entering into the distress of others. The slight hesitation of his voice was very much against him when he endeavoured to enforce a truth or make an appeal to the reason of

his hearers; but in this case it imparted a touching
gentleness to all he said, and his efforts to overcome
his natural reserve, and his evident anxiety lest he
might disturb instead of soothing her, were more
grateful tokens of his fellow-feeling than any
attempts he might have made at consolation.

But he made none. All topics of consolation
had been exhausted on her, all reasons why she
should bear up suggested, all alleviating circumstances pointed out long ago. Her friends had
been very anxious that she should see the man who
was now appointed to be her spiritual guide, thinking that he might be able to say still more than
they had done to comfort her. But now that she
had overcome her strong reluctance, he sat beside
her, offering few admonitions to submission or
patience. His manner seemed to express a consciousness that *he* could not lighten the dark valley
through which she was walking, at the same time
that it gave evidence of his willingness, if it were
possible, to enter it with her by sympathy and walk
for a while by her side.

There was no intruding, *but* in his consolation ;—
he seemed to admit at once the greatness of her
trial.

Her sisters and friends had said, " It is true
that your trial is great, *but* would it not have been
greater if pecuniary difficulties had been added ?
It is certain that you are greatly to be pitied, *but*
what would it have been if you had felt no comfort

as to the state of his soul? It is not to be denied
that your circumstances are distressing, *but* they
might have been far more so. It is a sad thing to
have lost your husband, *but* no tears will bring him
back, and you must endeavour to be resigned."

No such reasons for resignation were urged by
the successor of her late husband. He showed,
indeed, by the tone of his voice, and the expression
of his countenance, that he understood and entered
into her trial; but his manner expressed a perfect
consciousness that no earthly voice could heal the
wound. He did not even remind her of the
undoubted fact, that time would *certainly* moderate
her sorrow,—that most true but least welcome
source of comfort that can be offered to a mourner.

This singularity of manner, this casting aside all
the usual phrases and subjects that form the matter
of conversation between the happy and the unhappy, often proved distressing to those who did
not know the real feeling with which he "wept
with those that wept." But in the case of Mrs.
Greyson, it afforded a welcome relief after listening
to the reasonings of well-meaning friends, who had
seemed to say, "Try to look at your misfortune in
the light that *I* do, and it will seem less hard
to bear." But this friend rather told her, " I
cannot remove the suffering, but I suffer with
you."

Soothed by his fellow-feeling, she turned, after
a while, to speak of the mercies that were still

accorded to her,—spoke hopefully of the peace she might yet have with her two children, and mentioned the kindness she had met with in grateful terms.

He replied: "I do not agree with those who complain that there is a want of *kindness* in this world, even among the worldly. Surely we have all met with much; and we should take it kindly as it is meant. If those who give us kindness do not truly understand us, and give sympathy besides, we must not blame them; they know it only by name, and have it not to give."

"I have felt the truth of the distinction," she answered, "and I hope it has led me to trust in something better than *human* sympathy; otherwise, during all my trial, I must have felt utterly alone."

With the same hesitation of manner, he replied, "Certainly, Madam; there are depths in the heart into which no human eye can reach. With its bitterness, no less than with its joy, the 'stranger intermeddleth not.' The soul lives alone, and it suffers alone. There is but One who can fully understand its wants and satisfy its cravings,—who knows all that we suffer, and fully understands all that we cannot express. Where should we look for help if it were not for the 'Son of consolation?' When the spirit with which we had held sweet communion is withdrawn, what interest, what end would remain, if we might not hear the whispers of His love who regards us with a yet deeper tender-

ness than we ever bestowed on the departed, and
who said, long ago, 'Let thy widows trust in
me?'"

Finding that she made no answer, he added,—
"How marvellous is the sympathy of Christ! We
suffer, and the Head suffers with us, even while we
are enduring the very affliction that His love sees
to be needful to make us meet for our heavenly
inheritance. We suffer in darkness, and sometimes
not seeing nor understanding the end, and not
being able to conceive the glory that shall follow.
But He sees the end from the beginning; He
knows how short these years of darkness will soon
be to look back upon. Yet in all our *present*
affliction He is afflicted, and mourns for us, and
with us, over the dangers and sorrows of the way,
though every painful step leads us nearer to the
place that He has prepared for us, where 'sorrow
and sighing shall flee away,' and the redeemed
shall rest with Him, 'whose rest shall be glorious.'"

At this moment the two children glided softly
into the room. They had been out for their walk,
and had brought some snowdrops for their mother.
During her long illness they had been taught
quietness, and all their movements had become
habitually subdued. But with all this gentleness
they showed a delight on seeing Mr. Raeburn which
touched her heart. She felt how great that kindness must have been which gave them confidence
to climb about him and importune him for the little

childish pleasures that he had promised to procure for them.

The spring of the year opened unusually early; the blossoms and leaves were out nearly a month before their usual time. April came in like May; and Mrs. Greyson recovered sufficient strength to be able to attend the church services, and walk along the quiet country lanes, talking to her children of their dead father.

CHAPTER II.

For the first few months of Mr. Raeburn's residence
in his new parish, he occupied rooms in an old
farm-house ; but at Christmas he took a lease of a
fine but rather dilapidated place, the garden of
which ran along by the side of the church-yard.
The children, who had free leave to follow him
wherever he went, took great delight in wandering
about through the grand old rooms and corridors,
and in watching the progress of the work-people.
The house was a red brick structure, but its original
brightness had become subdued to an umber hue.
The west front was half covered with branching
ivy, which climbed over some part of the roof, and
mantled the chimneys. . The lawn was adorned
with a fountain and a sun-dial, from which, as from
two centres, a multitude of small flower beds
branched off. There the children spent many an
hour watching him, while he pulled up the worth-
less plants, and put in bulbs and young trees. But
the part of the garden on which he bestowed the

greatest pains, was that which lay before the windows of one particular sitting-room in the south side of the house. It was a pretty room, opening by French windows into a terrace, which led down by stone steps into the garden. There was a long balcony over the terrace, supported on stone pillars, over which beautiful creeping plants were trained ; and their slight pleasant shade cast a gloom over the room during the afternoon, when it would otherwise have been oppressively hot. This apartment was wainscotted with oak. The floor was partially covered with a square of Turkey carpet, and the cornice and chimney-piece were carved in a rich pattern, representing bunches of grapes twisted with ears of corn, and tied together with a carved ribbon, on which was written the motto, "I Dreux to me honour ;" for the house had formerly belonged to an ancient Norman French family, of the name of Dreux, and in almost every room their arms were quaintly carved in oak of deep rich colour, very few shades removed from black. Mr. Raeburn furnished this room in the taste of two hundred years ago. Even the plants in pots, which he set on the steps of the terrace, were stately and old-fashioned, and consisted principally of large hydrangias, tall hollyhocks, princes'-feathers, coxcombs, campanulas, and myrtles.

By the middle of spring the house was as neat and clean inside as a single gentleman's housekeeper could make it. But Mr. Raeburn, though as good a master as ever lived, was not perfect—who is ?

and one of the qualities which. in his housekeeper's opinion, stood between him and perfection, was his terrible untidiness. He stained the carpets with red mud, for want of care in wiping his shoes; he left her beautiful bright pokers in the fire till all their polish was burnt off; and he had a bad habit of opening any book he chanced to see, and putting his bands into it, as often as not with the strings hanging out. Besides which, he continually mislaid his papers, books, and other possessions, and thought nothing of turning out the contents of his drawers on the floor in his search for them. But untidiness, the housekeeper knew, was a failing common to most bachelors; so she put to rights after him with great resignation, merely remarking to her subordinates, when she found a more than ordinary uproar among his papers, "that to see how he went on, one would think he expected nature, or Providence, or some of them fine folks, to put to rights after him, instead of a lone woman that had but one pair of hands."

Every Monday evening, Marion and Wilfred came to drink tea with Mr. Raeburn. Immediately before their arrival they proceeded straight into the kitchen; for it was a kitchen after all, though as clean as the study, and ornamented with a square of Kidderminster carpet, as well as with several gaudy tea-trays, the special property of the housekeeper, one of which was the subject of unceasing admiration to the two children. It represented a striped

tiger issuing from a small pink temple, and making
its way towards a remarkably blue pond, whereon
floated a thing like a Noah's Ark, made of wicker
work. In this thing, supposed to be some kind of
boat or raft, sat two ladies, with their heads on one
side, fanning themselves with things like battledores,
while a fiery gentleman was taking deliberate aim
at the tiger with a weapon something like a spud.

When Marion and Wilfred had sufficiently
admired this tray, they proceeded to toast three
rounds of toast—one for each of themselves and one
for Mr. Raeburn. This duty over, they amused
themselves with the cat, and watched the cuckoo
clock in the corner, sometimes pulling down the
weights to make it six o'clock the sooner. When
things got to this pass, Mr. Raeburn always came
out and took them into his study, to sit with him
till the tea came in, with the three rounds of toast,
one for each of the company. Marion always made
the tea. At first, when they began to spend their
Monday evenings with Mr. Raeburn, she required a
great deal of assistance, and did no more than put
in sugar and milk at her own discretion. He was
extremely careful on other points to make things
fair between the children, but in making the tea he
admitted of no such thing as turns,—or what came
to the same thing, it was always Marion's turn.

Marion paid great attention to his instructions,
and by the time she was eight years old she had
arrived at a proficiency in the art that was quite

marvellous for one so young. Indeed, she was so
much at home in exercising it, and looked so sweet
and happy, that as he sat gazing at her during this
particular period of his life, he often conjured up
another image in her place—the image of a lady
whose cheeks were not so blooming, but whose
clear dark eyes and brown hair would not have
suffered by contrast with hers.

One night, when tea had been over some time,
and Mr. Raeburn had already concocted with his
pocket-knife a whole fleet of ships cut out of walnut
shells, and had also drawn a succession of landscapes
in the blank leaves of his pocket-book, each consisting of one cottage in the distance, with two doors
and one window, and a pond in the foreground full
of ducks and ducklings, each quite as large as the
cottage.—And when he had altered them to suit the
fancy of the possessor, by filling the atmosphere
with flying ducks, and when he had told them
several stories, and they had began to get rather
sleepy, he took Marion on his knees, and while she
rested her head on his shoulder, and began to sing
some nursery rhymes, he allowed his fancy quite to
run away with him, and transport him, like the
gentleman in the song, "over the hills and far
away." The particular hills he went over in this
excursion were the Malvern hills, and he alighted at
the door of a pretty house, where in a parlour
reading, sat the same young lady with dark eyes.

She was very much younger than Mr. Raeburn,

for she could scarcely have reached her twenty-
third year; but the vision went on to show that
she was delighted to see him; and it is impossible
to say how far he might have pursued it, if Marion
had not suddenly lifted up her fcae and said, "Uncle,"—he had taught her to call him so,—"Uncle,
who makes tea for you on other nights, when
we are not here? What do you do all by yourself?"

The words entered his ears and changed the
scene of his reverie, though they had not power to
wake him from it. He immediately recalled the
sweet image of his little tea-maker, with her childish
pride in the office, and let her features change and
give place to those of the dark-eyed Euphemia, whom
he hoped soon to see at his board; he imagined himself reading to her in the evening, and fancied how
pleasantly she would speak to the cottagers and the
children. Then he began to consider the fourteen
years' difference between her age and his, and
wondered whether they would make it less easy for
her to enter fully into his pursuits and for him to
make her happy. He was going out the next day;
in three weeks he hoped to return; by that time
the country would be looking its best, for the
orchards would be in full blossom and the hedges
in their first fresh green. Marion had dropped her
head when she found he did not answer, and had
gone on softly singing to herself; but presently the
same thought struck her again, and she repeated

her question,—" Uncle, what do you do all those nights when we are not here?"

Mr. Raeburn woke up from his reverie with a start, and, smoothing her hair, inquired, "What did you say, my pretty?"

Marion repeated her words once more, upon which Mr. Raeburn replied, that he certainly had been obliged to spend a great deal of his time alone,—a great deal more than he liked, and he often felt very lonely. He then went on and gave such a dismal picture of his solitary life, his sitting at tea alone, and being obliged to make it himself, that Marion's little heart was pained for him, and her eyes filled with tears.

Didn't he think he could get some one to come and make tea for him every night? she inquired.

Mr. Raeburn, as if the idea was quite new to him, took a minute to consider of it, and then said, he thought he could; he was almost sure of it. In fact, he intended to see about it very soon.

So Marion was satisfied, and did not trouble herself to ask any more questions, merely remarking, that if he did not remember to tell the new tea-maker (who was at present a mere abstract idea in her mind)—if he did not tell her to be very careful with the cream-jug she would certainly break it, for it was cracked already.

But Mr. Raeburn, to her great surprise, replied, that it did not matter about that, for he had sent to London for a new tea-pot and cream-jug made of silver, and that she should see them some day and make tea in them herself, if the new tea-maker liked, which he thought she would.

They were still discussing the new tea equipage when their nurse came to fetch them home; and Marion, whose sleepy feelings went off in the open air, related the conversation to her mother with great glee.

"Mamma, Uncle Raeburn says, that *perhaps* I shall make tea out of his beautiful new tea-pot."

"Did he tell you who was coming to make tea with it every night?" asked her mother, with a smile.

"No," said Marion, shaking her head; "but I dare say she is much older than I, for he said, if *she liked*, I might; and he thought she would."

This was on the evening of Easter Monday,— Mr. Raeburn was going out after morning service the next day. Easter had fallen very late this year, and the weather was unusually fine for the season; the trees had already put out their leaves, and the lane sides were yellow with primroses.

Mrs. Greyson lingered in the church after service with her children till the last of the rustic congregation had withdrawn, then, going out with them to the two cedar-trees, she sat down to wait for Mr. Raeburn, close to her husband's grave.

It had never been a sorrowful place for *them;* the dead father was not connected in their minds with any mournful images; they thought of him either asleep in his grave,—a smooth place and green, and quiet within; or else sitting in heaven in the presence of the Redeemer, and of all the good men and women whom they had read of in the Bible.

Exceedingly inquisitive, like many other children, about the employments and happiness of the separate state, they had listened with earnest wonder to every symbol put forward in Scripture to give an impression or image of the peace and the aspect of that land which is very far off.

They had no painful knowledge of death to make it a mournful subject; they knew that the dead in Christ should rise, for it was written on his tomb, and had often been explained to them from their earliest years; thus, when they thought of him in his deep, narrow bed, it was always as he had looked when he was alive, lying in a sleep from which he was to be awakened by that voice which will reach the dead. From year to year their thoughts became less distinct about him and their recollections more vague, but still he was always the same dear papa who had loved them so much, —who had liked to have them with him, and had prayed God to bless them a few minutes before he died.

To their mother, time, which softens all sorrow, had brought something more than the passive acquiescence which visits their hearts who look upon the dispensations of God's providence simply

as misfortunes which they must bear as they best
can; she had learned to consider all God's dealings
with her, even the most afflictive, as the evidences
of a heavenly Father's love, who has promised his
children that all things shall work together for their
good.

It was a beautiful morning, and as she sat watching her two children, the treasures of her life, and
looking at the beautiful landscape spread out before
her, she pondered on the text which had been the
subject of the morning's sermon,—" All things are
yours." It recurred to her first, as she observed
the extreme beauty of everything around her.
There is a kind of natural gratitude which arises
spontaneously in the heart when it is impressed by
any unusual beauty or grandeur in the face of
nature, and the natural mind often mistakes this
feeling for true devotional aspirations after the
great Maker and Founder of nature; but, in the
renewed mind, such indefinite delight and awe are
exchanged for grateful love to Him " who giveth
us all things richly to enjoy," and who has not
only in his revealed Word taught us many things
by symbols drawn from the external world, thus
making every season and every scene testify of
Him, but has made the place of his children's
pilgrimage beautiful, and filled it with objects that
delight the eye, as if his bounty could never be
satisfied with pouring out kindness on those whom
his love has redeemed, with heaping upon them the

treasures both of nature and redemption, and saying to them, "All things are yours."

Pondering on this subject, she forgot to observe how silent the children were, and how intently they were watching her face; but at length the striking of the church clock recalled her to herself, and she asked if they were tired, and whether they wished to go home. They were very happy, they said, and they wished to stay till Mr. Raeburn came: they knew he would soon pass through the church-yard, for the groom had been leading his horse up and down the lane for some time; he was going to a village about five miles off to meet the north coach, and though they had taken leave of him, they wished to see him again.

Marion and Wilfred were tying up some little bunches of daisies for their mamma; when they had finished they laid them on her knee, and Wilfred ran off to play; Marion watched him till he disappeared behind the church; then turning to her mother she said, as if the subject had puzzled her for some time—

" Mamma, what are toilsome years?"

" Toilsome years," repeated her mother gently, and wondering where the child had met with the expression.

" Yes, mamma, I read it on Miss Dreux's monument, that young lady who was an heiress. I always read the monuments when I go into the church with Uncle Raeburn."

" What is written on that one ?" asked her mother.

Marion repeated the lines which had perplexed her—

> " God comfort us for all our tears,
>   That only He has seen,
> And shortly end the toilsome years,
>   Us, and his rest between.
>
> " The love from earth with thee departs
>   That thou didst with thee bring ;
> Thou wert unto so many hearts
>   The *most* beloved thing.
>
> " But who remembrance would forego
>   That thy loved face had seen,
> Or let his mourning cease, nor know
>   That thou hadst ever been."

" Do you know who Miss Dreux was ?" asked her mother.

" Yes, mamma, it says on her tomb, ' Elinor, the beloved and only child of Colonel Dreux and Maria his wife : who died in her sixteenth year.' But what made their years toilsome ?"

" Did you never hear this life compared to a journey, Marion ?"

" O yes, in the ' Pilgrim's Progress,' mamma."

" If you were setting out on a journey with delightful companions, and friends to love you and take care of you, the little trouble and weariness of the way would not seem very hard to bear—you would not mind being tired, perhaps, in playing and talking, you might forget that your feet ached a little ; but if you had to go by yourself, and these pleasant companions were all gone away, and the road was very lonely and dark, then you would begin to feel the toil of the journey and to wish it was over—don't you think you should, Marion?"

Marion glanced at her father's grave, and then looked earnestly in her mother's face. During the last few moments she had dimly perceived, with the sympathy of a child, that the sadness of her mother was not all occasioned by the fate of the beautiful girl, whose marble statue with its listless features lay so quietly reclined upon her tomb.

Kind and affectionate feelings had very early exhibited themselves in her conduct and that of her little brother—the same feeling of longing desire to "show some kindness to the dead," which had often prompted them to come (as if to some duty which must not be neglected), to sit by their father's grave to bear him company ; and had often filled them with remorseful sorrow, if they had neglected to do so for a longer time than usual— that same feeling which, in older hearts, gratifies itself in spending care and love upon their living representatives, now sprung up in her mind towards her mother, and touched her with a tender regret, such as will sometimes visit a child's heart at the sight of habitual melancholy, or any continuous sadness—a state of mind which is always mysterious to them, and of all others the least easy to understand.

Marion perceived some application in her mother's words which she could not express, and began to wonder whether her mother's were toilsome years, because if they were, she thought when she was grown older she would comfort her.

The "desire of a man is his kindness;" this is still more strikingly true of the desire of a child; there is something lovely in the dim anxiety that haunts them when some fancied evil, some dreamed of danger hangs over the head of a father or a mother.

The morning was slipping away, Marion soon forgot her anxious speculations and began to make a daisy necklace. The starlings and rooks that lived in the steeple were busy and noisy, the one darting backwards and forwards in a straight, steady flight,—the others poising themselves and floating in the air with sticks in their beaks. The noonday air became warmer and more still, the red buds of the chesnut-trees began to unfold their crumpled leaves, and Mr. Raeburn's favourite horse, as he was led up and down with Wilfred on his back, ceased altogether to expect his master.

But he came at last in a great hurry, and waded through the long grass to wish Mrs. Greyson good by : he had lingered in his house till the last minute, and was afraid he should miss the coach; but he was in very good spirits, and told Marion, as he lifted her up to kiss her, that he hoped in three weeks to bring back the new tea-maker.

The three weeks passed very happily with

Marion and Wilfred. They took long walks with
their mamma, and made collections of out-of-door
treasures,—hoards of fir-apples, red catkins which
strewed the ground under the poplar-trees, cup
mosses, and striped shells. There was a hollow tree
in Mr. Raeburn's garden, where they were in the
habit of depositing these natural curiosities, together
with balls of packthread, last year's nests, bits
of empty honey-comb, and any other articles of
vertù which it was not lawful to carry into the
house. The children thought the new tea-maker
was a long time coming ; they went with their
mother in Mr. Raeburn's house to inspect the arrangements for his return ; they admired the plants in
pots which had been set all along the terrace, and
the cold collation on the table, but most of all,
they were delighted to see the servants in their
white gloves and white ribbons, and the housekeeper in her green silk gown.

It was about five o'clock in the afternoon : every
cottage door was open ; for if there had been no
wish to welcome the Rector home, it is certain that
no cottage girl or cottage wife would miss the sight
of a bride. So all the doors were open, and all the
gardens were full of flowers, bright ones, and large,
such as cottager's love, borage for the bees, tall fox-
gloves, cabbage-roses, peonies, lilacs, wallflowers,
crown-imperials, and guelder-roses.

Little Marion, with a white muslin frock and
satin sash, was standing with Wilfred at their

mother's gate, under the shade of a hawthorn tree, a soft shower of the falling blossoms kept alighting on her hair, till it looked as if it had been sown with seed pearls. The air had given a more than ordinary lustre to her fair complexion, though her blue eyes retained their usual expression of serenity and peace.

The church clock was striking five when the Rector and his young wife turned the slope of the last hill which divided them from the village, and as the carriage advanced, saw it lying beneath them half buried in trees, with the church spire and the two cedars, and the long sunny lane which led down to them. It was a beautiful evening ; never had the scattered village looked more picturesque, the meadows and pasture-lands greener, or the little winding river more tranquil.

The chesnut-trees were in blossom, and the lane was chequered all over with the rays of the afternoon sun slanting through them. No snow had ever made the hedges whiter than they were now in the full pride of their millions of blossoms—white as the bride's veil, they seemed almost weighed down with the multitudes that adorned them. All the orchards were white too, and a slow shower kept perpetually falling from the branches to the grass below.

Through the light foliage of lime-trees in their first leaf the bride caught her earliest glimpse of her new home, watched with earnest and pleased attention every change in the beautiful landscape, and looked at the far-off range of blue hills, so faint in outline that it was not easy to say where they melted into the sky.

She uttered no word as they drew nearer, but kept her eyes fixed upon the lovely scene; the hanging woods and hop-gardens, the corn-fields and apple-orchards; nearer at hand the sloping glades, where dapple cows were chewing the cud in the evening sunshine, and for a background a group of pure white clouds, small and distinct, lying as quietly in the deep sky as a flock of lambs on a green hill-side.

The Rector watched her face as she gazed on the neighbourhood of her home, and he read in her dark eyes their tribute of admiration for its beauty; but not a word she spoke; her face, always pale, looked paler from the agitation of her feelings, and made her long dark hair seem darker than before.

So going slowly on they soon passed out of view of Marion and Wilfred, and turned into the garden-gate which led to their own house, drawing up at the porch, where all the servants, with the old housekeeper at their head, were waiting to receive them.

She was a sweet lady, the Rector's wife; they all said so before she had been long among them. She soon paid visits to some of the cottagers with her husband, and then they too said she was a sweet lady. Marion and Wilfred quite agreed with them.

for she spoke to them so gently and tenderly ; she wished them to come and drink tea as usual on Monday evening, and she gratified Marion's desire to make tea out of the new teapot. Afterwards, sitting under the balcony with Mr. Raeburn, she let them water the flowers which were ranged upon the stone steps. But she was very silent, and her face was generally grave, though sometimes a quiet smile stole over it and lighted it for a moment. Her voice was low, and she had a habit of contemplating the faces of those about her, sometimes dropping her work on her knees, and looking for a long time together at her husband or her little guests with affectionate and pleased attention. There was a great deal of repose expressed in her features, and the same trait was equally obvious in her character.

Her dark eyes were clear, but not sparkling ; all her movements were quiet. Her affections were strong and absorbing. She was one of those not very uncommon people who supply every defect in the character of those they love from the fair ideal they have formed of them in their own minds.

Her happiness was relative rather than positive. As the moon has no brightness of her own, but shines by light reflected on her by the sun, so she seemed to have no happiness of her own and from herself ; her happiness was reflected on her from others, and waxed and waned with theirs.

After Mr. Raeburn's marriage his reserve became very much modified, and he gradually dropped many of his singular habits. His wife proved truly a helpmeet for him. Under her influence he unconsciously became more animated, and both in his parish and at home his character seemed to assume a different aspect. Marion and Wilfred, however, saw less of him than before his marriage. They were instructed not to haunt his footsteps nor importune him to take them with him. This they felt a great privation, especially as their mother's increasing delicacy of health, for some months after the bridal, confined her entirely to her couch. As long as the summer lasted they could scramble about alone among the coppices and wooded dells with which the neighbourhood abounded. But fate, in the shape of a tutor, separated them before the autumn was half over, and every morning the boy was mounted on a shaggy little pony, and sent off to the neighbouring parish, where lived a gentleman, Maidley by name, who had several sons, and was glad to receive Wilfred among them as a day-boarder.

Thus he was fortunately preserved from becoming a dunce, and his sister from becoming a romp.

Will. Greyson was a very droll little boy, quite a character in his way. He had an inexhaustible fund of good humour, a vivid red and white complexion, and a face which was such an odd compound of simplicity and shrewdness, that it was almost impossible to look at him without laughing.

From his earliest years he had shown a strong bent for mechanics, and great curiosity about screws, locks, wheels, &c. Before he was six years old he had made himself personally acquainted with the inside of almost every cuckoo clock in the parish, and he had two incorrigibly bad old clocks of his own, which were an endless source of amusement to him, and which he made to perform all sorts of strange evolutions, and, by means of belts and wires, to peal all hours with alarming vigour.

As he grew older he soon extended his knowledge of what he called the "insides of things" to the church organ, and could not only tune musical instruments, but play upon several. He also concocted several rude alarums, and invented a sun-dial, which, in the shape of an old clock-face, might often be seen protruding from his bed-room window on a sunny day, to the intense astonishment of passers-by.

The winter passed very cheerily to the two families; but in the spring, as Mrs. Greyson's health did not improve, a visit to the sea-side was recommended for her. The children were delighted with the prospect of going to the sea, and the more so as one of their aunts, with her children, was to meet them there.

They looked forward to this their first journey with the vague delight which arises from ignorance of what the splendid sea will be like, and a wonder how it can be possible to walk beside it without danger of being drowned, when the great waves are rising and foaming as they do in pictures.

The sea, after all, did not answer the expectation they had formed of it. Strange to say, they declared that it was not so big as they had expected; and they wrote word to Mr. Raeburn, when they had been there a week, that they had seen no breakers yet, nor "anything particular."

The first month they were very happy, though they missed their gardens more than they had thought possible. The second month was extremely fine, and their aunt, Mrs. Paton, arrived to visit them, with her four children. This was more delightful than can be imagined by any but country-bred children brought up in quietude and exclusion. They were delighted with their cousins,—they almost worshipped them,—particularly the two elder girls, Dora and Elizabeth, who were clever, and older than themselves. The two little ones were delightful playthings, and they spent many a happy hour with them in collecting sea-weeds and shells, and washing and arranging their spoils.

At the end of the second month, their mother one morning received a letter which seemed to give her so much pleasure, that, though they were ready dressed to go out, they lingered in the room till she had done reading it. They knew it was from their uncle (so Mr. Raeburn was always called), and they thought it must be to tell some particularly good news;—either that he had found some wild bees' nests, or perhaps that the gooseberries were ripe in the garden, or, better than all, that he was coming to see them.

They did not mistake the expression of their mother's face; she was greatly pleased, and with better cause than any they had assigned to her, for this letter was to announce the important news of the birth of twin children, a son and a daughter.

For several days after this nothing was talked of but the two dear little babies, and the post-office was visited daily for tidings respecting them. These were always favourable, and written in high spirits. The carpenter's wife, who had had twins in the winter, had been sent for to come and see them, and she had declared (a rare instance of disinterested generosity) that they were finer children than hers, by a deal !

Mr. Raeburn himself, who was allowed to be a tolerable judge of infant humanity, gave it to Mrs. Greyson as his impartial opinion that they were very satisfactory children, and had eyes as dark as their mother's.

Marion and Wilfred were delighted ; here were some children for them to pet and patronize when they were parted from their little cousins. They were urgent with their mother to go home directly, but this was not to be thought of, for she was now gaining strength, and as the weather became warmer, ventured out daily to saunter on the beach

with her sister, and sit under the shadow of the
cliffs.

Another month passed. Their mother began to
grow quite strong ; sometimes she had a colour ; she
seldom lay on the sofa, and could walk out with them
every day.   She had the society of their aunt also ;
but they began to observe, that in spite of all this she
was not in good spirits.   She often sighed deeply,
and their uncle's letters always made her shed tears ;
yet when they asked about the twins she said they
were well ; and as they could think of no other
reason for this change in her, they thought it must
be that she was longing to go home.

Nothing but their desire to see the twins could
have made Marion and her brother willing to leave
the sea and their cousins ; as it was, the parting
caused many tears on both sides, though it was a
consolation to be promised that the next summer, if
all was well, their cousins should come and visit
them at their own home.   During the long journey
the conviction that their mother was unhappy
forced itself again upon their minds.   She did not
seem to participate in their delight when they
talked of Mrs. Raeburn ; on the contrary, they saw
several times during the day that she had difficulty
in restraining her tears, and that when they spoke
to her, she answered with peculiar gravity.

It was on the afternoon of a lovely October day
that Mrs. Greyson returned home.   The yellow
leaves in continual showers kept falling from the

trees ; the lane was so thickly covered, that as they passed along the sound of the carriage wheels was deadened.

The air was perfectly still, and everything was steeped in the yellow sunlight peculiar to the finest hours of our autumnal day. There was a thin warm haze over the distance, which gave a dreamy tranquillity—a kind of sleepy repose to the landscape, and while it shed a slight indistinctness upon it, left the power for imagination to work upon deepening the hollows, lagging along the course of the river, and throwing the woods with their changing lines to a greater apparent distance.

Marion and Wilfred saw with delight the multitude of horse-chesnuts, acorns, and fir-apples that lay among the leaves, and they had no sooner alighted at their own door, and spoken to the servants, than they ran into the garden to collect some of these treasures, and see how their plants were flourishing. Presently, while they were running about, with the utmost delight examining every nook and cranny where they were accustomed to play, their nurse came out and told them that Mr. Raeburn was come, and their mamma wished them to leave off playing, and come and see him.

They ran in at once, and, amid their caresses, began to overwhelm him with questions about Euphemia and the children, asking whether they might see them to-morrow, whether they might nurse them, and what were their names.

Mr. Raeburn answered all their questions with a quiet gravity, which soon checked their glee. There was a tone in his voice that they were not accustomed to—something in his manner which they did not remember and could not understand. He seemed pleased to see them, and evidently meant to stay and take tea with their Mamma. Marion began to ask whether Mrs. Raeburn was coming too, but a glance from her mother checked her ; upon which Mr. Raeburn said, " It is of no consequence—the question was a very natural one : " and then, drawing her towards him with his usual tenderness, assured her that she should see the babies to-morrow.

Marion and Wilfred were soon sleepy and tired ; they went to bed shortly after tea, leaving Mr. Raeburn sitting in one corner of the sofa, with his arms folded, and his eyes fixed upon the ground. He had not said one word since tea, either to them or their mother ; and perceiving that something unusual was the matter, they were quick to observe that, as the housemaid carried away the tea-urn, she cast upon him a look of pity that could not be mistaken.

This same servant, who was a widow, came shortly afterwards into the nursery, and while the nurse was attending upon Marion, began to talk to her in mysterious whispers. Marion caught a sentence here and there, which filled her with wonder.

E

"Never takes any notice of them now, poor little dears—quite out of her mind."

"Mistress told her something of it while we were at the sea," said the nurse.

Marion looked up, and they talked of something else, but soon fell back upon the old theme, and spoke in whispers.

"Yes," Marion heard, "they sent for me that night to see if I could persuade her to give up the little girl. She had it on her lap. They had set the bassinet beside her, in hopes she would put the baby in, and as soon as she saw me, she says, 'Watson, everything seems to be floating away.' 'Oh, you'll be better, Ma'am, when you've had some sleep. Give me the baby; I can take care of it. You know I am a mother myself,' I said. 'No,' she says, 'I'm afraid if I give it to you I shall never see it again.' So she looked into the bassinet, and she says, very quiet-like, 'I thought I had two of them; perhaps it was only a dream; but I love this little one that's left!'"

"Hush!" said the nurse; "Miss is listening."

They then paused for a while, till she seemed attending to other things, and the next thing Marion heard was, "Dr. Wilmot kept making signs to me to do all I could, so I said, 'Let me set the bassinet by you on the sofa, Ma'am, and then you can lay her in, and watch her.' Well, she laid the child in it, and as soon as she looked another way, they carried it out of sight."

"Very strange she should know you, and not her own husband," said the nurse.

"Yes," returned the other, "and he so changed in a few days that you would have thought he had had a long illness"

Then followed a few sentences that Marion could not understand. "Never takes notice of any one now; quite out of her mind." "Then it all seemed to come on in a few days," said the nurse.

"Yes, and they only six weeks old, poor little dears."

"Does Mr. Raeburn take much notice of them?" Marion did not hear the answer to this question, but part of the housemaid's next remark reached her.

"He said, 'O my dear Euphemia, do you know me?—can you answer me?' And I took up her hand, and turned her face gently towards him. She looked like a person in a dream; and I said, 'Look, Ma'am, don't you see Mr. Raeburn?—don't you see your husband?' I thought she looked at him rather earnestly; at last she said, 'That's the clergyman,' and fell to thinking. In a few minutes she says to herself, 'And yet,' she says, 'I must have had them once; I think I heard one of them cry this morning.'"

"Poor dear!" said the nurse; and then Marion went to bed, and dreamed of the two sweet babies whose mamma was forgetting them.

The next morning, when Wilfred was gone to

school on his pony, Mrs. Greyson told Marion she
was going to the rectory, and she might come with
her. Mr. Raeburn met them in the garden, and went
up with them to the nursery, which was at the top of
the house — a large white-washed room, with casement
windows, half-covered with trailing ivy. Marion's
delight at sight of the two children asleep in their
pretty cradles, aroused him from his despondency,
and he said to her mother in a cheerful tone, "I
have been very anxious for you to see them; I hope
you think they look well and thriving."

Mrs. Greyson's reply was satisfactory, and in a
short time he asked her to come down with him and
see his wife.

Marion was left in the nursery, with the infants
and their nurses : presently one of them awoke, and
she was too much absorbed in watching the process
of dressing it in an embroidered cloak and satin
bonnet to notice her mother's protracted absence.
She came at last, and taking Marion down stairs,
stood still for a few minutes in the hall to wipe
away her tears. The child asked no questions, but
remained looking from her mother to Mr. Raeburn,
till the latter said, "I wish you would leave Marion
with me for the rest of the day, my dear Mrs.
Greyson. I think I should like to have her."

"Certainly," returned her mother, who had quite
regained her composure, "and I will send for her in
the evening.

Marion was pleased to stay, and walked to the

garden gates with her mother and Mr. Raeburn, amusing herself with watching the fall of the poplar leaves, which lay in such masses in the lane, that the movement of her mother's gown as she walked raised a little crowd of them, to flutter round her like a tribe of yellow butterflies.

All through the morning Marion asked no question about the unseen Euphemia, but while Mr. Raeburn sat writing in his study she amused herself with books in one corner ; after which she went out with him as of old, and they called at several cottages : but though he met with a very warm welcome, and the health of the twins was inquired after with great tenderness, no direct questions were asked about Euphemia, though there was that in the manner of some of the poor women which said plainly for him, as Job said for himself, " O that it was with thee as in months past, as in the days when God preserved thee ; when his candle shined upon thy head, and when by his light thou didst walk through darkness."

After their return from this walk, Marion went into the nursery again, and, to her great delight, was permitted by the nurses to sit in a little chair, and nurse each of the twins in turn.

Two o'clock was Mr. Raeburn's dinner hour, and then a servant came to fetch her down, saying that her uncle was waiting. Marion wondered whether Euphemia would come and dine with them, or whether she and her uncle were to be quite alone.

She lingered at the door of the dining-room, half
hoping, half fearing that she should hear the sound
of her voice. But Mr. Raeburn, who had been
standing at the window, turned when he heard her
step, and leading her in, said, as if he had read her
thoughts, " There is no one here ; come in, my
pretty ; it was very kind of mamma to let you stay
with me to-day."

Marion came in, and during dinner began to talk
of the sea-side, of the ships and the shells, till Mr.
Raeburn was beguiled of some of his heaviness by
her gentle companionship, and afterwards sat listening to her conjectures as to how soon the twins
would begin to know her, and when they would be
able to walk, till the old servant, who was watching
his master's face, blessed the day that brought her
home again. This went on till the dessert and wine
were cleared away, and till the sunbeams had crept
round to that side of the old house, and were playing on a pair of lustres which were held up by bronze
figures on the sideboard, and covering the ceiling,
the walls, and Marion's white frock with fragments
of little trembling rainbows. Mr. Raeburn took out
his watch, and finding it nearly four o'clock, glanced
at Marion, as if trying to decide something. At
length he said, " I am going now to sit for a while
with your aunt ; would you like to come with me,
Marion ?"

Marion assented instantly, put her hand in his,
and let him lead her through the well-ordered

garden, till they approached the morning-room by the stone terrace outside. Mrs. Keane, who had been Marion's nurse, opened the French-window when she saw them ascending the steps, and then retired into a corner and took up a piece of needle-work.

Marion cast a hurried glance round the room, and seeing Euphemia seated on a sofa, looking much as usual, was about to start forward and speak to her, when something in the calm face arrested her steps, and, while Mr. Raeburn walked forward and sat down beside her, she stood within the window, gazing at her with anxious perplexity.

It was obvious that she was perfectly unconscious of their presence; her lips were moving, but no sounds were audible; the expression of her face told of a calm abstraction, a depth of serenity and blindness to external things which nothing could possibly reach to disturb. But she had something in her hands,—she was twisting (strange sight for an intelligent child)—she was twisting a long skein of silk in and out and backwards and forwards among her fingers.

Marion looked at "her uncle," and he beckoned her to approach. It was a low sofa on which Euphemia sat, and she was reclining on one elbow upon the pillows; a large ottoman stood close to her feet. And when Mr. Raeburn spoke to Marion, and said, "Come close to her,—see if she will know you," Marion came and knelt on the ottoman, and, putting her arms round Mrs. Raeburn's waist, said, in her soft sweet voice, " Aunt, aunt, look at me ; I am come home again."

" Call her *Euphemia*," said Mr. Raeburn.

Marion's attitude had a little interfered with the movement of Euphemia's hands, as she went on twisting the skein, and she put out her hand and gently tried to push her face away. As she did this their eyes met, and hers assumed for the moment a less dreamy expression. She dropped the silk, and taking Marion's head between her hands, looked at her with great attention, and then uttered her name in the inexpressive tone of a person talking in sleep.

" Euphemia," said the child, as the two small hands drew her still nearer, " listen to me ;—do listen to me. I have been to see the babies."

But Euphemia's mind was sinking again into one of its long, listless reveries, and, having drawn Marion's head on to her bosom, she remained gazing out of the windows at the sunset clouds ; then folding one arm round the child, as she knelt beside her, she presently began with the same dream-like tranquillity to pass her hands among the long waves of her luxuriant hair. At last, to the astonishment of her husband, she lifted up her face, with an expression of evident pleasure, disengaged a yellow poplar-leaf, which had doubtless fallen on Marion's head as she passed through the garden, and held it out to him with a smile.

It was a long time since he had seen her smile, and it sent a thrill of pleasure to his heart. Wishing, if it were possible, to rouse her sufficiently to make her speak to him, he then addressed her with the utmost tenderness, entreating her to look at him, and saying, " Let me hear the sound of your voice once more, even if you say no more than my name. Let me hear my name from your lips once more."

But the voice to which she was so well accustomed seemed, by its very familiarity, less capable of penetrating through the deep dream of her existence; for when Marion lifted up her face and added her entreaties to his, she was again aroused to attention, and said, in reference to her words, which had been a repetition of Mr. Raeburn's entreaties that she would look at her husband :—

" My husband's dead." And then added, with a sigh and a touching tone of quiet regret, " It was a pity they laid him in the grave so soon. I should like to have kissed him, before they took him away."

Mr. Raeburn hastily arose and paced the floor with uncontrolable agitation. He had endured for weeks past to sit by her side and hold her hand in his, while she remained unconscious of his presence and uttered not a word; but now, she had been on the very brink of resuming some kind of intercourse with him, and it appeared to him that if he could only find the right chord to touch she might be won back to him. It was an additional bitterness to him, and one that he had not hitherto suffered, to find that his influence was even less with her than that of a happy child, who felt little pain at the sight of her malady.

Forgetting for the moment his usual self-control, he again returned to her, and entreated, commanded, adjured her, if possible, to give him some sign that she was conscious of his existence. Marion wept and trembled, and the nurse said what she could to calm him, but the silent object of all this pain sat still in her place, and resumed the coloured silk which she had thrown aside, turning and twisting it among her fingers.

It was not long before he recovered some degree of self-command, came up to his wife, and kissed her passive cheek; then he hastily drew Marion away from her, took her out of the room, and left her alone in the dining-room to dry her tears and wonder at the strange scene she had witnessed.

She had looked back as she left the room, and the image of Euphemia's face as she then saw it could never be forgotten;—the peaceful features, the quiet attitude, the sealed-up senses,—not to be reached by love or fear, or touched by the passionate entreaties of the husband who had hitherto been so dear to her.

That night Marion made tea again, as she had so

often done before Mr. Raeburn's marriage. She was quiet, and he was much more silent than usual, but he liked to have her with him; and from that time, whenever he felt more than commonly desolate, he used to send for her to spend the day with him and talk to him about his children.

CHAPTER III.

THE TWIN CHILDREN.

MARION became now again the constant companion of Mr. Raeburn's walks, and as the twin children grew older they were often added to the party.

They were both very lovely infants, and strongly resembled their mother, having the same soft, dark eyes, and long lashes, and the same tranquillity of expression. Never having had a day's illness from their birth, they delighted their father by their rapid growth and dawning intelligence; and, as he held them one on each knee, he often pictured to himself the comfort they would be to him when they grew older.

During the first year of their lives their mother seemed occasionally conscious of their existence; and as Mr. Raeburn took care that they should often be carried into her presence, he comforted himself with the hope that, if she ever should recover her reason, they would not look upon her as a stranger.

But from month to month her remembrance of

them diminished, her mind became less quiescent, and she would hold long conversations with herself, or with imaginary companions, always wearing the same rapt expression on her face.

Place and scene were supplied by her fancy,—she saw no passing changes; even when one of her own children was held up before her and would smile in her face, stroking her cheeks with its tiny hands, she would suffer, but never return, the baby caress, nor take the least notice of the little open mouth, with its rows of pearly teeth, and the calm dark eyes so like her own.

Thus matters continued with her till they were two years old, when her condition seemed slightly to improve. This improvement was shown by her following the children about the room with her eyes, and seeming to take some slight pleasure in the beauty of the little Euphemia, whose long hair fell in soft waves upon her neck.

Mr. Raeburn had been in the habit of reading to her every morning since her illness, and though he continued the practice for many months without her taking the slightest apparent notice, it was afterwards evident that she retained some expectation of it; for one morning, when he did not pay the usual attention, she manifested considerable restlessness, and at last spoke to her attendant and desired her to call the clergyman,—for since her mind had been disturbed she had always called her husband by this name.

When he entered she seemed to awake for the moment from the deep trance in which she lived, and as he sat down beside her she laid her hand upon his arm, and addressing him, with the grace and politeness which in her better days she might have shown to some stranger who had shown her a kindness, she thanked him for what she called his attentions to one who had no claim upon them, and requested that, if possible, he would never omit to read to her again.

But here this improvement ceased. He read, but could elicit no remark from her on the chapter, nor any appearance of interest in the prayer with which he generally concluded. Her two children, as soon as they could speak, were taught to call her "Mamma," and early began to manifest considerable affection for her, often attempting to draw their father to the door of the morning-room, and, if they could succeed in inducing him to take them in, standing before her hand in hand, looking up into her face with mingled tenderness and awe, and softly repeating her name.

In the spring of this year Dora and Elizabeth came to visit their cousins; they were very sprightly and clever, but had not the innocent gentleness of Marion, nor her serene spirits. They were scarcely at home again before she and the twins were attacked with hooping-cough, but of the mildest type, and in spite of the backwardness of the season none of the children seemed to suffer much.

By the end of May they all seemed perfectly recovered. The twins had been removed, at Mrs. Greyson's request, to her house, that she might watch over them more carefully, for their two original nurses had left them, and they were confided to the care of a less-experienced woman. They had returned home about a week, when one morning, while Marion was learning her lessons, Mr. Raeburn came in, and said to her mother,—

"I wish you would come and look at my boy; I do not think he is so well as when he left your house."

"Perhaps the warm weather makes him a little fretful," she answered.

"Yes; I dare say it is that," he replied, as if half-ashamed of his own uneasiness; and then added, with a smile which seemed to deprecate her *ridicule,* "The fact is, he has given me a peculiar glance several times the last few days. I think he looks as if he saw something."

Mrs. Greyson went up stairs and put on her bonnet immediately, but felt that, in all probability, he was enduring perfectly needless anxiety, though she could scarcely wonder at it, considering the circumstances of his case. As they walked towards the rectory she tried to give him this view of the matter, and he appeared so much restored to ease by it that he was even unwilling to allow her to proceed.

She, however, went up with him into the

nursery, where the little Euphemia, who had just awoke from her morning sleep, was laughing on the nurse's knee, and playing with a toy made of revolving feathers.

She bent over the crib where the other child was sleeping, lifted up his dimpled hand, and remarked to his father that he looked perfectly well. She reminded him that it was but four days since the children had returned home, and that she had seen them twice without remarking any apparent delicacy.

" When did you first observe that he seemed unwell ?" she inquired.

" Not till the day before yesterday. No doubt it is only my fancy."

" How very soundly he sleeps," she remarked.

" O, very indeed, Ma'am," said the nurse, who was now dressing her little charge for a walk. " The trouble I've had to wake that child these last few days nobody would believe ; but he always wakes so good tempered when I do get him roused."

Mr. Raeburn smiled at this new proof of the health of his boy, but happening to glance at Mrs. Greyson, was disturbed to see her colour change, and her face assume an expression of at least as much anxiety as he had ever felt.

After a momentary pause, she said, quietly, " Does he wake with a crowing noise ?"

" He has done, Ma'am, the last few days ;

no doubt that's the remains of the hooping-cough."

The nature of his mother's illness flashed across Mrs. Greyson's mind, and she wished for a medical opinion ; but fearful of needlessly disturbing his father, and thinking that, after all, she might be mistaken, she stood a short time irresolute, looking at the sleeping child. It was, however, quite needless for her to tell him her anxiety : he had already seen it ; and, as if he had instinctively guessed her fears, he said, hurriedly, " I hope you do not think there is anything the matter with the brain ?"

" I have no defined thought on the subject," she answered ; " the symptoms are so very slight that it would be quite unreasonable to dread the very worst, when we have not even heard a medical opinion."

She had scarcely done speaking, when the child awoke with a sudden start, and the peculiar noise the nurse had mentioned. He seemed good-humoured, but rather heavy. Yet when his father hinted at the propriety of sending for Dr. Wilmot, the physician who attended his mother, Mrs. Greyson assented with a readiness which gave him pain, adding, with assumed cheerfulness, that if there really was nothing the matter, it would be a relief to their minds to hear him say so.

Dr. Wilmot was accordingly sent for. He arrived without much delay, and, after examining the child attentively, and listening to the symptoms, declined to give any opinion for the present. But Mr. Raeburn saw the glance he exchanged with Mrs. Greyson as he sat at the nursery table writing his prescription, and felt that if he abstained from exciting his fears, it was more out of compassion than from any doubt in his own mind.

For the next week or ten days the symptoms did not, to an inexperienced eye, present anything unusual, but at the end of that time the sleepiness increased to such a degree that it was scarcely possible to rouse him even to take his food, and the child began to exhibit all the distressing symptoms of water on the brain.

His little sister, who at first had seemed to wonder why he did not get up and play with her as usual, used to come to the side of his bed and stroke his head with her hand, telling him to wake up and have his frock on ; but after a few days, finding this a hopeless entreaty, she contented herself with standing opposite and gazing at him, saying, in a sorrowful tone, "He very tired ; he can't get up no more."

Marion, who had free access to the nursery, was deeply affected. Day after day her mother sat on one side of the bed, and Mr. Raeburn on the other. He seldom said anything ; and since the day when he was told the name of the complaint, seemed to have given up hope, sitting always in silent despondency, watching the face of the dying child.

At length, one afternoon there was a perceptible

alteration. The intervals of wakefulness had lately been very short, and a languor was spread over the baby features, which told plainly of the near approach of dissolution.

Mr. Raeburn left the bedside, and unable to endure the thought of his child's dying without being again seen by his mother, went to her apartment to persuade her, if it were possible, to come into the nursery and look at him once more.

She had, ever since her illness, shown the greatest possible reluctance to leaving this room, and when he entered was sitting in her usual position on the sofa.

She took no notice of his approach, but the agonized tones of his voice when he spoke seemed to reach even her beclouded brain; and looking in his face with something like anxiety, she asked him whether anything was the matter.

"Are you ill?" she inquired, laying her hand upon his arm.

He shook his head.

"What then? are you unhappy?"

The slight quivering of the compressed lip, and the look of anguish which passed across his face answered her question, and she repeated, "What is it? what is the matter?"

Fixing his eyes upon her earnestly, and speaking with laboured distinctness, he answered, "One of my children is very ill; you must come and see him before he dies."

Euphemia sighed deeply, but it was not for her dying boy. She was far from understanding how truly she was to be pitied. She sighed because the effort of leaving her accustomed place and using any kind of exertion was almost more than she could endure ; nevertheless, she suffered him to raise her and lead her, half reluctantly, to the nursery, which she had never entered since the first day of her illness.

The child was lying perfectly still, his pale features retaining much of their infantine beauty. His eyes were open, and he seemed to look about him with more intelligence than he had lately shown. His mother looked at him when she came in, but neither recognised him as her own, nor even as the lovely child whose play she had watched when he had been brought with his little sister into her room.

His father, on whose arm she was leaning, entreated that she would kiss him ; and after a pause of irresolution, she kneeled down and pressed her lips on those of the child.

This short interval of consciousness was not yet over, and as she lifted up her face again and saw his languid eyes looking at her, she said in a tone of tender regret which added another pang to those who watched them, " Pretty child ! " Marion wept bitterly, and the little Euphemia gazed upon them all with a mournful face. The mother and child continued to look into each other's eyes ; at length the latter lifted up his wasted hand, and, touching her cheek, smiled faintly and murmured the word, "Mamma." Euphemia then started up with a strength and energy which astonished them, and for a moment the real circumstances of her lot seemed fully present to her as, pressing her hand to her forehead, she seized her husband's arm and entreated him to pray for her dying boy.

"For he is my child," she exclaimed in a tone of agony and horror, "and they never told me that he would die." But here her hand dropped down again : she murmured, " O that I could but remember ; " and then begged they would tell her what was the matter.

An effort was made to recal her to the scene before her, but it failed, and the dreamy look returning, she gazed forlornly about her, and desired her husband to take her down again.

Thinking his child had not many minutes to live, the father hesitated, and signified his wish that she would put her arm under his head. She accordingly sat down on the side of the bed, the child was lifted up and put into her arms, and in a few minutes he breathed his last upon his mother's bosom.

That was a sorrowful night for the members of the household, and for those who had so fondly watched the child from his earliest infancy—a bitter night for the bereaved father, and perhaps the echo of some sounds of grief, or some slight remembrance of his loss might reach Euphemia's heart, for she was restless and uneasy; but for three days after his death she said nothing by which they could gather that she remembered the circumstance, not even when the passing bell was tolled, though the sound of it generally disturbed and irritated her.

On the afternoon of the third day she evinced a desire to leave her usual place, and while her husband was sitting beside her, went up of her own accord into the nursery. The little Effie was lying there, fast asleep in her pretty bed, her dimpled cheek reclining on one hand and her eyelids partially open.

Her mother looked at her, and put her finger into the little hand, which quietly closed upon it. She seemed pleased, but this was evidently not what she was seeking, for after looking at the other little empty bed, she left the nursery, and, her husband following her, went straight to the dressing-room of what had been her own bed-chamber while in health. He did not make any attempt to check her, and she opened the door and entered.

The child was lying in his coffin, which was lined with white satin, and strewed with the buds of white flowers; a lily of the valley was laid upon his breast, which, though daily renewed, had already begun to droop and fade. His face was perfectly pale, and, though calm and lovely, had a touching expression of sadness spread over it. Two or three soft locks of hair were lying on his marble forehead, and the lace cap and embroidered robe gave him an appearance still more infantine than he had presented during his short life; but the baby features being settled in death, the child had never looked so like his father before, and it would seem that Euphemia observed this, for in a low voice she repeated her husband's name, and, taking up the lily, pressed it to her lips and put it in her bosom.

Mr. Raeburn watched her as she sat gazing long and intently at her child, while every now and then a forlorn expression of regret, which seemed a reflection of the dead baby's aspect, stole over her face. At length, with a heavy sigh she arose as if satisfied, and returning to her old place took no further notice of the change, of the closed shutters, or of her mourning dress on the day of the funeral.

As for his father, when he had laid him in the grave, and seen everything that had belonged to him returned to the dressing-room, his toys, his clothes, and even his little bed, he never willingly mentioned his name again or alluded to his loss, but seemed to concentrate all his affection on his little daughter and Marion, who was his cherished companion and her playfellow.

Since his wife's illness he had almost entirely withdrawn himself from society, and, but for Mrs. Greyson's unfailing friendship, must have been entirely alone in the world. His love for her children and for his little Euphemia, together with the pleasure he took in his pastoral duties, seemed all he was capable of enjoying, and for the sake of com-

panionship he often allowed his little child to
spend whole hours playing about in his study,
strewing the chairs and footstool with her dolls and
their various gay bonnets and gowns, till, tired with
her many journeys across the room, she would hide
her face in his bosom and fall asleep in his arms
while he was writing.

Two years passed on. Marion and Wilfred grew
tall and strong, and both manifested considerable
ability. They inherited from their father a great
love of music, and would spend many an hour
playing on the church organ. They were about
thirty miles from a cathedral town, but as there was
a railway across the country, their mother procured
for them a regular instructor from thence both in
singing and instrumental music.

Marion was now thirteen years of age, and gave
promise of everything that her mother could desire.
Her face retained its infantine tenderness and
serenity, and being rather small for her years she
generally passed for younger than she was; while her
endearing manner and confiding nature caused her
to be treated like a child by Mr. Raeburn, who
regarded her with scarcely less tenderness than he
bestowed upon his little daughter.

Marion and Wilfred had never been brought forward in their childhood, nor taught to assume any
other manner than that which naturally belonged to
them. They had both been rather encouraged than
otherwise in their child's play, and could amuse

themselves after their own fashion without the least
fear of being laughed at. Solomon, the wisest of
men, when he said, " There is a time for all things,"
doubtless made no exception excluding the time to
be a child, to think as a child, and to be delighted
with childish things. It is entirely a modern invention to make men and women of creatures not
twelve years old, to give their games a philosophical
turn, and make their very story-books science in
disguise.

Marion and Wilfred had never been cheated into
learning in this clandestine way; but, like the boy
in " Evenings at Home," when they worked they
worked, and when they played they played.

Their moral feelings had been carefully cultivated
from their infancy, and all that one human being
can do for another, in the way of religious instruction, had been imparted to them both by their
mother and Mr. Raeburn. But they had never
been encouraged to display their knowledge, or take
any part in religious conversation; and like most
children who really feel the importance of serious
religion, they evinced a sensitive shrinking from
anything like an explanation of their feelings.

There was one amusement reserved for Marion
which was not childish; it was to teach the little
Euphemia to read. This was at first thought a
great honour and privilege, both by mistress and
pupil,—the former, because it gave her the opportunity to exercise a little patronage; the latter,

because she looked upon the lessons as a new kind
of play. But in a very short time the little creature
found out that this play was different to all others,
inasmuch as she was obliged to play at it whether
she would or no. She therefore began to rebel, and
Mrs. Greyson was obliged to interpose her authority
to prevent her from making Jack's house of the
letters, or creeping under the table to nurse a sofa
cushion by way of doll. Neither teacher nor pupil
looked upon these daily lessons with much enthusiasm after the first novelty had gone off; but with
a little superintendence, they proved of essential
benefit to both; for the pupil was a warmly affectionate child, and having a passionate temper, was
more easily controlled by love than by severity. On
the other hand, her quickness and cleverness kept
the faculties of her always gentle teacher in a state
of salutary activity.

CHAPTER IV.

A JOURNEY IN A FOG.

ANOTHER year passed ; a quiet, happy, uneventful year. Since his wife's illness, Mr. Raeburn had never left home, but now he consented to the entreaties of his only sister to come and spend the autumn with her and her family in the Highlands.

Change of air and scene were of so much benefit to his spirits that he was easily induced to prolong his stay, and take a yachting excursion down the west coast. He had constant letters from Marion and Mrs. Greyson, giving good accounts of his wife and child up to the period of his commencing his excursion ; yet he did not approach his home without a restless feeling of agitation. He had so long been accustomed to watch over his wife, and delight in his child, that he could not return without a half wonder lest either he or they might be changed by the absence ; lest he might feel less able to bear with his poor impassive wife now, that for some weeks he had been emancipated from her, or lest his child might have learned to do without him.

He travelled alone inside the coach towards home. The day had been fine and bright, but towards evening a heavy fog came on, which gradually became so thick that the coachman was compelled to slacken his pace, so completely were hedges, fences, and open common enveloped in thick white mist, which seemed, as it grew more dense, to press up to the very windows.

Night came on : there was a full moon, but it only gave light enough to show the density of the fog. As they approached the cross roads, where he expected some vehicle to meet him and take him on, he almost feared the coach would pass it. He let down a window when they stopped to change horses, and the fog poured in like smoke ; it seemed to stop his breath as he put his head out to inquire whether they could not put up better lamps, to show their whereabouts to any travellers who might meet them on the road.

"Is that Mr. Raeburn?" he heard the landlady ask, as she stood with two candles in her hand, giving directions about a post-chaise which had gone on before them, "for the fog," she observed, "deadened sound as well as sight."

He was about to speak to the woman when he heard her mention his name, and retreat towards the house with an exclamation of pity, which struck upon his ear with a strange sensation of surprise and annoyance.

He had never asked for sympathy ; the condition

of his wife was never alluded to by him unless it was
absolutely necessary; and he had so full and true a
belief that all the events of his life had been appointed in love, and for his good, that he had taken
all possible pains to be not only resigned, but cheerful. His feelings were so well understood by his
friends, that he very seldom heard them allude to
his lot in tones of pity, and the words of this woman,
which evidently were not intended for his ears, cast
a damp upon his spirits which he could not throw
off—" Is that Mr. Raeburn? Ah, poor gentleman !"

It was midnight when they reached the cross-
roads ; he saw two dim lamps gleaming at the
road side.

" Is that my carriage ?" he exclaimed, springing
out. " Is Porson there ?—tell him to look after the
luggage."

It was quite a relief to speak ; and by the sound
of his own voice break in upon the constant mental
repetition of those words,—" Is that Mr. Raeburn?
Ah, poor gentleman !"

He advanced hastily to the carriage-door, and
was surprised to see the schoolmaster standing
beside it.

" You are very late, Sir," said the man, with
peculiar gravity.

" Is all well ?" asked the Rector, startled by his
manner.

" In the village, did you mean, Sir ?" asked the
man slowly, and as if reluctantly.

" No, at home ?" He waited for an answer.

The face of the schoolmaster was not very distinctly visible. It was some time before he spoke. At length he said,—" Did you wish to know *now*, Sir ?"

" No," replied Mr. Raeburn, springing into the carriage ; " drive on. Tell them to be quick. Don't speak again,—I cannot bear it."

The man got in also, and sat down opposite to him. The coach had gone on. There was some little delay in getting the luggage on to the roof of the carriage.

Mr. Raeburn had covered his face with his hands. Delays are dreadful to the wretched. With the impatience of agitation and suspense, he looked up, and said, vehemently, " Why don't you tell them to make haste ? I want to get home quickly."

The man answered, in a tone so desponding that it sounded like the echo of his own fears,—" It is of no use !"

The next instant the carriage started at as rapid a rate as even he could have desired. The journey was made in silence. He went through the thick fog with his arms folded and his eyes fixed upon the shrouded landscape. But he failed to recognise any of its features, and did not even know when he entered his own gates. It was not till they stopped suddenly at the door that he was aware of his arrival at home.

The hall-door was open, a lamp was burning,

and several servants were standing within. He saw a lady pass rapidly down the stairs. She met him on the steps; but her face was so utterly devoid of colour, so much changed, that for the moment he did not know her. Presently he remembered that it was Mrs. Greyson. She did not speak at first, and he advanced into the hall and demanded to see his wife.

The servants looked at one another; and Mrs. Greyson said, "Your wife is in her usual state;— she is asleep."

With a strong effort he went on into the study, and laid his hat on the table. It seemed impossible for him to ask the next question, and as he stood, amazed and pale, Mrs. Greyson sunk into a chair, and Marion, frightened and trembling, stole into the room and sheltered herself beside her.

Her presence seemed to recal him to himself. He turned to her mother with startling energy and sternness, and said, "Where is my child? I want her,—I must see her. Why don't you bring her to see her father?"

Mrs. Greyson looked in his face. It became paler and paler. She knew it was needless to prepare his mind when he already foreboded the worst. He repeated faintly, "Why don't you bring her to see her father?"

She answered slowly, "Your child has another Father. He has sent for her, and she is gone."

He had sunk upon the sofa as he asked his ques-

tion for the second time; and when the sound of
her voice reached his ears, he shuddered, and shrunk
back, as if to escape from the intolerable pain it
gave him. But he uttered no word of grief or
horror, and never changed his position excepting to
fold his arms tighter across his breast, and set his
lips, which grew more and more white.

Mrs. Greyson sat motionless, gazing at his countenance with unutterable pity. But she offered no
word of consolation, and for a long, miserable hour,
she and Marion retained silence, till the sound of
footsteps overhead startled him from his enforced
calmness. He looked up, and seeing the tears
stealing down Marion's pale cheeks, passionately
entreated her mother to send her away, and fainted
while he was endeavouring to explain his wish to
see his beloved child.

How shall we expect others to sympathize with
us when we know not how to sympathize with ourselves? Why, indeed, should we expect our friends
fully to understand our sorrows, and make allowance for our bending under them, when the very
soul which but yesterday, it may be, was stricken
down to the dust, to-day is able to cry for help,
to-morrow may be able to help itself, and the next
day may wonder that it was so utterly cast down?

If we cannot sympathize, neither can we understand ourselves. When the paroxysm of pain or
the storm of grief is over, we forget how great an
influence it exerted for the time, and with the

undisturbed, calm reason of health and composure, we look back upon our conduct and are hard upon ourselves;—we condemn our own folly, and forget that the faculties which sit in judgment now were then more than half dethroned.

Every parent can feel for a man when he loses a beloved child, especially if that child was his only one,—still more if it was the solace of a life otherwise lonely and marked by misfortune.

Every one felt for the Rector when he committed his only child to the grave. Many tears were shed for him when he first appeared afterwards in the church and at the cottages. But after a while it became an ordinary thing to see him wandering through the lanes alone; the people became accustomed to his smile, which played so brightly about his mouth, but could not reach to dissipate the gloom of his eyes, and vanished so suddenly with the short sigh of a person whose heart is heavy. People shook their heads when first they observed how much the dark-eyed children were always his favourites; but after a while, they only said it was very natural, and even the carpenter's wife soon began to think nothing of it when she saw him turn round, half unconsciously to himself, and watch her sturdy little twins as they walked hand in hand along the road.

Mr. Raeburn never once alluded to his loss after the first few weeks, and would not bear to hear it spoken of in his presence. He was, after a time, so perfectly calm and self-possessed, that the care buried in his own breast could scarcely have been detected by others; and but for his sensitive shrinking from certain topics, from the mention of some few names, and of the year of good promise which had succeeded his marriage, he might have been supposed to have got over his loss altogether, and to have " ceased to send sighs after a day that was past." But the few who knew him well were conscious that such was not the case, and of those few none knew it better than little Marion.

As has been often before mentioned, the nursery at the rectory was a long room in the slope of the roof, with casement windows, partly shrouded by ivy. These windows were the only part of Mr. Raeburn's house which were visible beyond the trees of its garden, an opening between them causing their diamond panes and bushy ivy to be distinctly seen from Marion's chamber.

As a child she had often laid awake watching these casements, lighted from within; and, with her curtains drawn back, could discern a person who might pass between them and the light, though the distance was too great for her to distinguish much more.

It had been a habit with her to watch this room before she went to sleep; and the dusky roof and dark outlines of the rectory, with the stars rising behind them, were among the most familiar objects that presented themselves in her dreams. After the death of the little Euphemia, it was some time before Marion took courage to draw back her curtains and look out at the blank, desolate nursery; but the force of habit prevailing, she one night did so unconsciously. The moon was shining full upon the windows, and their cold, blank appearance made her hide her face in the pillow and weep, till she started up, half-asleep, at sight of some one bringing a light in the nursery, setting it down near the central window, and then beginning slowly to pass up and down.

Marion looked a long while, and fell asleep before the light was withdrawn.

Every night, as she had watched the place where her little playmates were, she now watched the return of their bereaved father, and saw the long falling of the shadow on the wall; but she never told any one of these visits, though they were not without effect on her mind.

She was now old enough to know that she herself was the greatest solace left to her so-called uncle, and she returned his tenderness with a settled intention of drawing him from his trouble, and humouring him in a disposition which he sometimes showed, of trying to make her a substitute for his little daughter, and cheating himself into the fancy that she was his own child.

So the time passed, with little variation, till Marion was sixteen. There was no sudden change in her, though now she looked nearly a woman.

Her affections had dawned early, and as she approached the borders of womanhood her face retained, in a great degree, the tender expression which had marked it in childhood; and though she was tall for her years, her figure was exceedingly youthful, and her manner, without affectation, was made up of an interesting compound of the woman and the child.

About this time Dora and Elizabeth, Marion's two cousins, came to spend a week with her; their father was about to take them a tour in Wales, and, as Swanstead was in their way, he sent them forward with an old servant, to stay there with his sister and her children till he was able to join them.

The cousins had not met for two years, and were all very much altered. Dora and Elizabeth were very unlike each other in person, manners, voice, and even in dress,—that minor circumstance which often gives an apparent likeness to sisters. Dora was rather tall, and had a very graceful figure; she was pale, had dark hair, dark grey eyes, and a grave expression.

Elizabeth, on the contrary, had brown eyes, a very high colour, a quantity of curling brown hair, and something remarkably lively in her manner and elastic in her movements. Dora was so very retiring and silent in society, that Elizabeth, without any intention on her own part, had been gradually drawn on to take the lead; and as she was very much at her ease in all situations she generally passed for a clever and interesting young woman, though her talents were decidedly inferior to her sister's.

Two years, at their time of life, was a long time to have been separated, and their fancy that they knew each other intimately because they now corresponded freely, melted away after the first half-hour's conversation. Marion could not help feeling, in spite of their familiar, sister-like greeting, that they were two strange young ladies. She could scarcely believe that Elizabeth was only two years older than herself; and if they had not begun to talk about their aunt would have been abashed by their earnest gazing at her.

"Does my aunt lie on the sofa every evening?" asked Dora, while Marion was taking them up stairs.

"O yes, always. Mamma has done so almost ever since I can remember."

"How much older you look, Marion," said Elizabeth. "I declare you are taller than I am."

"Yes," said Dora, thoughtfully; and then added, "My aunt looks much older, too."

"I hope you don't think mamma looking ill?" asked Marion.

"O no," exclaimed Elizabeth, laughing. "Dora,

how grave you are; you frighten this little thing, —look how she colours. You don't think my aunt looking ill?"

"No," said Dora, turning from the glass and drawing her bonnet-strings through her fingers, "but she certainly looks much older."

"Well," said Elizabeth, giving her sister a gentle push, "and of course she is older, you silly thing! You know my aunt was not young when she married. You are getting fearfully old yourself. Marion, did you know that Dora was out of her teens?"

Marion had not time to answer when Elizabeth, who had sauntered to a window, exclaimed, "Here is Mr. Raeburn coming up the drive, and Mr. Maidley with him. How I disliked Mr. Maidley when I was a child; he used to tease me so. Marion, how is that clever son of his?"

"Frank? Oh, he is very well."

"Is his hair as red as ever?"

"Quite; and he never sees me without asking after you, Elizabeth."

"The dear youth! The time before last that I came here, we were devoted to each other. I remember I thought myself quite a young lady, and was offended because I had to come down one morning and see Mr. Maidley in my morning pink gingham frock with short sleeves. Frank was with him, and gave me some delicious toffy. I remember the taste of it to this day."

"They will stay to tea," said Marion, "and I must go down and make it, dear Elizabeth. Mamma will be tired if she is left alone to talk to them."

"Oh, we are quite ready, my dear; let us all come down together. Then my aunt is easily tired, is she Marion?"

"Yes," said Marion, disturbed to perceive that they both observed a change in her mother which had escaped her own observation; but, during tea, she could not help thinking her cousins had alarmed her needlessly. Her mother was in high spirits, and seemed quite amused with Elizabeth's lively conversation. Their guests, also, were inclined to be more than usually talkative, and had a great many questions to ask.

Elizabeth's letters had lately been very full of the praises of a certain Mr. Dreux—quite a young man, —who had lately come to the town. His personal appearance she had described with minute accuracy; and in the same page with the laudits upon his delightful dark eyes, and his fine voice, was a great deal about High Church and Low Church, and several other things, which Marion did not know very much about.

Marion was very curious to hear something more about this said Mr. Dreux. She was therefore pleased when his name was mentioned to hear Elizabeth launch out in his praise, though she observed that Mr. Raeburn listened without much enthusiasm. That might be, she thought, because he did not like to hear young ladies talk in that high-flown style of panegyric about a clergyman. But Elizabeth continued to descant on Mr. Dreux's various excellencies for some time with great animation, till, happening to observe that she was sure he merited a higher sphere, and she hoped he would not long be a curate, the grave manner of Mr. Raeburn's bow, in reply, caused it to flash across her mind that Mr. Dreux had an uncle in that very neighbourhood, who, it was said, had promised him the next presentation to a certain living. " Now, if it should happen to be this living," thought Elizabeth, " what an awkward mistake I have made !"

She was rather confirmed in the idea that this might be the case, by observing that Mr. Maidley immediately began to talk to her about her native place, and about her friends and occupations, with great apparent interest.

" ' Religion walks in her silver slippers ' at Westport," he observed, in answer to one of her remarks.

Elizabeth smilingly assented.

" In fact," she said, " the clergy are all in all there ; their opinions are consulted even on indifferent subjects with the utmost deference."

" It was so when I served my first curacy there," remarked Mr. Raeburn, composedly sipping his coffee. " Westport is a very priest-ridden place."

" Very what ?" asked Mr. Maidley, laughing.

Elizabeth thought the assertion so extraordinary that she did not attempt to conceal her amazement; and as Mr. Raeburn chose to appear quite unconscious that he had said anything remarkable, and she could not make up her mind whether he was in joke or earnest, she glanced at her aunt with an expression of annoyance.

" I think my niece would like some explanation," said Mrs. Greyson, smiling. " I am sure she has never heard the term priest-ridden applied to Westport before."

" No, indeed," said Elizabeth, laughing, but with the slightest possible shrug of contempt.

Mr. Raeburn did not seem disposed to comply with the request.

" Tiresome man !" thought Elizabeth; " he was always prosy; but I never heard him talk in this ridiculous way before."

" Will you favour us with a definition of the word, Miss Paton, as you take so much exception to it ?" asked Mr. Maidley.

" Oh, I know perfectly well what it means, of course, Mr. Maidley," said Elizabeth; " but I always thought it applied exclusively to Roman Catholic countries, particularly to Ireland."

" If it simply means, governed by priests, I think you ought in conscience to forgive Mr. Raeburn; but perhaps you objected to the expression because it is generally used to denote not simply govern-

ment by priests, but bad government by priests,—
not because it is a reproach to any people to be
under subjection to a priesthood."

Elizabeth again replied that she did not like the
expression, because she had heard it applied to the
Irish, and it implied pity for them. "Now, the
idea," she added, "of our being pitied at Westport!
We who have such active and excellent clergymen,
whose churches are all crowded. I have often
heard strangers say that Westport was quite a
model place. The people are so remarkably moral,
and evangelical religion has made such great
advances."

"And who are at the head of it all?"

"Oh, the clergy, of course," replied Elizabeth.

"Then you do not at all wish to qualify your
assertion, that they are the governing spirits of the
place?"

"No," said Elizabeth, anticipating what he
might have said further; "but who so fit to
preside—who would lead better? I think," she
added, quite forgetting that she was taking the
wrong side of the argument,—"I think it is a very
good thing, and we ought to be extremely thankful
that we have such excellent men to guide us, and
tell us what we ought to do, and to save us the
constant trouble of thinking for ourselves; besides,
we are expressly told to "obey those who are set
over us.'"

"Certainly," said Mr. Raeburn, taking up the

conversation; "but you are also commanded to 'try the spirits,' which, I presume, means something entirely opposed to unhesitatingly adopting any line of conduct or principle pointed out, just to save the trouble of thinking for yourselves."

Elizabeth blushed, and felt annoyed—not because her faith in the strength of her own position was shaken, but because she felt that her admission of want of thought must have weakened it in the eyes of her opponents. "I cannot see," she said, addressing Mr. Maidley, "how it can be otherwise than good to be swayed as we are by the clergy, provided they always sway us in the right direction. They must preside, for instance, at all the religious meetings."

"To be sure," said the Rector, looking pointedly at Mr. Maidley. "What's the use of asking a layman to speak?"

"I cannot speak fit to be heard," said Mr. Maidley, evidently parrying a personal thrust. "I should make the best cause ridiculous by my way of advocating it."

Mr. Raeburn laughed, but almost instantly sighed heavily, and beckoned to Marion to come and sit beside him on the sofa; presently, after saying, in a half bantering tone, to Elizabeth, "I am afraid you are in a terrible state of bondage, Miss Paton, like the other good people at Westport."

"So he really means it," thought Elizabeth. "What a queer old gentleman he is!"

" So we are a priest-ridden set!" she said, half laughing, to Mr. Maidley.

" Remember that the expression was not mine, Miss Paton," was the reply. " I by no means adopt it as the expression of my mind. I, for my part, should be sorry to convey the slightest reflection upon the clergy of Westport ; for the defects of that place (and I certainly think it has great defects,) I entirely blame the people, principally the young people, and among the young I think the greatest offenders are the young ladies."

" There, Elizabeth !" said her aunt ; " now I think you have an undoubted right to demand an explanation : this is bringing the matter very near home."

" Really, I cannot in the least understand what we have done ; I do not feel at all guilty. First, you seem to say that we are governed by our clergy ; secondly, that it ought not to be so ; and yet, thirdly, that it is not their fault if they do govern us, but everything amiss is the fault of the young ladies."

" No, I must alter your propositions a little. First, it was *you* who said you were governed by your clergy. It was, secondly, Mr. Raeburn who said that ought not to be ; and it was I who intimated that I blamed the conduct of the young ladies."

" Well, *I* think everything is right and delightful at Westport. So when you have told me what you find amiss, Mr. Maidley, I do not promise to be penitent."

"Remember that I am far from imputing it to the clergy as a fault that they take the trouble to rule. In this instance, as they happen to rule well, there is little to regret."

"As they *happen* to rule well?"

"Certainly; for when people have been in the habit of implicitly receiving as truth what has been set before them, thus, however unconsciously, giving the attribute of infallibility to their spiritual guides; where they have been accustomed to allow themselves to be led blindfold, even in the *right* way, they must, by this voluntary humility, this disuse of their own reason, have so much weakened it, that if a time comes for judging and discerning,—if the man who had led them one way is taken from them, and another stands up in his place who wants to lead them in the opposite direction,—the habit of dependance and reliance on another mind may very likely have become so strong, that, as they gave up the helm to the one to guide them right, they will leave it with the other to guide them wrong."

"Yes, perhaps so; but that applies both ways, Mr. Maidley."

"So it does, it is of universal application; but I do not think it is therefore the less to be deplored. If it is the fashion in any place to make a profession of serious religion, crowds will profess; and whichever party is the fashion will have plenty of so-called adherents so long as it remains in undisputed possession of the field. But let another party come up,

—no matter whether a good or bad one,—opinions change like a tide, and long-cherished sentiments melt away like frost-work; and this must be the case where people follow, not a system of doctrine, but a favourite preacher. Instead of holding to the one eternal standard, they go to Mr. So-and-so's church, and there, they think, 'whatever *is*, is right.'"

"And do you seriously think that people who have been accustomed to truth will not at once detect error and reject it?"

"Those would, undoubtedly," said Mr. Raeburn, "who had loved truth for its own sake, knowing it to be such, having a reasonable conviction of its power, and a personal certainty of its goodness. But in a large congregation, principally composed of the young, where the minister himself is young, popular, and amiable, and well calculated to attract regard, I should expect to find great numbers who hear with so little discrimination, so little exercise of their minds, that if he were some day to get up and advance something quite different to his usual teaching, they would scarcely remark or attend to it. And if we add to these (the perfectly thoughtless), that mass of people who hear the man, not for the sake of his message, but for his own sake,—those particularly among the poor to whom he may have become personally endeared for kindness done to them in times of sickness and distress, and who adopt and detail his opinions, even the most unimportant, simply because they are *his;* and those among the young, who actually excite one another to believe that they are deeply attached to the ministry of this man or that man, making their very profession appear ridiculous by their forgetfulness how much personal regard and admiration may have to do with their religious raptures,—if we add all these together, how few will be left whose intelligence on religious matters is sufficiently alive to enable them to discern error, if it should be taught by any whom they have hitherto looked up to. Only imagine what would be the state of the church where your favourite Mr. Dreux officiates, if anything so lamentable should occur as his taking up erroneous doctrine. It is difficult for a popular man to prevent his people from setting him up as a standard; they think less of his opinions than of himself. How many people would change, do you think, if Mr. Dreux should change?"

"Oh, I don't know, Mr. Raeburn; perhaps half of them."

"And yet you would not blame the clergy so much, where this is the case, as the people," said Dora.

"No, because the best teaching is nearly useless (humanly speaking) where there is a want of intelligence in the learners; people would be ashamed to remain in as much ignorance of politics, literature, or even science, as they do contentedly of religion—I do not mean of the practical part of religion, of devotional feelings, or moral maxims, I mean of what may be called the *theory* of religion —those *principles* without which no practice of outward duty can avail. There are thousands of well-educated people in this country who could not give a correct, distinct account of the difference between the English Church and the Church of Rome; and there are thousands more who know nothing, or at least could give no intelligent account of the great parties which exist within the Church of England, and which are divided as by vast gulfs from one another."

" I suppose you mean the High Church and the Evangelical, and the old Moral school; but as all these are called Church people, it seems natural to conclude that they are nearly alike."

" To be sure it seems natural, as you say; but don't you think the Church people in this country ought to know enough of the doctrines they profess to uphold, to be able to say whether their ministers are faithful or not. The Church, as an institution, is for the people; the clergy minister to and for the people, not for themselves. If they cannot discriminate in what good teaching consists, they are scarcely the better for it. The misfortune is, that they often consider it an act of presumption to judge of it, instead of an act of duty."

" But if people are to be encouraged to judge."

said Elizabeth, "surely it will encourage a censorious spirit—surely it will make them presumptuous."

" My dear, you are differing from me *now* on a subject of some importance."

"Ah, but it is only in conversation; you know all clergymen do not think with you, Mr. Raeburn."

" To be sure not; so now I have brought you to a point where you must presume to judge for yourself."

Elizabeth laughed, and said, " Ah, but it has not the consequence which need make me fear so much to judge for myself."

" Now there we differ again, for I say it is a matter of great consequence."

" Go on, Elizabeth," said her aunt, " you see you are encouraged to have an opinion of your own."

"I must say," proceeded Elizabeth, " that I think in some congregations they are very fond of judging, and are always criticising some clergyman or other."

"There we come to a point of agreement. I have known several cases where a censorious spirit has been manifested, but I almost always found that it exercised itself about trifles. ' This man's voice was harsh; that man's manner was offensive; this sermon was too long, and that was badly delivered ;' but if the true spirit of discrimination was abroad, if people considered it in all cases their duty to know whether they heard what was true, and

H

to know why—then, I think, the censorious spirit about trifles would nearly disappear; it is only a man incapable of appreciating a fine picture who draws your attention to a spot of dust on the frame. Those whose attention is absorbed by the important matter of a sermon, are the least likely to quarrel with its manner. You must not try to put off your own responsibility, you know. You cannot really shift it to any one else's shoulders."

"Then," said Elizabeth, half laughing, "it is still not our fault; we ought to be taught a little more self-dependance: and perhaps it would save our clergymen a good deal of anxiety in the end, and trouble too."

"The trouble, for instance, of leading you all your lives in leading-strings. Well, but if instead of so much religious enthusiasm and excitement, there was a more steady, serious, and reasonable value for the great truths of Christianity, I do not think the clergy would find themselves deprived of any of the respect which is due to their office; on the contrary, I should expect to find those who hitherto, from want of talent or from natural manner, had never been acceptable, though faithful and devoted, would meet with regard for their works' sake; and those now popular would still possess the love of their people, but it would be given from a better motive."

"Well, Elizabeth," said her aunt, "you and Dora are both come to years of discretion; do you mean to take any part of this censure to yourselves—does it apply to you?"

"Yes," said Elizabeth, in a doubtful tone, "it does in some degree; but that does not make us the chief offenders; I know of nothing particular that we have done."

"What! nothing particular!" exclaimed Mr. Maidley; "do you call adulation nothing particular? Is there nothing dangerous to a young man in the flattery and admiration of your sex?"

"Oh," said Elizabeth, "I cannot think *that* would have any effect; I am sure Mr. Lodge and Mr. Dreux, and a good many others whom I could name, are quite above any such influence. The idea of such excellent men feeling flattered and pleased by the attentions of a few girls seems to me quite derogatory."

"I don't mean to say," returned her antagonist, "that I think any man of sense can be pleased at the *way* in which these feelings sometimes show themselves. I know a man who told me he had had six and thirty pairs of slippers given him, some of them lined with white satin. I heard of another, who had thirteen pocket-handkerchiefs given him, worked in the corner with hair."

"Oh, Mr. Maidley," said Mrs. Greyson, "are you quite sure that anecdote is authentic; it sounds very like a malicious invention."

"Quite true, I assure you, and the same man had

a bouquet of flowers sent him every morning for his table."

Elizabeth blushed and looked uncomfortable ; perhaps she remembered one or two things which had taken place at Westport which were uncommonly like the above anecdote. She, however, repeated her assertion, that she was sure, quite sure, Mr. Dreux was not in the least influenced by the admiration his character could not fail to excite ; that, in fact, he was so superior to young ladies of any rank or order that he could not possibly be hurt by their attentions (if he ever observed them), or tempted in the least to alter his course for the sake of pleasing them.

" Oh," said Mr. Raeburn, rising, " if he is such a paragon as that comes to, of course we have nothing more to say. If this excellent, handsome, and devoted young bachelor is quite beyond all earthly temptations, if he is above the reach of flattery which has tempted and swayed the highest potentates, beyond that influence which stole away King Solomon's heart and lost our first father his place in Paradise— "

" Oh," exclaimed Elizabeth, interrupting, very much vexed, " I did not mean to make such an assertion. I only intended— "

" We'll hear his defence to-morrow. Maidley, we are late already."

" What a provoking man Mr. Raeburn is," said

Elizabeth, turning to watch the two gentlemen as they walked briskly down the drive. "The idea of his calling Mr. Dreux a handsome and devoted young bachelor! A paragon, indeed! I am certain he meant to infer that I at least thought him one. However," she added, laughing, and recovering her good humour, "he need not be afraid lest people should make an idol of *him !*"

"I am not so sure of that. The people here are more than commonly attached to him."

"Ah, just the poor, because he is so good to them, takes notice of their children, and talks to them all familiarly by name."

"Well, perhaps it was jealousy then that made him speak in such a slighting manner of popularity," said her aunt in an ironical tone. "Do you think that will account for it, my dear ?"

"No ; but really, aunt," said Elizabeth, laughing, "it was very provoking. I am sure he was laughing at me ; I saw his eyes twinkle, though his face was so grave."

CHAPTER V.

THE COWSLIP PICKING.

THE next day was hot and rainy; the three girls had their work carried to a thatched arbour in the garden, and followed themselves, with umbrellas.

There they could talk at their ease; and very much they amused Marion, and surprised her not a little; they had a piquant way of relating things, and detailed a great deal of religious gossip for her edification; for everything they said was, as it were, tinctured with religion, and yet in a way which conveyed more the idea that they lived in a religious atmosphere, than that their own minds were deeply imbued with its solemnities.

Mr. Dreux was described over again with minute accuracy, and old Mr. King, his Rector, who was also a very good man, it appeared, only he had a wooden leg—a cork one at least—which had a joint at the knee, and this joint creaked sometimes, and made foolish people laugh.

Marion was very much amused with her two cousins, but began to perceive that she had not

much in common with them, and liked their con_
versation best when they talked least about religion.
This was wrong, she supposed, and she tried to overcome it, but without much success, and as, in spite of
these differences between them, the three cousins
were very much attracted towards each other, they
easily found conversation which was equally pleasant
to all.

The next morning was more than commonly fine,
and they rose early to walk in the garden before
breakfast.

"Well, Marion," said Mrs. Greyson, when she
came down, "have you thought of any plan for
amusing your cousins to-day?"

"We can have a drive in the evening, mamma;
but for this morning Dora and Elizabeth have
thought of something for themselves."

"What is it, my dears?"

"Marion told us yesterday that the maids from
the rectory and two of your servants were going to
join at a grand cowslip picking for cowslip wine;
we thought we should enjoy of all things to go and
help, for it is not very hot."

"And we could choose the meadows along the
side of the wood," said Marion, "where there is a
long line of shade, and afterwards sit in the open
air under that great clump of lime trees, and pick
out the blossoms."

"That will be a very good plan of spending the

morning, and if you like, you shall have your dinner brought out."

Directly after breakfast the maids sent in word that they were ready, and Dora and Elizabeth went into the hall to look at them. Each had got a large bag fastened in front of her apron to hold the blossoms, and the gardener was going to carry a clothes-basket into the meadow for the " pips," as the flowers are called by the cowslip gatherers.

The young women looked very happy in the prospect of their annual day's pleasure ; each one had brought a basket of provisions on her arm. The young ladies also looked all the more blooming for their delight, as they tied on the largest bonnets the house afforded and set off, under Marion's escort, about half an hour after the maids.

"What an enchanting day !" they exclaimed, as they emerged from the garden and entered a broad meadow covered with cowslips, orchises, and the beautiful meadow-sweet. "We shall soon fill our baskets here."

But Marion said it would not do to stay there, the sun was too hot ; they must go through this meadow and several others, till they reached the skirts of Swanstead-wood.

It mattered very little to Dora and Elizabeth where they went, or what they did, so long as they were under the open sky in the meadows. They wandered along with a sense of freedom and delight which increased as the morning advanced, and amused themselves with observing how the rich landscape changed with their change of position.

At length they reached the meadow by the wood, and found that the maids had already gathered quite a rick of cowslips, which were ostentatiously heaped up, and made a great show in the shade.

Marion and her cousins now set to work to gather a rival heap; but there were so many things to be seen, so many trees to be admired, and so many little points of view which each must call the other to see, that their rick made a very poor figure beside that of their more industrious contemporaries, who kept at first a sufficient distance to enable each party to talk without being overheard by the other.

"How happy they look!" said Marion, turning to look at the maids, wh were evidently enjoying the change from their ordinary occupations.

"Yes, and how happy everything looks, Marion. We must go down to the river's brink; there must be such a delightful air there, and we can keep in the shade nearly all the way."

The river wound along one end of this meadow, and went through the thickest part of the wood. It was brimful of water, and as smooth as glass.

They stood for some minutes beside it, listening to the lapse of the water, and looking down the long arch of trees which met over it in the wood, where it became a perfectly green river in the clearest shade imaginable.

" If there was but a boat," said Elizabeth, "how delightful it would be to sit on the water under that arch of trees, and there pick out the cowslip blossoms !"

" There is a boat somewhere in the wood," said Marion, "and if the path is not very much overgrown I can find it. But we must let the maids know where we are going, that they may tell mamma how to find us when she comes."

The maids entered with great cordiality into this scheme of the young ladies; and as the latter had not gathered more than a peck of cowslips altogether, these generous rivals proposed to carry a quantity of their own booty into the boat for them.

The wood was alive with birds; and when they had made their way to the water's edge, they had some difficulty in finding the low, flat-roofed boathouse, so completely were the banks overgrown with six-feet-high bulrushes.

At last the dairy-maid discovered it, and then the next difficulty was to float the boat out, and get it clear of the rushes. This the same young woman effected, previously emptying her apron-full of cowslip-blossoms into it, and receiving the contributions of her companions. The boat was moored to the shed by a rope, and now the dairy-maid had to be pulled back that she might land. This the inmates of the boat easily effected; and the rope being only about five yards long, was no sooner fastened, than the slight onward movement of the water turned the boat's head gently down the stream, and they commenced their pleasant task, completely over-canopied by the green ash and maple trees on each side of the river.

" This really is felicity!" said Elizabeth, as she looked up among the thick branches, and saw the sunbeams shooting aslant in the tree-tops of their roof.

Marion took off her bonnet, and the delightful air moved her luxuriant hair.

"Look down into the water, Dora," she said; " see how full it is of tiny little fishes. I am glad we thought of coming here. It must be very hot by this time in the open meadows. See, Elizabeth, here is a nest!"

Marion said this with the composure of a person who can see a nest any day; but Dora and Elizabeth were wild with delight.

" Oh! don't stand up in such a hurry!" cried Marion. " See how you have made the boat rock!"

There was a branch of maple hanging down over Marion's head, quite into the boat, with a white-throat's nest depending from it. It was formed without of hay and grass, and lined with horsehair and a few tufts of wool. When she had gathered some of the leaves it was distinctly visible.

" Look at the beautiful eggs!—pink, with brown

veins. If we sit perfectly still, I dare say the mother will come back. Whitethroats are very bold birds."

They did accordingly sit perfectly still for some time, and picked a basket full of "pips;" but after a while they forgot themselves, and began to talk and laugh without any reference to the supposed terrors of the bird.

"The poor little creature!—how frightened she must have been," said Elizabeth, in a tone of regret, when she remembered her broken resolution. "I am afraid her eggs must be quite cold by this time."

Marion laughed. "Look up, Elizabeth," she said, "and do not make any exclamation."

Elizabeth looked up. "I see two black eyes peeping out at me," she said. "Oh! the beautiful little creature! But how keenly she watches us, and how fast she turns her head from side to side."

"Take no further notice of her," said Marion, "and she will sit on. I wish mamma would come. What a long time she is!"

"Can my aunt walk so far from home?"

"Oh, no!" and again Marion felt troubled. "But she will have the pony. There is a bridle-path through the meadows; she will only walk through the wood."

The morning wore on more quickly than they were aware. It was enlivened by the light species of work in which they were engaged, and diversified by such slight incidents as the playing of a larger fish than ordinary about their boat, the sudden splash of the water when a pike made a spring after the flies, or the leisurely floating towards them of a whole family of sleepy-looking waterhens, and their precipitate rush into the reeds when they beheld the human faces.

As the sun got high the reflection of the trees in the water became greener and more distinct, and the round spots of sunshine more yellow and bright.

Many country sounds floated down the river and made the solitude quite musical. There were the thousand voices of the rookery, so distant that any little wren who chose to perch near could drown them with his merry chirrup. There were the thrushes singing, and the jays chattering in the wood, the water-rats splashing, and every quarter of an hour there was the striking of Swanstead clock.

"It struck a quarter to one just now," said Elizabeth, beginning to fan herself with her straw-hat ; "if we are industrious we shall finish these flowers in a quarter of an hour."

"Of course we shall dine here," said Dora ; "there would be room for six or eight people in such a boat as this."

It may be observed of the said boat, that it had neither seats nor oars, so that the inhabitants could recline in its flat bottom with great elegance, as in a canoe.

At the moment the clock struck two the party became aware of a little creaking sound in the wood, as of some one treading down dead twigs. The sound approached, and presently Mr. Raeburn appeared, making his way among the trees and talking to himself as he wandered, with his hands in his pockets, towards the boat. He was in a fit of abstraction, and evidently had not come into the wood to look for them.

The girls looked at each other and smiled, as they just caught a word here and there of his soliloquy. He was just passing, when a clear merry laugh caught his attention and caused him to turn hastily.

" Well !" exclaimed the Rector, in a tone of perplexity, " I could have declared I heard some one laugh."

The girls made signs to each other to be quiet.

" Very odd," he continued, looking up into the trees, as if they were his last resource. " I could have declared it was just at my elbow."

" So could I," replied a voice from the water.

But the sound had to pass through the stalks of so many reeds that he was still undecided as to its direction, and gazed about him some time before he saw the white dresses of the girls and their bright hair, which they had decorated with chaplets of the idean-vine, some wreaths of which hung down from the trees.

"Do come in, uncle," said Marion, "we are going to dine here."

"My dears, you don't want me," he replied, looking down on their smiling faces with affectionate admiration.

"O yes, indeed we do, Mr. Raeburn," cried Elizabeth; "pray come and join us."

Mr. Raeburn turned and saw a cavalcade advancing slowly through the wood, with the dairy-maid at the head and the gardener behind, bringing various baskets covered with vine-leaves, and presenting a tempting appearance. Presently Mrs. Greyson appeared, and seemed rather dismayed when she saw the floating nature of their asylum. She, however, consented to dine on board with them; and, with Mr. Raeburn's help and the dairy-maid's, the embarkation of herself, a cold fowl, a cold custard-pudding, a basket of strawberries, and sundry knives, forks, and plates, was easily effected, after which Mr. Raeburn joined the party, and they commenced their noon-day meal with infinite relish.

The dairy-maid, who remained standing on the bank, was dismissed, with an injunction to bring a quantity more cowslips to be picked. And the girls showed their nest to the new-comers with as much delight as if it had been "treasure trove" of a kind never before seen in those parts.

"O the delightful sky!" said Marion, looking up through a gap in the trees; "how blue it is."

"O the delightful child, how happy she is,"—

"Dear uncle, you are always so pleased with us for being happy. You seem to think it a kind of merit in us to enjoy ourselves. But, uncle—but, mamma," continued Marion, appealing to her mother with more gravity and earnestness than the occasion seemed to call for, "don't you think it is quite time my uncle left off calling me a child, considering that I am sixteen; and considering"—

"Considering that I am already as tall as my mother," said Mr. Raeburn, taking up her words.

Marion, who was seated close to Mr. Raeburn, and supporting herself on her elbow, looked up at him, and answered:—"No; but really, uncle, if people always hear you say, 'My child,' they will never remember that I am nearly grown up."

"So you are sixteen, my dear," said the Rector, taking up one of Marion's small hands and spreading out the fingers upon his own large palm. "Well, I suppose you think it is something to be sixteen. Why, I shall be eight or nine and forty in a few days, and I do not expect to feel at all proud on the occasion."

Dora looked at Marion as she still continued with her blue eyes fixed on the Rector's face, and thought she had never seen anything more exquisitely

childlike than the tender expression of her guileless
face.

" O no, uncle," she answered, with perfect simplicity ; " I am not at all proud; but I think you
talk to me more as if I were a child than you do to
other girls of my age."

" If I do, it is because I love you more."

" When you are a few years older, Marion," said
her mother, " you will wish you could have people
who are .fond of you say as they do now,—' We
must excuse her for this or that little act of folly,
for she is but a child.' "

Marion smiled a half-incredulous smile, and held
out her hand for a leaf full of strawberries which
her mother had selected for Mr. Raeburn.

" So you young ladies have actually brought
books with you," said he, as she gave them to him.
" This must have been your doing, Miss Paton, for
I cannot give Marion credit for being so studious."
As he spoke he brought up two large volumes from
the bottom of the boat.

" Yes, I acknowledge that I brought them," said
Dora, " but they have never been opened."

" Something about Nineveh, and 'Modern Painters.' Well, I suppose you preferred to study the
book of nature this beautiful day." He continued
to turn over the leaves, and presently read aloud
the . following sentences from the last-mentioned
book :—

" ' The noblest scenes of the *earth* can be known

I

and seen but by few. It is not intended that man should live always in the midst of them. He injures them by his presence; he ceases to feel them if he is always with them; but the *sky* is for all. Bright as it is, it is not "too bright nor good for human nature's daily food." It is fitted in all its functions for the perpetual comfort and exalting of the heart. . . . And yet we never attend to it—we never make it a subject of thought but as it has to do with our diurnal sensations. We look upon all by which it speaks to us more clearly than to brutes—upon all which bears witness to the intention of the Supreme, that we are to receive more from the covering vault than the light and the dew, which we share with the weed and the worm— only as a succession of meaningless and monotonous accident, too common and too vain to be worthy of a moment of thought or a glance of admiration. If in a moment of utter idleness and insipidity we turn to the sky as a last resource, which of its phenomena do we speak of? One says it has been wet, and another, it has been windy, and another, it has been warm.'

" Sweeping censure this, Miss Paton. Do you plead guilty?"

" No," said Dora; "but I do think the study of the beautiful for its own sake seems very little thought of, especially the looking for it in simple external things."

" The spirit of the age is certainly very matter-of-fact, both in a religious, social, and political point of view. Marion, my dear child—my dear young woman, I mean—what are you about? you must not lean over so much to my side ; you make the boat rock. Actually, while we talk about the spirit of the age, that child thinks of nothing but cowslip stalks ! "

" I am listening, uncle, indeed," said Marion ; " but here come the fresh cowslips."

" Listen or not as you like, child ; I don't know that our talk was worth hearing."

" There are some interesting passages in that book about the clouds," said Dora ; " do you remember them, aunt ? "

" Yes ; but I do not agree with the author, that mankind in general are unobservant of the appearance of the sky. Perhaps we have not so many persevering cloud-gazers as star-gazers ; and there are certainly a vast number of people who go through the world with their eyes shut ; but I think all who do observe, observe the sky."

" I cannot recal any beautiful landscape that I have seen," said Dora, " without also remembering what kind of sky made up its background."

" And how full the poets are of cloud-and-sky scenes," remarked Elizabeth. " Do you remember, aunt, in those lines called ' Mathew,' how beautifully, after describing the feelings of the old man on going out with his fishing-rod, Wordsworth makes the presence of a certain cloud hanging in the sky remind him of an April morning thirty years ago, and he says—

> " ' My eyes are dim with childish tears,
>   My heart is idly stirred ;
> For the same sounds are in my ears
>   That on *that* day I heard.'

And then he goes on to compare ' yon cloud with that long purple cleft ' with the cloud seen in his youth, and treasured in his memory for so many years."

" And what can be more exquisite than that cloud, which we all fancy we must have seen, in Wilson's sonnet, beginning—

> " ' A cloud lay cradled near the setting sun,
>   A gleam of crimson tinged its braided snow.'

Surely every line of that sonnet is beautiful ; but our sense of its beauty is chiefly derived from our all having observed and delighted in such a cloud. But whether or not, we may be justly accused of neglecting to derive instruction and pleasure from the sky : it is certain that, in general, we do not pay sufficient attention to the beauty of natural objects."

" But, aunt, I thought the prevailing fault at present was said to be a kind of worship of nature. In fact, to hear some people talk, one would almost think that if we only listened with sufficient reverence to the teachings of nature, there would be no need of revelation at all."

" I was not thinking of such persons, my dear ; it is some of those who recognise the highest principles that I think deficient in a due acknowledgment of the beauty that surrounds them. If we shut our eyes to the beauty which lives and breathes around us, we act ungratefully, and do not enjoy all the happiness intended for us."

" Mamma," said Marion, " look."

Mrs. Greyson turned and looked down the smooth river. Sunbeams slanted across it, and here and there touched the water or the leaves. Some water-hens were diving at no great distance, and the green reflection of the trees lay in vivid distinctness all around them. But it was not to any of these things that Marion had wished to call attention. Through the gap in the branches one pure white cloud was visible, lying, small and distinct, in the deep sky, and its image, like a white swan, was reflected down into the water.

It was too beautiful to talk of, Elizabeth said ; and they continued to watch it till it was gradually withdrawn.

" I shall add the recollection of that cloud to the list of my possessions," said Dora ; " it will be a pleasure to me in future that no outward circumstances can take from me—something absolutely my own."

" In addition to your harp, your watch, and your work-box, Dora," said Elizabeth, with her usual gay good humour.

" You are not at all romantic, I see, Miss Paton,"
remarked the Rector, with a smile.

" A good thing for me," returned Elizabeth, " for
I shall suit the better with the spirit of the age."

" I hope something better for you than that you
should suit with the age in most of its character-
istics," returned the Rector, speaking with his
accustomed hesitation ; " with its characteristic
industry, for instance, which, though it cannot
be happy unless it gets through a great deal of
work, wants to cast aside the labour of hand and
heart, and do it all in a delegated way, and, as it
were, by machinery.

" We even carry this desire into our religion, and
having set a great deal of religious machinery to
work, we are inclined to wonder that it does not
produce the regenerating effect we expected.

" But we are in a great hurry ; we cannot stop to
inquire the reason. We must have something to
exhibit for our trouble, and we must have it quickly.
Certainly our machinery has produced a great effect,
and if we have our misgivings as to whether it is a
good one, we are obliged to keep them to ourselves,
for there is so much to be acted that the time for
reflection is wanting.

" I should also be inclined to accuse the age of
imitating machinery in another way. A few ma-
chines will do the work of thousands of men ; they
act as agents and delegates, and take the labours
from human hands. Now, in our religion we have

come to think that we will have agents and delegates also. Great masses of people consider it too much trouble to think for themselves, or to undertake the duties, and study the principles of Christianity in their own persons. Virtually, they say to their priests, ' Do the labour of religion for us ; pray you the prayers we ought to offer up ; be our substitutes ; believe for us, act for us ; and in return we will give you a portion of our gold, which we will lay like a sacrifice upon the altar. We do not pray that fire from heaven may descend upon it, for the age is not superstitious, and we know that the days of miracles are passed.' So they satisfy their consciences. And as for that hidden influence which comes down like dew upon the tender herbs, it is unseen and unobtrusive, therefore often overlooked and forgotten ; for we have not time to look deeply into anything."

"My dear Mr. Raeburn," said Mrs. Greyson, "you are surely severe upon the age."

"Am I?" he answered, taking out his watch. "Yes, and there sits Marion, in a state of amazement ; she cannot tell what I mean. Do you know how time is slipping away ?—it is nearly four o'clock. I believe I must take my departure ; but can I first help you to land ?"

The girls reluctantly consented to leave their boat, but the heat of the sun was now moderated by a soft breeze, and as they had finished their cowslips they had no excuse for staying longer, so they stepped on shore, previously sending all the cowslip stalks floating down the river. The maids were quite delighted with the great mass of flowers that they found heaped up for them in the boat.

Mrs. Greyson rode home on a rough little pony, and Dora walked beside her. They passed the maids at the corner of the wood: they had lighted a fire, and hung their kettle to the branch of a tree, in true rural fashion. Elizabeth thought she should hardly have known the landscape, it was so much altered by the opposite direction of the shadows and the different lights on the water. She also began to feel her old liking for Mr. Raeburn revive ; and as he walked home with herself and Marion, one on each arm, his affectionate tenderness for the latter touched Elizabeth with a regretful interest, and imparted so much more gentleness to her manner, that she seemed altogether a different person ; and Marion could not but admire her face, so greatly were her eyes brightened and her complexion heightened. Mr. Raeburn took his leave after bringing them to their own door, and Marion asked her cousins to be quick in changing their morning dresses. " We are going to drink tea with the Maidleys," she said ; " we always do on alternate Thursdays."

" All your fashions in this part of the world are unchangeable," said Dora. " Are the Maidleys as fond of clever talk as ever ; and do they still always have Devonshire posset for supper ? "

" Mr. Maidley is very fond of instructing, and I

dare say he will show you either some geological specimens, or talk about botany: you know he has made a collection of dried plants. Mrs. Maidley is proud of her Devonshire cream ; so I dare say you will spend the evening much as you have done several former ones."

" 'I dare say !' Dora, how cautiously this little thing expresses herself ! ' Mr. Maidley is fond of instructing,' quoth she. Why don't you say at once, Marion, that he is determined to cram one with his learning, and that he is a great bore ?"

Marion laughed, but made no answer.

" I wish you would imitate her caution," said Dora.

" I did not intentionally speak with caution," replied Marion, and was going to add, " I do not dislike to be instructed," but remembered that she should thereby imply a reproach to Elizabeth.

Mr. Maidley was a brisk little man, with a light active figure, and restless observant eye, and such a love of acting the schoolmaster that he had educated both his own sons, and young Greyson also, though his means would very well have admitted of his sending them to school.

Mrs. Maidley was also a small person, and had a neat, delicate figure, and very quiet manners. This couple were blessed with five towering sons and daughters, two of the former and three of the latter ; they were magnified images of their parents, but their gait was less brisk, and their voices were louder and deeper. They all had red hair, easy, good-humoured manners, and imperturbable self-possession, which latter quality they certainly had not inherited from their mother, who sometimes looked a little flurried when they were all moving about round her ; their heads came so near the tops of the doors, and they so completely filled up their cottage home, that they gave her much the appearance of a nervous hen in possession of a turkey's brood.

But she was proud of them, and with reason. Never was a milder, more docile set of young giants. They were clever, too ; and both physically and intellectually they made Dora and Elizabeth look small.

They received their guests with vociferous joy ; but Frank had evidently forgotten his childish partiality for Elizabeth, and talked of nothing all the evening but some new chemical experiments, by which he declared he could blow up the world itself, if he could only get far enough into it. He was obliging enough to take a great deal of trouble in explaining the matter to the girls ; but they looked upon him as a tiresome, uninteresting youth, and did not even affect to care for his wonderful experiments.

As Dora had expected, they had some Devonshire posset for supper ; it appeared in a bowl suited to the dimensions of the young people, one of whom, however—namely, Peter, the younger son—was absent the greater part of the evening.

The wheels of Mrs. Greyson's phaeton were heard at the door before supper was quite over, but the whole party rose at once and proceeded to assist in cloaking and shawling, and what Will Greyson called the stowage of the craft. Mrs. Greyson and Will sat in front, the latter being steersman, and the three girls got in behind, together with a music-book that Dora had borrowed, and three pots full of choice young calceolarias, struck by Frank for Marion, also some geraniums, with their roots tied up in cabbage leaves, and some quinces,—for the Maidleys were bountiful people ; and they liked apple-pie for supper, and apple-pie flavoured with quinces ; so as Mrs. Greyson had no quinces in her garden they always provided her with an abundant supply.

The girls were wedged into the back of the carriage and had scarcely room to move, when Peter made his appearance, quite out of breath, with his straw hat full of nuts ; these he handed over the back of the carriage to Marion, a pair of crackers lying on the top of them.

" O Peter," exclaimed Marion, almost in despair, "Peter, do please take these back ; what am I to do with them ? It was extremely kind of you to get them, but you had better eat them yourself."

Peter was Marion's age, and was supposed to be tenderly affected towards her.

" No, Marion, keep them yourself," he gallantly answered, as he held on by the back of the carriage, which was already in motion, and going on at a foot's-pace with its load. "I went to Swanstead wood to get them. You can't think how milky they are. Eat as many as you can yourself, Marion. I'll come for my hat to-morrow. I've put in a pair of crackers, in case you and the Miss Patons would like some on the way home."

So saying he took his leave. Elizabeth made room for the plants, and Marion, with her lap full of nuts, commenced cracking them.

"What are you about, my dear?" said her mother, turning round. "What is that noise? I hope the springs are not giving way. What are you all laughing at?"

Elizabeth explained the cause.

"Ridiculous boy!" said the mamma, in a tone of some annoyance.

"But it was a chivalrous action," said Dora. "He rose from his untasted supper and darted off when we remarked that Marion used to be fond of nutting when she was a little child."

"Yes," said Elizabeth, "it really was something for *him* to do. What a pity it is those Maidleys should be so fond of eating!"

"Devoted to it," observed Will Greyson. "Do you know, mother, I have observed that almost all very clever people are fond of eating."

"Have you, my dear? I should not have thought you had many opportunities of judging."

"Now you mention it, Will, I really think I

have observed the same thing," said Elizabeth. "How can it be accounted for, aunt?"

"The fact must be established, my dear, before we need account for it. My boy, if you do not keep at a foot's-pace we shall certainly break down."

So at a foot's-pace they went home in the starlight, Marion cracking her nuts the while, and distributing them to the rest of the party.

"Elizabeth," said Dora, when they were alone in their room, "what a happy lot Marion's is; so free from all care and responsibility."

"Responsibility," repeated Elizabeth, laughing, "why, my dear Dora, she does not differ in that respect from you and me."

"Indeed, I don't agree with you. How can the eldest daughter in a large family be free from responsibility? She has at least her example to answer for. But the reason I think Marion so happy is that she is the first object of interest to several people; they think for her, and are as tender over her as if she really were a child. How serene she evidently is, and no wonder, so secure as she must be of affection, and such a life of quiet happiness as she has before her."

"But my aunt is in very delicate health," observed Elizabeth. "I am sure she was very different the last time we were here."

"Yes, she could walk with us. We shall see how papa thinks her looking when he comes."

Mrs. Greyson had a cold the next day, and did

not go out for an airing as usual. Dora recurred to her idea that her aunt was changed, but she could see no reflection of her anxiety in the faces of the old servants, and neither Marion nor Mr. Raeburn seemed to think anything particular the matter.

Their father arrived in a few days, and Dora resolved not to be an alarmist. The first time he was alone with his daughters he remarked upon her altered appearance.

"It was strange," he said, "that at her age she should be so infirm."

"My aunt has long been in weak health," said Elizabeth, "but if she was worse than usual her children would have mentioned it."

"True, true," he answered, and seemed glad to take his daughter's view of the subject; but it did not quite satisfy him, for he presently remarked that it would be very little out of his way to return to Westport by Swanstead and take another peep at his sister. "Besides," he added, "you are doubly related to these cousins, and I should not like you to grow up in ignorance of one another."

The girls were pleased with this plan; it made their parting with Márion quite a different matter, and their aunt brightened up so much during her brother's visit, that they left her without any apprehensions.

It was a brilliant morning. The dew lay thickly on the grass, for it had not struck five, when Dora and Elizabeth stole into their aunt's chamber to kiss her and take their leave. Marion was up and dressed; she made breakfast for them and packed strawberries and cake in a basket for their refreshment on the journey. The phaeton was at the door. Mr. Paton had persuaded his sister to let her son accompany him and his daughter, and Will Greyson, full of joy, was heaping it with luggage.

He ran softly up stairs to take leave of his mother.

"Now, my dears," exclaimed their uncle, "no more last words, or we shall certainly miss the train. Three weeks hence you will see us again, Marion. Come, my dear, let the boy go."

"I am coming, uncle," cried Will, getting up behind. "Take care of mamma, Marion; and mind you see that all my creatures are fed."

And so they drove off, leaving Marion standing in the porch, looking the picture of serenity.

"She is certainly born to be happy," thought Dora.

Both the girls were delighted with Marion, and they might have talked and thought about her more if they had not been in the full enjoyment of their first tour. The weather was faultless, and their father was so determined that they should see everything worth looking at, that they thought they had never been so happy before.

In three or four days they got a letter from Marion, inclosing a note from her mother to Will. She was delighted that he was enjoying himself so much, and thought she was all the better for the little peep she had had of her brother and his children.

"Now you will see, Dora," said Elizabeth, "that papa will not go home by Swanstead. I know he wishes to go up by the lakes, and my aunt's cheerful way of writing will determine him that there is nothing the matter."

The event proved that she was right. Other letters followed, all cheerful; and Mr. Paton gave out one morning at Chester, that he had changed his plans, and meant to travel northward.

"Poor Marion," said Dora, "she will be very much disappointed."

"Oh, papa will let us visit her in the winter," remarked Elizabeth; "and you know, Dora, you would not like to give up the lakes for the sake of seeing her again now."

"Certainly not. We are not required to do so. What is this scheme of papa's about Wilfred?"

"Have you not seen him since he wrote to my aunt? Oh, it is to ask her if she will let him go abroad."

"My aunt will not like to part with him while he is so young."

"But papa thinks he ought to see a little of the world,—he is such a child for his years; and no wonder, always living in that country-place. Besides, Mr. Lodge is going abroad with his three pupils, and told papa he should like to take another.

My aunt cannot fail to see what a good opportunity this would be for Will to go with safety and advantage; and they are only to be away two months."

Two or three days after this, as the party were strolling on the borders of Windermere, Mr. Paton drew Will aside and informed him, with a little stately circumlocution, of a letter received that morning consenting to the plan above mentioned. Wilfred was wild with delight; a tour in Switzerland was a hitherto unhoped-for bliss. He could not be grateful enough to his uncle for having planned it.

He set off that same night with a letter of introduction from his uncle to Mr. Lodge, previously writing home to his mother to thank her for her kindness.

The Paton family then pursued their tour, and it must be confessed that they enjoyed it more now their restless cousin was withdrawn. Dora felt it a "responsibility" to have him with them, for he was a daring, inquisitive boy; he loved climbing among ruins; and made her very nervous by his determination to see all he could of the machinery whenever they took him with them over a manufactory.

They returned to Westport, having heard several times from Marion during their absence. In the first letter she said her mother was much as usual, only that the hot weather made her languid; in the next she spoke of her as poorly, but said nothing to excite alarm.   Dora, however, was of an anxious disposition, and though Marion said so little she began to wish they had not sent Will Greyson away ; but the sight of her mother, her brother and sister, and her cheerful home, banished these thoughts for a while, and she and Elizabeth retired to rest very much fatigued.

It was late when they awoke the next morning and saw their old nurse, who still lived with them, quietly opening the shutters.   She let a little light into their room to awake them more effectually, and then said, coming up to the side of the bed,— " Did you young ladies know how late it was ?   It wants but five minutes to ten."

" What will papa say ?" said Elizabeth, half rising ; " why did you not call us before, nurse ?"

" Your papa gave particular orders that you were not to be disturbed.   Miss Paton, are you awake, my dear ?"

" O yes, nurse ; you make too much noise for me to sleep.   I wish you would ask papa for my bunch of keys,—our boxes must be opened."

" Your papa is out, Miss."

" Out so early ?"

" You heard no noise in the night, then, my dears ? you did not hear the carriage come round ?"

" The carriage !—papa go out at night in the carriage ?   Why, nurse, what can it mean ?"

" You look frightened, Miss Paton."

"Yes, I am frightened. What do you mean, nurse?"

"Your papa and mamma were sent for in the night to go to Swanstead."

"O my aunt,—she is very ill then, and Wilfred away! O Elizabeth, how very sad!"

"What was the message, nurse?" asked Elizabeth; "I wish to know."

"I did not hear the message, Miss. Your mamma left her best love for you."

"Let us be alone, nurse," said Dora, with a trembling sigh; "we shall get up presently."

"Poor dear Marion," said Elizabeth, with tears; "I hope my aunt is not in danger."

But when they did get up and leave their room, they found the blinds of the house drawn down and the shutters shut.

CHAPTER VI.

THE LIGHT IN THE IVYED CASEMENT.

MARION was so completely exhausted by fatigue
and wakefulness, that when she had seen her
mother die, and felt that all motive for exertion was
now over, she sunk at once into a torpid state, and
was several days before she seemed fully to realize
her loss. The body had subdued the mind, and it
was not until its imperative demands for rest were
answered, that she perceived the bitterness of the
trial.

"Marion, my dear child," said her aunt, endeavouring to soothe her after a paroxysm of weeping,
"do let me see you at least trying to be resigned;
you are only exhausting your health and making us
miserable. What good can this violent grief do?"

Marion rested her aching head against the cushion
of the sofa, and thought she should never be happy
again. She became worse as the time of the funeral
approached, and exhibited all the peevishness of
over-wrought feeling. But the most sorrowful
eyes cannot weep for ever. On the day after,

having passed a sleepless night, she came down into the breakfast-room much calmer than usual, and her aunt being quite alarmed at her paleness, caused her to lie down on the couch, where, to their great relief, she presently fell into a deep heavy sleep; and they closed the window shutters, hoping that she might wake refreshed.

There were many things to be transacted in the family, and they were glad to be able to leave her for a while, which they did, setting the door open, and going in from time to time to look at her.

Mr. Raeburn had been appointed joint guardian with her uncle, and the two gentlemen were now in the library.

It had been agreed that it was useless to wait for the return of Wilfred before reading the will, and as it was absolutely necessary that Mr. Paton should return to Westport the following day, the two guardians decided that it should be done that same afternoon.

Mrs. Greyson had expressed a wish that her brother should take the charge of her son, and that he should finish his education at Westport: Mr. Raeburn was therefore not without hope that the other child might be left with him, but when he mentioned the subject to her uncle and aunt, he saw at once that it was a thing they had not contemplated; and Mr. Paton said he had intended to provide a home for his niece in his own house, considering himself as of course her natural protector.

Mrs. Paton, however, seeing how much pain this proposal gave, observed that perhaps there might be something in the will which would direct them.

"I can scarcely think it," replied the Rector, "but I cannot but feel that if Mrs. Greyson had been able to speak, she would have directed me to take her daughter, for she knows I have always loved her as my own."

"In our character as guardians we are, of course, equal," said Mr. Paton, politely but determinedly, and then added, "Marion is an unusually happy young person, to have two homes ready to receive her; but my near relationship to her mother seems to point out so clearly to which she should go."

"Certainly," interrupted Mr. Raeburn, "in relationship we are not equal, nor as parents, for you possess all your children, and I have lost both mine."

"Let me beg of you to leave the question till the will has been read," said Mrs. Paton.

Mr. Paton consented coldly. He could not be said to feel any particular fondness for Marion, whom he had never seen since her infancy till this mournful occasion; but she was his sister's child and only daughter of his wife's brother, and it seemed to him rather derogatory that she should reside with those who were not of her kindred, when he was so well able to receive her.

However, during the next half-hour he reflected

that Mr. Raeburn was a man of property, and that by taking Marion away he might deprive her of a handsome fortune,—he therefore determined that at least he would not do so ungraciously, and that if there was nothing in the will to decide the matter, he would agree to his wife's proposal, that it should be left to Marion's own choice whether she would go or stay.

"I have just been to look at Marion," said Mrs. Paton to the Rector, as he rose to take his leave. "I find she is awake, and if you would go and talk to her I should be very glad; perhaps you might inculcate a little more resignation, and if she is to be present at the reading of the will, she should be prepared for it beforehand."

"Certainly, I will go to her," he replied, "and see what I can do; though," he continued to himself as he went down the long passage, "I want some one to inculcate resignation to me if I am to part with her."

The door of the breakfast-room was ajar; he entered quietly and shut it behind him. The shutters were still closed, and two long sunbeams slanted through the heart-shaped holes into the room. Marion had dropped asleep again. There was a vacant chair at her head, and he came and sat beside her to wait for her waking. Her face was very pale, and looked still more so by contrast with her golden hair and deep mourning dress. Her attitude and expression told of the weariness of exhausted feeling, and her sleep seemed disturbed, for she started often and spoke hurriedly. At length she woke in a state of great agitation, and started up entreating him to do her some kindness, which she did not sufficiently explain. Her feverish manner disturbed him; and supposing her to be scarcely awake, he spoke soothingly to her, trying to calm her excitement, but in the tone of a person enduring so much himself that it struck upon her sharpened senses; and with the unreasonable irritation of over-wrought feeling she said, "Why do you talk to me, uncle? it only makes me worse. I am tired of their telling me to be resigned."

"My dear," he answered, with a heavy sigh, "comfort is from God. *I* do not try to comfort you. You and I are companions now in suffering."

Marion did not let him go on, but burst into a passion of tears, and hid her face in her hands, sobbing out, "Do not say *companions*, uncle: have I not lost my mother?" But the words were scarcely uttered before she began to reproach herself, and wondered how she could have repelled his kindness.

"And do you think I have no fellow-feeling, my dear child?" he replied. "Are you saying to yourself, 'there is no sorrow like my sorrow?'"

"I did not mean to be ungrateful, dear uncle," said Marion, attempting to cease weeping and collect her thoughts; "I know what your sorrows are."

"You *know*," repeated Mr. Raeburn in a low voice, which seemed not meant for her ears. "No, dear child, the heart *only* knoweth its own bitterness ; but you will soon know of another trial which even now hangs over me."

Marion's convulsive sobbing was not stopped by this ; it seemed quite to overpower her. She tried to recover herself, and heard Mr. Raeburn reproach himself for having made her worse. At length, with a violent effort she subdued it, and said, with passionate earnestness, "I should be better if I could sleep. Oh, the misery of my nights! I cannot bear it, uncle, and how can you? I did not think that anything could have added to my grief the last fortnight, but that does."

"What does?" inquired Mr. Raeburn, surprised.

"I have watched it for so many years," sobbed Marion, scarcely knowing what she said ; "every night I saw the light in the nursery. It used to stay only a little while, but since mamma died it shines nearly all night. Oh, dear uncle, I cannot bear it, and how can you? Do not break my heart, —what is it, then, has made you so miserable?"

As he did not answer, she turned to look at him, and was astonished at the effect her words had produced. She had never alluded to this subject before to him, even in the most distant manner. He believed that his nightly visits to the deserted chamber were unseen of any human eye, now he found they had been fully known, and that to the only person who could in any degree make up to him for the loss of the dead.

His face became pale, and he set his lips with a steady effort to bear down the outward expression of his thoughts, and then started up and paced the room with rapid steps.   Marion sat up, and watched him, subdued by the sight of the struggle which she herself had caused.   At length it ceased.   He came and sat at the foot of the couch, and covering his face with his hands, gave way to an agony of grief, such as it awed her to look at.

In all the misfortunes that he had gone through, she had never seen him shed a single tear ; she had heard nothing more than the short, suppressed sigh which often interrupted his conversation.   She was now subdued and terrified by the strong character of his passion, and his unsuccessful struggles against it.   It frightened her for the time from the remembrance of her own loss, and she sprung from the sofa, stung with remorse for what she had done, and throwing herself on her knees before him, tried to draw away his hands, and entreated his forgiveness, as if she had really done him some grievous wrong.

" Only this once forgive me," she urged in a supplicating tone ; " I will never be so cruelly thoughtless again."   But he only clasped his hands the tighter, and seemed incapable of making any answer.

Marion pressed her pale cheek against his hands

and continued, "Do not think of it, my dear, dear
uncle, I did not know what I was saying; do not
love me any the less for it; O do speak to me! Am
I not your child? have I not always loved you like
a——"

She hesitated to go on, for Mr. Raeburn's sudden
resumption of his self-command startled her—
he hastily dashed away his tears, and drew her
nearer as she knelt.   The room was not so
dusk but that she could see his eyes intensely
fixed upon her; she knew what he wished her
to say, and went on with her sentence: "Have
you not always made up to me for my lost father?
and have not I always loved you like a daughter?"

The sigh of relief with which he let go her
hands, told her that she had found the right clue
for subduing the emotion she had caused; but she
did not venture to say more, and remained in her
kneeling position, while he arose hastily and again
walked about the room to recover himself.

Marion turned half round and watched his face
as it rapidly changed to its ordinary calmness; for
the first time since her mother's death her thoughts
had been forced into another channel, and now
occupied themselves with the friend for whom she
had always felt a filial affection.

She had not had time yet to think as to what
might be her future destiny, the idea of leaving
this old home had never presented itself to her,
nor the question of what provision might remain

for her and her brother. She considered, as she continued to watch the Rector with her eyes, that she would certainly devote herself to making his future life as happy as possible, and did not remember that anything could separate them, though as her thoughts became more distinct she recollected that he had spoken of some fresh trial, and wondered whether his wife was ill, for she had not lately inquired after her.

At length, as she still knelt, he began to talk to her, and to her surprise, of his family misfortune, which he mentioned with a kind of desperate composure, which Marion dreaded to hear, though she could not interrupt him. He seemed as much impelled to speak now as in general to be silent; his natural reserve was gone for a time, but at the first pause she began a reply, and was unconsciously led on by the desire to soothe, till she had produced the tranquillity she wished, by her evident anxiety to do so. The sound of her voice, as unusual in its earnestness as his own, surprised him into silence; she spoke with such energy as he had never · given her credit for, he was astonished and touched to find that the dear child whom he had loved so long, had become a woman in soul when he most wanted her support. But in proportion as he grew calm, Marion's self-possession deserted her, and tears began to drop down her cheeks. Mr. Raeburn had stood still, the better to listen to her, and when she ceased to speak, he returned to his place on the sofa, and took her head between his hands.

" Dear uncle," said Marion, " there is no one left now but you and Wilfred, and how can I ever be happy again if I see one of you miserable ?"

" No one left but me and Wilfred ?"

" No one whose happiness matters in comparison with yours; why do you look at me so intently, my dear, dear uncle ? you always knew that we both loved you next best to mamma."

" Yes, I know it," was the reply ; " therefore call me father, it is a long time since I heard that name applied to myself, and I shall know that you are not quite orphaned if you can use it to me."

" I do call you my father," said Marion, taking up his hand and laying it on her head, " I have called you so in my heart many times, but O father, I never wanted your love so much before."

She put her arms round him, and heard him pray for her, as his hand rested on her head ; they were very low words, she could not distinguish half of them, but she perceived that he spoke of her as if she had truly been his own child, and when he ceased, and raised her from her kneeling position, there was an expression in his smile that she had not seen for years ; but she had scarcely time to remark it before he told her that he must return home for a while, and begged that she would go out into the open air, and take a short walk in the garden. Marion assented; he took leave of her for the present, and promised to seek her aunt to go out with her. Being now left alone, she opened the shutters and threw up the window. The weather had been showery, but the sun was out, and the garden had never looked more beautiful: she stood looking out on the green lawn and the rose beds with a more tranquillized heart; for the first time since her misfortune she had been roused out of herself, and her over-excited feelings had been relieved by sympathy with another.

When her aunt came in with Marion's crape bonnet in her hand, with its long black veil, she received them very calmly, and went out with her to walk in the more retired part of the garden. The Rector had signified to Mrs. Paton that he had not mentioned the intended reading of the will to Marion: she therefore opened the subject, and as Marion expressed herself quite able to be present, went on to hint that many things connected with her future life would be discussed afterwards and left to her own decision. " And I have no doubt, my dearest Marion," she continued, " that you will act as your uncle and I could wish."

" Certainly, aunt," said Marion wearily; for she could not at present take much interest in business matters, and such she supposed them to be.

" And it is a most fortunate circumstance," her

aunt went on, wishing to lead to the subject of her future home, "that the lease of this house is up at Christmas."

Marion started, and for the first time the certainty that she must leave the beloved place flashed across her mind. She instantly began to question her aunt, and when she spoke with anguish of leaving the spot where her mother lay, Mrs. Paton could not help blaming herself for having proposed that her lot should be left in her own hands; but she declined to give Marion any information, telling her that these matters would all be decided after the reading of the will.

Marion was very soon fatigued, she had so long been accustomed to a darkened room, that the dazzling sunshine oppressed her, and she was glad to go in and lie down on her couch to rest.

At four o'clock her aunt, Mrs. Ferguson, came, and led her into the library, where were two gentlemen, besides her uncle and Mr. Raeburn. She felt too much confused and agitated to listen to the document, scarcely gathering from its wordy sentences the fact that it secured a very sufficient provision both for herself and her brother. This trial to her fortitude being over, and the two solicitors withdrawn, Marion, who felt no inclination to shed tears, attempted to collect her thoughts, for her aunt reminded her of their conversation, and remarked that the most important part of the proceedings was yet to come.

Her uncle was seated at a table near the window, and her aunt beside him. Mr. Raeburn, with his arms folded, was leaning against the window-frame. Mrs. Ferguson was the only person who spoke. She began by reminding Marion that her uncle and Mr. Raeburn were appointed her joint guardians; and then, after telling her that her brother would now be sent to Westport, related to her what had passed in the morning, and the decision that she should have her own choice with whom she would remain.

During this time Mr. Raeburn did not look up or change his attitude.

Marion's face varied several times from red to pale. She had great difficulty in speaking; but mastered her agitation, and gratefully thanked both him and her uncle for their goodness to her.

"And you will understand, my dear," said Mr. Paton (quite sure, however, of what her choice would be), and speaking with a certain grave stateliness which never forsook him on any occasion, "that whatever you decide, it will make no difference in the kind feelings of the other party towards you; and there is no need for you to make up your mind to-day unless you please."

"No," said Mrs. Ferguson, who felt sure that Marion's calmness would not last long; "I think it a great pity that Marion should have a night of anxiety; she must be already aware with whom she would wish to live. Let her give her decision now,—it will spare her the harass of another discussion. Come, my love," she continued, pitying Marion's paleness, "it now wants ten minutes to six; we will give you till the clock strikes."

Marion was grateful for the permission to decide so soon, but she would not appear too hasty; and her own mind being already made up, she sat with her eyes fixed on the clock, the colour gradually fading out of her face. Her uncle, Mr. Paton, also looked at the clock, and nodded to his niece with a kind of stately patronage. And Mr. Raeburn looked at it, but never changed his attitude or glanced towards Marion. He had quite made up his mind, in spite of her affection for him, that she would go with her aunt and uncle; and when he thought of his own dull home, and, on the other hand, of the kind-hearted, lively cousins ready to welcome her, he almost wondered how he could have wished to keep her from them.

At last the clock struck, but not before both the ladies had fretted themselves into a perfect fidget.

Marion, who had been seated with her hands pressed together and her face quite colourless, now started up and made a few hasty steps towards the window, then turned towards her aunt and uncle, as if still irresolute; not that she felt so, but their unmerited kindness overpowered her.

"Now, my dear," Mrs. Ferguson began, trying to reassure her, "it is time for you to speak, Marion."

" Dear aunt," said Marion, addressing Mrs. Paton, and speaking in a scarcely audible voice, " how very good you have been to me! I shall love you as long as I live, both for mamma's sake and your own.   Dear uncle, I am very grateful."

" Tut, tut," said Mr. Paton, now looking on the matter as settled, " all very natural and proper; only my duty, my dear."

Marion then came up to Mr. Raeburn, took his hands in hers, and attempted to speak, but could not for her tears.

The action and her grief were very like a farewell, and he evidently so understood them.   But Mrs. Ferguson was not of the same opinion, and was determined that there should be no mistake.

" Your decision is yet to come," she said, in a calm, distinct voice, as Marion still wept and held by Mr. Raeburn.   " Do you decide to go, or do you decide to stay ?"

" My dear madam," said Mr. Raeburn, speaking in the same suppressed manner as in the morning, " your niece has already given her decision.   I have nothing to say against it.   May the blessing of God go with her !"

He laid his hand upon her head.   But Mrs. Ferguson still pressed the point.

" If it is given, let us hear it, Marion.   What do you decide?"

" I decide to stay," said Marion, and a short pause of surprise from all parties followed.

" Very well," said Mrs. Ferguson, breaking this awkward silence; " then we will not prolong this scene any longer." So saying, she advanced, and taking Marion's hand, led her away, adding, in a reassuring tone, " And now you shall come and take some rest, for it makes us quite anxious to see you looking so ill."

Marion had scarcely ever felt so grateful as for this considerate kindness. She stood in great need of quiet, and could not make her appearance again that night.

The light never appeared in the nursery again; and the Rector's face, as he sat in his study, looked more cheerful than for a long time past. When he came home that evening, he told his mother, who now resided with him, that she would soon have Marion for a companion; and the old lady, being very fond of her, was greatly pleased.

The news soon spread among the servants, who were also glad, the presence of a younger inmate promising to relieve the dulness of their home. And as Mr. Raeburn sat writing in his study, he heard the unexpected words, " I decide to stay," repeated as the echo of every sound which broke the silence.

The following morning Mr. Paton left Swanstead, and took a kind leave of Marion. The two ladies were to remain for another fortnight. There were many things to be arranged; the house and furniture were to be sold; but various little personal possessions of the late Mrs. Greyson had to be selected as memorials for her relatives and friends; while Marion found it enough for her weak spirits and little strength to select the books which had been her mother's favourites, to be divided between herself and her brother.

Mr. Raeburn saw but little of her during this time, being naturally anxious to leave her to the society of her aunts.

He had desired his housekeeper to prepare a room for her, and to give her the choice as to which she would prefer.

It wanted but three days to the time when she was to take up her abode at the Rectory, when one evening, as old Mrs. Raeburn sat dozing in her easy chair, while the Rector mused in silence over the events of the day, the housekeeper came in to inform him that she had been over to deliver his message; that Miss Greyson seemed tired and in low spirits, and she thought must have made a mistake in the room she said she wished for.

" However, Sir," continued the housekeeper, " I thought I'd mention it to you; you said you thought she would like the blue room."

" Which does she wish for ?" inquired the Rector.

" Miss Greyson did not name any particular room," returned the housekeeper, " but said she should like to overlook the church-yard, which seemed very natural, Sir; and, if possible, she should like to be able to see her old house."

"And there is no such room, you say?" observed Mr. Raeburn, considering. "No, I do not think there is." And he actually began to revolve, in his over-indulgent fondness, whether he could not open a window for her in the blue room.

It was very evident to Mrs. Mathews, when she spoke to Marion, that the latter wished to have the nursery, for she was far too well acquainted with the house not to know that no other room commanded both these aspects; but thinking that it would pain her master to have it so occupied, she had gently remonstrated, and inquired whether no other room would suit Miss Greyson as well. But Marion persisted in her choice, adding, that if she might have that room she would not ask for anything to be altered in it; and then left Mrs. Mathews, saying, "Give my love to my uncle, and say, that if he would rather I did not occupy that room, I will have any other that he pleases."

"Sir," said the housekeeper, waking up her master from his brown study, "if you don't think it reasonable that Miss should have that room, she particularly told me to say that she did not mind about it; only she would *rather* have it if she might. The nursery, I mean, Sir," she continued, seeing that she had failed to insinuate her meaning.

"The nursery!" repeated Mr. Raeburn, then first

struck with Marion's real meaning. "Is that the room Miss Greyson wishes for ?"

"Not unless it's quite agreeable to you, Sir," the housekeeper began ; but she soon saw, by the flush of pleased surprise which spread over her master's face, that he was far from needing an apology for what had seemed to her the unreasonable caprice of a wayward girl.

"Say no more about it, Mrs. Mathews," said the Rector, "but let the room be got ready for Miss Greyson exactly as she wishes, and tell her that no other choice would have pleased me half so well."

"Very well, Sir," said the functionary, curtseying and leaving the room, a little nettled to find, for the fortieth time, that Marion understood her master so much better than she did.

"I am coming to be his daughter," Marion had thought. "I shall see my mother's house from those little casements ; I shall remember her best there, and I shall be to my uncle in the place of the little lost Euphemia. He will walk upon the lawn as he used to do when she slept there, in the summer evenings, and he will see my light shining through the curtains ; he will know that the room is just the same as he has seen it through these years, with the child's picture over the chimney-piece, and the bed with the white hangings, and he will know that I am there. After a while he will forget that I am not his real child. I shall be his daughter grown up, and attending upon him, and he will not feel so lonely."

Marion put off leaving the home of her childhood to the last minute; when her aunts were gone, and all was desolate and empty, Mr. Raeburn sent his carriage for her. The distance was not more than three or four hundred yards, and she knew she should see the place every day; yet when the carriage stopped, and Mr. Raeburn led her into the house, and welcomed her, she could not thank him, or even speak, and with her veil let down over her face, ran up to her new apartment, where she could weep without restraint.

The most gloomy part of the year was coming on, and for the next three months Marion made but a sorrowful companion to the Rector; though, after a while, being urged by the old lady to resume her usual occupations, she roused herself from her inactive sorrow, and soon found the benefit of exertion, both to mind and body. She began to consider what she could do to make herself useful and beloved in her new home; and took upon herself various little offices, such as are generally performed by the daughter of a family. She made breakfast and tea, and paid a daily visit to the apartment of the poor invalid, taking care that she should always have beautiful fresh flowers before her. She also began to superintend the needlework in the girls' school, and to arrange the lending library. Moreover, she performed the part of a set of tablets to the Rector, reminding him of all his engagements; and above all, she read "The Record" to the old

lady,—a task which her son had hitherto thought
it his duty to perform, and which he specially disliked. She also talked to her and amused her, with
a great deal of tact, and contrived to turn the subject to something else when she teased her son about
his health and his parish,—a fruitful source of irritation to him. For it may be doubted whether any
other old lady, of an affectionate disposition, and
very proud of her son, could have been supposed
capable of unconsciously tormenting him to the
degree that she did. She had a habit of alluding
to the loss of his children in a very distant manner,
but with sufficient meaning to distress him. If the
younger Mrs. Raeburn was not so well in health as
usual, "she was sure she would not last long, and
indeed it would be a blessing if Providence would
take her, if some people could but think so." This
never failed to agitate her son; for throughout his
wife's long illness, he had never given up the hope
that she might one day be restored to him. If
Marion came in from a walk with a bright colour,
the old lady would privately take occasion to observe
that she hoped she was not consumptive, but that,
for her part, she did not like those lovely com-
plexions.

"Marion has very good health," the Rector would
reply, disturbed, in spite of his better reason, by his
mother's hints. "I really do not see any cause for
anxiety; she has a good appetite, and I never hear
her cough."

"Very true, my dear," the old lady would reply, "and these consumptive people often are very strong till they catch cold."

The feeling of anxiety thus caused, whether the supposed disease was consumption, spinal complaint, overgrowth, or indigestion, was generally half dissipated by the next sight of its object, whose face, naturally fair, and now again serene, presented no reasonable ground for anxiety to the fondest parent.

"And how is Wilfred?" the next attack would begin; "I suppose it cannot be helped, but really it seems unnatural to separate those two young people."

"Why unnatural, mother? The boy must finish his education, and he is to spend the vacations here, so that his sister will be with him three months out of the twelve."

"Ah, well, I suppose it's all for the best, but only think, if anything was to happen, what a long way they are apart. Well, it's a great responsibility to adopt a child, especially when one lives so far from all her relations. But I don't think myself," the old lady would proceed, in a musing tone, "that if they could see her now, they would remark any change; to be sure, we who see her every day cannot so well judge, but I should not say she was any thinner; I see no bad symptom excepting that bright bloom."

"That's a comfort," her son would reply, in rather a fretted tone; notwithstanding which his mother's remarks often annoyed him, and sometimes produced

more effect than the old lady had intended.   However, as she was naturally an affectionate woman,
and loved to extend her motherly protection towards
all young things, she soon found Marion's presence
a real boon, and, moreover, as she clung more and
more to her adopted father, and her dutiful manner
towards him came under the old lady's observation,
she began to consider her as a substitute mercifully
provided for the children that were lost.   Marion
also flattered her pride unconsciously by making all
Mr. Raeburn's opinions and wishes of so much importance.

" Why don't you go out, child ? " she would say,
rather testily.

" Oh, because I think my uncle would like me to
wait, and see whether he has any letters to copy."
Upon which the old lady's next remark was sure to
be made in the best of humours.

The garden and the gardener were under Marion's
special care, and she spent a good deal of time in the
greenhouse, occupied in the mysteries of striking,
potting, budding, and forcing, so delightful to florists.
It was of no use trying to teach the old lady to
appreciate the beauty of certain specimens ; a rose
was a rose, and a tulip was a tulip, and she did not
choose to see that one was better than another.   As
for your " white superbs," and " Prince Alberts,"
and " beauties of Britany," she thought it great
nonsense to spend so much time in rearing them.
It happened that Mr. Maidley, who was a great

florist, said one day, "Pray, Miss Greyson, why do you plant all your finest seedlings at the side of the house, where nobody can see them?"

"Nobody!" repeated Marion, looking up with a radiant smile of wonder; "why, Mr. Maidley, those beds are opposite the study windows."

"Oh, I beg a thousand pardons," returned the young gentleman, "for having made out our worthy Rector to be nobody, when it appears that he is everybody; but might I just venture to inquire whether he appreciates these flowers,—these superb calceolarias now? Do you think he could give a tolerable guess as to which is the best,—this one, stained and spotted with the deepest amber, or this pale, sickly-looking yellow one?"

"Perhaps not," said Marion, laughing; "but he is extremely fond of flowers; and if he does not know it himself, I at least know that his are of the very best."

"And very right it should be so," said the old lady, briskly, for she thought nothing too good for her son, and was not particularly fond of Frank Maidley, whose remarks on the ignorance of the former did not please her, though she felt their justice.

Many an hour, when the weather was fine, Marion spent in this garden with her small rake and watering-pot, tending her favourite petunias, and training the new varieties of fuschias on their wire supports; even the dreamy Euphemia took pleasure, such as

she was capable of, in watching her graceful movements, and the Rector was often called from his
books to admire the wonderful beauty of some new
specimen; for Marion, like most other flower
fanciers, had a great weakness in favour of what
was new.

As the spring advanced, the old lady, who had
become much attached to Marion, used to give her
a great deal of sage advice, and as they sat together in the small drawing-room in the front of
the house, would endeavour to improve her mind by
almost endless anecdotes respecting the fashions of
her youth, the behaviour and manners of her
various children deceased, and the last illness of her
lamented husband; also, as Marion grew daily more
graceful and pretty before her eyes, the old lady
took care to mingle with her discourse certain sage
remarks respecting the fleeting nature of beauty,
not by way of direct admonition, but rather as if
they arose naturally out of the subject. By this
manœuvre her hearer obtained possession of the
fact that she considered her very handsome, and
was not more impressed with the certainty that
beauty fades than might have been expected.

The room in which their mornings were spent
had a deep mullioned window, with stained glass,
and commanded a view of the flower-garden. Like
the apartment occupied by the younger Mrs. Raeburn, it was wainscotted with oak, and fitted up
with very old-fashioned furniture; the walls were

enriched with several family pictures, and in the window stood a fine old walnut-tree table, at which the old lady and Marion sat, the latter generally listening with great respect to all the old lady's advice and remarks respecting her various occupations, but pursuing her own plans notwithstanding, and following her own fashions in work, drawing, and music, though constantly assailed by such remarks as the following :—" When I was a young woman we never thought of playing on the harpsichord of a morning ;" or, " When *I* learnt drawing we never copied from such huge ugly heads as those, or splashed in our landscapes with a brush almost as big as a hearth-brush ; but times are changed. Ah ! "

" And what are you about now, my dear ?" looking up from the everlasting knitting.

" Stitching bands, madam," said Marion, holding up her work.

" Stitching, my dear ! you're always stitching. You 'll wear your eyes out.   Why don't you give it to the housemaid ?   I 'm sure she has little enough to do."

" Oh, I really could not think of such a thing," returned Marion.   " I have always stitched my uncle's bands since I was seven years old, I am sure the housemaid would not take so much pains with them."

" Well, they certainly are very beautiful bands,"

said the old lady, "and who's that coming up the drive, my dear?"

"Dr. Wilmot. I think he is coming to see aunt Raeburn. He generally does on Monday."

"Oh, does he," replied the old lady, "he very seldom comes to see me I know. How very consequential the Doctor looks this morning, to be sure; and there's my son going out to speak to him, without his hat too. He might know better than to go out in the east-wind, catching the rheumatism."

"East, Mrs. Raeburn! Oh no; the wind's in the west; quite a warm wind. Look at the vane."

"Well, child, east or west, it's all the same thing."

"I'll run out to him with his hat," said Marion, quite delighted to find an excuse for rushing into the sunshine.

"Miss Greyson, I declare," exclaimed Dr. Wilmot, as Marion came up, the soft wind playing with her long hair and heightening the bloom on her cheek. "Ah," said the old man, gently touching her shoulder with the silver head of his whip, "she's very nearly eighteen years old, and what a little time it seems to look back upon!"

"Now that's what I call real golden hair," said the old lady, as she looked through the window and saw the Doctor take his leave, and her son put his hat on and walk back towards the house with Marion on his arm, the wind, after having played various freaks with her locks, finishing at last by tossing them on to Mr. Raeburn's shoulder; but they did not return at once to the house, that gentleman being persuaded to come into the back garden to look at two little owls.

"Owls, child!" said the Rector, "I did not know you had any."

"Oh, yes, uncle," returned Marion. "Frank Maidley brought them on Saturday. He's going back to Cambridge, and they don't like the trouble of them at home. They always forget his pets, so he begged me to take them."

"And how are they to be fed?"

"Oh, Frank brought a bag full of mice for them, and gardener says he can get me plenty more. Here they are, in the tool-house," continued Marion, approaching the door. "I thought one of them was lost yesterday, till I saw its bright eyes peeping out from the shavings. They are fern owls, uncle. Look at them. Are they not pretty?" So saying she took out one of the impish-looking little things, and the Rector regarded it with strong disfavour; and when Marion added, "Frank wished me to take his silkworms too, but I said I had rather not," he said with great decision, "If Frank Maidley brings any of his nasty unwholesome silkworms here I'll have 'em buried."

"Alive, uncle?" said Marion, looking up from stroking one of the owls with her finger. Mr. Raeburn had uttered the threat in a sanguinary spirit, but not with any very definite ideas; besides,

burying alive was not in his way ; so he remained
silent.

" Because," persisted Marion, "if they are to be
buried *alive* that will be very little use ; for Frank
buried quantities once, and they came walking out
of the ground again by dozens, and crept on to the
lettuce-beds, as if nothing had happened."

Mr. Raeburn had been observed for some time
past not to look with a very favourable eye on
Frank Maidley; indeed he had been known to
speak of him as a " conceited young upstart." He
certainly had an uncommonly high opinion of his own
abilities, and was at no pains to conceal it ; but as
he undoubtedly was extremely clever, and was,
moreover, very ready at repartee, it was not so easy
to put him down. But probably this circumstance
would not have induced Mr. Raeburn to speak so
slightingly of his pets. The fact was, that Frank
Maidley constantly walked over to service at
Swanstead Church, and as constantly walked home
with Marion ; not that he cared about Marion
further than as a familiar friend of his childhood ;
but it was not much out of his way to come to the
rectory, and he was naturally of a social disposition.
If Mr. Raeburn had known this he would not have
looked upon the owls with such a jaundiced eye ;
but as it was, he declared that they reminded him
of pictures of demons, and declined to stroke them,
though Marion held up the largest on her finger,
saying,—

"Mr. Maidley says he wonders Frank should be so fond of pets, now he is so old, and so tall."

"Yes, I hope he is tall enough," replied Mr. Raeburn. "He must be six feet three, I should think, and nearly all legs and arms."

Marion laughed, and said,—

"Wilfred says he reminds him of scarlet runners, with his red hair."

"Oh," thought Mr. Raeburn, "at any rate I don't think it is reciprocal." "Well, my love, put the birds in and come away. After all, he is a young man of decided genius, and let us hope his peculiarities will wear off in time."

"Oh, no doubt," said Marion, wishing to say something kind of her old friend, "and so will his want of politeness."

"What, is he not polite to you ?"

"Not particularly," said Marion with a merry laugh. "He says he cannot help it ; he cannot be always thinking of his manners."

"Oh, indeed," replied Mr. Raeburn. "Well, my dear, as you have undertaken these owls, mind they are not neglected. Young Maidley really has many good points, my dear ; so you must not mind his odd ways ; and by the bye, remind me to ask him to dinner before he goes."

"Very well, uncle," returned Marion, carelessly, and they then walked back to the house, when the Rector, having shut himself in his study, took two or three turns, and indulged in a hearty fit of laughter; after which he sat down and indited an invitation to Frank Maidley, who in due time arrived, and behaved with most satisfactory bluntness, which pleased his host so well, that at parting he gave him several letters of introduction, so that they parted mutually delighted. Frank Maidley was guiltless of any attentions; in fact he took but little notice of Marion, and altogether conducted himself much more like an overgrown schoolboy of brilliant parts than a young man in his last year at college, and talked of as likely to take high honours.

It had always been intended that Marion should spend two months of that autumn at Westport, but just as the time was fixed for her coming the scarlet fever broke out in her uncle's house, and though it proved to be of the mildest kind, they did not think it advisable that she should be exposed to it.

On recovering, the girls were taken out for change of air, and did not return till so late in the year that the visit was deferred till the spring.

Marion often saw her brother, and kept up a frequent correspondence with him, as well as with her cousin Elizabeth; for, despite the great difference in their characters, the two cousins felt a considerable affection for each other. Elizabeth's letters often contained very life-like descriptions of places she had seen and conversations she had held; but after a while Marion observed that a certain Mr. Bishop often figured in them, being introduced at first as " Mr. Bishop, a friend of papa's," and often afterwards appearing in Elizabeth's letter as " Mr. Bishop came in to take a walk," or, " I was saying to Mr. Bishop."— " I wonder who this Mr. Bishop is," thought Marion ; " I think I shall ask, for Elizabeth would scarcely mention him so often if she did not mean to provoke inquiry." She accordingly did so, and Elizabeth's next letter contained the following postscript :—

" P.S. What do you think I did with your last letter ? It was so entertaining, that I read it aloud to Mr. Bishop. He was excessively amused at your inquiring about him. I hope you will see him soon, and like him for my sake, Marion. He really is a very agreeable young man, and a great deal too good for me. He is sitting opposite now, and very impatient for me to have done. He sends his kind regards. The next time I write I will give you a description of him."

" What a very odd way of telling me that she is engaged," thought Marion ; and a few days after came a letter from Mrs. Paton, containing a formal announcement of Elizabeth's engagement " to a very worthy young man, whose father is a great friend of your uncle's. He is not so decidedly serious as we could wish." The letter went on to say :—" But he has been piously brought up, and, as well as our own dear child, seems very attentive to his religious duties ; and he and Elizabeth are sincerely attached to each other."

Marion accordingly wrote to congratulate her cousin; and from that time, though Elizabeth's letters were as affectionate as ever, there was a certain coldness and restraint in her manner of speaking on religious matters which she had never manifested before; and after a while such a shrinking from them altogether, that her letters, though very amusing, gave Marion on the whole more pain than pleasure.   Marion sometimes asked questions about the various charities and Societies of which Elizabeth had hitherto written in such glowing terms, and in whose cause she had been so active, often concluding her letters by wondering how her cousin *could* live in such an out-of-the-way place as Swanstead, where she scarcely ever either saw or heard anything of the "religious world."

The questions asked by Marion she passed over in a very off-hand manner:—" As for the industrial school that you ask about, I don't think one would answer in your village; but I really have had no time to visit it lately, so I know very little about it.   I ride a good deal on horseback now.   Fred Bishop says he thinks my health requires it."   Or, " I forgot to mention that it rained at the time of the last Church Missionary Meeting; and Fred Bishop says I ought never to go out in the rain." Or, " I rather wonder you should have admired that book; it seemed to me uncommonly dull,— quite what Frederick would call a 'Sunday-book.'"

CHAPTER VII.

GENEROUS REGRETS.

MARION did not mention to Mr. Raeburn the change she had observed in Elizabeth's letters; and, in thinking them over, tried to believe that Elizabeth being now engaged, might, without impropriety, withdraw a little from those plans of usefulness in which she had hitherto taken so much pleasure. If she had ceased to write, or had written short, uninteresting letters, Marion could easily have referred it to the new tie which had sprung up to occupy her mind. But this was not the case; Elizabeth's letters were as frequent, and longer than ever, and sometimes contained a kind of apology to Marion for entering so much into her own affairs, such as —" You will excuse my telling all this to you, but I have no other *young* friend to consult, and it is very natural that I should wish to make a confidant of some one. Besides, you know, dearest Marion, that though Dora and I have always been most affectionate sisters, we have not many ideas in common; and lately Dora has withdrawn herself so much among her own friends, that she scarcely has time for any conversations with me. And as we grow older, our opinions getting more unlike, I assure you we often sit nearly silent to avoid discussion and argument, which are things I never could bear."

On the other hand, as Elizabeth seemed inclined to drop the subject of religion altogether, Dora as suddenly began to take it up; and Marion, who liked to write about what most interested her, was very well pleased to have it so.

In a former chapter mention was made of Mrs. Ferguson, a sister of Mrs. Paton's. That lady, who had no children, had been left a widow early in life, and had married a few years back a widower, with one daughter; this young lady, who was about Dora's age, was clever and sensible, and had a great deal of enthusiasm in her character; she and Dora had formed a strict friendship, of which many proofs were perceptible in the letters of the latter, who constantly spoke of her dearest Helen in terms of the most high-flown panegyric, blessing the day when her father came into the neighbourhood, and speaking of the religious knowledge she had acquired, and the light which had broken in upon her from reading the books she had recommended. Marion was greatly surprised at all this, particularly as Dora began to mingle her self-gratulations on the possession of such a friend with lamentations over the state of the town and the carelessness of the clergy on many important points, mingling the whole with certain expressions, over which Marion could scarcely help laughing. She had not thought it right to go to the Horticultural Exhibition because it had been held on a Friday, and she and Helen always went on that day to the church of the blessed St. Bernard. At another time Dora was shocked to find that Mr. King had fixed the 30th of January for the annual dinner to the Bluecoat-children; she hoped it was not an intentional insult to the memory of "our martyred King." She and Helen were making a collection for an altar-screen for the church of St. Bernard, but she was sorry to say, people did not treat the matter with the seriousness it deserved.

Elizabeth's letter of the same date contained the following sentence, which stood next to the information that Fred Bishop's father had given her a set of garnets:—" Young King is just ordained, and is now acting as his father's curate instead of Mr. Dreux, and a very poor substitute he makes, I assure you. We ought to be very thankful that we can still hear Mr. Dreux sometimes; for the Rector of Pelham's Church, who is extremely aged, has induced him to become his curate, since which the poor old gentleman has become quite bed-ridden, and Mr. Dreux has the complete control of everything, far more than the Rector ever had. The church is the largest and finest in the town, excepting St. Bernard's, and what with Mr. Dreux's popularity and his fortune, he carries everything before him more completely than ever."

" Mr. Dreux seems to be the only person about whom Elizabeth has not changed her mind," thought Marion, folding up the letter; " she still evidently thinks him ' quite a paragon.' "

By and by Dora's letters began to contain various panegyrics on a certain Mr. Allerton, who had lately been presented to the living of St. Bernard's, on the demise of a clergyman of opposite sentiments. He was doing an extraordinary amount of good, according to Dora's account; but many of the people had left his church, because they did not approve of his opinions, and had chosen to go and hear Mr. Dreux instead, which had occasioned a breach between him and Mr. Allerton, the latter of whom had preached a masterly sermon to Churchmen, on the danger and presumption of leaving their parish church. This sermon he printed, and as people thought it alluded pretty strongly to Mr. Dreux's conduct in taking no notice of the sin of the fugitives, they were greatly disappointed to find that he did not seem disposed to answer it.

In fact, Mr. Dreux not only never answered the said sermon, but he appeared quite unconscious that it was directed against him, and for anything the author knew might have never read it; for upon his sending him a copy, with " the author's compliments" on the cover, he received a note the same evening, which ran as follows :—

"DEAR SIR,

"I beg to thank you for a pamphlet bearing your name, which I found on my table this afternoon. I have not yet had time to open it.

"Believe me, dear Sir,

"Yours faithfully,

"ARTHUR C. DREUX."

Whether Mr. Dreux *ever* found time to open the said pamphlet, or whether he found it unanswerable, or whether he did not choose to take any notice of it, were matters which the Rector of St. Bernard's could not ascertain; but the public observed that he did not alter the manner of his bow, by lifting his hat one iota more or less, when he met his opponent in the street; neither did he bear in his face the slightest expression of consciousness, confusion, or offended pride. But the Rector of St. Bernard's having made up his mind that, if once he could draw his rival into argument, he should certainly get the better of him, was not likely to let the matter rest; accordingly, having waited a reasonable time, and no "Strictures on a Sermon delivered at St. Bernard's, &c.," appearing, he began to offer remarks on Mr. Dreux's speeches at Public Meetings, sometimes in the most gentlemanlike manner requesting him to repeat some expressed opinion or sentiment; or, with an excess of candour, declining to put their full meaning "on the last remarks of his Reverend brother," as scarcely thinking he meant them to bear a construction involving sentiments so novel.

Mr. Dreux had a calm temper, and used to let him go on and finish his speech, then get up, and, appearing to suppose that Mr. Allerton had really mistaken his meaning, quietly repeat his first sentence, and, declaring that it quite expressed his real opinion, would add a few reasons for supporting it, and sit down, as if he had not the least idea that anything like controversy could have been intended.

All this afforded great amusement to the gossips of Westport, who sincerely hoped something would come of it, and liked to see Mr. Allerton's handsome face flush with annoyance at the impossibility of getting his rival to come out and give him battle.

Mr. Allerton never attempted to try his power with any of the other clergy of Westport; indeed, being a man of unquestionable talent, and Rector of the church, which, from its beauty and position, was always called the Cathedral of Westport, he probably felt that his influence was already greater than theirs. But Mr. Dreux, a man about his own age, his undoubted equal in talent, and one with whom he could not but be sensible that he was constantly being compared, sometimes to the disadvantage of one, and sometimes of the other,— it was most natural that he should wish to try his strength with *him*, particularly as he firmly believed himself to be in the right; and moreover, as Mr. Dreux was only a curate, he often teazed himself by thinking it was particularly annoying to find that he possessed (quite unconsciously to himself) more influence in that parish than the Rector himself could boast of.

In the meantime, having tried several slight engines of attack without avail, he began to feel considerable resentment against the influence possessed by the Curate of Pelham's Church, and, by degrees, suffered his naturally generous mind to look on him solely in the invidious light of a rival. But Mr. Dreux, who was in reality keenly conscious of his feelings towards him, took especial care not to afford him the slightest real ground for finding fault with his proceedings; and it was observed of the two champions, that from month to month their opinions seemed steadily to become more and more contrary,—Mr. Allerton supporting his tenets more steadily as he got settled in the parish and found the people could bear it, Mr. Dreux becoming more distinctly Evangelical in his preaching as the consequences of his rival's teaching unfolded themselves.

Notwithstanding this constant opposition, there was something too noble and honourable in the character of each to admit of any *petty* manifestations of hostility; only on one point the Rector of St. Bernard's had decidedly the worst of it. He was of a very hasty, passionate temperament, and his rival was equally remarkable for his great command of temper.

Matters were in this state, when an aged lady died, leaving a sum of money for building certain schools in Mr. Dreux's parish. A Public Meeting was called to consider the locality in which they should be built, it having been thought advisable to erect them on a waste piece of land belonging to the Corporation. This plan was acceded to. The next Resolution proposed, that as there was not room at the parish church for the scholars, they should attend St. Bernard's. In consideration of this the parish of St. Bernard's was to have forty children educated in these schools.

As might have been expected, the pastors of both these churches were annoyed at the arrangement. Mr. Allerton, because it would leave his children under the absolute dominion of his rival the whole week; Mr. Dreux, because it would withdraw *his* on all occasions of public worship. But neither liked to say anything, though the dissatisfaction of one at least was obvious to the whole assembly.

It did not, therefore, excite much surprise when, after the business of the Meeting was concluded, Mr. Dreux came forward to propose an Amendment to one of the Resolutions, which was no other than a proposition on his part to provide proper accommodation in his own church for the scholars, which (after remarking that he did not wish to include the forty extra-parochial children unless agreeable to their own minister) he easily showed could be done, as he himself would provide the funds, and the additional seats would not at all disfigure the church. This arrangement, he contended, would be far more convenient than sending the children to a church at a considerable distance from the school-rooms. "And I think," he continued, turning towards the Rector of St. Bernard's with a courteous smile, "that however much my colleague and myself may occasionally differ, I shall be sure of his concurrence in a plan which will enable these young Church people to attend their parish church."

Mr. Allerton, who had intended to express his willingness to receive the children, looked up, and felt himself completely foiled, and that with his own weapons. He felt the colour mount to his temples, but to object was impossible. Through the obnoxious sermon he had given his rival an opportunity to gain a great advantage over him, and at the same time to show that he was not in the least afraid of alluding to it, though he did not seem to think it worthy of an answer.

The tact with which Mr. Dreux followed up this slight advantage was a considerable annoyance to the Rector of St. Bernard's, who now felt that he must either waive his claim to the education of his forty children, or leave them wholly under the influence of the former,—for the middle course he could not reconcile to his mind. He therefore chose to waive his claim, and set to work to build such an addition to his own parish schools as would accommodate forty extra children.

Things continued in this state till the first anniversary of his coming, when it appeared that his opinions had already gained so much ground as to have become constant matter of discussion and comparison.

Religion and its profession had long been the fashion at Westport; it was now taken up by a new set of people, who attended all his services, and adopted many of the practices he recommended. At first sight the duties imposed by Mr. Allerton on those of his people who desired, as he phrased it, to be " true sons of our holy mother the Church," were rather of an onerous kind; yet it appeared that to many they were a welcome relief after the requisitions of the other party. Moreover, they were of a *certain tangible* nature, and having been all duly attended to, enabled the performer to say, " I have repeated my prayers, gone through my devotional reading, attended service, given alms, &c., therefore I am a good Christian,"—or rather, a good Churchman; for Mr. Allerton taught much more of the Church than about the Head of the Church.

There were in Westport, as in most country towns, a great number of single ladies. Many of these made a Christian profession, and from the leisure they possessed, and their willingness to

devote it to the service of God, were looked upon
by the clergy as their natural allies. In almost
every parish there were several of these ladies,
more or less active. Among others, there were
three sisters of the name of Silverstone, who lived
in Mr. Dreux's parish, and managed most of his
charities for him,—that gentleman having been
heard to say that three old maids were as good as a
curate.

It may be greatly doubted whether this assertion holds good in general; but the three Miss
Silverstones were no ordinary old maids, and were
always treated with all possible consideration by
Mr. Dreux, though he did bestow on them the afore-
said disrespectful appellation.

These three sisters lived in a good old-fashioned
house near the church, but owing to the circumstance that their deceased father had been a linen-
draper, they were not visited by the " *élite*" of the
town, though it was admitted that they were, without doubt, among the excellent of the earth. They
were all past sixty, and two of them still extremely
active. The second, Miss Dorothy, was slightly
deformed, but her countenance retained, despite the
invariable expression which marks the faces of persons so afflicted, a peculiar sweetness. This old
lady was Mr. Dreux's favourite, and was so highly
esteemed by him that it was said he never undertook anything of importance without consulting her.

She was as useful in her quiet way as her two sisters in their more active path.

Miss Dorothy Silverstone used to go in and out of Mr. Dreux's house whenever she liked, and was far more at home in it than any other lady, whether old or young; besides which, he paid her great attention, and humoured her fancies, which was considered an amiable weakness by some other ladies, who decided that *they* never could see anything so particularly heavenly about old Miss Dorothy; while others remarked how excessively chary he was of his attentions to young ladies, and thought that at any rate *she* could not possibly mistake them, and wondered whether she had any chance of becoming Mrs. Arthur Dreux, the wife of the most popular and admired man in the town.

Besides these ladies, there was another set, who had always professed themselves "very fond of religion and all that sort of thing," and who yet contrived to enjoy such of the pleasures of the world as were within their reach, in connexion with this sort of half profession. These were among the first to declare themselves "greatly edified by dear Mr. Allerton's excellent discourses," in proof of which edification they always abstained from giving tea-parties on Fridays—took care to attend service on every saint's day—talked about the Anglican branch of the holy Catholic Church— wore slight mourning during Lent—spoke of the

Reformation with a shake of the head—talked with rapture of the ancient custom of confession, and hoped that "privilege would soon be restored to us."

These ladies caricatured all Mr. Allerton's opinions, and caused him infinite vexation. They were a set of retainers whom he would fain have been rid of. They had a book club of their own— most of the books had decorated margins; and to hear some of them talk, one might have been led to suppose that they conceived the distinction between them and their late friends, the Evangelical party, to lie chiefly in some such trivial peculiarities as dress, form, and fashion. They had never troubled themselves much with the doctrines of either party; consequently, when they apparently came over to Mr. Allerton's side, they had no better way of deciding to "which set" a clergyman belonged than by observing whether he preached in his black gown; and of certain people they would affirm that it was impossible they could be High Church, because they had no fish on a Friday.

It is not to be supposed that in Dora's letters to Marion she gave any such account as is here presented to our readers; it was only incidentally that she became aware of the very great change in the aspect of affairs, and the corresponding change in her cousin's views. There was no hint of the disputes, separations, and heart-burnings which had divided people, till Elizabeth, happening to mention

that Mr. Allerton had got a curate of the same
sentiments as himself, went on to say: " Mr. Dreux
has had a severe illness, and people do not scruple
to say that it was occasioned by over-exertion and
anxiety of mind. We are all very sorry about it.
Mr. Dreux is not now nearly so exclusive as he
used to be, and is far more kind in his general
manners. He was always very handsome," proceeded Elizabeth, lapsing into the old theme, " and
since his illness he looks more so than ever; but
Dora will not allow that he is to be compared with
Mr. Allerton; and as for the new curate, she and
Helen make themselves quite ridiculous about him;
but he goes such lengths that mamma will not
allow Dora to go to that church any more; in fact,
she has long disapproved of it, but Dora spends so
much of her time with Helen that it could scarcely
be prevented hitherto. The new curate is really
more than half a Roman Catholic, and has given
great offence to some of Mr. Allerton's people.
Mamma was lamenting the other day to Mr. Dreux
the divided state of the town, and the dissensions
these new doctrines have caused, and he actually
said that he did not think it so particularly to be
regretted. He thought it would ultimately do more
good than harm, for there were many things we
might copy from them with great advantage, he
thought; and if controversy did no other good, it
would at least oblige people to look into and
investigate the truths they contended for; and he

believed there were many people here who could not give a reasonable account 'of the hope that was in them.'"

Mr. Dreux's illness was of so serious a nature as for a few days to place his life in the utmost peril; and when all danger was over it was some time before he recovered his health and strength.

When it was supposed that he would not recover, the strength of affection which really existed for him began to be touchingly manifested, especially by the poor, and his door was daily and hourly besieged by inquirers after the last report of his physician.

Mr. Dreux had been very much over-tasked lately, having had not only that whole parish on his hands, but also the management of what had now become the open controversy between his own party and the growing one of his rival. The new curate had not shown himself so moderate as his rector, and his attacks had been so persevering and his charges so grave, that it was thought advisable they should be answered. All this fell upon Mr. Dreux, who had the treble duty of declaring what doctrines he did hold, defending them from the charge of being unscriptural, and showing that they were in accordance with the formularies of the Church,—no easy task, particularly with so keen an antagonist as Mr. Hewly, the new curate. There is no doubt that the harass attending this contention was very great; and when he fell ill

there were not wanting those who said they hoped
Mr. Allerton would take it to himself, for he alone
was to blame for it. They had peace and quiet
before he set his foot among them, " and there had
been nothing but dissension since."

Mr. Allerton, though he had not gone such
lengths as his curate, had not in any way dis-
couraged him; on the contrary, he had felt pleased
to find some one who was willing to set to work
more decidedly than he liked to do himself,—for he
was a thorough gentleman, and had no idea of
taking unfair advantage. His curate was troubled
with no such scruples. Mr. Allerton, nevertheless,
could not help feeling from the day of his arrival he
had never omitted an opportunity of harassing his
rival. He had persuaded himself to think of him
as such. His whole influence had been directed
towards undermining his power, destroying his
popularity, and throwing contempt upon his principles. One of his greatest hopes had been that
something might occur to remove this obnoxious
member of society away from the town, but nothing
was further from them than that death should effect
the removal, and that death be laid to his door.

Such being the case, he was shocked one morning
when he went to inquire after him to be told that
there was scarcely any hope of his recovery, and he
went home feeling as wretched as if the dying man
had accused him of being his murderer, and wishing
a thousand times that he could recal what he had

written and said against him. He was naturally an
amiable man, and in spite of his constant opposition,
he had really felt a considerable respect for his rival,
and, strange as it may seem, a kind of admiration
for his eloquence and pride in his talents. It was
something to have "a foeman worthy of his steel;"
and he would have been mortified if Mr. Dreux had
come short of the estimate he had formed of him—
for then where would have been the glory of his
hoped-for victory?

Apart from their religious differences, there were
many grounds of sympathy between them. They
were both young, talented, popular, energetic. And
as Mr. Allerton walked back to his own house, and
recalled their intercourse from the first, and remembered how needlessly and vexatiously he had opposed
him, he shrunk from the review of his own conduct,
and the many provocations he had given him, and
which he had tried to make most suited to chafe his
lofty spirit. On the other hand, he only remembered a few hasty expressions of momentary vexation and irritation; and he believed he would give
all be possessed to recal the past.

As he sat alone in his study, he made a solemn
resolution, that if ever Mr. Dreux recovered, he
would ask his forgiveness, and solicit his friendship;
but in the meantime he inquired at his house many
days before the answer was such as to give him
much hope that he should ever see him again. And
as anxiety began to tell upon his appearance, and

make him look pale and haggard, people ungene-
rously commented upon it. "Ah, now he sees what
he has done; he begins to be afraid. Ah, he'll
never have an opportunity of doing poor Mr. Dreux
an unkindness again."

However, after causing the utmost anxiety to his
friends for ten days, the unconscious subject of all
these remarks began to recover, and in another ten
days was able to leave his room for the welcome
change of his library sofa.

Mrs. Dorothy Silverstone, who had nursed him
through this illness with the tenderness of a mother,
was almost overcome with joy when she saw him
again in his favourite room; and when she had
drawn the curtain half-way across the window, so
as to cast a slight glow on his face, she pleased herself with thinking that he did not look quite so pale
as might have been expected.

Mothers and nurses are agreed that grown-up
sons are far more difficult to nurse than grown-up
daughters,—the former generally exhibiting a
refractory disposition when they begin to recover,
speaking disrespectfully of medicines and doctors,
and contemning their aliment, which they designate
"slops." Mr. Dreux, though an easy man to nurse
on the whole, according to Mrs. Dorothy Silverstone's account, was not exempt from this infirmity
incidental to mankind; and he showed it very
strongly when he found that he had escaped from
his bed-room, and was once more in the room with

his books, for he had not been many minutes lying there before he requested his watchful friend to bring him a certain heavy volume which he pointed out. This the old lady declined to do, remarking that he could not hold it if he had it, and requesting him to try to sleep; upon which he said if he might not read, he wished she would bring him a pen, for he should like to amuse himself by writing a little. Mrs. Dorothy elevated her eye-brows, but finding that he really was in earnest, she brought him a pen and propped up his head with pillows, while he tried to use it; but finding that his hand shook, so as to make the writing quite illegible, the invalid gave it up, as he said, "till the afternoon," and fell asleep, previously throwing out a hint of going down the garden to-morrow if it was fine.

Waking up after an hour's refreshing sleep, he amused himself for a little while by observing the stripes in Mrs. Dorothy's knitting, and counting the colours; then he watched the gardener, who was potting out some plants into the borders; at last he bethought himself of having something to eat, as a passable way of spending the time.

"Yes, that you shall, Mr. Dreux," said his nurse, "and glad I am to hear you ask for it." So saying, she trotted to a table, and brought him a beautiful bunch of grapes and a biscuit. "These grapes came from Mr. Allerton's greenhouse," she said, as she arranged the pillows; "he sent them this morning."

"Very kind of him," returned the invalid. "I should not know they were not the same as I have had all through my illness."

"They are the same," replied the old lady. "Mr. Allerton often sends them, and he constantly inquires after you."

"I will see him to-morrow if he calls," said Mr. Dreux.

"The day after," suggested Mrs. Dorothy, by way of amendment; and he submitted quite peaceably, for he knew that, as he could scarcely walk alone, he was quite at the mercy of any old lady who might choose to take him in hand.

It was, however, several days before his physician gave him leave to see his friends, and after that, Mr. Allerton happening to be one of the first persons who called, was shown into the library, where he found him lying on the sofa, alone, and forgetting for the moment that his change of feeling could only be known to himself, addressed him with a warmth of friendliness which evidently astonished Mr. Dreux, who had certainly been pleased at his kindness in so constantly inquiring after his health, (though it was no more than he would have done himself if their circumstances had been reversed,) and expected nothing less than to see him come in with a face of the utmost solicitude, and address him with as much interest as if he had always been the object of his warmest regard.

Though much better, and perfectly capable of

entering into conversation, he was still very weak; and happening to turn towards the light, his guest was betrayed into an exclamation of regret at his altered appearance. The slight flush of surprise that passed over his face on hearing it, instantly reminded Mr. Allerton that there was no reason to suppose his own change of feeling would find a corresponding change in the mind of his late antagonist. Being a man of very quick feelings, he was nevertheless hurt to see that his unexpected manner had flurried him, and felt as if he had been intentionally repelled, when he, after thanking him for his kindness, and answering his inquiries after his health, turned the conversation again to the most ordinary topics, half afraid lest anything of nearer interest might lead to a discussion.

Mr. Dreux had indeed felt a sensation of wonder at the expressions of regard, almost amounting to affection, with which his new friend had commenced; but his own perceptions being extremely keen, he saw that this involuntary feeling had given pain. He accordingly attempted to assume an answering tone of voice, and seem unconscious of anything unusual. But Mr. Allerton could not recover from the first check, and after several topics of conversation had been tried without the possibility of dragging it on any further, he stopped short, with his arms folded, and various painful emotions working in his face; and his host, almost as uncomfortable as himself, lay still, looking at him, and wondering what was to come next.

It was very obvious that something unusual must have happened since they had last met ; and as he lay watching the pained expression of Mr. Allerton's face, who sat with his lips set, intently gazing out of the window, and a flush overspreading his features, which completed the contrast between them, he began to be troubled with one of those uncertainties which often beset the minds of those newly recovered from fever. He wondered for an instant whether there really had been any differences between them then, as some of the bitter expressions in his last pamphlet occurred to him: he next wondered whether this man, who now sat before him with so much suppressed feeling visible in his every glance, had not come to his bedside, or at least seen him since they parted at variance, and held out his hand to him, hoping they might be friends. He could not be certain that he had not, and if so, how cold and restrained he must think his present conduct.

He knew that in his restless hours of fever he had often mentioned Mr. Allerton's name ; he had fancied himself compelled to hold long, weary arguments with him, and in his delirium had entreated him to desist ; but he did *not* know that this trivial circumstance was perfectly well known to his late rival, and at that moment was present to his mind.

When this fancy passed away, he was certain he

had not seen him in any other way than as an uncompromising antagonist; and with feverish anxiety he began to consider whether some misfortune might not have happened to him during his illness, and that Allerton was come to tell him of it; and accordingly he watched his countenance with an intensity of attention which must surely have forestalled his evil tidings, had any such existed.

At length, with a short, quick sigh, Allerton changed his position, and looked him full in the face.

His expression of anxious interest could not be mistaken, but there was an appeal in his eyes which his late rival scarcely knew how to answer, though he thought he knew its meaning; but raising himself up, and holding out his hand, said, with a cordial smile, "Pray do not be uneasy about me, I am much better."

Mr. Allerton took the offered hand, with a painful perception of how white and thin it was; but this only added to the troubled look of his face, which struck upon the sharpened senses of the invalid, who said hurriedly, "Or if you know that I am not better, if you have been charged with any message from my physician, speak it; I am not afraid to hear. Not that? Then my sister is ill."

"No, no; nothing of the kind," cried Allerton, starting up, really alarmed. "I am charged with no message; I have nothing of consequence to say,—of the least consequence to you I mean."

The invalid, sitting upright, had seized his arm,

as if to prevent his going away before answering his question. Now, without appearing reassured, he sunk back exhausted on the pillows, but did not let go his hold, saying faintly, "Whatever it is I must hear it now, something must be the matter. If it is of consequence to any one in whom I feel an interest, it must be of consequence to me."

"What have I done?" thought Allerton, now doubly disturbed. "I do beg, I entreat you, to be calm; it was only about myself that I wished to speak to you—only myself I do assure you."

Dreux was satisfied, and made a violent effort to recover his outward appearance of calmness, but his nerves being weakened by illness, required a longer time than he was inclined to give; and the veins in his temple throbbed wildly, while his guest continued to beseech him to think nothing of his inconsiderate awkwardness, and in a tone of bitterness against himself, said, "The matter is, that I have been making myself miserable during your illness, with the remembrance of how much I have harassed you in your work. I know what your people think. I am afraid I am partly to blame for this illness."

"Pray do not say any more," returned the invalid, holding out his hand and attempting to stop him, "I am grieved that such an idea should have suggested itself to your mind: do not let it disturb you for a moment. I have never thought that I had anything to complain of."

" Not of defeat, certainly," replied the Rector of St. Bernard's ; " but," he added with a sigh, " though controversy was inevitable, though I could not endeavour to spread my own opinions without opposing yours, I have wished very much lately that I had done it in a different way. I have said and done many things, which on reflection have given me great pain." He said this with such deliberate earnestness, that it was impossible to check him, and concluded by frankly acknowledging that his late rival's friendship was a thing that he greatly coveted. This was tendered at once with the greatest cordiality.

" And I earnestly hope the day may come when we shall both think alike," continued Mr. Allerton.

" So do I," was the answer, " most heartily desire it. I shall make it one of the subjects of my prayers."

Allerton rather winced at this, as if horrified at the supposition that a change on *his* part could be thought possible. Nevertheless, being strongly drawn towards his late antagonist, he forbore to express the contempt he felt for his tenets ; and perceiving that he had now quite got over his late excitement, contented himself by saying, " And as for these pamphlets, which I heartily wish had never seen the light, I hope you will consent to discontinue them. I am sorry I ever tried to unsettle the minds of *your* people ; and if we could in a friendly way discuss our points of difference, I have great hopes that—in short, I mean to say, that if you would investigate these matters—you would soon come over yourself to the right—I mean to the other side, and prove a far better advocate for it than I can ever hope to be."

He had spoken earnestly, and leaning forward, heard the subject of these good wishes say, in a very low voice, "God forbid."

"Respecting these pamphlets," he presently said, "you have nothing to answer for them, your curate and I must manage them as well as we can. In my opinion he has not conducted them in the most gentleman-like manner possible, but that we neither of us have anything to do with. I MUST write one in answer to his last attack, or people will think there is nothing to be said on the other side."

Mr. Allerton was apparently examining the hearth-rug during these remarks, but from the involuntary confusion he betrayed, it became evident that he must have had more to do with these pamphlets than his rival had been led to suppose; but being anxious not to disturb their newborn friendship, the latter concealed the discovery, and went on in the same tone. "I shall be glad if he will be prevailed upon to drop this mode of warfare, for I always disliked controversy. Not that I complain of his statements, for I have had a fair opportunity of answering them, and I sincerely

believe that the cause I advocate has been rather
advantaged than otherwise; for several matters
have been brought into notice on both sides,
opinions about which people have been compelled
to *think*, to choose, and distinguish for themselves,
which they will call *truth* and which *error*. For
as this controversy has touched upon the very vitals
of religion, and we take opposite sides, I need
make no difficulty in taking for granted that one
of us must be utterly in error. As for the manner
in which Hewly has conducted his side, I do not
wish to complain of it. No doubt it is difficult
to keep one's temper. I am afraid I shall lose mine
altogether, if this goes on much longer; in fact,"
he added, with a sigh of excitement and fatigue,
" it makes my head ache to think of it."

" Yes, yes," returned his guest, perceiving that
in his weak state the very mention of argument and
mental labour of any kind was a trouble, "these
things shall be arranged as you please. I ought
to have known better than to have talked of them."

He then altered the cushions, partially darkened
the room, and brought some refreshments from the
table, expressing considerable anxiety lest his new
friend might have over-excited himself, and would
have taken his leave but for an urgent request that
he would remain another half-hour.

" I am afraid of fatiguing you," he replied;
" you are not able to bear the least exertion."

" Anything is better for me than being left

alone," urged the invalid. "I am not able to read, and cannot prevent my mind from wearying itself with all manner of abstruse speculations—little trivial things disturb me. The church bells agitated me beyond expression this morning when they chimed; and if you can credit anything so absurd, I have been annoyed all the morning by those two pictures opposite, because they hang awry."

"That source of annoyance at least may be spared you. I shall take upon myself to alter them. What is this beautiful village church— is it a fancy picture? What a spire! and what fine cedars!"

"I have not seen the original since my boyhood, but this view scarcely does it justice. It is Swanstead Church."

"Has it any particular interest for you beyond its beauty?"

"It may probably have the deepest interest, if I am spared to middle life; the living is in the gift of my uncle, Colonel Norland."

"The east window is very fine," remarked the Rector of St. Bernard's, who was an enthusiast on the subject of church architecture. He then went on to describe some alterations then in progress in his own church. But before taking his leave, he said, with some hesitation, "I do not know what you will think of me, after hearing what I am about to acknowledge; but I really cannot take my departure without admitting that

I am myself responsible for the greater part of those pamphlets. I do not mean to say," he hastily explained, "that *I* wrote any of those odious personalities. I despise such modes of attack, and did what I could to dissuade Hewly from them; but I sketched out *all* the rest for him, and you best know how bitter it is. Nevertheless, I do not choose that you should remain ignorant of this, still less that any one else should tell it you."

"You are perfectly right to defend your cause to the utmost," returned Mr. Dreux, who seemed lost in thought.

"You are not offended?"

"O no."

"But I see very plainly that you never expected a covert attack from me."

"I am quite sure that I need never expect another," was the answer, given with a smile.

Still it was evident that he had formed in his own mind a higher estimate of his opponent's character than the result seemed to justify.

Allerton felt mortified, but answered calmly, "The only thing I wish to urge on your consideration is, that your views had had time to gain ground; I was, therefore, so far at a disadvantage. Still I *am* sorry that I should have drawn so many of your people away."

"I said before," was the reply, given however with the greatest gentleness, "that I can scarcely think so much harm has been done to the side

o

I advocate, as you seem to consider. Indeed, I must
tell you plainly that I do not believe one person, who
was a true· convert to the doctrines which we call
Evangelical, has been induced to leave us and
go to you. I do *not* believe it," he repeated, seeing
the incredulous look directed to him. " I do not
deny that the proceedings of the past year have
made my path far less easy, but it has shown
who really were for us, which before we could not
know. The scheme of salvation as set forth by you
and by us is a totally different thing. We declare
that faith, having been vouchsafed by God, the
sinner no sooner exercises it than he becomes
completely justified. And that, according to the
promise, 'whom he justified, them he also sanctified,'—the work of sanctification by the Holy Spirit
then begins. This is directly opposed to your
belief, which sets sanctification first, and when
it has reached a certain point, admits that the
sinner becomes justified.

" You also deny that change of heart which we
call conversion, and declare to be essential. I do
not say this to remind you how widely we stand
apart, but to account to you for my firm belief, that
no person who has experienced this conversion—
who had been taught the impossibility of doing
anything himself to forward his own salvation,
taught the deadly nature of sin and the fulness
of Christ, a knowledge which can only be imparted
by the Spirit of truth—would ever be permitted by

that same Spirit permanently to decline back upon the belief in any other scheme of salvation, and turn his back (for ever) upon the Lord who bought him, acknowledging that any outward sign or sacrament, or any holiness of his own, could save him."

"Go on," replied Allerton, whose penetrating eyes seemed as if they would search his very soul. "I will bear you out in some of your assertions, strong though they be. If one of us is right, how great must be the error of the other! If one is a true son of the Church, the other is scarcely worthy of the name. The only thing for each to consider is, which that one may be. And I hope," he continued, reflecting for an instant how strongly they had both spoken, "that you will permit me in future to call you my friend, and that we shall be able to preserve a personal regard for each other without any compromise of principle."

As might have been expected, he met with a cordial response to this, and took his leave, pleased on the whole with the interview; though the momentary change which had passed over Mr. Dreux's face when he acknowledged how much he had written of the pamphlets, rankled in his mind and subdued in some degree the peculiar regard he felt for him.

"He has the advantage of me in everything," he reflected, as he walked down the broad pavements of the streets leading to his rectory. "His temper is not half so warm as mine, and he does not so easily forget himself. I must get him to drop this pamphleteering,—but that new one, which he has not yet seen, what will he think of it? He *must* answer it. I hope I shall not be provoked into a rejoinder. Well! I would go great lengths to get him for an ally, but I suspect his principles have taken deep root. I went great lengths to-day, and I do not think he met me half way. I would not have endured that last speech of his if he had not looked so ill, and if I had not remembered what I have suffered the last three weeks. I am afraid my popularity will decline if we become friends. Nothing but this rivalry keeps us equal. I suspect he is more than a match for me. However, I have done this thing with my eyes open and of my own free will. If he has one spark of generosity he will be very careful now not to do me more harm than he can help; and, for the rest, perhaps the Vicar of Swanstead (whoever he is) may obligingly die, and so help me out of the difficulty."

A few days after this he called again on Mr. Dreux, and found him astonishingly better, and sitting at a table, with a paper-knife in his hand, which he was using on the pages of a new pamphlet, reading a piece here and there as he went on. He was beginning to look like himself again, and came forward with a most cordial smile to meet his visitor.

" So, I see you are commencing work again," said the Rector of St. Bernard's.

"Yes; but at present I am not equal to much exertion. I believe, however," laying his hand on the pamphlet, "that I must answer this. I have been looking it over, and fancy I can trace more of *your* style than usual in it."

"I did assist a good deal with it," was the reply. "I hope it does not offend you?"

"By no means. I think it fairly written, and not so difficult to answer as some of your former ones."

"Indeed! Well, whatever the answer may be, I will keep in mind that I began this contention; and I hope it will leave our newly-formed friendship unimpaired."

"What makes you doubt that? Is it the recollection of those words—'how shall two walk together except they be agreed?'"

"No; for our walking together may lead to our becoming agreed, which is 'a consummation devoutly to be wished.'"

"Not more by you than by me; but I will tell you what I am much afraid will prevent any close friendship between us, if no such change takes place. I am afraid our people, if they see us acting together,—seeking each other's society, and by constant communication sanctioning, in *appearance* at least, each other's proceedings,—may come to think that we consider the differences between us trivial and of no account,—that we think one set of opinions as good as another."

" And that I could not permit."

" No, we could not permit our conduct to give ground for such a supposition; and, therefore, my chief hope of anything like a permanent friendship between us is, that, as you have said, by the blessing of God, we may become agreed."

" And yet you seem quite confident that that agreement is to come from no change in your own opinions? Now" (laying his hand upon the arm of his late rival, and laughing) " don't begin again about conversion and all that sort of thing. I never could bear that exclusive doctrine, and yet I suppose you would tell me, that unless I pass through all its supernatural influences we shall never be agreed? No, no; I hope for better things. Why, what does our holy and perfect Church bestow baptism for on her infant members, if they are afterwards to be called upon to be converted, as if they were no better than Heathens?"

Though Mr. Allerton had spoken good-temperedly and as if half in joke, there was a contemptuous tone in his voice, when alluding to the tenets held by his friend, strangely at variance with the regard he expressed for him personally; and Mr. Dreux, as he leaned back in his chair and listened to all this and a great deal more, could scarcely reconcile the two together. He, however, showed both feelings strongly, and at the same time talked of his own plans with most perfect good faith, and made himself completely at home, insisting upon remaining for the morning to give his help with some accounts belonging to the secretaryship of the Pastoral-Aid Society, which, since Mr. Dreux's illness, had got into some confusion, and which that gentleman had been fretting himself to extricate from their tangled state.

If there is one thing that most clergymen agree to dislike it is accounts; the fraternity have a natural horror of them. And their curious habit of making memoranda on the backs of letters, making notes in pencil on any bit of paper that comes to hand, and then confiding the said paper to any drawer that happens to be open, makes the time for balancing very troublesome; so that when they *come* right (which expression is a most appropriate one) it seems to be by a happy accident, or, as it were, of their own accord.

Mr. Allerton hated accounts, like most of his brethren; nevertheless, he spent no less than two hours over the Society's books, and then, having got them into order, did not scruple to tell his obliged friend, with the most perfect *bon-hommie*, that he considered the Society a horrid Dissenting sort of thing, and it would give him great pleasure to see it knocked on the head!

"Then, how can you reconcile it to your conscience to help it forward so zealously?" was the rejoinder. "Your help has been the same thing as a five-pound note to it, for I should never have discovered that I had not paid my own subscription if you had not pointed it out to me."

"I wish the Society all manner of misfortunes, notwithstanding," replied the Rector of St. Bernard's, laughing, and buttoning up his coat preparatory to taking his leave; "and among others your speedy withdrawal from it."

"Don't you know the old saw,—'Love me, love my dog?'" inquired Mr. Dreux, calling after him as he was about to shut the door.

"Don't speak so loud, Dreux," said Allerton, putting in his head again, "it's enough to throw you into another fever. With regard to your dog, which you seem to think I ought to pet; I'll act by it as one of the boys in my school did this morning by another. I found two of them had been fighting when I went in, and I insisted that they should shake hands. They were a big boy and a little fellow; so the big boy turned round with his back to me, and just as they shook hands the little fellow burst out crying. 'What's the matter now?' I said, 'you little rascal.' 'O please, Sir,—please, Sir, just as Wylie shook hands with one hand, Sir, he fetched me a back-handed slap with the other.' Now don't laugh, Dreux; it's extremely bad for you. Keep calm." So saying, he shut the door, and left Mr. Dreux to meditate at leisure on his amiable eccentricities.

CHAPTER VIII.

THE HEROINE WITHOUT ADMIRERS.

THE Rector of St. Bernard's, partly in consequence
of his warm-heartedness, and partly in consequence
of his fiery temper, was very much influenced by
his friends, and neither acted nor thought for himself half so much as might have been expected from
a man of his talents and position.

As long as Mr. Dreux continued to retain the
slightest appearance of delicate health he kept himself under strong restraint in his intercourse with
him, but this appearance, with God's blessing on
an excellent constitution, soon vanished, and then
Mr. Allerton began to " come out in his own proper
colours."

He was one of those people of whom it is jocu-
larly said that they are always in hot water with
somebody. He could not help quarrelling with his
dearest friends ;—always putting himself in a passion whenever he was thwarted, and apologizing in
the most generous manner when his short-lived
anger had blown over.

On an average he quarrelled with Mr. Dreux about once a fortnight; sometimes going the length of declaring that he never would speak to him again, at others contenting himself by banging the library-door after him, with a noise that resounded through the whole house.

By the time he had got to the bottom of the stairs, he generally paused to consider; with consideration came regret. By this time Mr. Dreux had followed him to the foot of the stairs, and finding him standing irresolute in the hall, would inquire whether he would like a turn in the garden, and then, without waiting for a reply, take him by the arm, and the two would go out together, Mr. Allerton's passion subsiding as rapidly as the unusual colour from his face; till, after swallowing down the remainder of his wrath, he would interrupt the discourse on indifferent subjects by suddenly breaking out into a violent invective against himself, declaring that he was not fit for civilized society, that his friends must have the patience of fifty Jobs to bear with him, that he did not care in the least about the matter in dispute, and that he now saw he had been perfectly wrong throughout (but this he generally said whether he had been right or wrong), and that he requested forgiveness for his unaccountable behaviour.

With Mr. Dreux he was safe when he made these admissions, as he never suffered him to go further than he thought he would approve when he became calmer, nor ever took the least advantage of his warmly affectionate disposition; but with Mr. Hewly, his curate and college friend, things were different.

No two men could have been greater contrasts to each other than the rector and curate, and, judging by appearance and manner, no person could have supposed that the former was in bondage to the latter.

Mr. Allerton was a fine man, with a fair complexion, an erect figure, and a face so extremely open and honest, that few strangers, looking into his clear hazel eyes, would have hesitated to confide in him. Generous to a fault, open-hearted, and contemning all meanness, he seemed incapable of believing in such a failing among others, at *least* among educated and respectable people, and often, as he put himself into a passion about some flagrant act of deception in those whom he had befriended, he never inveighed against "the rascals" for cheating him without expressing as much surprise as if it had never happened to him before. As he walked in the streets, with his regular, firm step, and business-like air, his manner said, as plainly as possible, "Good people, I am not afraid to look any of you in the face. I am going about my lawful calling, and I have no doubt you are going about yours."

Mr. Hewly, his curate, was as different a man as

it is possible to imagine. He was about the middle height, extremely slender, had deep-set eyes, very smooth black hair, and used to walk with an air of deep humility, his eyes generally fixed on the ground. He seldom looked any one in the face, spoke in a low, internal voice, and often sighed deeply. He was not by any means without his admirers, but most even of *these* were afraid of him. He generally conveyed his wishes by insinuation, and exercised his influence in an underhand way.

But the most startling novelties in doctrine (and he held many which were such to his flock) he would advance in the calmest manner, as if they had been familiar truths which our Church plainly taught, and which no man in his senses would deny ; and if any one expressed astonishment at them, would affect anguish of mind, with indignation, not against the person objecting, but against his or her spiritual guides, who, he said, had much to answer for before God and the Church for their daring impiety in wilfully concealing the truths she taught. And then would follow an exhortation on obedience to the commands of the Church (as expounded by himself, of course), together with various promises as to the safety, comfort, and repose which should attend those who practised such obedience.

With this gentleman Mr. Allerton had formed a

friendship at college, and, when he found himself
settled in his living, had written to offer him the
curacy.

At first rector and curate got on amicably
enough, though Mr. Hewly, even in his friend's
opinion, went great lengths; and he sometimes
ventured to hint to him that he thought he was
drawing uncommonly near Rome.

But Mr. Hewly always replied, that he hoped to
see him following in the same path when more
light had been vouchsafed to him, and generally
contrived to follow his own track by means of the
concessions Mr. Allerton made after they had quarrelled.

By this means he got several innovations introduced into that church (and innovations they truly
might be called, as it had been built since the
Reformation), and set up several customs which his
friend reluctantly gave into, though he considered
them unnecessary, not to say highly imprudent.

" We shall certainly get into some scrape," said
the Rector, going one day into his curate's study,
and throwing down a newspaper, which contained a
letter full of severe strictures " on the manner in
which Divine service is conducted at St. Bernard's."

This letter, after commenting on the changes
lately introduced, went on,— " And do the officiating clergymen of this church really mean to
tell a congregation of intelligent English people,

that all this bowing and reverence towards the
table of the communion,—these senseless imitations
of the worship of the corrupt Church of Rome,—
have anything in them of the nature of true godli-
ness? Do they mean to impose upon the people
this double absurdity?—for what is this but a copy
of the priest's bow of reverence to the host, which,
in a Catholic church, stands upon the altar? But
to bow to an empty communion-table is worse than
folly,—it is a pretence of a sin that they cannot
commit, when the host (the idol) is not there to be
adored!"

"There," exclaimed Mr. Allerton, flinging the
paper across to his curate, "see what you have
brought upon us! Did not I tell you that your
preaching would be quite as effectual without all that
—that (he was going to say "mummery," but was
checked by his curate's eye),—" and would not
arouse half the suspicions?"

Mr. Hewly took up the newspaper, and having
doubled it to his mind, read the letter through
twice with great deliberation, and scrutinized it so
long as tenfold to increase the passionate impatience
of his Rector. He then said, quietly folding it up,
" I always said that fellow Dreux was a false friend
to you, but you never would believe it."

" What has that to do with it?" exclaimed Mr.
Allerton, turning short round upon him, fretted
almost past bearing by his quiet way of taking the
thing, and his daring allusion to Mr. Dreux.

"No more to do with it," pursued Mr. Hewly, "than that this is wonderfully like his style. However, as he is your sworn friend, I suppose nothing must be said against him; but if he does not get us into some scrape or other I am very much mistaken."

Now Mr. Hewly knew perfectly well that the letter was no more like Mr. Dreux's style than it was like the Pope's; but after he had made the above remarks he took up his pen and began to write again, as if his mind was made up on the matter.

"*His* style!" cried Mr. Allerton, snatching up the paper with more than his usual impetuosity;— "if I thought he had written this letter, holding me up to ridicule in an underhand way, I'd never speak to him again as long as I lived."

Mr. Hewly smiled. "You ought to be a good judge of his style, I should think," he said; "he is always writing something or other against you."

"Not against *me*, and not lately, either," interrupted Allerton; for, angry as he was, he perceived the injustice of this remark.

"But I suppose you must like it," Mr. Hewly proceeded, as if he had not heard the interruption; "or at least, you must have changed your opinions since you knew him, for you are always quoting them. He insinuates them so cleverly that you will soon be over on his side if you let him get so completely the upper hand of you. Why, he can wind you round his finger! And then he pretends to be attached to you! Bah! I hate such dissimulation!"

"Change my opinions! go over to the Evangelicals!" cried Mr. Allerton, "and be ridiculed by him behind my back! No, that I never will. Give me the paper this instant." So saying, he snatched up his hat and posted off to Mr. Dreux's house, boiling over with passion,—the most bitter ingredient in the dose his curate had administered being the insinuation that Dreux only pretended to be attached to him in order to bring him over to *his* side.

In the meantime, Mr. Hewly, well content with his pious fraud, sat awaiting the result full of hope that his Rector, being far too angry to explain himself, would begin his interview with such an outbreak of invective as Mr. Dreux never could forgive.

There was at the end of Mr. Dreux's garden a high wall with a door in it. Mr. Allerton had a key of this door, for the garden was at the back of the house, and was much his shortest way of reaching it, which was an object, as they had now almost daily intercourse.

Though very angry he did not forget to take this key with him, and, having let himself in, proceeded up the walks in a towering passion, and ran up a flight of steps to the verandah, into which the library windows opened. The weather was fine, and Mr. Dreux, looking up from his writing, close to the open window, was astonished at the vehement passion exhibited in his face, and which was too great to suffer him to speak at his first entrance.

He came into the room, and taking out the newspaper, flung it towards his supposed enemy, struck his hand violently on the table.

" What *is* the matter?" exclaimed his host.

" If—if ever I come into this house again," he stammered.

"Which I hope you will to-morrow," replied Mr. Dreux, without the least appearance of anger, for he was quite used to him.

" Will you listen to me, Sir?" stammered Mr. Allerton. " Do you see that newspaper?"

" Yes, I see it," he replied, pushing a chair towards him. " Come, my dear Allerton, sit down, and try to be calm."

" Calm!" repeated Mr. Allerton. " Sit down in your house! If—if ever I do—" and here he gave the table another blow.

"Give me your hat," said his host, rising and taking it from him, at the same time giving him a gentle push towards the chair.

" Will you read that letter?" cried Mr. Allerton, more angry than ever, and at the same time throwing himself into the chair which he had so vehemently abjured.

" Yes, to be sure I will," answered its supposed writer, speaking in the most soothing tones of his pleasant voice, and quite disturbed at the painful excitement he manifested. "What am I to read? the letter on this page?" He took up the paper with such perfect coolness, and read it through as if it was so utterly new to him, that Mr. Allerton already began to think there must be some mistake, and when, after finishing it, he looked up for an explanation, he felt ashamed to give it him.

He was a man who of all things detested ridicule; he now began to feel that he really was in a ridiculous position; but if his friend thought so too, he had the delicacy not to betray the slightest consciousness of it. And was it likely, whatever Hewly might have said, that *he* would hold him up to derision in an anonymous letter? That this same man who now sat opposite to him with the honourable uprightness of his soul so plainly stamped upon his noble features could be such a master of dissimulation as to be capable of looking up and saying, "I shall be glad of an explanation, Allerton. I do not see what this letter can have to do with your anger against *me*."

"Against *you*," repeated Allerton, aroused to renewed irritation partly against himself, partly against his curate, and partly against his friend for taking it so coolly;—"Against *you!*" Look at it again. Can you tell me you are ignorant from whose pen it proceeded? Do you think I can be so familiar with your style and not recognise it there?"

He paused when he had got so far, astonished at

the effect of his accusation. He had been accustomed to see him so perfectly unmoved when he tried to quarrel with him, and so ready to excuse any ebullition of anger when it was over, that the glow of incredulous indignation which mounted to his very temples, was no less new than startling.

It was however not for long—though long enough to banish every vestige of suspicion and completely calm his passion—that he had to wait before it subsided. After a struggle to regain his composure he took up the newspaper, which in the first moment of offended pride he had thrown from him, folded it, and returned it, saying, with tolerable calmness,—

" The warmth of your temper has been an excuse for many past accusations, but this is a suspicion which no passion can possibly justify."

Perfectly silenced, and feeling deeply hurt, Allerton took the paper, and his host, still struggling to prevent any further outbreak of displeasure, got up and took a few turns up and down the room, the glow gradually leaving his features, but leaving such an expression of mortification as could not fail to pain the person who had caused it, who, notwithstanding the reckless manner in which he had wounded him, had in the bottom of his heart more regard for him than for any one else in the world.

But when Dreux came up to him again and with something like his usual manner proposed that they should go down into the garden, instead of his ordinary vehement apologies when they had had a difference, he simply said, "I am sorry I have hurt your feelings," and went down into the garden far more pained at his keen sense of the accusation brought against him and his struggle to preserve his usual manner, than he would have been at any display of irritation, however violent.

"I am sorry I have hurt your feelings," he repeated, when they had reached the bottom of the garden and were turning towards the house again.

"Do not think of it. Pray do not allude to it again," replied Mr. Dreux, wincing at the very mention of the thing.

"I did not mean to annoy you by allusions to what I am thoroughly ashamed of, but you must let me at least express my contrition," was the reply.

This garden, which was beautifully laid out and adorned with several fine elm-trees, was a very favourite resort with its owner, particularly when his temper was at all ruffled by little petty vexations, and to Mr. Allerton it was a real boon, saving him from many an intemperate outbreak, for when he felt himself getting hot in an argument, he used to go out and walk for a while, and return all the better for its fresh air and cool shades.

On the present occasion it had a healing influence, and after a few minutes' walk, the two gentlemen began to converse very amicably on subjects about which they were not likely to disagree, till, on a sudden, Mr. Dreux exclaimed,—

"Allerton, do answer me one question. It was not your *own* idea that I wrote that letter? Surely some one else must have put it into your head?"

"Since you ask, I have no hesitation in saying that I never should have dreamed of suspecting you if it had not been suggested to me."

"By whom? Was it not by Hewly?"

"Yes, it was," replied Mr. Allerton, and partly from a sensation of irritation against him, partly by way of retribution, he related the conversation they had held that morning, not even omitting the hint that Dreux only *professed* friendship for him, held up his opinions to ridicule, and would gladly get him into a scrape.

Instead of being angry, Dreux laughed at this, and said,—

"Why did you not tell me that at first? Do you suppose I care what *he* thinks of me? Here have I been fretting myself for the last half-hour, and making a great merit of forgiving you, instead of which, if I had known what you have just told me, I should have thought nothing of it. But, my dearest Allerton, what a pity it is you should be so much at the mercy of those with whom you associate; how can you allow yourself to be played upon in this way, and made a tool of? You surely know that Hewly cannot bear me, and can scarcely speak civilly to me. Nothing would please him better than to set us at variance. As to my trying to bring you over to my side, *that* is a proof of my friendship and sincerity, which, even if it were any business of his, ought not to surprise him. Besides, he knows perfectly well that the attempt has been mutual."

Allerton replied by violently inveighing against the conduct of Hewly, and declaring that he would not be influenced by him in future.

"And as to your being got in some awkward predicament by *me*—let me use the privilege of friendship, and entreat you to be more cautious. I am quite sure that you scarcely approve of some of the alterations which Hewly has induced you to sanction. And if serious notice should be taken, who will be to blame? Not I, Allerton. Nor Hewly either, so much as yourself, for suffering your better reason to be overborne by him—a man so much your inferior in intellect and uprightness of mind."

"I ought to have a man like you for my curate; you never take advantage of my temper, you always advise me for the best, and after every quarrel we are better friends than ever."

Mr. Hewly, who long before this had expected the return of his Rector, began to feel rather uncomfortable at his protracted absence. He could not account for it; and as the evening wore on, he wished he had not ventured upon his bold suggestion. But his uneasiness was nothing to what it would have been if he could have seen him after dinner sitting with Mr. Dreux in the library, discussing the letter, his curate, and the said curate's opinions, with most perfect confidence in his honour and good faith,—actually he would have thought taking counsel of the enemy.

"I am astonished," said the over-generous Mr. Allerton, "that I could, for a moment, have thought this trumpery letter resembled your composition. It is very badly written."

The answer was—"Yes, very badly written, but the worst of it is that it's TRUE. It begins by remarking that you always preach in your surplice."

"Well, what of that? Surely that is a thing of no consequence!"

"Not the slightest consequence in the world; then why do it, in this place, contrary to immemorial custom?"

"People call it the badge of a party, and they have no right to do so; it is very unjust."

"Not unjust to *you*, certainly, for you have always openly acknowledged your party. If I see a man in the uniform of a soldier, how am I unjust if I take it for granted that he serves in the army?"

"I choose to follow the ancient custom of the Church."

"What! even contrary to her expressed desire? I do not wish to go into any question as to what *is* the ancient custom, because our Church expressly tells us that every particular Church hath authority to change ceremonies and rites. Grant, then, that the ancient custom has been changed: you are not an obedient son of the Church if you restore it, for she says, ' He ought to be rebuked that doth willingly and purposely break the traditions and ceremonies of the Church (and here she must surely mean the *existing* ceremonies), as he that offendeth against the common order of the Church.' "

" Well, let that pass," said Allerton, impatiently.

" As to the latter part, it certainly contains a much more serious charge; and I must ask you, my dear Allerton, where you find any warrant in Scripture for such observances—such bowings and prostrations?"

" I find plenty of warrant in the ancient practice of the Church."

" What Church? But not to go out of our way to argue about that, we here touch upon one of our chief grounds of difference. *You* honour the Scriptures so far as they seem to uphold the Church, *I* honour the Church because she holds the doctrines of the Scriptures."

" And pray," said Mr. Allerton, " how do you reconcile it to your conscience to contemn the accumulated wisdom of ages, and despise the traditions of the early saints?"

" Are, then, their accumulated wisdom and holy traditions so contrary to the spirit of Scripture that I cannot uphold both?"

" Don't argue unfairly, Dreux. Is not the Church

the only true interpreter of Scripture? has not she herself the best right to say whether or not they agree?"

"I demur to your proposition—the Holy Spirit is the true interpreter of Scripture; but if I agreed with you, tell me what the Church is?"

"If you mean in whom is this authority of the Church vested, I say, in the three orders of priesthood—the bishops, priests, and deacons—of this and past ages."

"Well, I will meet you on your own ground: and I ask, being possessed of this authority as well as yourself, where do you find that the Scriptures require us to be subject to any such traditions as those you think you ought to honour? Where do you find it laid upon this generation as a duty to be subject to the souls of past generations? Besides, has not each generation in its turn been the present? If, then, the generation of hundreds of years ago was born to follow tradition, and was not able to judge for itself, how can it be able to judge for me, so that I should be subject to its laws? How can you say you are so bound, for *I* can find no such law; on the contrary, I find that the Scriptures assert their own exclusive authority. And as for the traditions of men and their 'fond inventions,' I find no warrant for them. But so far from it, I find this injunction, 'Add thou *not* unto *His* words, lest He reprove thee,' and, 'If any man shall add unto these things, God shall add unto him the plagues that are written in this book, and if any man shall take away from the words of the book of this prophecy, God shall take away his part out of the book of life.'

"However, no doubt you will tell me that you deny the authority to a solitary individual, though you grant it to the whole body. To that I can only reply that we are both in the same case: if one has no right to say, 'This is the meaning,' the other has no right to say, 'No, it is not.'"

Allerton, who with his arms upon the table had been earnestly listening to his friend's remarks, said, when he had finished, "There is one thing, Dreux, and only one, in which I wish you would follow my example."

"What is that?"

"Since the first few weeks of our acquaintance I have never obtruded my opinions upon you, and I should be very glad if you would treat me with equal forbearance."

"Impossible! Do we not differ in the most essential particulars, and with that belief can you really expect me never to try to convince you, or, if I did not, could you believe in the sincerity of my regard?"

Allerton coloured on hearing this, and said, "By that remark you call in question the sincerity of mine."

"I had no such thought, nor do I in the least question it."

"Then," persisted the other, "you *must* either

excuse me from the belief that I do not consider religion of half the importance you do, or you must think I hold my views of it in a very half-hearted manner."

Finding that he waited for an answer, Dreux replied, " I do not think that any man who professes that he has never suffered under the burden of his sins, nor caught at the free grace and mercy of God as his *only* refuge, can, in the nature of things, attach so much importance to his religion as the man who *has*. It cannot be so present to him, or so real."

" Well, I suppose I must take that for an answer," said Mr. Allerton, rising up with a sigh, " but I *do* wish you could let me alone."

After this they went into the garden. He was in a tranquil, thoughtful humour, and his friend took this opportunity to press on him the more careful study of the Scriptures, to see " whether these things were so." He listened with patience, almost with pleasure—for it gratified him to find himself the object of such persevering solicitude; and besides, the tones of his friend's voice always exercised an agreeable influence over him. He listened to it as to " a lovely song of one who has a pleasant voice ; " and sometimes permitted a wonder to rest in his mind for a moment, whether his affection for this last-made friend might not in time sufficiently master him, to induce him to adopt *his* principles, just as his late lamented friend at college, who found him a thoughtless, worldly young fellow, had so influenced his whole character as to induce him to take up *his*. If it were not for the sake of consistency, he felt that such a change might take place. His was a religion more of feeling than principle, and having no solid basis, might easily be moved. However, he roused himself at last, and took his leave, as usual, after a fresh quarrel, more bound to him than ever. He went home, and the next day had a dispute with Mr. Hewly, which he did not make up with half so much cordiality as usual; and carefully avoiding the least intimation as to what had passed in Dreux's house, peremptorily insisted on several slight alterations being made in the manner of conducting service; and then preached a sermon which verged in a very slight degree towards evangelical doctrine—not so much so, however, as to be detected by any but the most discerning of his flock, and was intended specially to intimidate his curate, and let him understand that he had better not push him too far, or there was no saying how far he might go the other way, on purpose to spite him. However, Mr. Hewly, though much alarmed by the said sermon, did not set it down to its true cause, and did not doubt it was all owing to Dreux's influence.

While all these events were taking place at Westport, things at Swanstead went on much as usual, the chief circumstance that occurred being that Marion had her picture taken, at the request of her brother, for whom it was done.

It was a much more tedious business than she had supposed when she gave her consent to sit for it, and the artist was a very ill-tempered old gentleman. Marion was thankful when it was finished and sent to Westport. She could not bear sitting for hours in one attitude, with her hands dropped upon her knees, and her eyes directed towards a particular flower in the wainscot carving, and it was a great pleasure to receive a letter from Wilfred declaring that it was a most speaking likeness. So Marion, having stipulated that it should not be hung in the ordinary sitting-room at her uncle's house in Westport, dismissed it from her mind, and went to see her different poor people, and take leave of them, for she was to go to Westport in a week, and stay away three months,—a long time to look forward to. Mr. Raeburn was to escort her there, and remain a day or two. It was expected that Elizabeth's wedding would take place before Marion's return, and she was to be one of the bridesmaids.

About the same time that Mr. Raeburn and Marion arrived at their destination, Mr. Allerton, who had been out for a short excursion, came home, and having business to transact with Mr. Dreux, proceeded straight to that gentleman's house through the garden. It was about eight o'clock in the evening. There had been a deluge of rain all day, and as he looked up to the windows of the library, which was lighted from within, they presented such a cheerful appearance that he quickened his pace, and running up the stone stairs, tapped briskly on the glass, as was his custom.

The footman, who at that moment was bringing in the tea-urn, knew the accustomed signal, and advanced to the window to open it. In the meantime Mr. Allerton had a full view of the room, which contained one more inmate than he had expected.

It had been a very late spring, and though already the second week in May, the evening was chilly, and a bright wood fire was burning on the hearth. Mr. Dreux was seated on a sofa beside it, with a Review in his hand ; and close to the sofa stood a table, with a lamp upon it, and before the tea-urn sat a young lady.

All this Mr. Allerton saw at a glance, and would have withdrawn, but his tap had been observed. " This must be Dreux's sister," he thought, as the young lady turned her face that way ; " her profile is very like his, and he said she was coming to visit him some time this spring."

" Come in, Allerton," exclaimed Dreux, as the window was opened, and Mr. Allerton's dripping umbrella taken from him.

' He accordingly came forward, with an uncomfortable feeling of awkwardness and embarrassment at his intrusion. He was introduced to Miss Dreux, feeling keenly conscious all the while that his appearance was not exactly " comme il faut," for his hair was in disorder, his boots splashed, and his whole outer man far from exhibiting that perfect neatness which generally characterizes a clergyman.

" If you'll allow me, Dreux," he then said, " I'll go to your dressing-room."

" Certainly," was the reply. " Joseph, bring a candle."

" That gentleman makes himself very much at home," said Miss Dreux. " So he is your friend Mr. Allerton."

Mr. Dreux laughed, and remarked that he had not made his first appearance under very favourable circumstances. His sister, then remembering that she had left her work up stairs, went to fetch it during the absence of the stranger. She had scarcely shut the door behind her when Mr. Allerton entered at another. He advanced with a candle in his hand, wearing a white cravat of unblemished purity, and a coat which seemed to attract the notice of his host, for he looked pointedly at it, and uttered the expressive word INDEED.

" Why, you see, my dear fellow," said Mr. Allerton, in reply to that short remark, " if I had sat all the evening in a wet coat I might have caught cold ; besides, I am naturally anxious to appear well before your sister."

His host admitted the reasonableness of both propositions.

Miss Dreux then returned, and commenced the duties of the tea-table. She behaved to him with a little distance and reserve at first, and he mistook her shyness for pride; but as the evening drew on, he altered his mind and liked her very much, though he once or twice detected a lurking smile about the corners of her lips, which he rightly attributed to the ludicrous stiffness and awkwardness of his movements, for his borrowed coat was too tight for him. She was several years younger than her brother,— that is, about nineteen, and though not nearly so handsome, bore a general resemblance to him in her air and expression. She was, however, by no means without her attractions,—had, like her brother, a very pleasant voice, and was, moreover, of a joyous disposition, with a keen sense of the ludicrous, though without anything sarcastic or severe.

Though not timid, she clung to her brother with most dependent reliance, and looked upon her yearly visit to him as the greatest pleasure of her life. In religion he had been her only guide, and she had imbibed all her views on that subject from him; but her unaffected piety was certainly not likely to enhance Mr. Allerton's admiration, for he found out in conversation, even during that first evening, that she was "one of Dreux's sort."

However, he thought it must be a very disagreeable sentiment indeed that a man could not endure from the lips of such a sweet young creature.

Elinor retired early, leaving the two gentlemen together, upon which Mr. Allerton divested himself of his coat, drew an easy chair before the fire, and having put a large block of wood upon it, and possessed himself of the poker, prepared for conversation.

" Well," said his friend, " and so you preached before the Bishop."

Mr. Allerton nodded. He was humming a tune, and did not wish to interrupt himself. When he had finished he continued looking at the fire for a few minutes, with a half-smile upon his lips ; then, having given it one or two scientific thrusts, turned round, and said, " I have got a new teacher in my girls' school,—who do you think ? "

His friend made several unsuccessful guesses.

" I found a note on my table before I went out from Miss Ferguson, saying that she should be happy to become a visitor, and that Miss Paton would take her class when she was out. They called almost directly, with old Ferguson. Miss Paton 's an elegant young woman."

" Yes," said Mr. Dreux.

" Very elegant,—a perfect lady. I thought her manners quite interesting ; she has a sweet smile. What's her Christian name ? "

" Dora."

"Ah, not a bad name either. Well, she's an elegant young woman, as I said before."

Mr. Dreux replied as before, "*In-deed.*" This word seems to have nothing particular in it, yet when uttered by some people, it expresses all manner of indescribable things.

"What do you mean, Dreux?" said Allerton, quickly.

"What do *I* mean?" inquired that gentleman, with an air of unconscious innocence. "Why, what do *you* mean?"

"Nonsense!" exclaimed Mr. Allerton. "I know very well what you have taken into your head; there's nothing in it, nothing whatever. I no more think of her than she does of me."

"Oh!" said Mr. Dreux, taking away the poker, and in his turn giving the log a few dexterous thrusts. "Then if any one asks me when it's coming off, I'd better tell them at once that there's nothing in it."

"Dear me!" exclaimed Mr. Allerton, ruefully, "I hope it's not reported in the town; I hope not. Most absurd, if it is. I never was in company with Miss Paton but twice. Surely, Dreux, it's not a common report in the town."

"Not that I know of," replied the person so appealed to, with the utmost coolness. "I never heard any one breathe a syllable of it but yourself, just this minute, and you may depend upon my not telling, Allerton."

The victim made a feint of being very angry.

" Well," proceeded Mr. Dreux, "so you preached before the Bishop?"

" Yes, to be sure, and dined with him on Monday."

" Did he say anything about your sermon ?"

"Not much ; I took care to choose a practical subject, and treat it what might have been called cautiously,—in short, to exercise ' the wisdom of the serpent;' but I don't want Hewly to know that. However, he sent to ask for my sermon, and I gave it. He was tolerably frank in conversation when I dined with him, but yesterday morning I called, and he received me politely, though I thought just a little coldly,—for you know I notice anything like coldness. I think he was not at all cordial, but perhaps as much so as I had any right to expect, he being rather one of your sort. However, he expressed himself pleased with the schools, and the restorations in the church, and then said, ' And pray how is your friend, Mr. Dreux ?' I thought he emphasized the word ' friend' very strongly, and I said you were very well, I was happy to say. ' And how do you manage your disputes, Sir ?' he said, in his slightly pompous way ; ' which is pupil, and which is master ?' ' Disputes, my Lord !' I answered. ' You take it for granted, then, that we have disputes.' ' Undoubtedly, Sir, undoubtedly ; or if not disputes, arguments and controversy,—for I take it no two men of honest minds can differ

without them.' 'We certainly have had a good
deal of controversy,' I replied, and I wondered
whether he had read any of it. 'So I presumed,
Sir,' he said. 'The great problem for human thought
is before you,—that question into which all religion
resolves itself, and you solve it differently.' What
question did he mean, do you think? 'What is
truth?'"

"I should rather think he meant the more defined
one. *How* shall man be just before God? that is
the all-important question to which we give such
different answers. The key-stone which supports
the whole structure of religion; the one momentous
problem on which hope and happiness hinges,—
How shall man be just before God?"

Mr. Allerton was silent for a few minutes, then
said, "By the bye, Dreux, what a crowd there was
at your church on the Thursday evening that I
went away. Was it any particular occasion?"

"The Thursday before last,—yes; there is an
annual sermon preached on that day to the sailors.
A sea-captain met with a great deliverance from
shipwreck, and left a small sum of money to have a
sermon preached on its anniversary for ever. After
service we give away the money to the sailors'
widows."

"O that was it! Well, as I went down the street
to the coach-office, I was a little too early, so I
stood a while in the porch, for it was full to the
door, and there was such a strong light thrown on

to your face that I could see every change of expression distinctly, though too far off to hear a word you said. It had a very curious effect;—there you were, thundering away in dumb show, conveying impressions without ideas. Some old seamen standing beside me seemed to think they were very much edified, and said it was a very fine discourse. One old fellow informed me, that 'that was Parson Dreux,—quite a Boanerges;' and some of them seemed quite impressed with your face and action. Now there you, who speak extempore, have certainly an advantage over us; for my own part, I am generally rather quiet in the pulpit. But I could not help laughing afterwards, when I thought how Hewly would have looked at that distance. Like an image, I suspect; for he stands stock still and pours out his words in a smooth, sleek stream, never venturing to turn his head lest he should lose his place; but sometimes he gives his eyes a sweep round in an inexpressibly penetrating manner. If anything is amiss he is sure to see it. If ever there was a deep, artful—Never mind, I'd better keep my opinions on that subject to myself; but he quite gets the better of me."

"Why did you stay at Chester so long?" asked Mr. Dreux, rousing himself from a reverie; "a whole week, was it not?"

"Yes. Why, the fact is, I happened to meet a poor fellow whom I used to befriend at Cambridge, a miniature-painter; he paints beautifully, but not being the fashion he can scarcely get his bread. I declare he looks as if he had not enough to eat, and he asked me so wistfully if I had nothing for him to do that I was fain to tell him I wanted my portrait painted."

"Just like you. But what will you do with it?"

"I don't know. I have neither kith nor kin, excepting my old cousin, who kept me a boy as long as he could, and seems to think I'm scarcely a man yet; and I think I see myself having my picture taken for him! Well, I had no idea what a business it would be; I gave him a long sitting every day, and heartily sick I was of it. One day I fell asleep, but he said it was of no consequence, he had only been painting the hair. I think it very like, though it has rather a sleepy expression; so, when it was done, I hung it by a black riband round my own neck, and what to do with it I don't know."

"Let me look at it."

The possessor disengaged the riband, and, handing it over, said, with the assumed carelessness with which people generally speak of their own portraits, "Has the fellow done it well?"

"Excellent!—capital! I never saw a more satisfactory likeness."

"Rather sleepy-looking, is it not?"

"No; it only looks calm,—that is an advantage. I cannot bear a grinning portrait." And having then inspected the picture thoroughly, he wrapped the riband round the case and put it into his own waistcoat-pocket, saying, very composedly, "You had better leave it in my possession ; you will only lose it if I give it you back. If you marry to my mind it is just possible that I may give it to your wife,—that is to say, if you wish it ; and I see no reason to alter my intention. In the meantime you know you don't want it, and I do."

Allerton laughed, though secretly much pleased, and said, "If I die unmarried, which I most likely shall do, it *may* help to keep me in your remembrance ; and one does not like the idea of being utterly forgotten in the world."

"You will never be forgotten in the world as long as I am in it," was the reply.

And the fire being nearly out and the clock striking twelve, the two gentlemen separated, Mr. Allerton taking with him a lively recollection of his friend's sister and wondering whether she was engaged.

"And what made Dreux take it in his head to quiz me in that way?" he thought. "*I* saw his quiet smile when I said I should most likely die unmarried."

It was natural that Elinor should ask several questions about him the next morning as they sat at breakfast, and that her brother should give her the history of the rise and progress of their friendship.

"So, then, you have only been friends a

year," she said, "and you seem as intimate as brothers."

"So we are," was the reply; "and I never cease to hope that the day may come when we shall agree on the one important subject about which we now differ, that we may believe alike and work together. I thought, last night, he seemed particularly anxious to avoid the topics on which we differ,—probably in compliment to you, my dear."

"In compliment to me!" said Elinor, laughing merrily. "Oh no, dearest Arthur; gentlemen never pay compliments to *me*. I scarcely remember ever to have received one yet."

"Why, my dear, you cannot be in earnest?" said her brother, with an incredulous smile.

"I assure you it is quite true," said Elinor, amused at his surprise.

"But you must have had proposals?"

Elinor laughed and shook her head. "If I had been a heroine in a book," she said, merrily, "I should have had three or four despairing lovers by this time. But I don't mind confiding to you, dear Arthur,—that I not only never had an offer, but no gentleman ever said anything to me which I could have twisted into a pretence of preference; and yet my aunt sees a great deal of society, and, as I am always with her, a great many people pass in review before me."

Mr. Dreux replied, that it was very odd.

His sister continued: "You never read of nay

young lady in a book who has not had at least one admirer,—some have three or four; and I have come to this philosophical conclusion, that if one have so many others must go without."

" Of course they must," replied her brother, in the abstracted tone of a person trying to solve a difficult problem.

Elinor burst into a joyous laugh, and presently said, " But what a very common-looking watchguard you have got, dearest; I must make you a better one."

" This is not a watch-guard," said her brother; " it's a portrait that Allerton brought here last night. I think I'll hang it in my dressing-room. Look at it,—is it not like?"

Elinor came close to her brother and took up the little likeness in her hand. " I should like to have such a one of you," she said, after inspecting it. " Really this Mr. Allerton has something inexpressibly candid and amiable in his face,—what a pity that he is so unsound in principle! Do you still carry on your pamphlet war?"

" Oh no, we dropped it long ago; but not before I began to think it did more harm than good, which I did not expect."

" How so, Arthur?"

" Do you remember my sending some to you?"

" Yes; and I liked yours very much, and I thought his extremely clever."

" So clever, my dear, that you said they half

carried you over to his side, till you had read the answer."

" Yes; but when I *had* read the answer, I was satisfied."

" But that remark of yours opened my mind to an evil which I had not suspected. I thought the result would be good, and so it was to the really intelligent; but I begin to be convinced that there are many people in the world who really have not the power to think. These people were shocked when they found that things which they had believed from their childhood *could* be called in question. And when it was asserted of certain dogmas, that they were the doctrines of our Church and of the Bible, they knew so little, theoretically, of the faith they professed, that they could neither refute the assertion, nor give any reason why they held a contrary belief, and so their minds got thoroughly shaken. If all those who adorn the profession of Christianity by their lives and practice were well versed in what may be called its theory, the case might be different."

" But all Christians ought to know the doctrines of their Church," said Elinor.

" Undoubtedly they ought; but it has been for a long time the custom here to dwell almost exclusively on the Gospel invitation and the first rudiments of Christianity. Several very successful clergymen here might have been compared to men standing on the steps of a temple and inviting

people to come in; they held out their hands to
them and helped them to enter the door, but when
once they were in, turned, and without troubling
themselves as to how the newly-entered would proceed, went on with their invitations to those without.   By this plan they left their converts very
ignorant of the deeper mysteries of religion, and to
this day they are distasteful to them; so that when
any of us preach on such subjects, which we are
impelled to do both by inclination and necessity,
particularly since Allerton and Hewly came, they
do not scruple to lament the days of 'good old
Mr. So-and-so, who never troubled simple-minded
Christians with much about election, predestination,
the corruption of the will, the nature of the sacra-
ments, &c., but fed them with the sincere milk of
the Word,'—never considering that by this com-
mendation they are actually accusing their late
pastors of not declaring to them the whole counsel
of God, and that ignorance is of all things most
likely to lead them astray."

As has before been mentioned, it was about eight
o'clock in the evening when Mr. Raeburn brought
Marion to her uncle's door. She soon found herself
surrounded by her brother and cousins, the two
younger of whom she had not seen since their
infancy.   Little more could be done that night than
to sit on a sofa in the drawing-room, answer all
inquiries, and endeavour to seem unconscious of the
scrutiny she was undergoing, and not to notice the

sotto voce remarks that went on around her as to whether she was grown and what she was like.

Mr. and Mrs. Paton were chiefly occupied in another room with Mr. Raeburn relative to the affairs of their wards. Marion retired early, a good deal fatigued with her journey, and Elizabeth took her to her room, which was connected with a small parlour—half drawing-room, half boudoir. It was wainscotted, and the moon shining through the stained glass in the window made it look almost like a chapel, so silent and grave did it seem.

Elizabeth perceived that Marion felt a little agitated after her introduction to her young relations; she therefore did not remain in her room, but kissing her affectionately, rang for her maid and left her to her meditations.

Marion had many subjects for thought; her uncle's house, familiar to her imagination from childhood as the first home of her mother, proved, as might have been expected, totally different to the idea she had formed of it. It was a fine old place, such as is still sometimes seen in a country town. There was a beautiful garden behind it, and its mullioned windows, oak wainscots, and wandering stone passages, gave it altogether an air of "pomp and ancientry."

Wilfred was very much grown since she had last seen him; he was also much more manly in appearance; he seemed quite domesticated among his cousins, who were evidently very fond of him.

Elizabeth and Dora, Marion thought, were both changed, but she scarcely knew whether for the better or the worse. Her third cousin, Rosina, was a perfect stranger to her, but even during that first evening Marion felt greatly attracted towards her. She was about fifteen, short for her age, and altogether childlike. She was the only one of the family who was fair, and so far she resembled Marion. It was rather remarkable that though the cousins were doubly related there was scarcely any likeness between them, each family resembling its respective father. Rosina seemed to be considered quite in a subordinate position by her elder sisters, who expected her to run up stairs for them, deliver their messages, and be attentive to their wishes; neither was she allowed to offer her opinion in the conversation. Her countenance was exquisitely modest and retiring, and her hair literally flaxen, and as she sat listening to the conversation of her elder sisters she looked as if she was born to admire the perfections of others and obey their wishes. Yet there was nothing unkind or exacting in the manners of the elder sisters. Rosina was not yet grown up, and they thought she *ought* to obey. Nor was there the slightest sullenness or unwillingness on the part of the sweet little girl, who treated them with a respectful deference not often bestowed or required. She admired her sisters and entertained the fond delusion that they were altogether her superiors, and she could never hope to be so interesting or so elegant.

As for the only son, he was about thirteen, and was alike the darling and the torment of his sisters; he was extremely like Elizabeth, had the same brown hair and dark eyes, with all her liveliness of disposition. He had a reckless good humour about him, and generally walked with his head on one side, as if in the enjoyment of some exquisite joke. One of his great peculiarities was, that he could not pronounce the letter r; another that he had a striking facility in finding out whatever his sisters most wished him *not* to know; it was impossible to conceal anything from him, and it was currently reported in the family that he knew of Mr. Bishop's partiality for Elizabeth some time before any one else found it out. It was a subject on which he took special delight in teazing her, notwithstanding which she was his favourite sister,—a distinction which she did not deserve, for she had done more to spoil him than all the rest of the family put together, even including his father, who rather enjoyed to hear him teaze Elizabeth by asking at table or other embarrassing times, "Pa, why does Fwed Bishop dine here so much oftener than his father?" or, "Pa, why does Elizabeth have so many letters now Fwed Bishop's in the Highlands?"

Marion found the whole family busily engaged in discussing a bazaar, which was to be held in the

Town Hall for the benefit of the infant-schools.
After breakfast, Mr. Raeburn having gone out
to call on some of his old friends, Mrs. Paton
reminded her daughters that they must give her
their help in ticketing the articles for sale, while
she and the other ladies of the Committee were
engaged in deciding on the position of the stalls.
Marion offered her help, and Elizabeth proposed
that they should adjourn to the little parlour before
mentioned, and have the articles conveyed up stairs
to them in large baskets, And there, Elizabeth
said, they should be quite free from interruption.

Rosina had a governess, with whom she was
engaged all the morning, so that the party only
consisted of Elizabeth, Dora, and Marion. Elizabeth
had many things to say about Mr. Bishop, who was
absent on a short tour in the Highlands, and Marion
had some questions to ask about her old friend,
Frank Maidley, who was spending the long vacation
at Westport, and making chemical experiments with
a very talented apothecary, who had the care of his
younger brother, Peter.

They were in full conversation when the door
was pushed open, and Wilfred and Walter entered
and inquired whether there was any admittance;
they had nothing to do, they said, for Mr. Lodge
(the clergyman who gave them lessons) was gone to
a Visitation, and they were quite willing to help
with the tickets. The offer was declined, but it was
evidently their intention to remain and be amused,

for they presently commenced looking over the fancy articles and making various disrespectful comments upon them. They were a considerable interruption, for they changed their position frequently, hovering about their sisters' work-baskets, snipping bits of thread to pieces with small scissors, and setting thimbles on the tops of their large thumbs.

"Why, Walter," said Elizabeth, "you seem quite grave and absent this morning?"

Walter murmured something about his "heart's being in the Highlands."

"Are his two little coots come back again?" said Dora.

"No, and I am afraid they never will. They should not have been allowed so much liberty. Walter had just got them perfectly tame. They looked very pretty yesterday splashing in the water, and this morning they were gone."

"Well, perhaps they will come back again, after all," said Dora, in a sympathising tone.

"O no, Dora," said the little boy, in what was a very grave and rueful voice for him, "I'm sure they never will; but," continued the youthful philosopher, "what's the use of sighing when coots are on the wing. Can we prevent their flying? No. Very well, then, let us merrily, merrily sing." Having uttered this quotation the young gentleman went away to look after some of his other pets.

" Is Frank Maidley coming to dinner to-day?" inquired young Greyson.

" No," replied Dora, with whom that young gentleman was no great favourite, " I am happy to say he is not."

Marion looked up surprised, and her brother exclaimed, " Oh, Marion, I quite forgot till now to mention that I wish, if you can, you will leave off calling him by his Christian name. He is very familiar now, and I think, if you called him Mr. Maidley, he might take the hint. He always speaks of you as Marion, and I do not like the idea of his calling across the table to you by your Christian name."

Marion smiled. Her brother was becoming a man sooner than she expected. Young Greyson was nearly eighteen, and though perfectly unaffected, and even retaining a good deal of boyish simplicity, had a great idea of the respect with which he should like his sister to be treated. " I will try to leave it off, dear," she replied.

" I don't mean to say that he's ungentlemanly," said Wilfred ; " but he does not care who he laughs at, and he is so very familiar."

" In not caring who he laughs at he presents a point of resemblance to the speaker," said Dora. " I wish you would leave off that improper habit, Wilfred."

" Why, Dora," was the reply, " you would not mind who I laughed at if I reverenced Mr. Hewly's absurdities. Besides, every age has its characteristic: one was called the golden age, some were the middle ages (I suppose for want of something better to distinguish them), some were the dark ages, and people call this the age of machinery, but I call it the age of jokes. I must make jokes; we all partake of the spirit of the age."

"And a very proper name for it," said Dora. "I often spend a whole evening without hearing one word spoken in earnest; everything is made ridiculous; you alter the meaning of words; you contrive to see something absurd in everything, even in religion."

"Even in religion," repeated Wilfred. "Why, Dora, if I were inclined to retort, I might say how absurd it is to suppose that the things I have laughed at in Mr. Hewly have anything to do with real religion."

"But you have no right to laugh at a clergyman."

"I can't help it," persisted Wilfred, "any more than I could help laughing when old Mrs. Browne said, 'Mr. Dreux was next door to an angel.' When first I came here I had the most exalted opinion of the religious people whom I met with. I almost thought that, like the Queen, they could do no wrong, and that everything they disapproved of must be improper. I must say that you all conspired to give me this impression. Even the gossip that goes on here is a sort of religious dissipation;—I thought myself extremely wicked to see its absurdity. But now I have learnt to distinguish between religion and the foibles of those who profess it. I know better than to think the nonsensical way in which some good people go on is any part of their religion, or owing to it; but this does not make me sceptical as to their sincerity. As for that Mr. Hewly ——"

"Well," interrupted Dora, who did not wish that subject to be introduced again, "we have discussed him so often that we know perfectly each other's opinions about him. But what I meant to say was, that you cannot see the foibles of religious people without respecting them less, and, consequently, respecting their religion less."

"I am willing to change the subject," replied Wilfred; "only I must say that I don't believe it was ever intended that any one person should respect another so much as to think all his foibles trivial simply because they *are* his."

CHAPTER IX.

A PATENT ANTI-TALKING SOCIETY.

In the evening of the same day the young people were all sitting together in the drawing-room. Mrs. Paton generally spent her evenings with her husband in his study when they had no company.

Wilfred had been playing a spirited march on the piano, and having brought it to a flourishing conclusion, he turned round on the music-stool, and said to his sister, " So, my little Marion, I am glad to see you so busy fixing those tickets. You will see a great many people to-morrow. I wonder what idea you have formed of the society here."

" Oh, a very brilliant one," said Marion. " Of course I expect a great deal, from all I have heard."

" Yes," said Elizabeth, in a tone of pique, " and I wish you would leave Marion alone to form her own opinion. And as to the parties ——"

" Now I'll just tell you, Marion," interrupted Wilfred, coming and sitting by Elizabeth, " what they *are* like. I shall never forget the first party

I went to. I'm sure I don't know why I should have been expected to enjoy myself, sitting on a cane-bottomed chair all the evening close to the door, with nothing to do and no one to speak to."

" But why did you not speak to some one?" asked Marion.

" Oh, they were nearly all old ladies, excepting a sprinkling of clergymen, who talked in knots of two or three. I overheard the conversation of two of the old ladies;—they talked of how the parish soup had been burned to the bottom of the copper, and what was the best way of stitching up tracts in wrappers. But, Elizabeth, you promised to play at chess with me to-night."

" Oh, do play with him, Elizabeth," said Dora, " it will stop his tongue."

" Why are you so much afraid of my talking? Marion will soon be able to judge for herself whether the parties are as delightful as I say they are or not! Oh, here are the men;—red or white, Elizabeth?"

" I always play with the white," said Elizabeth.

" Oh yes, since Mr. Bishop said he always gave the white to a lady, because white was the emblem of innocence. But for myself, Marion,—(though I sincerely hope *you* will profit by the delightful society here),—for myself, I think of giving it up, for I feel that it is quite time I began to think of some plan for the benefit of my fellow-creatures;

and unless I give up the enthralling pleasures of society I do not see how I can perfect one."

" What might the plan be ?" asked Marion.

" Why, my dear, I don't mind telling you, as you are my relation, that I intend to invent another Society. I think I shall call a meeting on the subject."

" Oh! no more meetings!" exclaimed Elizabeth ; " we have one now more than once a-fortnight, besides all the little private District Meetings and Teachers' Meetings. I shall not patronize you if you have any more meetings."

" Yes, I must have a meeting for my Society ;— I mean to be President of it myself. I think of calling it the Hold-your-tongue Society, or the Total-abstinence-from-talking Society, and I hope it will do a great deal of good here ; for besides putting a stop to all the scandal, all the flattery, all the talking about other people's concerns, that now goes on at the parties, it will also prevent bad grammar among the lower classes and inelegant diction."

" Then the members are never to talk any more ?" said Dora.

" Certainly not. *I* must talk of course, or else how am I to make speeches to the members in praise of silence ? But I shall not allow any one else to speak. It's very trying, Marion, to see you laughing at my honest attempts to benefit my fellow-creatures."

"I would join the Society," said Elizabeth, "if I did not think it would put a stop to social intercourse."

"My dear madam," said the self-elected President, "your remark can only proceed from a total ignorance of what social intercourse really is (in Westport, I mean). Social intercourse is neither more nor less than a meeting for the express and avowed purpose of dining or drinking tea;—sometimes a friendly cup, sometimes a quiet cup, sometimes green, and sometimes black,—but always tea; and generally, but not constantly, accompanied by bread and butter. The members of my Society shall meet frequently for this purpose, and their faces will beam with the expression of every social and silent virtue."

"And a very sweet picture they will present, I have no doubt," remarked Elizabeth; "but I do not see how they are to communicate their sentiments."

"I shall invent a set of signs for them," replied the President. "For instance, a gentle closing of the right eye might say, 'How do you feel yourself?'—a similar movement of the left might express, 'Dear Mr. Dreux was very powerful last night, wasn't he?'—a tender moan might express sympathy,—and a slight skip on the floor, accompanied by a brilliant smile, hilarity. I shall not allow of any more complicated signs than these. Marion, don't laugh; Elizabeth, you can't move,—you're in check."

"I hope the Society will prosper," said Marion; "but I wish to observe, that *I* do not mean to be a member."

"But I thought," observed Dora, "that you had involuntarily an opportunity of trying this very plan at Mrs. Browne's party. I thought you said no one spoke to you, and that you did not like it?"

"I did not like it at the time, but being one of those excellent people (check) who can find sermons in stones, and something or other in everything, I soon began to turn my painful circumstances to good account by moralizing upon them. 'Now, Wilfred, my dear boy,' I said to myself, 'we all have our trials, and I wish you may never have a worse than this which you are now labouring under. It's true, my dear fellow, that you're very hungry, being what's called a growing lad, and having had nothing to eat but one three-cornered bit of muffin, and I don't see any prospect of your having anything more till supper-time, when perhaps you may get a sandwich and a strawberry ice, which you will like very much, being cold yourself, and the wind through the key-hole so silently blowing into your ear, will soon provide you with an earache.' Well, after I had reasoned with myself for some time, I found it had done me a great deal of good, so that I began to feel a sweet resignation stealing over me. So being restored to good temper, I began to look out for something to amuse myself with. First, I counted the spots in the carpet, and made out how much money they would bring in if they were pounds in the Three per cents. After that I considered whether I could live on such a sum if I had it, and I decided that I could, and that I should have something over for charity. When I had exhausted that subject, I took a view of Mr. King's wooden leg, and considered what I would do with it if it was mine."

"There, you're checkmated," cried Elizabeth in triumph.

The President stopped for a moment, and looked rather ruefully at the board, after which he resumed his discourse, and began to set the men for a fresh game.

"Well, all this time the gentlemen were talking together in a corner, and the ladies—never mind what they discoursed about,—so I went on with my thoughts. I thought if I were Mr. King I would have my cork leg hollowed out, and divided into three compartments, each with a little door, and a lock and key to it. In the lowest compartment, about the instep, I should have a musical-box like the musical snuff-boxes, and when music was desirable, I should wind it up for the amusement of my friends. 'Foot it featly,' should be one of the tunes."

"And the leg-acy?" suggested Marion, amid the laughter of her cousins.

"Well, in the second compartment, about the ancle, I should carry a knife and a few pamphlets, a pair of bands, and a card-case, with some other trifles, besides one or two of my best sermons, so that if I were to be asked by a clerical friend to preach for him on any sudden emergency, I could produce a sermon at once out of my leg. In the third compartment, the calf, I should carry my prayer-book and hymn-book; and as you see some people unlock little boxes in their pews and take out their books, I should unlock my leg and produce mine.

"Then only think what a man I should be for a pic-nic! I could carry all the knives and forks and the corkscrews in my leg. As for you, girls, I should convey your books, fans, and sal volatile bottles from church with the greatest ease. I should, in fact, be quite a treasure."

"No gentleman shall carry my books from church again," said Elizabeth; "I never knew one yet who did not forget to give it back at the right time."

"Ah!" said the President, "and the number of little square parcels that used to come on Monday morning with Mr. Fred Bishop's compliments, and he was sorry he had accidentally carried Miss Paton's books home with him. I always used to think there was a note inside as well as the book."

Elizabeth laughed. She rather liked to be rallied on that subject. "Mr. Bishop always wanted to carry my parasol too," she said, "but I told him the other day that I really could not allow it any longer, for as soon as he gets warm in conversation he begins to flourish it about and whisk off the heads of the thistles by the road-side in the most reckless manner, so that either the hook or the handle is sure to be snapt before we get home. Since we have been engaged, I have never had a parasol with a handle !"

Walter, who had often accompanied Elizabeth in these walks, here burst into a chuckling laugh. He had been so perfectly silent during the last half-hour that they had quite forgotten his presence, and had talked with less caution than they ever used when aware of his neighbourhood. Being perfectly conscious of this, he was extremely quiet, and thus collected several little things to torment them with on future occasions; but being now reminded of his existence, they immediately changed the conversation, and finished the evening with music, to his great chagrin.

The breakfast cloth was not removed the next morning before Mrs. Paton left the room, anxious to complete her arrangements for the coming bazaar. She left some employment for her daughters, which she said would occupy them about two hours at home, and they were then to come and help her. She had not been long absent when a lazy-looking Mayor's officer made his appearance, with a message to the young ladies: they were to send their mamma a quantity of cut evergreens and some flowers.

The girls accordingly went out to give orders to the gardener, and returning, found young Greyson with his elbows on the table and a book before him, with which he seemed perfectly absorbed.

"Wilfred," said Marion; but he was so intent he did not hear her.

"Let him alone, Marion," remarked Elizabeth; "he is always quite absent when he has an interesting book. What has he got now?"

"Some learning or other, no doubt," said Dora, gaily; "he's always either reading a learned book or else talking nonsense."

"What did you say?" inquired young Greyson, looking up.

They repeated the last remark.

"The reason is obvious," he replied; "I read to please myself—I talk to please *you*."

"If you would read us some of your books aloud instead of talking, we think it might be more improving—begging your pardon for the remark," said Dora.

Young Greyson instantly began to read aloud from his own place: "The contrary of glaring are 'clandestine instances,' where the nature sought is exhibited in its weakest and most imperfect state. Of this, Bacon himself has given an admirable example in the cohesion of fluids, as a

clandestine instance of the nature or quality of con-
sistence or solidity.   Yet here again the same acute
discrimination which enabled Bacon to see the
analogy which connects fluids with solids through
the common property of cohesive "——

"That will do," said Elizabeth, hastily.   "Now do
put the book away—we want to ask you about the
evergreens for the bazaar."

"Is there not a great quantity of evergreen in
the garden?"

"Not half enough; we mean to erect a complete
bower, a kind of triumphal arch, behind our own
stall."

"What do you want me to do towards helping?"
said the philosopher, stretching his arms.   "You
ought to have growing plants, as they will not be
seen till to-morrow.   I dare say my aunt would let
you take some out of the conservatory."

"I never thought of that," said Dora; "let us go
on to the assembly-rooms and hear whether mamma
would like the plan."

No sooner said than done.   The young ladies,
entering in a body with Wilfred, were warmly
greeted by the possessors of the different stalls,
who, hammer in hand, were superintending the
labours of some half-dozen Mayor's officers and
public servants, who were knocking nails into the
walls for faded election banners to hang upon, and
appearing to have about as intelligent an idea of the
effect intended to be produced as the poodle dogs

belonging to some of the ladies, who sat looking
on in blank amazement.

At the lower end of the room were three ladies,
who had got a large blue banner hanging like a
curtain at the back of their stall. It was very
handsome, but the words " Cobden and Free-trade,"
depicted on it in huge letters, did not look particularly appropriate, and they were accordingly in
course of being hidden by some long wreaths of
holly and idean vine. Next to them were some
Quaker ladies, whose stall was very badly arranged
in point of taste, though their articles for sale were
far more costly and better manufactured than those
of their gayer neighbours.

At the upper end, the farthest from the entrance,
was Mrs. Paton's stall. It occupied the whole end
of the room, excepting where some large folding
doors opened into the reading-rooms, behind. None
of the other ladies could compete with her, either in
the quantity or taste of her goods. At the back of
her stall were two large looking-glasses, which were
to be decorated with the orange and white flags
belonging to the Tory party. The girls set to work
to make garlands of green corn to twist among the
folds; and Elizabeth suggested that two beautiful
mimosa plants, which had been brought from the
conservatory, should be hung all over with little
articles, till they resembled Christmas trees. Two
Azalias, about six feet high, one white, the other
orange, were set behind them, ornamented in the

same way, and certainly presented a beautiful appearance when covered with their exotic fruits.

Mrs. Paton had a great advantage over the other ladies in her conservatory, which was more than despoiled to form a background for her stall. The beautiful Azalias standing among the rich silk banners, with heliatropes, geraniums, and even some of the creepers, which had been carefully disengaged from their trellis-work, had an enchanting effect; one in particular, a Cobæa scandens, many yards in length, had been pressed into the service, and hung in long festoons across the glasses and over the curtains, in all the glory of its pale green cups, some of them changing to a splendid purple.

"Is it not beautiful?" they all exclaimed, as the lovely plant, which seemed to suffer nothing from the twisting of its flexile runners, was drawn backward and forward like a drapery, over the stall.

"I think it would be a good plan," said Dora, "if we were to give out that all persons who purchase at this stall to the amount of five shillings, shall have a bouquet presented to them."

"Dora, my dear, I give you great credit for the suggestion," said her mother; "you must rise early and cut the flowers."

"And get them beautifully made up," said Dora. "How I wish we might serve at the stall."

"There will be many things you *can* do to help me," said her mother, half regretting, as she looked at Elizabeth and Marion, that she could not permit them to stand behind her stall,—for she was sensible that they would be a great ornament to it,—but their father had positively forbidden such an exhibition. " You will be present," she said, " all day, and can supply me from the reserved fund of articles whenever my stall begins to look bare."

" Ann Paton, can thee lend me one of thy helpers?" said the elderly Quaker.lady. " Thee sees I am sadly behind-hand."

Marion came forward immediately, and with her usual gentleness began to give her assistance.

The Quaker lady was making a wreath, and Marion went to her aunt to ask if she might adopt some of her rejected evergreens, for Mrs. Paton had quantities lying before her stall, enough, in fact, to decorate two or three of the tables of her less fortunate neighbours. Marion had been some time busily employed when Elizabeth came up. " Dearest Marion," she said, " what are you about? how dull you must be!"

" No, not particularly," said Marion: " but, Elizabeth, what a pity it is you allow these fine branches to lie wasted on the floor. I am sure some of the ladies would be very glad of them; only look what a contrast your mamma's stall is to the rest of the room. Do offer some of these laurels to the old ladies opposite."

Elizabeth cast a gratified glance towards her mother's end of the spacious apartment, and said, " Certainly there is a great contrast, but then mamma's stall *ought* to be the most attractive in all other respects, as she is to have no young ladies, except Helen Ferguson."

"But if your mother's is made so conspicuously attractive, it will really injure the sale at the other end."

"So much the better," said Elizabeth, laughing.

"But I meant," said Marion, "that if all the visitors crowd to that end, fewer things on the whole will be sold than there might be otherwise."

"But mamma's stall will be pre-eminent," replied Elizabeth.

"Oh, I understand," said Marion, with a quiet smile. "I thought the bazaar was for the Infant Schools, but it seems—"

"Marion, don't be moral," exclaimed Elizabeth, laughingly interrupting her. "I don't like the severer virtues. Ah, here comes that stupid Joshua, with a great basket full of babies' shoes, and little nonsenses. I must go and help to set them out, so good by, Marion."

Joshua was a young servant in the Paton family; he was renowned for his stupidity, but as it was so great that it made him quite an amusement to the family, it kept him his place when more estimable qualities might have lost him it.

"Good by, Elizabeth," said Marion, "but I give you fair warning that I shall make the Quakeress's stall look as well as I possibly can."

The two cousins then parted, and each advanced

to her own end of the room,—Elizabeth to add a
finishing touch here and there to what was already
the admiration of all the stall-keepers; and Marion
to twine the tendrils of an azure-flowering creeper
among the folds of the blue banner, Mrs. Paton
having rejected it as not harmonizing with her other
colours.

After suggesting and planning the whole afternoon, and making use of her aunt's refuse, Marion
had the pleasure of seeing the Quaker's stall really
beginning to present an appearance of great beauty,
though still not at all comparable to its *vis-à-vis*.

She had drawn the blue folds of the silk into less
formal festoons, and finding that the Quaker ladies
placed implicit reliance on her taste, she ventured
on several other innovations, which were all taken
in good part. In the midst of the preparations, one
of the Quakers began to lament over a basket of cut
flowers, which she said a friend had promised to
bring her. "I wonder they are not come," she said,
addressing Marion, "for friend Cowley always passes
this way at noon; thee understands."

Marion offered to go down stairs and look in the
great hall if the flowers were come, observing that
perhaps the people of the place had neglected to
bring them up. The great staircase and the hall
had been as quiet as those of a private house when
she entered in the morning, and it never occurred
to her that she might find them otherwise now.

She saw several sleepy-looking Mayor's officers in

the vestibule, from one of whom she learned that
some flowers had arrived, and been put in a room
at the end of a long passage, to which he pointed.

As it did not seem to enter the head of this
worthy that it might be a graceful little act of con-
descension if he fetched them for her, Marion went
down the passage as directed, passing several open-
ings and staircases.   She found the basket,—a flat
one of moderate size, containing some exquisite
geraniums, all arranged as if they had been intended
for a horticultural show.   She took up the basket,
and being rather in a hurry, ran quickly up stairs
and along a very lengthy lobby, passing several
doors in search of the Bazaar-room.   " How different this place looks coming up to coming down," she
thought, in her unsuspicious heart.   She next came
to a door on which was painted " Committee-room,"
then to a Magistrates' room.   In the same way she
passed several others, and was surprised at the
noises she heard within, at the slamming of doors,
and passing in and out of policemen.

She now began to think she must have taken a
wrong turn, in which suspicion she was confirmed
by seeing two young gentlemen, who had been in
conversation close to one of the doors, looking at
her, and amusing themselves with her perplexity.
If they had behaved in a gentleman-like manner she
would not have hesitated to accost them and inquire
the way, but as it was, the fragments of their
discourse which reached her only added to her

confusion. " Very pretty creature," she heard one
of them lisp, as he tapped his riding-boots with his
whip, and then they both laughed, turning round to
watch her movements ; while the other expressed a
wonder whether she had lost her way on purpose.
Marion turned hastily round, and at the same time
the door of the Committee-room opened, and a
young gentleman of very different appearance came
quickly out, and looked at her for a moment with
surprise, but instantly observing her annoyance, and
appearing to divine the cause, he bowed politely, and
said, " You have lost your way, I believe, madam ;
will you permit me to conduct you ?"

Marion gratefully assented, and he brought her
up a little staircase, which gave into the great land-
ing, close to the door of the Bazaar-room.

She presently perceived where she was, and turned
with her natural grace to thank her conductor, who
merely opened the door for her, and having bowed,
took his leave.

Short as had been her interview, she had had
time to observe several things respecting this young
man which made him stand out in favourable contrast to her two tormentors.   In the first place, he
had evidently come out of the Committee-room in a
very great hurry, but he checked himself, and conducted her with perfect deliberation, though the
instant after he had shut her into the right room,
she could hear him clattering down the stairs again
at a tremendous pace.   Then the two other young

men, perceiving her alone and unprotected, seemed to have taken delight in making her feel that such was the case, and that her intrusion had placed her in a ridiculous situation; but this agreeable unknown, though he only glanced at her face for an instant, seemed to have perceived her sensations by intuition, and had treated her with more deference than he might have thought it worth his while to bestow on a damsel under more favourable circumstances.

When she returned she found that her aunt had completed her arrangements, by having an arch formed of evergreens over the folding-doors, it having been agreed that they should be thrown open for the day of the sale, that the visitors might pass through the reading-room down stairs into the museum and conservatory, which belonged to the town, and were all under the same roof.

"Oh, I am so tired," said Elizabeth, throwing herself on to a sofa as soon as they got home. "I wish it was all over. Marion, you look quite pale; pray sit down and rest."

"I am not so tired that I cannot tell you a little adventure which I had this morning," said Marion, reclining, as directed; "it made me very uncomfortable at the time." She then related how she had lost her way, the rudeness of the two young men, and the sudden appearance of her knight-errant, who rushed out to the rescue just at the right moment. Tired as her cousins were, they seemed completely roused by their curiosity to find out who this gentleman could possibly be.

"Was he handsome?" asked Elizabeth.

"Yes, I should say decidedly so."

"Do you think he was an officer?" asked Dora. "Captain Manners is a very handsome man, and just the sort of person to help a damsel in distress."

"No, there was nothing military in his appearance. I should say he had rather a Grecian nose," she added, in answer to a question of Elizabeth.

"Then it was not Mr. Calvert, for his nose is hooked!"

Marion laughed, and inquired whether they expected to recognise him by description. "Perhaps he does not live in the town at all," she said; "he had evidently been sitting on some Committee, for I saw into the room when he opened the door, and there were ten or twelve grave-looking people within sitting round a green table, with papers and letters before them. Some of them looked like clergymen."

"Did your friend look like a clergyman?"

"Well, now you mention it, he was dressed in black, and I think he had rather a clerical air about him."

"Then, Marion, I think I know who it was," said Elizabeth, gravely. "I am sorry to bring your romance to an end; but if it is the gentleman I mean, he is married!"

"I can bear that intelligence with great equanimity," said Marion.

" Well, then, I think it was Mr. Beckett, the
Vicar of Maston, a village about ten miles from
here; he called a few days ago, and said he should
be in the town during the week of the bazaar, for
he was going to sit on a Committee for inquiring
into the drainage of Maston fells and marshes,—
a fearfully unpoetical subject, Marion; but he is
just like your description."

" Then we will say it was Mr. Beckett," said
Marion gaily; "and *I* say that Mr. Beckett is a
gentleman, and certainly both handsome and considerate—he was quite young, Elizabeth."

" He looks young, but I think he is past thirty."

" He certainly did not look more than five-and-
twenty."

And so the conversation ended, and the young
ladies retired very early that night, that they might
rise betimes to tie up the bouquets.

Mrs. Paton left soon after breakfast; but her
daughters and Marion remained at home till noon,
fastening up the bunches of flowers with riband.

" There," said Dora, looking round at the
denuded green-house, when the last detachment
of bouquets had been sent off, laid upon flat
baskets, "mamma never does anything by halves;
no other stalls will be at all comparable to hers;
I am sure she will have by far the largest .col-
lection."

The young ladies were then dressed to go to the

bazaar. Their father had stipulated, that as they must needs be in the room a good deal to help their mother, their appearance should be as simple and inconspicuous as possible. Accordingly they and Marion were dressed exactly alike, in white crape bonnets, black velvet scarves, and white muslin gowns.

It was past one o'clock when they arrived, and the rooms were already almost full of visitors, who crowded to their mother's end. Elizabeth and Marion, who kept together, had so thoroughly seen all the articles for sale beforehand, that they scarcely cared to walk up to the stalls, but went forward to the top of the room to observe the general effect. Mrs. Paton's stall was magnificent, the bouquets lying among the articles gave a brilliance of effect that the other ladies could not hope to attain, and the delicate scent, for they were all made of the choicest flowers, completely filled the upper end of the room. Mrs. Paton had been rather annoyed at her husband's insisting that his daughters should be plainly dressed. She was therefore delighted, when Marion and Elizabeth came in, to observe that, with the proximity of the rainbow colours all round them, their own simplicity of appearance was a great advantage; in fact, if they had been gaily dressed among all that splendour of tint, they would have looked absolutely vulgar.

" Marion, there's the *lion*," said Elizabeth,

jogging her cousin's elbow,—"I mean that gentleman passing through the folding-doors into the library."

"I see a gentleman's back," said Marion carelessly, "does it belong to Mr. Dreux?"

Marion and Elizabeth then passed down the other side into the refreshment room, where ices and pastry were sold, all for the benefit of the same Charity. In the meantime Mr. Dreux, who had been teazed to come and just show himself in the rooms, in token of his approval, took two or three turns, and then came and leaned against the pillar of the folding-doors, amusing himself, or rather beguiling the time, by watching the humours of the groups around him.

Elizabeth and Marion, having passed through the refreshment room, came into the library, and being satisfied with their view of the bazaar room, sat down upon a sofa in a window, and established themselves for a conversation.

Mr. Dreux, as they came leisurely up the room, was struck with the beautiful contrast they presented to each other, and Mrs. Paton being just then disengaged, he went up to her and inquired, who that *fair* young lady was, sitting with her daughter.

"That is my niece, Miss Greyson," said Mrs. Paton; "she is come to pay me a long visit; she is a very sweet girl."

"She has a very sweet face," thought the *lion,*

" and 'more serene than Cordelia's countenance.'
I think I know where I have seen it before."

Mrs. Paton was soon occupied with other pur-
chasers, and Mr. Dreux having paid his compliments to the other ladies at her stall, went through
the folding-doors to speak to Elizabeth, or rather
to be introduced to her companion, and Marion
looking up beheld her champion. He endeavoured
to banish all recognition, from his bow, though
he had come up on purpose to decide upon her
identity with the unknown lady of the day before,
and though he saw by Marion's face that she recognised him.

" I see you have entitled yourself to a bouquet,"
said Elizabeth, glancing at a combination of helio-
trope and scarlet geraniums which he held in his
hand.

" Yes, I have bought this thing," said he, drawing a long winding riband out of his pocket.
" Mrs. Paton said I should find it of great use;
but I cannot say I know exactly what it is."

" Oh, it is a knitting stirrup," said Elizabeth,
smiling.

" One feels rather foolish carrying such a thing
about," said the young divine; "but if I could find
a lady who would do me the honour to accept it?"
and so saying he held it out to Elizabeth, with one
of those smiles which the ladies of Westport thought
so fascinating.

Elizabeth laughed, and accepted the knitting

stirrup. He knows perfectly well that I am going to be married in a few weeks, she thought, so I will not be so prudish as to make any difficulty about it.

Having thus smoothed the way for a further offering, he turned to Marion, before whom he was standing, and with a peculiar smile playing about his lips, and lighting up his dark eyes, said, with slight hesitation, as if doubtful how she might like it, " You have no flowers *to-day*, I think, Miss Greyson. Might I have the pleasure to present this bouquet, to be worn in honour of the day, which you have assisted to make so brilliant ?"

Marion wished to thank him for his politeness of the previous evening; she therefore held out her hand for the flowers, saying, with a slight blush, "I would rather wear them in honour of yesterday."

" Yes, the bazaar-room looks brilliant indeed from here," said Elizabeth, who was rather surprised at what her cousin had said.

" The little pomps and vanities are set out in very tempting array," replied the young clergyman.

" What, Mr. Dreux !" said Elizabeth, "after sanctioning the thing with your presence, will you still object !"

" I don't know that I decidedly *object*," was the reply; " but I should not like to see my sister behind the stalls. I should most decidedly object

to *that*, and that reminds me that I must go and
bring her here to see the bazaar, as I promised."

So saying, he bowed himself away.

"Elizabeth," said Marion, the moment he was
out of hearing, "that is the very gentleman I told
you of."

Elizabeth was quite astonished that Mr. Dreux
should never have occurred to her before. "It could
only be because he was generally so very much the
reverse of attentive to ladies, that she had not
thought of him," she observed.

"I thought he was quite attentive enough
to-day," said Marion.

"You talk of him and his attention as coolly
as if he were any other man," said Elizabeth,
laughing. "You forget that he is a lion! . . Yes,
he was uncommonly agreeable, but in society he
sometimes has the *appearance* of being afraid to
pay any attention to a lady, for fear it should raise
her hopes!"

Elizabeth laughed; but Marion perceived that
she actually meant what she said, and answered,
rather indignantly, "Well, I think a man must
indeed have a high opinion of himself, if he thinks
there is danger of his being too agreeable, when
he does not try to make himself so."

"Oh, I dare say he knows that he might marry
almost any disengaged lady in the place," said
Elizabeth; "in fact, I do not see how he is to help

knowing it, and I by no means wish to intimate
that I think him a conceited man ; on the contrary,
I am often surprised at the graceful manner in
which he gives way to the elder clergymen, though
he is so much their superior in talents and position.
Besides, he is a man of good family and fortune,
and the most idolized clergyman in the place. Who
that was disengaged would not like to be married
to such a man ?"

Marion might have answered, " I should not," for
Elizabeth's remarks had made her champion seem
much less interesting.   However, she contented
herself with saying, " Of course, if the fancy that
he might marry any lady he likes is very obvious,
the young ladies here take care to keep him at
a distance."

Elizabeth laughed merrily at this remark, but did
not answer, and just then young Greyson came up to
them, saying, " I have been looking for you all
over ; the rest of our party have gone down through
the museum into the conservatory.   Will you join
them ?   They say they are quite tired of the
bazaar."

Elizabeth and Marion each took an arm and went
down through the Committee-room, of which the
latter had had a glance the day before, and then
across a lobby in a museum full of rather musty
specimens of stuffed birds and forlorn-looking
animals, with their teeth sticking out in formidable
array.   The museum terminated at one end in

a broad flight of stone steps leading down to the conservatory, which was not so much of flowering plants as of botanical specimens, medicinal herbs, and foreign plants used in dyes and pigments.

" There they are, on a bench at the far end," said Greyson, " and Frank Maidley with them." They all came to meet the new-comers, and Marion was surprised at the height of her late companion, who, when they were seated on the bench, stood by them, and leaning his elbow on the mantel-shelf, looked down upon them with an easy smile.

" Now we'll show you what we've bought," said Greyson, taking up a tangled mass of articles from one end of the bench.

" That's mine," said Frank, as a lady's white knitted carriage-cap was held up. " I bought it of Mrs. Paton."

" This is mine," exclaimed Greyson, drawing forth a large anti-macassar. " The Quaker woman made me buy it. I told her it was of no use. ' Then,' she said, ' thee may give it to a friend.' "

" And that's my property too," cried Frank, as a muslin apron, worked with coloured crewels, was handed up in a woefully crumpled condition. " Old Miss King made me hand it all round the room, and because nobody would buy it of me, she made me take it myself."

" You seem to have been cruelly used," said Marion.

" But I really should have thought you might

have made more appropriate purchases," remarked Dora, endeavouring to disentangle a heart-shaped pincushion, stuck full of pins, from the fringe of the apron.

"Appropriate to what?"

"Why, to your condition as gentlemen.   There were some beautiful slippers and braces, and some very handsome waistcoats, worked in lamb's-wool, and ready made."

"Do you think I would demean myself to wear a waistcoat made by a woman and worked with cabbage-roses?" exclaimed Frank Maidley, with ineffable scorn.

"There, this is mine," cried Greyson, as Elizabeth handed up a very elegant work-bag,—" *Quis?* "

"I'll have it rather than it should be wasted," replied Dora.

"You ought to have answered, *Ego*," said Frank.

"Greyson, hand me up my cap that I bought; I'll put it on and see how I look in it."

There was a very large mirror over the chimney-piece, so tilted as to present a beautiful reflection of the climbing plants hanging from the roof.   Frank Maidley arrayed himself in the cap, which he tied under his chin, and then turned round to be admired.

"Your head reminds me of a dish of carrots and turnips," said young Greyson.

"My hair being the carrots.   Thank you for the

simile.   Miss Paton, may I trouble you to pass up my apron."

" Why, you don't mean to say that you are going to put it on ? " said Greyson.

" Yes, I am.   When the people are tired of the bazaar some of them will come down here, and perhaps I can dispose of these articles to them at half price.   Besides, why should not I make myself ridiculous if I like on behalf of this pious cause ? "

" You had better take the Macassar as a shawl then, I think," said Elizabeth.   " It will make a very tasty finish to your dress."

"I will," said Frank, receiving the article and spreading it out over his shoulders with the inimitable awkwardness of a man.

" Now would you mind obliging us by standing a little farther off ? " said Marion, with perfect gravity.

" In order that you may not seem to belong to our party, you know," added Elizabeth, to make the meaning of her cousin's remark the more obvious.

" O certainly, with pleasure.   I'll go and stand at the other side of the chimney-piece, and if any people come down I'll look at you through my eyeglass, as much as to say, ' I wonder who those people are ? ' "

" Here *are* some people coming," said Elizabeth. " Now, pray unrobe, Mr. Maidley."

"Thank you, I don't at all mind this style of

dress. Yes, here they come,—old Dr. Hubbard and three young ladies; just look at the old gentleman."

Dr. Hubbard was a short, stout man, rather bald, and very good-tempered in appearance. He went down the side of the conservatory, examining the plants and commenting on their properties aloud, till he came to Frank Maidley, before whom he paused with a comical expression of surprise, looking up at him with his head on one side and his hands behind him; he then came to speak to the Miss Patons, the three young ladies, who had come down with him, resolutely turning their heads away, as if afraid of laughing. This party withdrew, and were presently followed by another.

"Here are some more people," cried young Greyson. "Would you believe it?—Mr. What's-his-name Brown, and his mother. Now, Marion, you shall be introduced."

"How came he by such an odd name?" asked Marion.

"There they are, examining the birds and beasts in the museum with the greatest curiosity, Brown as discontented as ever, and his mother trotting after him, admiring and wondering. Why, Marion, his real name is Athanasius, and people say that during his father's lifetime the place was so full of Browns that there was no distinguishing them one from another; there was Brown the doctor, and Brown

T

the butcher, and a retired man who went by the
name of Gentleman Brown; then there was a tall
man whom they called Long Brown, and this
Brown's father, who, being a little man, was called
Brownie.   However, he was determined that his
son should have a name which should distinguish
him from all other Browns whatsoever, so he had
him christened Athanasius.   He had made a pretty
little property, so he sent his son to College and
made a clergyman of him; but behold, when he
entered upon his duties the people of the parish, not
being of the learned sort, could not compass such a
hard name, and as to have called him Mr. Brown
would not have distinguished him at all, they always
called him Mr. What's-his-name Brown; they even
sent petitions to him directed in that style and title;
at last it got to the ears of the upper classes, and now
nobody ever thinks of calling him anything else."

Mr. What's-his-name Brown, who all this time
had been examining the museum, now began to
descend the steps, his mother following him.   She
was a tall, stout woman, not much like a lady, and
not pretending to be one.   He was a puny man,
with rather a discontented expression, very straight
black hair, a pale complexion, and precisely that air,
manner, and appearance which in society is almost
sure to cause a man to be overlooked and accounted
a nobody. Everybody, however, said he was a very
good man.   But it has been remarked before that

people are very fond of finishing any observation of
a disparaging nature by remarking that the subject
of it is a *very good man.*

" He preaches a marvellously dry sermon ; " or,
" he is terribly dull in conversation ; " or, " he spoke
as if he was half asleep ; " or, " nobody could make
out what he meant ; indeed, I don't suppose he
knew himself, ' but I dare say he is a *very good
man !* ' "

Mr. What's-his-name Brown having reached the
foot of the steps, began to examine the plants with
an air of inquisitive discontent.   Mrs. Brown, his
mother, the pride of whose life he was, now came
forward to speak to the young ladies, and cast
a furtive glance at Frank, who, catching her eye,
bowed politely.

" Me and my son were led to expect something
worth seeing here, ladies," said the worthy matron,
"but I can't say the plants are particularly handsome.
Dr. Hubbard certainly said there was a very fine
specimen near the *chimley*-piece."

" Yes," said the Rev. Gentleman, " he said a
plant of stately growth."

" Did he ? " cried Frank Maidley ; " then he must
have meant me."

Mr. Brown accordingly looked up at Frank
Maidley, but did not appear to derive much satisfaction from the sight ; on the contrary, he had the
air of a man who felt that he had been deluded and
ill-used by false representations.

" Could I tempt you with any of these little articles?" said Frank, in his blandest voice, pretending to think he was examining his toggery with a view to purchase.

" Frank," said Greyson, " here are half a dozen people coming down the steps. Do take that rubbish off."

" This is a fine room," remarked Elizabeth to Mrs. Brown, for she did not like to see her standing there and being taken no notice of.

" Yes; a fine room, indeed, Miss 'Lizabeth," said Mrs. Brown; " and the whole building is very handsome. They tell me it is in the *Elizaberian* style."

Elizabeth tried to give an air of courteous assent to the smile which she could not repress, and the whole party found it difficult to help laughing, when she went on to observe,—" that everybody praised the proportions of the magistrates' room, and said that really the *cemetery* of those pillars was perfect."

" Marion, I think we had better come away now," said Elizabeth, blushing; " there are some more people descending the steps; and really Frank Maidley makes us quite conspicuous."

Marion gladly assented, and, having taken leave of the rest of the party, they went back to the Bazaar-room, where they found employment in replenishing Mrs. Paton's stall.

Though none of the young people liked to

acknowledge it, they were heartily tired of the bazaar, and longed for the time when they might go home again; it came at last, and they entered their own house with real delight. Then came the time for regretting the spoilt appearance of the conservatory, and all for the sake of *one day*. Through the evening the plants kept arriving, but most of them were very much shattered, and all were denuded of flowers. They were quite grieved to see the miserable appearance they made.

"I wish we had remembered our own dinner-party," they said, "before we destroyed all the flowers."

"Oh, by the bye, my dears," said their mother, "I have invited Mr. Dreux and his sister to come to us on that day; he brought her up to be introduced to me, and I thought he seemed rather disappointed that none of you were there. You must be polite to Miss Dreux; she knows no one here, and I dare say he will be very glad for you to take her about a little."

The next day Mr. Raeburn was to take a journey, and, as he did not know whether he could call at Westport before going home, Marion stayed at home to wish him good by. She had nothing to do, and offered to assist Elizabeth in adding up the accounts of a Club for the poor, in which she had formerly taken a great interest.

"And I shall go out, and take a ride with mamma

into the country," said Elizabeth, "for I am sure she wants a change after the fatigue of that bazaar; it took her a week to prepare for it, and I am sure it will take another week to put all the things away."

"Where shall you go?" asked Marion.

"Mamma says she really must go and call on old Mrs. Brown," said Elizabeth, "for she has never been to see her since she and her son took part of a farm-house about two miles out of the town, that he might walk in every morning. By the bye, Marion, what did you think of Mr. Allerton?"

"Mr. Allerton," repeated Marion, "have I seen him?"

"Yes, to be sure. Don't you remember, when we came out of the bazaar we passed through an open space like a lawn, with trees round it, and I told you it belonged to the almshouses,—Mr. Dreux was walking up and down there with another gentleman?"

"Oh, yes, I remember him perfectly, if that is the gentleman you mean,—a tall, Saxon-looking man, who walked school-boy fashion, with one arm over Mr. Dreux's shoulders."

"That was him."

"Indeed! I thought him a very agreeable-looking person."

"Dora used to go to his church," continued

Elizabeth; "you know I have often told you of it."

"Yes," said Marion. "What a pity it is that Dora should be so much changed."

"Well, good by for the present, dearest Marion," said Elizabeth, turning from that subject, as usual. "I do not like to leave you, but I hope, when Mr. Raeburn is gone, you will come out for a walk. Dora and Rosina will be down immediately."

Dora and Rosina presently came in, as Elizabeth had predicted, and Walter with them. And as there were presently some morning visitors to be attended to, Marion had not much time for her accounts; so that when she had seen Mr. Raeburn off, and sent messages to his mother and to her favourite children in the school, she had not been seated over the books many minutes before Elizabeth came back into the drawing-room after her ride, with her hat and habit on. She had been riding beside her mother's carriage, and inveighed against the idleness of her sisters in staying in-doors.

"Well, where have you been?" said Dora.

"To call on Mrs. Brown."

"Was she at home?"

"Yes, and so glad to see us. She was excessively anxious that mamma should 'do her the honour to stay to dinner. She had got the best end of a loin of veal at the fire, and she was sure we should have a hearty welcome.' But, Marion, how industrious you are over those Club-tickets; what pains you take in checking them off by the book. I am sure I ought to feel very much obliged to you."

"One,—Martha Perry, ought to feel obliged to me," returned Marion, laughing good-humouredly; "for, do you know, Elizabeth, by your way of adding up her card you had cheated her out of threepence?"

"You are not in earnest, surely?" said Elizabeth, in a voice of dismay. "I hope the good woman has not found it out. I hope she does not think I abstracted that sum for my pocket-money."

"It does not appear what she thinks," said Marion; "but seriously, Elizabeth, she is not the only sufferer, though you certainly seem to have an idea of poetical justice, for in adding up some of the cards you have cheated yourself; and as, of course, I cannot abstract from them the surplus sums, you will have to pay what is deficient yourself."

"How much does it come to?"

"One and tenpence," said Marion.

"Well, it is very hard," said Elizabeth, "for I'm extremely poor just now. I think, as it is your doing, you ought to advance the money."

"I am not sure that I can trust you," said Marion, laughing. "What have you done with all the money you had yesterday?"

"All!—it was only nine shillings. I'm sure I

don't know where it's gone to. Let me see,—two
shillings for stamped envelopes."

" Two shillings for stamped envelopes," repeated
Marion, writing it down on a piece of paper.
" Well, what else ?"

" Eighteenpence for a blue calmia in a pot—Oh,
Dora, you'll be sorry to hear that Athanasius has
got a very bad cold."

" I wish you would leave off calling him so," said
Dora. " I am sure, if you get such a habit of it,
you will do it some day when you will be very
sorry. And *you* particularly, ought not to laugh at
him."

" Why *Elizabeth*, particularly ?" asked Marion.

" Oh, because,—poor little man,—we used to
think he admired Elizabeth, before Fred Bishop
declared himself."

" And I am sure I don't know how he ever
showed it," said Elizabeth, " except by paring apples
for me at dessert. But it *is* wrong to laugh at him,
particularly now he's unwell ; however, his mother
hopes fiddle-strings and paregoric will soon set him
right again."

" Did she say so ?" asked Dora, quietly, and with
a slight glance at Walter.

" No ; you know she didn't, Dora. But is not
playing on the fiddle the solace of his life ? Because
you never laugh at anybody, is that any reason why
I never should ? I wish you would let me alone."

" I'll choose another theme on which to give you

good advice," said Dora.   " You had better take off
your hat and habit."

" Yes, I will, when Marion has made out my
list.   I saw such beautiful blue salvias in the
cemetery to-day,—I wish it was not a sin to steal.
Ninepence, Marion, for a purple salvia, which I
fully believe will turn out a scarlet one; there's a
very red hue about its buds: and eightpence for a
globe-fuschsia,—that's all?"

" That comes to four shillings and elevenpence,"
said Marion.   " Four and elevenpence from nine
shillings,—how much remains, Elizabeth?   I shall
not lend you anything, for you have enough to pay
your debts, and threepence over.   Now, do go and
take off your habit."

" Yes, presently.   Dora, has any one called?"

" Only young Mr. Morton."

" What did he say?"

" Oh, he said just what all gentlemen say during
their first call.   He observed that the neighbourhood was very beautiful; that some of the churches
were fine specimens of the florid Gothic; and that
the society seemed agreeable."

" Does he live by himself?"

" He does, madam," said Walter, who was sitting
at the table making a fishing-net, " and all the
bwead and cheese he gets he puts upon a shelf."

" You impertinent child," said Elizabeth, laughing at this sally, " how dare you meddle with *your*
remarks?   Was that all he said, Dora?"

" Yes, I think so. Oh, I remember, he asked if we were going to observe the eclipse of the sun next week, and said, if we were, the best place would be that elevated field near the cemetery."

" Ah!" said Elizabeth, " how I do wish I could get some cuttings of those blue salvias! Marion, I must take you to see the cemetery."

" Do, if you please," said Marion;—" you talk so much about it that I should think it must be an interesting place."

Elizabeth laughed. " Do you remember that old lady who sat in the pew before us this morning at prayers?—an old lady in a striped knitted shawl?" she said.

" Yes, perfectly."

" Well, she's Frank Maidley's aunt."

" Indeed!"

" Yes, she has only lived here a few months, and one day Frank took her to walk in the cemetery gardens. ' And what's written on that sign-board, my dear?' she said, when they got in, for she's very shortsighted. So Frank read, ' The public are desired not to tread on the borders, not to pluck the flowers, and not to sing "Away with melancholy," in this cemetery.' ' And very right, too,' said the old lady; ' I'm sure they could not sing a more inappropriate tune.' But oh! how angry she was when she came close and found it was all his own invention! She declared she would cut him out of her will for making game of her, and I don't believe she has ever forgiven him to this day."

"Now, Elizabeth," said Dora, "there is another knock at the door; you had better go and change your dress, or you will have to stay and entertain these visitors."

CHAPTER X.

ROSINA.

MR. BISHOP'S father (one of the most sweet-tempered and simple-minded old gentlemen that ever lived) seemed to think it part of his duty to pay attention to his son's intended during his absence; and finding Marion almost always with her, soon began to include her in his kind recollection.

He was a short old gentleman, rather stout, and bald; he generally wore a long great-coat, and took very short steps; he had a pair of twinkling black eyes, expressive of the most paternal tenderness, and always called his son "my dear child," and Elizabeth "my pretty dear."

One morning Mr. Bishop had brought the two girls a pretty offering, in the shape of a fairy rose-tree in a pot, and they had taken it up-stairs to Marion's little parlour, where they were admiring its beauty, when young Greyson came in, and said,

"Elizabeth, my aunt told me to remind you of the District Meeting to-day at Mr. King's."

" How tiresome!" exclaimed Elizabeth ;—" I wanted to take Marion out to-day ; and now I shall have all the way to go to Mr. King's, and then to return for her."

" But cannot I go with you, and wait till the Meeting is over ?" said Marion.

" Oh yes, if you will, dear Marion," said Elizabeth ; " but I wonder where the district books are ?"

" Rosina has got them, no doubt," observed young Greyson ; " she is often going out with tracts or a little bag in her hand. I see her go past the study-window almost every day while I am at my writing."

" I thought it was Elizabeth's district ?" said Marion.

" Yes, so it is," replied Elizabeth, blushing ; " but really I begin to feel it too much for me. The little houses are so hot that they always give me the headache, and then the poor women have so many grievances to relate that it makes me quite low. But Rosina likes going, and besides, she keeps the books very neatly, so that I have only to make an abstract of what she has done when I have not been able to go myself."

" Which abstract runs thus," said Wilfred :— " ' Mrs. Black—Groats and sugar, 9d. ; child has the measles ; husband out of work ; promised her a hat for her boy.—Mem., not to forget it. Mrs. Reeve—Very impertinent ; wanted to know why

I gave so much more to her neighbours than to her; gave her child a pound of beef for tea; declined to take the tract; said she would see about it next time. Mrs. Collet's father ill; gave her tea, sugar, and sago, for him; heard him whistling before I opened the door; when I came in he began to groan audibly, and declared his cough was "killing of him." Found the Wilsons toasting muffins; did not give them anything.— Mem., not to take my gloves off there; eldest child has the ringworm.'"

"How came you to be so well acquainted with my district-books?" said Elizabeth, who, though she could not help laughing, had tried to stop him several times without success.

"Don't I go into the school-room whenever I like?—and don't I find Rosina poring over the accounts? Of course, I help her. You'll see my name down as a subscriber, 'W. F. Greyson, Esq., one pound a-year.' I help her, too, to cover the tracts, for I like to make myself useful. I know all about it, Elizabeth, my dear! You have not been into your district for five months. Rosina says, 'Dear Elizabeth is so kind as to let me take it for her.' She thinks it quite a treat and a privilege to have it, poor little dear! And the people are so fond of her,—they say she talks so prettily to them!"

"Well, I am sure she may have it altogether

if she likes," said Elizabeth, in a tone of pique,
" for I have a great many other things to
do."

" Yes, of course, and she does not like going to
the meetings," said Wilfred, " which is a part you
do not so much mind. She has no time for them,
because all the morning she is at her lessons with
Miss Woods; and then Dora's schools, which she
used to be so fond of, Rosina says, ' Dora is so kind
as to let her go to them when she has other things
to do.' I think she goes most days to the girls'-
school, to teach them arithmetic. She says they
are getting on very nicely. Dora used to be wild
about those schools when first they were built, but
now she seldom goes to them;—she lets Rosina
have that treat, as well as take her class at the
Sunday-school. Mr. Dreux says she is a capital
teacher."

" You seem to know all Rosina's plans," said
Elizabeth, rather tartly ; " perhaps you can tell me
where these district-books are ?"

" Yes, I will bring them," he replied, " and then
I must go, for I am rather late."

When he had left the room, Elizabeth said
nothing to Marion. She felt vexed that Wilfred,
in his joking way, should so plainly have let her
see that he thought too much was left to his
favourite Rosina. However, the little girl presently came in herself, with the books in her hand,

knocking first at the door, and entering with her usual charming modesty.

" Well, Rosina," said Elizabeth, looking up with rather a heightened colour.

" I asked Miss Woods to allow me to bring the books myself, dear Elizabeth," said Rosina, " because I wanted to remind you of that dispensary ticket which you said I should have for old Larkins."

" Oh, I forgot it," said Elizabeth,—" how tiresome! Well, he must wait till next month."

Rosina looked disappointed. " And there are several subscriptions due, Elizabeth; would you mind calling to ask for them, or if I might call myself for them, with Miss Woods?"

" No," said Elizabeth, " I do not wish you to do that,—I will call for them myself; perhaps not to-day, for I am busy; but I will lend a sovereign to the district purse in the meanwhile. It is a great deal of trouble collecting those small sums."

Rosina gratefully received the sovereign, and put it into her little purse.

Elizabeth thought she had spoken rather sharply to her, so, as she gave her the money, she drew down her face and kissed her.

" Why, there is not one penny in your purse, Rosina," she said; "what a wasteful little thing you must be, to have spent all your money so soon!"

Rosina trifled with the tassels of her purse, but said nothing, and Elizabeth began to examine the books, to see how much had been spent.

"Why, Rosina," she said, "the district money will never hold out if you spend it so fast."

"Oh, but there is my own subscription," said Rosina; "I subscribe half-a-guinea a quarter."

"What! half your allowance? Well, you must do as you please about that; but *still* you are spending too much; you know you must not get my district into debt."

"But papa always gives me a sovereign on my birth-day," said Rosina, "and Mr. Raeburn said he meant to give two guineas a-year, if I would remind Marion to ask him for it."

"But how came Mr. Raeburn to know that you had anything to do with the districts and schools?"

"I don't know," said Rosina, blushing, "unless Wilfred told him."

Elizabeth coloured deeply; but whatever she might think, she said nothing. "Well, that is all," she observed, when she had finished the abstract of the month's proceedings. "You may go now, Rosina; I will not forget to ask for the ticket."

"And will you ask for a new book for your coal club?" said Rosina, lingering at the door; "the old one is quite full."

"I will see about it," said Elizabeth, in a fretted and rather ungracious tone, and Rosina withdrew.

"Now, Marion," said Elizabeth, "we had better put on our bonnets; it is quite time to go."

The District Society was a partnership concern

between Mr. Dreux and Mr. Lodge, and the subscriptions were equally divided between them.

When the two girls entered, they found twelve or
more ladies already assembled, and talking with
volubility on various subjects, but all in some degree
tinged, as it were, with the phraseology of the Evangelical school. Marion was astonished at the ease
with which they alluded to some of the most awful
truths; talking of conversions, death-beds, prayer-
meetings, all in a breath and without the reverence
which such topics would seem to demand, and the
next moment bringing in some trifling anecdote
about a favourite clergyman,—mingling the whole
with the gossip which always prevails in a country
town. At length the two clergymen came in. Mr.
Dreux was evidently in a hurry, and wished to begin
the business immediately; but his colleague was instantly assailed with questions as to why he had put
a stranger into his pulpit on Sunday, and patheti-
cally requested not to do so again, various strictures
and criticisms being offered on the stranger's sermon, which made Mr. Lodge laugh. He was a
much more easy man to deal with than Mr. Dreux,
who often appeared not to understand implied compliments, or was so reserved and dignified that it
seemed taking a liberty to pay him one.

The actual business of the meeting could easily
have been transacted in a quarter of an hour; but
there were so many compliments, which rendered
so many disqualifying speeches needful, so many

digressions, so many anecdotes related, and so many appointments to meet at different places, made before it began, that it was more than an hour before Mr. Lodge declared that his accounts were finished, and paid over the money to his colleague as treasurer, who immediately after rose, and bowing all round, took his leave with alacrity.

"Dreux is excessively busy just now," said Mr. Lodge, when he had left the room.

"Something like you in that respect, I imagine," said an elderly lady, who had shewn herself well versed in the art of flattery.

"Well, I really do sometimes wonder myself how I contrive to get on, beset as I am; I never have a moment to myself. Then there are my pupils, and I have visitors from morning to night," said Mr. Lodge, half laughing.

Marion stole a glance at him, and thought he looked none the worse for his work, whatever it might be.

"Well," said one of the most fashionably dressed among the ladies, "a minister's time is never his own. I do not see how it can be otherwise; if people are always coming to you for advice, it is no more than you ought to expect, who are so well able to give it."

"And so willing, I am sure," said another lady.

Elizabeth then rose to take leave, and Marion followed, half wondering what sort of adieu Mr. Lodge might give them, and whether he counselled them to abstain from worshipping the creature more than the Creator; at the same time she was surprised at the active benevolence of those ladies, who seemed to spend the greater part of their lives in doing good, visiting the sick, teaching the ignorant, and organizing clubs and provident societies. After this several days passed without any acquaintance on Marion's part with the society of Westport, but she heard Mr. Dreux preach twice, and, to her surprise, found it superior to her expectation; its masterly earnestness astonished her, so that she felt very serious the rest of the day, and could not understand the levity of her cousins, nor approve of the way in which they spent their Sunday.

Not that they talked on absolutely secular subjects,—their conversation always bore on religious matters, more or less remotely,—but there was something so ready-made and so fluent in it; they talked with so little feeling and so much ease, as could not fail to suggest to a stander-by the idea that they had been brought up with the understanding that they were to hold certain opinions, and possess a certain character, and they had the dialect of those who did, whether or not they were truly of their number.

Rosina was apart from the rest of the family, no less on Sunday than on other days. She was completely occupied with her Sunday-school class; and young Greyson, who also was a teacher, escorted her there. On Sunday evening, as she had a very bad cough, her mother desired that she would remain at home, and Marion wished to stay behind and read to her. Her cousins seemed to think it most unnecessary, but as she evidently wished it, they did not oppose her. So Marion went up stairs to her cousin's room to tell her of the arrangement. Rosina was lying on her bed, reading; she looked very poorly, and Marion persuaded her to come down to her own little parlour. "I am going to read to you," she said, "for your eyes are weak, and you must keep them closed." The little girl blushed, and did not like to give her cousin so much trouble; she, however, followed her advice, and lying down upon the couch, and putting her arm round Marion, laid her head upon her shoulder to listen. Marion read to her for some time, and she was so still that she thought she must be asleep; she put aside the book, and looking down upon her face, she opened her eyes, and Marion said, "I thought you were asleep, my sweet Rosina."

"Oh, no," replied the little girl, "I was only thinking," and then, without either affectation or bashfulness, she began to talk about the evening lessons which Marion had been reading, as if she was sure that her cousin could both understand and sympathize with her.

Marion was not slow to fall in with the strain of conversation, and they continued to converse till it was dark.

Rosina said nothing brilliant, but the childlike

sincerity and simplicity of her religion struck home
to Marion's heart with a delight that she had not
felt since she left her village home, and this oneness
of feeling increased tenfold the affection which from
the first had drawn them together, and made the
time pass so swiftly, that Marion could not repress
a sigh of disappointment when she heard her cousins'
footsteps in the gallery.

" Is it possible the service is over ?" she said, as
they entered. " What a little time you seem to have
been away !"

" My dear Rosina, do sit up," said Dora ; " you
must tire Marion very much, I am sure."

" Oh no, she does not," said Marion, preventing
the little girl from rising ; " do not move, my dear."

" How is your cough ?" asked Elizabeth. " You
should have told me, Rosina, that you were not well,
and I would have taken the class myself."

" Oh, my cough 's better now," was the reply ;
" and, besides, the last time you took it, don't you
remember you said it gave you the headache ?"

" Yes, I—I am rather subject to the headache,"
said Elizabeth, blushing, as she stooped to kiss her
sister's forehead.

The next day Mr. Raeburn passed through Westport on his way home. It was evening, and he
found the ladies of the family, and two or three
strangers, assembled after dinner in the drawing-
room. The guests were all uninteresting people
(at least so Dora and Elizabeth said,—people whom

it was necessary to invite now and then), always with the bright exceptions of old Mr. Bishop, Mr. Dreux, his sister, and Frank Maidley.

The gentlemen soon entered the drawing-room, and as soon as possible Mr. Raeburn took young Greyson aside into the little study before mentioned.

The drawing-room was a spacious, old-fashioned apartment, opening by French windows into the garden, and on each side of it, and divided from it by folding-doors, was a little room about ten feet square. These two rooms (each of which was furnished with a heavy curtain, which was seldom drawn over its entrance) had merely the appearance of wings to the main room. One of them was fitted up with china, and in the other stood the harp and piano.

Into the former of these little rooms Marion and Elizabeth had retired. They were going to play a game of chess, and while the former was setting out the men, Elizabeth said to her, " Well, Marion, what do you think of him now you have seen him in a room ?"

She spoke in a low voice, but it unluckily chanced that Mr. Dreux was sitting on a sofa near the entrance of the room, and hidden from them by the folds of the curtain. He was languidly listening to the conversation of one of the uninteresting people, who sat beside him, pouring her nonsensical nothings into his ears.

Marion made a movement of impatience when the question was asked, and as he turned involuntarily he caught a glimpse of the smile that played about her lips as she answered, " I shall soon begin to wish him the fate of Aristides, Elizabeth, to be banished (for a while, at least) from the conversation. I am *a little* tired of hearing about him."

Of course Mr. Dreux had no business to think the conversation related to him. He tried to give a listening ear to the talk of the old lady.

" Well, but," said Elizabeth, " I really wish to know what you think of him."

Either his hearing must, in spite of himself, have been very acute just then, or Marion must have spoken during a pause. He distinctly heard the answer, given in the softest tones of her sweet voice,—

" Think of him ! Oh, I think he was worthy of a better fate."

" Better than what ? " said Elizabeth.

" Than to be spoilt and made an idol of," said Marion, in the same subdued tones.

" Than to be spoilt ! " answered Elizabeth ; " why, you don't mean to say that he is spoilt ? "

" I wish this old woman would talk louder, or let me go," thought Mr. Dreux, as he resolutely turned away. Of course he could have had no idea that they were talking of him,—at least, so he said to himself,—but he did not relish being an eavesdropper, and they had no reason to suppose any one

was so close to them. In spite of this, his ears
would not shut themselves—they would persist,
against his will, in hearing Marion's answer, which
was floated softly to him through the folds of the
silken curtain.

" Considering the laudable pains people have
taken to spoil him," she said, " perhaps they have
not succeeded quite so well as might have been
expected."

The old lady happily here came to a pause, and
Mr. Dreux left her, feeling greatly dissatisfied with
himself and her. " Am I spoilt, then," he thought ;
" is my demeanour really the worse for the flattering
speeches that continually reach me ? Do I show in
manner or words that I *know* they make an idol of
me ? What a mortification ! I do not care for the
good opinion of *any one* person who has thought
proper to flatter me ; and yet their flattery in the
aggregate must have done me mischief if its effects
are visible to an almost stranger. Well, I am
vexed. I wish Miss Greyson were not so discerning. I had rather have heard of my faults from
the lips of any other person whatsoever ! But,
after all, why should I think they were talking of
me ? "

The Paton family were moderately fond of music.
The two elder girls played very fairly—just well
enough to entertain their visitors when music was
desirable,—but neither of them sang. The gentlemen had no sooner joined them than old Mr.

Bishop demanded that the piano should be opened,
and Dora and one of the uninteresting ladies played
a duet by way of commencement.   They had no
sooner finished than he attacked Elinor, and asked
her for a song.   Now Elinor, though she had high
spirits, and was very much at her ease in society,
could not endure to sing before strangers, especially
if she thought they were good judges of music.
She accordingly excused herself, and offered to play
instead.

"Oh, no," said the old gentleman, "we will not
be put off in that way. I know you can sing like a
nightingale. Come, Miss Dreux, what will you
favour us with?"

"Indeed," said Elinor, "I assure you my singing
is not worth hearing. I scarcely ever sing."

"All a pretence of modesty, to make it sound the
sweeter when it comes," said one of the uninteresting gentlemen. "Mr. Dreux, I appeal to you; your
sister sings exquisitely, does she not?"

Being thus appealed to, Mr. Dreux was obliged
to confess that his sister did sing, though when he
looked at her face suffused with blushes, he wished
he could have withheld the fact. Elinor now felt
far more uncomfortable than ever. She knew this
delay would greatly raise their expectations. She
began to turn over a portfolio of music which Dora
handed to her, and her hand trembled visibly.
Marion, who during this conversation had entered
the little music-room, plainly saw the state of things,

though no one else appeared to notice it, excepting
her brother, who feared that when she began to sing
her voice would tremble so much as to be scarcely
audible, so he sat, feeling exquisitely uncomfortable.

" I really do not see anything here that I know,"
said Elinor, turning over the song; " this music is
far too difficult for me."

Marion, who was accustomed to sing every night,
whether alone or in society, was, partly from that
circumstance and partly from natural constitution,
perfectly free from that miserable feeling called
nervousness which very much afflicts some young
ladies, and is made up of bashfulness and an over
desire to please. She easily perceived Elinor's
feelings, and generously wishing to relieve them,
made a step forward, and producing another portfolio, said, " Or perhaps you would prefer to sing a
duet ? "

The grateful assent with which this proposal was
met assured her that she was conferring a real
benefit. Elinor felt that it was quite a different
matter to sing supported by another voice. The
audience could have nothing to say against it; and
Marion, though she would rather not have put herself forward when not asked, felt indemnified by
Elinor's evident relief. She let her choose any duet
she preferred, and she fixed on some common-place
air. Marion gave her a splendid accompaniment,
and humoured her voice to perfection, managing her
own so as not to overpower it.

Elinor had neither a powerful nor a fine voice, but its tones were sweet, and with these advantages, and the confidence inspired by feeling herself in such good hands, she sung her part extremely well, and the audience applauded both performers at its conclusion.

"After all," thought Mr. Dreux, looking at Marion's serene face, "I think I am not sorry you are so discerning. You have saved Elinor from a very ridiculous exhibition."

During the closing strain Mr. Raeburn and young Greyson returned, and entering the music-room and seeing that Marion was one of the performers, cast a look of amazement at each other. When the duet was finished Elinor withdrew, and Mr. Raeburn coming up to Marion, and looking at the title of the song, said, in a subdued voice but with infinite expression, "What rubbish is this that you have been singing, my love?"

Marion was still sitting on the music-stool, and Mr. Dreux (of whose relationship to one of the fair singers Mr. Raeburn was by no means aware) was standing beside her, having been occupied in turning over the leaves.

Marion was sure that he could not have failed to hear the remark, and as she rose she gave a gentle admonitory look to Mr. Raeburn, which was intended to silence him, and said, with a blush of uneasiness, lest her innocent little *ruse* should be discovered,

" Dear uncle, you are singular in your disapproval;
our duet has had great success."

" I never heard such stuff in my life," proceeded
the discomfited amateur, and Mr. Dreux went
away and joined his sister, to whom Mr. Bishop
was talking gaily, rallying her on her disinclination
to sing, and declaring that it was only that she liked
to be pressed.

" Marion's voice sounded very poor to-night,"
whispered Dora to her mother.

" I cannot think what was the matter with it,"
replied the discerning Mrs. Paton, " I never heard
her sing in that style before. Perhaps she is not in
voice."

At this moment Mr. Paton came in, and said to
Marion, " Well, my dear, I hope you are going to
favour us ? I never hear any singing that delights
me so much as yours."

Not wishing to sing again so soon, lest the contrast between her first and second performance
should be remarked, Marion made some slight
excuse, and her aunt said, " Well, then, Rosina
shall play her last new piece,—where is she ?"

The little girl, who, as usual, was quite in the
background, came when she was desired, and
played her piece remarkably well for her years,
Mr. Raeburn standing by and testifying his
approval.

" Rosina will play very well, I think," said young

Greyson, addressing Elinor; "her style is very pure, and she has excellent taste."

Elinor could never hope to play as well as Rosina did already, and she said so.

"Now, Marion, you will sing, my dear?" said Mrs. Paton.

Marion came up to the piano, and her brother prepared to accompany her. Mr. Raeburn chose a splendid song of Handel's for her, pointed out a passage which he said must be sung more *piano* than when she last sang it, and desired her not to dwell too much on the closing strain. It had been very evident to him, from the remarks on Rosina's playing, that there was no one present who really understood and could appreciate good music. He was sure they would not appreciate her singing, however much they might be delighted with the beauty of her voice. Such being the case, he did not much care to have her sing beyond the pleasure of hearing her himself, and he sat down to listen in a place where he could see her face.

Truly beautiful voices please all ears, however uncultivated; and on this occasion both the interesting and uninteresting people testified their delight by the most breathless silence. When she sunk her thrilling voice to the softest audible sound, in the passage which had been pointed out, she glanced rather timidly at Mr. Raeburn; and when he smiled and nodded she gathered courage, and went on triumphantly to the end.

" Oh," thought Mr. Dreux, " I see Miss Greyson is singing to Mr. Raeburn,—not to us."

The audience declared that they had not had such a treat for a long time, and protested that, though they did not know much of the science of music, they knew very well what pleased them, upon which a slight smile quivered about Marion's lips, which rather increased when old Mr. Bishop remarked, that no doubt that song of " Wise men flattering " was very fine, and so was that other Italian air, and no doubt Miss Greyson knew best, but *he* should have thought nothing would have suited her so well as a good old English ballad, such as " Alice Grey," or " The woodpecker tapping," which were very popular songs in *his* youth.

" It is very evident," thought Mr. Dreux, " that we are all mere nobodies." He had listened with far more real delight than any one else, but did not venture to commend, from the feeling that he did not quite understand what had so much enchanted him, and should not like to betray his ignorance.

Marion then left the piano to Elizabeth, and went and sat down with Mr. Raeburn in the little China-room, where they were presently joined by Mr. Dreux, Wilfred, and Dora. The rest of the party had dispersed themselves about the main drawing-room,—some playing at chess, and some amusing themselves with books and drawings.

On their entrance Dora and Mr. Dreux were still

talking of music, though at sight of Marion they dropped all reference to her particular performance.

" If there is anything that I *ever* feel inclined to quarrel with in music," said young Greyson, " it is that it agitates the feelings so much."

" It is certainly a direct appeal to the feelings," rejoined Mr. Dreux.

" And I do not like to have my feelings appealed to," said young Greyson. " I had rather be let alone, or appealed to through my reason ; and though I cannot help being affected and distressed when people attack me with touching appeals, I often experience a kind of resentment against them afterwards."

Mr. Raeburn smiled, and said, " I agree with you, my boy, in not liking to have my feelings aroused,—at least, in an agitating manner. But music has a different effect upon me ; I never willingly pass an evening without it,—it is both soothing and elevating."

" Most probably it is uniformly delightful to those who have studied it as a science," observed Mr. Dreux ; " but us, to whom it is almost like a beautiful foreign language, as far as its structure and the means of its power are concerned, it must be regarded as holding more completely in its thrall. We receive each sensation obediently, and do not know what feeling it may arouse next. It sometimes takes us thoroughly by surprise. Among the. uninitiated, a man of joyous disposition and

x

cheerful temper will not at all dread to hear the
most pensive music, provided his sensibilities are
not acute; it does not do more than gently rouse
the even surface of his mind and touch his slumber-
ing sensibility with a pleasurable excitement. But
a man of an excitable temperament, strong and
keen sympathies,—one, with high hopes, who has
yet many regrets, will seldom dare to put himself in
the way of music when these last are uppermost.
His ignorance enables it to subdue him; he per-
ceives neither the science nor its artifices, but finds
himself suddenly living over again among passionate
regrets which he is always trying to tranquillize,
and recollections which he hoped had faded into
oblivion. He resists the appeal, but not till it has
had its will, and perhaps betrayed him to some
before whom he would fain keep a calm face always;
and betrayed to himself, moreover, unfathomed
deeps which may never have been thoroughly
tested yet, in their capacities either for sympathy or
suffering."

Mr. Raeburn's face became troubled, and Marion
cast a slight glance towards the speaker, which had
the effect of checking him.

"I am inclined to think that music is a wilful
thing," said Dora, "and generally goes by contraries; those who are in high spirits it lowers, and
those who are depressed it soothes."

"Perhaps so," remarked Mr. Raeburn; "human
minds are often not so easily acted upon by their

like as by their contraries. In fact, I think contraries attract us all."

"One may see that in a man's choice of his friends," said Mr. Dreux; "and even of his wife."

Dora laughed, and said, "I have certainly observed that in external things. A fair man's wife has generally dark eyes. You seldom see a tall couple; or a clever man with a clever wife. And how often the most lovely, brilliant women, marry taciturn men."

"I do not know whether one might found a theory on what I must now advance," said Mr. Dreux, "but I have known more than one man of fine feelings and great sensitiveness who has preferred to marry a woman conspicuous for nothing but the repose of her character, though her sympathies might be too obtuse to admit of her thoroughly understanding or appreciating him, and though, by the face, she could fathom his thought no further than he chose to reveal it to her; because, I suppose, he was willing to give up the pleasure of being fully understood, for the sake of the soothing influence her unbroken repose would have on his own sensitiveness."

"I must say that I like to be surrounded by calm and quiet things," said Dora.

"I sometimes fancy you may form a guess as to a man's character by the pictures he hangs about on his walls," remarked Mr. Dreux, with a smile. "You find some men pleased to have before their

eyes pictures of bustle and strife and action,—
battle-pieces, perhaps, or even the representations
of the martyrs' legendary sufferings; other men
have plenty, both of action and passion, in their
own minds to make them wish to be outwardly
surrounded by stillness and tranquillity."

" Then I suppose you would infer that the first
man was of a sluggish disposition, and that excitement was pleasurable to him ?"

" The first man *might* have some other reason for
such pictures," was the reply; " but I think I could
pronounce on the character of the second."

Mr. Raeburn thought this very fanciful, and
Dora was surprised to hear Mr. Dreux talk so
openly of his theories and imaginings,—he who
generally conducted himself with such gravity and
reserve, and whose opinions were so difficult to
fathom.

Marion, who, not knowing him so well, saw
nothing unusual in this scene, sat tranquilly looking
from one speaker to the other, till, as they arose to
leave the room, Mr. Raeburn said playfully to her—

" So you see, my sweet child, no person can be
both calm and sensitive."

" Oh," interrupted Mr. Dreux, " I do not admit
any such heretical doctrine. I only intimated (for
I did not assert it) that the two things were rarely
combined."

" You did not *assert* that the pictures in your
study were of the tranquillizing order," said Marion;

" notwithstanding which, *I* assert it as an undoubted fact."

" Be so good as either to confirm or contradict that statement," said Mr. Raeburn.

The person thus appealed to laughed, and seemed well pleased to be the subject of such a remark; but he parried the question, and the conversation was just then brought to a close by the entrance of a servant, who told him that Miss Dreux was waiting for him.

He accordingly took his leave, rather surprised himself at the open manner in which he had been talking, but perfectly satisfied that Miss Greyson, though there was no particular appearance of penetration in her unusually serene face, knew more about him than he had incidentally unfolded that night, and this had been the idea that had made him talk. Where was the use of silence? he thought,—she had read his character through and through.

His character, in fact, was of that kind the full extent of whose *power* will always be felt by others, but the depths of whose sensitive affections will remain in the deepest secrecy to all common observers, as well as its weaker points and temptations, from the great and successful efforts made to conceal them.

The next morning the eclipse of the sun was (as Walter phrased it) to "come off." The great luminary was to rise partially eclipsed, and all the young people had agreed that it was well worth taking a walk up-hill to see it.

Very early, indeed, Greyson and Walter were astir, invading the slumbers of the girls by violently knocking at their doors. The only two individuals who obeyed the summons were Rosina and Marion, who came down just as Frank Maidley was ringing at the bell, with the intention of going with them.

The morning was very grey and dull, and there was something falling without which Wilfred declared was not exactly rain,—he thought it was dew; so they set out, but found it had much the same effect upon their clothes as if it had been rain.

Dora and Elizabeth heard the street-door shut, congratulated themselves that they were not of the party, and then went to sleep again. They came down at the usual time, and found the hungry party enjoying their ham and eggs.

They looked unusually blooming, and the stay-at-homes had the inhumanity to hope they had had a good view of the eclipse, though they knew it had been drizzling all the morning.

The sun had risen partially eclipsed, and they had only caught a short glimpse of him, yet they declared they had enjoyed the walk very much.

" We went into a house on the hill," said Wilfred ;—" you know it, Dora, it is not yet finished. The indoor workmen were there, painting and papering. They cleared away the shavings for us before some of the windows; but what amused me most was the curiosity of a builder's boy about it. I was behind the others, and he showed me which room they were in, and said, 'You'd better make haste, Sir!—they're all doing the eclipse there with a long tube.' I have not the slightest doubt, that whatever he might think was the matter with the sun, he firmly believed it was something that we were helping in! The workmen scarcely looked at the sun, only at us;—they thought we were concocting the eclipse up there."

"Yes," said Elizabeth, "and I should not wonder if they demand a little more rent for the house in consideration of there having been an eclipse in it."

"'Fragments of which are visible to this day,' they may assert," proceeded Wilfred; "for we left numbers of pieces of smoked glass on the chimney-piece, which they seemed to regard with some veneration;—they were Irishmen."

In the middle of the day, as Marion declared herself not at all tired, Mrs. Paton proposed to take her and Dora a drive through a beautiful park a few miles distant.

Marion, being dressed first, was sitting alone in the drawing-room, when Joshua, the stupid servant, came in, with a beautiful bouquet in his hand, which he gave to her, saying that a gentleman had left it for her.

"Mr.—Mr.—I forget his name, I'm sure," said this model footman.

"It does not matter," said Marion, holding out her hand, and not doubting they were from Frank Maidley, for they had talked a good deal about flowers that morning.

"'His compliments to Miss Greyson,' Mum, he said," proceeded Joshua, first smelling the flowers with an admiring air, and then saying, with the greatest composure, "Lawk! how sweet they are!"

Marion's astonishment was great. However, she took the flowers, and remained ignorant of an important fact; for though Joshua could not recal the name, yet if Marion had encouraged his rising talents, and drawn him out, he would have characterized the gentleman as "him as preaches at Pelham's church, and dined at *our* house yesterday."

And here let it be observed, that though Mr. Dreux's church had, as tradition said, been built by a grateful inhabitant of the town some centuries before, in consideration of the fortune he had made in it, and had been called after his name, the common people generally put *St.* before it; for, indeed, no doubt Pelham was as good a saint as some others that have had churches called after them, and the name *Pelham* had got corrupted into "Plum." It was often called "Plum's Church," or "St. Plum's."

But to return to the bouquet. The cause of this offering was, that the day before, Mr. Dreux being seated between Marion and Elizabeth at dinner, they talked of a visit which they had paid that morning to an old lady in the neighbourhood, who had a most beautiful conservatory, and described their sensations, when, while mentally lamenting over the ruined appearance of their own, she said,— " I am sure I need not offer *you* any flowers, you have such nice ones at home,"—and thus had permitted them to leave her, hopeless of obtaining any.

They particularly regretted some myrtles in full flower, and a certain azure-flowering creeper, with long pendant flowers, which neither of them had seen before.

" It is very difficult not to covet sweet flowers," Marion had said, " and even at this moment I cannot help wishing I had some of those !"

Mr. Dreux called upon the old lady next morning, perhaps scarcely acknowledging to himself why ; and when he beheld the flowers, the temptation was too great for him, and he asked her point-blank to give him a bouquet.

" Well," said the old lady, " as you are bent on having some, I suppose I must indulge you. Let me see,—which do you wish for ?"

Mr. Dreux pointed out the myrtle and azure-flowering creeper.

The old lady cut some flowers of each, and said, "There, now mind you don't give that bouquet to a fair lady!"

"Why not?" asked Mr. Dreux.

"Don't you know the language of flowers? If you were to present those to a lady she would say you had tendered her your heart!"

Mr. Dreux laughed; notwithstanding which he took the offered flowers, which he carefully conveyed homewards, and, reckless of consequences, rang at the Patons' bell; and when Joshua opened the door, handed them down to him, as he sat on horseback, and desired him to give them, with his compliments, to Miss Greyson.

If he had gone in and presented them himself, like a man, there is no saying how much future uneasiness he might have been spared. But he made a great mistake. He did not like to come in and face her aunt and cousins, and he was afraid she herself might think it odd to bring her such an offering on such short acquaintance.

So he made off, and took care not to let his sister know where he had been, and what he had been about.

Marion never knew who had brought her the flowers; and the next day, when they were blooming in water in her little parlour, her cousin Elizabeth coaxed her out of them to wear at a *fête* for poor children, which was to be rather a grand affair. The children of all the parish-schools were to meet, and be treated to a cold dinner, which was to be spread under some tents.

Mr. Dreux and Elinor were there. As his school children were figuring at the collation, he presently came up to speak to Elizabeth, who was standing, leaning on old Mr. Bishop's arm, with *his* bouquet in her hand, and he instantly recognised it. Marion was there, but she was at another table with her aunt and the rest of their party. He could not come near to her, but he particularly noticed that she had no flowers ; indeed, she and Dora were in riding-habits, ready to go out when the children's feast should be over. Mr. Dreux had therefore the choice of three suppositions respecting this celebrated bouquet ; either that Joshua had given it to the wrong lady, or that Marion had given it to Elizabeth (which supposition was not a pleasant one), or that this was not the same bouquet, but another exactly like it, which supposition he preferred.

All the *élite* of the place were there, and several of the noble families from the country round. Some of the ladies assisted in waiting on the children at dinner, and afterwards superintended the giving away of the prizes.

Mr. Dreux, with his sister and Mr. Allerton, retired early from the scene of action, for the former had, as usual, a good deal to do, and the latter kept more with him than ever since Elinor's arrival. She had made what is popularly called a complete conquest of him ; but like other gentlemen (as she herself had told her brother), he paid her no compliments, and his love, from the first, had made him much more quiet and grave than usual. He had never addressed a word of admiration to her, but everything she said and did pleased him ; and Elinor was beginning to be aware of that fact, though, from her unusually slender experience, she could scarcely fathom the reason.

She had perceived from the first how unusually anxious he was to possess her brother's regard,—to be important and necessary to him: her brother, unconsciously to himself, seemed to exercise a kind of fascination over him ; he felt that he did not perfectly understand him, and erroneously thought the principal affection was on his own side. She therefore *determined* to think that his pleasure in her society was only a part of the regard which he extended over everything that belonged to her brother, who, in speaking of him on the second day of her visit, had said, " I never knew a man with such a warm heart as Allerton, and he has not a relation in the world. An only child, left an orphan in childhood, no near relations,—he was taken up by a distant cousin, handed from one school to another, his property shamefully mismanaged, and himself not kindly treated. He told me himself some time ago, that if he were to die he did not know of one individual who would go into mourning for him. Who can wonder, then, if he feels the

same affection for his few friends that other men
bestow on their most endeared relatives?"

Mr. Dreux was not the only person who made a
mistake about this time. For it so happened that
Frank Maidley called on Wilfred that afternoon, and
not finding him in the usual sitting-room, went into
the little room before mentioned as being dignified
with the name of a study, and sat down to wait for
him. He no sooner entered than his eyes were
attracted by a picture of a young girl, seated on a
bank, and dressed in white, with what is usually
called a shepherdess hat on her head, with a long
white feather depending from it; her hands were
dropped rather listlessly on her knees, and the face
was turned slightly toward the shoulder, so as to look
full at the spectator. "It's Marion!" he exclaimed,
as he came nearer. "Dear me, how pretty! and
yet it's not at all flattered."

He drew a chair, and sat down opposite to it.
The eyes, with their sweet, tender expression, seemed
to speak directly to his heart; and a crowd of recollections swarmed upon him, of days and times when
her face had worn that tender look. Her living self
had never struck him with that sudden astonishing
sense of how desirable a companion she was in herself, and how sweet a girl. The soft blue eyes had
become inexpressibly touching, and he was amazed
to think that he had hitherto seen nothing in them
to distinguish them from other eyes, beyond their
colour and shape. For the first time, the thought

which Mr. Raeburn had imputed to him flashed upon his mind, and he did not at all like it when young Greyson came in and called him away.

The living original met him at the drawing-room door, and held out her hand as usual. He perceived that she was quite as charming as her portrait, and that her eyes had that same expression,—facts which he had doubted while gazing at her picture; for if it were so, he thought, I should surely have found it out before.

Marion was mindful of her brother's request, that she would not address him by his Christian name; and as she entered the drawing-room, leaving the two young men in the hall, she said, " Good morning, Mr. Maidley."

" Mr. Maidley !" repeated Frank, very much disconcerted, though he had heard her say so several times before, with perfect indifference. " How very ceremonious the air of Westport makes my friends!"

Marion looked gently at her brother, as much as to say, " You see he does not like it," and then said to Frank, with a little, not ungraceful embarrassment, and with a smile, " One must not speak too familiarly to a gentleman about to take a double first class."

" Am I to do so ?" asked Frank, quite indemnified for her distant manner.

" So it is said," replied Marion; " let us hope the prediction will prove a true one."

" It shall not be my fault if it fails, *Miss Greyson,*"

said Frank, laughing. "In the meantime I do not venture, you perceive, to speak familiarly to a lady who has already achieved a double conquest."

"What does he mean?" thought Marion; but she did not ask for an explanation, and as he offered none, she took up her work, and remained no more conscious of the change in his mind than of that other change which had occasioned the gift of the flowers.

Elizabeth presently came in; she was in high spirits, and told Marion she had got a note from old Mr. Bishop, to say that he expected Fred home that very night.

Marion congratulated her, and was glad to hear that she should see him so soon.

"Yes," said Elizabeth, "and I am so glad he will be in time for our large dinner-party."

"Why, you had one yesterday," said Marion.

"Ah, that was a small affair; but this is partly in your honour, Marion. Papa thinks you ought to be introduced to some more of his friends, and Mr. Athanasius Brown and his mother are to be here. Mamma says she is quite ashamed of the length of time it is since she invited them; no party can be dull when they are present."

Fred Bishop came in the evening. He was introduced to Marion, who perceived at once that he was a gentlemanlike young man, and rather good-looking; but after some hours spent in his society, there was nothing more to be said respecting him.

He was rather silent, but evidently devoted to Elizabeth, who behaved to him with the acknowledged preference generally expected from their relative position.

Marion rather wondered at Elizabeth's choice, but she had not much time for speculation, as her uncle asked her several times to sing ; and knowing it gave him pleasure, she never thought of declining.

CHAPTER XI.

NOTHING particular transpired after this for two or three days. Fred Bishop made no change in the house beyond withdrawing Elizabeth from conversing much with the other members of the family, to talk to him, and walk and ride with him.

When Marion came down on the day of the dinner-party, ready dressed for dinner, she found no one in the drawing-room but Frank Maidley and Walter, the latter of whom ran into the hall, and presently returned with a bunch of late violets in his hand, saying, " Look, Marion ; are not these pretty ?"

" Lovely," returned Marion: " do you think I might venture to adopt them ?"

"I should think you might," said Walter, " as they were brought from Fernly on purpose for you."

Marion took the violets and fastened them into her sash. She knew that Walter and old Mr. Bishop had been to Fernly that morning, and supposed the latter had brought them for her ; she therefore said,

in a grateful tone, " How kind of the dear old gentleman !"

" No," said Walter, laughing, " it was not an *old*
gentleman."

" How kind of the dear boy, then !" said Marion,
looking at him, and smiling.

" It was not a boy, either," said Walter, shaking
his head.

" What ! you are grown too proud to be called a
boy. Well, I am determined to have it right. How
kind of the dear *young* gentleman ! Will *that* do ?"

" Yes, very well," said Walter, "but it wasn't
me."

Now Marion had found out that her myrtle bouquet had not come from Frank Maidley, for when
she thanked him for it, he stoutly denied having sent
it ; in fact, he declared, with a bluntness not unusual
with him, that he never should have thought of such
a thing. Subsequently to this his hint about the
double conquest had puzzled her, and though she
could not make out who had sent the flowers, she
coloured, and was silent, feeling secretly annoyed at
having called the unknown " a dear young gentleman," and wishing she could find a pretext for
taking them out of her sash.

Now the fact was that in their walk Mr. Bishop
and Walter had overtaken Frank Maidley, and
when they got into the wood Walter said, " How
delighted Marion would be with these violets !"
upon which the old gentleman advised him to

gather some for her, but to his lasting disgrace, he
replied that he did not like stooping on a hot
afternoon, and, besides, if he did gather them they
would all wither before he got them home.   Upon
this Mr. Maidley applied himself to the work with
great alacrity, groping among the leaves with his
spectacles on, with an earnestness that it did one
good to see.   However, as he left them in his hat
instead of bringing them in and giving them to her
himself, he had no right to have felt piqued at her
obvious annoyance, which he did notwithstanding,
accusing her, mentally, of affectation in pretending
not to know who the violets came from.

"Are they not pretty?" said Walter; "don't
you wonder who brought them, Marion?"

"Not particularly," replied Marion coldly; "I
shall find it possible to wait till you tell me."

"I dare say you would never have put them on
if you *had* known," said young Maidley, in a tone of
pique, as Walter left the room.

Marion looked up, surprised.   "Why not?" she
inquired.

He made no answer, but looked sullen.

"Perhaps you would advise me to take them off
again?" she added, still thinking about her last
offering, and curious to find out where they had
both come from.

"I think you had better," he replied; "I am
sure you put them on by mistake."

"What does he mean," thought Marion.   However, she was relieved at the turn the conversation had taken, and unfastening the violets she gently tossed them towards the table near which she was sitting. If she had thrown them with a little more force they might have rested there, but as it was, they dropt over the edge and fell on to the ottoman at her feet.

" The person who brought them seems to have fallen under your displeasure," she said, after a short pause.

" Only because he is a great fool," replied young Maidley, who had no sooner made her take out the flowers than he repented it.

Marion felt much puzzled, but a slight glimmering of the truth reached her mind as she rose from her place and went to a sofa in the window.

Womanly curiosity was not to be resisted, and as Walter had left the room, she could not help saying, " After all, Mr. Maidley, I should be glad to know who gave me those flowers. Perhaps you will favour me with his name."

" How oddly Frank behaves," she thought, as he looked about him, as if he felt ashamed of himself. " Who brought me those flowers, Mr. Maidley ?"

" I did."

Marion paused for a moment, scarcely knowing what to reply, but her natural tact coming to her aid, she presently said, " I am surprised you should think so slightingly of a person for whom I feel so much regard, still more so that you should hurt my feelings by calling any friend of mine a fool. However, as you are probably the only person in the world who thinks he merits such an appellation, perhaps you will oblige me by picking up the flowers again, and bringing them here."

Frank Maidley did as he was desired, and brought the flowers with the air of a rebuked school-boy. Marion took them and reinstated them in their former place, saying, with as much composure as if she had really been speaking of some other person, "I hope you will never speak ill of my friends again, particularly of those whom I have known from my childhood."

While he stood before her quite undecided whether to feel reproved or flattered, and before he had made up his mind, a bevy of Miss Patons entered, and immediately after the dinner company began to arrive.

But neither the presence of many strangers, the necessity of talking to them, the singular traits of character displayed by some, nor, to crown all, Mr. Dreux's conversation, which was chiefly addressed to her,—not all these things could keep her from pondering on the sudden change in Frank Maidley's behaviour, and perceiving, with many uneasy sensations, what it must portend. She was still thinking on this subject, when the ladies retired to the drawing-room, and started when Elizabeth laid her hand upon her arm and asked where those beautiful violets came from.

"Come with me, dearest," she said, without awaiting the answer to her question, and leading Marion to the little wing of the drawing-room before described as the china-room; "I want to tell you something."

Marion followed her cousin, and they established themselves on a couch, with a sofa-table before it, while Elizabeth, with great animation, began to detail various particulars relative to her own prospects.

Marion did her best to seem amused, and succeeded. Elizabeth continued to talk till the increased sound of voices announced the return of the gentlemen, and immediately after, Fred Bishop drew aside the partially-drawn curtain and established himself beside Elizabeth.

He was followed instantly by the Rev. Athanasius Brown, who was in the middle of a sentence when he entered, on the subject of the prospects of the turnip crop; and if he expected Fred Bishop to answer it he must have been surprised as well as disappointed, for that gentleman seemed no longer conscious of his existence. In a few minutes Frank Maidley came into their sanctuary, and leaned his broad shoulders against the doorway. Mr. Brown, who for the last few minutes had been looking forlornly about him, searching for something to do, now espied a chess board, and inquired of Elizabeth whether he might have the pleasure of a game at chess with her.

Upon this Fred Bishop looked a good deal annoyed, and Elizabeth was about to give a reluctant consent, when Marion said, "Dear Elizabeth, you know I am the family champion!"

"O yes," said Elizabeth, looking gratefully at her, "you play so much better than I, Marion, that it will be best to leave our reputation in your hands."

"So if Mr. Brown has no objection," Marion began.

Hereupon Mr. Brown gracefully signified that it was all the same to him which of the ladies he played with, and drew a chair opposite to Marion, and began to set the men, the narrow sofa-table serving for the board to stand on.

The Rev. Athanasius Brown, whether he moved a resolution at a board of gentlemen or moved a pawn at a game of chess, was equally in earnest and equally absorbed in what he was about. After the first few moves he became perfectly abstracted from all around him, and incapable of hearing the conversation or remarking the movements of the various guests who passed in and out of their little retreat, and laughed and talked on all sides of him, while, with his brows knit and his eyes intent upon the board, he weighed all the consequences of some impending aggression on the part of his adversary, or hovered with uneasy fingers over the piece which he intended to move.

Elizabeth and Mr. Bishop could talk quite at their ease, though sitting so near the combatants: it was

quite obvious that he was utterly absorbed; and
Elizabeth, as the evening wore on, felt increasingly
obliged to Marion " for her obliging self-sacrifice."
Mr. Bishop also remarked, quite fearlessly, that he
had often heard of heroines in humble life, and he
now had the pleasure of seeing one belonging to the
upper classes,—one, he continued, who deserved to
have kings, queens, and knights at her disposal, and
to be unchecked in her progress through the game
of life.

" I find a Bishop the only thing that troubles me
at present," said Marion, casting an admonitory
glance towards him, of which he took not the
slightest notice, but waxed yet more incautious in
his remarks, feeling perfectly secure in Mr. Brown's
state of oblivion.

At length, after a pause of at least a quarter of
an hour, he made his move, and Marion, who had
had abundance of time to consider what she would
do, whatever piece he advanced, moved almost
instantly, and Mr. Brown relapsed into another fit
of abstraction.

It was certainly not a very lively occupation
playing at chess with Mr. Brown, and as the time
wore on Marion began to wish for a little change.
The game had lasted more than an hour when this
was afforded her by the entrance of her uncle, who
beckoned away Fred Bishop, and bore him off among
the gentlemen who were talking in the main drawing-room. At the moment of his disappearance

Frank Maidley took his place, and Mrs. Paton came into the room, with Mrs. Brown, Wilfred, and Dora.

" Why, Marion, my dear," said her aunt, " I wondered what had become of you. What, at chess ? Ah, I know you are a famous chess player."

Marion looked up and tried to seem amused, and Mrs. Brown, observing her son's abstracted air, and that he seemed quite unconscious of her presence, nodded mysteriously round, and whispered to Mrs. Paton that " she believed if you were to tell him that the Parliament itself was burnt down you would not rouse him till he had made his move."

" Dora, my dear," said her mother, " why have we had no music ? Go find Rosina, and play those new duets of yours."

The obedient Dora needed no second bidding.

" Don't you think Athanasius is looking better the last few days ? " said that gentleman's mother, addressing the standers-by generally.

" Oh, much better," said Frank Maidley, in a tone of the deepest interest.

" Ah, it's the country air. Dr. Tring always said he ought to have a good walk every day,—and to do the Doctor justice, I must say, Mr. Maidley, he practises what he preaches, and takes a long walk every day with Mrs. Tring. I met 'er and 'im this morning on the Fernly road ; or at least I should say, 'im and 'er. Ah, there's nothing like the country, Mr. Maidley!"

" No," replied that gentleman. " Let me wander not unseen by 'edge-row elms and 'illocks green."

Mrs. Paton turned quickly round on hearing this quotation, and looked with astonishment at young Maidley, under the impression that he had actually dared to ridicule her guest before her face, but seeing the benevolent smile that lighted up his broad, good-humoured countenance as he looked up at Mrs. Brown with an air of respectful interest, she thought she must have been mistaken, and the notes of the harp and piano beginning to sound in the distance, the two elderly ladies went away together.

" Pray take a seat," said young Maidley, looking at Wilfred. " You had better settle yourself comfortably, for we—that is, my excellent friend and myself (nodding towards Mr. Brown)—*we* have no intention of going home till morning, ' 'till daylight doth appear.'"

" You seem determined to make us acquainted with the writings of the poets," said Marion, turning towards him. " You are particularly rich in quotation this evening, Mr. Maidley."

" I'm inspired by your presence."

" I like you much better," replied Marion, " when you are not in a state of inspiration."

" I know Miss Greyson wishes me to go," said

Frank, addressing Elizabeth. " I wish I might be allowed to enjoy myself in my own peaceful way."

" Don't you think you should find the society of the gentlemen more improving than ours?" said Elizabeth, smiling. " I see papa and Mr. Ferguson talking on what seems to be a very interesting subject."

" No, I can't go to old Ferguson, for I know he would patronize me, and I hate to be patronized."

" Well, you may stay here then, provided you promise not to laugh at your betters any more."

" Which are my betters?" inquired Frank, looking round with an air of innocent bewilderment.

" Every one here present," replied Elizabeth, laughing.

" Perhaps, then, one of my betters will propose some improving theme on which we may discourse with advantage to our young minds. I do so love to hear people hold forth on virtue and morality."

" Check," said Mr. Brown, in a deep portentous voice which made them all start.

Marion moved her piece out of danger, and the conversation went on.

" After all," said Frank, " when one ridicules a good man it's not *him* or his *principles*, but merely some little oddity in his manner or appearance that one laughs at."

" Well," thought Marion, looking anxiously at

her *vis-à-vis*, " I know he does not hear, poor man ;
but I wonder at their daring."

" And it does not at all lessen the respect that
one feels for such a man to be able to see that in
some respects he is open to ridicule; besides,
' censure is the tax that people pay to the public
for being eminent,' and so ridicule is the tax they
pay for being better than their neighbours."

" Very bad morality, and I don't agree with you
that it does not lessen the respect one feels for such
an one."

" Besides," continued Frank, " ridicule is a kind
of tacit avowal that the man has something excellent
and exalted about him ; for if he were altogether a
mean or commonplace character there would be
nothing out of keeping in those very points which
are now, in consequence of their incongruity, felt to
be laughable."

" Exactly so," said Elizabeth, following on the
same side. " The little blemishes of a fine character
are more conspicuous than the grave faults of a
common one.   Think of the splendour of Dr.
Johnson's genius ! and yet, because he was a great
man, his putting his fingers into the sugar-basin
when he went out to tea is remembered to this day,
because people wondered that a man who could
write a dictionary, and use so many fine words that
scarcely any one else understood the meaning of,
should not know how to use a pair of sugar-tongs ;

whereas, a man who only just knew how to read and write his mother tongue might have done the same thing all his life, and the world would not have taken the slightest notice."

" The more eminent a man is," said Frank, " the better target does he present for the shafts of ridicule. Ahem, I hope Miss Greyson hears that."

" I hear," replied Marion, in a tone sufficiently subdued not to interrupt Mr. Brown's cogitations; " but I think, though what you say may hold good with respect to men of genius, it does *not* with respect to men who are only eminent for piety and a desire to influence others for their good; if you make them ridiculous you take away half their power."

" Certainly," said Frank. " But we were not talking about MY making them ridiculous, but about their making *themselves* ridiculous."

" Ah, I think if they make themselves ridiculous," said Marion in the same soft voice, " we should do our best to think charitably of them, remembering that very likely *we* are as absurd in their eyes as they in ours."

" Marion is getting very severe," said Elizabeth, undauntedly, " but let us try to think charitably of her, for she has had enough to try her temper this night."

Marion blushed deeply, from fear lest the remark should be heard by her partner, and Elizabeth happening to turn her head, saw Mr. Dreux leaning against the doorway, apparently an amused spectator of the scene.

"Checkmate," said Mr. Brown.   The event had been so long expected that when it did at last take place they were quite surprised.

"I hope you have had an interesting game," said young Maidley.

"Very much so," replied the Rev. Gentleman. "Miss Greyson plays extremely well, and I should have been very happy to have given her her revenge, but unfortunately I have an engagement at home which will oblige me to take my leave early."

Marion turned away her face to conceal a smile which she could not repress, and Mr. Brown bowed all round with his usual stiff formality, and took his leave.

"I hope you have been amused with our conversation, Mr. Dreux," said Elizabeth, turning half round.

"Very much so," he replied.   "I did not agree with the speakers, but I perceived that only one of them uttered her real sentiments."

"Of course," began Elizabeth, a little abashed, "we should not *seriously* defend the practice of laughing at any good man, particularly at a clergyman."

Mr. Dreux bowed, but in a manner which seemed to express neither assent nor dissent, but simply informed her that he had heard what she said.   He seemed occupied in looking at Marion, who was putting away the chess-men, and whose face was still rather troubled, for she fancied Mr. Brown must surely have heard her cousin's last remark about her temper.

Elizabeth began several sentences relative to her not wishing to defend the practice of laughing at others, but she could not finish them; and, as Frank Maidley showed not the slightest inclination to help her, she was not sorry when Mr. Dreux joined the rest of the party in the main drawing-room.

"I wonder how all the nonsense we have been talking would look in print," said Elizabeth, in a tone of vexation.

"Luckily," said Wilfred, "there is no one present who will be likely to give it to the world. I can only say, that if I ever become sufficiently celebrated to have my biography written, I shall begin to talk in the most elegant periods possible, and always in praise of all the cardinal virtues and the discouragement of vice, and all that. I shall also fill my letters with sentences that will do me credit, and all the moral axioms I can think of; for of course I shall wish to improve my age. As for Athanasius and his mother, nobody shall ever hear *me* make game of either 'er or 'im,—or, at least, I should say, 'im or 'er." This last remark was so precisely in the old lady's voice, that they all burst out laughing.

"Yes," said Elizabeth, spitefully, "it's very well

to laugh at us. By the bye, your portrait must be in your biography, and in profile, of course, to display the proportions of your nose."

" No ; I think I shall not have a portrait," replied young Greyson ; " but let it be said of me,—' He was about the middle height. We have no objection to admit that his nose was large, but otherwise he was good-looking and well-proportioned.' "

" I am afraid you scarcely reach the middle height, dear," said Marion.

" Well," said Elizabeth, " there's not the slightest chance that his biography ever will be written ; but if it should be, I think they'll say, ' rather below the middle height,—all but short.' "

" Then I won't have it written at all," was the reply.

" Come to facts," said young Maidley,—" what is your height ? "

" Why, five feet nine."

" Very well, then, let that be stated, and leave the invidious world to judge for itself."

" He has a habit," said Elizabeth, " of saying of rather tall people,—' Oh, he's a fellow about my height.' But he never says so of any one who is even a shade shorter than himself."

" As for you, Marion," remarked Wilfred, turning the conversation, " I really should like to know what a biographer would say of you."

" He shall say whatever he pleases," said Marion.

" Let him describe her as she now appears,

beginning with—' Miss Marion Greyson was a young lady possessing moderate talents and a serene temper. At the time when this biography commences she was seated at a table with one of her accomplished cousins, who, like herself, was occupied in tossing little balls of brown braid over her fingers whereof to make watch-guards. She was arrayed in a lilac silk-gown, with flounces snipped at the edges.' "

" Pinked, you Goth !" interrupted young Maidley. " Don't you know that those wriggles are called pinking ?"

" Well, it's all the same thing. ' She had round the top of her dress an article which I understand is called a berthe, and round her arm a bracelet in the shape of a snake, with its head dotted with blue stones (she chiefly valued the latter because it was a present from her justly esteemed brother). Now for her face."

" The eyes good," interrupted young Maidley. " Let the biographer compare them to stars."

" He shall compare them to two blue stars on a misty night. As to her nose—I should be sorry to hurt your feelings, Marion,—but don't you think it has just a slight leaning towards the genus of pugs ?"

" Nothing of the kind," said Elizabeth ; " it's quite a straight nose."

" Well, I should have said it was a mild pug ; but I don't wish to be contentious."

" Then we'll have her portrait put into the biography," said Elizabeth ; " and if the world says it is not a Grecian nose, I shall think the worse of the world's discernment."

" Let it also be said in her favour, that she has a great respect for the Church, and never laughs at clergymen, in which respect she does *not* resemble some other young ladies whom I could mention."

" Why *will* you talk about that again ?" said Elizabeth, " I am sure you might have seen that I was sorry for what I had done."

" O yes ! very sorry that Mr. Dreux heard you laughing at one of your father's guests."

" Well," said Elizabeth, in a tone of levity which was not unusual with her when she was in high spirits, " then, ridiculous people, and people whose mothers cannot speak their own language properly, have no business to go into the Church. If all clergymen were like Mr. Dreux, I should never think of laughing."

" No, I am sure you would not, Elizabeth," said Marion, looking up with a smile, " for you seem quite afraid of him."

" Because he is so grave and so silent ; and then he has so much dignity about him, that it's quite natural *he* should meet with respect."

" Yes, as a man he will no doubt meet with more deference than most others ; but you know, Elizabeth, we ought to respect a clergyman for his work's sake."

"I can easily respect Mr. Dreux, both for his own sake and his work's; but Athanasius is very different."

"How, different?" said young Maidley. "Now I should have said that in all points that ought to command respect they were exactly alike,—they both preach the same doctrines, are each equally devoted to their work, and each equally anxious to set a good example. So far from being very different, I can see no difference at all between them."

"I admire your remonstrance, Mr. Maidley! Why, you were the principal offender in our late conversation; you did far more to make our friend appear absurd than I did."

"That's perfectly true," said the accused party; "but though I do so, that's no reason why I should approve of it. I do *not*. On the contrary, I know it's very wrong, and I am now confessing my fault, on the principle that 'he who acknowledges an error has gone half-way towards correcting it.'"

"But that proverb was never meant to apply to a case like yours. Every one present has seen you commit the fault, therefore there can be no merit in acknowledging it."

"It's impossible to please you, Miss Paton. Shall you be satisfied if I promise to call on Mr. Brown to-morrow evening and propose a game of chess with him, by way of penance?"

"I am not sure that I should," replied Elizabeth;

" but if you like to call on him, and explain how
we laughed at him and his mother, and how wrong
we feel that it was, I think that will quite set my
mind at ease. There will be no need for you to
mention names, you know, but merely say, ' Myself
and one of the young ladies.' "

" No ; I have too much respect for the Church
to show a clergyman that his presence has been felt
to be tedious. Besides, when I asked him,—' Will
you forgive me for having laughed at you ?'—
perhaps he would answer, ' Are you sorry you did
it ?' And then I *might* feel it necessary to say
' Yes.' I am almost sure," continued Mr. Maidley,
in a musing tone, " that I should say yes ; and how
very wrong that would be. It would hurt my conscience. In fact, it would be telling an untruth."

The party could not help laughing at this sally,
it was so gravely uttered, and with an appearance
of so much good feeling.

" I remember," said Wilfred, " that when I was a
little boy I used to bite my nails, till one day Mr.
Raeburn promised me that if I would leave it off,
he would give me five shillings and a fishing-rod ; so
I began the cure by restricting myself to the little
finger of each hand. Now, don't you think it would
be a good plan to leave off laughing at our betters
in the same way, confining ourselves strictly to one
or two people, and not making jokes on any others
on any pretence whatever ? "

" I don't know that it would be a bad plan," said

young Maidley, "if one could keep to it. So, as Miss Paton told me that you were all my betters, I think I shall choose herself and you to be, as it were, my two little fingers, and from this time I shall laugh at you only."

" Then I hope you will at least always have a good end in view in your ridicule, Mr. Maidley," said Elizabeth.

" Yes, there will always be a good moral in my sarcasms, which I will tell you myself, in case you should not find it out. Now I am going to begin ! Ahem. The absurd opinion which Miss Paton expressed—namely, that there was a great difference between the respect we owe to our two clerical friends (about whom we have been talking the whole evening)—proves, I think, that her mind is like a picture out of keeping, or as it were out of perspective. She puts together all things that go to make a clergyman in equally prominent positions; such as his piety, and his voice, and his gown, and his character, and his creed, and his bands, and his features, &c. Now this is a mistake against which I must direct my sarcasms; for it often causes her to form wrong conclusions."

" Please to observe," said Marion, " that this is invective, not sarcasm."

" It does not matter what we call it," said Frank, "if it does good. Now listen to me, Miss Paton. I am going to tell you a pretty little story, to illustrate my meaning. It is about the Church."

" Oh, I am not afraid to hear it," said Elizabeth. " I dare say it will not shake *my* principles."

" That would be very undesirable in a lady who destines the honour of her hand to a Bishop."

" What a wretched pun, Mr. Maidley."

" Shocking: but will you hear my story?"

" Oh yes, certainly, if it is not too grave."

" Well, Miss Paton, once upon a time there was a nation of fairies, who having reached a highly civilized state, were told by a mortal who was in their confidence, that all the most refined nations of mankind professed the Christian religion.

" ' And I would strongly advise you to do so also,' said the confidante.

" ' But we have no souls,' said the fairies.

" ' Oh that does not signify at all,' replied the mortal; 'to see how a great many of my country folk go on, you would never find out that they had souls either.'

" ' Well,' said the fairies, 'then you may bring us down a bishop to-morrow, and if we like him, we'll profess your religion.'

" So the next day he brought them down a bishop, dressed in his gown and lawn sleeves, you know, and his prayer-book on an elegant cushion."

" How *can* you talk such nonsense, Mr. Maidley!"

" I find it comes as naturally as possible. Well, before he introduced the bishop to them, he muttered a spell over him, by the power of which he became as small as the fairies themselves.

" ' Here is my Lord Bishop,' he said, bringing him up to the fairy King.

" But the fairies were not at all pleased with him.

" ' A very pretty bishop indeed!' they said. I dare say he's only an old worn out one that your King has done with—why, look at him, all the gilding is rubbed off his mitre ! ! !'

" ' So it is,' said the mortal, ' I never observed that before; but, you know, nothing human is perfect, and really in a matter of such *very* small importance—'

" ' Small importance !' shrieked the Queen ; ' only hear the impudence of mankind !'

" ' Small importance !' said the fairy King. ' How dare you tell me such a falsehood ! Why his mitre is the most conspicuous part of him. Take him up again directly, and if you don't bring us down a better one to-morrow, a large gooseberry-bush shall begin to grow out of the top of your head.'

" Well, the next day the mortal presented himself again, with a very rueful countenance, for he was in a dreadful fright.

" ' Now,' said the fairies, ' have you brought us a better bishop ?'

" ' I told you, good people,' said the mortal (shaking very much, and looking very humble), ' that nothing human is perfect. All of our race have some defect, and I have looked in vain for a bishop who has no blemish whatever.'

" ' Let us see him,' said the King.

" So the bishop was brought in, and they all walked round and round him.

" ' How white his robes are !' said one.

" ' And how beautiful his mitre is !" said another.

" ' And what curious buckles he has in his shoes !' said a third ;—' he looks quite perfect.'

" ' Now,' said the King, ' you have brought us down a very different bishop to-day. Understand, that the fairies are not a people to be trifled with ! But if he *has* any defect let us hear it.'

" ' All the beginning is torn out of his Prayer-book,' said the mortal, trembling very much, and thinking that now something dreadful would certainly be done to him.

" ' Is it ?' said the King, looking at the bishop with his head on one side. ' Well, I don't think that will matter particularly, for it does not show on the outside ; and as the defect is so very trifling, you shall be forgiven this once, and nothing shall be done to you.' "

" A very pretty story indeed," said Elizabeth, " and well suited, no doubt, to my infant mind. People who are going to take high degrees are certainly very conceited. The moral is so obvious that I think I need not trouble you to tell it me !"

CHAPTER XII.

MAIDLEY'S EDIFYING CONFESSION OF HIS FAULTS.

MR. ALLERTON all this time had never allowed a day to pass without seeing Elinor, and yet he never spoke to her on any but ordinary subjects; and having never been alone with her, had not ventured to be very explicit, even in looks of admiration.

"How late you are!" said Mr. Dreux to him one evening when he entered the library;—"what can have been detaining you?"

"It was neither man, woman, nor child," replied the delinquent. "It was nothing more than the button of a wristband! Buttons and button-holes are the plagues of my life!"

"Ah!" said his friend, "when buttons won't go right, then's the time to feel the power of woman. The misery they can inflict by means of such things is astonishing!"

"The number of passions I have been put into by them," pursued Mr. Allerton, "is dreadful to think of. Why, look here,—how does my laundress suppose I am to get a button nearly as big as a cheese-plate through a hole scarcely visible to the naked eye?"

"I don't know; my buttons are never bigger than half-crowns,—hardly so big, I should say."

"You must have been talking of something very amusing," said Elinor, as they entered the drawing-room.

"We have been inveighing against women, my dear," replied her brother. "I know we shall be late. Allerton has lost his riding-gloves and whip, my love; he says he left them here this morning, but the servants know nothing of them."

"I think Mr. Allerton took off his gloves in the verandah, and laid them on the bench, Arthur."

"You have a good memory," said her brother, going out, and presently returning with them in his hand; "women are of some use, after all."

"And my whip,—I wonder what I did with that?" said the Rector of St. Bernard's, beginning to look for it in the most improbable places; for he was very careless with his possessions, and generally laid them down wherever he happened to be standing.

Elinor, who was at work on the sofa, cast a glance here and there in search of the missing whip, and presently drew it out from behind the sofa-cushion; her brother was already at the door, when she held it out to its possessor, saying, with a smile, "Is there anything else that I can find for you, Mr. Allerton? pray have you lost anything more?"

Mr. Allerton took the whip, and said, with rather an embarrassed smile, "Why, yes, I have; I have lost my heart. Can you tell me what has become of it, Miss Dreux? for I think you must know."

Elinor looked up, astonished and confused; and her brother's voice calling to Mr. Allerton from the foot of the stairs to make haste, he took his leave in a great hurry, and left her to her meditations.

It would appear that they were not altogether of a pleasing nature, for as she stooped over her work a few tears dropped from her eyes and fell upon her hands. She felt ashamed that she should have been so much taken by surprise, and alarmed as she confessed to herself how much Mr. Allerton's implied affection had for the moment delighted her. Then she was angry at her present emotion. "His remark," she argued, "was nothing but a passing compliment. If he should go abroad to-morrow, and I should never see him again, I could not blame him for those few words. He thinks it necessary to say polite things to Arthur's sister; but if he had felt anything more than ordinary kindness for me, he would not have addressed me as he did to-day for the first and only time."

After all this reasoning, Elinor was still not satisfied; and as she sat with her work before her, and her hands dropped upon her knees, she remembered, with a painful kind of shrinking, certain remarks, slight in themselves, but containing allusions to some of the principles she held most sacred, and which, by an indescribably slight smile, or some peculiar tone of voice, he had contrived to show her that he held in contempt. That he was exceedingly attached to her brother she could not doubt; but in spite of his occasional efforts to conceal it, she had always seen that, though he endured to hear him speak on religion, it was only his affection that made it palatable, and prevented him from openly expressing his disapprobation.

This he had shown strongly a few days before, during one of the very few arguments they had held in her presence. As long as her brother had said, "*I* think so and so," Mr. Allerton had treated the matter in hand with gravity and respect; but on his happening to quote a remark of King's on the subject, Mr. Allerton had thrown himself back in his chair, with a burst of laughter, exclaiming, "Now, don't, Dreux; now, don't. I really cannot listen to the absurdities of the whole fraternity; and as for that wooden-legged old fellow, I always thought him one of the greatest spooneys that ever breathed."

Her brother, who did not join in the laugh at poor Mr. King, had replied, "I quoted the remark because I quite agree with Mr. King." Upon which Mr. Allerton looked at him with that curious mixture of pity and respect which he often exhibited,—pity for his supposed delusion of mind, and respect for that species of personal dignity which many fear, but none despise.

Her brother then went on with his own ideas on the subject, Mr. Allerton's face gradually becoming grave. Elinor had seen from the first that they strove with each other for the mastery, but that Mr. Allerton knew *he* should never get it. It is impossible for two minds in constant communication to preserve a strict equality; the one must give in, and as the other gains power, it must begin to bend that one, and make it revolve around it.

Mr. Allerton had brilliant talents, but he wanted tact; he lost his own advantage, and was not clever in catching at his adversary's weak point. He was equal to her brother in most respects, but he wanted his masterly energy and steadiness of principle. They were both remarkable for strength of feeling, and each had a warm temper; but the one had struggled with his temper and mastered it, while the other was the slave of his.

Elinor, who had all her brother's penetration, and a good deal of womanly tact besides, soon perceived that Mr. Allerton was playing a losing game. She also saw that the contention in which they were engaged was, with him, head work only. It was obvious that he was never disturbed with the idea of what would become of *him* if "these things were so." Their arguments, when *he* was vanquished, and admitted the fact, did not lead to any change in his proceedings; it scarcely seemed to occur to him that the matter was one which involved practical consequences.

" I 'll tell you what," he one day said to his friend,
"I wish I could hear you having a good tough argument with Hewly; you 'd find it rather a different
thing, I fancy. He would put you in a passion before you knew what you were about."

" I don't desire the honour," was the reply, with
a laugh. "One of you is enough; besides, I like an
antagonist who is sincere, and whom I can respect.
I do not consider Hewly an honest man."

" You don't?"

" No, nor manly either. He has not sufficient
respect either for himself or his principles to state
them openly and without shuffling; and he takes
underhand means to accomplish his ends. He pretends to be very much attached to *you* before your
face."

" No, he doesn't," retorted Mr. Allerton. " He
does nothing but scold me, as if I were a school-boy;
he wanted me to bear him out in all his plans, and
let him go whatever lengths he likes."

" Well, but I mean he *appears* to be devoted to
your interests."

" To be sure, and so I suppose he is."

" He takes a singular way to prove it, then," said
Dreux, deliberately, " for he does not speak so well
of you behind your back as I could wish."

Mr. Allerton's sudden change of countenance made
Elinor particularly attentive. He looked indignant,
and coloured with mortification, as her brother, leaning forward, said, " Listen to me, my dear Allerton;

I do not tell you this without regret; I would not willingly point out a man's failings to his friend, but I consider it a duty to tell you of this, because it makes Hewly quite unworthy of your future confidence."

Mr. Allerton changed his position, and nodded to her brother to go on. Elinor wondered how he could care for the friendship of a man like Hewly, for she had met with him *once*, and found the interview quite enough to make her fear him a little, and dislike him a good deal.

Her brother went on,—" You know something of the Paton family and their principles, therefore, of course, it cannot be new to you that they are very much disturbed that their eldest daughter should have taken up some of your views, and wished to join herself to your congregation. Yesterday I called there : only Mrs. Paton was at home, and she said to me, 'I wish you would speak to my eldest daughter, Mr. Dreux ; you once had considerable influence over her.' Just then she happened to come in, with a Prayer-book in her hand ; she had been to Hewly's morning prayers.

" I immediately entered on the subject of her having in a great degree left my church, and in the course of conversation she advanced several of your opinions, and advocated them much as you do. At last she said something that I was quite certain she had never learned from you, and I answered, ' But Allerton does not sanction any such proceedings, nor

do I believe he would consider you right in leaving
your parish church and attending his, particularly
against the wishes of your parents.' ' Oh,' she said,
in rather an embarrassed manner, ' but Mr. Hewly
thinks it quite right, and he says Mr. Allerton is a
very weak man, and I must not be too much guided
by what *he* says,—for he is afraid of giving offence,
and is not willing to bear the reproach of the Cross
openly; he only cares about having a large congregation, and being talked of as a popular man.' At
this instant she recollected that I was your friend,
and stopped short, looking much vexed. I was so
surprised and angry that I could not answer for a
moment, and she tried to qualify what she had said.
' Hewly does Allerton gross injustice,' I answered,
not in the best possible temper, ' and he knew perfectly well that there was no truth in what he then
told you. But,' I went on, ' whether true or otherwise, Miss Paton, he told you this of a man for
whom, in public, he professes (and you must often
have heard him) the very strongest feelings of
esteem, friendship, and brotherhood; therefore I
submit to you—and I hope you will bear in mind
what I say—that a man who is capable of such
meanness as to stab his friend in the dark, to serve
his own ends, is quite unworthy of your future confidence; he is either a disgrace to the principles he
professes, or, if he is acting up to them, he proves
them to be vile. But,' I said, as I got a little cooler,
' I do not wish to pour contempt on any principles

which you have adopted. Of course, I should be thankful if I could see you happy in the belief of those in which you have been educated; but it is of no use my declaring to you how much *I* dislike Hewly's principles; all I have to do is, if possible, to show that they are not worthy of *your* approval. I do not wish to argue so unfairly as to insinuate, that because Hewly has proved himself dishonest, that others professing the same belief are not likely to be honest men; but I do say this, that your duty is now made plain. And I think, Miss Paton, as it is Allerton's church which you have attended, and Allerton's influence which first brought you there, you should at least have so much deference for the judgment of him whom you call your spiritual guide as to yield to his so-often expressed opinion, that it is an evil to leave your parish church; and as in your case that has been done contrary to the known wish of your parents, you should retract that error, and return to your place, *at least* till Mr. Allerton shall testify his disapproval.'"

Allerton heard him to the end, and then broke out into severe expressions of disgust against his Curate, which would have been stronger still if it had not been for the presence of Elinor.

Her brother then said, "Did Miss Paton ever speak to you on the subject of attending your church?"

"Yes, several times. She asked me whether I thought she ought, and I distinctly told her no. She

A A

began by saying that she greatly wished it ; that
she had had several conversations with her parents,
and they strongly disapproved, but that it had ended
in their saying they did not *command* her to continue to go to church with them, but they should be
grieved if she did otherwise. She had then said,
'May I go to the week-day services ?' and *that* they
did not deny her. So I told her that her duty to
her parents was always paramount, unless they
desired her to do anything sinful, and that she must
content herself with coming to us during the week,
which she did at first, but now she frequently comes
on Sunday."

"Which is Hewly's doing, of course ?"

"No doubt of it ; she always came with Miss
Ferguson. Do you think she will come back to
you ?"

"I cannot tell, but I incline to think she will.
She was most deeply hurt at what I said about
Hewly ; I could see tears in her eyes, and I wished
to prolong the conversation, but one cannot do so
with a lady unless she chooses to permit it. She
intimated that she would give her best attention to
what I had said, and then began to introduce other
subjects, so I presently took my leave. Mrs. Paton
had told me she did not wish to force her daughter's
conscience, and thought that a proceeding more
likely to do harm than good ; so it is left to herself.
But I was surprised at the degree of influence
Hewly had obtained over her, and could not help

thinking that, though she disliked to hear me hold forth on his meanness, she was more sorry to have betrayed it thus accidentally to me, than shaken in her own exalted opinion of him."

Elinor pondered on this conversation during the evening with pain and anxiety, because it had opened her eyes more fully than ever to the fact that her brother and his friend were not only opposed in principle, but that they both fully acknowledged that it was so, and conducted their intercourse accordingly. It did not disturb her at the time to know that it was so, but she now looked back on the matter in a different light; and as she reflected on Mr. Allerton's affectionate heart, his agreeable manner to herself, his talents, and his great regard for her brother, the tears filled her eyes again, with the earnestness of her wish that it might have been otherwise.

It was quite a relief to her when at last her brother came in, and enabled her to cast off these uneasy thoughts for a while, by occupying herself with him.

"How late you are, dearest," she said, as she met him at the top of the stairs.

"Late!" he replied. "Why, I told you that I should not be home till ten."

Elinor rang for tea. "Then you walked home," she said.

"Yes; don't you remember my telling you that Allerton was going to drive me to the church where

I was to preach, and that you said the long walk
home would do me a great deal of good?"

"O yes, I remember it now," said Elinor.

"What a forgetful little thing you are, my dear!
what's the matter with your eyes? You have been
reading in the dusk!" he exclaimed, answering his
question himself. "Never do so again, Elinor,
it is a most injurious habit. Why, if you had not
often told me how happy you are here, I should
almost have thought you had been shedding tears!"

"You know I am happier with you than anywhere else, Arthur," said Elinor, earnestly. "I wish
we could always be together."

"And so we will when you are of age," said her
brother; "then don't read any more in the dusk."
And so saying he lifted up her face to inspect her
eyes, permitting her to return to the table just
in time to conceal the fact that they were filled
with tears again.

"Did you call at the Patons' as you came
home?" asked Elinor.

"Only at the door, I had no time to go in; the
message was, that Rosina's cough was rather better
—she had quite lost it till yesterday, and now it is
more hollow than ever. I do not at all like the
sound of it. I hope they take care of that sweet
little creature."

"You really must find time to call there with me
to-morrow," said Elinor; "the Patons are very
polite to me, and I owe them a visit."

"I will see what can be done," replied her brother; but the next day he was very busy, and the next—the next day, to her great annoyance, the Patons called on her, with Marion and Fred Bishop, leaving her to make the best apology she could for her apparent neglect. They asked her to go with them to a certain wood in the neighbourhood, where they meant to spend the afternoon, and from the outskirts of which they would show her a very beautiful view.

Elinor gladly consented. Rosina was with them: she said her cough was much better, but she looked pale and delicate. The wood was about a mile and a-half from the town, and the path to it lay principally through wheat-fields.

It so happened that Frank Maidley had got up early that morning to enjoy a long day with the fishing-rod. His brother Peter was with him, and after breakfast they both set out with a basket of provisions and their fishing-tackle. The wood was principally on elevated ground, and sloped gradually down to the margin of the river, the ash and chesnut trees, which composed its western border, descending to its brink and overhanging it. On the opposite margin was a towing-path, but it was scarcely ever used, the river after passing through the town taking a sudden sweep in the form of a horse-shoe, and becoming so shallow and narrow, that it had been found worth while to connect the two ends of this waterloop by digging a canal across, from one to the other; thus saving two or three miles in distance, and leaving the loop or river in a state of absolute seclusion. It was about the middle of June, and the wheat-fields on the opposite side to the wood were green and in full flower, but much too gay with red poppies and blue cornflowers to please the husbandman. Near the one-arched bridge, which led over the river into the wood, grew a fine ash-tree, its trunk for two or three feet upwards concealed by the leaves of the yellow flags among which it grew. Underneath this tree the two youths prepared to enjoy their morning's sport, and sat for several hours, talking of home, old scenes, and past fishing parties.

The day was perfectly cloudless, and the air perfectly still. The massive foliage of the wood made a pleasant resting-place for the eyes, and the soft lapse of the water had a sleepy, idle sound. The songs of the skylarks, whose nests were in the wheat-fields, were so delightful to listen to, that they gradually left off talking: their sport was not good enough to be very exciting, and as the heat of the day increased, they moved under the arch of the bridge; for it was considerably wider than the stream, and cast a broad distinct shadow, from under the shelter of which they could watch the gradual changes of light on the landscape.

Frank never went out without a small library of books and pamphlets in his pocket; he was not a very ardent fisherman, and on this occasion he laid down his rod, before noon, and took out a book of poetry, as being more suited to his mood than the somewhat lazy sport of fishing.

Peter grumbled a little at first, but the peaceful influence of the scene stealing over him, he left off wishing to talk, and amused himself with watching the swallows, whose nests under the arch were almost within reach of his hands. The mother birds, with their bright black eyes, kept looking out at him with a suspicious air, and their mates dashed backwards and forwards, making the thick chattering noise peculiar to the swallow tribe.

The shadow of the bridge fell distinctly over the clear water. They could look down into it and see shoals of tiny fish glancing round the stems of the rushes: the chattering of jays in the wood came across to them, as an evidence that the spirit of activity and restlessness had not utterly died away out of the world. But with the sound came also the soothing notes of the wood-pigeons and cuckoos, making Peter feel so sentimental that he began to think he should like to write some poetry ! and with that view had taken out the back of a letter and begun to bite the end of his pencil, when he was surprised to hear several voices near at hand, and a laugh which was familiar to him.

" The Miss Patons, I declare !" he exclaimed, " with Marion and Greyson, Mr. Bishop and Walter."

Frank hastily put away his books, and declared that nothing could be so lucky.

The two emerged from their hiding-place, and met the party of new-comers just as they reached the brink of the river. Fred Bishop was carrying two or three books under one arm, and had Elizabeth on the other.

Walter and Wilfred were lagging behind: the former looked hot and cross,—he had got a large basket to carry, which Peter was glad to see was full of strawberries. Marion, whose bonnet-strings were untied, was walking with Elinor; her face wore its usual serene expression, and she evidently enjoyed the beauty of the scene. They meant to spend the whole afternoon in the wood, and had brought the strawberries at Fred Bishop's suggestion. Dora hoped Mr. Maidley would join them, for they wanted a good reader. Wilfred wanted to make haste, for Rosina was fatigued, and he was sure she ought to sit down and rest. Walter thought it was very odd Marion should wish to come to the wood when she had so many woods at home; and how any one could wish to see a wood instead of a pin manufactory he could not think! At any rate he thought it was extremely unfair that he should have been obliged to carry all those strawberries; and, as was usual with him when he was cross, his pronunciation was more defective than ever. Frank released him of his burden, and offered his other arm to Marion. Peter was in high good humour, and ran with characteristic gallantry to fetch his own basket of provisions, to be added to the store, assuring Dora and Rosina that it contained some sandwiches of the most delicious tongue she had ever tasted.

Thus the cavalcade proceeded into the wood; for the first hundred yards the ground sloped upwards, but when they had gained the top of this little elevation, it descended suddenly into a very deep dell, the trees being principally chesnuts and planes, and the ground free from underwood. Walter, however, objected to this place as a resting station, and proposed that they should go down deeper into the wood, where there was a slope quite covered with Muscovy violets, and where the trees were thicker overhead. There were many more birds in that dell, he said, and the last time he went through it "the blackbirds were singing like mad."

" Like what, did you say ? " asked Frank.

" Well, like charity children, then, if you like that better," replied Walter, with some heat.

" In all my experience I never heard of any birds that could sing like charity children," exclaimed Frank.

" Excepting in the ' Pilgrim's Progress,' " remarked Greyson, " where the birds sing, ' He that is down need fear no fall.' "

" No, that song belongs to the shepherd-boy, who wore the herb called heart's-ease in his bosom," said Dora.

" This is the place," cried Walter, suddenly recovering his good humour, and dashing up the

bank; "I know it by those two larch-trees, where
we found the cwoss-bill's nest last year."

"What a delightful scent of violets," said
Marion. "I commend your taste, Walter, as to
resting-places."

"This is the only place in England," remarked
Dora, as they sat down on the bank, "where Muscovy violets grow wild; at least, so it is said."

"Yes, but I suspect the first roots must have
been planted here years ago by some public-
spirited individual, for you see they have only
spread down as far as the spring; it would seem as
if they stopped there, for there are none on the other
side."

Wilfred was very anxious that Rosina's place
should be sheltered and shady, and when she was
established to his mind the other girls took off their
bonnets, and Peter being mindful of their fatigues,
and thinking they must want refreshment, immediately began handing a little glass of lemonade to
one after the other, greatly to their amusement;
but Peter always treated the fair sex as if he
thought their feet were not meant to walk with,
nor their hands capable of holding anything heavier
than a fan or a smelling-bottle.

Frank let him alone, and he presently began to
hand round the fruit, while the girls amused themselves by decorating each other's hair with the blue
cornflowers which they had gathered in the wheat-
field.

" Now if we only had a flute," said Marion, " how delightful it would be."

" I really have a great mind to go and fetch mine," said young Greyson.

" What, to go back a mile and a half! Why, politeness is really uppermost to-day."

" Yes, if you will promise not to stir from this place I really will. I shall not be a quarter of an hour getting home, and I shall come back in the pony-gig, and put it up at the little inn just by here, and then, if Rosina likes she can ride home."

No one could object to his plan, so he set off with the plaudits of the assembly. He had not been gone more than ten minutes when two gentlemen were seen making their way towards them.

" It is Mr. Allerton and my brother," exclaimed Elinor, as they came nearer. " How remarkable that they should have chosen this path out of so many !"

But when the thing came to be explained there was nothing remarkable in it. Elinor, when she left home, had desired a servant to tell her brother that she was going to Fernly Wood with the Miss Patons. He happened to come in very soon, having made time to go with her to pay her call. It was very natural that he should decide to follow her, thinking it most probable that Marion was of the party. It was also very natural that Mr. Allerton, who met him in the street, should wish to go with him. And extensive as the wood was, it was far from wonderful that they should have found the group they were in search of, for they had met Wilfred at the entrance, who had given them such minute directions as could not fail to ensure their success.

Elinor blushed deeply when she saw Mr. Allerton, who, coming up the knoll, was introduced by his friend to such of the party as were not acquainted with him, and then took his place between Dora and Elinor, while Mr. Dreux secured a seat where he could see Marion.

When people have taken a long walk on a very hot day, and have just found a delightfully cool resting-place, they are, generally speaking, not much disposed for conversation, excepting of that desultory kind which consists of passing remarks on what they have before them. Agreeably to this observation, very little was said by any one for the next half-hour, the two new-comers not taking any pains to enliven the others, who sat quietly happy, waiting for young Greyson and his flute. Mr. Allerton gathered some flowering grasses for Elinor, confining himself, however, to such as were within reach of his arm, and Marion twisted corn-flowers together, by means of the said grasses, to make a wreath for her hair.

Rosina, as usual, sat a little withdrawn, and Walter beside her. He was cutting a pop-gun out of a bit of wood with his knife.

Marion made an exquisite wreath for Elinor, and

when she had put it on, Mr. Allerton declared it was almost as lovely as the wearer. He spoke in a low tone, so that no one heard but herself, and for the moment she was pleased, but she presently lifted the wreath from her head, and asked Marion to wear it for her. Marion was a little surprised at her earnest manner, but perceiving that she really wished it, submitted very quietly to have it placed among her long silky curls. It looked extremely well in its new destination, but Mr. Allerton felt that he had received a check, and that Elinor was much less lively and open than usual.

" How quiet we are," thought Dora, " and how dull these two poor gentlemen must be. I dare say they are wishing for an excuse to get away. If I could only get Marion to sing. But I am afraid she will not."

Now it happened that some of the same thoughts had been passing through Marion's mind, for though extremely happy herself, she had an idea that their two new friends could scarcely feel so well content as they looked, knowing how remarkably active and energetic they both were. As for Mr. Dreux, the fact was, that, besides the pleasure of being in Marion's society, he was luxuriating in the un-wonted bliss of an idle hour. Leisure was a thing he knew so little of that he regarded those who possessed it with somewhat of the same interest with which one looks upon the lives of the normal tribes. There was from its very rarity quite a spice of romance in reclining on mossy grass in a wood, and having nothing particular to do.

"Marion," Dora ventured to say, "would you favour us with a duet? You have taught Walter several, and it would be delightful to us to hear one now."

Marion consented with her usual tranquillity, and Walter said he did not mind singing if Marion would beat time for him.

"No, young man; that's rather too much to expect," said Mr. Allerton. "Look at me—I'll beat time for you with this little bough of alder."

"I know I shall laugh," said Walter. "What are we to sing, Marion?"

"Suppose we begin with 'Come, ever-smiling liberty!'" said Marion; "you know that duet perfectly."

"Then you must look at me exactly when I am to say 'come.'"

Marion smiled, and began. Her thrilling voice sounded better without the accompaniment, and Walter, who had a considerable taste for music, forgot everything but the anxiety to do his part aright, for he was exceedingly proud of being thought able to take a part with her. He had a very sweet child's voice, and the defect in his pronunciation was less observable in singing than in speaking.

Mr. Allerton had never heard Marion sing before, and his earnest delight, which he expressed with characteristic energy, brought a pang to Elinor's heart, which was not unmixed with self-reproach. She could no longer conceal from herself how desirous she was of his good opinion, and of how much importance he was to her.

They asked Marion to sing again, and she did so with perfect ease and grace, receiving the thanks of her hearers in a manner which marked her own pleasure in being able to please. In answer to a question of Mr. Allerton's, as to whether she did not feel very proud of her voice, she laughed, and said, " I often feel very grateful for it; it makes up to me in some degree for the want of conversational powers; besides, it always pleases my uncle."

" And what may you be pleased to mean by conversational powers, Miss Greyson?" he replied. "I don't like to hear ladies hold forth on law, physic, and divinity. But perhaps you mean those delightful conferences which we men often overhear between ladies, as to their knitting and crotchet work,—I think that's what they call it. Dear me! the quantity of talk I have heard about worsted work and lace work has often made me wish the fair creatures had no conversational powers ! Why, you have paid yourself the highest possible compliment."

" I had no such intention," said Marion, with a gentle smile.

" Here comes Wilfred," cried Walter, dashing down the slope to meet him.

"But he is not alone; I see some other people behind the trees," exclaimed Elizabeth, in a tone of vexation. "Oh, how provoking! Actually Mrs. Brown and her son!"

Mr. Allerton's look of amazement on hearing this was not lost on Dora, who cast a glance at her sister expressive of her wish that she would be more cautious.

Greyson came walking up the slope, looking at his cousin Elizabeth with steady gravity, while old Mrs. Brown, leaning on his arm, panted up, and her son followed, looking as discontented as ever.

"And how do you do, ladies and gentlemen?" said Mrs. Brown, with a countenance redolent of good humour and heat. "Very kind of Mr. Wilfred, I am sure; he met me and my son on the road, and told us where you was, and, in short, he took us up, and brought us on in the pony-gig."

"And very kind of you to join us, I'm sure, Mrs. Brown," said Frank, casting a peculiar look at young Greyson. "How pleasing are these little social *réunions!*"

Wilfred with his disengaged hand was holding a small hamper, out of which they speedily unpacked a cold fowl, a loaf of bread, some cake, wine, and water, and plates, besides the flute and music-books, —for young Greyson had represented to his aunt that they would like to stay two or three hours more, and she knew they had left home before luncheon.

Wilfred and Frank began to busy themselves in distributing this refreshment to the assembly. Mr. Athanasius Brown seated himself as near Mr. Dreux as he could, for he had a dim idea that something like ridicule often mingled with the smiles of these elegant young ladies, and fancied that he should do well to get under Mr. Dreux's protection. But being a restless little man, and not feeling quite at his ease, he had no sooner demolished his cake and strawberries than he got up and wandered away in search of ferns. He was no sooner out of sight and hearing than Frank Maidley signified to Marion that he intended to draw Mrs. Brown out, and would not stop till he had made her laugh; in pursuance of which object he came and sat next that worthy matron.

Marion immediately turned away, and began resolutely to talk to Mr. Dreux,—that gentleman not feeling so much flattered by the attention as he might have done, if he had not distinctly seen that she was determined not to lend any sanction to the conduct of Elizabeth and Frank.

" So you don't understand philosophy, Mum," she heard Frank say during a pause.

"No, I don't, Mr. Maidley," replied the good woman, "at least not that I know of, for really things are called by such fine names now-a-days that one can scarcely tell what one knows and what one doesn't know."

Mr. Dreux kept his countenance, and made some remark, but Marion could not answer.

"Exactly so, Mum," proceeded Frank. "As the immortal Newton says—you've heard of Newton, of course, ma'am?—he was a very great philosopher. Have you read any of his works?"

"Yes, I 'ave, Mr. Maidley," replied Mrs. Brown, complacently, "but I was not aware that he was a philosopher. Dear me, what things people do find out. You mean 'im that used to preach at St. Mary Woolnoth?"

"To be sure, to be sure," replied Frank, after a moment of perplexity. "Newton was a very great man. 'Ah, Diamond, Diamond, thou little knowest what mischief,' &c. You know that little anecdote of course, Mrs. Brown?"

"Can't say I do, Sir."

"Read his 'Principia?'" inquired Frank, coolly.

"No, I've not, Sir; but I've read a good many of his writings. I've read his 'Cardiphonia.' Principia is Latin for principle, I suppose?"

"You've exactly hit it, Mum; that's just what it does mean. Well, he was one of the greatest philosophers that ever lived."

"Only to think!" said Mrs. Brown, "and I'm sure I never knew it when I read his works."

Frank Maidley by this time being in excellent spirits, now began to impart some still more extraordinary pieces of information to Mrs. Brown, and

the party were edified with the singular opinions
she expressed in reply.   Mr. Allerton no sooner
perceived what was going on than he leant his hand
to this good work with a diligence worthy (to use a
common remark) of a better cause, and between
them they contrived to make the old lady so perfectly
absurd, that even Marion could not help joining in
the laugh, though it annoyed her to be compelled to
do so.

Frank Maidley had begun in apparently the
sweetest spirit of humility to confess his faults to
Mrs. Brown, and also to ask her advice about his
studies, upon which the unconscious and gratified
victim favoured them with a wonderful amount of
valuable information as to how Athanasius used to
go on when he was at College, and the advice she
used to give him on his health and morals.   "For
you know," she said, appealing to the assembly,
"he was but a lad, about Mr. Greyson's age, as I
should judge, and it's a lucky thing he had me
to advise him, for, dear me, he knew no more of the
world—in short he'd never been to London."

Frank Maidley listened to all this without relaxing
from the usual benevolent smile that played about
his lips, and reclining his lengthy limbs upon the
grass, gazed at the worthy matron as with laudable
zeal she began to favour him with many a moral
maxim that he might have attended to with advantage, but instead of which he looked up with an

air of respectful deference, mingled with admiration at the excellence of her sentiments.

Going on with the catalogue of his faults, and willing to show how far he dare go, Frank presently said with a sigh, "I have such a sad habit of making game of people, Mrs. Brown, you can't think how I reproach myself for it afterwards; but it grows upon me. If you could hear me sometimes you would be quite shocked."

"Indeed!" said Mrs. Brown, in a tone of condolence, "that's a bad habit, Mr. Maidley; it's a great pity when people give way to it."

"So it is," said Frank, "but it's so strong upon me, that even if *you* were to say or do anything absurd I couldn't help laughing at you."

Mrs. Brown seemed to have difficulty in believing this, but Frank assured her it was a fact. "I say IF you were to behave in a ridiculous way (though of course you never do), but IF you were, I could not help laughing at you."

"Why, of course. I understand you, Mr. Maidley," said Mrs. Brown in a complacent tone; "but as I often say to my son, depend upon it, Athanasius, there's nothing so absurd as a person pretending to be what they are not. Why, my dear, I often say when he talks about it, why can't you let me alone? I behave in a very proper manner, and if I was to pretend to the breeding of a lady I should only make myself ridiculous; but as it is, I say to 'im, there's nothing ridiculous in me, and it must be your mistake that the ladies and gentlemen laugh at me."

" What does she mean?" thought Elizabeth, colouring, and exchanging a glance with Frank.

" Laugh at *you*, Mrs. Brown!" said Frank, looking at her, apparently quite aghast.

" Ah, you may well be surprised, Mr. Maidley. Only to think of his taking such a fancy. But (sinking her voice) Athanasius thinks a great deal of these sort of things. Why, my dear, I say to him, if my breeding was thought not good enough for gentlepeople's society I should not be invited to go and see them. Why, bless me, I often say, do you think, my dear, that people of quality would invite anybody to their houses on purpose to make game of them? That would be a downright breach of hospitality."

" To be sure," said Frank, a little abashed. " But what made him think of such a thing, Mrs. Brown?"

The colour mounted to Elizabeth's temples, when the unsuspicious old lady replied,—

" Well, I can't justly say, Mr. Maidley, but somehow he does think so. It was only the other night— was it last night?—no, I think it was the night of Mrs. Paton's party—well, however, he said to me, ' Mother, we should 'ave been a great deal 'appier if we'd kept in our own sphere."

Elizabeth and Marion both blushed to their temples as they exchanged a glance with Frank

Maidley, which seemed to say, " So, then, Mr. What's-his-name Brown was not so oblivious as we thought him, after all."

But Mr. Allerton, who could not understand this by-play, seemed inclined to go on with the conversation, and had already got it back to the confession of faults and foibles, when Marion, quite hurt and ashamed, started up hastily, and looked as if she would have liked to walk away, if she had not been afraid of losing herself among the trees.

Mr. Dreux easily perceived her wish, and, rising, offered his arm, at the same time inquiring whether Rosina would not accompany them in a walk through the more open parts of the wood.

Marion's face was coloured with a soft carnation, and her eyes filled with tears of vexation. Mr. Dreux said nothing for the first few minutes, but as they got further away from the party she recovered her spirits, and they began to converse on various subjects, Marion saying that this wood reminded her of one in the neighbourhood of Norland House, where she very often went when at home.

"And in that wood I believe I once had the pleasure of seeing you, Miss Greyson—at least I imagine it must have been you," said Mr. Dreux; " but I dare say you do not remember it."

Marion admitted that she did not.

"I was quite a boy," he proceeded, " and was staying with my uncle, Colonel Norland, when one day, as I was nutting in the wood I saw a little girl riding on a grey pony; she had a broad leghorn hat on her head, with some long white feathers in it. Since I have seen you here I have often thought that little girl must have been you, the more so as Mr. Raeburn was holding the bridle of the pony."

" Yes, I think it must have been," said Marion, "but I do not remember seeing any youth whom I could imagine had grown up into Mr. Dreux in those woods; most of the boys who frequent them are truants from my uncle's schools, or the children of farmers round, who go there for nests or nuts."

They had now reached the top of the rising ground, which was covered with fern, thick grass, and heath. A good many trees had been felled in this particular locality, and seated on one of them was Mr. Athanasius Brown, with a book in his hand.

When they saw him Mr. Dreux said to Marion, " It must be of course quite evident to you, Miss Greyson, that some of the conversation of a few nights past must have been overheard by Mr. Brown. If you are inclined to show him some little politeness now I think it might gratify him. He is a man of very quick feelings."

Marion and Rosina gladly assented, and they went up and joined Mr. Brown upon his tree, which commanded a delightful view of the still green wood, under whose trees the sunbeams dropped in tiny fractions, broken by the leaves, and quivering as they wavered in the light air.

Mr. Dreux helped the young ladies to begin a conversation, which was very stiff at first, but he dexterously led it to a subject on which he knew the Reverend Gentleman felt an interest, and then they got on extremely well, and found that Mr. Brown was anything but a stupid man, very well informed, and by no means wanting in either inclination or ability to defend his own opinions.

At length, after half an hour's conversation, during which Marion displayed so much tact that Mr. Dreux was more than ever amused at her lamentations for the want of conversational powers, she rose to join her cousins; and Mr. Brown, who had nearly lost his stiffness of manner and a good deal of his awkwardness, offered his arm to Rosina, and discoursed on their way back with all possible politeness.

Their return was the signal for breaking up the party. There had been a good deal of singing and flute-playing, but the girls began to look rather weary, and Dora, perceiving that the thing grew flat, began to thank those who might be considered their guests for their company, and inquire who would like to ride home, and where they should agree to separate.

Mrs. Brown, in the kindness of her heart, pressed Mr. and Miss Dreux and Mr. Allerton to come on to the farm, and take a substantial tea with Athanasius and 'er. Mr. Dreux, having a leisure evening, accepted. Mr. Allerton's agreement followed, as a matter of course. The host was secretly much delighted; and Mrs. Brown bore them off, taking a brilliant leave of the Miss Patons, and thanking Frank Maidley for his obliging conversation.

The Maidleys then said they must go home by the river, for they had left some line and part of their fishing-tackle hidden in a clump of yews. So it was agreed that Walter should drive Rosina back in the pony-gig, and that the others should walk home through the fields.

"I do hope that old lady will not remember enough of what we talked about to-day to give her son a connected account of it," said Elizabeth, in a tone of the deepest vexation. "I had not the most distant idea that he knew we laughed at him."

"If she remembers anything, I hope it will be what Mr. Allerton said," remarked Fred Bishop, "for that *we* have nothing to do with."

Fred Bishop himself had not had much to do with the matter beyond enjoying the jokes of the others, who now seemed rather out of spirits, and walked without any further conversation till they were clear of the wood and had crossed the bridge into the fields.

"What a fine, handsome man that Mr. Allerton is, Dora," said Elizabeth. "Did you observe what a face he made when Mrs. Brown asked him whether it was true that clergymen '*of his persuasion*' thought it undesirable to marry?"

"Yes, I observed him," replied Dora, who had included in her observation a glance which he cast towards Elinor, as if he thought it would be the most desirable thing in the world to marry if she were the bride.

"I know Mr. Hewly thinks it wrong for priests to marry," said Fred Bishop. "I remember his writing a pamphlet in which he advanced that and some other of his nonsensical opinions."

"Mr. Hewly does not think so now," said Dora, hastily; "I believe he has changed his opinion on that point."

Elizabeth and Marion looked at each other, and a dead pause succeeded to the conversation.

Dora presently observed it, and immediately made some slight observation on the beauty of the wheat through which they were passing. Nobody answered. She was nettled, and asked why they were so silent.

"Dear me," said young Greyson, pretending to wake up from his reverie, with a great start, "were we silent, Dora? I beg your pardon. It was very inconsiderate of us. 'The wheat is very fine,' I think you said. Yes, it is a very fine crop; I don't know that I ever saw a finer. When people make awkward little mistakes you should never appear to notice it," he continued, addressing the others in a loud whisper. "Yes, Dora, it is a remarkably fine crop. Now, why don't *you* say something, Elizabeth?"

Being thus appealed to, Elizabeth said: "It's a remarkably fine day."

"So it is," echoed Fred Bishop.

"There, now we are getting on beautifully," proceeded Greyson. "Marion, what are you laughing at? You needn't hold your handkerchief to your face, for I'm certain you're laughing. I say, Dora, this wheat's fuller of poppies than any I ever saw. Dear me, how very awkward!—what can you all be laughing at? I should not wonder if it's ready for the sickle in a month, Dora."

"In a fortnight," said Fred Bishop, who now really wished to let the matter drop.

Marion then put in a remark, and among them they contrived to keep up a conversation, now and then venturing to put a question to Dora, and receiving a very tart answer. So that it was quite a relief when they got home and could separate to dress for what was called in the family a tea-dinner, Mr. and Mrs. Paton having dined in their absence.

A few evenings after this Wilfred remained in the drawing-room after Mrs. Paton and the ladies of the family had withdrawn, and, setting down his candlestick, said to his uncle,—"Were you aware, Sir, that Mr. Hewly always escorts Dora home after the daily morning service?"

Mr. Paton lifted up his head in surprise, and desired him to repeat what he had said.

"Does he, indeed?" said Mr. Paton, deliberately. "And pray how do you happen to know it?"

" Why, you know, uncle, the shortest way from here to Mr. Lodge's is down Horsemonger-lane,—a very quiet lane. I go down there often, and meet Mr. Hewly walking along it with Dora till it joins this street."

" Very well, my boy. Have you anything further to communicate?"

" Nothing, uncle."

" Then I will not detain you."

It ought here to be observed, that Dora was rather in a different position to the younger daughters of the family, as she had an independent fortune, which had been left to her by her godmother; and though Mr. Paton was supposed to be rich, he had an expensive family, and it was always said that he meant to make a great difference in favour of his son.

The next day, just at the time when he thought Dora would be coming from church, her father took up his hat, and, walking leisurely down the lane before mentioned, he met Dora and a strange gentleman with her.

Dora started, but stopped, and with a grace peculiar to her introduced Mr. Hewly. Her father took off his hat, as if he thought nothing of it, passed on, and, taking the first turning, came back to his own house.

When he came in he asked no questions, and the affair passed off without remark; but the next day Mr. Paton met them again in the lane, bowed, and passed on. The third day he did the same thing. And the fourth, as Dora was coming out at the church-door, she found her father's footman, waiting to escort her home (not Joshua, but the old servant who had been long in the family).

"Is it possible that my father thinks it necessary to have me watched?" thought Dora, blushing, and inwardly hoping that Mr. Hewly would not offer to accompany her, as he must know her father had some motive for meeting her daily.

The servant, who had been waiting in the porch, touched his hat, and said, "Master sent me, ma'am, because he thought the town would be rather noisy to-day after the cattle-market."

Dora set out, and Mr. Hewly did not follow. Perhaps he had heard the colloquy with the servant.

When she got in she quite expected to be sent for to her father's room, but no notice was taken. And the next morning she did not go to morning service. The following morning it rained, and in her inmost heart she was glad of the excuse for keeping away.

The morning after this her father, to whom all the letters were generally taken, and distributed by him to their owners, when he had selected his own, came into the drawing-room, where the girls were sitting, and gave a letter to her, saying, quietly,— "Dora, my love, this letter, I believe, is for you."

She thought he looked at her attentively as he

gave it. She saw at a glance that it was a West-port letter, and took it out of the room to read it in quiet.

In less than half an hour she knocked at her father's door and brought the letter in to him.

"Well, my dear?" he said, as she gave it into his hand.

"I thought I ought to show you this, papa," said Dora, colouring.

"Very well; put it down. Have you anything else to say to me, my dear?"

"Not if you are busy, papa."

"I shall be at liberty in ten minutes. Sit down, my dear."

Dora did so, and her father calmly wrote on at his own letters. She knew he had given her these few minutes to consider what she had to say; and when he looked up and remarked that now he was quite at liberty, she said,—"I wished to tell you, papa, that I am sorry I have permitted Mr. Hewly to walk home with me so often, unknown to you."

Mr. Paton bowed. He generally preserved a certain air of politeness even in talking to his own daughters.

"I am the more sorry, papa," Dora went on, "because you have always been so extremely kind and indulgent to me, and have never seemed afraid to trust me."

Here she stopped.

"Is that *all*, my dear?" asked her father.

"And I have brought this letter," Dora proceeded, "for you to do whatever you please with it, entirely as you think proper."

Mr. Paton opened the letter. Dora felt that she had rather not be present while he read it; and as she rose to leave the room her father kissed her. He seemed pleased with her apology, but he said nothing further, and, having opened the door for her, permitted her to leave him. Having read over the letter five or six times, he buttoned it up in his pocket and walked, not to Hewly's house, but to Mr. Allerton's. That gentleman was writing, when Mr. Paton was shown into his study and observed, with his usual stately but always courteous manner, that he was come on particular business. Such being the case, Mr. Allerton was a little startled when, on a letter being handed over to him, with a request that he would read it, he observed that it was in Hewly's handwriting, and that it began, "Ever dearest Miss Paton."

When he had finished it, he folded it up and laid it down with an appearance of considerable contempt.

"Well, Sir," said Mr. Paton, "may I be favoured with your opinion on that piece of composition?"

"If you wish for my opinion, Sir," said Mr. Allerton, turning very red, and speaking with uncompromising firmness, "I think it is a mean, shuffling, despicable letter; quite unworthy the writing of any man calling himself a gentleman. I do not at all wonder that it should have been at once given up to you. A young lady of Miss Paton's pretensions is not much in the habit of being addressed in this style, I should imagine."

" I am glad you concur with me, Sir," said Mr. Paton. " You may perhaps think it strange that I should come to you for advice and information in this affair."

" Not at all,—not at all," interrupted Mr. Allerton. " I shall be happy to answer any questions you choose to ask."

The old gentleman bowed, and said, " In the first place, then, I must inform you, that it is by no means thought probable in this place that *my* daughters will be portionless ; independently of which, Miss Paton has a fortune of her own,— eleven thousand pounds. I am, therefore, parti- cularly anxious that my eldest daughter should marry a man who loves her for her own sake, not a mere adventurer, to whom her fortune may be an inducement. Now I ask you as a gentleman, to tell me whether Mr. Hewly is, in your opinion, a proper man, in point of morals, family, fortune, and amiability, to marry a lady whose honest uprightness of mind has not suffered, I hope, from his teaching, who possesses a good fortune, is of respectable, I may say, of ancient family,—who has never been used to anything but indulgence, and is by far too gentle to assert her own rights ?"

" If she were my daughter, Sir," said Mr. Aller-

ton, striking his hand on the table, as he often did
when he was heated, "I'd as soon see her throw
herself away on any sharper in the town as on
Mr. Hewly, my curate.   It's the height of presumption in him to aspire to Miss Paton's hand ;—
he is no more deserving of her, in point of amiability, or fortune, or position, or anything else ——"

"But as to that," interrupted Mr. Paton, "I
shall be very glad if you can tell me whether this
letter contains an offer of marriage *or not?* It is
expressed with such extraordinary ingenuity, that
it is next thing to impossible to say.   It implies
much love and admiration ;—the writer wishes he
could be always with my daughter.   He then goes
on to express a hope that his society is not distasteful to her,—a sigh that he is not more worthy of
her.   Finally, he hopes she will consider what he
has said, and not too hastily reject him.   Reject
him, Sir! why how can a woman reject what has
never been fairly offered to her acceptance?   At
the first reading it seems impossible that any man
in his senses could look upon that letter in any
other light than as an offer; but I confess that the
religious advice and counsel is so singularly blended
with it, that if my daughter were to answer it by a
decided negative, it would not at all surprise me if
he were to reply that she had mistaken his meaning,—he only meant to offer her spiritual counsel!
I think very meanly of the man, Mr. Allerton,—I
disapprove of his principles ; but as my daughter

has adopted them, I would not have opposed her marrying a man who professed them provided he was suitable in other respects."

"If Hewly is suitable, Sir," said Mr. Allerton, "the suitability must be consistent with his having written a mean, shuffling letter; with his being the son of a village butcher; with his having no fortune but his curacy!—that *I* know of; and with his having violently inveighed against matrimony till within the last three months."

"That is sufficient, Sir," said Mr. Paton. "You remarked that your curate was no way deserving my daughter. Now, in case she *may* feel inclined to favour his suit (which, however, I do not expect), there is still one ground on which it may prove that they are equal,—I mean, regard for each other. Have you reason to suppose that his regard for my daughter, though recent, is sincere? or if you have any reasons to entertain a contrary supposition, will you favour me with them?"

Mr. Allerton reddened; he felt what mischief he was doing to his cause by speaking so meanly of one of its chief advocates before Mr. Paton. "I have often heard Hewly speak of your daughter, but oftener still of her fortune," he replied. "He does not appear to me to entertain a very exalted opinion of her understanding,—indeed he showed that by his proposition of this morning; *but* I have also reason to think he makes himself agreeable in other quarters,—that, in short, he aspires 'to have two strings to his bow.' So that, I fancy, if he is disappointed here, I could name a lady whom he expects to find more willing. Is that enough, Sir?"

"Quite enough," said the old gentleman. "Will you favour me with his address?"

Mr. Allerton did so, and he wrote it down, saying, "I shall write and desire Mr. Hewly to call upon me this evening, and you may depend on my not giving the slightest hint as to whence my information came."

"Indeed, I beg you will not think of such a thing!" exclaimed Allerton, hastily; "I should scorn to speak thus of him and not to have him know it. I beg you will tell him that you got your information from me; that I expressed to you that I thought his letter mean and shuffling; and that I said I believed he was trying to make himself agreeable in other quarters."

And now, thought Allerton, when his guest was gone, Hewly will come to me to demand an explanation; we shall have a regular quarrel, and I shall get rid of him. Of course he will throw up his curacy, and never again, as long as I live, will I make an engagement, as I did with him, for two years!"

Mr. Paton had told him that in the evening he should have an interview with the delinquent. Accordingly the Rector of St. Bernard's sat at home, from hour to hour hoping that he should hear Hewly's knock at the door,—that they should have a rupture, and a final parting. In this idea he was mistaken,—Mr. Hewly never came. And the next morning, it being his own turn to read prayers, he saw nothing of his curate. He soon after walked on to his house, but the servant said Mr. Hewly was gone out, and she did not know when he would be home.

Perhaps he acted on the remembrance, that

> " The wise will let his anger cool,
> At least before 'tis night ; "

and was carefully cooling *his* before he went to his Rector ; or perhaps he knew his man so well as to be certain that he longed for a good ground for a quarrel, and knowing that his anger would soon evaporate, in spite of himself, was resolved to wear it out.

At eight o'clock the next evening he called on his Rector. His manner was perfectly calm and very pensive. He took great care not to rouse Mr. Allerton ; but after a while, said mildly, that he had been deeply hurt at something which had been communicated to him an evening or two ago, but that he wished to cherish a forgiving spirit, in consideration of their long friendship, &c., &c. ; and as Allerton made no reply, while he sat determined not to quarrel, and looking as meek as a lamb, he concluded by murmuring a few words of pardon, and holding out his hand.

Nothing was further from his Rector's wishes

than to be forgiven. He was astonished. He was certain Hewly must have some special motive for trying to ward off an outbreak. He tried very hard to work himself up into a passion, but could not manage it; and when he was cool he did not know how to say severe things to any one.

Hewly observed that his offered hand was scarcely touched, and that his Rector and late friend looked on him with smiling contempt. Notwithstanding which, he introduced another topic of conversation; and after several expressions of regard and forgiveness, took his leave, having conducted the interview so admirably that there had been no outbreak at all.

As soon as this unsatisfactory visit was over, Mr. Allerton put on his hat and went to see Mr. Dreux, related the whole affair to him, and inveighed against Hewly's art in not giving him an opportunity to say a single irritating thing. " So now I am tied to him for another year!" he exclaimed, in a rueful voice ;—" I declare it is scarcely endurable."

" Yes, it must be highly unsatisfactory to work with a man whom you cannot respect."

" I declare I am sometimes inclined to throw up the living. Why should I be tormented with his whims, and his company ?"

" Have you heard anything further of the affair between him and Miss Paton ?" inquired his friend, diverging a little from the matter under discussion, as he often did when Allerton got irritated.

"Not a word, but Miss Paton has not been to morning service for several days. By the bye, here's this book of yours, ' The Force of Truth.' "

" Have you read it?"

" Why, yes, I did, as you wished it. The author, Dreux, is of the same school as that Newton who preached at St. Mary Woolnoth,—quite a philosopher of that style. Ah! that was a pretty little scene in the wood, Dreux!—your religious young people shone on that occasion. I'm glad they got a fright, though; to be candid, I helped as well as I could; and I think, after you were gone, the old lady began to perceive their sarcasms."

" I was extremely hurt at their conduct. I certainly should have told them of their fault if I had not been afraid of letting Mrs. Brown know they were ridiculing her."

" I thought some of them seemed annoyed," replied Mr. Allerton. " To do him justice, young Greyson was very silent, and as for his sister, she was evidently quite ashamed. What an elegant girl!—she is a perfect lady."

Mr. Dreux admitted the fact.

" Very lovely too," proceeded Mr. Allerton; " but I don't care for beauty. I'm no connoisseur in it, but I admire that finished grace." (Elinor, by the way, had no pretensions to beauty.) Mr. Allerton went on, not at all aware how much he was disconcerting his friend: " There is something in the courtesy of a perfect lady, and her tranquil

ease, which charms me very much, I confess."
(Elinor had charming manners, and did the honours
of her brother's table with remarkable propriety.)

"Then," said Mr. Dreux, perversely thinking of
any person but the right one, "in my opinion,
unless you're suited already, Allerton, you'd better
see whether a letter from you would not do better
in the Paton family than the celebrated epistle from
Hewly; for I think I have heard you remark before
that you did not know a more elegant and lady-like
girl than Miss Paton."

This observation put an effectual stop to the conversation. Mr. Allerton was so grave for some
time after, that his friend thought he actually must
be pondering the matter over; accordingly he began
to rally him again, upon which he took out his
watch and declared he must go. (He knew Elinor
was gone to drink tea with the Miss Silverstones.)

"So you can give me no advice as to Hewly," he
said, as they walked across the lawn together.

"He will not leave you, merely because he knows
you wish it," was the reply; "and as you have
made an agreement for two years, I do not see what
is to be done. As long as he has any hope of Miss
Paton he never will stir, and if that should be put
an end to, I think I should venture on the experiment of inclosing him a cheque in a letter for one
or two hundred pounds, and advising him to travel
for the benefit of his health,—for you say he is anything but strong."

Allerton greatly admired the ingenuity of the proposal, and declared that he would certainly put it in practice if Hewly did not succeed in obtaining Miss Paton's hand; after which he went home, and wished he could have summoned courage to tell Dreux how much he admired his sister, and was very angry with him for being so blind, or pretending to be so, and for continuing to teaze him about a lady for whom he did not care a straw. However, he comforted himself with the thought that unless Elinor loved some one else, which he shrewdly suspected she did *not,* there was very little doubt about his ultimately succeeding.

CHAPTER XIII.

A CHARADE ACTED TWICE.

It would be rather difficult to describe how the next few weeks were spent by Marion; she herself could scarcely tell in looking back upon them. She went to a good many dinner-parties and tea-parties, these last being described irreverently by her brother as consisting of three courses: tea, twaddle, and tarts. She took many rides and walks into the country, and she made a friendship with Elinor, generally seeing her every day. Mrs. Paton had asked Elinor to come and spend the mornings with her niece and daughters whenever Mr. Dreux was engaged,—accordingly, many a pleasant morning they all passed, sitting out in the garden under the shade of some tall elm-trees which grew close together on the lawn. Mr. Dreux generally brought his sister on these occasions, and often felt considerable reluctance in leaving her,—a bevy of fair girls sitting in the open air in delightful shades, occupied with their needles and pencils, being just what some men most like to join themselves to, especially as they are generally welcome, and can give piquancy to the group by reading aloud. Mr. Dreux read remarkably well, and two or three times he stayed for half an hour, and in leaving, detected himself envying Frank Maidley, who contrived to lounge away the greater part of each morning in Mr. Paton's garden. He was trying to make himself agreeable to Marion, and in so doing afforded an immense deal of amusement to her cousins, especially to Dora, who wanted something to divert her mind from the letter, which she had never mentioned in her family. Frank's wooing was quite in the gay style, and did not seem to proceed at all the worse for being carried on under the eyes of other ladies. He used to complain bitterly, but with a slight air of banter withal, that he could make no impression on his fair one; and as Marion resolutely refused to be flirted with, he used to appeal to her cousins what he should do next, upon which Dora would set him to read poetry in an impassioned tone, sometimes to write it, which he did very nicely, and, as Elizabeth said, it kept him quiet.

"I can't make any impression, I see," he one day said to that young lady, with a sepulchral sigh.

Marion began to feel a little annoyed.

"I think," said Elizabeth mischievously, "it may be as well to try to excite jealousy! Suppose you direct your attentions to me for a while!"

" Ah, Miss Paton, you are doubtless very charming," replied Frank, " but—but I heard some talk
yesterday about wedding-cake."

" Well, try Dora," said Elizabeth, laughing.

The despairing swain immediately did as he
was desired, and Dora humoured the joke.

" How do her eyes look now ? " said Elizabeth.
" Any chance of jealousy ? I'm afraid they are as
blue as ever."

Frank turned round to look at Marion's eyes.
" She seems much better pleased than usual, and I
delight to please her," he remarked ; " therefore,
Miss Paton, if you please, let us proceed as
before."

With all this he was so good-humoured and droll,
so amusing and clever, that it was impossible to be
really angry with him, and Marion, having fully
made up her mind that nothing on earth—no,
nothing should ever induce her to become Mrs.
Frank Maidley, was quite pleased to see his attentions directed to her cousin, first in joke, and afterwards, as she could not help fancying, sometimes in
earnest.

Mr. Allerton, finding that Elinor spent so much
time with the Miss Patons, easily got up an
acquaintance with their father, whose call upon
him made a good beginning ; and as Mrs. Paton
was generally engaged in assisting with various
preparations for her daughter's wedding, and
ordering the furniture for her house, she was

absent a great deal from home, and not quite aware of the extent to which he stretched her husband's invitation, which had merely been couched in some such ordinary terms as these, that he was sure Mrs. Paton and the young ladies would be glad to see him when he liked to call.

Mr. Allerton accordingly liked to call very often when Elinor was there, and used to join the party under the trees, and take part in whatever occupation or amusement was going on. As Elinor always looked pained when he said anything of a complimentary nature to her, he had now altogether ceased to do so, confining himself to attentions of a different kind, but not less flattering. She certainly got dearer to him every day, and he could scarcely believe he was indifferent to her, yet she did not look so happy nor so blooming as when he had first met with her, though this, he tried to persuade himself, must be nothing more than his own fond fancy.

As for Mr. Dreux, he had often been in Marion's company, and often heard her sing. He had long made up his mind that he greatly preferred her to any one whom he had ever seen, but his affection had come on by degrees, and partook of his natural character,—it was not demonstrative, but it was deep and patient, quite beyond the power of any circumstances to overthrow, partaking of all the energy and intensity of his character, and, unconsciously to himself, most carefully concealed from view. Such being the case, it was not strange that he should have been greatly perplexed by the unaffected ease of her manner—the complete freedom from embarrassment with which she met his eye. And as he had seen early in their intercourse that she perceived the peculiarities of his character, he wondered at an ignorance which he sometimes fancied must be feigned, so completely oblivious did it seem of his preference, his intentions, or his hopes.

Elinor and Marion being now much together, became attached to each other; and as it was now the Midsummer holidays, Rosina was admitted to be present at most of their conferences, while Elizabeth began to be fully occupied with the arrangement of her new house, and Dora, who had entirely given up attending the morning service, nobody at home exactly knowing why, was often occupied with Frank Maidley, who contrived to engage her attention to an extent that soon became perceptible to her father, who resolutely shut his eyes to it, which was his general habit when he did not disapprove. As for Marion, she sunk again into the background as suddenly as she had risen out of it; and it soon became obvious enough, that in this new affair, though the lady might be half in joke, the gentleman was quite in earnest.

It is highly probable that she would soon have forgotten the affair in which Mr. Hewly had figured if it had not unluckily happened that just at this time Mr. and Mrs. Ferguson, with their daughter, came home, after a few weeks' absence at the sea-side. The latter came the next morning to see Dora, who, after being closetted with her for two hours, came down with unequivocal symptoms of tears about her eyes and in very low spirits.

"So he's the son of a butcher," said Helen, during their conference, for Dora had told her the whole affair by letter. "Well, certainly that's a pity."

"Yes," said Dora, sobbing. "And only think, Helen, Wilfred says—"

"Oh! *he* knows of it, then?" said Helen, hastily.

"Yes; and he says he knows his brother is a butcher in Staffordshire to this day, and that Mr. Hewly himself used to wear a blue apron and carry out the meat when he was a little boy?"

"But if there is no better reason than *that* for your not accepting him," argued Helen—

"But papa said it was a mean, shuffling letter, and no one could tell whether it contained an offer or not," replied Dora, weeping still more.

"He's incapable of such a thing," exclaimed Helen, with enthusiasm. "What, that dear, good man, with his holy countenance,—that dear Mr. Hewly,—write a mean, shuffling letter! I can't believe it."

"Papa said so," said Dora.

"Then did your father strictly forbid your entering the church again? Did he desire you never to speak to poor Mr. Hewly, nor to receive any more letters?"

"No," said Dora, who had not had the satisfaction of being persecuted; "but he said he should think me *very imprudent* if I ever went there again, so of course I could not do it; and that he should trust to my good sense not to answer any letter without showing it to him."

"Good sense!" said Helen, scornfully. "Trust to your good sense,—when your soul is bowed down with grief, and when you love a man like that dear, deserted, excellent Mr. Hewly!"

"Papa said he did not believe that I did love him." And really she seemed to have some doubts herself, if we may judge by her dubious tone. "He said it was a Jesuitical letter, and—oh! Helen, he said he did not believe that Hewly really cared for me. And, besides, papa has UNFORTU-NATELY found out that Mr. Hewly is very much in debt;—dear, good man, it must be from his charities, or something of that sort. But papa thought he wanted to marry me for the sake of my fortune."

"Well, never mind, dearest Dora," said Helen, soothingly, "we cannot expect to be understood by those of opposite sentiments. If your papa *will* discountenance Hewly, and if he *will* look coolly on you on account of your religion—"

"He doesn't," interrupted Dora, testily; "he is the same to me as ever,—more kind, if anything.

And, oh! Helen, I am sure it is true that Mr. Hewly is in debt,—and—and, oh! how—how unhappy I am!"

Helen wept in sympathy. It was quite clear that Dora was not persecuted in any way, nor watched, nor even suspected,—her father "placed perfect confidence in her good sense." There was a subject for regret and condolence! Why, he must have concluded that her feelings were but little touched; indeed he had said as much.

"What have you done with his invaluable letter?" asked Helen.

"I think I put it in my desk."

Helen opened her eyes:—" You *think* you put it in your desk!" she exclaimed. "Why, don't you know where it is? If it had been mine I would have carried it about with me to the day of my death."

Dora blushed for her forgetfulness. "I remember now," she said, "I gave it back to papa."

"Then he did not insist upon your burning it?" asked Helen.

"No; he never insisted on anything. He only said he was thankful that his dear child had confided in him, and given him an opportunity to investigate Hewly's character before he had had time to make any impression on her heart. So nothing can make papa believe that I like him or care for him. But *you* still go to St. Bernard's, Helen?"

"Oh, yes," replied the confidante, with a peculiar twitch of the head. "I am thankful to say *my* father makes no objection."

Thus the conversation ended, and for several days after, Dora was out of spirits; but, as Helen did not come to see her again that whole week, she soon began to recover herself, and take part in all the little arrangements and preparations for the coming wedding, though for consistency's sake she still tried to keep up an appearance of dejection before her cousin Wilfred, because he was the only person besides her father who knew of the affair; but even this soon wore off, and Dora was herself again, as kind and good-humoured as ever. She was one day standing alone in the little china-room, when young Greyson came in and, looking in her face, smiled good-humouredly.

"What are you thinking of, Wilfred?" said Dora.

"I was thinking," he replied, "how pleasant it is to meet with young ladies who permit their fathers to decide important matters for them, and afterwards turn their thoughts from the subject, and behave as agreeably as if nothing had happened. And though, to be sure, in some cases there never could have been any real *affection* between the parties ——"

"How do you know that?" exclaimed Dora, thrown off her guard.

"I know it because the lady has far too much

good sense really to care for a mean, sneaking character, and I am not afraid the gentleman should break his heart. By the bye, of course he has to walk home every day from church with Helen; because the London-road, you know, is such an intricate neighbourhood,—there are so many almost impassable fords to get over, so many gangs of highwaymen (as one would naturally expect should be the case), and so many dangerous bogs, that she stands in great need of protection, as, indeed, I told her to-day, when I met her walking to church by herself. I said to her:—' Helen, it grieves me to see you going through this perilous country alone, but I hope some one conducts you home, at least as far as the turning, where,' I said, ' he would naturally leave you; otherwise he would be seen from your father's windows, and that would seem like a designed reproach to your father for not providing you with a proper escort, and thus throwing you on the mercy of a benevolent stranger.' "

" What did Helen say to that?" asked Dora, surprised at Wilfred's speech and all that it insinuated.

" Why, really," replied her cousin, with unabated good humour, " her reply was so little to the purpose that I have almost forgotten it. I think I have a recollection of her using the word ' impertinent,' and also the word ' boy,' but I cannot tax my memory beyond those two disconnected expressions. I often go down the London-road now, Dora, I am so fond of that road. You would be quite surprised if you could but know how fond I am of it, and of that little lane at the back of the Fergusons' garden."

Dora smiled, in spite of herself.

"The other day," pursued Greyson, "I happened to meet Mr. Hewly walking there, with his eyes fixed on the ground, absorbed, no doubt, in pious contemplation. I know a little of him, for he and I both collect insects, and sometimes exchange a rare specimen or two. 'How do you do, Mr. Hewly?' I said, with a pleasing suavity of manner; 'I hope you are quite well this fine evening?' 'Quite well, thank you. I hope your family are well?' 'Thank you,' I replied, with intense friendliness of manner; 'I am happy to say, with the exception of my cousin Rosina, who has still a slight cough, they are all remarkably well, particularly my eldest cousin,—I don't know when I have seen her looking so well.'"

"You did not say that, Wilfred?" said Dora.

"Yes, I did. And if you had seen his face!—it was quite a treat to me to look at it. But it seems he did not wish me to have that pleasure, for he kept it turned away towards the Fergusons' garden-hedge. 'Oh!' I said, 'if you are looking for Miss Ferguson, she is just gone down the garden,—I saw her myself; she came out with her garden-bonnet on.' 'Looking for Miss Ferguson!' he exclaimed, in extreme amazement. 'Yes,' I said, standing on tip-toe to look over the hedge, and pretending to misunderstand him; 'she is sitting in her usual place in the arbour,—good evening!' There is a little gap in the hedge near there, Dora, and I should not wonder if they talk through it sometimes, like Pyramus and Thisbe, you know."

Dora was silent for a few minutes, then she looked into her cousin's good-humoured countenance, and said, "I am glad you mentioned that I was quite well, not that he particularly cares to hear it, I dare say." She accompanied this remark with a slight toss of her graceful head.

"To say the truth, I don't think he does. He looked at me as if he would like to have set me under a tumbler, like one of his moths or butterflies, and exploded a lucifer-match under it. Well, we don't care what he thinks, that's certain."

"I'm sure *I* don't care what he thinks," said Dora.

"No," said Wilfred, "and I must go now to practise with Frank Maidley; he wants me to bring my flute with me. I saw him just now; he desires his most particular regards."

"Did he?" said Dora; "I wonder what he means by spending all his mornings at our house; it really gets quite troublesome."

"Yes, it does; and when he's at home he's always playing on the flute. He told me (not that *that* has anything to do with it,—O dear, no!) but he told

me you were fond of a flute-accompaniment to your
duets."

"Silly boy," said Dora, "how tiresome he is!"

"Oh, very; 'boy' he's not, though; he'll be
twenty-four next September. And as to that flute,
if it does not lose him his honours it's a pity; for he
deserves it should, squandering all his vacation in
this way. But if he does, it won't matter to either
of us, I should hope,—of course it won't."

Dora, however, looked as if it would most particularly matter. "I never liked a flute-accompaniment," she said, carelessly; "in fact, I think a man
never appears to advantage playing on such a little
instrument."

"Humph!" said young Greyson. He was stooping down, looking out for some music to take for the
practising. "Then I think I had better tell him
so."

"You can do as you please about that," said Dora.

The next day Dora and Helen met, and had a
grand quarrel; not about Mr. Hewly,—his name
was never even mentioned,—but when two people
are bent upon breaking friendship, it is easy to find
something about which to disagree.

After this Dora became quite herself, and entered
into the family amusements with right good-will.
Her father treated her with marked tenderness, and
one day presented her with an elegant bracelet, "in
token (as he phrased it) of his approval of her conduct for some time past."

While these things were going on, the intercourse between Elinor and Marion became daily more intimate; but Mr. Dreux could not help seeing that his sister was neither well nor happy. She also seemed restless, and he thought a change might do her good.

On imparting this idea to her, and telling her that he thought he could spare a few days to take her out for a short tour, he was surprised at the earnestness with which she caught at it, and smoothed down all difficulties in the way of the project. It was accordingly soon arranged, and the next time he met Mr. Allerton he told him of it.

"I hope you will not be away long," was the reply.

" O no, but I wish Elinor to see something of this beautiful country, and I think a change will do her good; I think of returning in time for my Thursday evening lecture."

Mr. Allerton went home, wondering whether his friend had observed his partiality for Elinor. He could not be sure, for he had never given him the slightest opportunity of being alone with her, and had seemed very silent and absent lately. However, he thought,—" On that head I have at least nothing to fear; Dreux would, of course, rather give her to me—a man whom he knows so well—than bestow her on a stranger; and as for his absence of manner lately, perhaps it was only put on to set me more at ease in my wooing, under pretence that he did not see it."

The time of their absence seemed unaccountably long to him, and he had a daily argument with himself as to whether he could with propriety intrude upon them on their return, before the evening service. At last he decided that he could not, but being determined not to forego the pleasure of seeing Elinor that night, he resolved to go to the church, and be shown into her brother's seat, "where (he thought) I shall certainly find her, and be near her during the service."

He carried his intention into effect, and found he had not miscalculated. Elinor was there, and, sitting by her, he soon lost himself in a delightful reverie. But the commencement of the sermon recalled him to himself. He had heard a great deal of his friend's eloquence, but had hitherto adhered to his resolution of not entering his church. The same voice which influenced him so much in private now appealed to him more powerfully, and so completely carried him away that he troubled himself very little as to whether the words it uttered were truth or error.

Of all pleasures that exist in the world there is none equal in power over an enthusiastic mind to the pleasure of listening to beautiful ideas, uttered by a fine human voice, in the impassioned words that befit them.

On this occasion he was completely enthralled, but not convinced; and though he now began to feel, or fancy, a greater distance than ever between them, as far as talent was concerned, he was too warm-hearted to be humbled by it, and too generous to envy.

After service, he accompanied Elinor to the vestry, where he found Dreux in some perplexity. The Clerk had just given him a message from a sick person, requesting that he would come and see him as soon as possible.

" Will you go to-night?" asked Allerton.

" O yes, I shall go directly; but I must just see my sister home first." He paused a moment, and then said, " Unless I might trespass on you to do that for me."

" Oh, I shall be most happy," was the ready reply, Allerton feeling only anxious not to express his pleasure too strongly.

The next morning, as they sat at breakfast, Elinor said to her brother, " Mr. Allerton told me last night that the Paton family had met with an adventure which might have led to serious con-sequences."

Her brother looked up, and coloured; she thought she knew the nature of his feelings in that quarter, and looked another way as she went on : " They were riding through Feynly woods the other day, in that little open carriage of theirs, when the ponies took fright, backed, and upset them all upon a bank; they were none of them much hurt."

" Who was in the carriage?" asked her brother.

" Dora, Marion, and Walter inside, and young Greyson on the box. Walter's face was very much bruised, and Marion sprained her foot; but it could not have been anything of consequence, for Mr. Allerton says he saw her sitting in the pony carriage yesterday, looking as well as usual."

Marion, in fact, had not been much hurt, though sufficiently to confine her to the sofa for a few days. The family physician had said she must give herself a week of perfect rest, and then he thought she would be as well as ever.

The house was now unusually quiet, for nearly half the members of the family fancied they were wanted to assist in preparations for the wedding which was to take place in a few days. On the morning after Elinor's return no one was left at home but Marion and Rosina. Walter and young Greyson were gone to a gardener, to order plants and flowers to grace the conservatory. Mrs. Paton and her two elder daughters were at Elizabeth's house; and Marion, looking quite as blooming as usual, sat in the drawing-room, with her foot on a hassock, sealing up Mr. and Mrs. Fred Bishop's wedding-cards. She had a candle before her, and a formidable array of white sealing-wax, and envelopes with silver edges. Rosina helped her for an hour, and then went to take her French lesson. Marion had enough before her to occupy the whole morning, and she was sealing away with great diligence when the old footman brought her a card.

"Mr. Dreux's compliments, ma'am, and calls to inquire how you are to-day?"

" My compliments, and my foot is nearly well," said Marion.

Presently the man returned, and said, "If agreeable to you Mr. Dreux will come in, ma'am."

Marion replied, " Certainly, I shall be very happy to see Mr. Dreux."

Accordingly he was ushered in, and an observant person might have read something in the earnest look of anxiety he gave her, as she half rose to give him her hand, and in his smile of instant relief when he had seen with his own eyes that she looked as well as usual. Marion had generally a very quick perception of what others thought and felt, but in the present instance she was wondering what Elizabeth would think of his seeing her occupation, and whether she would mind this early exhibition of her wedding-cards, for Elizabeth had so many fancies as the wedding-day approached that it was quite a difficult matter to please her.

She decided, while asking a few questions about the journey and about Elinor, that as time pressed she must not be too fastidious; accordingly, after the first few minutes, she gently resumed her occupation.

As Mr. Dreux did not help her much, she was incessantly obliged to think of something fresh to say, and the conversation flagged several times, and was highly uninteresting.

Marion began to fall back upon her favourite regret that she had no conversational powers. At

last, notwithstanding all her attempts, matters came
to a dead pause. He did not answer her last
remark at all, and, while quietly sealing the notes,
she looked up at him, and became conscious that
something must be coming.

Mr. Dreux had taken up a piece of the white
sealing-wax and snapped it in two. Marion could
not think why his face was touched with such a
peculiar expression of agitation and embarrassment.
At length, with an exceedingly deep sigh, as if he
had just contrived to screw his courage to the
sticking point, he turned suddenly towards her,
looked in her face, and in an instant the whole
truth flashed upon her mind.

Mr. Dreux, who generally looked as if nothing
short of an earthquake would frighten him, and as
if he would not mind getting up at a moment's
notice to make a speech before the Queen, Lords,
and Commons, the assembled Bishops, and the
Peeresses in their robes, was evidently, for the time
being, a different person. He was so very much
afraid of saying anything that would not be well
taken, that he absolutely could not open his lips
at all.

Nevertheless, when he saw by Marion's manner
that she understood the state of the case, he recovered himself, and having previously snapped the
sealing-wax into twenty little pieces, and his usually
calm features being coloured with an emotion which
was evidently a very hopeful one, he began several

sentences relative to his admiration of her character, &c., &c., and having got himself into a dreadful mess, broke them short, and in two minutes had made her an offer in due form.

Marion's astonishment was so sincere, so unfeigned, and the blush which suffused her face to the temples was so sudden, that when she drew back her hand he started from the sofa, and said, in a tone of the deepest mortification, "Is it possible that I take you by surprise, Miss Greyson?"

"So much so," Marion replied in her usual gentle tone, but with obvious agitation, "that I assure you, Mr. Dreux, it is difficult for me to believe what I hear."

If she could have seen the change which came over his face when she said this,—his instantaneous perception of the mistake he had made, and the sudden lowering of his hopes,—she would have pitied him; but she did not raise her eyes, till after a painful silence he said, "I hope that at least what I have said is not displeasing to you, Miss Greyson," and while she hesitated to find an answer, he intreated her to give him some slight encouragement, and even pressed her for an answer to his proposals.

Marion replied, "After the confession I have made that your offer took me perfectly by surprise, I need scarcely remind you, Mr. Dreux, that there can be but one answer. However much I may feel the honour you have done me—"

Mr. Dreux, as if afraid to hear her finish the sentence, said hurriedly, "I have made a great mistake. I believed you to be perfectly aware of my feelings and of my hopes."

"His hopes," thought Marion. "Did he really think I both knew it and gave him encouragement?"

"I beg you will excuse my folly," he proceeded, venturing to resume his place on the sofa, "it was the strength of my regard which misled me."

His confusion and bitter disappointment struck Marion with the certainty that he had scarcely contemplated the possibility of a refusal; even now he seemed scarcely able to believe it; but as she really felt nothing for him but esteem and admiration for his talents, it was comparatively easy for her to express herself, and she said, "I cannot feel otherwise than grateful for the preference you have shown me, Mr. Dreux, but as I have before assured you that it is a preference of which I never had the slightest idea—I have really never thought of you otherwise than as a friend, I hope this assurance of my unconsciousness will acquit me in your mind of any trifling with your feelings. Still more, I hope you will soon see that no woman can be worthy of you who can give only esteem in return for regard like yours."

In reply to all this he only repeated, "I have made a great mistake; I hope you will forgive me."

He folded his arms, and appeared to be gazing

out of the window.   Here the interview ought to
have ended, but Marion, being a prisoner to the
sofa, felt very much embarrassed.   Any occupation
was better than sitting with her hands before her.
So she ventured very quietly to go on with her
sealing-wax, and now and then cast a stealthy glance
at her companion.

The restless flashing of his eyes and the slight
compression of his lips were all the tokens he gave
of the pain he was enduring.   His fine features
expressed not only disappointment, but something
like shame. Perhaps he inwardly inveighed against
the folly which had so often whispered, loud enough
for him to hear, that he was quite irresistible;
perhaps he wished he had never heard any of that
soft flattery which, though he generally rejected
and always despised it, had yet by the frequency of
its appeals to his vanity, made him almost take for
granted that he must possess some slight title to the
perfections it ascribed to him.

Whatever he thought he said nothing, till Marion,
who could not rise, happened to drop some slight
article, the fall of which attracted his attention.

Some faint hopes might perhaps have been growing up during the silence, for when he arose and
she held out her hand to him, his eyes certainly
expressed an appeal, but the answering look only
told of the most gentle womanly regret.   She said,
" Good morning, Mr. Dreux," and he took his leave,
for he saw it was of no use.

Now it so happened—and unfortunate things will happen sometimes—it so happened that Mrs. Paton, Dora, and Elizabeth no sooner entered the door on their return home, than they asked the old servant whether any one had called.

" Only Mr. Dreux, ma'am," replied the man, who had his own thoughts on the subject, " and he did not stay very long. I should say," he continued, carrying his eye slowly along the cornice of the hall, as if to assist his memory, " I should say Mr. Dreux did not stay over three quarters of an hour, ma'am."

Now three quarters of an hour is a long time for a morning call, and that the old servant knew quite as well as they did; nevertheless, when the young ladies entered the drawing-room neither of them said a word to Marion on the subject nor alluded to anything connected with it, though they watched her as she went on sealing the notes with great diligence and a brighter bloom than usual in her face.

Their mother thought this call rather a pointed thing, and that if Mr. Dreux did not mean something by it he had no right to sit three quarters of an hour with her niece, but that this had been the end of his wooing instead of the beginning she had no more idea than she had of what he was suffering at that moment.

In the evening, Elizabeth, having dismissed the last milliners, and given the last sitting to the

artist who was taking her miniature, seen the
garden of her new house finished to the last bit
of trellis-work, and heard Fred Bishop call himself
the happiest of men, was in such a high state of
hilarity that she wanted some active amusement,
in short, some mischief "for her idle hands to do."
So she proposed that they should act charades, a
favourite amusement of theirs, and one in which
she particularly excelled, though it must be owned
that she often called in the aid of mimicry, and
often indulged in something personal in her charades.

Frank Maidley was present, and was always an
invaluable helper. They were to perform the charade
in the little music-room, there being a curtain and
all things conformable, and the audience was to sit
in state in the main drawing-room.

The audience, as is usual on these occasions,
was extremely impatient. At length the curtain
was drawn back, and Elizabeth was seen, with a
large cap on, a pair of spectacles, a black stuff
apron, and at her side a huge bunch of keys.
Maidley, as butler, stood at the sideboard.

Elizabeth. "So he's not come down yet!—sleep,
sleep, sleep, for ever. What a lazy fellow he is!
Never mind, sleep costs nothing. Where's my
straw bonnet, Pinch? I'll go into the garden."

Pinch. "Please, ma'am, the 'osses is hungry,
and this morning, as I was laying cloth for breakfast, Neptune, he looked in, and saw your bonnet

lying on the chair, and he ate it up, ma'am. If they aint to have no hoats, poor dears, they must have something."

E. "You must be more careful in future, Pinch. That bonnet cost 6*s.* 6*d.* when it was new, and there was a great deal of wear in it still. I've only had it—let me see! how long has my poor dear sister been dead? Why, seventeen years. How time flies! Well, she left it me in her will, and her turned black silk gown with a train to it. Ah! she was a saving woman,—an excellent woman, Pinch."

Enter Wilfred.] "Good morning, mother;—a beautiful sunshiny morning."

E. "Sunshiny, indeed! Ah! boy, boy, you never consider how the sun fades the curtains and blisters the paint on the house-door."

Greyson sits down to the table.] "What! a partridge again, mother! I declare, we never have anything but game, mother! I've not tasted anything else at breakfast, dinner, or tea, since I came into the country;—game and little birds, thrushes and sparrows."

E. "To be sure, my dear. Why, you don't consider that birds cost nothing,—at least, nothing but the bullets they shoot them with."

Pinch. "Lawk! ma'am, we don't shoot birds with bullets! Why, dear me, it's nothing but shot."

E. "Remember your place, Pinch, and don't be

disrespectful. Well, I mean shot, of course;—it's all the same thing. I hope, Pinch, you're careful not to waste the shot: the number of shots I sometimes find in one wing is really quite distressing. The age is grown very extravagant! Instead of pouring in the shot in that reckless manner, you should count how many birds there are in a covey, and put in one for each of them."

Pinch. "I always does, ma'am; and then I shuts my eyes and lets the gun off. But sometimes all the shot gets into one of them, and I'm sure I can't help that;—I lets the gun off very straight."

Wilfred. "And that's the reason you get so few birds, eh?"

Pinch. "I reckon myself a reasonable good shot, Sir. I shot five partridges this very week, not counting three as I took in the nest, and that dear one that I found under the hedge; and then I got two goslings, and ever so many blackbirds, besides a polecat."

E. [*Looking very hard into Wilfred's plate, which is, in fact, a china basket, full of visiting cards.*] "My dear boy, I see several shots on the edge of your plate;—one, two, three. Why, dear me, there are six of them. Here, Pinch, take these and clean them,—they'll do again."

Pinch. "Yes, ma'am." [*Brings a hat by way of waiter, into which Wilfred drops several cotton balls.*]

E. "My dear boy, how very large your appetite

is! I'm sure you'll have an illness if you live so high. Let me feel your pulse. Ah! very feverish indeed!"

Wilfred goes on eating.] "What's this, mother?" [*Draws a straw work-basket towards him.*]

E. "Why—why that's a meat-pie, my dear. Don't you think it would be as well not to cut it to-day?"

Wilfred. "Why, the crust's so hard I can't cut it. Oh, that's right,—it's all come off in a piece. Pretty pie-crust, truly! What's this, mother?" [*Draws out a short ivory knitting-needle.*]

E. "That's—that's—why, dear me, how foolish cook is! I told her particularly not to put their tails in."

W. "Tails, mother? Rabbits' tails are not so long as this!"

E. "How can you be so undutiful, my dear? I hope you don't suspect me of anything, I'm sure! The pie is very good,—I saw it made myself."

W. "Suspect what, mother?" [*Turns it about with an air of disgust.*] "I hope it's not made of anything nasty. What's this pie made of, Pinch? If you don't tell me I'll toss it out of the window."

Pinch. "Rats, Sir, and very good wholesome food too. I hope, Sir, you'll never come to the workhouse for despising of them. Cook and me would no more think of objecting to eat 'em, if there wasn't cold meat and ceteras which requires speedy eating, than we should think of ——"

E. " Pinch, don't forget your place. Why, my dear,—the fact is, my dear, and I don't mind, as you now are getting old, letting you know a few things that are done in *all* families,—*all*, my dear, though they may pretend to the contrary. Don't look at me in that undutiful manner. The fact is, my dear, that on Saturday Jowler killed six or seven fine tender young rats, and I really thought it would not be right to waste them. They are very good indeed smothered in onion, and stuffed with sage and fennel. The clergyman called here yesterday, and I had one served up to him fricasseed, and he declared it was excellent."

Wilfred. [*Fishing out a knitting-shuttle.*] " And what's this, mother, I should like to know ? "

E. " Oh ! what a sad thing it is to have an undutiful, spendthrift, extravagant son ! " [*Puts her handkerchief to her eyes and sobs.*] " Why, my dear, can't you tell by the shape of it that that's a fish ? One of the gold fish died yesterday, and I had it put into the pie ;—it's quite fresh."

" Oh, my work ! " cried Dora—the owner of the basket, as Wilfred, drawing it towards him, stirred up a tangled mass of threads and worsted with his penknife, the weapon wherewith he was eating his breakfast.

" Oh ! Dora," said Elizabeth, " now that really is too bad. We can't go on if the audience is to interrupt us in that way."

" Well, only let me come and get my work-basket. There, really, the shocking confusion your hopeful son has made in it!"

"Come for it, then; and we had better draw back the curtain, and call this the end of the first scene. Come, Frederick, you said you would help us with the next. And, my dear son, you may go, and let a mother, in parting, beg you to practise economy."

"Oh, I know what the word is;—don't you, Dora?" cried Walter. "So we don't want to see any more of that scene. It's either *save* or *shot*, I'm certain."

Frederick Bishop went into the little room, and Wilfred came out and sat down among the audience. And now was heard a vast deal of tittering, and whispering, and running out of the little room. The audience, at first, were so occupied with chattering together that they did not observe it. At last, however, they got impatient, and began to exclaim, that if the show did not begin directly they should amuse themselves in some other way.

Upon this the curtain was slowly drawn aside, and Elizabeth was seen seated among a number of flower-pots, hastily brought in for the purpose. She was completely dressed in Marion's habiliments,—shawl, bonnet, gown, even parasol,—and held a few flowers, to make it more impossible to mistake who she was intended to represent. She held a book in her hand, and began to read as from its pages: "They *Drew* him in such fair colours, that it quite Drew my admiration—his robes as white as a Dru-id's, and his smile as sweet (oh, far sweeter, *I* think!) than that of a Merry An-drew."

Marion, on hearing this breathed quick, and began to tremble for what might be coming. Walter whispered to her that the word was *drew*. She looked anxiously at Wilfred, but he seemed to see nothing strange in the scene, so with a flushed cheek and trembling heart she bent her eyes again upon the actors. She could not expostulate, for that would have betrayed her.

(Enter Fred Bishop in a white apron.) "Please, ma'am, a gentleman has called to see you."

E. "Oh! show him down the garden to this arbour."

(*Exit* Fred, with half-a-dozen silver spoons and a great piece of wash-leather in his hand, to show that he personates a footman.)

E. "Dear me, I feel quite nervous. What shall I do till he comes? Let me see. I'll be reading." (Snatches up a book, which happens to be 'The Rambler,'—opens at random, and begins to read aloud.) "Others may be persecuted, but I am haunted. I have good reason to believe that eleven painters are now dogging me, for they know that he who can get my face first will make his fortune. I often change my wig, and wear my hat over my eyes, by which I hope somewhat to confound them. I have, indeed, taken some measures for the preservation of my papers, having put

them into an iron chest, and fixed a padlock upon
my closet. I change my lodgings five times a-week,
and always remove at the dead of night. Thus I
live, in consequence of having given too great proofs
of a predominant genius, in the solitude of a hermit,
with the anxiety of a miser, and the caution "——

(Enter Maidley, with his hat on, a pair of bands
made of silver paper, and a white neckerchief:
rushes up to Elizabeth, and without more ado goes
down on his knees): "Do I behold the fair image
which ever lives in my heart?"

E. "Oh, really, my dear Sir, I feel quite confused—so very awkward that you should happen to
overhear my little efforts to—to improve my mind
with the writings of our classic Johnson. Pray,
rise."

"No, ma'am, I will not rise till you promise to
accept this little offering, which I am proud to—if
I may say it—to lay at your feet" (takes off his hat
with gravity, and looking steadily at her, draws out
of it a red pocket-handkerchief, in which are tied
up quantities of damsons; he unties it, and pours
the contents into Elizabeth's lap, saying, with his
hand on his heart),—

> "I give thee *all*, I can no more,
>   Though poor the offering be;
> My heart and PLUMS are all the store
>   That I can give to thee."

*Elizabeth receiving the plums graciously, and
beginning to eat them*—"Oh, but I am afraid this

plum is not quite ripe yet. Pray, let me beg of
you to rise."

But as if her entreaty had taken effect on others
besides young Maidley, almost every one in the
outer drawing-room rose also. Wilfred had dexterously turned down the lamp, and all was darkness
and confusion. Fred Bishop tumbled over a settee
in groping his way to the bell to call for other
lights; and it would seem as if the charade was
forgotten, so completely was the subject dropped.

When the lamps were again lighted, Elizabeth
saw by her mother's face that she was seriously
hurt and annoyed. Dora also looked flushed, and,
as usual, took upon herself to propose some fresh
way of spending the evening, and to see that
matters were put in train for it. The two gentlemen had sense enough to see that they had by no
means made themselves acceptable by their little
scene; and Elizabeth, seeing that Marion had
slipped out of the room, took the opportunity to
follow her.

Elizabeth ran up into Marion's little parlour, and
there found her sitting by the window, looking out
into the moonlight. She ran up to her, half afraid,
half laughing.

"Really, Marion, I assure you I had not the very
slightest idea you would be annoyed,—and if you
are, I am very sorry."

Marion made no answer.

"I assure you, my dear, if I could have known

it would have put you so completely to the blush——
but how did you get up stairs by yourself?"

"Wilfred helped me," said Marion.

"Ah! well, I see you are displeased. As for
Wilfred, I am certain it was he who caused that
sudden ending to our little scene. It would have
been a good one if you could just have waited.
Come, I will take off your bonnet. Why, Marion,
I only wanted to call your attention to a little
fact."

"What little fact?" asked Marion.

"Why, that Mr. Dreux looks at you when he is
here a great deal oftener than at any of us."

"I wonder whether they have found anything
out," thought Marion, and she arose hastily and
stood by the window.

"My dear Marion," said Dora, coming in, "I am
sure Elizabeth is really sorry."

"How ridiculous you are, Dora," said the
thoughtless Elizabeth. "Yes, I really am sorry,
of course; but what a fuss about a trifle!"

Marion still stood in the window, and made no
answer. The two sisters looked at each other;
then Elizabeth came up to her cousin, and drew her
arm round her neck. "I really am very sorry,
dearest Marion," she said, kissing her.

"But before Frank Maidley, Elizabeth," urged
Marion, for Elizabeth still laughed in spite of her
protestations, "how could you do it?"

"Frank Maidley, Marion! Why, I declare he

was the first person who put it into my head. He
came in the other day, and said, with the greatest
coolness, ' So Mr. Dreux has been here. Well,
how 's Mrs. Arthur Cecil ? ' "

" It was excessively impertinent of him, then,"
said Dora, gravely. " I could scarcely have believed
he would have done such an ungentlemanly thing."

" There," thought Elizabeth, " now I have got
myself into another disagreeable predicament."

" I do hope you will never couple my name with
Mr. Dreux's again," said Marion.

" No, I really will not. But why not? there's
nothing in it ! "

Oh, because I don't like it," said Marion ; " and
besides, it is extremely wrong. What right have
you to take it for granted that he has any such
intentions with respect to me, or to make him
appear so ridiculous ? "

" *Intentions!* Marion. Why, how seriously you
take the matter up ! I never thought anything of
the kind. I only think he is perhaps a little
smitten, and comes here rather oftener than he
used to do. But why do you stand? Don't you
know you ought not? How is your foot to-
night ? "

" Oh, it feels nearly well this evening," answered
Marion, relieved by the last remark, which showed
her perfect ignorance of what had happened.

" Well, you won't bear any malice, Marion ? "

Marion laughed, and kissed her cousin, but she

could not quite recover her composure, so she did not come down again that night.

Nothing more was said to Elizabeth, for as she was to leave them so very soon, no one of the family liked to shadow her *after-recollections* of those evenings with anything unpleasing. But though Elizabeth was not to be teazed, her mother could not possibly do without some one to whom to repeat over and over again how deeply she was hurt by this extreme impropriety, this very great want of delicacy, &c., &c. So poor Dora, who had been summoned to her mother's dressing-room, could only regret the past, and hear her mother predict that *now* she was certain nothing ever would come of what might, if undisturbed, have ended in a union, but *now* it was not likely Marion could get over this annoyance sufficiently to like Mr. Dreux. Dora said what she could to palliate her sister's want of discretion, and to soothe her mother, but she was seriously annoyed herself, and the more so, because Frank Maidley had been the aider and abettor in this unlucky charade.

CHAPTER XIV.

DISUNION.

MR. DREUX, after his interview with Marion, walked home, like a man in a dream. Whatever pain, disappointment, or vexation he might have felt, he had retained till the last moment, a kind of secret incredulity, a lurking hope, that she would not permit him to leave her without one word that he could construe in his own favour. This hope did not utterly forsake him till she held out her hand at parting, with that look of gentle regret for the mental suffering of which she had been the innocent cause, but without anything in her whole expression which seemed to wish for a renewal of his attentions.

He always kept a strong constraint upon his feelings. His face, as he walked along the streets, bore little evidence of what was going on within, beyond a more settled gravity than usual ; but as soon as he reached his own house, he went hastily up stairs to shut himself up in his library, and as he entered the room his face, already changed from its enforced calmness, looked anxious and restless.

But silence and solitude, the relief he so much needed, were not awaiting him. There was some one in the room; Allerton was walking up and down in it; and as he came forward to shake hands with him, with his usual hearty cordiality, he said,— "You see, Dreux, I have invaded your premises, for the fact is, I want to have some private conversation with you. I thought you would never come in. But what's the matter?—you look ill."

He felt disappointed, but only answered, "I have rather a sharp headache," and threw himself upon a sofa near the window, pressing his hand upon his forehead.

"Ah, that's the consequence of working so hard; I knew you would exert yourself more than ever after that short holiday. And why have you placed yourself in this glare of light?—a strange remedy for a headache!" So saying, he drew down the green blind, and going up to the couch, said,— "Come, let me see what sort of a pulse you have got."

"Oh, there is really nothing the matter with me, Allerton, beyond this headache; I only want a little rest."

The look which was directed to him, in reply, said so plainly, "I am certain there *is* something the matter," that he added, in explanation, "I mean that I am not ill, but something has happened which has disturbed me very much."

Allerton did not wish to be inquisitive, and a pause ensued, during which he walked up and down the room, as he always did when excited, either pleasurably or otherwise.

His host watched him a while, thinking that he had no recollection, during all their intercourse, of ever having wished him away before. Now his desire to be alone made him so restless that he could not keep two minutes together in the same position. At length he said, "I believe you said you had something to tell me, or that you wanted some private conversation." Allerton did not cease to walk, and it was difficult to divine the meaning of his half-pleased, half-embarrassed manner; but, as if he wished to make it more difficult still, he presently broke silence by relating a variety of particulars respecting his parentage, his past life, his prospects,—giving an exact account of his income from various sources, with a short digression to explain his expectations ; and all this he did like a man performing some duty which must naturally have been expected of him. At first, Mr. Dreux was so preoccupied, and so wide of the mark, that he thought he was going to ask him to lend him some money, and he was just on the point of declaring his willingness to do so, without all this preamble, but checked himself; and Allerton went into various details, each one more perplexing than the last,— his bewildered auditor getting more and more confused, and feeling an uneasy consciousness that he ought to know what was coming, he ended his communications by saying, " And you agree with me, of course."

Dreux, without much consciousness of what he was talking about, answered mechanically, " Of course."

Thereupon followed a short silence. "Well, I wish he would help me through," thought Allerton, glancing towards his friend, whose restless agitation became more apparent; he looked thoroughly dispirited, and what is popularly called " cut up."

"I wonder what can have happened to disturb him so much; I have chosen a peculiarly unlucky day." He waited a while, but no answer was forthcoming,—indeed, his friend was quite unconscious that one was expected of him; but at length, looking up, and meeting rather an earnest glance, he forced a smile, and trying to appear interested, asked if he had any more to say.

" Any more?" repeated Allerton. "Why, I do believe you have not heard the half of what I have said, Dreux. Well; I know you are not fond of finances, but of course I thought it was my duty to give you a notion of my prospects, though you have always treated me with a generous confidence, which has been highly gratifying to my feelings; and I really do feel most grateful to you for your conduct throughout the whole affair." (Mr. Dreux upon this lifted up his eyes from the floor, and gazed at him with the most unfeigned astonishment.)

"And," proceeded Allerton, "for always permitting me such free access to your house, and for not appearing to notice how things were going on; for really, though I can fight my way tolerably well through the world, I feel quite—I am such a diffident man as regards ladies, that I believe I should have fretted myself nearly into a fever before I found courage to speak, if you had not so kindly given me the opportunity by asking me to walk home last night with your sister."

"With *my* sister!" repeated his auditor, speaking more to himself than his friend. "Is there no mistake about this?"

If Allerton had not been so preoccupied with his own pleasant thoughts, he must have remarked the sudden change of countenance which followed this remark, and the intense attention which now awaited every word he uttered.

Mr. Allerton explained that he had offered his hand to Elinor, and had elicited from her the avowal that she was not engaged.

Not a word was spoken in reply, but he perceived that his friend's powers were stretched to the utmost, either to subdue some new emotion, or to discover what *he* was expected to say.

"Did Elinor accept your proposal?" he presently asked, with tolerable self-command.

"Not exactly; one feels rather foolish when it comes to such a thing as saying that a lady testifies the reverse of indifference. I do believe your sister is not indifferent to me, but she would not give me any answer herself; indeed, when I urged her to do so, she wept, and seemed very much moved, and I began to get into a dreadful fright. However, at last she told me she would leave the answer entirely to you, and desired me to tell you that she was resolved to abide by your decision; so you may easily imagine, after that, that I felt easy, for she could not fail to know what your decision would be."

In the full confidence of his trusting nature, he stopped short, and coming up, held out his hand, saying, with a smile, "I felt for you all the affection of a brother long before I thought I should ever be one to you in reality."

Instead of taking the offered hand, Dreux made a movement which seemed to entreat his forbearance, and shrinking back, covered his face with his hands. This unexpected movement was an evident shock to Allerton, and for a moment his face darkened. But he resolutely fell back on his idea that it was illness; he was determined to distrust him no more; and when he saw how wildly the pulses were throbbing in his temples, he was confirmed in his first belief, in spite of some words which might have shaken it, "Entirely to me!—what right could she have—how could she do so, Allerton? Give me a few minutes to collect my thoughts."

His face had become so colourless that again wonder and distrust arose in Allerton's mind; but he rallied instantly, and said, "I know you are ill, Dreux; you cannot conceal it from me. I am certain something more than ordinary is the matter; you have hardly been able to attend to what I said; I have been very inconsiderate; I forgot." Thereupon he hastily threw up the blind, and opened the glass-door.

"There," he said, "come and sit here in the air, it will refresh you,—that's right. What an inconsiderate fellow I am, I have made your head worse. But, though I am very impatient, I will not ask you to think of all this at present. I shall wait for what you have to say till to-morrow morning."

His manner, always affectionate and friendly, and the expression of his face, which was full of solicitude, affected his friend almost beyond control or endurance; but he had two great causes for depression, and, as first one, and then the other, rose up before him with bewildering rapidity, he was not mastered by either, though he would doubtless have been had either existed alone.

Suddenly Allerton exclaimed,—"My groom tells me you were thrown yesterday in riding from the railway,—is that true?"

"Yes. I was not hurt."

"Not at all? Well, but how did it happen? I thought you had such an uncommonly good seat on horseback."

"I was quite off my guard. We were passing some hay-wagons, and I turned in the saddle to look after them. He had me off in an instant. I mounted again; but, having once thrown me, I suppose he thought he always could, for he made several attempts in that short distance. I must part with him."

"Yes, sell him, Dreux, and at once. I only wonder you have kept him so long; but you are such a reckless rider. I wish I could see you more careful. Have you not a funeral to take to-morrow?"

"Yes; I promised to do the occasional duty at Wigton while Loyde was out."

"Then I'll send my horse round for you. Don't think of mounting your own, particularly as that will be the same road on which he threw you yesterday. Well, at ten to-morrow shall I come? Shall you be ready for me then?"

"Yes; at ten."

"Well, good by, then, and take care of yourself."

Allerton, whose head was running on proposals, thought he looked like a man who had just been rejected, but most fortunately he did not say so, and took leave of him, repeating his assurance that he should come again the next day at ten.

He ran down the steps into the garden, and had reached the centre, when he turned and looked back. The windows were already shut and the library-curtains pulled down. "Poor fellow!" he said to himself, "I wonder what can have happened." And he crossed the lawn, thinking, but in the generosity of his heart reproaching himself for the thought,—"If I had been in his place, I think, whatever private sources of care might be distracting me, I could have found some pleasure in the idea of giving my sister to my most intimate friend."

But while these thoughts and many more were passing through his mind he had no more idea of the struggle which was going on between principle and feeling in the heart of the man he had left,—no more conception of the bitter reproach, the protracted conflict with himself, the long review in which HE and all his generous friendship came before him each time in better and in brighter colours, and his perfect consciousness of what would and must be the termination of that next day's interview,—than he had that what he had told his friend of his attachment to his sister was as new and unexpected as the sudden termination of his hopes with reference to his own.

He remained alone all the afternoon, and then Elinor came into the room, saying she wished to speak to him. She had been shedding tears, and her cheeks were pale, but, with a woman's quickness, she soon discovered that it was not for her sake alone that he was so oppressed; she was certain there must be something more. He related somewhat of their interview, and then, drawing her towards him with almost impetuous earnestness, entreated her to release him from the obligation she had put upon him.

" You must, Arthur," she replied, " *I* cannot give him a refusal."

" *You* cannot, and yet you believe it should be done. Is he to be refused because you honour what Christ said: ' How shall two walk together except they be agreed?' and because you know that, from opposing principles, no true harmony could result and no happiness? Or is it that you do not feel any very great interest in him? Think of this, Elinor; consider how short a time you have known Allerton. If he had not spoken out last night, should you not, on returning to your aunt, soon have forgotten any preference you might have felt? And if this is so, Elinor,—if you do not love him, cannot you tell him yourself that you do not feel a sufficient regard for him to accept his hand?"

Elinor made no answer.

He went on: " But why, in any case, leave it to me? Oh, Elinor, it is cruel! Do you not know that scarcely anything in the world could give me so much pain as to have to refuse you to my dearest friend, and to tell him that my principles demand it of me?"

" Ought I to refuse, or ought I to accept?" said Elinor.

" If you do not love him—"

" But if I do,—if you can advise me to accept, oh! pray do; there is nothing about him I do not love, excepting that smile that hovers about his face at the mention of many most sacred things. He used only to smile so when you were speaking, but lately he has treated even his own professed belief in the same way. He even said to me, that, at least, you had found him sincere in his creed; and now, without teaching him to believe yours, you had shaken his faith in all."

" Elinor, you frighten me,—Allerton a sceptic!"

" Ah, I knew he never said such things to you; and yet, Arthur,"—she looked in her brother's face and saw what he thought,—" but if, when he offered me his hand, I struggled with myself and gave no word of reply; if I mastered myself sufficiently to refer him to you, and to promise, in his hearing, that I would abide by your decision, surely you will not ask me again to encounter such a scene. I have not courage to tell him in so many words that I prefer him to any one else, but that to accept his offer would be inconsistent with my profession. Even now I waver between duty and regret. I almost regret the power I have given you over me. If you give it me back again—"

" No, my dear Elinor, I do not give it back. If it might have been otherwise I should have been thankful; but if this must be so, I will give up my friend rather than subject you to this trial."

" *You* give him up?" said Elinor, surprised.

" He knows that it is to rest only with me. Do you think he will feel anything but anger and resentment against me, when I might have made him happy and have refused to do so? If he despises my principles now, he will detest them then, for having compelled me to withhold you from him, when natural affection and every feeling of friendship and gratitude would call for their being set aside. No, Elinor, if one of us gives him up the other must also, and, as the decision is left to me, I decide to do it. And yet, Elinor, if you could spare me this,—must I lose all the influence for good that I hoped I had acquired? Must I make this cause detestable to him which I have laboured so hard to recommend? You cannot see him; I do not ask it. But if you could write?"

But no, Elinor was inexorable; she would not see him, and she could not write.

" I am sorry if I have said too much about it," he said, when he found she was not to be persuaded. " I reproach myself for my carelessness in so constantly letting him have access. I might have known,—I ought to have foreseen what was sure to happen. But why did you give me no hint of it, Elinor? If you had, though ever so darkly, I could in great measure have prevented all this."

" I did not feel sure about it," faltered Elinor. " He never said anything decisive. Sometimes I thought I would mention it to you, or even that

I would hint to him that I should prefer a different manner. But if I had done so how deeply abashed I should have felt if he had said, as he might have done, that he was sorry I was annoyed at what he had only intended as proper attention to the sister of a friend in whose house he so constantly was, or if he had rallied me with that half playful, half respectful manner which he always assumes towards ladies."

As she stood, her colour coming and going, and her whole manner evincing the deepest regret, yet not giving way to any of those transports of sorrow, nor using any of those vehement expressions so often resorted to to express disappointed feeling, her brother remembered what she had told him of her never having been accustomed to the language of adulation, and he reproached himself for his unwillingness to endure his part of the privation, when she was so quietly resigned to hers.

"Elinor," he said gently, "you are not looking forward to any change on Allerton's part? You cannot. And you must not deceive yourself. We shall certainly part in anger to-morrow. No care on my part, no desire to conciliate can possibly prevent it, and after that we shall see him no more. Strange as it may seem, Elinor, I am certain that he expects what is coming; I saw it in his face; but I saw at the same time that he would not suffer the thought to start into prominence; he was determined not to acknowledge to himself that it existed; and when we parted, and I looked earnestly at him, his expression seemed to say, 'I am resolved to trust you, and resolute that you shall not read the shadow of a doubt in my eyes of your affection, or of your being willing to follow it up as I now give you opportunity.' You know Allerton's character, my dear, and you must not hope, Elinor, that we shall be reconciled again. He might hate me for a while and then come round again, but by this I shall make him despise me. He has hinted to me before now, that in his belief our most sacred feelings were instincts given us whereby to correct and govern our principles. It is clear to me that in this case he will think principles ought to give way."

"Why do you say all this to me, Arthur?"

"Partly, dearest, because you have got that little portrait of Allerton in your possession. You asked me for it nearly a fortnight ago to fix a chain to it for me."

"Well, I will give it back," said Elinor, with a sigh. "I shall bring it to you to-morrow."

"Yes, and we will not talk of this any more, my dear Elinor; it only distresses. Without doubt you have made it a subject of prayer, and you will feel resigned and even happy. We must leave these things in the hands of our Heavenly Father. The commandment is plain, to marry only in the Lord. Let us obey in faith and trust Him with the consequences."

" And I am not to see Mr. Allerton any more?
You will not ask me to take leave of him?"

" Certainly not. You shall not be distressed. I
will do all I can to save you needless pain."

The next morning, punctual to the minute,
Allerton came up the garden steps and rapped
at the library window. He looked earnestly at his
friend as he opened it. He was greeted by a sudden,
and what seemed to be an involuntary smile, for it
instantly disappeared, and left his face pale and
overshadowed with gloom.

" Well," said Mr. Allerton, resolutely keeping to
his last thought, " and how is your head?"

" It still aches; but, my dear Allerton, surely
you are going to sit down!"

" Sit down! of course I am," and he threw himself upon a chair, and leaned his arms upon the
table with an earnest, steady expression.

Elinor had brought down the little picture and
laid it on the table. His eye lighted upon it; he
pushed it a little further off, and said hastily, " Well,
Dreux, I am come to hear your sister's decision
—yours rather. She confirmed what I told you,
did she not—that she left the decision to you?"

" Yes, she told me that it rested only with me."

Allerton looked at him, and his face darkened
and his brow lowered, but he went on in a steady
voice.

" And she admitted that I was not entirely

indifferent to her?" He paused for a moment, and then added, more firmly still, "Dreux, the head-ache does not make a man's lips tremble."

For the time they seemed to have changed natures. The passionate man was so firm and self-possessed, and had assumed so much higher ground than the other, who shrunk from his steady eyes, and seemed to have difficulty in answering,—

"Will you let me speak on another subject, Allerton, before we enter upon this? I have some-thing to explain to you, or rather to remind you of, which I should have thought would not have come upon you quite unexpectedly."

Though he had believed in the bottom of his heart, since the past day, that this would come, he had so strenuously kept the unwelcome conviction down, that this confirmation of his worst fears struck him with a feeling like astonishment, which was increased by Dreux's manner, which even seemed to appeal to his compassion, and to dread the utterance of his next sentence still more than he did to hear it.

"What," he said, "is it possible you are going to put me off as you did yesterday?"

He was excessively angry, and yet he felt some-thing like pity for the pain and agitation betrayed by his companion till he had heard his answer, and then every gentler feeling was gone. It was a pity these words were said; they added fuel to the fire ; but the speaker for once was so distraught, that he scarcely knew what he was talking about.

" I only ask a few minutes for explanation, Allerton. I hope you will bear with me. If my principles—"

" Your principles ! " repeated Allerton, burning with anger, and scarcely believing what he heard. " Is it possible that you want to speak to me about your principles now ? Don't you know what I mean ? Don't you know what I came here to ask, and that with all your vaunted principles you will never make woman a more loving husband than I would make *her ?* Don't you know that the decision rests with you, and that, considering the intimate friendship which has subsisted between us so long, and all the professions which have arisen from it, you would be one of the meanest rascals living if you refused ? Don't you know all this, Dreux ? and that if I were the most patient of men I could scarcely endure this delay. What do you mean, then, by thrusting in your detestable principles ? I have to hear enough of them at all times, without being tormented with them now."

" Hear me. Only let me speak, Allerton," pleaded his auditor.

" Hear you ! " repeated Allerton, in a towering passion. " I 'll hear nothing but this :—will you give me your sister, or will you not ? Answer me, —yes or no."

"I must and will speak to you. Allerton, hear me, I entreat of you, I beg of you, if you have any remembrance of our friendship, which has been as strong a bond as brotherhood—"

"Brotherhood!" repeated Allerton, starting up from his seat, and speaking with such intense scorn that it sent the blood up to his friend's face. "T'cha! don't talk to me of brotherhood. Let that rest with your detestable principles. You need not debase yourself by any further explanations. I shall know what to think in future of them and you." And he went on with such a torrent of reproach and invective as showed the height of his excitement, being, however, not so transported with passion that he could not see the torture he was inflicting, for at every fresh accusation this man, who was generally so calm and self-possessed, shrunk back as if he had been struck, while his very features were altered by the violence of his efforts to restrain himself. He lifted up his face as soon as there was any hope of being heard, and made another attempt to speak.

"I entreat you, Allerton, in justice, not to go away without suffering me to speak, not in self-defence or with any hope that friendly feeling toward me should ever revive in your mind again. —I know that all that is over and gone,—I only wish to express my sorrow at what is inevitable, and beg you, when you are calmer, to admit that you at least believe I have preserved my consistency at the expense of what has long been one of the best blessings of my life."

"That's enough," interrupted Allerton, who, if he had in some degree mastered his rage, was far more bitter and determined than ever; "I only ask you to answer that one question—will you give me your sister, or will you not? Say no, if you will, I shall not tell the world of it; you will only have made yourself despicable in the eyes of one man—you will have fallen lowest where you did sit highest of all—I emancipate myself from your yoke for ever; I have often thought this day would come—I thought *I* might some day provoke you past your bearing, and go out at this door to return no more; but I never thought I should go despising you so deeply, as to conquer a regard which I thought stronger than death. As for our past friendship"—he took up the little miniature case, flung it upon the ground, and struck it with his heel—"as for our past friendship, I fling it aside without regret; there is no such man as he whom I called my friend, he IS NOT, and he never has been." He pushed away the crushed fragments from under his feet, and laid his hand upon the glass door, when Mr. Dreux sprung towards him, and held him so firmly by the wrists, that he could not disengage himself.

"Not yet, Allerton, and not so—don't leave my house for ever thus!"

"Will you give me your sister?—not one other word will I hear, not one."

"Allerton, stay one moment—are we really to part in this way?"

"Leave go," cried Allerton, irritated at the strength with which he held him. "The sooner I go the better; and if ever you think of me again, make up your mind that I remember our past friendship, and how you performed your part of it. I shall think of you and your principles, and everything connected with you, with utter detestation and contempt. If the whole world had leagued together to warn me of you, I would not have listened—if a voice from heaven had denounced you, I would have heard it with distrust! You have awakened me rudely from my dream, and now I know you as you are and as you have been!!"

Exerting all his strength, he wrung asunder the detaining hands; and without his hat, without the slightest look or gesture of farewell, turned his back upon the house, went deliberately across the garden, and disappeared. His late friend looked after him till he was gone, and then shut the window and let down the blind; he picked up the uninjured miniature from the remains of its broken case and held it in his hand, while he slowly collected all the articles about his room which belonged to Allerton, or that he had given him. There was the seal, cut with his crest, with which he sealed his letters when he wrote them there;—there were several books in which he had written notes, and others inscribed with his name; he had left his gloves upon the table. Having brought all these things together, he opened a drawer and buried in it the memorials of their dead friendship—there

were no memorials of his other loss to hide. And
now the ideal wife seemed to come and stand beside
him, looking at him with her sweet eyes: she was
lost, and with her all his future changed as he
looked into it—he made his appeal again, and again
met that look of womanly regret; but dear as she
was to him, the second loss was the one that
belonged most to actual life—the one which would
empty his home of the face he had been accustomed
to greet with so much pleasure, and the loss of
which would overcloud his sister's brow, and so cast
a gloom on the life of every day.

He held the small picture pressed between the
palms of his hands, and now all the circumstances
of their friendship rose up before him. He felt
not the slightest resentment against Allerton, but
was tortured with regrets over his own blindness,
and became constantly more aware how great a loss
he would be to him, for he could not make friends:
he had plenty of popularity, plenty of applause,
many acquaintances and well-wishers; but his
reserve had not suffered him to make a single
intimate friend. He had always shrunk with
a sensitive dislike from the outward display of his
feelings; he always had great difficulty in expressing them, however strong they might be, and now
he was sensible that, for anything he had said to the
contrary, Allerton might easily think he cared but
little for him.

In the hurry of his excitement, he thought first
of the ideal wife, then of the lost friend—and all

the time struggled to master his emotions. It is strange how, when the feelings are more than usually strong, and the habit of self-control has become habitual, a man will battle with himself from mere habit, even when he is far too miserable to care whether his emotions master him or not. He walked about the library, still holding the picture in his hands, and struggling with a suffocating sensation in his throat; at last he looked at it, and happily for himself, was subdued by its tranquil smile, laid it down, and covering his face with his hands, threw himself upon his couch, and gave way to a passion of tears.

He thought, and thought a long time, and at length, between exhaustion and excitement, he fell into a troubled dream; but it seemed to himself that he could scarcely have closed his eyes before he was aroused by a brisk knocking at the door: his servant had come to remind him that it wanted but a quarter to three, it was quite time to set off for the funeral, and his horse was at the door.

What wonder if, in his hurry and excitement, he forgot the injunction never to mount him again, and set off far less able to control him than usual?

END OF VOLUME I.

G G

ALEX. MACINTOSH,
PRINTER,
GREAT NEW-STREET, LONDON.

ALLERTON AND DREUX;

OR,

𝕮𝔥𝔢 𝖂𝔞𝔯 𝔬𝔣 𝕺𝔭𝔦𝔫𝔦𝔬𝔫.

BY

THE AUTHOR OF "A RHYMING CHRONICLE."

IN TWO VOLUMES.

VOL. II.

LONDON:

WERTHEIM AND MACINTOSH,
24, PATERNOSTER-ROW.

IPSWICH: HUNT AND SON. DUBLIN: CURRY AND CO.
1851.

MACINTOSH, PRINTER,
GREAT NEW-STREET, LONDON.

CONTENTS.

CHAPTER XV.

THE FUNERAL BELL.

It was a beautiful afternoon, about three o'clock, when Marion and her brother went out by the North-road for a ride; Marion's foot was not yet quite strong enough to admit of her walking, but Elizabeth had lent her her horse, and none of the home party had proposed to accompany the brother and sister, as they wished to give them this opportunity for conversation together.

After riding for about two miles, they turned down a by-road with tall hazel hedges—the leaves of which were already beginning to wear the autumnal tint—and threaded it as it wound along at the foot of the hills, and by the sides of corn-fields and copses. The yellow sunshine lay softly on the landscape, and there was that thin, dream-like haze hanging over the distant woods, which often gives such an air of quiet to an August afternoon. They rode on for several miles in this by-road, talking principally of their friends at Swanstead, and relating various little things to each other, which

never would have been told but for an opportunity
like this. At last the road took a sudden turn,
almost straight up a very high hill, and when they
had reached its summit, they involuntarily stopped
their horses, to gaze at the beautiful rich country
spread out at their feet—white cottages, with vines
trailing over walls and roof, what happy abodes
they seemed! but who could tell what passions
might fret, or what cares might cark the hearts
of those who dwelt in them!—farm-houses in the
sunny hollows—groups of hop-pickers, crowding
round the prostrate poles, in their white aprons—
cattle, knee deep in the rich grass, and by the margin
of a little river, which turned and twisted itself
in and out and here and there, wasting its time
(if time were any object) in a thousand doublings
and returnings, sometimes floating softly along,
without a ripple on its surface to show at what
rate it went, in other places so thickly and completely overgrown with rushes, that it was quite
an invisible river—a green riband winding through
the corn-fields which, where the reapers had not yet
entered them, looked like acres of rusty-coloured gold.
All perfectly still, steeped in sunshine, as quiet as
a picture or a dream. The sunbeams dropt through
the hedge, and chequered the road at their feet
in patches that did not waver; the clouds stood
still, as if the wind had gone forward and left them
behind; even the red poppies, growing so thickly
in the fields, stood upright and never nodded their

heads. There was no movement and no sound, but that inner humming which the ear itself supplies when it is empty of all sound—that slight, soft ringing, like the music in a sea-shell—a witness that "the ear is not satisfied with hearing," that it is restless for some of the sweet voices of the earth, and failing them, brings up the echo of sounds that are past.

But this silence was not for long: they had not been conscious of it many moments, when a musical note floated towards them, softened by the distance, but regular and clear; they lost it when it had been repeated twice, then a slight breeze sprung up and wafted it to them again more fully and distinctly— it was the tolling of a funeral bell.

Marion and her brother looked across the valley and up the opposite hill. There was a village church near its summit, with a slender white spire; the rest of the building was nearly hidden by a group of chesnut-trees crowded before it and sloping down the side of the hill; but the porch could be distinctly seen, and a few scattered gravestones in the church-yard. It was from this spire that the sounds proceeded, passing over the valley to the height where they were, which appeared nearly level with it. They heard the bell much more distinctly now that they had got accustomed to its tones; and as they went at a slow pace along the ridge of the hill, they saw the rustic funeral procession winding through the valley, the mourners (chiefly women) with heads bowed down, and white hoods, which showed the youth of the deceased, the black pall with its snowy border glancing out from time to time in its slow progress between the trees.

They went on for another half-mile in silence. Many thoughts had been aroused by this scene. That state of feeling, which has been well called the " still sad music of humanity," was awakened in their hearts, and the funeral bell kept time to the strain.

We cannot fathom our own souls; and, especially among the young, there are many who have never considered how much they may be made to suffer. But sometimes—quite unexpectedly, it may be, even to themselves—their serenity is disturbed, and even in the happiest circumstances. The sight of human grief,—the flashing conviction of some approaching sorrow,—the sudden, though but momentary perception of a vague trouble hanging over the heads of some beloved objects—an insight, though but for a short time, into the wearing anxiety that haunts the paths of so many,—sometimes even a glance at a stranger's face, will give a pang of sudden fear and shrinking before the pains, the troubles, and the separations, which are even for them most surely and steadily approaching; and the young heart, sheltered as yet under the shadow of protecting love, begins to count over the number of its gourds, and wonder which of them will soonest wither away.

But it soon passes, this feeling. Early, happy youth is so incredulous; it believes only in theory that this is a world of woe. It easily forgets the short glimpse it has taken, and even though it should ponder with dutiful consideration over the complainings of some aged friend, or stretch its powers of fellow-feeling to enter into the misfortunes of all whom it loves, there is still a kind of luxury in the bestowal of this sympathy. There is something sweet in tears shed for others,—unselfish tears, and not divided between another's sorrow and one's own. In a case like this, oh! how much more blessed it is to *give* than to *receive!*

The funeral bell went on, but the funeral procession was out of sight. THEY had not seen the face of the dead,—they could not hear the bitter sobs of the mother!

The afternoon sun shone upon the long road stretching up to the church; the spire looked white and beautiful, and the sound of the bell floated through the sunny air, divested of its sadness, or retaining only enough to give sentiment to the scene.

But what was this? They had reached a turn in the lane, and come in view of two cottages a little further down, when a labouring man darted through the hedge just before Marion's horse, and cried out some unintelligible warning. The next instant a saddle-horse dashed past them at full gallop, the stirrups flying in the air. The man had already seized Marion's horse by the reins, and was trying to quiet it. The lane was so narrow that it was a marvel how any thing going with such speed could have passed between them without unseating either. Her brother, who had now dismounted, came and took the reins from her unknown friend, who speedily helped her down; and in a cloud of dust, and between two frightened horses, Marion found herself holding the labouring man by the wrist, and begging him to tell her what was the matter.

The man took the reins, and called to Wilfred: " Get the lady up the bank, Sir."

There was a high grass bank at the side of the lane. He had scarcely time to comply with this command, which was given in the most peremptory manner, when back came the runaway horse, wild with terror, and one of their own horses was struggling in the dust. It was up again in an instant, and tugging at the reins, with a cut and bleeding head.

There was another man helping, and the first was chiding him, in no very measured terms, for having tried to stop " yon mad brute," by which, it seemed, he had sent it down again upon them.

Marion, half-fainting with fear, held by her brother. She had seen something carried into one of the cottages by two men,—something perfectly passive and motionless,—and she knew it must be the unfortunate rider of the runaway horse, whose progress could now be marked by a rapidly advancing cloud of dust.

"What is the matter?" exclaimed Wilfred,— "and what is all this?"

"The clergyman, Sir,—him that came from Westport to bury poor old Maxwell's grand-daughter."

"Thrown!" cried Wilfred. "Where is he, then?—hurt or killed?—or—what have you done with him? Can't we help him?"

"Thrown, Sir;—looked back just as he come to that first cottage;—horse shied, frightened, I reckon;—pitched on his head, poor gentleman."

"Oh! Wilfred," cried Marion, quivering with terror, "do, pray, go and see."

"Yes, my dear,—I will, indeed, Marion; but I can't leave you in this state."

"Put the lady on your own horse, Sir," said the labourer. "I'll engage to lead him; he's quite quiet. Bless you, Sir, she can't walk! We'll take her to the other cottage."

"No," said Marion, ready to faint, "not into that cottage."

"No, no, we're not a going to Maxwell's cottage," said the man, his rough voice instantly assuming the tone in which he might have spoken to a pretty child; "we're a going to t'other cottage, yonder, with the porch. Don't be frightened, Miss, there's a dear."

So saying, he took her up in his arms, set her on

Wilfred's horse, and held her on. It was not fifty yards to the cottage.

"Did you say it was a gentleman from Westport?" asked Wilfred.

"Yes, Sir. Be you from Westport?"

"Yes; but who was it? Don't you know his name?"

The man glanced at Marion. "You may as well go and see him, Sir, yourself first."

"Thank you for your consideration," said Marion; "but it's not at all likely to be any one I know. Poor man! Oh! I hope he is not very much injured."

The man shook his head, and answered Wilfred's question: "It's Mr. Dreux, Sir. Our parson being out, he came over to take the funeral. They've carried him into Maxwell's cottage."

Marion caught the name, and instantly begged her brother to let her go with him.

They were now at the cottage door. The man lifted her down, and set a chair for her. Her tremor had entirely subsided, but she wept violently with dread and excitement, while the funeral bell still sounded softly over the valley.

"Marion, you may come in afterwards, if you will let me go in first;—you may even be of use."

Marion promised to wait.

"So you do know the poor gentleman?" said the labourer. "Well, keep up heart then, Miss. Why, if he's not past everything, he'll be main glad to have somebody about him that's not strange. So keep up heart, Miss."

" Oh, yes," faltered Marion, very glad of this rough kindness. " Indeed, I am trying to be calm."

All was perfectly still within the cottage. Marion listened with sharpened senses, but there was no questioning voice of sympathy, and no answer; no sound like complaining, not a groan, not a sigh.

Presently her brother came out.

" He is not killed!" whispered Marion, shuddering. " Oh! don't tell me that he is killed!"

" No, Marion, but quite insensible. You may come."

He led her through the small front kitchen, which was quite empty, and opening the door of a very low, whitewashed chamber on the ground-floor, beckoned her in.

He was lying on a narrow pallet bed, with his eyes shut, and the usual expression of his face not much altered. There were no signs of external injury beyond a bruise over the left temple, but he was breathing uneasily, and there was a convulsive quivering about his lips.

Greyson stooped to loosen the white handkerchief about his neck.

'· Have they sent for a surgeon?" said Marion, hurriedly. " Oh! I hope they have."

" I know nothing. Can you watch beside him

while I go and see about it? Be calm, Marion;
remember we are responsible for everything that is
done."

"Oh, yes; indeed, I am calm. Leave me with
him."

As her brother hurried out of the room, she first
observed the presence of a miserable old woman,
who was sitting on the only chair the place afforded,
at the right side of the bed.

"Oh! my girl, my poor girl!" muttered the
palsied creature, when Marion looked at her;—
" who's to bury her? Oh! my poor daughter!—
she'll break her heart this day!"

There was a close, oppressive feeling in the air
of the chamber, and there was nothing on the low
bedstead but the mattrass. The feather bed, the
clothes, and even the pillows were gone, and she
felt conscious that this must be the chamber, and
this the bed, from which they had just carried the
coffin. She hastened to open the window, and as
she stood watching the utterly insensible form, her
excited fancy was busy with the funeral. She
wondered what the people would do, now there was
no one to bury the dead. Would they bring the
coffin back, and think to lay it there again? The
funeral bell kept tolling on. Oh! that it would
cease! She thought it disturbed her patient, for
he sighed deeply, and his face assumed a touching
expression of sorrow and perplexity.

Marion knelt down by the low bed, and gently

drew off his gloves. Then she stepped out into the
little garden at the back of the cottage, and brought
some cold water from a pump, with which she bathed
his forehead and the palms of his hands. She
thought he could not be perfectly unconscious, for
he muttered to himself, and often threw up his arms
as if he would have touched his head, but easily
allowed himself to be thwarted by her, as she took
hold of them and drew them away.

Scarcely daring to breathe, she knelt and watched
his face, which gradually assumed a look less and
less like its own. It was not a look of pain, nor of
fear, but rather of indescribable forlornness, which
took possession of his features. There was a disturbed and yet helpless restlessness about the slight
movement of his head, and when he whispered, as
he often did, they were broken and incoherent
words, but always seemed to express trouble and
perplexity.

Her brother came to the door and beckoned the
old woman away; Marion was left alone to watch
him. The funeral-bell kept tolling on, so clearly
and distinctly in the silence, that it marked by every
stroke how fitful and irregular, how hurried and
tremulous was the breathing of the injured man.

The afternoon sun streamed in upon the clear
white-washed walls, through vine-leaves and flowering plants, which were trained outside the casement;
the soft slight air came in, and moved the hair upon
his temples. As she held his hand, she fancied

there was a change again for the better. He was breathing more freely; she stooped to listen, and he started and uttered her name distinctly, but in a whisper. He had never opened his eyes; but Marion, forgetting that if he had been really conscious of her presence, or sensible enough to be aware of what he said, he would not have addressed her by her Christian name, was relieved by what she took for a token of returning consciousness, and answered soothingly, "I am here, my dear Mr. Dreux; what can I do for you?" But he took no notice of her voice; his breathing again became quick and heavy, and his restlessness increased so much that she had great difficulty in holding back his hands from his head. While inexpressibly touched to find herself the subject of his impressions at such a time, when he seemed incapable of actual thought, she wept bitterly, and watched every movement and every change with a beating heart.

In the meantime the labouring man before mentioned had been sent by Wilfred upon his own horse, to a village two miles off, where the nearest surgeon lived. The road lay by the church, where the people were waiting with the dead woman. He was to tell them of the accident, and go as quickly as possible on his errand. There was no one left in either cottage but this poor old woman, and Greyson hoped some of the mourners would return, and render some assistance or advice as to what should be done for the patient.

To the restlessness of feeling himself responsible was now added anxiety at the non-return of his messenger. It was three-quarters of an hour since he had started, and there was no appearance of him yet, though he kept pacing about the road before the cottages, looking out in all directions. He came back to the bed-side, agitated and flushed. Of the two men who had carried in Mr. Dreux, one was of weak mind, and not capable of taking a message; the other had gone off in pursuit of the runaway horse, and had not made his appearance since.

"Oh, this waiting is dreadful," said Marion; "and every moment we are losing may be of the utmost consequence."

"Yes, Marion, but what can be done? Shall I set off to run to Westport?"

"If I only had some leeches," murmured Marion; "I am sure that must be a proper remedy, and I cannot endure this inaction any longer."

"Marion, he looks a great deal worse; I saw a great change when I came in. Oh, what shall we do!"

"If so be as you want leeches," said the palsy-stricken woman, who had followed Greyson into the chamber,—"if so be as you want leeches, and *would take some o' me?*"

"Where are they? O yes, of course, we'll take them."

The old woman hobbled to a closet in the wall, and brought out a bottle with a great number in it.

" The Doctor ordered 'em for my poor dear, the night afore she died," she said, holding out the bottle; " but, hows'ever, she was dead afore they comed into the house, so you 'll pay me for 'em, dear ?"

" Yes, O yes," cried Marion, hastily laying aside her hat and veil, and preparing to use them.

The old woman could give no assistance, but care and tenderness made up to Marion for her slender experience. As soon as they were on, she entreated her brother to return to Westport for a physician. It was eight miles off, and he would be obliged to go on foot, as her horse was hurt; but then their messenger was not returned, and they could think of nothing else to be done.

With a hurried glance at the patient, he left the room, closing the door after him. He had not been gone ten minutes when Mr. Dreux opened his eyes for the first time, and looked Marion full in the face. It was a look which expressed neither surprise at seeing her there, nor recognition, nor consciousness, —nothing but a vacant stare. His eyes soon wandered from her; he began to talk hurriedly, and used several incoherent expressions of pain, making repeated attempts to throw up his hands.

Fully occupied now, Marion knelt at his head, sometimes speaking to him, at others listening sadly to the quick, restless breathing, which was accompanied by a sound like low, suppressed sobbing. There was something terrible to Marion in the

responsibility of her situation; every change, every
start, sent the blood to her heart. But at length
she had the inexpressible relief of seeing his eyes
gradually close again, and the forlorn expression
which had so much alarmed her fade by slow and
almost imperceptible degrees. She could scarcely
tell when and how the change had been effected,
but the dreaded look was gone, and in its place was
a quiet natural expression, only clouded by weariness and pain.

In a little time longer his breathing became regular
and soft, his lips ceased to tremble, and the burning
hand, which had been so restless and quick in its
movements, now closed languidly upon hers. The
old woman was sensible of the change, and as she
hobbled to Marion's side, to give what little assistance she could with her palsied hands, she whispered
that she was main glad the leeches had done so well,
and did not add anything this time about her desire
for payment.

At this instant the sound of voices was heard in
the outer room; the old woman opened the door, and
left her alone; she closed it after her, but Marion
could distinctly hear the sobbing of some person in
great sorrow, while several others were trying to
comfort her.

She knew these must be the returned mourners,
but was just then so fully occupied as to have no
time for thought on the subject, beyond a wish that
they might not come in and interrupt her. This

wish, however, was not gratified, for in a few minutes a decent-looking woman, in a black gown and white hood, came in and closed the door after her. She had evidently been crying bitterly, and her eyes were red and swollen; but the moment she saw how Marion was occupied, she applied herself to assist her, with great skill and tenderness. In the deepest silence the next half-hour passed, though not without many cheering hopes on Marion's part. Her patient seemed now to have sunk into a natural easy sleep. He was perfectly quiet and calm,—so very calm and still, that but for a slight movement about his parted lips, she might easily have thought he had ceased to breathe. She watched him intently, almost breathlessly. The noble features were perfectly colourless, their expression touchingly pensive. She thought the room was too light, and arose to draw the remains of a tattered curtain across the casement.

The rest of the mourners had left the front room, and gone over to the opposite cottage, and there was no sound but the cautious footsteps of the woman, as she passed in and out, bringing what Marion required. She had lighted a fire in the front room, and set on a kettle; she seemed not at all surprised or distressed, and asked no questions, but applied herself at once to the business in hand; and when at length their task was over, and all signs of it cleared away, she set a chair for Marion, and left her to watch for the waking of the patient. The time had seemed very long to Marion, but on a reference to her watch she found her brother had only been away an hour; it was therefore another hour before he could be expected back; but Mr. Dreux's perfect tranquillity made her feel sure she had been doing right, and she sat down to watch him with recovered composure. She had taken off her hat and veil, and now that the heat of the afternoon was moderated by a slight breeze, the colour began to return to her pale cheek.

In a short time the kind cottager returned, and brought her a cup of tea, begging her not to mind being left alone, as she had sent her neighbours to the opposite cottage with her mother and grandmother, lest they should make too much noise.

Marion detained her to ask, " Was the poor young woman who is dead your sister ? "

" Yes ; and mother takes on much worse than ever now "——

" Because there was no one to bury her ! What, then, have they done with the body ?"

" Two neighbours stayed in the porch, ma'am, to watch the coffin. Mr. Clay (the Vicar of a neighbouring village) will be home at nine o'clock to-night, and she's to be buried then."

" I feel the more grateful for the help you have given me, as you are in so much trouble yourself."

" Ah ! Miss, we shall get on badly in this world unless we're willing to help one another."

Marion took the cup, and thanked her. It might

have been the sound of their voices, or the closing
of the door, that aroused the sleeper, for when she
looked again his eyes were open.   He looked at her
with some slight surprise, but presently he closed
them again, saying, in a faint voice, "Only a
dream."   Sinking to sleep again, Marion watched
him with the cup in her hand.   She had greatly
hoped that when he next awoke he would be
sensible, and it was a great disappointment to find,
as she believed, that this was not the case.   She
resumed her kneeling position, and held back his
hands.   In a few minutes he awoke again, with a
sudden start of pain, and uttered a few uneasy
words about not liking to be left alone.   Marion
held the cup to his parched lips, and as he drained
the welcome draught, she said, in the softest tones
of her sweet voice, " *He* has said, ' I will never
leave thee nor forsake thee.' "

Her attitude as she leaned towards him, and the
earnest expression of her eyes, seemed to arrest his
attention, but still, not quite satisfied as to the
reality of her presence, he lifted up his hand, and
as if wishing to try whether she was sensible to
touch, took one of her long soft curls in it, and
remained gazing at her with a kind of tranquil
wonder.

But Marion had endured too much anxiety, and was
too free from any other feeling towards him than desire
for his recovery, to be much abashed by this scrutiny,
and gently disengaging her hair, she said a few quiet

words to him expressive of her hope that he would not attempt to move (for he had tried to raise his head), and going to the door she asked for some more tea, as she thought it had refreshed him.

Gradually as he looked round the room, after she had returned to her seat, he seemed to understand what had happened, and when she had given him the tea, he was perfectly collected, and appeared easy, or at least free from any acute pain.

Marion sat perfectly quiet, scarcely venturing to change her position, for she saw that now he was satisfied of her actual presence it excited him,—the pulse in his temples became more rapid, and his veins swelled and throbbed. She wished him to sleep again, and hoped at first that her silence might enable him to do so, but she soon found that his mind was now painfully awake, and at work; and sensible that nothing would be more likely to soothe him than the idea that his recovery was a subject of great solicitude with her, she ventured to talk to him in a calm, gentle tone, with the acceptable tenderness which women know so well how to bestow on invalids. Then, finding that her words had their desired effect, she went on to speak gently to him of the sympathy of Christ. The subdued tones of her voice, and the solicitude expressed in her face, gradually calmed his excitement, and he presently sunk again into a deep but tolerably quiet sleep.

And now Marion's watch was over. She heard the

sound of carriage wheels at the gate, and the next
minute her aunt, with Wilfred and two physicians,
entered the little chamber.

Marion was not aware, till the necessity for
exertion was over, how greatly she had been
excited. As soon as she saw her aunt the tears
began to flow fast from her eyes, and she became
very faint. They took her to the little open casement, and as soon as she recovered herself she
inquired nervously whether what she had done was
right.

" Quite right, my dear Miss Greyson," said the
elder of the two physicians, turning from the pallet;
and then advancing to Mrs. Paton, he said, as he
felt her niece's pulse, " You will be glad to hear
that there is no fracture."

"Aunt," said Marion, " where is Elinor? and
have you brought a nurse?"

" Mrs. Silverstone is coming, my dear; she
is to tell Elinor of the accident, and bring her
here."

" Oh, we shall do very well for a nurse," said the
physician, " and you are no longer responsible, my
dear Miss Greyson, so don't make yourself uneasy;
you have done wonders."

But it was so obvious that she was uneasy, that
as her aunt arranged her hair, and assisted her
with her hat, she reminded her in a low voice
that her staying any longer was quite out of the
question.

"O yes, I know, aunt," said Marion, glancing at the patient.

"But, my dear," returned her aunt, "if it would be a satisfaction to you, *I* will stay and attend to Dr. Grainger's directions, till Mrs. Silverstone comes, and Elinor."

"Oh, thank you, aunt," said Marion, drawing the gloves on to her trembling hands. "If you would, I should be so thankful."

"And now come, Marion," said her brother hastily, "and when you get into the air you will feel better again."

Marion turned to kiss her aunt, and suffered herself to be led away, her boy-brother being in an agony lest she should appear too much distressed, though he probably might have forgotten her dignity on such an occasion, if the unlucky charade had not been fresh in his mind.

She had scarcely reached the carriage, when the woman who had rendered her so much assistance came up and pulled her by the sleeve. Marion looked round.

"I beg your pardon, Miss," said the woman, who did not much like her errand, "but grandmother will keep worriting about the leeches. She seems to think you owe her for 'em. Grandmother's old and childish, Miss," she added, colouring deeply as she observed Marion's perplexed look, "and she would not be satisfied without I told you of it."

"Oh, I know what she means," said Greyson,

drawing out his purse and giving the woman some silver   "Yes, you're quite right; I am sorry I forgot it."

"You are still there, my dear," said Mrs. Paton, coming up to the carriage door; "I am glad of that.   Come back for a moment—I want you, Marion."

Marion followed her aunt into the chamber. Mr. Dreux was awake; and Dr. Grainger, who was feeling his pulse, waved his hand towards her, and said, encouragingly, "There, my dear Sir, you see you are not so bad as you thought; it was no delirious fancy.   Are you satisfied now?"

Whatever Dr. Grainger might say, or however light he might make of the patient's condition, his expression of countenance was anything but satisfactory, and when Mr. Dreux lifted his eyes to Marion's face, he looked at him in a manner which betrayed a good deal of uneasiness.

"Are you content now?" he asked, in the same soothing tone, in which a little very gentle banter was mixed; "or are we to say it was only a dream?"

Marion saw the same uncertainty in his face which had before prompted him to touch her, and wishing to remove it, she drew nearer, and laid her hand upon his as the Doctor held it.   It was burning hot, and even in the short time she touched it she felt the rapidly-going pulse,—yet the desired effect was produced, for though he said nothing, his face instantly became calm, and, as if he dreaded the least excitement, he turned away and closed his eyes.

The physician made a sign to her that she might go, so after taking a last hurried look, she left the cottage, threw herself into a corner of the carriage, and gave free course to her tears.

But not for long. She soon began to listen to her brother, who kept industriously plying her with consolation, as is the custom with many kind people, who, if they see you in distress, contrive to find so many alleviating and comforting circumstances in the case, that at last they seem to make out, to their own satisfaction (if not to yours), that on the whole it was rather fortunate than otherwise that the distressing circumstance occurred.

It certainly was a consolation to find she had done right, and it was another that her aunt was going to stay at the cottage a few hours longer, and would bring tidings in the evening as to how the physicians thought their patient. So Marion dried her eyes, and looked out of the window, trying very hard to be calm and composed.

The sun was getting very low. It illuminated the windows of the church on the hill, so that they looked as if they were lighted from within with burning torches. It streamed through the thick foliage of the trees, and made of the dark clouds on the horizon a fine background for the white spire. There was the little river winding through the valley—the reapers and the hop-pickers were coming home through the corn—the poppies were waving in the soft evening air,—but there was no funeral bell now to startle a serene heart with its unwelcome forebodings.

The landscape before her was toned down, its colours had lost much of their brilliance; but the tone of her feelings was also lowered, they had changed very much since she rode between those hazel hedges glowing in the broad sunshine of an August afternoon, and on reflecting, she almost wished that secure feeling of happiness which she had felt during the beginning of her ride might never come again; it would be better, she thought, never to rest at ease and in such tranquil quietness than to be so rudely startled from it. The sorrow and anxiety would be easier to bear if they were not so utterly unexpected.

Soon after Marion left the cottage Elinor arrived, with Mrs. Dorothy Silverstone. She behaved with wonderful self-possession, and when she had seen her brother, and observed the slightness of the external injury, she was evidently greatly relieved; and though Dr. Grainger said nothing in reply to her expressions of thankfulness that the accident was no worse, she was too much absorbed to observe it.

Soon after the physicians were gone, the invalid awoke suddenly, and said, in a hurried whisper, " Where's Allerton ? " Mrs. Dorothy put him off with some slight answer, and Elinor's emotion seemed to her the natural consequence of hearing him speak for the first time. It was a trial she had to endure many times during the night, for he never awoke without asking the same question, being generally satisfied when she came up to him and laid her hand on his, or held some cooling drink to his parched lips. She felt quite sure that they had parted in anger, and a few broken words which he uttered now and then confirmed her in this conviction. Having her own private sources of sorrow added to her anxiety for him, it was no wonder that she exhausted herself with weeping, and that every repetition of the question cost her a renewal of her tears.

In the morning Dr. Grainger came and a surgeon with him. Her brother was awake, and, though feeble, did not seem to be in pain. Elinor was struck by their gravity, and watched them as if her life hung on their words. They took seats close to him, and asked one or two questions, which he answered collectedly. Then the surgeon said, in an abstracted tone, "Let me see, what day is this?"

"Ah, what day?" repeated Dr. Grainger, as if he could not remember it either.

Mr. Dreux answered, with a movement of irritation, "It's Thursday."

"Is it?" said the Doctor, composedly and slowly; "yes, I think it is; and what day of the month, I wonder?"

" Sunday was the 16th," said the invalid, turning his head restlessly on the pillow, " so this is the 20th."

Upon this they seemed pleased, and presently went into the outer room to confer together.

After a short interval Elinor followed them. " We think the patient somewhat improved," said the senior physician in answer to her appealing look. " His mind is clearer than could be expected. He has certainly a great deal of fever."

" I hope he is not in danger," said Elinor, the idea occurring to her for the first time.

" I shall come again in the afternoon," said Doctor Grainger, without answering her question.

" But he is not in danger ? " repeated Elinor. " Oh, don't tell me that he is ! "

" Why, there is a certain degree of danger attending all illness," said the physician, slowly.   Elinor shuddered.   " We shall hope to find him somewhat better to-morrow," he continued, soothingly.

" And if he is worse ? "—

" Oh, we must not distress ourselves with such a fear.   Sufficient unto the day is the evil thereof."

Elinor returned to the room and gazed at her brother with a sinking heart.   He was just sufficiently sensible to be aware that if he talked he should talk nonsense ; but a confused recollection of his quarrel with Allerton continually tormented him.   He was divided between his desire to see him and a half-recollection that he ought not to talk of

him. In spite of this he found himself often asking
for him, and his kind old friend increased his perplexity by promising that he should see him soon.
Towards afternoon he became less restless, and hope
strengthened again in Elinor's heart. She needed
some encouragement, for her mind was exhausted
with anxiety as well as her bodily strength. About
four o'clock the physician came again, and said he
was much the same.

Mrs. Dorothy then wished Elinor to go to bed,
and though she could scarcely endure to leave her
brother, she had not strength to resist long, and had
but just laid her head on the pillow, when she fell
into a heavy sleep.

It was hours before she awoke, which she did at
last in a fright, and hurried down to her brother's
room. It was the middle of the night, and the
place was still as nothing but a sick man's
chamber can be. The nurse and Mrs. Silverstone
were sitting up, the former dozing in her chair:
the latter nodded encouragingly to Elinor, and
pointed to her brother, who was lying in a deep
sleep. Elinor recovered from her nightmare terror
and gratefully kissed the old lady, who urged her to
retire till morning, reminding her that she would
have to sit up the next night, and entreating her
not to waste her strength needlessly. Elinor could
not comply. She sat watching with the other two
attendants through the rest of the night, and was

still close to her brother, holding his feverish hand, when the physicians arrived.

"He is rather better to-day," they said, "but he must be kept extremely quiet and nearly in darkness."

Elinor followed them into the next room, and said, with a face of terror, "But he did not speak collectedly to-day. Is he delirious?"

"That confusion is partly the effect of opiates," was the reply; and again she was put off with a hope of the favourable things they thought they should have to tell to-morrow.

She felt relieved of a part of the weight which had pressed down her soul; but though she believed they really thought him better, it frightened her to hear him talk at random, especially as the one theme of his rambling thoughts was still Allerton, an endless succession of regrets that he was not there, and entreaties that he might be sent for.

"Which we can't do, my dear," Mrs. Dorothy said with a sigh, "for Dr. Grainger tells me Mr. Allerton's ill—confined to his room, I think he told me."

Elinor knew that whatever her brother might say, they could not send for Allerton, and anxious as this information made her about him, she was glad that, in the old lady's eyes, there existed a sufficient reason for his absence.

In the evening they again came to see their

patient, and still said he was better,—decidedly
better, and were obviously both surprised and
pleased to find him so.

Elinor sat by him that night, and in the morning
she felt that he now really was better; his face had
resumed its usual expression, and, owing to the
shortness of his illness, his features were very little
changed.

She met the physicians with a tranquil face, and
read their favourable report in their eyes before
they left her brother.

"He really is better now, I am sure of it," she
said, as she joined them in the front room.

" Yes, really better, and there is now little fear
of a relapse."

They then desired her to take some rest, and
went away, she feeling now as unduly elated as
if her brother had not another peril to encounter,
and might expect to go home in a day or two.

He was awake when she returned, and leaning
over his pillow smoothed it tenderly, and spoke to
him with all her own gentle hopefulness.

" Am I better ?" he inquired.

" Yes, much better, dearest," she replied, "but
you will be very quiet, will you not ? You will
not move, nor even *think ? "*

"Very well," he answered, and shut his eyes to
ponder on something which had been puzzling him
for several hours.

The influence of the opiates was now completely

spent; the nurse and Elinor had retired, leaving
him alone with Mrs. Dorothy. He knew she would
not be induced to talk to him, and therefore there
was nothing left for him but to speculate over and
over again on the same puzzling subject. His fever
was rapidly subsiding; the furniture, which hitherto
had seemed to spin round him, every object invested
with a dazzling halo, had now settled down steadily;
his thoughts were becoming distinct, and his
recollections defined; he was perversely disinclined
to sleep, and an event or a dream of the night presented itself to him in vivid colouring. It must
have been in the night, for he remembered that
a small lamp was burning on the floor, shaded with
an open book, that the light might not come near
him. The nurse was in the front room, dozing, no
doubt; and his sister, who was alone with him, was
sitting on a cushion at the foot of the pallet-bed, and
resting her head on a pillow; he could see her face,
which still bore the traces of tears,—her dishevelled
hair had fallen back from it, but sleep had restored
the bloom to her cheeks, for he remembered that
she certainly *was asleep*, and that he had tried to
calculate how many nights she had sat up with him.
After this he had shut his eyes again, and got
entangled in the meshes of a half-delirious dream,
till a slight noise startled him, and he had awoke
with his oft-repeated exclamation, " Where's Allerton ? "

His sister still slept. He had spoken in a con-

fused whisper. He was conscious of the presence
of a man standing near him, and when he could
collect his thoughts he saw that it was Allerton;
but looking dreadfully pale, and gazing at him with
an expression of agony which had caused him to
close his eyes and turn away, for he could not bear
to be disturbed.

What happened next he could not recollect. He
thought it must have been some time after this that
Allerton had said, "Do you know me, Dreux?"
and that he had tried to answer, but had failed.
After this, by degrees, as he thought on the subject,
his recollection recovered the confused interval of
delirium which had followed. He remembered
putting up his hands, under the impression that the
ceiling was falling upon him. This interval seemed
an hour, but it might have occupied but two
minutes. Then he remembered seeing Allerton
kneeling by his bed, that he was holding one of his
hands, that his head was bowed down, his chest
heaved, and he wept with such bitterness of agony
as none but natures so loving and so passionate
can. He saw that his sister still slept, and remembered that, as Allerton knelt by him, he poured
forth against himself the most bitter reproaches and
uttered the most poignant regrets. He thought
that, at every pause, he had tried to answer him,
but without success, he supposed; for, when Allerton lifted up his face and looked at him, he had
certainly addressed him, but not as a man who was

capable of observing him or at all conscious of his presence. He had known, at the time, that this was a mistake, and that he was quite collected. He had tried once more to speak to him, and had said, " Don't distress yourself, I am better."

He remarked that Allerton had looked at him with almost incredulous hope when he said it, and had bent his head to listen, upon which he had repeated the sentence, adding a desire that he would stay a while, and a wonder that he had never been before.

He had scarcely said this when he remembered their quarrel, and all the circumstances respecting his sister came clearly back to him. He tried to raise his head, and, as he did so, Allerton put his arm under it, and said, with deep regret, but not as if addressing him,—" Is it all forgotten?—and so soon. Oh, the dreadful cause !"

Upon this he found strength to answer, in a low, faint voice, " I remember it now ; and how we parted."

He had not intended to give pain by this remark, but he observed that Allerton shuddered on hearing it and lowered his head again. He did not feel any answering emotion, and again became very much confused.

As he now lay awake in the broad daylight, he did not recover these slight circumstances and their sequence without a considerable effort ; he was still weak enough to be wearied by it, and sunk to sleep.

It was afternoon when he awoke. Elinor was sitting by him; she gave him some jelly, and then, it being a very sultry afternoon, she opened the door, which led into the garden, and he instantly remembered that he had seen the man enter by that door before he knew who he was.

As he lay awake, looking out into the green shady garden, he began to speculate as to whether this visit of Allerton's was a reality or a dream. He now recollected various other circumstances, but whether his active imagination had suggested them during this last sleep, whether he had dreamed them during the night, or whether they were waking truths, he could not decide. He carried down his supposed recollections, step by step, to the point where he had left them in the morning. He thought, after this, he must have talked confusedly, for the next thing he recollected was Allerton's voice, in its lowest tones, trying to soothe him; he had mastered his emotion, and was looking earnestly at him, as if waiting for an answer to some question.

" Can you ever forgive me," he repeated, speaking in suppressed tones. " If you can, oh, let me hear you say it before we part, perhaps for ever."

He had answered to the purpose, though he did not know what.

Allerton went on:—" The last time we were together you called me ' brother.' I did not care for it then, but, oh! how happy it would make me to hear you say it now!"

He knew he had exerted himself to say the required word, upon which Allerton embraced him and went away, he supposed; for when he next awoke, his sister was close to him, holding him by the hand, and telling him what a delightful sleep he had had.

He replied, as she thought, at random: "And if he was really here, of course he will come again?"

His sister kissed him tenderly, and said, "Dearest Arthur, you always awake so much confused." As she handed some lemonade to him, she said, "Where is the ether?"

Elinor's eyes filled with tears when he answered, "Allerton put it on that chair."

The ether was standing on the chair.

Elinor said, "No doubt nurse put it there, dear." She was going to add,—"I wish you could spare me the constant mention of Mr. Allerton's name," but she saw that he was perplexed, and tried to divert him from the subject by remarks on indifferent matters. This would not do. He presently said:—

"*You* did not see him, of course, my love; you were asleep."

"I asleep, Arthur!" said Elinor, with an incredulous smile. "O no; try to think of something else,—Mr. Allerton will not come; it was only your wish to see him that made you dream of him. Don't you remember telling me that we must both learn to do without him?"

"But he did come."

"Why, it's not yet dawn. Would he come in the middle of the night, dearest? Well, but, Arthur, if he came once, he will assuredly come again."

"Yes, I suppose he will."

"Then, if he does not come to-day, you will try not to be always thinking about him and expecting him."

Elinor now hoped she had shaken what she considered a half-delirious fancy, and went on, in a soothing voice: "And you never ask after your other friends, Arthur. Don't you remember the Greysons, how kind they were to you? Are there no people in the world that you care for besides Mr. Allerton?"

"Yes, I suppose so. Tell me their names."

"Dear Arthur,—well, I am one of them."

"Yes; come and lay your head on my pillow. Don't cry, Elinor,—this confusion in my head makes me say inconsiderate things."

This short conversation with Elinor did not form a part of his present speculations, but he now began to remember his duty, and inquired whether a Sunday had passed during his illness, who had served his church, and who had undertaken his various other engagements.

Mrs. Dorothy Silverstone was always with him in Elinor's absence, but she would not give him much information, and advised him not to talk. But the crisis was passed, and though he still felt extremely feeble, he was already beginning to suffer from the peculiar restlessness attending convalescence. In the afternoon Elinor came again, and his kind old friend left him for a few hours. He then tried what he could do with his sister, and nothing but her perfect ignorance of what had been going on since his illness prevented her from answering any question he chose to ask. He then wished her to read to him, but she had scarcely found a Bible when Doctor Grainger came in. Again Elinor saw the expression of surprise, as well as pleasure.

He beckoned to her to follow him, and said, "We find Mr. Dreux remarkably well this afternoon. We are inclined to think the injury to the brain must have been much slighter than was at first apprehended; it is not by any means sufficient to account for all this fever."

He then questioned her as to her brother's previous state of health, and asked whether anything had lately happened which was likely to have shocked and distressed him. Elinor said nothing, but her face was a sufficient answer.

"Well, then," said the friendly physician, "if Mr. Dreux has another good night I shall hope to pronounce him out of danger; and, probably, in about a week or ten days he may be able to return home."

How light her heart was during the rest of the day, or how happy she felt, it would be impossible to describe; the absorbing nature of her trial, and the great personal exertion it had involved, had, for the time, thrown her previous sorrow into the background. If she had lost her brother, she felt that this additional loss would almost have weighed her down, but now she incessantly repeated to herself,—"If God will only spare *him* to me, I think I can bear the other loss very well."

Completely absorbed in watching him and waiting on him, the next few days passed quietly enough with her; she almost forgot to be sorrowful while observing his gradual restoration. They were too far from Westport to allow of more than a very few inquirers after his health, and the cottages were situated in such a secluded lane that there were never any passers-by.

The people who had lived in the cottage they now occupied had been easily persuaded to give it up, by a present of money; they had taken away what little furniture they possessed, and some of a better description had been sent on to them from Westport. The woman who had assisted Marion had been retained in the character of servant; and a square carpet, a sofa, a few chairs, a table, and some few books, had completely altered the aspect of the front kitchen. The chamber in which her brother lay was equally improved, and through the open door and window he could see the long narrow garden, with its garniture of tall sunflowers, holly-hocks, its bed of thyme, sweet marjoram, and angelica, edged with double daisies, and its two "pleasure borders," filled with heart'sease, pinks, and cabbage-roses.

How happy was Elinor the first time he was able to leave his room and lie on the sofa! One of the strongest traits in her character was its hopeful-ness; she was always the first to see every good symptom, always determined to make the best of every drawback, always ready to echo his ideas when he was cheerful, and to soothe and reassure him when he was tormented with restlessness and gloom.

When Doctor Grainger came that evening he found his patient lying on the sofa, and Elinor sitting at work by the little table; she had that morning indulged herself with a walk, and the room was garnished with a number of field-flowers which she had brought in with her. Mrs. Dorothy had placed a few in her hair to please her brother, and as she moved about, her manner, though retain-ing the quietness so pleasant to invalids, was so expressive of happiness that, according to the old saying, she seemed to tread on air.

" All this morning I have fancied I heard bells, a peal of bells," she said, addressing the Doctor.

" Notwithstanding the interest that young ladies take in wedding-bells," said the old gentleman, good-humouredly, " I hold it to be impossible that you

could have heard the bells of Pelham's Church seven
or eight miles off, Miss Elinor, though they are
ringing, no doubt, at this moment, for Miss Elizabeth Paton was married this morning."

" Elizabeth married this morning !" said Elinor,
surprised. " How strange, when I was to have
been present, that I actually should never have
remembered the day !"

" You have had so many other things to think
of, my sweet Elinor," said her brother, taking up
her hand; "but I hope you sent to excuse yourself."

" Oh, yes, a week ago ; but I am sure I did hear
bells," persisted Elinor.

" You are fond of the sound of bells ; you were
happy this morning, and your imagination supplied it."

" Well, at any rate it was a good omen, Miss
Dreux," said the physician, " and I think you might
have really heard them, without either the help
of imagination or such acuteness of ear as to
distinguish them eight miles off; for I now
remember that Mr. Paton has a small estate about
three miles from hence, and I think it very likely
his tenants might set the bells ringing on such
an occasion."

" I cannot possibly believe in that version of the
story," said Elinor, laughing ; " it is so very common-
place !"

" Then we shall be obliged to fall back on th

old superstition, Miss Dreux; don't you know that
when a lady hears a peal of bells, it is a sure sign
that she will be married within the year?"

He saw in an instant that he had made an
unlucky remark, for the tears came into Elinor's
eyes in spite of herself; her spirits were still far
from settled, and this unfortunate speech was too
much for her.

" And now let me see how we are off for
medicine," he said, instantly rising and turning
his back to them, while he examined the contents
of a small corner cupboard.

He made his scrutiny last as long as he could;
when he turned round again Elinor was gone; but
she returned when he had taken his leave, with
no other traces of her tears than served to give
a still softer expression to her sweet face.

CHAPTER XVI.

THE RING.

THE next few days were spent very quietly by the inhabitants of the cottage; Elinor found plenty to do, and her brother, not being allowed to read or write, amused himself as he lay on his couch with watching the movements of others.

It was quite impossible in such a house that they could have a regular servant: the woman who waited on them sat during the day in the opposite cottage, and there she did all the cooking; she came over when they beckoned to her, but she was an awkward personage, and Elinor found it less trouble to wait on herself than employ her. So, among other things, she took to washing the tea-things, and after each meal setting them in array upon the chimney-piece.

It amused her brother to see these operations, and she easily found others which she made it appear must needs be done. He liked to see her flitting about, for she did everything gracefully, and it was something new to see her come in out of the garden

with a basketful of apples, which she pared with
her silver knife and sliced into a pie-dish, sitting
down to the task with deliberate care, and then
sending the dish over to have the crust manufactured in the opposite cottage. She took care to have
something of the kind to do every day; sometimes
she shelled peas for dinner, or sliced French beans
upon a wooden trencher, or printed little round pats
of butter with extraordinary care, and garnished
them with sprigs of parsley.

The next day Mrs. Dorothy Silverstone was
to leave them: she had bestowed unbounded care
upon her nursling, and shed tears of delight when
she saw him able to raise his thin, lengthy figure
from the couch, and recreate himself with a walk
to the gate of the tiny cottage-garden; on his part,
he repaid her affection with a kind of filial preference, which sometimes made Elinor just a little
jealous, though this was a feeling that she would
not have acknowledged for the world, even to herself.
She sometimes wondered what it was that made her
services so peculiarly acceptable; it was not certainly that she was amusing, for she never said
a word—she did not even inquire of her patient
whether he wished or whether he wanted anything;
all *that* she knew by intuition, in spite of which
she never seemed to be watching him. It might
have appeared that her mind was not occupied about
him, if she had not come to his side just at the right
moment.

As for him, he submitted to her mandates with a kind of pleased docility; even during his greatest weakness, he revolted as well as he could from the hired nurse; he would, when at all delirious, refuse to let her bathe his temples, sometimes would command her imperiously to leave his chamber; but everything Mrs. Dorothy did was acceptable—he did not want to have Joseph sent for—he did not want even Elinor to take the old lady's vocation out of her hands; she brushed his hair for him, and he was not at all contumacious; she cut up his dinner and gave it to him with a fork; she called him "my dear,"—that was right too; the most delightful unanimity subsisted between them, a taciturn friendship, very peculiar, but very sweet. He was excessively sorry to part with the old lady, but one of her sisters was ill and had a superior claim to himself. She promised him, as she might have done some favourite child, that she would certainly come and see him again very soon, and he lifted up his pale, hollow cheek to be kissed at parting, much as he might have done if she had been his mother.

Upon her departure, he tried very hard to throw off the invalid and resume his more manly occupation, but it would not do, and in consequence of sitting too long writing a letter, he was so much fatigued, that for the next two days he could scarcely lift his head from his couch.

As long as he had been in danger, young

Greyson had ridden over daily to inquire after him; now that he was better, the family contented themselves by sending over a groom.

By this man he sent a message that he was very much better, and would be most happy to see Mrs. Paton, if she would favour him with a visit.

There were many reasons why it fretted him to be without tidings from Westport, and without a sight of any of the Paton family. He wished, if he never saw Marion again, at least to convey his thanks to her, and he knew she was to return very shortly to Swanstead. He was very restless for want of tidings respecting Allerton's movements, for he had never sent to inquire after him, never been to see him,—unless, indeed, it was true that he had been with him that midnight; it was still scarcely possible to give up that belief, unlikely though the circumstances seemed.

As might have been expected, Mrs. Paton called after this message, and Marion and Dora with her: the latter did not get out of the carriage, but Mrs. Paton came in with her niece. They had been sitting at home all the morning to receive calls of congratulation, and Marion was dressed in all her bridal decorations. Always lovely and interesting as he had thought her since their first meeting, she had never appeared to him with so many attractions as during this farewell visit, while she sat almost entirely mute, and scarcely daring to lift up her eyes. The soft slight bloom fluctuated in her cheek, and as she moved, the golden locket hanging from her neck was sometimes in shadow and sometimes glittered in the sunshine cast upon it through the cottage casement. That same sunshine covered her dress with a wavering lattice-work of shadow, mingled with clear imprints of vine-leaves.

A strong constraint seemed to be hanging over them all. Mr. Dreux could not speak to Marion; Marion could not speak to any one. Mrs. Paton was very uncomfortable, from uncertainty as to how they felt towards each other. At length Marion looked up; her glance met Elinor's; the two girls looked earnestly at each other, and their eyes filled with tears. Marion's did not seem, in their appealing gaze, to ask for gratitude, but rather to deprecate reproach.

Mrs. Paton saw that a very little thing would overpower Elinor, and did what she could to bring indifferent subjects before her mind. She talked of Elizabeth's wedding; remarked on the beautiful weather she had for her wedding-tour; she had heard from her son-in-law that Elizabeth was enchanted with the lakes; she was delighted to find that they (Mr. and Miss Dreux) hoped to be able to return to Westport the next week; finally, she hoped Mr. Dreux would spare his sister to spend a short time with her before she left that part of the country. She should be very dull now that dear Elizabeth had left her, especially as her dear Marion was to leave her to-morrow.

This remark brought matters to a crisis. Elinor was sure that Marion had refused her brother's hand. Their eyes met again; and between gratitude for the tenderness which had watched over him, and pain at this refusal, Elinor burst into a passion of tears, and sobbed violently.

Mr. Dreux half raised himself on the sofa, took his sister's hand, and looked entreatingly at her.

"Now is my time," thought Mrs. Paton, "and if these young people have anything to say to each other, they shall have an opportunity to say it."

"Elinor, my dear girl," she said, soothingly, "don't distress your brother; pray try to command your feelings."

Of course, Elinor could not command herself. Marion, trembling, rose and came up to her. She took her other hand, bent over her as she sat, and kissed her forehead.

"Marion, I am not ungrateful," said Elinor, whispering; and withdrawing her hand from her brother, she held Marion closely.

Low as the answer was, it reached his ears. "You mistake if you think there is anything to be grateful for."

These words were commonplace, yet they confirmed Elinor's conviction, and renewed her pain. She released Marion, turned from her, and wept more hysterically than ever.

"This will never do," said the politic Mrs. Paton, and taking Elinor's hand, she said, kindly, "Come, my love, I think we should do well to take a turn in the garden till you are calmer; indeed, your brother should not be disturbed."

Elinor gladly yielded, and there was nothing for it but for Marion to remain. She saw Mr. Dreux about to rise and bring her a chair,—about to make the attempt rather, for this little scene had very much agitated him. She made a gesture to prevent it, and sat down near the couch, her heart beating so painfully that she could scarcely distinguish the first few sentences he addressed to her. He continued to repeat, in an altered voice, which faltered a little, his sense of her goodness, which, he said, could never be repaid, and which in all probability had saved his life.

Marion ventured to lift up her face, and encountered his eyes, but the change she saw there took from her what little courage his voice had left her; they were hollow, and had lost much of their brightness. His forehead was still slightly discoloured; there was a very small scar under the hair; she knew precisely its situation; apparently it was healed. His face, owing to a somewhat dark complexion, was not very pale, but it was thin and wasted. As she glanced at his altered lineaments, they were suddenly illuminated by that rare smile; its sweetness and beauty made the change in them the more conspicuous, but in passing away it left the traces of suffering, both mental and bodily, more distinct and plain.

Marion tried to find some reply to his acknowledgments. Her confusion was obvious ; and as she sat before him, modestly silent, he showed the interpretation *he* put upon her behaviour by saying,—

"Do not fear, Miss Greyson, that I can so forget myself as to try to make the obligation under which you have laid me a plea on which to urge my former suit. I do not say that if this had never happened I might have refrained from further appeals, even though ultimate success was scarcely to be thought of, or hoped for. But though I can scarcely suppose it possible that I could ever have ceased to love you, how much less now that—"

Marion looked up when he said this, and he paused, but perhaps it was more from agitation and the effects of his illness than anything else, for he proceeded, quite unconsciously, to drive his blunder home.

"But I have no right to disturb you by any allusions which point to you as being the cause of pain, however innocently. I wished only to remind you that I have now, from another cause, a full right—one which you will recognise—to think of you. This emboldens me to ask if you will permit me to retain something of yours which is now in my possession ; it would be an inexpressible pleasure to me to have it. I believe I have seen you wear it."

He took from his waistcoat-pocket a ring with hair in it, and explained that a few days after his accident it was found in the saucer of a china cup, which had been set aside in a cupboard.

Marion instantly remembered having taken it off; it was in her way; but how it had happened to be set aside thus, and forgotten by her, she could not tell.

"If you could possibly permit me to retain it, Miss Greyson?"

Marion looked at him, quite surprised, and did not know what to say in reply. She could not help thinking this was rather a curious way of relinquishing all further claim,—all further attempts to found one.

It was a ring that she was always in the habit of wearing; it had been worn by her mother, and contained some of that beloved parent's hair, and some of her own hair when she was a child.

"If you would permit me to retain it," Mr. Dreux proceeded, "I would found no false hopes on the gift; I would look on it only as a memorial of *that* day."

Marion had put on the ring, but he still kept urging her to return it, exhibiting in his manner a good deal of that nervous sensibility so common in recovery from severe illness.

"If you would only let me have it, Miss Greyson," he said at last, "I would look on the gift in any light you might choose to indicate."

The voices of Mrs. Paton and Elinor were heard approaching. Marion drew off the ring, and giving

it back, said, " I ask you, then, to consider it simply
as a proof that I do not like to refuse you anything
for which you wish so earnestly."

If he had had his wits about him, he could surely
have made something of this. As it was, he took
the ring gratefully, raised her hand to his lips, and
easily allowed her to withdraw it, while he tried,
without much success, to control his excited feelings,
which, in his present state of weakness, were often
on the point of mastering him.

Mrs. Paton entered with Elinor, only to take
leave, she said, and bring Marion away, which she
did at once, without observing the look of unutterable regret with which his eyes followed Marion as
she left the room.

Elinor and Marion took an affectionate leave of
each other ; and Dora, who was quite tired of sitting
in the carriage, telegraphed several questions to her
mother during the ride home, but could not make
much of the answering signs.

And now the cottage began to get very dull.
The letters came to it irregularly ; sometimes the
newspapers were forgotten. Vague rumours reached
it, however,—wafted by chance callers,—that Pelham's church and parishioners were getting into a state
of anarchy and confusion ; that the churchwardens'
meeting had been a stormy one ; a window which
was out of repair was being mended after a barbarous
fashion ; some peculiar ornaments thereto pertaining
were under the hands of a modern glazier : now this

window was dear to the heart's core of the Curate
of Pelham's church; it was of far more ancient date
than the edifice itself, and had been removed to it at
considerable cost; it was one of those rare and
curious specimens of early art called a "Jesse window." These various circumstances made it quite
impossible to stay much longer. Accordingly Dr.
Grainger, with a very bad grace, gave his patient
leave to go home, on condition that he would be
extremely quiet for some time to come,—not think
of preaching, go to no meetings, and amuse himself
as much as he liked in superintending the repairs of
his Jesse window. His patient kept to the letter of
their agreement, but contrived, notwithstanding, to
get himself so tired by the evening of each day that
he could not creep up stairs to his library sofa without the help of his servant's arm. Many were Dr.
Grainger's warnings and threatenings, but they were
of small avail; and day by day, as his natural strength
and sound constitution triumphed, the old gentleman
gave them up. He saw that it was no more use
trying to persuade him to be quiet, and let things
take their course, than it would have been to try to
make Hercules (supposing that worthy had been
living) lie on a sofa all day, and read fashionable
novels!

Elinor's aunt now began to get very urgent with
him to let her return. It was only by repeated
representations of how ill he had been that he had
induced her to spare his sister so long; now he was

resolved, if possible, to retain her for a short time
longer. Her spirits were often oppressed; she began to suffer from anxiety at Allerton's protracted
absence,—not that she seemed to expect any renewal
of intercourse, but he had gone on a journey, and as
no one seemed to know anything of his whereabouts,
she had a vague fear lest some evil should have
befallen him.

The same feeling haunted her brother's mind.
One of his first visits was to Mr. Hewly, but here
he could get no further information than that
Allerton, having been unwell, had made up his mind
to take a tour in Wales.

Mr. Hewly could not tell how a letter ought to
be addressed to him; could not say whether he
were yet in Wales; had, in fact, thought of calling
on Mr. Dreux for information, not doubting that *he*
knew everything about his movements.

He was so evidently surprised at this proof that
he knew nothing about him as to put Dreux on his
guard, and make him give up all hope of a communication in that quarter.

He took leave, and called on Allerton's banker,
but there he heard nothing encouraging. Allerton,
he said, had taken a sum of money with him, quite
sufficient to last a long time, and had not written to
be supplied with any more, nor said anything as to
the length of his intended absence.

These questions had to be asked with caution,
lest they should injure Allerton, or in any way

compromise him. The information they elicited
only added to his anxiety. He thought it very
strange that he should have no correspondent at
Westport.

At last, one day when he came in, Elinor told
him that Mr. Hewly had called for a few minutes,
and had said he had received a letter from his
Rector respecting some arrangements in the church ;
that he was still in Wales, and well in health, or, at
least, had said nothing to the contrary.

Though very tired, he forthwith went to Mr.
Hewly, but could obtain no further information.
That gentleman was now confirmed in his former
suspicion, that they were no longer friends ;—the
very circumstance that Allerton had *still* not written
fully proved it.

Hewly was glad at heart. He saw that the
influence he had so greatly disliked was withdrawn. He received his visitor coolly, spoke of
his call with condescending suavity, was sorry he
could not give Mr. Dreux the address, believed he
must have inadvertently destroyed the envelop, so
that the post-mark could not be produced.

In reply to the question, whether he expected to
hear again, he replied, that though no doubt Mr.
Allerton was very much engaged, he could find
time to write to his friends if he chose ; *consequently*, he had no doubt he should hear again,
the more so as Allerton had requested him to pay
all bills and demands upon him, that he might not

have the trouble of attending to them where he was.

This was enough. Mr. Dreux saw that the address was purposely concealed from him, and believed it was at Allerton's own request. He arose to take leave, keenly conscious of the secret pleasure the Curate felt in letting him see that he knew the strong bond which had bound them together was broken.

When he came in, Elinor questioned him, and he admitted that he had failed in obtaining the address.

She was evidently distressed, and he began to fear that her feeling of preference for his late friend was not of so transient a nature as during his illness he had flattered himself that it might be.

"At any rate, my dear Elinor, we now know that Allerton is safe and well. I really had began to have my fears. Now they are relieved, and the rest we must leave."

He was very tired with his day's work, and lay down on the sofa to rest. Elinor came and sat by him. Whenever she saw him fatigued, or looking ill, she forgot her own anxieties for a while.

She began to tell him about his habit of over-exerting himself, and entreated him to be as quiet as he could when she had returned to her aunt.

"I am not exerting myself too much," he replied; "and I believe, if my mind were at ease, I should soon be as strong as ever. I want Allerton's society more than I can describe. It pains me very much—inexpressibly, sometimes—that he should think of me, meanly too. And I am uneasy about you, Elinor. I feel that my want of observation and my imprudence has cost you, for the present at least, your peace of mind, and it has removed Allerton from my influence, which I fondly hoped was for his good."

Elinor replied, like a woman, that though her intercourse with Mr. Allerton had certainly been the cause of her present unhappiness, she would not wish to be restored to peace of mind by forgetfulness of him. " I know I shall never see him again," she added, " but at least I can pray for him ; and, Arthur, since I cannot cease to think of him, I hope, when you write, you will always tell me all you hear of him. I knew, when I gave him up, that I was doing right, but I did not know, dearest, how strong the hope, indeed the belief, was in my heart that it would lead to a change. I had, almost unknown to myself, a kind of superstitious expectation which swayed me and buoyed me up,—an idea that I should surely never be the worse for that sacrifice."

" Nor do you think so now. You do not regret ? "

" No : but what I thought simple submission and faith in God was really superstition ; at least some such feeling was mingled with the others. The feeling clung to me that he was certainly to be restored to me, better than he was before."

"Because you had made that sacrifice?"

"I don't quite know,—I incline to think so."

"My dear, we all have a great many of these unacknowledged superstitions, and, as long as it can, the heart will cling to the idea;—no, I mean the sensation—impression,—(instinct I would call it, if it were not false,)—that obedience to the will of God is to be rewarded by the prospering of our wishes in this world. I hope, whatever painful thoughts you may have, you do not *really* regret what you have done. The command is so plain: ' Be not unequally yoked together with unbelievers.' You believe God has called you out of darkness into light. You have heard Allerton say many times that such a call does not exist. And however highly you may think of his many estimable and most amiable qualities, you cannot suppose that he has experienced the change he contemns."

"No," said Elinor, "and I must not regret it; I cannot, and—I do not."

"You have obeyed the dictates of conscience, and we must leave the rest with God."

Elinor was silent for a while. Then she said, "Mr. Allerton never said but one thing to me which inspired me,—or has done since, with the slightest doubt."

"What was it, my dear?"

"You remember that text: 'We know that we have passed from death unto life, because we love the brethren?' We were walking in the garden one day with Mr. Allerton; I think you had alluded to the necessity of a change of heart, and I remember you spoke of the Holy Spirit's influence. After some time you left us, and went up into the library to fetch a book that he had asked for. As you ran up the verandah-steps, Mr. Allerton looked after you, and slowly repeated that text to me. He smiled when he had finished, and asked me whether his affection was not a proof that he was one of the brethren? We had then been acquainted a very short time, but it disturbed me to hear him talk so lightly. I said, 'I know you have a great affection for my brother.' He laughed, and said something about the two people he loved most on earth being both of 'your sort,' as he generally called it. And there was something in his manner which pressed the conviction upon me, that he meant me to believe myself one of those two. But I put that aside, and answered, 'I think we should inquire, when we love "the brethren," whether we do so because we believe them to be such, or *in spite* of our belief that they are such.' 'Ah,' he said, 'you all talk alike. That very thing Dreux said to me himself when I was talking on that subject once. But there is nothing of the kind in the holy Scriptures to which he is everlastingly referring: it there simply specifies, "*Because* we love the brethren."'

He went on, still laughing, 'He is a horribly uncharitable fellow, but, in one respect, he resembles the great Napoleon!' 'What is that?' I asked. 'Oh,' he replied, 'did you never hear it said of Napoleon, that he had the *genius* to be loved? There is something like that about Dreux. He contrives to attach one to him without taking any particular pains to ingratiate himself,—in fact, without much troubling himself about it. Why, if any other man were to dare to say the things to me that he does, I would never speak to him again. But as for him, when he opens a battery upon me, and calls me to account for any of my goings on, I rather take a secret pleasure in seeing how intensely he annoys himself when my proceedings are not to his mind. It shows that I am of consequence to him. I know he prays for me, Miss Dreux,—far more, in fact, than ever I do for myself.'

"I was so surprised at his making such an avowal, that I believe I showed it, for he instantly looked mortified, and tried to palliate it as well as he could. 'You know I'm no saint, Miss Dreux, though I try to do my duty. My notions of the standard one ought to aim at are not so high as his, but I don't nearly come up even to that; and sometimes as I'm walking home, on a fine moonlight night perhaps, after I've been with him, I have, under the clear heavens, an uneasy suspicion that I'm rather a good-for-nothing fellow. Then I admit that there is inexpressible repose in the sensation that a better man than myself is "besieging heaven" for me. I should be ungrateful if I did not at least *wish* that they might be answered,—I should be a madman if I did not trust rather to those prayers than to my own.'"

"No more, Elinor; you bring his voice too vividly before me."

"There is no more to tell, dear."

"But what was there in that conversation to make you doubt, my sweet Elinor?"

"It has not done so—not quite—not exactly; but that word 'because' haunts me sometimes."

"Allerton, in spite of his hot temper, which, in truth, was one of the sources of my influence over him, has always seemed to me the most amiable of men,—but I do not think he said those words to you without an object. He honourably informed you that he thought such a change all a chimera, but he would have had you believe that even if there was such a thing, that 'because' proved that he (unconsciously) was a subject of it."

Elinor did not wish to continue the subject—she only said, "Promise me, Arthur, that whatever you hear concerning Mr. Allerton shall be communicated to me, even if it is of an unsatisfactory nature?"

"I am afraid I shall not hear anything; it is now nearly five weeks since my accident."

"Strange that he never came to see you,—never even sent to inquire!"

" My dear, he did come once, at midnight ; don't you remember my telling you of it ? "

" Yes, Arthur; but I am sure that was only a delirious fancy of yours. He never did come, or I should have surely heard something of it."

" I feel convinced he *did* come, Elinor ; but in proportion as I return to health my recollections of the interview become more vague. You feel convinced he did not ? Well, I can oppose no reason to that — nothing but my own contrary conviction."

Elinor sighed, and wished he might be right. Her brother had never told her anything of his interview with Allerton on the morning of his accident. She was afraid, almost certain, that they had quarrelled, and nothing but the fear of having this confirmed prevented her from asking the question.

It was not without deep regret and many tears that Elinor prevailed on herself to part with her brother, for she saw he was still far from strong, and since this last illness, was much more sensitive than before, and not so well able to cope with difficulty and annoyance. She even urged him to write to her aunt, and beg her to let the winter be passed with him ; but as this relative had brought her up, and always made much of her, he did not like to do that, though he was far more unwilling to part with her than he had ever been before.

Elinor accepted this as a sufficient reason for

letting her go. There was a vague report floating
about Westport which might have supplied her
with another reason. Her ears were, however, the
last that it was likely to reach, and she stayed the
time out in peace, leaving him at last surrounded
with comforts and with assiduous servants.

She saw he was depressed. She knew of one
cause, and there was, or might be, another which
had never been mentioned between them, but such
a thing as pecuniary anxiety never occurred to her
as likely to reach him,—he had an ample income,
and had been born and bred in elegance and com-
petence.

On the morning of her departure they were walking in the garden. He was absent and depressed.
She was going to leave him, and with her departure
another evil seemed to draw nearer and take a more
distinct outline.

She was begging him to have a certain passion-
flower differently trained. If the branches were
supported, she said, they would cover the trellis-
work of the verandah, and climb over the roof.

"By next summer, when I come, it would be a
complete canopy, Arthur."

Her brother sighed, but at her request he spoke
to the gardener about it. She occupied herself for
a while with twining the most luxurious branches
over the woodwork.

"Now we shall see," she continued, "that by
next spring it will look beautifully."

" Shall we see ? " he answered, in a tone of regret, but observing that it pained her, he went on more cheerfully : " well, at any rate the plant is worth training, and I have no doubt, as you say, Elinor, it will be beautiful next summer."

" Yes, my dear Arthur ; and then you can go up and down under a complete canopy."

She remembered afterwards the expression of his face when she said this, but he made no reply, and went on twisting the passion-flower through the railings ; and at last he permitted her to leave his house, gave her the last kiss, and shut her into her aunt's carriage, with her maid, without allowing her to suppose he had any further causes for depression than those she knew of.

CHAPTER XVII.

ABOUT A HEDGE AND A HAYSTACK.

SINCE Elizabeth's wedding, Marion and Dora had been more together than during all the previous weeks which had been spent by the latter in her uncle's house.

When Marion returned from the cottage, the effects of anxiety began to show themselves, and for two or three days she was very unwell—obliged to keep her room. She was with difficulty able to appear at the church as bridesmaid, and after that she required rest and quiet.

"And where," she asked, "was Frank Maidley?"

"Oh," Dora said, "he had been sent for in a great hurry on the very afternoon of Mr. Dreux's accident to come and see his aunt—she was dying."

"Had he been heard from since?" Marion asked. Dora trifled with her watch-chain, but made no answer. She had seemed happy, that is, cheerful, enough the past few days, but she was restless; it was a pleasure to find some one on whom she could lavish kindness and attention. Marion naturally came under her superintendence, and both nurse and patient were all the better for the companionship.

Dora wanted a *confidante*, at least, some one to whom she could tell all that had passed about Mr. Hewly, and how she had quarrelled with Helen, and what she supposed were the intentions of her former lover with regard to that young lady. That there was anything further to tell no one could have guessed from the conversations of the two girls. Dora was very anxious to set the matter in such a light to Marion that she might be quite sure she never had loved Mr. Hewly, only " felt flattered by his politeness," as she phrased it. Even that seemed remarkable; and there was an evident reason for this confidence,—it was that she might excuse herself from all inconstancy, and that Marion might excuse her to others, should she at any future day (which day, perhaps, she thought near at hand) engage herself to another. The name of this said " other " was never mentioned or hinted at; the one was too delicate, the other too discreet, for that.

After several conversations Marion asked Dora if she would return with her to Swanstead. Mr. Raeburn had desired she would invite one of her cousins to stay with her. She had wished to have Rosina, and had planned in her own mind that she would go on with her lessons if any difficulty was made in allowing her to come; but Dora having mentioned how very much she wished to be away

from Westport for a time, she did not hesitate to
give up this cherished wish, and pressed Dora to
come and stay the winter at Swanstead, in which
she was so warmly seconded by Mr. Raeburn that
Dora gladly consented,—partly, no doubt, for the
pleasure of her cousin's society; partly that she
might get away from the scene of that little episode
in her life which she so much disliked to think of;
and partly,—who knows?—that she might be in
the neighbourhood where Frank Maidley would
spend the Christmas vacation, which would be, she
could not but know, with his parents.

Mrs. Paton gladly spared Dora, and the day after
the visit to the cottage, when many affectionate
things had been said on both sides, Mr. Raeburn
set off to take the two girls back to Swanstead.

They arrived on the afternoon of the next day,
several hours having been occupied in seeing a
cathedral which lay in their route.

Mr. Raeburn was delighted to see Marion's joy
on returning home; she had been so pensive for
several days past that he had feared this visit to her
cousins would make the old rectory look lonely and
dull.

Marion, however, was almost childish in her
delight; she ran over the house and garden with
the interest of a person who had been away for
years. "Everything looks just the same," she said,
with a happy smile; "I was afraid it would be
altered."

" What, the house, my dear, and the garden ?
Did you expect to find them altered ? "

" Not exactly ; but I scarcely thought they would
seem to welcome me home so pleasantly, just as if
I had never been away. It has always seemed as
if the little gap I used to occupy must have been
filled before I returned,—no one is missed long.
Dear uncle, I have had so many untrusting thoughts
even of you. I have thought, ' Now that I am
away he must discover how little I ever do to make
him happy,—how little consequence I am in his
world.' In fact, you know, uncle, I can really do
nothing for you beyond loving you."

" Perhaps, my dear, you have not quite understood that it is something as needful to the happiness
of the human mind to be able to bestow kindness,
protection, and affection, as to receive it. Granting
that you can do nothing for me to make me happy,
—which, I confess, is a view of the case in which I
do not quite agree,—you are still always at hand
to—"

" To be made happy by you, uncle. Ah, I never
thought of that ! "

" Then, my dear, you must keep it in mind for
the future. It is much more likely, humanly speaking, that you should forget me than that I should
forget you ; affection descends. Sons often forget
their mothers ; mothers never forget their sons. You
are to me instead of a daughter ; you receive from
me the attention and tenderness of a father. If you

were withdrawn, my affections would be restless for want of something on which to fix themselves."

" But if I were withdrawn, uncle, do you really think I should forget you ?"

" No, my dear; not soon, not quite, and not consciously; but I think some other person would soon step in to bestow a much higher degree of tenderness, and in receiving it again, would make the image of your doting old father dim and indistinct."

" Never, uncle !"

" Very well, my pretty; then you never mean to marry, and leave me ?"

" Leave you ?—No. Marry, perhaps; most people do."

" And what will you do with your husband ?"

" Oh, I shall make him come and live with us."

" Make him !—a wifely speech, indeed. And pray what is he to do in this quiet place ?"

" Can't he be your curate ?"

" Curate ! Why we get on fast. He's not an abstraction, then; he's a real man, this husband, and in orders ! Well—"

" Dear uncle !"

Mr. Raeburn laughed, first gently, and then as if he felt an exquisite appreciation of the joke,—the best of men now and then take a delight in teazing girls. Marion made protestations,—he only laughed the more; she begged, she entreated; her eyes filled with tears. At last he left off; she had the art to remind him that she had not yet been to see Mrs.

Raeburn, and that always made the lonely Rector
quiet and sad.

Mrs. Raeburn the elder was gone to spend a year
with her married daughter in the Highlands, so
Marion and Dora had the house to themselves, and
very cheerful they made it with their practising and
laughter, more especially as Mr. Raeburn thought,
by their manner of running up and down stairs, to
which he had a particular pleasure in listening, as
well as to the little scraps of tunes sung the while.
They were careless creatures, as the happy often
are; and, as they generally left part of the things
they went up for behind them, in the shape of
skeins of silk, netting-needles, bits of lace, or cotton-
reels, he had this pleasure a great many times
during the morning. He often, now, wrote and
read with his study-door partially open, for he was
extremely fond of everything cheerful, youthful,
and lifelike.

Dora and Marion were excessively anxious for
all sorts of news from Westport, and had charged
Wilfred to write them a true and detailed account
of all that transpired. Their first packet of letters
inclosed a note which Mrs. Paton had received from
her daughter, saying how much she enjoyed her
tour, and demonstrating the fact, that the young
matron was trying very hard to assume a wifelike
dignity and a certain staidness of style, as well as
moderation in the use of epithets.

The letter was a good one, but stiff; it did

not even remind them of Elizabeth, who had been
celebrated in her little world for her exaggerated
language. Everything with her was either dreadful,
exquisite, horrible, enchanting, or inconceivable.

The next letter was from Wilfred, and contained
so much family news that we shall give it entire :—

" My beloved Marion, and my dear Dora,—

" As I know you always show your letters to
each other I shall write one long one to you both,
instead of two short ones in separate envelopes.

" Mr. Dreux is much better ; I saw him yesterday. Mr. What's-his-name Brown and his ma'
were calling. Mr. Dreux was very polite to the
old lady, and thanked her for coming to see him.
Mrs. Brown described to Miss Dreux her feelings
when she heard of the accident, and declared that
Athanasius ' cried like a child.' For my part,
Miss Dreux and Mr. Greyson, the first words I said
were,—' Why, if that excellent gentleman is to lie
on the brinks of Jordan's flood, what's to become of
the poor ? and who will attend to their perishing
offsprings ?" ' I looked at Mr. Dreux,—he didn't
laugh at all ; his sister did. He asked me if we
had heard of your safe arrival, and desired to be
remembered to you both. Miss Dreux sent her
love, and she is going to write soon. After this
Mr. D. walked round the garden, leaning on my
arm ; he seems to consider himself quite well, only
a little weak. He has a tight ring on his little
finger, which reminded me a little of a ring Marion

used to wear; it certainly was something like it, perhaps rather more valuable; but the value of a thing is in the owner's opinion of it, more than its price in a shop, and comparisons are odious."

Dora, who was reading aloud, stopped here, and said, "What *does* he mean? He always puts all sorts of odd things into his letters." She read the passage over again, and, as Marion said nothing to explain it, went on :—

"I go down the London-road now almost every day, and generally pay my respects to my Aunt Ferguson. You know it is such a pleasing trait in the character of a young man to be attentive to his elders. Besides, by the time I get to the house I am almost always hungry, and, as I naturally wish to show Helen that I don't bear her any malice for calling me an 'impertinent boy,' I go smiling into her father's house, and there eat some bread and cheese.

"You know those meadows at the back of the house? The pond there is capital for moths. I often go prowling about there. My aunt compliments me very much on my industry. The other day she said she knew there were very often beautiful dragon flies there. 'Then why don't you go sometimes and look at them, aunt?' I said. 'Oh, my dear, I'm afraid of treading on some slimy grub or craunching some snail that might be hiding there.' 'Exactly so,' I said, 'and then there would be an end of all his schemes for ever, and all the tender flutterings of his insect

thorax (which means breast). How afflicting to
think of his widowed mate drooping her head ever
after in the shadow of the arbour, and he never
coming back to whisper to her behind the haystack.'

" ' What stuff that boy does talk ! ' said Mr. Ferguson, and Helen coloured to the eyes; for you
must know, my dear Marion and Dora, that the
evening before that I was in the meadows with my
butterfly-net, lying in wait behind an oak for a
certain humming-bird sphynx which had jilted me
the day before (such a beauty she is, I've got her).
All on a sudden I thought I heard some one near
me in the meadow give a cough ; so I went softly
towards the place,—for you know I could not tell
but that it might be a fellow-creature in distress.
There are two haystacks close to the hedge, and
when I had looked well about them twice and seen
nothing, I was disgusted with myself for my suspicions, and said aloud (for unluckily I have con-
tracted a horrid habit of talking to myself), ' Now,
W. G., I hope you see your mistake. It was the
pony who coughed ; there's nothing clerical in this
neighbourhood, my dear boy, so you 'd better walk
off, and learn to be less suspicious in future.' I had
scarcely said this, when I heard a loud, violent
sneeze, so near me that it made me jump and drop
my butterfly-net. The thing sneezed again twice,
evidently against its will. I walked quickly up to
the hedge, and there, jammed in between the hedge
and the stack, stood Mr. Hewly, with his arms, as it

were, pinned to his sides, and his face gazing at me
with its usual solemn, earnest expression. The
thorns must have pricked him very much, and
no doubt that helped to make him look melancholy.
'Good gracious, Mr. Hewly,' I said, 'how happy I
am to have found you! How did you get into that
unpleasant position? Can I help you out?' 'Thank
you,' he said, his face subsiding into a miserable
smile, 'I—I don't particularly mind it; it's—it's not
at all unpleasant, Mr. Greyson.' (Of course he had
worked himself in there to hide from me.) 'Shall I
call somebody to help?' I said; shall I see if I can find
Mr. Ferguson?' 'O no, thank you, Mr. Greyson.
O dear no,' he said, forcing himself out, and scratch-
ing his face and hands very much. The instant he
was out I climbed up a small elm, growing on the
hedge, and there in the arbour sat Helen, looking
unutterable things. I did not say a word to her,
but merely remarked to Mr. Hewly that it was fine
weather for the late crops, and went home."

Dora and Marion paused, and laughed heartily
when they came to this place.

"How I could ever have suffered that man to
walk beside me and talk his nonsense I really cannot
think," said Dora. "Wilfred certainly spares no
pains to make him ridiculous in my eyes, and I
think, even if I *had* loved him, what he has told me
to-day would have worked a cure."

"Do you really think Helen will accept him?"
asked Marion.

" Oh, I am sure of it; and as she is of age her father cannot prevent their marrying."

" But he can forbid it and say he disapproves."

" Ah, Helen will not much mind that, and Mr. Ferguson has always indulged her to such a degree that he will be obliged to give in; he is proud, though, and he will feel most the idea that Hewly is the son of a butcher."

Dora went on reading:—" The next day my uncle told me that Mr. Ferguson had been with him—in a great passion he seemed—and told him it had been hinted to him by an acquaintance that Mr. Hewly—a man he did not know even by sight—was trying to make an impression on his daughter. My uncle says he told him several things that he happened to know about Hewly (of course keeping one particular thing to himself). He told me Mr. Ferguson was coming again in the evening, and that he wished to see me, for he knew I was acquainted with Hewly.

" So in the evening I saw him. I was cautious what I said, for fear he should wonder what interest I could have in watching him. He then asked why I had not told him before. I replied that as he allowed Helen to go to St. Bernard's, and knew that she constantly consulted the clergyman there on religious subjects, I had no right to suppose that he disapproved of him, though I *had* certainly thought he could not be aware of what was going forward.

" ' Disapprove,' he retorted; ' why, I know nothing

about the man,—never saw him in my life; besides,
I may think a man very proper to instruct my
daughter in her religious duties, and yet most improper to be my son-in-law.'

" Well, he put himself into a pretty pet, and went
away, declaring he would soon put a stop to the
stupid affair. If he does, or if he can, I shall be very
much surprised."

After this followed various matters connected
with the writer's amusements and studies, and then
the letter concluded with a promise to write again
soon, and give a particular account of how matters
were progressing.

It was remarkable that from that day Dora gave
up her last lingering preference for the peculiar religious opinions that Hewly had taught her. Yet her
cousin had never mentioned the subject of religion;
he had merely set the man before her in a mean and
ridiculous light, and he went down and all his
dogmas with him.

And now autumn advanced, Dora was by no
means idle, but entered heart and soul into all the
plans for the good of the poor which had been set
on foot at Swanstead, while the visiting in the
neighbourhood and the letters from home served to
enliven the country rectory and make the time pass
pleasantly away.

She and Marion wrote frequently to Westport,
and chided their correspondents for not entering
more into details in their descriptions of what was

going on at home. Accordingly after this came a letter from Wilfred, full of circumstantial matters which entertained them very much :—

" My dearest Marion and Dora, — What you mean by saying we don't enter into details I can't think. Rosina and I wrote a long letter together about a week ago, in which we told you how we went to dine with Elizabeth and Fred after their return. How we had a melted ice pudding on the occasion and some very cinnamonny blancmanges. And didn't we mention that Elizabeth was quite grave, and tried to seem old and formal, but couldn't ? Of course we did. And after that we told you how my uncle had got a whitlow on his thumb. And then Rosina told Marion how one of her Sunday school-girls had come to church in curl-papers, a cap full of bows of blue ribbon, and an old green veil. I looked over her and saw her write it. The girl's name was Clementina Clump. Don't you call all that details ? What would you desire ? But to proceed. The Fergusons gave a grand dinner-party the other day, and Mr. Hewly was there. I will tell you how that was. Mr. Ferguson came into the study while Frank and I were busy with our crucibles. He told us Hewly had got an intro-duction to him, and had been so excessively, so blandly polite during his call, that he had not been able to treat him otherwise than courteously, *which he regretted.* Frank then said, ' I wish, Sir, you'd invite him to dinner.' (Frank knows all about the

affair, he's always at the Fergusons'.) ' I am sure the
more Miss F. sees him in ordinary life, the less she
will like him. So invite him, and me to meet him.'
Only think of the old fellow's consulting two young
men like us ! Well, he said he would, and the day
before yesterday we went. The party was in
honour of the bride and bridegroom. Elizabeth
wore her wedding dress of white satin. I never
saw her look so well. She was evidently trying not
to be in her usual high spirits, but to seem indifferent and tranquil. At first it did very well.
She was a very elegant, distinguished kind of bride,
but in the middle of dinner she forgot herself, and
laughed heartily, for Frank and I drew Mr. Hewly
out in a way that does one good to think of. You
know he is always a very grave man, and as he was
desirous that day to be agreeable, he was then
intensely so.

" The solemnity with which he asked Helen to
take wine was glorious ; the earnest *empressement*
he imparted to his great black eyes, when he
inquired whether she preferred the liver or the
gizzard-wing, was something delicious to behold ;
the sombre gravity with which he besought her to
take some woodcock almost petrified her,—there
was something tragic in the tone with which he
assured her that ' it was excellent, and very
young.'

" His helping her to cheese was perfect. He did
it as if it was a matter of life and death. Some

ladies, he observed, in his slow, solemn voice, preferred the blue mould; but for his part, he agreed
with Mr. Bishop (here a low bow) that the brown
was better.

" All this he did himself; afterwards we helped
him a little. We hoisted him on to one of his
hobbies, and he rode it gloriously.

" He began to talk about himself, and extolled
the practice of self-denial, in which all present
could join without joking; but he went on to
remark, that he always made a point of denying
himself some elegant little luxury, excepting upon
the festivals of the Church.

" ' Upon those days, the better to bear them in
remembrance,' he said, ' I always drink lump sugar
in my tea.'

" ' On other days, I suppose, you take moist ?'
said Frank Maidley, with an expression of deferential interest.

" ' I used to do,' he replied, flattered to be so
noticed, ' but lately I have thought it better to
make a still more marked difference by abstaining
altogether.'

" ' How interesting !' said Frank, with a deep
sigh.

" From one thing to another we drew him. He
felt himself a lion, a person of interest, and ' roared'
for our entertainment ' like any sucking dove.'
But unfortunately, just as he was opening out,

Elizabeth helping us, and Helen looking completely annoyed and ashamed, my uncle asked some question about the draining of those stupid marshes that all the gentlemen think so much of, and before we could get him round again, the ladies left the room.

" The rest of the evening Helen was excessively cool to us, but as there were several strangers present, she was partly occupied with them.

" However, I've no time for any more of this. Do you know, it is said in the town that Mr. Dreux has lost his property. I saw him yesterday,—he certainly looked out of spirits. He saw I observed it, and told me, by way of a reason, that his sister was gone, and Mr. Allerton out. It was in the evening that I called, about some gas that Frank and I want to concoct. He had promised to lend us an apparatus. He asked me to stay and drink tea with him;—he has always been extremely friendly to me since his accident. I think there must be some truth in these reports, for he told me he was going to London in a day or two on business, and probably should not be home for a fortnight. He asked me to re-direct his letters for him to an address in London.

" After tea he got me to play to him on the piano, while he lay on the sofa. He asked by turns for almost all Marion's favourite songs, and I played them for him with variations.

" I suppose we did tell you that he is come home.

" Well, they all send their love.

" And with mine to my Uncle Raeburn,

" Believe me ever,

" Your affectionate brother and cousin,

" WILFRED GREYSON."

Here followed a postscript to the said " Uncle Raeburn." So the letter was carried to him, with permission to read it all, for he had been sufficiently enlightened on certain points not to see any mystery in it.

" Poor Mr. Dreux !" said Marion ;—" I hope it is not true that he has lost his property, or is about to lose it; he does so much good with it in the town."

Dora said nothing. She was occupied in wondering whether Helen would overlook the absurdities of her admirer, and whether Mr. Ferguson would suffer the affair to proceed. After that she sat down and wrote to Wilfred, desiring still further details, and then she and Marion prepared to receive some visitors.

CHAPTER XVIII.

THE PUPIL.

Two days after Elinor's departure her brother went to London, and then the reports before mentioned began to take shape and distinctness.

It was said that his absence was in consequence of the failure of a certain banking-house in town; that all his property was in the hands of one of the partners, not precisely what would be called capital in the business, but so involved with this gentleman's concerns, owing to his own carelessness, or some informality, or, perhaps, the ignorance and temerity which make some men always certain of their own success, that his downfall would be Mr. Dreux's ruin.

Some people would not believe that a man of sense and undoubted talent would have left his property so insecure, or the whole of it in the hands of one house ;—it was absurd, an unusual proceeding. At last they went to his lawyer, and being met with a shrug of the shoulders, the rumour went forward triumphantly. Then all his acquaintance said, "Why hadn't he bought an estate?" excepting those who said, "Why hadn't he invested it in the funds? It was excessively foolish!—wonderfully imprudent!"

Most people said he would now certainly give up his curacy, for it was not to be expected that he should continue to live in the town in such different style to what he had always been accustomed. On the contrary, others sagely argued that it would be grossly imprudent to leave a place where he was so popular, and where he had so good a chance of succeeding his present poor childish old Rector.

At the end of a fortnight Mr. Dreux came home. He looked harassed, but not otherwise altered. He found his library-table covered with tradesmen's bills, though it still wanted two months to Christmas. By way of paying them, as well as meeting all other demands upon him, he advertised his house and furniture to be sold, and set to work to consider his position.

He had lost everything. His curacy brought him in a hundred a-year, and a lectureship in the afternoon, not connected with it, though in the same church, about forty more. This lectureship was his for life, if he chose to hold it.

This was his whole maintenance, and seemed a miserable pittance to a man who had been accustomed to spend from eight hundred to a thousand a-year, and knew absolutely nothing of economy.

His house was of a good size, and very hand-

somely furnished ; for when he came to the town
he had given orders to an upholsterer to furnish it
properly.   The bills came to a good deal more than
he had expected, but he supposed they were all
right ; and with the same good faith he had listened
to his housekeeper, gardener, and groom, suffering
them to carry out their notions of what was proper,
and supposing, that, as the matters under discussion
were such as belonged to their respective depart-
ments, they ought to know more about them than
he did.

He was a man of so careless a nature as regarded
money, that it was not so much what he spent upon
himself that made the items mount up in the account
(for his personal habits were simple and inexpensive
enough), but what he gave away, and threw away,
on unworthy objects and useless, thoughtless charity.
He supplied his Sunday and infant schools with three
times as many books, slates, maps, and pictures as
were needful, not considering the undoubted fact,
that great abundance almost inevitably leads to
waste.   As he paid for them all himself, mistresses
and scholars never spared. When they were out of any
article there was no meddling, scrutinizing committee
to interfere,—they had only to send to him for more.
They accounted him a *real* gentleman,—he bowed to
each mistress as if she had been a lady. If, when he
was present, the school-room fire wanted mending,
he did not allow the females to lift the heavy coal-
pans, but mended the fires himself ; consequently,

of course, they would not knowingly and willingly have wronged him—of course they repaid this respect and consideration with interest a thousand fold. He could not have been more implicitly obeyed if he had been an autocrat. Nevertheless, they used twice as many articles connected with their craft as any other school-mistresses, and though they would have risked their lives to serve him, they remorselessly wasted *his* pens, ink, copy-books, slates, coals, and " kindling."

He was a charming master to his servants, for he was no trouble to please in his own house, and he looked over the household accounts in such a care-less fashion, that he might just as well have let it alone. He never asked any awkward questions, seemed oblivious of cold joints, was very unobser-vant of the disappearance of old clothes, and would often leave about a good deal of loose money.

He now resolved to give up his house, sell his furniture, his horse, and all his effects, excepting his books, and go into lodgings. Several other curates in the town lived very comfortably on as small a sum as he should now possess, he argued, and why could not he?

But he quite forgot that these several other curates had been brought up in the country on small means, had been allowed at college only just enough to carry them through respectably, and were thoroughly used to economy. Besides, he never calculated on the difficulty of retrenching in his charities. It was comparatively easy to deny himself,—he would walk instead of riding, he would leave off buying the expensive books, the reviews, and periodicals with which he had been accustomed to load his tables; he would take no more tours, he would not keep servants. This he thought and found easy, but it was extremely hard, most bitter to his feelings, to be obliged, in common honesty to his tradesmen, to give up his subscriptions to many of those charities in the town of which he had hitherto been one of the chief supporters—it grated upon his feelings to be obliged to refuse money to some among the poor to whom he had been most generous—it pained him to the quick to hear the ill-suppressed murmurs of those to whom he had hitherto made a weekly allowance, and whose behaviour now seemed almost a reproach to him for having led them to expect it, as if the years of comparative comfort they had derived from it had better never have been enjoyed than that they should be so suddenly deprived of it.

He took small apartments in the town, near the church, and moved to them the books that he had in constant use, his wardrobe, his family plate, and one family picture. Then he went back to his old house to make arrangements about his papers, and to go over the different rooms with the broker, who was making out a catalogue of everything preparatory to a sale.

" And these books, Sir," asked the man, " what is to be done with them ? "

" Oh, I cannot think of parting with my books ! " He might have added, " They are all I have to look forward to for interest and relaxation."

" Very good, Sir ; then where are they to go ? "

" To my rooms, of course."

" Sir, you don't consider the size of that little parlour ; it's not a third as large as this library, and, besides, you have a book-case in one of the bed-rooms."

" I cannot possibly get on without my books," said Dreux, quite dismayed.

As he did not seem to know what to do, the man said, " Perhaps, Sir, you would not object to hiring a good large room ? they would all go into one room, I think, if they were properly arranged."

" No, I cannot do that."

" Well, then, suppose we were to step on and measure the lodgings, Sir. Perhaps one or two of these book-cases might stand in it."

The measurement was effected : not one of the book-cases would stand in either the bed-room or sitting-room,—if it was set against the chimney-piece it blocked up the bed-room door, if against the opposite wall, it blocked up the window.

" Well, leave this room for the present," said the owner ; " I will see what can be done when the sale is over."

The sale of household furniture, &c., was effected

a few days after ; it did not realize nearly so much as he had expected—absolutely not enough to pay all his bills.

He was standing in the empty library of his old house, all the furniture of which was gone, the very book-cases sold, and the books left in heaps on the floor.

He was thinking with dismay at the sum brought in by the sale, when the man who had valued the furniture, said, in a careless way, " Colonel Masterman came to see the house the day before the sale, and spent a long while looking over the books. He said they were a capital collection, and seemed quite disappointed when I told him they were not for sale. I told him, Sir, you wouldn't part with your books on any account. He said he had understood the contrary, and would have taken them at a valuation. He's building a library, you know, Sir."

Dreux had sent some fifty or sixty volumes to his new abode. They filled two small shelves in his parlour. He now selected about half a dozen more, which had been great favourites, sat down and wrote to Colonel Masterman that he had altered his mind, and wished to part with his library.

The next few days he was very busy, and did not feel the want of them much. The transfer was easily effected,—and having now no servant to send on his errands, he walked himself to pay the remaining bills, and brought home exactly twelve pounds as the residue of his property. He was very tired, and threw himself on the couch in his little parlour, surprised and vexed to find that day by day he felt the loss of his property more and more.

And then came to light by degrees various things connected with his past charities, which made *them* no longer pleasant things to reflect on.

He had no intimates, and he unburdened his mind to none of his fellow-labourers in the town, though very friendly with them. Yet he did hint to one or two that he suffered from the importunities of the poor; it gave him great pain to deny them, and he did not hide it. Thereupon, by way of consolation, followed a long list of instances, which seemed to multiply at will, of how he had been cheated and imposed upon by the recipients of his bounty—how the beggars, trusting to his well-known careless generosity, had been heard to boast that they could go twice a week for a month to " Saint Plum's," and each time with a different story—that he always gave them something or other, and being in a great hurry, seldom either listened, or looked at them. " Oh, he's the real gentleman ; he wants no certificates." " He was a deep one when he liked, but had an absent way with him ; and if a woman had but the sense to bring a squalling baby with her, he was took quite aback, and seemed as if he'd give anything to be rid of her."

These good-natured friends had never told him before how shamefully his bounty had been abused; now they sagely observed to each other, "It was best he should know it, as it might keep him from regretting what he could no longer accomplish."

Then again, strange to say, Mr. Dreux became of far less consequence in the town than heretofore.

A short time after his loss of property a relation of his died in India, and was reported to have left him ten thousand pounds. There was no truth in the report, but it caused the poor to besiege his door again, or rather his landlady's door. "Here was a pretty parson for you!—here were fine doings, denying the poor their crust! Mr. Dreux was saving his money. His rich Huncle that had died in the Hinjies had left him as much money as filled two mackerel boats, in which it was landed, as they were told, at the post-office,—and they should hope the post-office people knew what they were talking about, and had the best of news. What a shame it was that he couldn't spare a sixpence for them that had none! He needn't hold up his head so high. He always walked like a millingtary officer. They wondered he wasn't ashamed of hisself."

Moreover, as Madame de Stael said of herself, that the men could not perceive that wit in her at forty-five which they ascribed to her at two-and-twenty, so Mr. Dreux might have said, "The people cannot perceive that eloquence in me now

I am poor that they ascribed to me when I was richer."

In his small, lonely lodgings,—Allerton and his sister away, his health not so good as usual, his mind harassed by many anxieties which he had never been accustomed to, and his books gone,—he spent the next few weeks, till autumn deepened into winter, and till, one by one, he had lost many of those distinctions which he had hitherto supposed belonged to him personally, but which he now found partly to have resulted from his property, partly from his hospitality,—the style in which he lived, and the money he gave away.

It was one consolation that Elinor was away, that she knew nothing beyond what he chose himself to tell her. She still lived in comfort and elegance, and he resolved that he would never give her one needless pain respecting him.

She knew broadly that he had lost his property, but all the harassing details were spared her. He only told her that he now had 140*l.* a-year, and that he lived in lodgings. He wrote to her once a-week, and her letters in reply were now his chief solace. He presented everything to her as cheerfully as he could. He had found it needful to give up almost all society, and her sisterly sympathy was very pleasant; it was all the sympathy offered, and all he would have endured to receive.

Of Allerton he could hear nothing, and had many an anxious hour respecting him. He could not

make a new friend. There were few persons whom
he could feel to be thoroughly congenial, and though
there were great and essential differences between him
and the Rector of St. Bernard's, there had been such
cordial regard that it fretted him more than any of
his other troubles to miss his cheerful steady step,
his voice,—for he had an inveterate habit of singing
about the house ; chant, song, or psalm came alike to
him,—even his short outbreaks of passion were a
loss, and so was his influence. He was the only
man who would think of such a thing as invading
him in his lair (as he called the library), shutting
his book, and dragging him out for a country walk ;
the only man who came uninvited to breakfast,
dinner, or supper, as the fit took him ; made himself
at home, railed at his host for his unsociable habits,
and made him both sociable and communicative.
However, that was over. Allerton's continued
silence seemed a proof that he still harboured resentment ; and as long as that was the case, he would
wish for no renewal of intercourse, not even if he
could know how acceptable it would be.

As might have been expected, though he believed
himself to be very economical, he soon found that
he was living beyond his income. Mrs. Dorothy
Silverstone was the only person he talked to familiarly, and he notified this fact to her quite coolly
one evening, when she had come in to drink tea
with him.

" And I'm sure I don't at all wonder at it," said

the quiet old lady, without the slightest appearance of discomposure.

"Why don't you wonder at it, Mrs. D.? You ought to have gone into hysterics."

"Lie down on the sofa, Mr. Dreux; you know you're recommended to rest after the day."

"I will; why don't you wonder?"

Mrs. Dorothy had got some description of outer coat in her hand; she was turning out the pockets most unceremoniously. "Is this the coat you wear every day, Mr. Dreux? Bless us! one, two, three, —here's no less than six pairs of gloves in it; black, lilac, grey, odd ones too,—some old, and some as good as new!"

"Yes, they accumulate. I suppose Joseph used to turn them out formerly. What are you going to do? You've been stitching all the afternoon, with your pearl buttons and your strings; I like to see you here. You're not going to mend those old gloves? I won't allow it, Mrs. D."

"You won't, Sir? Well, I *am* going to mend them, sort them, smooth them, and then they'll do perfectly well to wear again. Why," proceeded the old lady, in her soft internal voice, "you spend a fortune in gloves, Mr. Dreux; no wonder you live beyond your income; and what will you do, Sir, to make up the sum you want?"

"I shall take an evening pupil."

"Ah! Will you have another cup of tea, Sir?"

" Yes, Mrs. D., and then come and sit where I can see you."

" What for, Sir ? "

" Because yours is the pleasantest face in Westport, and I like to look at it."

" Well, I'm sure ! Now, if I were you, I shouldn't take a pupil. I should just make it up instead with my uncle, that great gentleman,—I forget his name."

" Impossible, Mrs. Dorothy ; I could not if I wished, which I do not. Do you know what we quarrelled about ? "

" No, Sir."

" Well, I'll tell you. What sort of a boy do you think I was ? I was the most mischievous young scape-grace that ever breathed. I had a brother once, two years my junior. I took delight in leading him and abetting him in all manner of mischief. It is a mystery to me how he came to die in his bed, which he did, of measles, when he was seven years old ; but not till I had carried him pick-a-back over all the dangerous streams (half torrents) within ten miles of my father's house in Wales, and also helped him to set fire to a stack with a burning-glass, and got him run away with by a wild, half-unbroken horse. I was fond of him, used to fight his battles with the housekeeper when our parents were out ; but I am certain that I endangered his life at least once a-week. Well, he died, and both my parents

died. I went to live with my uncle. At first he
liked my daring habits, but my love of mischief
grew, and I often got into dreadful scrapes. At
last,· one day I thought I should like to see how
many trout there were in a large deep pond he had.
I laid a plan to turn the water off to within a foot
of the bottom, and thought what bliss it would be to
wade about among the fish. There were two grat-
ings, one at each end of the long pond. I first, with
infinite pains, dammed up the higher one, through
which a little stream ran; then I went to the lower,
which allowed a regulated quantity of water to flow
off into a drain. This would not do for me; I
quietly set to work to dig a hole in the bank. I dug
and dug till, all on a sudden, out rushed the water
in headlong haste; the bank gave way, and mud,
water, and I with my spade, were tumbled down
into the field of standing corn. I rushed back to
my dam, but I had made it a very secure one, and
before I could loosen one sod, the pond was drained
of every bucket of water, the corn-field flooded, and
the corn full of dead fish. As many as filled a cart
lay at the foot of the hole; they were carted away
in the afternoon, and I after them. The pond
covered nearly an acre. Well, Mrs. Dorothy, what
do you think now of reconciliation?"

"How old were you then, Sir?"

"Nearly fifteen."

"Well, Sir, I shouldn't like to have had the managing of you."

"No, but I'm easily managed now,—don't you think so?"

"Pretty well, Sir, when you can't stir hand or foot! What makes you in such good spirits, Sir?"

"Your being here. I never see anything cheerful within doors now. You ought to have pity on me, and take me in hand."

"So I will, Mr. Dreux."

"For better and worse?"

"Now, Mr. Dreux, how you talk! It does me good to hear you laugh though," and the old lady stopped her needle and looked fondly at her nursling. He was rather a large one for such a frail little nurse; yet, as he stretched his six-foot limbs on the couch, he looked at her with a kind of smile which seemed in some sort to express dependance on her, for at least the present hour's tranquillity and good spirits.

A pupil was soon found in the person of young Greyson. He was to go to Cambridge in a few months, and in the meantime Dreux undertook to "coach" him for two or three hours in the evening. It took away all his time for relaxation; but his pupil was so determined to give as little trouble as possible, and so droll and good-humoured, that he soon began rather to enjoy the lessons than otherwise. Besides, young Greyson's character just suited him; he was so utterly free from any description of embarrassment, or reserve, and had such a quaint kind of humour about him. Moreover, he still retained a good deal of boyish simplicity, and was remarkably shrewd, having all his sister's insight into character, and perception of the wishes and feelings of others.

While he worked he was a man, when he amused himself he was still a boy; he at once made himself completely at home in Mr. Dreux's small lodgings, and used often to stay and amuse him, when the lessons were over, with odd sketches of character, and accounts of the adventures of the day.

Hewly often figured in these descriptions; the whole account of that gentleman's *second* courtship being detailed, and various other particulars respecting him; Helen's determination to abide by her choice; and Mr. Ferguson's weak submission to her will. One morning in November he came in to excuse himself from attending in the evening as he wanted to dine at Mr. Ferguson's. Mr. Dreux made some difficulty about it, and reminded him of several other occasions lately, when he had absented himself. The pupil, however, was very urgent,— he gave his consent, and, after a very busy day, was extremely glad of the evening for letter-writing. To his surprise, about eleven o'clock Greyson came in, looking anything but lively,—told him he had met Mr. Hewly at dinner, and he had mentioned something "which I hope," he continued, "is not true; but if it is, I am afraid it will be a great annoyance to you, and even a great inconvenience."

He then told his dismayed auditor that he had heard Hewly relating to his aunt how he had been that afternoon to the house occupied by the master of the schools, before mentioned as having been lately erected, and to his surprise had found that the evening before he had given the children a whole holiday; that the neighbours had said they supposed it was by Mr. Dreux's orders; that the schoolmaster was out—he went out that same night; and had said he should be home on Saturday morning.

"I never gave him leave to do anything of the kind," interrupted Dreux. "I have not seen him since Wednesday."

"I was afraid so," proceeded Greyson; "but it seems certain that he *did* go away on Thursday evening. I had better tell you what Hewly went on to say, though I fear it will greatly annoy you. As he means to call on you to-morrow morning early, it is best you should be ready for him. He went on, 'I always thought that man was a hypocrite. I never liked his high professions; but Allerton and Dreux thought they had got quite a treasure,—for you must know that though Allerton has no sort of power in the direction of these schools (all that belongs to Mr. Dreux), he was complimented by the parishioners with the office of Honorary Secretary. I am happy to say Allerton had nothing to do with the choice of this man. However, they both used to trust him to do all manner of odd jobs for them. Mr. Dreux chose him, and he must take the consequences if he has run off, as I half suspect he has.'

" ' Why, if he *has* taken himself off,' my aunt said, ' surely he is not such a treasure that his loss cannot be supplied; there must be many masters equally well qualified, who would be glad of so good a situation.'

" If you could have seen Hewly's face then, I think you would have seen the most villanously sinister expression you ever set eyes on. It nearly put me in a passion. He went on, in his blandest voice, in which I could easily detect his secret satisfaction,—

" ' I was the more sorry when I recollected that Mr. Dreux has always employed the man to collect the pew-rents of his south gallery and the rent of those two or three fields which belong to the almshouses, so that I am very much afraid the fellow has a large sum of money in his possession, not less than three or four hundred pounds. The almshouses are half in our parish and half in his. Of course he will have to refund. I am very sorry, but if people will do such imprudent things as to authorize a man like that to collect money for them, they must take the consequence ; the poor must not suffer.'"

" Four or five hundred pounds ! " said his auditor, quite aghast.

" Yes; but is it possible that all this can be true ? "

" I am afraid it may be."

" But it is not near quarter-day, Mr. Dreux."

" So much the worse; the rents are only paid half-yearly, so are the rents for the almshouse fields, and some few tenements,—and that in November, because then the new nominations take place."

" And is the weekly allowance of five shillings to each person paid out of this sum ? "

" Yes."

" Well, the man *may* come home to-morrow morning, or, in the next place, he may not have got any money in his possession."

" Oh yes, he has; I gave him the usual note last Saturday, authorizing him to collect it."

" And then pay it into the bank ? "

" Yes; and it is Hewly's business every Monday morning to draw out a sufficient sum to pay the pensioners."

" But at any rate, whatever has happened, half the amount ought to be paid by Mr. Allerton, for half the pensioners are in his parish and of his parish."

" No, Hewly was right, the choice of the master was entirely mine; it is all my doing; but we have trusted him several times before and found him scrupulously honest. How could I imagine such a catastrophe as this ? "

" But what will you do? You will not surely take for granted that the man is a rogue and pay down the money ? "

" I must try to think of some means of borrowing the sum. I really feel bewildered at present." (He leaned back in his chair, looking weary and harassed, and laid his hand upon his forehead.)

"Dear Mr. Dreux, nothing is more easy than to borrow the money; any one would lend it you."

"Any one, my dear fellow! But how am I to pay it again? How am I to pay even the interest?"

Greyson had tact enough to see that his reserve did not extend to pecuniary matters; these were externals, and he might venture to push him on the point for further information.

"What is the weekly outlay in payments to the pensioners?"

"Twenty pounds. There are eighty of them."

"Then you have to produce that sum next Monday?"

"Just so; and, thanks to these lessons, I can pay the first week, and that only."

Greyson sat for some time, lost in thought. He was struck by the weary composure of his host's manner, who looked harassed and utterly perplexed. It annoyed him exceedingly to have been the bearer of such evil tidings. The great church clock striking twelve roused them both. Greyson started up and buttoned his coat; Dreux pushed his papers from before him and sighed heavily; he remembered that Greyson had taken a long cold walk, and as he thanked him for his visit he moved mechanically towards the bell to order refreshments.

"Don't ring," interrupted Greyson. "I can let

myself out, and I think the people of the house are in bed."

The host remembered that he was in lodgings, and desisted.

"What will you do?" said Greyson, looking at him with real anxiety. "Indeed, it is not idle curiosity that makes me ask."

"I know not at present what to do," was the answer. "I have no reasonable expectation of being able to pay that sum if I could borrow it."

"But the interest? It would not be more than twenty pounds a-year. Yet you say you must pay the sum yourself—you must take the responsibility on your own shoulders, the whole of it?"

"Yes, the whole of it if I have any regard for my future usefulness and respectability. It would be exquisitely painful to me to lay myself under an obligation to any one; and if I loaded myself with a debt of four hundred pounds I should be harassed. I could struggle with anything else—but the idea of living in debt and dying in debt would be *subduing*,—it would embitter my days."

"But you have some family plate and two or three pictures?"

"They are not nearly worth four hundred pounds."

"Will you promise me one thing?" returned Greyson. "I ask it as a great favour. I should not have told you all this, nor asked how you thought of meeting the demand, if some idea had not come into my head which I think, if properly worked out, bids fair to lift off the load; but I cannot possibly explain it at present. If you could trust me without an explanation I should be so very glad."

"What do you want me to do?"

"I have no hint at present as to where this fellow is gone; that was not my idea, though by judicious management we may yet find out and recover the money, IF he has taken it. But will you let me beg of you to give Hewly the money for next Monday, and then will you *promise* me to take *no further* step till Monday evening, when I shall come in again?"

It instantly occurred to Dreux that Hewly must have dropped some hint as to Allerton's whereabouts. He could not endure the idea of *his* being applied to even to pay half the amount, and he said so.

"I never thought of such a thing, it never entered my mind," was the reply; "but if you could promise not to take any steps till I come again!"—

"You are very mysterious, and your interest is very pleasant. I certainly, under any circumstances, should have taken several days for reflection before I stirred in such a matter as this, therefore I will give the promise, provided *you* promise not to commit either yourself or me."

"Oh, yes; never fear that. Thank you."

"You make me smile. Come, shake hands;

don't burden yourself with my troubles. Go home,—you are young yet for schemes to raise money."

" But you have promised ? "

" O yes."

" Ah, I see you are quite convinced that I can do no good ! "

" I fear you cannot, without either disclosures, which at present would be imprudent, or committing me, which I ᴋɴᴏᴡ you will not do."

" You consider me quite a boy,—you don't know what I've been trusted to do before now. All sorts of things have been confided to me, partly because I found them out ! Why, my cousins tell me all manner of things. As for Fred Bishop, he made his offer through me—fact, I assure you."

" And your sister — are you in *her* confidence ? "

" She's very fond of me, of course, and I know as much about her private affairs as I can find out —no more."

" Indeed ! "

" Don't you think I'm very like her ? The image of her, *I* think—face, manners, and all."

This question was asked so suddenly that it seemed to take his auditor quite aback. · He had some difficulty in meeting young Greyson's eyes. He cleared his voice, and said, calmly, " No, I confess I don't see much likeness ; in fact, I never observed any."

" Well, Marion rather piques herself on the idea that she is like me ! "

" Will you go home, or am I to sit up all night to listen to your nonsense ? "

" Oh, I'm going now ; good night, Mr. Dreux."

" Yes," thought that gentleman, as he listened to young Greyson's foot on the stairs, " and I wish you had gone two minutes before. If I had continued to think you were ignorant of my inmost thoughts I should have been more at my ease with you. Well, you are amiable, and a most decided oddity, but no more like your sister than I am. I wonder how much you *do* know,—not the truth, certainly, with all your shrewdness, or you would not have talked as you did just now."

CHAPTER XIX.

THE ALMSHOUSE PENSIONERS.

ON the following morning, Mr. Raeburn, as he sat at breakfast with Dora and Marion, was very much astonished to see the latter dart suddenly out of the room and run into the garden, without her bonnet, to meet a gentleman, whom she straightway kissed, and brought in triumph to the house.

" It's Wilfred!" cried Dora, lifting up her glass.

" I'm glad to hear it, my dear," was the answer; " otherwise I might have thought Marion's conduct a little strange."

He accordingly went out to meet his adopted child at the foot of the steps, gave her brother a hearty welcome, and herself a hearty chiding for going out in the frost with no bonnet on.

They brought him into the room, and looked on while he ate such a breakfast as none but growing young men can eat,—at least, so it seemed to the girls, who wondered what could have brought him so suddenly, and knew it was no use asking him till his hunger was satisfied. They saw a mischievous little smile about his lips. He wanted to teaze them. They affected great indifference—asked coolly " how were all at home?"

" Oh, they were very well."

" Had he brought them any messages or letters?"

" No, for they did not know he was coming; no one but his uncle had the least idea of it."

In reply to further questions, he said he had been travelling all night by railroad, and had walked from the cross roads. He had come on business—business of his own. His uncle gave him leave, and had sent his kind regards to Mr. Raeburn, and his love to Dora and Marion. His uncle did not know why he had come.

The curiosity of the two girls was now raised to the highest pitch. He further said he should stay over Sunday, and then go away in the middle of the night.

Mr. Raeburn being here appealed to, declared he did not know why the boy was come; he supposed he soon should do.

" Oh, of course, we shall all know soon," said Marion.

" Ahem! We shall see about that.—Uncle, I've done.—You may make your minds quite easy on one point, my dears, which is, that you'll never find out what brought me here, not if you try till Christmas.—I've quite done, uncle."

"I'm glad to hear it, my boy. I should be sorry if any harm came to you from an over-hearty breakfast in my house."

"May I come with you into your study, there's a green baize door to it?"

"What do you mean by that?" said Dora.

"Nothing insulting; only the housemaids might be listening outside."

Marion and Dora sent several messages to the study, informing young Greyson that it was a very fine morning for a walk; also that there was skating on the pond in Swanstead Liberty; notwithstanding which, it was twelve o'clock before he came out, which he did at last looking very joyful, and declaring he should like a walk of all things.

All lawful means having been tried without success to make him divulge his secret, the trio set out, leaving Mr. Raeburn writing his sermon. There was a sparkling hoar frost, and the trees were spangled with a light fringe of snow. They set out in high spirits, and there was no lack of conversation by the way: such a torrent of questions respecting Elizabeth and Fred, Maidley, Mr. Dreux, What's-his-name Brown, and his mother, Mr. Hewly, and Helen, being poured forth by the fair ladies, as fully entitled them to the reputation of being what is commonly called "true daughters of Eve."

"Mr. Brown was going out to be a missionary, and his mother with him."

" Extraordinary! Good little man! what a disgrace that we ever laughed at him. Where's he
going?"

" To Smyrna, or somewhere in the Levant."

" Oh, then we don't think so much of it."

" And what do you mean by saying that we are
not good correspondents?" said Greyson. " I write
every week, and tell you all sorts of things. I
thought I entered into enough details to please
anybody. Didn't I tell you last week that I had
taught Mr. Dreux to bake potatoes on the hob,
wherewith to regale himself when his landlady's
gone to bed? and that she had got a little closet on
the stairs, where she keeps his coals, butter, eggs,
meat, and all his eatables, and a little old black tea-
pot for his tea?"

" Well, let that old feud rest now; you have
harped on those *details* since we mentioned them.
How's Mr. Dreux,—is he quite well?"

" O yes, I think so, *ma cousine;* but he has been
very much harassed lately, and his old Vicar is very
poorly, so that now he has to go and see him every
day. The old gentleman is perfectly childish. I
think he is ninety; but he is very cheerful and
happy. I went one day last week with Mr. Dreux
to see him. He takes the oddest fancies into his
head. He thought I was a foreigner of distinction,
—an Ambassador from the Turkish Porte. He
said I did him great honour, and then asked me
how the Jews' Society flourished. Then he asked

Mr. Dreux how old he was; then he told me he
was his son, and asked if I did not think he was a
very fine young man. Notwithstanding that he
knows he is his curate, he also thinks he is Lord
Arundel, and generally calls him so. After that he
told us what he had had for dinner, and stopped
himself to ask again,—' Well, my Lord Arundel,
and how old are you?' 'I'm eight-and-twenty,
Sir.' 'Eight-and-twenty! You always say the
same thing over and over again; no variety at all.
I'm sick of hearing you say you're eight-and-
twenty.' Then he dozed a little, woke up, and
said, in quite a sensible tone, ' Well, brother, shall
we read a portion of Scripture together?' Then he
drew a great Bible to him and read a short psalm
quite well and reverently. And inquired whether
I was a Mahometan, and whether I should mind
joining them in prayer: ' The Church of England,
Sir,' he said, ' has been accused of ignoring the
existence of other bodies; on the contrary, she not
only prays for all who profess and call themselves
Christians, but also,—you will forgive me, Sir,—
for all Jews, Turks, Sir, Infidels, and heretics.
Brother, you had better pray, my memory rather
fails me.' So Mr. Dreux prayed for a short time,
very simply. The poor old man professed himself
greatly edified, and began to tell me how happy he
was, and how kind everybody was to him. ' My
dear son, particularly,' he said, ' is always kind, and
he comes and administers the sacrament to me every

month. So, you see, I have nothing to do but to wait till my change comes.' Then he forgot himself, and said, ' Well, my Lord Arundel, and how old are you?' This time Mr. Dreux varied the answer: ' I shall be nine-and-twenty, Sir, in a few months.' "

" Poor old gentleman," said Dora ; " he was an excellent man before he became childish."

" Oh very, and he is quite happy now. When we went away he pulled out his watch and made me a present of it. I accepted it, and made a speech in return. He said he hoped our friendly relations with the Porte would never be disturbed. I echoed the sentiment, and said, I thought Britain the finest country in the world. Then he gave Mr. Dreux his snuff-box, and we took leave. And on the stairs we met the housekeeper, to whom we gave the two articles back. He gives his snuff-box to Mr. Dreux every time he sees him."

" I wonder," said Marion, " what made him give Mr. Dreux that particular name."

" Nobody can tell. He calls his housekeeper the churchwarden. The other night, just as my lesson was finished, a message came for Mr. Dreux to go to the old gentleman, as he had something particular to tell him. I offered to stay and let him in, for there is no such thing as a latch-key. When he had been gone an hour, I went to his little closet, took out four potatoes, which I cooked in the ashes ; then, when they were nearly ready, I frizzled some

slices of bacon on a fork, laid cloth with some
green-handled knives and forks and the cruets, and
when he came in, at eleven, all powdered with snow,
there was a bright fire and a sumptuous supper, not
to mention some hot wine and water with which we
caroused. He declares my society does him a great
deal of good. He generally sits up till one o'clock,
writing, and will certainly follow the hint of the
baked potatoes instead of going supperless to bed."

"But why did the old gentleman send for him?"

"Oh, I don't know,—some nonsense or other."

"What does he teach you?" asked Marion.

"Principally mathematics. I like him extremely
now I know him. He always was '*somebody*,' you
know, and he is now just the same; but, in spite of
his dignity, I am on uncommonly good terms with
him. I ask him all sorts of questions, and he seems
rather to like it. I suspect he tells no one else
what he tells me. But really, you know, I have
such a winning way with me,—havn't I, Dora?"

"You conceited boy!"

"I am. Well, he told me, the other day, that at
first his landlady used to come up every day and
teaze him about what he would have for dinner,—
he never could think of anything; so at last he told
her that whatever dinner she had sent him up the
day before he would have till further orders; this
was some mutton-chops and a batter-pudding.
Well, he had this for three weeks, and then he got
so tired of it that he told her she might change the

mutton for a veal-cutlet. 'Veal, Sir?' she said, quite aghast; 'why, Sir, veal's a penny a pound more than mutton. The price of veal, this time of year, is awful, Sir,—quite awful, in particular of cutlets.' 'You may send up what you like,' he said. So she sent him eggs and bacon, and that he has had for a fortnight."

"Poor Mr. Dreux!" said Dora, "the idea of his dining off eggs and bacon and eating baked potatoes for his supper."

"Well, he does," said Greyson; "and what's more, I don't believe he cares much about it. In fact, he is so busy he has no time to care for anything. He often comes in to give me my lesson so completely fagged, that when he has set me something to do he falls fast asleep; and when I have done it I am obliged to wake him to tell me if it is right."

"And how are the Fergusons?" asked Marion, anxious to change the subject, for the last few sentences had fallen on her ear very painfully.

"Oh, tolerable. Hewly has ingratiated himself so well, that he is now allowed to visit at the house as an acknowledged admirer of Helen's, but her father will not allow of an engagement; so they choose to call themselves bound in honour to each other, but not engaged."

"Ridiculous! What is the difference?"

"None at all, my fair cousin; but you needn't be so warm about it. Helen is of such a very,—*very* fickle disposition, that her father thinks she will very likely change her mind if she is not opposed."

" Yes, she certainly is the most fickle person I ever knew," said Dora, and then suddenly checked herself, for she remembered that she was not exactly the person to say it.

" One can hardly hold too fickle a hand to a bad cause," was the reply. " However, Hewly is constantly there, and now I trouble myself very little about the business. I have taken care that Helen should know what kind of a man he is, and, if she chooses to marry him after that, I have nothing more to do with it. Helen gets more fond of her forms every day. My aunt says she has got a little ivory crucifix in her dressing-room, which was a present from Hewly ; and she has a picture of a saint kneeling a little way up in the air. The legend is, that her prayers have such power they actually draw her a little way up from the earth before she has done."

" Poor Helen !"

" Her velvet prayer-book is adorned with a great gold cross. Mr. Dreux said to me, the other day, ' It is surprising to find how fond the age is of symbols. We put the sign of the cross everywhere now that it is no longer either a burthen or a reproach to bear it.' I repeated that to Helen ; she was very angry, and said she would not be without the protection of that cross on any account (What could she mean ? Does she trust to it as a charm ?)

And she went on,—' Father Macauley says we ought to sign ourselves with the cross, at least during our worship, else there is nothing to distinguish us from the world.' "

" Father Macauley, who is he?"

" The new Roman Catholic Priest; don't you know the chapel? There are a great many poor Irish at Westport. Mr. Hewly knows the Priest, he is a very different man to the vulgar, fat old Father Dennis. Hewly introduced him to Helen, and she says he is a polished gentleman and very devout. I said nothing when she told me, but I thought, 'if Hewly is so impolitic as to divide his influence with another—one so very, very much his superior, an upright man, who has no nonsense about him, as is said to be the case with this Roman Catholic gentleman—he is leaving himself very little chance of ever being master of Helen's fortune.' "

" Very little," repeated Dora; " Helen can scarcely have been long in the habit of familiar intercourse with Mr. Hewly, without perceiving his real insignificance; besides he is not open, nor honest; not that I charge that upon his principles, I should be sorry to be so uncharitable."

" If his principles are *not* bad, his conduct is; have you not often heard him advocate his doctrine of reserve,—' We must not preach all that the Church holds,' he says, 'lest we offend and startle; we must unfold truth by degrees.' "

" Well, if the principle is allowed at all," said
Dora, "it may be allowed in other things besides
religion. He has advocated to me before now
keeping back that part of the truth which might
be for one's disadvantage—to *his*, as he thought,
and *mine*. I'm much obliged to him ! Mine, indeed !
I blush to think that I listened !"

" Does Helen often see this Father Macauley ?"
asked Marion.

" I suspect she does rather often ; he is very
much with Hewly : they don't look well together.
Hewly is at such great disadvantage, he is rather
a shabby little man ; the other has quite a military
air compared with him ; he is certainly no sneak,
and evidently takes the upper hand ; it is said that
he told Hewly it was something for a priest of the
true Church to acknowledge or hold any intercourse
with one of a rebellious community like his !"

" Well ! So he is better-looking than Hewly ;
so much the worse for that gentleman's prospects."

" Is he young ?" asked Marion.

" About forty."

" Helen will turn round again," said Dora, very
much annoyed. " How's Frank Maidley ?"

" How you slip from one subject to another !
Oh, he's very well, he's at Cambridge ; he is going
to spend the winter vacation at Westport ; but all
that I have no doubt you know better than I do,
Dora."

" Indeed I know nothing about him."

Her cousin paused, and she was sorry she had inadvertently betrayed a fact which evidently surprised him.

"So you hear often?" she said, carelessly, unable to control her wish to know something about him.

"Oh yes, frequently; he writes such odd, droll letters sometimes; he declares he's far gone in misanthropy, and totally sick of the world. The other day he declared he was blighted! but one never knows whether he's in joke or earnest; do you, Dora? Perhaps some fair lady has done something to him. I don't allude to any lady in particular, of course."

"Perhaps some fair lady has," said Dora, calmly; "and perhaps not."

"Humph!" said Wilfred. "It is so droll to read his letters; he does rail so against fortune (you know that old aunt of his left him not a penny; but I think he needn't make such a fuss about it); then he reverts to his favourite theme, and declares he's breaking his heart, that his good spirits are only put on,—only on the surface, and so on; and then he launches out about his chemicals."

"Marion," said Dora, gently, "let us cross the fields and look at the skaters."

The brother and sister looked at each other with some rue, and more surprise; they dropped the conversation, and went to look on at the sides of the pond. Marion then began to rally her brother upon his secret, by way of diverting Dora, but it was quite without success; and though they both returned to the attack several times that evening, they were obliged to confess at bed-time that they had not obtained the slightest clue.

After a quiet Sunday, he took his leave of Swanstead, setting off to walk to the cross-road about ten o'clock at night, in order that he might reach Westport by the middle of Monday.

During his absence things had gone on much as had been expected; the schoolmaster did not return, and at nine o'clock there was a crowd of children in the street before the locked doors, clamorous for entrance; there soon collected a crowd of parents, idlers, and above all, alms-house pensioners, among whom the direful news spread like wildfire.

Mr. Hewly came down about a quarter-past nine with a face of dismay, sighing over the folly of those whom he did not name, in trusting a man whom he declared bore the stamp of his hypocrisy on his forehead.

The crowd agreed. Mr. Hewly looked "cut up;" he was a good gentleman, and pitied them; *he* would never have been guilty of such an impru- dence.

Mr. Hewly sighed, accepted the compliment, but hoped that even the imprudent were honourable and honest. "Oh yes, there could not possibly be a doubt of it."

The crowd seemed to think there was a doubt;

they must not fear, of course the money would
be refunded; they would not be robbed of their
rights. The crowd perceived the difference between
his word and his manner, and augured no good.

Worthy, kind man, he promised that he would
go and call on Mr. Dreux (who had authorized the
schoolmaster to collect this money), and see whether
he was prepared to refund it; "and if not, my
poor friends," he went on, "we know to whom
we must look in all times of danger and adversity."

After this pious address the old women wept,
and the lookers-on said it was a shame.

Mentally they saw Mr. Dreux in the dust, under
good Mr. Hewly's feet, who proceeded forthwith
to give them some more excellent advice, and then
set off on his pious mission.

Almost the whole of the crowd followed him
to Mr. Dreux's lodgings, making a great commotion
in the street. He was not at home, he had been
called up in the night to witness the quiet death
of his old Vicar, who had died in peace, after a few
hours' illness.

He had presented his snuff-box for the last time,
his Curate was now coming home with it in his
hand. He paused, surprised when he saw the not
very orderly crowd before his lodging; they were
gazing up earnestly at his window—some of them
in a low voice were expressing an opinion that
he had run off too. He was seen advancing, they
instinctively became quiet—*that* fear was dissipated.

He looked sad and weary; they hoped he was penitent for having thrown so many poor creatures out of bread! Dear good Mr. Hewly (as kind a man as ever drew breath) was upstairs, talking to his landlady; they hoped when he came in he would be told what they thought of the matter.

He came on, and by his face showed no consciousness that they were gathered together on his account. They let him pass through them, and as he reached the door, they greeted him with a volley of groans,—good ones, and deep,—for they had soldiers, sailors, and numbers of low Irish among them by this time, who had joined for the sake of the fun.

At the same moment, the children began to cheer, not that they meant anything by it beyond the pleasure of making a noise. He had his back to them, and they were valiant; but he turned suddenly round on the door-steps, and took off his hat, as if he meant to speak to them.

They fell back in a great hurry. Fifty little boys cried out, "It wasn't me, Sir;—Oh, Sir, I didn't do it." The old women sobbed, but curtseyed; the old men subdued their cry of shame into a gruff cough, and tried to look respectful; and the soldiers and sailors, tickled by this sudden change, wrought simply by a commanding gesture and a piercing eye, roared with laughter, and cheered him vociferously.

He saw that this was not the moment to make

himself heard, and, after a moment's hesitation, entered the house, and shut the door behind him.

There was a dead silence without for about five minutes; the crowd became dense, and all eyes were fixed on the window. It was furnished with a little balcony.

At length the window-blind was drawn up, and the sash flung up by Mr. Dreux, who stepped out into the balcony, and looked at them with grave self-possession. Mr. Hewly stood a little drawn back, looking, both morally and physically, very small.

With a gesture of his hand he demanded silence, for his appearance had been the signal for a storm of cheers. They stopped as soon as they could. Then he took out his watch, and informed them that it wanted but a-quarter to ten; that if the almshouse pensioners did not immediately repair to the Town-hall their money would not be paid till the following week, for they well knew that the Mayor granted the use of the room for one hour only. He lamented that the schoolmaster had decamped, and informed them that he himself was the only person who would be a loser. Then he ordered all the children to go back instantly to the school, where, he said, he would meet them, and make the best arrangement he could. Having said this, with an aspect of authority which completely calmed them, he turned round, entered his room, and shut the window, leaving the people rushing different ways;—the almshouse pensioners to the Town-hall, the children to the school, where a man was speedily procured to perform the part of master, he having already officiated in that capacity during an illness of the missing master.

As for Hewly, he went and drew the money, feeling like a sneak, as he was. He was greeted with most unceremonious requests to "look sharp," together with several compliments of a very equivocal nature ;—they were whispered near him, and made his cheeks tingle. They had nothing whatever to do with the matter in hand, but were not the less galling on that account. They seemed to take note of his hands, and pronounced them coarse; of his height,—he was a "shabby little chap," they said, "a whipper-snapper,"—"a poor-spirited sneak ;" Mr. Dreux would make two of him. "There were shoulders for you ! and didn't he walk upright, for all the world like a Lord High Admiral !"

Poor Mr. Hewly ! Was not this unfair? Could he help it, if nature and education had combined to make him stoop and turn in his toes?

But he had his revenge. The Mayor came, and a respectful silence followed, during which Hewly was heard to whisper mysteriously, "All well at present, my good Sir; but wait till this day week ! However, *perhaps* he may be able to pay the debt ; or if not, *perhaps* the public may do something ; or, perhaps, I may be able to think of some plan."

This speech sunk the spirits of the audacious crowd, they scarcely knew why; and the popular opinion again began to waver, the more so because the Mayor, who was a very grave man, shook his head sagely, and looked as if he did not know what to make of the matter.

In the meantime young Greyson got back to Westport, and, at the usual hour, went to Mr. Dreux's lodgings to take his lesson.

The pupil was excessively restless and uneasy, the tutor no less so. The room was full of old silver plate, all the six chairs covered with it, and the sofa, as well as with several other sorts of antique finery, silver models of tombs, with cross-legged knights upon them, costly snuff-boxes, &c.

The lesson being over, Greyson ventured to ask whether the plate had been valued, and what it was worth.

"One hundred and fifty pounds is its value," was the reply, "and no more."

"One hundred and fifty pounds," repeated Greyson, in a low voice; "and have you really nothing besides, Mr. Dreux?"

"Yes, I have a diamond ring, which I had overlooked. I am glad to find that it is worth, that is, it will *sell* for fifty pounds."

The pupil breathed more freely, and looked about him at this display of old-fashioned splendour. He supposed Mr. Dreux had forgotten his hints, or, at any rate, expected no result from them.

After a pause, he stammered out a hope that he was not intruding, and seeing Mr. Dreux's eyes fixed on him with surprise, he went on: " I came here to-night on purpose to tell you of something which is on my mind ; but it makes me so excessively uncomfortable to have to say it, that I hope you will make allowance for my mode of doing so."

The heightened colour, and the deep sigh of embarrassment and excitement with which he said this, made his auditor look intently at him, and lay down his book on the table.

" I heard you say the other night, that you could not bear the idea of being in debt."

The auditor winced as he said it. But he went on, hastily—

" These things, it appears, are worth more than one-half the sum you want ?"

" Yes, if any one would buy them. But who wants plate stamped with another man's arms? and who cares for the monuments of another man's ancestors ?"

" If it has been valued at that sum, no doubt it is fully worth it. But that was not what I wanted to say. I wanted to tell you that my guardian pays all my bills, and allows me to spend what I think reasonable. So that, without having any money in hand, or any fixed allowance, I have all that I require."

Mr. Dreux now knew that something must be coming, but he did not look half so uncomfortable as his pupil, who had far more the air of a person about to ask a favour than one desirous to confer one.

" Well," he said, in a low voice, " what else have you to tell me ? "

" Only this : that if you could borrow the sum, or half of it, from a person who does not want it, and, consequently, without laying yourself under the slightest obligation "——

" There is no such person," was the quick reply. " Do not propose to me anything so exquisitely painful as that I should take advantage of the generosity of a very young man ;—I could not endure it, indeed. I am very much indebted to you, and touched by your kindness, but I could not do it. Besides, Greyson, you are a minor."

Greyson paused to allow his excitement to subside, and then went on more boldly on another tack.

" Well, but you told me that these things were worth something more than 200*l.* Now, if you would sell them to any one else for that sum, why not to me ?"

" That is a different thing. But what could you do with them ?—they are not worth that sum to you."

" Very true ; neither is 200*l.* worth much to me ; because whatever I want is paid for by my guardians. If you would sell me these things for 200*l.*, which sum I have now in my possession, I should have no object in converting them again into money until I came of age, and by that time it is possible you might be able to buy them of me yourself."

Mr. Dreux made no answer; he sat lost in thought. Here was a way by which he might clear off one-half of his debt; and painful as it was to do what seemed to his sensitive mind the taking advantage of the generosity of a mere boy, he did not think his conscience would acquit him if he declined.

His pupil left him some time to his cogitations, and then proceeded: "This plan, if you will accede to it, will place one-half of the sum required at your disposal; before the rest is wanted we may trace this man, and recover something; or Mr. Allerton will return, and of course he will insist on paying the other half."

"I selected this Master."

"But I believe I have heard you say that it was his idea to permit him to collect the field rents; the fields are in his parish too. This has nothing really to do with the *school*. Besides, if the cases had been reversed, and you had been absent, would not Mr. Allerton have felt himself bound in honour to pay the whole?"

"I dare say he would."

"And would you, on your return, have suffered it?"

"No, certainly not; I believe you are right." And thereupon followed another long pause, which was broken at length by the tutor remarking that he supposed Mr. Paton was acquainted with Wilfred's wish.

"No human being knows anything of it but myself," was the reply.

"Then, my dear fellow, how came you to be possessed of such a large sum of money?"

"When I left you last I told my uncle Paton that I wanted to go to Swanstead for a day or two. He treated it as a whim, and did not ask me why; no doubt he thought I wanted a peep at my sister, and let me go.

"When I got there, I told Mr. Raeburn I wanted the sum of 400*l.* I reminded him that I had always been very moderate; I had not even spent so much as my guardians would have been quite willing I should. Then I asked him whether he would lend me that sum, though I could not possibly tell him what I wanted it for.

"He said he was not empowered to lend it me out of my own property without the consent of the other guardian, my uncle Paton. I told him that would not do, for no one but himself must know that I had borrowed it. I am sure he believed that I wanted it to lend Frank Maidley, for his chemical experiments. He thought a little, and then said he would not lend me 400*l.*, because he knew I could not pay him the interest, but he would give me 200*l.* for a present, if that would do. I declared I had rather pay it when I came of age; but he only laughed, and said, if I was too proud to have it as a present from him, I should not have it at all. So I took it, and he promised not to tell *any living soul* that he had given it me."

"And why did you make that stipulation?" asked his auditor, touched by this evidence of his generosity. "Did you think it would lessen the obligation?"

"I don't exactly know; I suppose I thought you would rather it was a secret between us; I wish that also. But obligation there never was. It was given me by a person who did not want it. It is now possessed by a person who has no use for it,— who has, however, a good use to which he is not allowed to put it, for I suppose, Mr. Dreux, you will force me to take a full equivalent for it. I did hope you would borrow it of me, and then sell your plate to make up the rest of the sum."

"You have lifted a great load from my shoulders. You have both thought and acted for me to far more purpose than I have done for myself."

"You see," said Greyson, "there is no doubt my uncle Raeburn thinks we are going to squander the money in our chemical experiments. He never expects to see any result, and will not ask where it is all gone. He only hopes we shall get ourselves into no mischief, for, as I was leaving him, he called after me to mind I did not blow myself up. So if you would borrow it of me, or, or "—

"Shake hands, and let things rest as they were. If you will take this rubbish of me, I will take the 200*l.* for it; and remember I *am* under an obligation to you (and I do not mind it), for you have told me you do not mean to part with the plate, consequently your taking it is only a *ruse* to prevent my paying interest."

" Such a thought never entered my head."

" No one else would buy it, Greyson, excepting to melt down as old silver. It's not entering your head proves that you are not experienced in such dealings. You are anxious to help me out of a difficulty in the way most pleasant to my feelings. Well, you have done so. I can breathe again, and I have three months before me, during which I hope I shall be able to make up the other sum, supposing we cannot recover it from this rogue."

Greyson saw that various feelings were working in the breast of his host. He had no motive for further continuing the conversation. It was plain that all this old finery, and these evidences of family pride, were to be left on his hands. He got up to mend the fire ; he then went to the little closet on the stairs, and took out some potatoes to roast in the ashes, and some eggs ; then he collected all the plate on the table, and began to examine it, commenting on its beauty, and now and then hazarding a conjecture as to the use of some of the more antique pieces.

" I think the best thing I can do with it will be to give it to Marion for a wedding present," he said. It was a bold stroke ; but his curiosity was excited, and he thought this would be a likely way of satisfying it. If there was anything between Mr. Dreux and his sister, what present could be more appropriate?

He heard a start, but did not look up. "Your sister is going to be married, then," asked a voice, not exactly like Mr. Dreux's. "Marion?" he asked, looking at a face not exactly like his either.

"What! Marion going to be married? Not that I know of; but I presume that some time in her life she will enter into the holy estate of matrimony, and all these gewgaws would look most elegant on her table, and perhaps delude the world besides into the idea that we are of an ancient family."

"Oh!" was the succinct reply. "How very, very cold it is to-night!"

"Yes, it seems quite to make you shiver. But, Mr. Dreux, supper's nearly ready."

"You odd fellow! The idea of your preparing it yourself,—laying the cloth too!"

"That's the best part of the fun. Now I'll go and get the pepper."

He got up suddenly, and the same instant a noise of retreating footsteps startled them both. They had been sitting with the door not quite shut, for the chimney smoked. Wilfred darted out, and distinctly saw the skirts of a man's coat, as he whisked into a small bed-room close to their sitting-room, and shut to the door.

"It must be the other lodger," said Mr. Dreux,

very much annoyed, " and he has been listening at
our door."

Wilfred said nothing. To his exquisite delight,
he perceived that the man had shut a piece of his
coat-lap into the door, and could not draw it
through; he must consequently be standing close to
it within, and could not fail to hear every word they
said.

The young gentleman had a skewer in his hand
with which he was about to toast some bacon; he
stuck it suddenly and securely through the bit of
coat, pinning it to the door, so that no pulling could
free it, and then proceeded in a high, raised voice,
not the least like his own, to harangue Mr. Dreux
on the impropriety of listening at doors.

" Listeners," he observed, "never heard any good
of themselves."

The lodger here made an ineffectual effort to
draw in his coat.

" Oh, my dear friend," said Wilfred, addressing
Mr. Dreux, and speaking through his nose, "what
a shocking vice is eavesdropping! How mean
and small in the minds of upright humanity! How
it lowers a man in the eyes of his fellow-mortals!
Yes, my hidden individual, the Rev. Arthur Cecil
Dreux, descended from a long line of Crusaders,
godson of a Bishop, grandson of a Lord, Curate of
Pelham's Church, and Wrangler, I forget in what
year,—also the amiable youth, W. Greyson, of this
town, have had their feelings harrowed up and dis-

gusted by your conduct, my hidden individual. Never forget that, henceforth, in their eyes you are little beyond all appreciable littleness. Ahem, you needn't try to draw your coat through, for I've got hold of it." This was said in his natural voice, through the key-hole, while the lodger made another desperate, but unsuccessful attempt, and was heard breathing hard inside; Mr. Dreux all the time standing by, laughing so that he could not check Greyson.

"Call the police," said that young gentleman, gravely. "Hi! let's break open the door!"

Upon this the hidden lodger uttered a cry, apparently of fear, and rent away his coat from the skewer, double-locking the door with frantic haste, while Mr. Dreux, with his hand on Wilfred's mouth, dragged him back into his room and shut the door.

"Will you be quiet?" he exclaimed, as soon as he could speak for laughing. "We shall have the whole house about us; and I am sure you have punished the poor man enough, he really seemed quite frightened."

"He's a coward, as well as an eavesdropper, then. What harm could we have done him?"

"It is very lucky for us that he is a coward, else he would have come out and confronted us. What could I have said then?—we have no proof that he listened."

Wilfred was sorry he could do no more, and

applied himself to his cookery, in a short time serving up an excellent supper of potatoes and bacon, with poached eggs. He was in such high spirits that his host had the greatest difficulty in keeping him within reasonable bounds; perhaps he would have failed in the attempt if he had not declared that he would not take the money of him unless he was quiet.

"Well, have we decided everything?" he asked, when supper was over.

"Yes; we decide that this plate is yours, and the money mine."

Wilfred was rather dejected; he made another attempt to make his host borrow the money. He declared the things were so old-fashioned that he was afraid they would make him feel old before his time; and then began to put them back into the chest from which they had been taken, commenting on them àll the time in a manner the most absurd, —he was sure he did not know where he was to keep them.

At last he said he would have them, provided Mr. Dreux would promise that he should be the first person applied to to advance the rest of the money. He declared, with boyish vehemence, that he could not bear the idea of Hewly's perceiving that there was any difficulty in procuring it, or that it put Mr. Dreux to the slightest inconvenience to lay it down.

His host, in very good spirits, assured him that he had removed a great weight from his mind, and proceeded to lock up the chest containing the plate and jewels, giving him the key, and telling him to write his name on the chest, which he did, and then, careless as he was, left the key on a little table and forgot it. He promised to send for the chest in a few days, and sat down to pay over the notes which Mr. Raeburn had given him.

"Now then," said his host, "let me give you a written acknowledgment that this plate, &c. is yours."

"What! do you think I wish to cheat? No; I assure you I really mean to take it quite honourably. I shall soon send for it. In fact, I will sell it if you wish. I don't want to lay you under the slightest obligation."

Mr. Dreux smiled at this novel notion of cheating, and explained that, in case he should die before Wilfred came of age, he wished him to possess a written agreement, by which it would appear that he had sold these articles and received for them their full value. Having made such a statement, he gave it to young Greyson and told him to put it in his pocket-book.

"And will you, as a favour to me, keep this affair and everything connected with it a profound secret?" asked the pupil, as he held out his hand, when about to take leave.

"Why?" asked Dreux, with a smile,—"because you think it will be pleasant to my feelings not to have it known?"

"Oh, I really have a reason,—two reasons."

"Well, I do promise."

He helped his pupil with his overcoat, and took up the candle to light him down the dark stairs; he went to the door with him (for the household were already in bed), and then returned, feeling lighter of heart than he had done for a long time. He shut the outer door and bolted himself into his bed-room, which opened into the sitting-room. He slept very soundly, and woke later than usual, for he had lately been too much harassed to sleep long. It struck him as very odd, when he was ready to leave his room, that his door was locked on the outside, and it could not be opened till he rang for his landlady. She seemed surprised, and declared that the door could not have been locked without hands. However, being very busy, he gave himself no further concern about it, contenting himself by remarking that the lock must have sprung.

His first care was to pay over the 200*l*. to the account of the almshouses; his next to inform Hewly of what he had done. It would be some time before the rest of the money was wanted; he thought he could take two more evening pupils, and make other arrangements, which would enable him to meet the emergency.

He had now leisure to think of his own prospects as regarded the probability of his remaining in the parish. He had written to the Patron, a descendant of old Pelham's, informing him of the death of the Vicar, and telling him that, his own salary being paid up to Christmas, he should continue to perform the duty as usual till that time. The Patron, Colonel Masterman, the same gentleman who had bought his library, wrote back to thank him for his communication, and remarked, that, as he hoped to be in the town in a few days, he would do himself the pleasure of calling.

In the meantime various considerations made him think it highly probable that the living would be offered to him. He had always been friendly with Colonel Masterman, and it had long been said in the town that the parishioners would petition the Patron to present it to him, at the death of the old Vicar. It was worth about 250*l.* a-year; and, in his former circumstances, he would have preferred to remain a curate, rather than burden himself with such a tie; but now he considered that he could not do much with his income as a curate, and he might effect great good, even with so small an addition to it. He thought, then, if it was offered, he would accept it, for it would in no wise increase his responsibility, and he could not be more tied down than he already was.

In the evening Wilfred came, and they set to work in downright earnest; for the last two lessons had been very spiritless affairs, and they wished to make up for lost time.

"And how is our interesting eavesdropper?" asked the pupil, as he rose to take leave.

"Oh, I have not seen anything of him. You must have put him quite out of countenance, for 'he hides his diminished head,' and keeps as quiet as if he really thought we had power to take him up for listening."

The next day young Greyson asked the same question, just before the landlady made her appearance with the kettle.

Mr. Dreux repeated the question to the good woman in rather different terms, and was informed that he had left early in the morning of the previous day, taking all his luggage with him.

"He only took my room for a week," she proceeded, swelling with anger, "and I don't believe he's no better than he should be. If *he* didn't steal them bath-bricks out o' my shop, I should like to know who did."

"Bath-bricks! What! things not worth a penny? Nonsense!"

"Begging your pardon, Mr. Greyson,—tenpence apiece, if you please."

"Not likely a man would steal anything so bulky and of so little value," said Mr. Dreux.

"Well, Sir, they're gone;—ten on 'em, all of a row. You remember 'em, Sir,—used to stand in the corner, by the passage?"

Mr. Dreux couldn't say he did; and the landlady left the room, having previously swept up the
hearth.

"That's my doing!" exclaimed young Greyson,
with a smile of delight. "He knew he could never
look me in the face again, so he's taken himself off.
Oh, Mr. Dreux, did I leave my key here? because,
if not, I've lost it."

"I've not seen it. What do you want it for?"

"Just to take a look at my old crusaders."

"You will do no such thing;—we are going to
work to-night. When you have finished we will
look for the key. But you are a careless fellow;—
how came you to leave it behind you?"

"Oh, I forgot it."

"Yes, just like you; and I wish you would send
for the chest, Greyson."

"I've told a man to come for it this very night.
I'm going to polish all the silver myself, with a
chemical preparation that I've made. I shall work
at it like any footman."

After the lesson, a search was instituted for the
missing key. The furniture was moved, the shelves
searched, but without success. They were still
looking for it, when the porter came for the chest, and
duly conveyed it to Mr. Paton's house, where, being
directed to young Greyson, it was taken up to his
bed-room, not without a good deal of grumbling
about its great weight.

When the owner of the chest came in, it was very

natural that he should wish to inspect his property. Accordingly, he bolted himself into his room, and proceeded to pick the lock of his box, intending to amuse himself with a sight of his old teapots and mustard-pots, &c., not to mention his diamond-ring, which latter he intended to have altered, and present it to his aunt, Mrs. Paton; and she well deserved it of him, for in every respect she had treated him like a son.

He picked the lock without much difficulty, and, on lifting up the lid, found a thick layer of silver-paper lying at the top of the chest, which he was sure he had not laid there; a good deal of fine white dust came up as he moved it. His heart beat quick;—he began to suspect that all was not right. He hastily tore away the paper, and found beneath it ten bath-bricks, a hearth-brush, some large pieces of coal, several heavy books belonging to Mr. Dreux, and two folio volumes of Foxe's "Acts and Monuments!"

He was so aghast at this unexpected sight that he knelt for some time before the chest without uttering a sound. Here was a pretty state of things! And yet he believed he must keep the secret, for if it came to Mr. Dreux's ears, he would feel that he had received the 200l. as a gift, and that would never do.

He then remembered the lodger. It was clear that he must be the thief. He had seen the silver lying about the room, and very likely had heard them descant on its value. His having left early the next morning seemed to establish the fact. He had never seen him, and if he had been willing to try to trace him, he could not do it without making the affair public.

He felt very much perplexed, and knew that in the course of time he should be compelled to tell the facts to Mr. Dreux; but he resolved to put off the evil day, hoping that before long he might be in such circumstances that it would not matter to him.

All the next day he kept changing his mind as to what was best to be done, but in the evening he found Mr. Dreux in such good spirits that he could not bear to damp them.

He had to endure a good deal of banter from him on the subject of the lodger, and the terror his harangue had inspired. The landlady had declared that he went away in such a hurry that he had left 6s. 8d. on his chimney-piece,—an unprecedented thing!—and also a very tolerable coat hanging up behind the door!

It suddenly occurred to Wilfred that he should like to go into this room, and see whether the man had left anything else behind him,—anything by which he might be traced, or any letters or papers by which his name might be ascertained.

The landlady just then appearing with a note which required a short answer, he asked her several questions while Mr. Dreux wrote; and she, being gratified at the interest he took in her affairs, was very communicative.

" He only went out at night," she said, " and he was as stealthy in his habits as a cat."

" I should like to see his room," said Greyson, carelessly.

" Well, Sir, I'm sure you are very welcome."

" But not now, my dear fellow," said Mr. Dreux, surprised at the oddness of the idea, " we have no time to spare at present."

Greyson gave in, and got through his lesson extremely well, considering how much his mind was occupied with other matters. As soon as it was finished, he declared his wish to go and examine the eavesdropper's room, and Mr. Dreux took up a candle and went with him.

He was amused by the curiosity expressed by his pupil, and stood looking on while he opened the closet and peered about in all directions.

" Come, Greyson, have you done?" he said at last. " I declare, you are as curious as the lodger."

The party accused made no answer. He was feeling in the pockets of the coat: most of them were empty, but at last he brought out a handful of Sunday-school tickets, and laid them on the bed, then drew out a common clasp-knife, and lastly, an envelop.

" This is in your handwriting !" he exclaimed, as he gave it to Mr. Dreux, " and it is addressed to the schoolmaster."

Mr. Dreux took it, and turned it round. There could be no doubt about it,—the words were as plain as possible: " Mr. Thomas Dickson, Schoolmaster, St. Clement's-lane."

" This, most assuredly, is my writing," he said.

" And here's an old crumpled note," proceeded Greyson,—" I found it between the pocket and the lining ; it is signed with Mr. Allerton's name :—

" ' MR. DICKSON,—You will be good enough to see that the boys learn the inclosed questions and answers. They must be ready with them by Wednesday.

" ' Yours truly,
" ' FRANCIS G. ALLERTON.' "

" What are we to think of this ? The lodger must have been Dickson himself."

" Impossible ! I saw the man several times, and I could not have been deceived. He was a much smaller, darker man, than Dickson. Besides, of all houses, Dickson would not have taken a room in the one in which *I* live."

The search having now become of the deepest interest to both parties, they set to work to examine every pocket again, and were rewarded for their diligence by finding a note signed A. C. D., and written not many days before the disappearance of the schoolmaster.

" That sets the matter at rest, then," said Wilfred ;

" the man was Dickson.   No wonder he was frightened when I talked of calling the police."

" I don't agree with you ; these notes are in a
place where no one looking at the coat could fail
to find them.   I do not believe it was Dickson,—I
am convinced to the contrary.   I cannot understand
the thing."

" If it was not Dickson, it is very clear he wished
us to think so."

" *No!*   Why, how could he possibly suppose that
we should search his coat ?   What interest could he
suppose it would have for us ?   Besides, we know
nothing against the man, and what object could he
have for trying to pass himself off for a supposed
thief ? "

" None, unless he *has* committed some crime, and
wishes to fix it on another man," said young Greyson, feeling his way.

" We know of no crime, unless you call listening
a crime.   Come now to my room, and wash your
hands after your researches."

" Your landlady says he stole her bath-bricks,"
remarked Greyson, trying to speak carelessly.
" He must have required a good large box to put
them in, nearly as large a one as your plate-box—
my plate-box, I mean.—Why ! here are two torn
letters, both addressed Mr. T. Dickson, and thrust
into the fire-grate.   What does this all mean ? "

" I cannot tell.   If they have been put here

designedly, it must be as a blind, and this man is
an accomplice of Dickson's.

To young Greyson's mind the thing bore quite
a different aspect: this thief wished to fix his crime
on another thief; the only mystery was, how he had
contrived to obtain these notes and the knife, which
was marked Thos. Dickson.

As there was nothing more to be discovered,
they returned to the sitting-room, and with a mind
more perplexed than ever, Greyson went home to
consider what was best to be done.

Mr. Dreux had laughingly remarked to him that
he still possessed some property in the shape of a
miniature of his mother set with diamonds, and a
picture, by a first-rate artist, of himself and Elinor,
when they were children; it hung over the chimney-
piece of his little parlour.

The boy was represented as about ten years old,
and the little sister perhaps two. He was carrying
her pick-a-back over a brook. His naked feet, seen
under the clear water, were considered remarkably
fine, and the dark eyes expressed a humorous
gravity. It was obvious that he knew he was in
mischief, and was happy in that consciousness.
The face, though childish, and shaded with a quantity of curling hair, still bore a strong resemblance
to the grown-up original. Elinor's was a sweet
cherub face, full of baby joy. The landscape was
lovely. It represented a break in a wood. Long

sunbeams slanted down to the water upon some watercresses. Elinor's arms were clasped round her brother's neck, and her cheek laid on his shoulder, his head turned slightly towards her, and was a complete personification of the beauty of boyhood.

This fine picture had been an especial favourite with Allerton, and this circumstance seemed to have given it additional value in the eyes of its owner. Wilfred, when he went home, spent an hour or more in thinking of it. Mr. Dreux had told him, that at the time of the sale he had been offered three hundred guineas for it. He dreaded lest if the affair of the bath bricks came to his knowledge he should send it to London to be disposed of, and force the proceeds upon him. Yet, if he did not confess to him what had happened, how could he trace this man, and how identify him? He thought and thought, till at last he fell asleep, and dreamed that Mr. Dreux recovered his property, and that the schoolmaster came back with all the plate in a sack, which he laid at the feet of its late owner, being rewarded for so doing with a present of three baked potatoes, and a number of old exercises, presented to him by the hands of himself, dressed in the identical coat with the torn lap.

CHAPTER XX.

MRS. BROWN'S MUSTARD-POT.

Young Greyson's hopes for Mr. Dreux were
destined to meet with a disappointment.

The next day happening to dine at Mr. Ferguson's house, he met Colonel Masterman, and
heard his host talk of Mr. Dreux in a very
slighting way, as a young man who held rather
wild notions. He thought he observed a peculiar
smile in Helen's eyes when this was said.

Mr. Hewly was present, and he observed that it
was Mr. Ferguson's intention to make him appear
as well as possible in the eyes of the Patron. In
fact, it was but natural, when one man believed he
must accept another as his son-in-law, that he
should try to raise him (if he could) beforehand.

Colonel Masterman's second son was present, and
Mr. Ferguson appeared to take a great interest
in him. He talked to him about India, where he
had spent the best years of his youth, and where,
he intimated, he had quite enough interest in
certain quarters to get an appointment in the house

with which he had been connected for any young man for whom he chose to exert himself.

Greyson was very shrewd; he saw there was an understanding between the parties, and that now the Curate of " St. Plum's " had little chance of the living.

He kept his ideas to himself, and in a few weeks they were confirmed: the living was presented to the Rev. Brigson Hewly, who read himself in on New Year's-day; and as the parishioners did not choose to offend *him* individually, they burnt the Patron in effigy, partly because they disliked his choice, but principally because he had taken no notice of their petition.

In the meantime, it was not natural that the new vicar should feel cordially towards the man whom they had wished to have. Nothing, indeed, would have pleased him better than at once to have told the late vicar's curate that he could dispense with his services, but he was a long-headed man, and did not choose to take such an unpopular step till he had got some hold in the parish. He resolved to ask Dreux to stay, hoping that he could make him so very uncomfortable that he would soon throw up the curacy of his own accord.

He called at his lodgings, and offered him the curacy. He was a little mortified at the unhesitating pleasure with which it was accepted; in fact, the present curate, and virtually late vicar, felt that there was scarcely any annoyance he would not submit to rather than give up all influence over the people, and leave them altogether in the hands of Mr. Hewly.

And now began the real tug of war. Hewly was determined that he never would dismiss his curate, and equally determined to make him so uncomfortable that he would soon go of his own accord. Unfortunately for him, if he did induce his curate to leave him, he could not prevent his preaching in the afternoon, for the lecturer was constituted such for life. So there was not much use in getting rid of him. But it was gall and wormwood to him to see the power that this circumstance gave. He felt that the church was only half his own; and in the morning he preached to empty benches,—for his adherents dared not follow him from his late church, as he had so constantly spoken against the wickedness of leaving one's parish church; and as for his new parishioners, some from good motives and some from bad ones, chose to absent themselves, so that from his lofty pulpit he could see the handsome woodwork of the benches very plainly,—there were few shawls and fewer coats to hide it from his view.

On the other hand, in the afternoon there was always such a crowd as could scarcely be accommodated; the people stood so thickly in the aisle, that they crumpled and crushed his clerical garments as he passed down it to read prayers, for it was an established custom that the vicar or his

curate should read prayers for the afternoon lecturer.
The lecturer's first act of conciliation was to do
away with this custom by reading for himself; but
it soured the vicar's feelings only to have done
it for him twice.

Mr. Hewly felt that he could not stir; his
curate's conduct irritated and perplexed him
to the last degree: from the slight knowledge
he had previously had of him, he had supposed
him to be possessed of far too high a spirit
to endure the most trifling impertinence; and
his dignified carriage, together with a certain
calmness in his voice, kept him at an unaccountable distance in spite of himself.

He now found his curate was not the kind
of man he had imagined; instead of firing up
at any little act of neglect, or any assumption
on his part of the tone of command, he seemed
not to notice the one, and to think the other quite
inadvertent, and treated his vicar with such polished
courtesy, as made that gentleman feel it almost
impossible not to assume his very best behaviour
in return. But it annoyed him to feel that he could
not act the gentleman half so well with his most
elaborate exertions, as his curate did without effort
and by nature. As to anything so ungentlemanly
on Hewly's part as an intentional affront, such
an idea never seemed to occur to him; and
after a short struggle, a few poor, spiritless
attempts to be rude to him, the vicar gave in,

and treated him with proper consideration, afraid
lest he might show him by his manner that he
felt his want of courtesy, but supposed he knew
no better !

Mr. Hewly at this time would have given something to have been born a gentleman; his manner
and address were by no means bad, but the consciousness of a certain difference between his own
manner and that of his curate, filled him with envy
and dislike. Without the slightest assumption on
the part of the curate, he received a great deal
of genuine respect and deference : the clerk's bow
and the pewopener's curtsey were quite different
things, as bestowed on the vicar or on his curate.
They were all alike : the poor spoke to him in quite
a different tone ; to the less familiar one they
reserved for Dreux; and the worst of it was, they
evidently did not do it on purpose; instinctively
and without effort, they entertained for the one
a deferential feeling, that no kindness, no pastoral
superintendence could teach them to extend to the
other !

It was very provoking, the more so as he was
obliged to keep it to himself. But he thought,
though he felt obliged to be polite to his curate,
he could still annoy him with a little patronage ;
he accordingly hid his discomfiture, and asked him
to come and dine with him ; but he detected himself
repeatedly during dinner, hoping that he was doing
the honours of his table in a stylish and gentleman-

like manner, and in wondering whether everything was set on the table properly. He had ordered an absurdly abundant and handsome dinner for two people; he now blamed himself for it, as it seemed to make his guest of too much consequence.

He tried to think of some of the pieces of good advice that he had intended to bestow on his curate; and some of the little patronizing speeches he meant to have made; but it would not do, he could not "screw his courage to the sticking point," and he actually found himself following his guest's lead, who being specially desirous to get over the evening without any unpleasant argument, was introducing, one by one, topics of conversation on which he thought they could agree and talk amicably, humouring him in his own house, where he wished to play the patron! and changing his subjects with great tact, as he deemed it necessary.

Mr. Hewly was acute enough to see this, but he could not help himself; and all the time the unconscious curate, who saw in the whole affair nothing but a piece of ordinary civility, irritated him by his unaffected ease. In fact, he considered this dinner rather a dull thing, but one which he must go through with, and that with a good grace. He was accordingly giving himself up, with amiable patience, to the task of purveying conversation and keeping things smooth.

Oh the annoyance of being with one's superiors! thought Mr. Hewly, as the conviction became more strong in his mind than ever, that this man, his own curate, was so far above him, that he actually could not feel at ease with him, even in his own house, unless he treated him with proper respect.

And yet Mr. Dreux preserved towards him, however slightly, yet constantly, a certain recognition of his superiority in point of relative position; he perceived this, though he could not define it; and the more he knew him, the more he saw that he had mistaken reserve for pride, and energy for a high spirit.

When a man, remarkable for uprightness and honesty of purpose, gets into contact with one of sinister disposition, not at all straightforward, and conscious of defective motives, he is sure to make him feel extremely uncomfortable; he feels acutely that he is not honest, and fancies the other feels it too.

Hewly was very glad when this unpleasant evening was over, and he mentally resolved never again to encounter a dinner *tête-à-tête* with his curate; he had not accomplished his purpose; he had not shown himself the patron, the great man, and he had not even felt at his ease. He began to be quite afraid of him,—he thought he should never be able to shake him off; he felt that he should lower himself by the exhibition of any petty act of meanness, and though he was intensely jealous of his curate, he could not bear that he should despise him.

So matters went on for several weeks. The curate read prayers, and the vicar preached in the morning, dilating on such matters as he thought of importance. In the afternoon the curate preached exactly as he had been accustomed, and set forth precisely the same dogmas as before, though he never advanced them in a controversial way. "In fact," said poor Hewly to one of his friends, "he speaks with no more hesitation as to his being in the right, than he might do if no man had ever differed from him: he never even alludes to my opinions, any more than if he ignored both their existence and mine altogether."

But though in public the curate lost no ground, he felt that everything his vicar touched he marred; they had both made a mistake, and though they were both accommodating, it was evident that they could not work together. However, by really mutual forbearance, they got on till the middle of February. Dreux did not care how much of the work he did; in fact, he had been accustomed to do it all; on the other hand, the Vicar had a delicate chest, and was very glad on cold snowy days to sit at home by the fire. Dreux was extremely accommodating about all points that he thought unimportant; but then he was tenacious of all others, and this must inevitably have led to a quarrel, if the vicar had not been so hoarse that he could scarcely speak, and the curate so busy, owing to an unusually sickly season, that excepting for a few minutes at a time, they scarcely saw each other.

For the present, as long as the dreary east wind blew and the frost froze his finger ends, poor Mr. Hewly had neither strength nor desire to disturb his curate, lest he should suddenly take leave of the parish and leave it on his hands, and then he would be in a terrible predicament. He got quite pleasant in his manners, and, having been long accustomed to weak health, was quite astonished to see his curate coming in day after day as well as ever, though he could see him from the vicarage windows standing over an open grave with the snow piled up on each side, and himself with a thick powdering of it on his head before he had concluded the service. Yet he was none the worse. He could stand anything in the way of work and weather. He seemed to bring an atmosphere of health into the house with him. His hands were always warm, his step always elastic; he knew no inconvenience from the east wind, and though he was very busy, he seemed rather to like coming in daily to see his vicar and tell the small unimportant pieces of parish news so interesting to clergymen, and to them only.

By the middle of February the weather suddenly changed and became remarkably warm and mild. This filled the churches with a continuous volley of coughs; the town was visited with influenza, but the mild weather released Mr. Hewly and put a stop to the friendliness which had arisen between

him and his curate. He could now put his head out
of doors, and they again began to pull different ways,
and that with considerable vigour.

Among the many who were laid up with influenza was Mr. What's-his-name Brown.   He sent
one morning to know whether Mr. Dreux would
take his week-day evening lecture for him; the
latter complied, and wrote to Wilfred not to come
for his lesson till nine.

Now Mrs. Brown bethought herself that she
should like to give Mr. Dreux a supper after the
lecture, and to that end she caused some sausages to
be fried and laid on mashed potatoes, and prepared
a dish with her own fair hands, called apple turn-
overs.

" And very glad he will be of it, my dear, no
doubt; for I dare say it's not often that he has
a good supper now, for they say he's as poor as
a church rat."

The Rev. Athanasius looked up with feeble
wonder.

" And what do you think, Athanasius, my dear,
of our sending him that fowl as hangs up in the
larder and a basket of our keeping apples?   Don't
you think that would be a pretty way of paying
him ? "

" Don't think of such a thing, mother," said the
fretful little man.   " Oh dear, I hope you won't
hint at it before him by way of payment.   What an
affront ! "

"Well, I'm sure, what a fluster you're in, Athanasius! You needn't colour up so. Isn't pride one of the deadly sins? A Christian man ought to be meek, and not above *excepting* a benefit."

"If he wouldn't mind it I should. Many and many's the time he's stopped at the vestry on his way from morning service and taken me back with him to dinner to save me the lonely, wet walk. He made me welcome to his books; and you know, mother, after I had that illness he came and drove me out every day."

"And yet you won't let me give him so much as an apple?"

"Not if I can help it."

Mr. Dreux presently came in, and perceiving the preparations made for him, did not like to disappoint Mrs. Brown. He accordingly sat down to supper, though it was very little past eight o'clock, and the good woman began to ply him with eatables and drinkables, being determined that for once he should have a good meal, for she laboured under the idea that in his lodgings he probably had but short commons.

Having done the greatest justice that he possibly could to the supper, he stayed a while to talk to Athanasius. The poor man looked most dismal, with his face swelled and his eyes dull and heavy, but Mrs. Brown observed that he soon cheered up as their guest continued to chat with him; she also observed that he watched the maid with considerable attention while she cleared the table, and put away two or three articles of plate in a corner cupboard.

As soon as he could he took his leave, came home, and gave young Greyson his lesson. When it was over he inquired of his pupil whether he had sold his plate?

Young Greyson, with some confusion, replied in the negative.

"Then," said Mr. Dreux, "something that happened to-night is the more unaccountable. I could have declared—I think I could have taken my oath, that among the plate I made over to you was a mustard-pot which I have used for years. It is made in the shape of a barrel, and has my arms and my motto upon it."

"Most assuredly there was such a mustard-pot," said his pupil, aroused to interest.

"Your remark only shows how much two disinterested witnesses may be mistaken, for this very night I used my own identical old mustard-pot at Mrs. Brown's, with my motto and cypher upon it."

"Are you quite certain—are you sure of the fact?"

"Quite certain. There could be no manner of doubt on the subject. So, my dear fellow, we are both wrong, and that mustard-pot must have been sold with my modern plate. If you look when you go home you will not find it."

"I am quite convinced it was in the chest," said Wilfred, abstractedly.

"And I am quite certain that it was on Mrs. Brown's table to-night. The moment I took up the old familiar thing, the motto stared me in the face, —'I Dreux to me honour.' You need not look incredulous. It is so."

"I'll go and ask the old lady where she got it, and whether she has any more. I not only can, but will, take my oath that that mustard-pot was *here* on the night when I wrote my name on the box."

"And do you mean to say you have missed it since?" asked his host, surprised at the vehemence of his manner.

Wilfred admitted that he had, and that his suspicions fell on the lodger,—adding that that was why he had been so anxious to find out where he was gone, and to examine his room.

"Then," said Dreux, "we must have left that mustard-pot about the room without observing it; for of course if he had opened the box he would not have taken that and nothing more."

Young Greyson made no answer.

"I hope you did not miss anything else, Greyson?" asked Mr. Dreux.

"Oh, I found the box quite full," returned his pupil, feeling his ears tingle and his cheeks burn. "But I shall go to-morrow to Mrs. Brown, and ask her where she bought that mustard-pot. With this clue we may possibly trace him and find out where Dickson is. What am I to prepare, Mr. Dreux, for to-morrow night ? "

But Mr. Dreux's suspicions being once aroused, he was not to be put off with any half-confidences, and he questioned Wilfred so closely, that at last he was compelled to confess how, when he opened the box, he found nothing within but some heavy books, ten bath-bricks, and a hearth-brush.

Mr. Dreux did not receive the communication with half so much equanimity as his pupil could have wished.

" I am extremely sorry," said Wilfred, " quite as sorry as you can possibly be ; but now that we have got a clue I shall take all possible pains to follow it up."

Mr. Dreux sat silent.

" I have already made many inquiries in an underhand way," proceeded Greyson, " and to-morrow I shall set to work in good earnest and try to recover my property."

" Your property ! " repeated Mr. Dreux, remarking the slight emphasis with which he uttered these words.

" Yes, to be sure," said Greyson, taking out the piece of paper, and reading from it the list of articles, " my property, which I bought, and which has been stolen from me."

" Your property, which you paid for and never

possessed. I blame myself exceedingly that I promised to keep the thing secret. What a position I shall be in if this man cannot be found! Give me that paper, Greyson."

"I shall do no such thing," replied Greyson, thrusting it into his coat-pocket, and hastily buttoning it up.

"But I desire you to let me have it back."

"Why, I am sorry to refuse; but how, without it (if I should get back this property), am I to prove that it really is mine, that the former owner really and actually sold it, parted with all interest in it, and received a fair price in return?"

In spite of his distress, Mr. Dreux could not restrain a faint smile when Greyson said this, and the boy went on, as composedly as possible,—

"When people are so excessively anxious to have everything made plain and distinct, and when they distrust other people's straightforward, honest intentions in trade and barter, and are afraid they shall have their goods thrust back upon them by means of some beggarly quibble or other, they sometimes find that, in self-defence, the purchaser becomes as deep as themselves; if they cannot trust their fellow-creatures without documents, the documents must be produced against them. That property is mine. If any one says it is not, let us go to law at once, and I will prove it in open court. Here is the list of the articles, with the signatures of buyer and seller. I should hope I'm not going to be cheated out of my property because I'm under age."

Mr. Dreux laughed, but so painfully that it forced tears into his eyes.

" Give it me," he said, "if you have any regard for my peace."

" I haven't the least "—

"No, don't joke; let us call this a loan, and let me pay interest."

" I can't think of it. Really I wonder, Mr. Dreux, that you should try to take advantage of my youth in this way. You don't consider the fun I shall have in ferretting out this lodger. Would you, now, have given it up at my age ?—tamely made over your rights to another, instead of setting out in search of your property yourself ?"

" Will you behave like a man ? "

" There's only one man present; if I imitate his conduct, I shall act in a most unreasonable manner. I think, rather than that, I will still practise the innocent simplicity so becoming my age."

" Well, if there is nothing to be done with you, go on with your problems."

Greyson did as he was desired ; but just as he had settled again to his work, there was a loud ring at the bell, and the landlady showed up Mr. Hewly. The fortnight of warm weather had completely set him up again. With health had come spirit, and he came in with his nerves or his temper evidently strung up for something more than common.

He had been to dine at the Fergusons'. This
young Greyson knew, and he thought, from his
highly irritable state, that something must have
greatly annoyed him. He thought it would be no
pleasure to him to see his tormentor that night, but
he did not go; he merely took up his compasses and
began an ornamental design upon a piece of paper,
while the vicar proceeded to unfold his mission.

This was soon done. He was evidently highly
excited. He produced a paper containing a list of
engagements, the duty for the week, funerals, &c.,
informed his curate that he was going out for a
week, and requested, or rather laid his commands
upon him to perform it.

Mr. Dreux bore his insolence of manner with
perfect calmness.

" There, Sir," said Hewly, tossing another paper
towards him, " and you will be so good as see this
attended to."

Wilfred looked up, amazed. Mr. Dreux took it
up and said, " This, I perceive, is a form of prayer
to be used by the mistress on dismissing the school."
Having looked it over, he laid it down, leaned back
in his chair, and began to mend a pen.

Hewly's irritation increased. " Yes, Sir, you are
right," he retorted, " it is a form of prayer; and I
suppose, though I have been called a formalist, I
should scarcely be justified in flinging aside forms
altogether."

The Curate made no answer, and only showed his

astonishment by a slight, involuntary elevation of the eyebrows.

But Wilfred was by no means inclined to let his insolence pass so quietly. He did not like him, but he despised him too much to be seriously angry with him. "Give him the opportunity," he thought, " and he'll soon make himself ridiculous." He accordingly said, with a smile of apparent good humour,—

"I believe, Mr. Hewly, it was one of our own old Divines who said, that while we 'cultivate the form, we must not neglect the spirit.' He was a nice old gentleman, but he afterwards fell into the hands of the Roman Catholics, who sweetly and piously burnt him alive."

"Greyson," exclaimed Mr. Dreux, astonished at his absurd remark, "do you ever think of the old saying, 'Let us be silent, for so are the gods?'"

"Sir," said Mr. Hewly, starting up, and speaking to Greyson, "I don't know what you mean. All I can collect is, that you mean to affront me, Sir. (Mr. Hewly was always very lavish of the title of honour when he was in a passion.) If you have no respect for me as your spiritual superior, I should have expected you might have shown some respect for yourself, Sir."

On hearing this, Greyson lifted up his compasses, and, having examined the point, began to design a figure, with an easy smile.

"Sir," exclaimed Hewly, addressing his curate,

and stuttering with passion, "your—your—your—
pupil's worthy of his master."

"I am sorry he has purposely annoyed you," was
the reply, "and if I understand him aright, I believe
he will apologize."

"I have much pleasure in apologizing," said Wilfred, looking up with the same smile, "since Mr.
Dreux wishes it; and I am sorry I have annoyed
him by annoying you."

"Greyson," said Mr. Dreux, in a low voice, as he
again went on with his figure, while Hewly stormed
at them both with surprising violence, "I cannot
consider that this is acting either like a gentleman
or a Christian."

"Sir," cried Hewly, "I'm much obliged to you,
but I don't want you to take up my quarrels."

"I beg your pardon, Mr. Hewly. I am sorry I
have annoyed you," said Wilfred, and then muttered
to himself, "particularly when I have such a different example before me."

"Ever since I first saw you, Sir," proceeded Mr.
Hewly, now too angry to care what he said, "you
have opposed and thwarted me by all means in your
power, even the most unjustifiable."

"Some people think the end justifies the means,"
replied Greyson, forgetting himself again, and
astonished that Hewly should have alluded to his
wooing. "I had a very good end in view."

Here Mr. Dreux, not knowing what would be
said next, started up, and taking a candle, said,

" Mr. Hewly, as my pupil has apologized, you will excuse my lighting him down stairs; it is long past his time. He ought to be at home, and the sooner the better."

" You have spoken the truth for once, Sir," replied Mr. Hewly. " Your influence tells quite enough upon him without his having more of it than usual."

" Spoken the truth for once !" exclaimed Mr. Dreux, for the first time thrown off his guard. " What do you mean by that ?"

" It's your turn to apologize now," said Wilfred, passionately, " and the sooner you do it the better. Will you, or will you not ?"

" I shall do nothing at the bidding of a boy like you," replied Hewly; " and I hope to make you repent of this before long. No, Sir; I will not apologize."

" Very well," said his curate, looking steadily at him, " I shall not urge it upon you ; there is no use in arguing with a man in a passion ; but you will excuse my remaining in your presence any longer." So saying, he took young Greyson by the arm, opened his bed-room door, and shut himself and his pupil in.

Hewly being thus left alone, stood for a few seconds irresolute on the rug, then he snatched up his hat and made the best of his way down stairs, slamming the street-door after him so as sufficiently to apprise them of his exit.

"There," said Wilfred, as they emerged again from their retreat, "what a fool I was not to hold my tongue."

Mr. Dreux's features were still flushed with the indignant feeling of surprise that his vicar's conduct had occasioned, but he sat down quietly by the table and said nothing.

"It was very evident," continued Greyson, "that he came here on purpose to annoy you; but I am sorry I gave him the opportunity. Hewly in a passion!—I wouldn't have believed it unless I had seen it. It's my belief he had taken too much wine."

"Well, think no more of it," was the reply. "You have now to think of recovering this stolen silver and the ring. You must leave this contention to me. In my opinion, the first thing you have to do is to obtain what information you can from Mrs. Brown as to the person from whom she bought the mustard-pot. The next thing is to tell your uncle all about this affair. I deeply regret that I permitted you to make the purchase unknown to him."

"I would not have made it on any other terms."

"Now, good night. Let me know to-morrow evening what success you have had."

The pupil then took his leave. The host sat up, lost in thought; he had now an additional weight on his mind; he believed he must leave his curacy at once. He could not stay without some apology from Hewly, and yet he was greatly attached to the people among whom he had laboured so long, and it was very hard to leave them to such a successor.

At ten o'clock the next morning he received the following note from Hewly,—its formality, no less than its contents, perfectly astonished him:—

" The Rev. Brigson Hewly presents his compliments to the Rev. A. C. Dreux, and sends him the books connected with the almshouse accounts.

" Mr. Hewly is sensible that the unchristian conduct of another party induced him last night to betray too much heat in repressing it. He therefore thinks it most consistent with Christian meekness to apologize, and to assure Mr. Dreux that the events of last night shall never be alluded to by him in future.

" *Tuesday morning.*"

Mr. Dreux's first impulse was to toss this impertinent apology into the fire. On second thoughts he resolved to put it away, but not to answer it. He saw that Hewly was determined he should not throw up the curacy, and have it in his power to say that it was in consequence of *his* refusal to apologize for having insulted him; at the same time he wished to word his apology so that it should rather widen the breach between them.

Notwithstanding, it *was* an apology; so he decided not to take any steps at present about leaving the curacy; and he anticipated one quiet week, at least, in the absence of his vicar.

In the middle of the day he called on Wilfred, and was shown into his little study. Both his injunctions had been obeyed; but the affair had only been laid before Mr. Paton upon his giving a promise of secrecy.

" I've found out why Hewly was in such a passion," said Greyson. " My aunt told me that, during the evening, it came out that Helen had been to confession,—at least it seemed so. My aunt did not give a very distinct account of it, nor could she tell how Helen, being still a professed Protestant, could confess to a Catholic priest; but it seems she must have done something tantamount to it, for they talked about her having received absolution from Hewly's friend, the Irish Roman Catholic priest."

" And this is the result of Hewly's teaching. I am not very much surprised "—

" But Hewly was; he had no idea she would go so far beyond him. He was horrified, as well he might be; for if she professes herself a Roman Catholic, she cannot do such an inconsistent thing as to marry him. And if he becomes one himself, he shuts himself out from marriage altogether."

" Poor man,—I pity him. I think I can excuse his rudeness of last night."

" I do not pity him, for I believe he is only

looking out for a rich wife. Helen now talks a great deal more about 'Father Macauley' than about him. While Hewly was ill, he very much lost his influence over her weak, fickle mind. She is so wild and headstrong, that, if she thinks she ought to become a Roman Catholic, she will profess herself one, however soon she may see fit to turn round again. Still, I think she has a strong liking for Hewly."

" Then, if he is engaged to her, he may very likely declare that he considers it his duty to fulfil the engagement."

" Ah, but they are not engaged," said Greyson. " Helen's father would not allow that; though it is an understood thing that, if neither should change, they may be married in a year from last November, which makes Hewly's chance small." He then proceeded to tell Mr. Dreux that, in case he could find any clue as to where the lodger was concealed, his uncle had promised to let him set out himself in search of him. Frank Maidley was to go with him. He painted the delight of such an expedition in glowing terms, and declared that the adventures he hoped to meet with would more than indemnify him for his loss. " In fact," he concluded, " if we are to find it at all, I hope it will not be for a good long while."

CHAPTER XXI.

MRS. THERESA DREUX.

It was not till the day before Mr. Hewly's expected return that young Greyson found out anything of the lodger which his uncle thought worth investigating.

Directly after breakfast the next morning he made his appearance at Mr. Dreux's lodgings, completely disguised by an enormous pair of whiskers, a light great-coat, and a red comforter.

"What is this absurd disguise for?" asked Mr. Dreux, when he recognised him.

"Why, of course I don't want him to know me."

"Know you,—he has never seen you."

"Oh, that does not at all matter; we wish to have a little fun. You should see Frank; I am certain his own mother wouldn't know *him*."

"Where are you now going?—tell me that."

"Oh, a long way; it's a secret *where*. In fact, we don't exactly know where we may have to go. Now I'm off,—don't you wish me success?"

" Most certainly. But I am just as certain what kind of success you will have, as—well, I do not wish to damp you. Pray let me hear often what you are about; I shall be very uneasy about you till I see you again."

" Oh, I shall write," cried the pupil, and he ran off in high spirits, while Mr. Dreux applied himself to his letters, which lay unopened before him. He hoped to find one from Elinor; it was so long since she had written that he had begun to feel uneasy. Instead of this, there was one in his aunt's hand-writing, which rather startled him, and he broke it open hastily, and read as follows:—

" MY DEAR ARTHUR,—

" I am sure you will be glad to hear that Elinor has had rather a better night; and Doctor King thinks her no worse this morning. So do not be alarmed; for, as I always say, when young people are ill, you know they have youth on their side. And I have said, over and over again, to Elinor,— ' My dear, why don't you write and tell Arthur how poorly you are?' but she doesn't like to distress you, which seems natural. And, as I said to her yesterday, ' What a mistake it is, my dear, for he must be far more anxious than if he knew the truth,—which, Dr. King says, should never be concealed from the friends of a patient.' And so I asked him point blank whether you hadn't better be told, and he replied,—' By all means. I am surprised it has not been done before.'

  " So I thought I would write, my dear Arthur, to relieve your anxiety, for I do not like to have all the responsibility myself; and as Elinor gets weaker every day, and takes nothing but rusks soaked in wine and water, don't you think it would be much better for you to come over and see her, for all the advice I have for her does not seem to do her any good; and if she *has* anything on her mind,—I'm sure I don't know why they should think so,—but perhaps she might tell it to you and feel relieved.

  " My dear Arthur, you know how weak and bad my eyes are, and Dr. King says they will never be any better, nor at my age is it to be expected; but as I had said to Elinor, ' My dear, I will certainly write,' I thought I would put myself out of the way to do it. And you have always been a very fond brother to her, though it is shocking to think how rude you used to make her when she was a child,—I never shall forget it,—and teach her to climb, and fish, and all sorts of things not proper for a girl. But, as I said, you could have the blue room, you know, and the little boudoir off Elinor's dressing-room for a study, just as you used to do when you were at college.

  " So I hope you will not disappoint Elinor if you can possibly help it, for now she is confined to her bed she is, of course, very dull.

  " She told me before she went to sleep to give

her dear love to you; and believe me, my dear Arthur,

"Your affectionate aunt,

"ELINOR THERESA DREUX.

"P.S. Dr. King says these slow fevers are often very obstinate. I told him I had asked you to come. He is a very disagreeable man, and says that ought to have been done a week ago."

He read this unaccountable letter to its close, and then, leaning back in his chair, a faint vertigo for a moment almost deprived him of his senses. He presently recovered himself sufficiently to rise and open the window; then a wretched half-hour passed before he could decide what was best to be done. That Elinor was ill was only too evident, but the extent of her illness he remained in doubt of. He knew his aunt too well not to be aware that Elinor might be at the point of death before she would take sufficient alarm to rouse herself to any decided line of action; it was a great deal to have herself written to request him to come to his sister. To go instantly to Leamington was his decision. Hewly would return in a few hours. He therefore wrote a letter, to be sent to his house, explaining his absence and its cause.

The journey was one of two hundred miles, but great part of the way was by cross country roads, so that he did not reach his destination till the middle of the next day. The nervous excitement caused by this ambiguous letter was almost past endurance. It was quite a relief, on looking up to his aunt's windows, to find them unclosed.

The servant who ushered him in volunteered the information that his sister was better.

"Bless me, Arthur, how pale you look!" cried his aunt, meeting him at the door of the dining-room. "Bring some wine, Gorden. Why, of course, my dear Arthur, you cannot go up-stairs yet, while Dr. King's here; so sit down, and don't think of such a thing."

His aunt's vague communication fretted him almost past endurance, and he threw himself into a seat to wait for the physician, looking so ill that the old lady began to ply him with questions about his own health.

The physician presently returned; was glad Mr. Dreux was come,—thought his patient no worse,— she had a great deal of low fever,—she was certainly in some danger,—he might presently go up and see her,—she had been got up, and was lying on the sofa.

"He must not go, Doctor, while he has that pale, eager look,—he would frighten her out of her senses," said Mrs. Elinor Theresa. "You look as if you had been turned to stone. Come nearer the fire, Arthur. Are you cold? Dear me, how nonsensical I am!—perhaps you havn't dined. Are you hungry, Arthur?"

"My dear Sir," said the sympathizing physician,

"I assure you I quite expect to see your sister better to-morrow."

"Ah! well, Arthur, I'm glad to see you beginning to look like flesh and blood again. Didn't I tell you when I wrote not to be uneasy? My dear Doctor, they were always so very fond of each other. As for Elinor, she constantly says, ' If I could only see my brother I should be happy.' "

"Well, Madam," said Dr. King, rather testily, " and she will see him directly, and be all the better for it, I dare say."

"I wish to go up at once," said Mr. Dreux; "I must see my sister directly."

"Not till you have taken a glass of wine and a biscuit;—it would excite my patient to see you looking so pale."

The glass of wine was hastily swallowed, and Mrs. Theresa Dreux showed her nephew up stairs. As she walked to Elinor's door she talked on subjects strangely at variance with his feelings.

"Wait here for a moment," she said, "I must just go into the room first and prepare her."

He sat down in Elinor's dressing-room while his aunt went into the bed-room beyond.

"You may come in, Arthur," she presently said, and he quietly entered.

Elinor was reclining on a very low couch, close to the window. She wore a wrapping white dress. Her face was pallid, and her features attenuated and tense. As he entered she half-raised herself into a sitting position, and he knelt down by the couch the better to receive her in his arms. Elinor laughed with hysterical joy as she put her thin arms round him; but presently his face sunk heavily, and as she held him, she fell back on the pillows, and said, with a terrified glance, " Help me, aunt, Arthur has fainted!"

Her aunt wrung her hands, and ran about looking for a smelling-bottle; the maid shrieked at the top of the stairs for a glass of water; but, happily for all parties, Dr. King came speedily up. He had been very doubtful as to the result of the interview, and fully expected to find Elinor in a swoon, instead of which he found her sitting up with a strength he had not given her credit for, supporting her brother's head, while her aunt and maid ran hither and thither, a perfect picture of helplessness and inefficiency.

He soon relieved Elinor of her burden, and, the proper remedies being applied, the patient opened his eyes.

" Bless me, ma'am!" exclaimed the maid, crying and sobbing, " I never saw a gentleman faint before!"

Elinor, sitting up on her sofa, watched their proceedings with the utmost anxiety. Her brother's face gradually resumed something like its natural hue, while her aunt, holding the smelling-bottles, exclaimed against the world in general for all the dreadful things that happened when nobody expected

them; and against Elinor in particular, for being ill
and frightening her brother; then against the said
brother, for causing her a palpitation of the heart,
and disappointing her expectations. "For I have
always said," continued this wise woman, "that if
there was a man in the world who possessed perfect
self-command, it was my nephew. I have said to
Elinor times out of mind, 'Elinor, my dear, if you
were to cut his hand off he would never shed a
tear; he wouldn't jump, not if fifty guns were to go
off close to him! Such nerves! Elinor, my dear,
don't you remember that review?' Why, bless me,
Morris, how the water trickles down this poplin
dress of mine. Make haste to get a towel and
wipe it."

The physician, who seemed to be a man of a
crusty temper, looked daggers at the good lady;
and then, his face suddenly changing, he said something kind and encouraging to Elinor, and gave her
brother leave to rise.

The two females had drenched his hair with
water; the physician took the towel from the maid,
without apology or remark, and began to dry it for
him.

"Now," he said, in a whisper, "don't imagine
that all this has done my poor little patient any
harm,—quite the contrary. I told her the other
day, that if the house were to take fire, she would
find strength to run out of it. She wants rousing.
I hope this will prove a little stimulus, poor child!"

"Are you better now, dearest?" said Elinor tenderly, as he stooped over her to kiss her; "but ah! how thin you are, Arthur—how cold your cheek is; you have been ill too!"

"No, I am quite well, Elinor; my fainting was nothing but a foolish mistake. I see you are much better than I thought."

"I shall be better now you are come, dear; but oh! I am so tired."

"And no wonder," interposed the crusty doctor. "Madam, I wish Miss Dreux to be put to bed immediately; she is exhausted, and quite hysterical. And you, Sir, come away at once. You are not to see her again till you have had a good meal and an hour's rest. Travelled all night, and eaten nothing to-day, I'll be bound; and then fainting away! Parcel of silly old women frightened him to death! Bah! Come away, Sir; I'll have no kissing and hanging over my patients. Done her a great deal of good, though,—but that's mum."

This speech was not all uttered aloud, and during its delivery the old gentleman looked with strong disfavour at the mistress and maid, who were still occupied with the purple poplin gown.

"Madam, are you going to undress that young lady; or must I fetch up the cook to do it?"

"Now really, Doctor King!"

"Will you do it, then, ma'am? Now, Sir, come away. What did you mean by going off in that style? A fine, strong young man like you! Did you do it for experiment—Eh?

"I don't know what I meant by it," was the reply. "If it was an experiment, I hope I shall never repeat it as long as I live. I found it anything but an agreeable one."

This conversation took place as they descended the stairs.

"I'll be bound that old woman mystified you nicely when she asked you to come here. I had great work to get her to write at all. Parcel of silly old women! I've no patience with them."

"My aunt's letter certainly tortured me a good deal; it was extremely vague."

"Well, the fact of the matter is, she's very poorly, there's no denying that; but, in my opinion, she has something on her mind, and if you can get her to talk of it, you'll do her a service—but not for the next few days, she's too weak at present. I dare say you hardly expected to find her alive when you got here."

"I scarcely knew what to think."

"Ah, I saw what kind of a demon had been gnawing and worrying at your heart! You shall hear the downright truth from me every day. Never mind what that old woman says; she frets me almost out of my life. I wonder whether that poor child's in bed yet. Well, Sir, good day. My advice to you is, that you eat a good dinner, take a

couple of glasses of port, and leave the rest to
Providence."

With these remarks the Doctor took his leave.

Elinor was too weak to see him again that day,
but while she slept he came and looked at her.
Her face was painfully thin—strangely altered, but
in sleep the anxious expression which had shocked
him so much was not apparent. Her small hand
lay on the counterpane; every little bone was
visible.   When in health it had often looked
whiter; for now through the too transparent skin
every purple and lilac and crimson vein was distinctly traceable.   She was wasted to a skeleton.
He thought he should scarcely have known her;
yet he took comfort from the maid's assurance, that
she was sleeping much more comfortably than
usual.

He saw her several times the next day and the
next: she seemed feverish, and could not talk.
His heart sank within him as he watched the
gradual failure of her strength, appetite, and interest
even in him.   They were never left alone, and she
seemed to care for nothing; yet she was dressed
daily, and laid on her couch, and seemed none the
worse for that slight exertion.

It was not till the fourth day that they were left
alone together.   Elinor had been more than usually
lethargic during the morning, but she no sooner
saw the door shut on her aunt and maid than she

seemed to revive. She was lying on her couch, and asked him to sit by her and hold her in his arms. She was so quiet that he fancied she was asleep. She had nestled close to him, and while he supported her hope grew strong within him; she was at length left to his influence: he thought he could soothe her. Now was an opportunity; but while he hesitated to begin talking to her, she showed him strongly the cause of her illness and the direction of her thoughts. She put her hand so gently upon his waistcoat pocket, that if he had not been alive to her motive he would not have observed it. That was not the right one. The thin fingers presently found the other, and very softly drew something out, and opened it. There was a very long silence. Elinor soothed herself with gazing at Allerton's picture. She seemed scarcely aware that he could see her. Tears began to fall upon it, then she sobbed, but still neither of them said a word.

It was too evident to him now what was the matter. He felt himself powerless, far more so than he really was. He drew her still nearer, and entreated her not to weep. The sound of his voice seemed to recal her to herself, and she asked him first, with a burst of tears, why he had kept his trials so much to himself—why he had concealed them from her, who loved him, or at least spoken so lightly of them? and then, why had he never told her anything about Mr. Allerton—never even mentioned his name.

It was bitterness to him to be compelled to admit that he had nothing to tell—nothing whatever, but that he had wrung out of Hewly that Allerton spoke of himself as active and doing duty, therefore he must be in health wherever he was.

To his surprise, Elinor received this scanty intelligence with lively gratitude. She did not want to see him,—she could do without even knowing whether he still cared for her,—if he was safe and well it was enough. She could live now, she could even be happy; but to go on week after week not knowing whether some long illness or some lingering death might have kept him away from Westport, was more than she could bear.

She lay silent for a while with the miniature in her hand,—something of the tranquillity of those endeared features seemed to pass to her own heart, and the manly affection they expressed soothed her as if the original had looked so at herself.

"I feel much better now—far stronger. I think it was hope that I wanted," she said, "and some one to love me and comfort me as you do, Arthur."

"My darling! what hope did you want, Elinor?"

"Not the hope of seeing him again. I wanted hope *for* him—hope that he might be happy—even hope that he might forget *me*, if that would make him happy."

Her fit of weeping, far from exhausting her, seemed to have brought relief and tranquillity. She would not let her brother leave her, but still retaining the little portrait, began tenderly to upbraid him for having concealed the state of his health from her. She confessed that she had written to Mrs. Dorothy when first he lost his property, and from time to time had heard from her a full account of all that had happened, and that he had endeavoured to conceal.

"We have each made a mistake, my sweet Elinor," said he; "we should have done better to have trusted each other."

"Ah, yes! I have drooped for months for want of knowing the whole truth respecting you and Mr. Allerton, and now you have endured a much greater shock than if I had told you frankly how ill I was."

Her brother said nothing; he felt that in his earnest desire to spare her he had inflicted a great deal. But though there was so little that was cheering to be communicated, Elinor was surprisingly the better for the conversation. She absolutely required sympathy,—her brother could give it, and she revived like a watered flower; it drew her thoughts in some degree from their aching pining after the absent to have something present to love. The mere sound of her brother's voice was healing to her—it calmed and comforted her; and when he came each night to pray beside her, however restless she might have been, she would drop away to sleep after it like a weary child.

This quiet sleep, to which she had long been a stranger, did her more good than medicines or restoratives. Each day she could sit up longer, and though still a mere skeleton, she had already lost the transparent whiteness which characterized her complexion when first her brother saw her. In the full confidence of being understood, she unburdened her mind of all the tormenting thoughts which had oppressed her nearly to death, and received from him an assurance that he would never conceal any of his trials from her again.

" And has nothing happened," she went on, recurring to the old theme,—" has nothing happened to give you the slightest clue to Mr. Allerton's feeling ? "

Her brother sighed ; he scarcely knew what to do for the best. It was evident she *could* not forget ; then, perhaps, it was better she should think favourably of his friend.

" I can scarcely think anything has happened, Elinor," he replied ; " and yet, if you would not lay too much stress upon it, I would tell you something which I fancied might be of his doing. Do not lay too much stress upon it, my dear ; it is but a trifle, and I fear lest the relation of it should make you fancy me more to be pitied than I really am. You know, Elinor, all our circumstances are of God's appointment ; ' He setteth up one, and putteth down another.' Things are changed with me, but that is no matter. You remember those two little cabinet pictures which used to hang in my dressing-room,— small landscapes ? "

" O yes, perfectly."

" And you know that all my pictures were put up for sale, Elinor ? "

" All your pictures ! What, the good ones,—even our old family pictures, Arthur ? "

" All, my dear. Well, these two little ones would not sell for anything like their value, so they were withdrawn, and I sent them to London to a picture-dealer. I heard nothing of them for some time. They were great favourites with Allerton, but he used to object to the frames ; he said they were not deep enough, and I had promised that I would shortly have them altered. Just before Christmas, word was sent me that they were sold, and I paid the last of my bills with the money. The night before I came here I found a box at my lodgings, directed to me ; on unpacking, I beheld my favourite pictures, in just such frames as Allerton had described. There was no note,—nothing but the direction for me to examine, the writing of which was not like his ; it was disguised. I tore the card off ; the name on the other side was carefully inked over."

" And why, then, do you think they came from Mr. Allerton ? " asked Elinor. " Let me hear all you know.   What a pleasure it would be to me if I could think so too!   It would be a proof that he still thought of you."

Her brother was surprised at the eagerness with which she caught at this slight hope, but he went on to tell her all he had reasoned out on the subject. "If any of my friends at Westport," he said, "had wished to give me some favourite possession out of my old house, they would not have thought of wait-ing so many months : and would they have chosen the only things which were sent away to be disposed of?   Besides, I do not remember telling to any one Allerton's fancy for these two pictures, nor the kind of frames he wished them to have."

"I know the kind you mean ; he had several prints so framed.   They were invented by a man whom he used to patronize."

"Yes ; so that, on the whole, I feel quite inclined to think they came from him."

Elinor fully believed it, and this shadow of a hope that he still retained a friendly feeling for her brother was enough for her imaginative mind to work upon. She might see him again, at least she might hear of him ; there was no such quarrel between them that it was impossible they could ever be reconciled,—no estrangement which time and change might not remove.

Elinor felt and acknowledged herself better.   Her brother's visit had been just in time.   She was sinking under the double anxiety of ignorance respecting Allerton, and certainty that he himself was concealing his real state from her.

He stayed with her a week, and though she had several relapses, she was so much improved that her physician said he might now leave her with safety. After their first conversation, they had many others. Elinor did not let her brother leave her till he had promised her that, as soon as she was well enough, she should come and visit him in his lodgings; but first she was to go to the sea-side, and as her recovery was slow, it would be some time before this could be effected.

Elinor bore the parting tolerably well, both from him and the picture. He thought it would be a cruel kindness to leave it with her, and as he did not offer it, she would not ask it.

She was far more hopeful than he was about herself; and when he had prayed with her, and commended her to God, she smiled, as he bent over her to kiss her, and said cheerfully, "Good by, dearest, I begin to be full of hope that we shall soon see happier days."

"If we can entirely acquiesce in the will of our heavenly Father, we shall see happier days," he replied; "there is no peace like that which arises from leaving all things in His hands, and saying, 'Undertake for us.'"

He left her feeling more easy, for he knew she would have every luxury and comfort that money could supply,—every indulgence but that of fellow-feeling, and every luxury but that of being understood.

He lamented this, but he could not remove her from her aunt, for he had no house to offer her; and during the old lady's lifetime she was entirely dependent upon her, though, by the terms of her grandfather's will, she was to inherit a very sufficient fortune at her death.

He had been away twelve days, and though he had written twice to Hewly, he had received no answer. He therefore feared that he might be ill, or that he might not have returned at the time expected. He took leave of Elinor, intending to travel all night, but he thought he must steal up stairs to look at her again. She was already asleep, and looked calm and happy. He touched her hand, and she moved slightly. He felt that he could now leave her with comfort; and not much relishing his aunt's letters, he called her maid aside, and giving her his address, desired her to write immediately, if anything should be amiss. When a great and new anxiety starts suddenly forward, it annihilates for the time those which had previously existed. Elinor's illness had banished for the time all his other difficulties; but now, as he journeyed homeward, they gradually returned upon him, and resumed their old sway.

First, there was his anxiety about Wilfred. He thought him by far too young, too full of spirits, and too careless to have been sent out on such a mission, and get, in all probability, among thieves and

ruffians. Secondly, he had by some means to procure the remaining 200*l.*, which in a few weeks
must be paid in for the use of the almshouses.
Thirdly, there was Hewly's conduct, which was a
source of endless trouble and annoyance, the more
so as for at least another month he believed it was
his duty to bear it. Fourthly, he would fain have
been able to return young Greyson the money he
had paid him, but there were other things to be done
before that; it was the least of his anxieties.

His eyes, as he drew near the scene of his labours,
became clouded, and his breast laden with these
various depressing thoughts. He had written to
his landlady to say at what hour he expected to
return, but he did not expect any one to meet him;
he was therefore surprised to find her waiting for him
at the station, as well as her son,—a lad of fifteen,
—and behind them Mr. What's-his-name Brown.

There was in the manner of this last a kind of
contempt, as he pushed the others back, seized the
carpet-bag, and gave it to the boy.

" Glad to see you, I'm sure, Sir," said his landlady, curtseying.

The bag was received with a humble, crest-fallen
air, and the Rev. Athanasius scowled at the obse-
quious landlady, as she rubbed her hands and continued to curtsey.

"If you'll allow me, Mr. Dreux," he then said,
with the slight air of deference with which he
generally addressed his brother clergymen, " if it's

not an intrusion, I shall be glad to walk home with you."

They soon reached the house. Mr. Brown came in, and, with a good deal of hesitation of manner, hoped he would not be offended, but his landlady, when that morning he had called to return a book which he had borrowed, had informed him that she never expected to see Mr. Dreux again, "which," she said, "is a great misfortune to me, Sir, for Mr. Dreux owes me a bill of 3*l.* 15*s.*"

"I thought, Sir," continued Mr. Brown, in his usual voice, at once discontented and deferential,— "I thought I would come with her to meet you and tell you this. She said you were supposed not to have any intention of returning. Now, Sir, you have evidently some enemy, for she never could have taken such a wild fancy into her head of her own accord. In fact,—I hope you will excuse my mentioning it,—but I found her with some silver forks and spoons, which, she said, you had in common use. She was going to take them to a silversmith, to ascertain whether they were worth the money."

Mr. Dreux felt excessively shocked and annoyed.

"I hope my having returned at the time I appointed will be supposed sufficient to exonerate me from this charge," he remarked, with a slightly bitter smile. "My credit in Westport must have sunk low indeed if any person here can think I went away to avoid paying my debts."

Mr. Brown did not make any answer; and having fulfilled what he considered a painful duty, was glad to take his leave.

Mr. Dreux thanked him, and, as soon as he was out of the house, rang the bell for his landlady, who presently appeared, looking rather frightened. He desired her to bring her bill, which she did at once, and he paid it out of some money that he had about him.

He did not think proper to ask any questions, and she left the room with many professions of sorrow, previously laying on the table a note in Hewly's handwriting, which he opened hastily, and read with no little wonder, not to say alarm. One remark of the good woman's rang unpleasantly in his ears as he went on: " She was sure she hoped he would not be offended, for she should never have believed the report if she hadn't heard it from them that ought to know."

The note began with several expressions of esteem, which, considering the source from which they came, were equally novel and alarming. The writer had heard with sorrow and amazement certain hints which he could not believe, and ought not to believe, of a man who had hitherto stood so high in public opinion; and to *quiet the popular clamour* against him, which, during his absence, it had grieved him (Hewly) to hear, the said Mr. Hewly had thought it best, in Christian kindness, to take vigorous measures; and as he had

no doubt of the perfect uprightness and honour of
Mr. Dreux, he could not suppose that he was
unprepared to meet the claims of the almshouses
against him.   He had no doubt, though Mr. D. had
left the town suddenly, without explaining anything, that the money on which these aged people
depended for their maintenance was ready, and that
Mr. D. would not fail to produce it, and save them
from beggary or the workhouse.   Accordingly he
(the said Hewly), as a proof of his friendship, had
paid the money out of his own pocket (which was a
little slip of the pen, for Mr. Ferguson had lent it
him to make some alterations with in the vicarage
previous to his marriage), to his curate's account,
and hoped, that as soon as possible after his return,
he would call on him and arrange matters, for it
was an inconvenience to a man in his circumstances
to lend the money, and it was only to save the
character of a brother clergyman that he had done
so, &c., &c.

As a foe, though a covert one, the curate was not
afraid of his vicar, but he shrank from him with
something like dread as he now saw him in the
character of a false friend.

It wanted a fortnight to the time for producing
this money.   Why, then, had Hewly been so hasty
in producing it, unless to get him into his power?
And as to popular clamour, what could he mean by
that and all the other insinuations contained in this
abominable note?

He hurried on his hat and coat, and went straight to the Vicarage. He was a good deal excited, otherwise he might have observed, that though Hewly attempted to assume a tone of patronage, he looked pale and nervous. But he contrived to check much outward expression of these feelings, and perceiving that for once his curate was both angry and agitated, he felt his advantage; and bringing up the subject of his note, he again hinted, with a kind of offensive mildness, that it had been a great inconvenience to him to advance the money.

"I am sorry for it," replied his curate, with some heat; "it is also a great inconvenience to me."

"What!" exclaimed Hewly, "you are sorry?— sorry? Do you mean to say you wish things had been suffered to take their course?"

"Most certainly I do," was the reply; "I should have been glad to have been allowed to manage my own affairs myself."

"You will please to understand," replied Mr. Hewly, trying not to be afraid of his curate's rising anger,—"you will please to understand, Sir, that, however unfortunately for me, this is, in fact, partly my own affair. I advanced the money, because, to have such things said of *my* curate, Sir, reflects, in some degree, upon *me*." ("Now for it," he thought. "Oh, do get into a passion!—you're near it, I can see. Fire up, and I have you.")

" *Such* things!" repeated his curate, in a voice of thunder.   " What things do you mean, Sir?"

Hewly felt a little nervous tremor; but he paused before he answered, and assumed an air of pious regret; he also put his hand to his head, as if it ached.

His curate repeated, passionately, " What things?"

(" Now you'll do," thought Hewly; " I *dare* say the rest to you now.   But when I've got you into a rage I hope I sha'n't turn coward.")

" What things?" he again repeated, lifting his sinister black eyes to his curate's face, and speaking with peculiar mildness, " they are things that do you no credit, Sir.   It is said that you cannot pay your debts."

" I have heard that.   What else?"

(" I wish you would take your eyes off my face," thought Hewly.   " And you're recovering your temper, worse luck!")   He folded his arms, and tried to meet his curate's steady gaze.   (" I'll make you wince before I've done, grand as you look. You shall not tower over me for nothing, with your birth, and your eloquence, and your beauty.   I like to excite you,—I like to see your eyes flash.   Now he's worked up enough.   Slowly and steadily,—I'll have him.")

" If you must know, Sir, it has been whispered in this place, that if you had not *known* where the schoolmaster, Thomas Dickson, was gone, you would probably have taken some pains to ascertain it."

An eager movement of astonishment and indignation was all the answer he got for more than a minute,—a wretched minute, he thought,—during which his curate never released him from his penetrating gaze.

" *If* there is such a report current, Mr. Hewly," he then began.

" *If,*" repeated the vicar, and began to quail, for he felt that he had not mastered him after all.

" I said *if,* Sir—*if* there is such a report current, I know of but one person who could have originated it."

" What do you mean by that, Sir," cried Hewly, now permitting himself the relief of a little bluster. " Do you mean to make *me* accountable for the reports that are rife respecting you? Is it my fault, if when a man in debt goes off people say he will never return? Is it my fault if people say you are in league with this villain and knave, Dickson?"

" Enough, — I have heard enough," cried his curate, starting up. " Be silent. I will not endure another word. If you could tamely listen to calumnies so insulting as these, and never even contradict them, they lie at your door as much as if you had yourself invented and propagated them."

" That will do, Sir," replied the vicar, also rising. " I rejoice that I can now without a breach of Christian forbearance dissolve the bond between us. Our connexion is at an end. An unblemished character, Sir, cannot be too highly valued; none can despise it with impunity."

Stung by this insult, his curate darted a look at him which brought the blood up even into *his* cheeks; but Hewly, though he felt a tremor through his whole frame, was cool. Nothing but compassion for the erring, and a mild reproval of his fault, was expressed in those virtuous lineaments. But it pleased him to see by the flashing eyes and quivering lips of his curate that he had him now sufficiently in his power to excite him to the utmost. Looking on, it was a balm to his heart to estimate the violence of the struggle by which he kept himself silent. He saw how indignation battled for the mastery, and that his face was colourless even to the lips, before it could be subdued.

" And what on earth is he staying for ?" thought the vicar ; but though a meek man, and, as he often said, desirous to forgive injuries, and not to exhibit pride, he felt extremely small when at length his victim rose, and with something of his own peculiar dignity, gave in his resignation, and, appointing to call on him the next morning, took his leave without deigning to notice his last remarks by a single word.

What Mr. Dreux thought as he walked home is impossible to describe. People do not think very collectedly when they have been first excited and then stunned. But why had Hewly been so hasty about this money, and was it a preconcerted thing this forcing him to leave his curacy? Was it true that such reports were believed respecting him? and if so, did not Hewly want to make him leave the town before he had had time to live them down and leave it in debt to his enemy, who had his character at his mercy. The bank at that hour was closed, but he determined at once to pay back the money to Hewly. He could borrow it, and must pay the interest as best he could; but then he must leave Westport. There was no curacy vacant in the place, and it seemed plain that his usefulness there was over, and his influence also.

It was getting dark, and he felt with poignant regret that perhaps the dusk sheltered him from insult—at any rate from the suspicious looks of those whom he might meet.

That he individually should have been despised he thought might easily have been borne, but it was hard to suffer patiently the certainty that every thing he had ever taught, all he had laboured for, would suffer and go down with him. This crowning fear sunk his agitated spirits. Tired as he was he turned away from his lodgings, and sought the square of grass before mentioned as belonging to the alms-houses, where in the gathering darkness he walked backwards and forwards, praying for direction in these new and overwhelming perplexities.

CHAPTER XXII.

LIGHT BREAKS THROUGH THE CLOUD.

Mr. Hewly sat at ease in his study, and sipped a cup of tea, while his late curate walked wearily up and down the square of grass under the black rocking trees. It was a wild, windy evening in March; the rain fell in half-frozen drops; the soaked grass did not rise after the foot had pressed it; the limes groaned and creaked like old fretful people; the gusty wind turned his umbrella, and he began to feel faint with fatigue and hunger, but no light seemed to dawn upon his path for all this thinking; and as he turned at last towards his lodgings he felt the necessity for quiet, warmth, and food, though the unsubdued restlessness of excitement craved bodily exercise still as a means of keeping it under.

He looked up to the window of his little lodgings; there he thought he could have quiet for the evening, to rest and consider what was to be done. He perceived the bright flickering of a fire within and the movement of a figure. He entered the house and walked slowly up stairs. Some one in his room was blowing his fire with a pair of bellows and singing most cheerfully. He entered, and the singer turned and disclosed the features of young Greyson.

"Hurra!" cried that young gentleman, rushing up to him, and flourishing the bellows. "Here I am at last—a hero returned from his first campaign. But how dreadfully tired you look," he added, seeing his faint smile and worn appearance. "I hope Miss Dreux is no worse. I beg your pardon, I ought to have known better."

"No, go on talking," replied his host. "I am indeed glad to see you again. I had begun to be quite uneasy about you. My sister is daily improving." This was in answer to young Greyson's inquiring expression.

"What is the matter, then?" asked the pupil.

"Let me forget it for a while. I cannot talk just now. I am worn out, body and mind. Do stay with me this evening. I do not think I can give you a lesson, but nothing would do me so much good as to hear your adventures."

Wilfred agreed, and immediately began to excite a great bustle. He piled the sofa cushions into one corner; insisted that his host should sit down; took away his over-coat; then he drew the curtains; made a cheerful blaze; called out at the top of the stairs for tea and candles; came back again; cleared the table; set the egg-glass, and boiled two eggs. The kettle and tea-things having by this time made their appearance, together with the little black tea-pot, he made tea, brought a tiny table to the sofa, and set a round of buttered toast, two eggs, and a cup of tea upon it.

"There," he exclaimed, delighted to see that his presence and his bustling had already wrought a wonderful improvement, "who cares for Hewly? *I* don't. Let him come in here if he likes, and I'll tell him so to his face."

"What made you think of Hewly?" asked Mr. Dreux.

"I am too hungry to tell you just now," was the reply.

"Because we have come to a final rupture," remarked Mr. Dreux, with the composure of complete weariness. "I am no longer his curate. He has aspersed my character, and he refuses to retract. And, moreover, he has taken upon himself to advance the remaining 200*l.* during my absence, and he demands immediate payment. I thought things had reached a climax when I came in just now, but your cheerfulness and this bright fire which you have made, and this rest make me feel quite different again. Well, you seem in very good spirits after your unsuccessful expedition."

"Unsuccessful!" repeated Wilfred. "Ah, well, never mind. I wish you would begin to eat. I must put some more water in the teapot and boil some eggs. Hewly"—

"Don't let us talk of him," interrupted Mr.

Dreux; "I am afraid of speaking uncharitably. With regard to the success of your expedition,—of course I know that you would have told me at once if you had met with any."

"We certainly set off on the most wild-goose chase that ever was heard of," replied young Greyson, cracking his second egg. "But, never mind; after tea I will tell you everything." As he spoke he produced from his pocket a small parcel, and, remarking that he always thought eggs were the better for a little cayenne-pepper, unfolded a pepper-box, the very counterpart of Mrs. Brown's mustard-pot, and set it down on the little table.

"Mr. Dreux took it up, and gazed at Greyson in considerable bewilderment. "Do you mean to say you have really and actually recovered the plate?" he asked, turning round the little article with intense interest.

"Not exactly. Didn't I go on purpose to recover the plate? Why, then, should you be so much astonished at my bringing some of it?"

"I never had the slightest idea that you would bring any of it back; I never entertained so wild an expectation for an instant. That you might return without getting yourself into any serious scrape was the utmost I hoped for."

Greyson laughed triumphantly, and declared that after tea he would explain all. Mr. Dreux sat quietly in his nook on the sofa, noting his face; he began to think he must have some good news to communicate, especially as he would burst into a short involuntary laugh whenever he caught his eye, and became suddenly grave again, declaring that it was no laughing matter.

At last he gave out that he had finished, rang the bell, snuffed the candles, put on two large pieces of coal, swept up the hearth, and ensconced himself in an arm-chair, with the poker in his hand and his feet on the fender.

The landlady had cleared away tea, shut the door, and Mr. Dreux had looked at him for some time before he evinced any inclination to begin; his face had become serious, not to say sad, and he seemed lost in thought. When he did speak, it was not at all to the purpose; he seemed still far from the matter in hand.

" So Hewly has insulted you," he said. " Well, the worse for him."

" My dear Greyson, pray let us drop the subject of Hewly," urged Mr. Dreux. " You seem anything but aware how completely I am in his power."

" Completely in his power," repeated Greyson, in a musing tone, and then sunk into another silence, which Mr. Dreux broke by inquiring whether he meant to tell him anything at all that night.

On hearing this, young Greyson roused himself, and, turning his ingenuous face towards him, said, " I only paused because I scarcely knew where to begin. I have a great deal to tell you, but I was thinking, just then, how many changes there are in people's lives, and how sudden they are. When you came in this evening you were miserable,—I know you were; before the end of it you will be so glad."

" Go on," said his auditor, " I cannot understand you; but I fully believe what you say."

" Then, if I am to tell you, you will promise not to interrupt me with questions?—you will hear me to the end?"

" I will do my best," was the answer, while the listener changed his position and stretched all his faculties to discover what this might mean.

Wilfred settled himself in the chair, and launched at once into his narrative: " The only real clue I had when I left this was given me by your land-lady, who described to me most accurately the trunk in which the lodger carried away his goods; it was covered with calf-skin, she said, with the hair on, and it did not look as if it had been made by a regular trunk-maker, for it was shaped like a coffin. She also described the lodger's person; that he was a small, spare, dark man, with black eyes; that he had lost the third finger of his right hand, and that he went away from hence by the Birming-ham Railway.

" Frank and I set off accordingly for Birming-ham, with a policeman from here. And we and the police at Birmingham searched in all the places where they bought old silver, to see if we could identify anything. We inquired at the railway offices whether they had seen anything of such a trunk, but it was of no use,—of course they could remember nothing. At last we were told that a person of the description we wanted had gone off to London two days before. We followed, not that we distinctly hoped to find him, but there was a curious kind of pleasure in the excitement of the chase. To describe the dens we went into with the police and the characters we met with, would, I suppose, surprise even you. I should think there are no such places anywhere but in London. We spent nearly a week of fatigue; sometimes the police thought they had got a clue, and then they lost it again. At last we got a summons to return to Birmingham, for they thought they had discovered the traces of a gang of thieves, some of whom they suspected were coiners. They contrived to elude the police, but it was believed they were still in the town, and we were advised by the magistrates to put an advertisement in the papers, stating that some weeks ago a robbery had been committed at Westport, and describing the stolen goods, stating that it was supposed the thief was concealed in Birmingham. They told us this was sure to be seen by the thieves, and that they would not dare to remain in the town, but would most likely try to get out by night.

"Well, we had several weary nights, haunting the railway stations, but though two men were taken up and proved to belong to this gang of coiners, neither of them at all resembled the lodger. After this we went about in all directions, wherever they told us there were people suspected of coining. We got into gipsy camps; we searched the prisons. We were both getting heartily weary of the affair. We knew we had no chance; the police had told us so; for no man in his senses would keep plate about him when it could so easily be melted down, and that, once done, no acuteness could identify it.

"Well, we decided to come home, and were within an hour of setting off. We had actually gone to York, where, we were told, a man had been taken up with plate in his possession. It all came to nothing. We had left the hotel and reached the railway-station, when a waiter came running after us with a letter,—it was from Marion. I had written to her the day before, and given her my address. She wrote to inclose a letter which had arrived for me at Swanstead, and to say that my Uncle Raeburn had got another, and desired that I would come to him immediately, for that it would be very little out of my way in going back to Birmingham."

"Back to Birmingham," said Mr. Dreux, "what was that for?"

"I could not tell till I had read the inclosed letter; it had been written at Swanstead, and stated that the writer was lodging there; that he had sent it to the parson to be directed to me; that he came from a poor dying wretch in Birmingham, who could tell me what I wanted to know, provided I would promise secrecy; that the writer would go with me to Birmingham, if I would go with such a person, or the parson might go instead. Of course Frank and I started off at once for Swanstead. It was a most bitter night. We had to do part of the journey by coach; and the consequence was, we were not there till twelve the next day.

" Marion met us at the cross-roads in the carriage. She told me my uncle had waited for me till ten, the last minute, and then, as I did not arrive, had gone on himself to Birmingham.

" She knew I was in search of stolen property, and told me the informant had urged my uncle to go immediately, or he feared the man would not live till he reached him.

" Unluckily, that morning he had disappeared from the village, taken fright probably. So my uncle was left to find out whereabouts in Birmingham this sick man might be, as well as he could.

" Frank was so knocked up, and so ill with influenza, that as we were within five miles of his father's house, I advised his going home; we put him into the carriage at once; Marion came with me into the inn, and as the country was so blocked up with snow, I told Frank not to attempt to send back the carriage that night, but to keep it at his father's.

"After I had had a hasty meal, it was time to start for the railway; but when we came to investigate matters, there was only one post-chaise to be had. Of course I did not like to leave Marion there alone, and I could not send her home without a chaise. So, after less than five minutes' deliberation, we agreed that she should come on with me to Birmingham."

"What, on that bitter day, and with no preparation!"

"Don't look so shocked. What could I do? She was excessively uneasy about my uncle, and did not like the idea of his going into such places as the man had described; she was well covered up with furs and velvets, and seemed quite relieved at being with me; but though we had only fourteen miles to go, the snow was so deep that we were three hours on the road.

"It was lucky indeed that she came, for at the station I discovered that Frank had got our purse with him, such a careless trick of us both! Marion had money, only one sovereign and a few shillings, with her. So I was obliged to take her in the second class; very cold the carriage was, and very dark for her; there was an oil lamp, by the bye, but it wouldn't burn; we had just enough money for the tickets. Marion made light of the

cold and everything else. I know she was delighted
at the thought of getting to my uncle, just as if she
could do any good, you know! or keep him out
of mischief. She was quite warm and happy;
so she said. It was sixty miles to Birmingham;
and of all the cold I ever experienced, I recollect
nothing to compare to that night; it soon silenced
us; the speed of the engine was very much impeded
by the snow, and I began to be afraid we should be
very late. I was so tired with travelling, that
I kept falling asleep, in spite of the cold. We were
quite alone, and Marion asked me to sit upon the
floor, with my carpet-bag for a hassock, and lay my
head on her knee. I had her muff for a pillow, and
was dreaming away at a great rate, when a tremendous jerk woke me; it was quite dark; we seemed
tilted over. I was on my knees, Marion was holding
my head between her hands, and wrapping her furs
round it, never thinking of herself. I had not an
instant to ask what the matter was, when, with an
awful creaking crash, the carriage turned over on
its side. Marion cried out, but kept my head still,
and held me tight. Don't be alarmed, she was not
hurt, not in the least. I perceived instantly that
we had stopped. Marion was perfectly still. I heard
distant cries and groans; the snow gave us a little
light, and I contrived to get the upper window open
and drag Marion through to the roof, from which
we scrambled somehow down to the ground, and
found that four carriages, with ours, and a coal

platform had broken away from the rest; the train had run off the line, and stopped half the field from us. There were four houses in the field; some of the inhabitants were already out, they seized us with frantic haste and hurried us indoors. It snowed so fast that we could not see the state of the train; but in our carriages not one person was much hurt; no bones were broken.

" Though the thing was so alarming and strange, I could hardly help laughing at the behaviour of these people; they crowded about Marion and the other females, and the women kissed and hugged them; oh, it was so droll! They were not exactly poor people, for they soon produced eatables and drinkables in abundance; and there was such a frying of bacon, drawing of beer, and toasting of cheese! they seemed to think we must all be famished.

" A great motherly woman stood over Marion, turning up her sleeves to see if her arms were bruised; she warmed her at the fire, and tried to bend her bonnet into something like shape. Marion behaved pretty well; she cried a little, of course; the woman wanted to make her eat, but she could not. She looked blue and almost frozen. In the meantime some men came in from the train; most providentially, not one life was lost. A pen of sheep had been overturned, and most of them killed; and a high bank stopped the engine before any further mischief was done.

" They said there was a farm about half a mile off, where we could get a gig; we were only ten miles from Birmingham. I wished to stay the night, that Marion might rest and recover from her fright a little; but she thought of my uncle,—she was sure he would expect me by this train, and hear of the accident by telegraph before we could arrive. I agreed to go on. I had not a shilling, but I said I should drive the gig back myself the next day. Not a word was said about payment; the women wrapped Marion in a rough, thick shawl, and we set out. Women seldom think of themselves in these cases: Marion braved the east wind and the snow extremely well. It was a good thing they lent her that shawl, else I think she would have been nearly frozen. It seemed a very long ten miles, however we reached Birmingham at last. I drove straight to the station, and, as I expected, there stood Mr. Raeburn waiting for me; for he had got news of the accident, and was anxiously hoping I might not be coming till the next train. I flourished the whip and called out to him;—how relieved he seemed when he saw me! but when he beheld Marion sitting beside me, I shall never forget his face—yours is nothing to it. How hard you are upon me, I couldn't help it."

" No, I am quite aware of that, my dear fellow."

" Then don't look so uneasy, I told you she was none the worse. Well, he took us to the hotel. It was midnight. He shook the snow from us, hugged us both, and cried in the corner while we ate a most excellent supper, for I can tell you we both did that. After that Marion began to cry. Here I made a speech to prove that I had done the best I could, and she said it was all her doing, coming in that way, and she hoped he would not be angry. Well, then we all went to bed.

" I know I'm spoiling this story in the telling, anybody else would have made a capital thing of it ! Well, the next day my uncle told me the history of his search for the supposed poor dying man, which was in fact the history of his defeat. He had had a toilsome day, and no likelihood of accomplishing anything. The only thing he had to guide him was, that this man was said to have been very much injured in a fire, and that he was lying in a lodging-house. He had been to numbers of lodging-houses, and had seen a great deal of misery. He had only asked for the sick inmates ; at some they had none, at others he went in and saw the sick, but perceived at once that they did not answer the description he wanted. They saw that he was a clergyman, and took for granted he came to visit them as such ; so he did not choose to leave them without reading and praying with them.

" After breakfast it snowed heavily, but we went out together, leaving Marion, who was only a little tired, lying on the sofa by the fire.

" We went to all kinds of places without the

least success, and came in after twelve o'clock, quite tired. Marion then told us that an hour ago a woman had called and begged to speak with the clergyman who was staying there, that the waiter had at first refused to come up with her request, but she was so urgent that at last he did, 'and as you were not within,' Marion said to my uncle, ' I went down to speak to her. She told me she came from a woman whom the parson had visited the day before, that she wanted to see him again to pray with her, and hoped he would come for the love of God. The woman said the poor creature could not live through the night, and had begged so earnestly to see the parson again, that she had agreed to bring this message. I told her that when you returned you should hear of it, and that I had no doubt you would come and see her. She then went away, thanking me most gratefully.'

" Marion gave us the address, and my uncle set off directly, for he said he could at least visit the sick, though his first object in coming was thwarted. I thought I should like to go with him. The lodging-house was not far off,—we easily found it, and there was a person outside evidently waiting for us. She begged my uncle would go directly to the dying woman, for she quite raved after him. He would not let me go up stairs with him, and while I sat below, doing nothing, I asked the woman if she had any other sick lodgers.

" She looked rather queerly at me, but after a

cautious pause, during which she seemed to be
scrutinizing my appearance, she said, ' Yes, she
had, but he was a poor wretched object, not fit for
a gentleman like me to see.' But I got up at once,
and said I should like to see him, if she had no
objection.

" So she took me out of doors into a broken-down
open shop, and up a ladder, into the most wretched,
dirty loft I ever beheld, with a hole in the roof,
through which the snow was drifting on to the floor,
and there, his face disfigured with patches of linen,
lay, covered with rags, and feeble and stretched
upon straw, not the man I had come to seek, but
the schoolmaster, Thomas Dickson ! "

He paused here, and remained silent several
moments. His auditor was too much surprised to
say anything. He went on, fixing his eyes on the
fire, and speaking in a deeply thoughtful tone.

" I have been too happy in the world. I have
not sufficiently considered the misery there is in it ;
and when I have thought of crime it has been too
distinct from its fearful punishment even in this
world. One side of his face was dreadfully burnt,
his limbs were maimed, he seemed wasted to a
shadow, and had nothing but a can of water standing by his straw.

" 'The woman left me with him, and as he could
not turn, it was only when I came close that he
recognised me.

" He did not seem startled or ashamed,—he was

past that; he only said, in a hollow voice, 'You have been a long time coming, Sir; I was afraid you would be too late.'

" I asked him if it was he who had sent for me. He said it was,—that he wished to make what reparation he could before he died.

" And then he told me a long story of all his guilt and misery. I cannot tell you the whole of it to-night, but it seemed to make me older as I listened, and I shall never forget the wretchedness it unfolded to my dying day.

" What he told me was in substance this: that *he did* steal that money, intending to carry it off, and go abroad—that he had an accomplice, a man more wicked than himself—that this man was the lodger—that after he had committed the robbery this man harboured him here, in this house, for the night—that he went early in the morning to a lonely place with him, for as he had threatened to betray him, there was nothing for him but to divide the spoil with him.

" In the grey morning twilight they went down into that open gravel pit on the London road to effect the division, and there the lodger proved the falsehood of that proverb that there is 'honour among thieves,' for he knocked Thomas Dickson down, and while he lay stunned and bleeding, he robbed him of the whole of the money, took his coat and watch from him, and when he recovered his senses, was nowhere to be seen.

" He was now miserable and destitute—all the fruits of his wickedness had been taken from him— he could not return to his situation. His character being gone, he told me he did not care what became of him, but went to Birmingham, where he got connected with a gang of coiners, and soon sunk into the deepest destitution and misery. At last, one day he met his former companion in the streets, and instantly threatened to give him up to the police if he tried to get away from him.

" The lodger, finding himself powerless, suffered himself to be followed to a stable, where he slept. He then declared that the notes he had stolen were worse than valueless to him, for their numbers were posted up at all the banks, so that he dare not attempt to change them, but that if Dickson would help him to dispose of a quantity of old silver which he had on his hands, they would make up their quarrel, and do the best they could for each other.

" Dickson told me that that night they set to work to knock the diamonds and pearls out of the old boxes and quaint old models of monuments. They collected them in a little leather bag, and then broke up some of the silver and melted it down. His heart smote him, for he saw whose they were, but he dared not remonstrate. They worked hard, and in two nights they had melted nearly all the plate, or crushed and defaced it.

" The next day, he says, the lodger met me and

Frank in the street, recognised us, and found means to ascertain our errand. He came back, and that night they together buried the notes, the jewels, and the remainder of the silver,—for some they had contrived to sell. They came home in the middle of the night, and laid down in the straw of their stable. They had struck a light, and he supposes a spark fell and smouldered among the boards, for shortly they were roused by a great light. They had made the door so secure that they could not undo it in a hurry. The lodger climbed out at one window, but before Dickson could rush to the other, a heap of straw took fire, and he was bathed in the flames. To use his own fearful expression, he crawled out of that stable blind and 'half roasted.'

"He told me that the lodger was unhurt, and that he conveyed him to that wretched house where I found him—that two days after he was taken up for breaking into some outhouse. The sessions were just at hand, and he was tried and sentenced to seven years' transportation.

"But when this poor, miserable Dickson found that he never could recover from his injuries, he wished to restore as much as he could of the stolen property, that, as he told me, he might not die with that sin on his conscience.

"When I looked at the poor dying creature, lying on that wretched bed, the snow drifting in about him, and nothing but some cold water to wet his parched lips, and when I reflected on all he had lost, and what he had got in return, I thought how true it was that 'the wages of sin are hard.'"

When Wilfred added that he had expressed a hope that his late patron would forgive him, and had said that without that he could not die in peace, Mr. Dreux started up, and declared that he would go himself to Birmingham, rather than Dickson should not be satisfied.

Wilfred did not wish that evening to damp his spirits by telling him that a few hours after that confession the poor man had died. "Sit down," he said, "I have not done yet. He told me, as well as his weakness would permit, the place where they had buried their spoil; it was in a barren field close to the railway; there, he said, we should see two poplar-trees, and we must walk, coming from the town, until the one trunk was hidden behind the other; that fifty paces from the nearest tree we should find the box in which they had buried the silver, and a tin case containing the notes, not one of which they had been able to change, so, as he had drawn only 25*l.* from the bank in gold, there was only that sum deficient. That very evening Mr. Raeburn and I, with a policeman, went to the spot, and two feet below the surface we found the box, and the tin case within it. The whole thing seemed so unlikely, so unreal, that I felt as if it must needs be a dream, I had so completely given up all idea that the original 400*l.* would ever be recovered;

however, here it is, as good as ever, and I wish you joy."

It would be impossible to describe the gratitude with which the pile of notes was received. Here was a most unexpected relief from the pressure of real pecuniary difficulty. Mr. Dreux, a few months before, could scarcely have credited that any amount of worldly possessions would have caused him such heartfelt joy and ease of mind. Now he looked upon the recovered money with a joy beyond what even his pupil could have hoped. He counted out 175*l.*, and handed over the rest to young Greyson.

"This two hundred is yours," he said.

"Mine," repeated young Greyson, "what do you mean?"

Mr. Dreux replied by thanking him, in the most grateful and affectionate terms, for what he had done, told him how relieved he felt on the very next morning to be able to pay Hewly what he had advanced; and then, reminding him that the plate was ruined, and most of the jewels gone, entreated that he would not pain him by refusing to take the money back again.

"I never tried to lay *you* under the slightest obligation," replied his pupil; "then why should you try to do it to ME?"

"Never laid me under the slightest obligation!" exclaimed Mr. Dreux. "You astonish me beyond measure! I am more indebted to you than to any person living. What can you mean, Greyson?"

" Oh, I meant pecuniary obligation; if you like to feel obliged to me for finding out where this money was, I do not mind. On the whole, though, I must say I rather enjoyed most of my adventures."

" Well, I see it is of no use talking to you; your notions of what constitutes obligation are, above all things in the world, extraordinary."

Greyson laughed, and said, "I was perfectly aware that you would try to cheat me into taking that money, so I propose that we lay the whole matter before an umpire, to be approved by both parties, and that we promise to abide by his decision."

Mr. Dreux agreed, and Greyson then began to question him about Hewly's conduct, especially as regarded his hints to the almshouse pensioners. If his host had not been unusually pleased, and tired withal, he might have observed a peculiar bearing in these questions, which revealed something more than common curiosity. As it was, he stretched his long limbs on the sofa, told everything his pupil chose to ask, and, too much occupied with his returning good fortune to see anything strange in the request, acceded at once, when Greyson asked if he might go with him the next day when he paid over the 200*l.* to Hewly.

"Certainly you shall, always provided that you will promise not to be rude to Hewly."

" Rude!" repeated Wilfred, as if quite shocked, "I should not think of being so mean."

" You were *not* rude, then, the other night, when he called here,—Eh ?"

" Oh, well, I was rather, but I never mean to be again. What an ass he was to be rude to you to-day ! "

" I suppose the diamond ring is gone ?"

" That is the best part of the story. They had pawned it for a mere trifle,—not a sovereign ; only imagine their ignorance. We may yet recover it ; but when we went to the pawn-shop, of course it was not to be found."

" Have you got the silver ?"

" No, it was all nothing but a mass of ore, excepting that pepper-box and a little model, not so big as a snuff-box, of your dear ancestor, Sir Gualtier de Dreux,—his tomb I mean,—and when Marion saw it, she said she should like to have it."

" What did your sister want with it ?"

" Oh, I don't know ; do you ?"

" How can you be so absurd ? Of course not."

" I now remember Marion gave me some elaborate reasons why she wished to have it ; the original is in Swanstead church. I think she wanted it, she said, because the real old fellow was opposite our pew. I remember she was afraid to sit opposite him when we were children, he looked so stern and so grim. She also said it was an interesting little work of art, and several other reasons she gave ; I forget them. However, I gave the thing to her.

It's very odd how family likeness descends; he is something like you, I declare."

"Nonsense; am I, then, so stern and grim that a child would be afraid of me?"

"I can't tell how you would look in chain armour. I asked Marion if she did not see the likeness."

"I wish, I do wish you would not talk in this strain," thought his auditor. "I am sure if you knew, you would be the last person to do it."

"So you have nothing left but the pepper-box, Greyson?"

"Yes, I've got old Gualtier, after all. Marion altered her mind, and wouldn't have him. He's the image of you,—she may say what she likes to the contrary. Here he is."

"Your pockets are capacious. How bright he looks!" remarked his descendant.

"Yes; we cleaned him up with plate-powder."

"*We?*"

"Yes, Marion and I; we had nothing to do in the evening. I think it's a beautiful thing,—a great pity little M. wouldn't have it. I always thought that hound, crouching with its head on his breast, and looking so earnestly in his master's face, had something peculiarly touching about it. How well I remember our asking Mr. Raeburn, when we were very little children, to lift us up to stroke that dog, and feel how cold the knight's forehead was!"

" Well, Greyson, shall we have supper ? "

The pupil willingly consented. The tutor, at his request, ordered oysters and bread and butter for that repast, that, as he said, they might finish the evening in a convivial style befitting the occasion.

" Now, about this umpire ? " asked Mr. Dreux. " I have been thinking, Greyson, that, if I may draw up the statement, you shall choose to whom it shall be submitted."

" Agreed. And I name Mr. Raeburn. Let us call ourselves Smith and Jones,—I am Smith."

" Very well. Then the statement begins :—' I, Jones, sold goods to Smith, for which I received 200*l.*' "

" No ; it begins before that. It begins :—' The sum of 400*l.* was stolen from Jones ; in consequence of which he sold goods to Smith for which he received 200*l.*"

" Well, be it so, if you please. I will draw it up to-night, and to-morrow, at ten, let us go to Hewly and pay down the money. I shall be very happy, my dear fellow, to have it off my mind."

" I do not care how soon we go," returned Wilfred. " So Hewly refuses to apologize, does he ? Ah ! well, we shall see."

Mr. Dreux smiled, and said, " You are very much mistaken if you think the mere proof of his being wrong as to my ability to return the money, will make him do so."

"I think no such thing," replied the pupil. "Good night; I will be here by ten."

Punctual to the moment young Greyson arrived the next morning, and found Mr. Dreux wonderfully improved by ease of mind and rest. He had got a letter from Elinor's maid, reporting good progress; and showed Wilfred the statement he had drawn up for the umpire, which the latter thought very fair.

They arrived at Mr. Hewly's house, and were shown into his study. He did not keep them waiting many minutes, and gave Wilfred a peculiarly sinister look when he saw him, for he thought he was come to try to accommodate matters.

He was obviously surprised when Mr. Dreux handed over the notes, and the more so as he observed that the numbers were the same as those of the stolen ones.

"My friend, Greyson, wishes to give you a short account of how he became possessed of these notes," Mr. Dreux said, turning to Wilfred, who now looked excited and ill at ease.

"As you please," returned Mr. Hewly, with his most unpleasant expression. "Then perhaps he will make haste and begin, for my time is precious."

"However precious it may be," replied Wilfred, "it will be as well to spare enough to hear what I have to say. You have heard nothing so important, Mr. Hewly, for a long time."

Dreux and Hewly both looked at him with unfeigned surprise; the latter, with a supercilious smile, requested him to proceed.

"I am ready," said Wilfred. Yet he paused and hesitated, with an embarrassment which was not usual with him, and which fixed the attention of both gentlemen, who involuntarily glanced at each other.

"I believe, Mr. Hewly," he at length said,—"I believe your parents are not in the rank of life which you—you occupy yourself"—

"My parents," interrupted Hewly, "what do you bring up that for, Sir? My father was as worthy a man as yours could have been, Sir."

"I have no doubt of it, Sir," proceeded Wilfred, in a tone of apology; "and, in most families, some members rise and others SINK."

"Well, Sir, to the point," said Hewly, testily; "I have heard enough of my parentage."

Wilfred then began to give an account of how he had discovered the poor, miserable schoolmaster, and repeated his statements as to how he, in his turn, had been robbed by another man, who afterwards, to complete his crimes, stole a quantity of valuable plate from the house where he lodged.

"Indeed!" replied Mr. Hewly, indifferently, not to say insolently.

"That man, Sir, lodged in the same house with Mr. Dreux," remarked Wilfred. "It was then that he stole the plate."

Mr. Dreux, at this point of Greyson's narrative, observed that Hewly turned very pale.

" He afterwards met with Thomas Dickson, the man whom he had robbed of his ill-gotten gain, and the two together melted down a great part of this plate, but the notes they dared not change. This man, of whom I spoke, became connected with a gang of coiners, and was suspected, while with them, of having committed murder; but they pursued their own wretched system of morals, and did not give him up to justice. In a few weeks he was taken by the police in the act of forcing open a door; he was brought to trial, convicted, and I saw him in jail. He sails for Australia this very day."

Mr. Hewly's face had become deadly pale, and the cold perspiration stood upon his forehead. The sinister expression was then in greater force than ever, but with it enough of terror to excite the pity of both his companions; and Greyson went on more gravely than before.

" I saw the man in jail; he was hardened and profane. He is a small, dark man, and he has lost the third finger of his right hand."

" Merciful heaven!" said Hewly, faintly, and shrinking back in his chair.

" Do you wish to hear his name?" proceeded Greyson. " The schoolmaster told me his real name; it was known in this part of the country to him only. He died in whispering it to me;

and he told me that the wretched convict came of
respectable and honest parents, but that he had
always shown himself a reprobate.   Hitherto I
have divulged the name to no one.   I returned to
this place intending to keep it a secret for ever, but
I have altered my mind, and must tell it now in
the presence of Mr. Dreux.   This wretched man,
who had been lingering about Westport, tormenting
you for money to bribe him away,—this double
thief, whom suspected murder has not brought to
the gallows, because his house-breaking was discovered first,—this coiner, and now convict, whose
crime has enabled you to—to—yes, I must and
will say it—to oppress a better man than yourself,
cannot now be *named* even without reflecting some
of his disgrace upon yourself, for he is your brother
—Michael Hewly."

With a cry, between terror and pain, Mr. Hewly
covered his face with his hands.   He had always
shown a nervous sensibility about his low origin,
and a great dislike to having it known ; and now
the disgrace of his brother, no less than some struggling remains of natural affection, battled for the
mastery, and made him truly a spectacle for pity.

Mr. Dreux's consternation at this *denouement* was
too great to admit of his saying anything.

Greyson paused till Hewly removed his white,
trembling hands from his face, and looked forlornly
at him.   Then he proceeded : " I hope you believe,
Mr. Hewly, that I did not give you this pain with

any mean wish to revenge Mr. Dreux upon you, or merely to let him see that all these difficulties have been brought upon him by a member of *your* family, but I acknowledge that I have an end in view."

"Greyson," interrupted Mr. Dreux, "I had rather—I wish you not to bring me into this affair."

Greyson looked at him, but went on addressing Hewly:—

"You will please to observe that this man was tried under a feigned name, and there is every reason to think no living persons know his real one but myself and Mr. Dreux. I do not know what use he may choose to make of his knowledge,—knowledge which I was determined he should possess, not that he was likely to revenge himself, but that he might have full opportunity to do so if he chose,—as for me, my silence is only to be bought in exchange for something which I have already fixed in my own mind."

What Hewly might have done, or to what depths of submission he might have condescended in the confusion of his thoughts, it is impossible to say, if he had not been arrested by the voice of his late curate, who said, deliberately: "Mr. Hewly, I give you my unconditional promise that, God helping me, I will never divulge what I have just heard to any living person."

He received a look in reply which expressed both shame and gratitude. Then the unhappy man turned anxiously to Wilfred; he was a mere boy to them, but they both looked at him with something like entreaty, for Hewly felt as if everything worth living for was at stake, and Dreux felt keenly that but for his sake this punishment would never have been inflicted; he could not but think there was something of unsparing hardness in the way in which the thing had been done, and yet he knew that he ought not to interfere, for nothing could be so galling to Hewly as that Wilfred should promise silence at *his* request, which was what he believed matters were tending to.

Greyson preserved a dogged silence for some minutes, in spite of the restless agitation of Hewly. At length he said,—" Mr. Hewly " (and he threw an accent almost of respect into his voice)—" Mr. Hewly, in looking back upon our past intercourse, I find that throughout I have not treated you as I could wish. I regret it the more, because I can now make no difference on this account in the conditions on which I will promise silence—utter, complete silence. I shall only insist upon *one* thing,—one which seems to me an absolute duty; and I most solemnly promise silence on that condition, and on that only."

" Name your condiion, then, at once," said Hewly; " there is nothing I will not do—no, nothing."

" My condition is, that you shall make a written apology to Mr. Dreux for the expressions you have used concerning him, which apology shall be dictated by me, and shown to the people in the almshouses."

The start of horror and indignation with which this proposal was received did not seem in the least to disconcert Wilfred.

"Greyson," exclaimed Mr. Dreux, much agitated, "I do not desire it. I beg as a favour to myself that you will dispense with it. If Hewly will apologize to me in private I shall be quite content."

"If the people have not *believed* Mr. Hewly's insinuations respecting you," remarked Wilfred, "his admitting them to be false will not lower their opinion of *him;* but if they have believed them, then it is necessary that you should be righted."

"But leave the thing to me, Greyson. Will you leave it in my hands? Consider,—a written apology,—what man could " ——

Hewly hoped. But he saw the pupil turn to the master, and give him a look of such calm, steady denial, that the latter was fain to bite his lips and look out of the window to hide his surprise and annoyance. He then looked at Hewly, and said, "Well, Sir, you have heard me."

"And I should be glad to know what I have done to make an apology necessary," replied Hewly, with his most unpleasant expression.

"I do not refer to what you have actually asserted," replied Greyson; "but I went to the almshouses this morning, and I found a very bad opinion prevailed there concerning Mr. Dreux,— one quite derogatory to him as a clergyman and a gentleman. I was referred to *you* to know whether he did not deserve it. A slight hint, a gesture even, an insidious doubt, or an ill-timed application of some common-place proverb, may be at the root of all the preposterous tales now current respecting him, but I know the mischief is done, and that you have been the doer."

" I will write an apology," said Hewly, looking daggers at his late curate, who rose and walked to the window. "I must, I suppose, as I am entirely at your mercy. But the injustice of the thing must be glaringly apparent even to you, when the very man who is to receive it admits that it is not required."

" No other man would," replied Greyson. " The apology must be written, or I take my leave."

" You are in a needless hurry," said Hewly, hastily; "I have said once that I would write an apology."

" You remember that it is to be at my dictation," said Greyson.

Mr. Hewly actually writhed in his chair. But what was the alternative? He took up a pen, and, with strong sensations of shame and disgust, wrote down as follows:—

" I, Brigson Hewly, Vicar of this parish, hereby

declare that I believe the Rev. Arthur Cecil Dreux to be in all respects an upright and honourable man; I also declare that I never had any reason to think otherwise; and I hereby apologize to the said Rev. A. C. Dreux for having given cause to others to suppose that I did.

(Signed)   " Brigson Hewly."

" There," said Hewly, now giving way to his temper, and tossing the paper over to Greyson, " I have paid dearer for your paltry promise than it was worth. Now I shall be glad to have it."

" Certainly," replied Greyson. " I do hereby solemnly "——

" You will please to swear," said Hewly, drawing a Testament towards him.

Greyson complied.

" And now, gentlemen," said Hewly, rising, and quivering with passion, " there is the door;—the sooner you go the better. Go, and make the most of your mean-spirited revenge."

The sneer with which he accompanied these words was quite electrifying.

Greyson folded up the piece of paper, and left the house with Mr. Dreux. He did not wish for a *tête-à-tête* conversation with him, and was thinking how best to break the silence, and take his leave, when Dreux stopped him just as they reached the garden-door of his late house, and holding out his hand, by way of thanks, said,—

" But after all, Greyson, if you had failed to get that apology."——

" I would still have held my tongue. Was that what you were going to ask ? Of course I would."

" And what are you going to do with the paper ?"

" It is mine."

" Yes, I know that. But be merciful, Greyson."

" Because I see that you really wish it, I will. I will take the trouble of carrying it round myself to the almshouse people, and they shall see it, but I will not make even so much as one copy for distribution. Surely that is kindness to him, and less than that would not be justice to you. Why do you smile ?—I know what you are thinking."

" Indeed, you do not."

" Yes, you were thinking how odd it was that a youth like me should have such important matters to arrange."

" You are telling me your own thoughts, not mine, for you are a friend and counsellor to me. I have nearly lost sight of the fact that you are a mere boy and my pupil. By the bye, how did Mrs. Brown get my mustard-pot ?"

" Bought it of a pedlar, to whom the thief must have sold it that same day."

CHAPTER XXIII.

THE VESTRY AND THE CLIFF.

AND now the gossips of Westport were destined
to have their hearts cheered with a little news.
Various versions of the apology got about the
town; then it was rumoured that Mr. Dreux was
going to leave, and had given up his curacy, though
not his lectureship; also it was a known fact that
Mr. Hewly was gone out for a month; finally, it
was observed that old Ferguson looked very glum,
and that his daughter seemed very much out of
spirits.

Mr. Dreux soon began to feel the good effects of
the apology. All his friends called on him, and
all expressed their sorrow at his leaving a place
" where he was so much respected." He was very
well pleased to hear them say so, but was too busy
to go out much into society. However, he found
time to write to Greyson, to beg him to come and
dine with him at his lodgings; and as the note
contained a pen and ink illustration, representing a
young gentleman playing on a flute, he understood

thereby that he was to bring that instrument with
him, which he accordingly did, and found his host
in excellent spirits, and looking quite well.

" In the first place, how is Miss Dreux?" asked
Greyson.

" I have a letter to say she is steadily improving,
and is to go to the Isle of Wight in a week."

" And I have got a letter from the umpire, which
I will read after dinner."

Nothing could be said till the servant had cleared
away the dinner equipage and withdrawn.   Greyson then produced Mr. Raeburn's letter, and read it
aloud:—

" DEAR WILFRED,—

" I have received your letter, containing the
complicated statement of the transactions between
Smith and Jones.   I fully understand that you do
not wish to consider what the *law* would decide on
this matter (as on that head there can be no doubt),
but you merely wish for the opinion of a third
party as to what is equitable, so that neither may
feel himself laid under an obligation, or that he has
taken an unfair advantage of the other.

" I shall state the case, in order that my opinion
may be plainer.

" It appears, that in consequence of the loss of
the original 400*l.*, Jones sold Smith 200*l.* worth of
silver plate, and this silver, after the money was
paid over for it and the receipt given, was stolen.

" But it appears that Smith, setting out in search of his silver, finds the original 400*l.*, which he returns to Jones, who then considers that Smith has a right to be indemnified for the loss of his silver, and wishes to share the 400*l.* with him. Smith, on the other hand, declines.

" Now it is certain, that in returning the 400*l.*, Smith only did his duty; but Jones, in requiring him to accept 200*l.*, desires to do *him* a favour, because he is of opinion that it was hard upon him that he should have enjoyed the property he had purchased for so short a time; for if it had not been stolen for a couple of years after Smith bought it, Jones would never have thought of repaying him.

" My opinion is this,—that the 200*l.* should not be accepted by Smith, he having no right to it; but that, as he spent a large sum of money in searching for his silver, which search led to the discovery of the 400*l.*, he shall receive from Jones the whole of his travelling expenses, and, if his time was of value, Jones may indemnify him for that loss also.

" This, my dear boy, is the best conclusion I can come to. You will observe, that Smith has no *right* to his travelling expenses, but he, having done Jones a benefit, may fairly accept one in return.

" Your sister sends her love to you.

" Your affectionate uncle," &c.

" There," said Greyson, when he had finished it, " I think, on the whole, that it is a very fair decision."

" I have promised to abide by it, and I will," was the reply; " but it gives me greatly the advantage."

" Here is the packet of notes," said Greyson, producing a parcel from his pocket, " and you are to pay my travelling expenses. Do you see that my uncle has put notes of admiration after the remark about Smith's time, and its possible value? Of course he knows quite well who Smith and Jones are."

And now that this affair was settled, the other arrangements were easily made. The late Curate of Pelham's Church, *alias* St. Plum's, found himself out of debt and free from his engagement with Hewly, while the possession of the rest of the recovered sum made it needless for him to accept any curacy without deliberation.

" Have you heard that Mr. Hewly is in treaty with a clergyman in Kent to exchange livings with him?" asked Greyson. " I believe he thinks St. Plum's will hardly do for him after that apology."

Mr. Dreux could not but acquiesce in the propriety of the step, and Greyson went on,—

" I really am sorry for Hewly; for my aunt Ferguson says Helen was so astonished, so horrified, when she heard of it, that it seems impossible she can ever get over it and like him again; and yet, you know, Mr. Dreux, I took all imaginable pains not to put a word in which was not absolutely necessary to make it an apology at all. I did not say 'humble apology,' or anything of the kind, for, in fact, I was afraid he might turn restive, and I should not get it at all; and if he had refused, and trusted to my generosity, I could not but have held my tongue."

The rest of the evening was spent in giving and receiving the lesson, and for several days after this Mr. Dreux was unceasingly occupied in going about taking leave of his old parishioners. He had made up his mind to spend two or three months in travelling for one of the great Evangelical Societies. The tour marked out for him would occupy three months, and as public speaking was no trouble to him, he believed he should find this engagement a positive relaxation, and find a relief from his regret at leaving his people, in the change and bustle of travelling.

Accordingly he preached his farewell sermon, took leave of his old pensioners, and set off one chilly morning at the end of March. It was six o'clock in the grey of the morning, and as he had kept the time of his departure a secret, there was no one at the railway office to see him off but young Greyson, from whom he was very sorry to part for more reasons than one.

The same day that he thus quietly withdrew from the scene of his labours and usefulness Mr. Hewly returned, but he did not appear in public; he had effected the exchange of his living, and he now advertised his furniture, paid his bills, and left the town to return no more.

In the meantime his late curate recovered all his wonted health, strength, and energy in the variety afforded by travelling and the pleasurable excitement of public speaking.

So passed the whole of April. It was an early spring, and the country grew more beautiful day by day. He travelled west and south, through South Wales, Dorsetshire, and Devonshire, till, on the 1st of May, he reached a small town in the wildest part of Cornwall, standing close to the sea cliffs. The trees were in full leaf and the day was almost sultry. He walked through the gaunt old-fashioned street to the vicar's house, and to his disappointment heard that the vicar was ill, but that the officiating clergyman could no doubt assist him, though he could not be spoken with at present, for the bells were already ringing for the Wednesday evening service. "But if Mr. Dreux would go down to the church," the vicar's wife said, "he would no doubt see him after the service, and hear what arrangements he had made for the meeting."

It was a glorious evening, hot as midsummer, but the east was already beginning to turn ruddy. There was a high steep hill rising directly behind the church. It looked wild and bushy, and it flung back the sound of the bells with such a strong echo as seemed to fill to overflowing the narrow valley in which the town stood.

The streets were very quiet, and the old-fashioned casements were full of flowering plants. He easily followed the sound of the bells, and found the church,—a fine old building, with a tapering spire, and windows glowing with the sunset red, but the ringing of bells was over, and the service had already begun.

As the sound of the reader's voice fell upon his ears, he stood for an instant doubting the evidence of his senses. He went up the side aisle and was shown into a pew, then turned to make conviction still more certain. The reader stood with his face full towards him—it was Allerton!

Yes, assuredly it was Allerton. As he read, the familiar tones of his voice struck with mingled pain and pleasure upon the senses of his sometime friend. The heart is very quick at divining the hidden history of those whom it loves. As he listened he perceived some unwonted cadences. There was a change, and who could tell what sorrow and pain had caused it, or whether it might not be referable to the disappointment he had suffered when they parted?

As he went on listening, the change became more perceptible. There was an earnestness of gravity and feeling not usual before. It was extremely touching to him to fancy, as he could not help doing, that this man who had taken such pains to hide from him had yet found no new friends to heal the pain of his rejected affection. He little thought who was listening, and he took no pains to conceal the altered expression of his face. He went through the prayers with grave simplicity, and ascended the pulpit. He was now still more distinctly seen, for the church had been lighted; but his late friend was sheltered in the deep shadow of a pillar, and was in no danger of being recognised.

He gave out his text,—" For old things have passed away, all things are become new."

A singular text for *him* to have chosen, his auditor thought; but as he went on and opened out his subject, a strange bewildering feeling came over and nearly overwhelmed him. It seemed as if this scene and all other things, nay, even existence itself, might be a dream and a mistake,—for with far more power and more emotion than he had been wont to exhibit before, he brought forward his opinions and unfolded the scheme of salvation according to the principles which he had once despised.

The sermon went on; the first impression had been correct; there was nothing which left room for a moment's doubt. Allerton was preaching to a small audience and from notes; he hesitated now and then, perhaps less from want of words than from the newness of the matters which he was bringing forward,—new to him,—but said without compromise, and evidently from heartfelt experience.

The hidden listener sat still in the shadow, and

thanked God ; but an irrepressible pang of regret shot through his heart as he wondered what could be the feeling which made him still hold himself aloof when, as it seemed, they should be far more to each other than ever they had been before, and when he ought no longer to resent what his sometime friend had done.

This excitement was almost too much to be borne, but still the thrilling voice went on, and now he wondered how they were to meet, and what must be done. It was evident that Allerton had been there some time, and that he was not setting forth anything different to his ordinary teaching. With what motive, then, or with what feelings did he still conceal himself from his best friend? But this question could not be answered, and the sermon was over before he had come to any determination as to how he should present himself.

He went out of the church with the rest of the congregation, and passed down the dusky street. It was strangely painful to him that Allerton should have made no effort to regain his friendship. He had got nearly as far as the inn where he intended to sleep when the desire to see and speak with him came back so strongly, that he turned at once and retraced his steps to the church, hoping to find it not yet closed, and to gain some information as to his residence.

He ran up the stone steps. The pew-opener, a

woman, had just put out the lights, and the church looked dark and large as he glanced down the ranges of pillars.

"Did you wish to see the monuments, Sir?" said the woman.

He explained his object, and she told him Mr. Allerton would soon return, for he was only gone to see a sick woman, and had ordered the light to be left burning for him in the vestry. She further volunteered the information that he often made a study of the vestry, for that their vicar (who was ill, poor gentleman, and had been all the winter) kept his books there. She took him into the vestry, talking all the time.

"Mr. Allerton was gone out at that door," she said, "and would not be long." In fact, the vestry door leading out into the wild rising ground before mentioned stood wide open. There was a square of carpet on the vestry floor, an old-fashioned sofa, and some high-backed chairs, together with a closet door standing ajar, where might be seen clerical vestments hanging against the wall.

"If you wish to see Mr. Allerton, Sir," said the woman, "perhaps you won't mind waiting here? He is sure to return."

"Not at all. I need not detain you. I will wait alone."

"Yes, Sir. Only, you see, I must lock you in, Sir."

" Indeed ! "

" Yes, Sir ; for Mr. Allerton has a key to let himself in by.

" Well, if you are quite sure Mr. Allerton will return "—

"Oh, no fear, Sir. Mr. Allerton can't get home without going through the church ;" and so saying, the pew-opener set him a chair, made him a curtsey, and withdrew along the dark aisle, locking the doors behind her.

He waited so long that he really began to fear there must be some mistake, and that Allerton would not return at all that night. With this fancy strong upon him, and not relishing the ridiculous position he should be in if left there all night, he went hastily down the aisle to try the strength of the great lock. Of course he could no more stir it than he could fly ; but he had scarcely tried when he heard the vestry door hastily opened and rapid steps crossing the floor. There was all the length of the church between them, and before he had taken many paces toward him Allerton had flung open the closet door, taken out a decanter of wine, and left the place as quickly as he came in, leaving the door open behind him. He seemed in urgent haste, and never turned round, or he must have seen the figure entering the moment after he left the vestry. Dreux hesitated a moment, disappointed at being so thwarted, and then looked out at the open door to see which way he had gone.

Apparently he must have turned down by the side of the church, for no trace of him was discernible. By his haste, and by his going away with wine, his late friend believed he must be about to administer the sacrament to some person in extremity, and, resolving to wait for him, walked up and down before the door for nearly an hour.

A low wooden paling, with a gate in it, divided the church-yard from the rugged hill. The moon was shining, and when the clock had struck eleven he began to get so impatient of Allerton's protracted absence that he resolved to climb the hill and try to find his way out into the town. At first he got on very well, but presently he came to a gravelly ascent, partially covered with trees, and so steep that he could not climb it without the help of his hands among the bushes. Though the moon had gone in, and it had become perfectly dark, he was still thinking of forcing his way up the ascent, when he heard a door at some distance behind him creak heavily, and immediately made the best of his way towards the sound.

To his mortification, the vestry-door was closed. He shook the lock with right good-will, but could not stir it; but as the lamp was burning, he fancied the wind must have blown it to, and if so, Allerton might yet return.

Still, it was wearisome and dispiriting to walk there alone. He wandered about, but could find no outlet, and at length tried the rugged, thorn-dotted

hill again. He dashed about blindly for some time
among the trees, but could not reach the boundary
line, nor see any path, the little light scarcely serving
to mark the different hues of grass and gravel. His
progress was slow; sometimes he came to a rock,
and had to go round it before he could ascend again.
At last he came to a smooth open space, where the
grass grew short. The ascent was as steep as ever,
but he set off at a quick pace, for he did not at all
like his position; he might be trespassing for anything he knew. On a sudden he heard steps behind
him, as of a man rushing up after him. He quickened his pace, and the man called out to him to stop,
and the next instant had seized him by the arm.
The ascent was so steep that he had greatly the
advantage of his assailant, who was so out of breath
with running that he could not speak, but closed
with him, and was evidently trying to throw him
down. It was but the work of an instant to throw
him off violently: the impetus sent him running
down many degrees faster than he came up. Before
an instant had passed he heard another man rushing
up towards him. He did not relish the idea of there
being two against him, and ran up the precipitous
hill, trying to distance this new pursuer, and deter-
mining, if possible, not to close with him till they
came to open ground. Violent as his exertions
were, they availed him nothing, for the man running
after him redoubled his own, and ran as if his life
depended upon it. The moon was gone in; he did

not know the ground ; the man was close behind him, crashing down dead boughs, and displacing the heavy loose stones in his reckless race. He was close at his heels, and would have him instantly. He seemed trying to speak, and was panting violently, when Dreux, trying to repeat his last experiment, turned upon him, and seizing him suddenly, wrestled with him with all his strength.

He was a powerful man, but his assailant was a match for him, though both were so completely out of breath with running that to speak was impossible. Dreux struck the man several times, and struggled desperately. The man tried to pinion his arms ; he strove to speak and to stop him, and when he found he could not,—for Dreux continued to drag himself further up,—he next attempted to throw him down, and, not succeeding, flung himself on his knees, and by his weight brought his assailant down also. He recovered breath as they fell, to cry out, frantically, " Stop, stop ; Oh, my God ! the cliff, the cliff ! " He held tightly by Dreux, whose foot slipped, and the two, still struggling, rolled over the edge of a descent of about four feet, and so steep that, when the latter recovered from a short giddiness which had seized him, he was astonished to find himself unhurt. The man, as they fell over together, had uttered a cry of indescribable horror. The word " precipice " suggested itself to his bewildered brain ; he heard an injunction to be quiet, and, as he became more collected, he found himself supported, in a half-upright

position, on a very narrow ledge of rock. He rested
on one elbow, but his feet were hanging over, and
he could feel no footing. He found that the man,
who seemed to be in a kneeling position somewhat
above him, was grasping him round the chest, and
that if this support was withdrawn, he must inevitably fall over.

It was intensely dark, but he was conscious of a
rushing, booming sound far beneath him. The next
instant the man said, in a hurried, faint whisper,—
" I am no enemy ; don't move ; don't stir a muscle,
if you value my life or your own." Low as the
voice was, it was too familiar to be mistaken. He
heard it with a start, which placed his life in additional peril. The man was Allerton.

His first impulse was to make himself known ; the
next instant he remembered the imprudence of such
a step.

"Now, listen to me," Allerton proceeded, more
calmly, for he had taken breath ; " do you see that
cleft of sky between the clouds ? "

He answered, in a whisper, " Yes."

" In less than ten minutes," proceeded Allerton,
"the moon will reach it, and we shall have an interval
of light. Don't attempt to move till then ; I can
easily hold you while you are still ; till light comes
we must rest." He paused a moment, and then went
on, " You are a stranger here, or you would not
have climbed this hill in the dark. I tried to stop
you,—could not speak for want of breath ; keep

still, I charge you. If I know where we are, I only want light to get you up safely."

"But this cliff, this precipice,—the sea "—

"Yes, the sea rolls at its base. If you struggle to help yourself you are lost,—we are both lost; but if you can be still, perfectly passive, I trust in God that I can lift you by main strength on to my ridge, without overbalancing."

"And if you should fail?"

"If I should fail. Don't think of that now; don't look over,—don't for your life look over; there are still a few minutes left for prayer,—call upon God."

The moon drew near the edge of the cloud, and they had a full view of their fearful position. Beneath them was the sea, with the face of the precipice shelving almost sheer down to it. Allerton felt a shiver run through the frame of the supposed stranger, and charged him once more to be quiet. He was becoming faint and sick, but had strength of nerve to obey. The ledge on which he was lying was too narrow to admit of his turning; he was held on by the strength of Allerton's arms, who himself was kneeling on a broader space, two feet higher up.

Both their hats had fallen off in the struggle, and the troubled water was tossing them about below.

"Now," cried Allerton, "*dare*, if possible, to be passive. I hold you; try if you can find any footing at all; take time."

"No," was the reply, "I can find none."

" Can you draw one foot up on to the ledge ?"

" Impossible."

" The instant I begin to raise you draw a long breath. Now !"

The moon was fully out. Allerton slightly changed his position, unclasped his hand, seized his companion by the wrist, and with a mighty effort raised him about a foot. Happily Dreux disobeyed his injunctions, and dared to help himself. He was no sooner half erect than he found footing, which lightened Allerton's task, and gave him time to breathe ; this was a timely rest, and he gathered coolness and the confidence which was beginning to waver, then with one more effort he dragged him on to the upper ledge, where they rested in comparative safety.

It was easy to climb the small descent down which they had rolled. They had scarcely accomplished it when the moon went behind the cloud again, and they were left in total darkness.

" Now, we must wait a while," said Allerton, and he threw himself into the long grass, almost overpowered with his exertions.

The man whom he had saved came up and wrung his hand, but did not speak. Allerton supposed him to be some artist or tourist, for many such visited that romantic neighbourhood. The momentary glimpse he had had of his appearance had assured him that he occupied the station of a gentleman, and feeling a strong interest in him, he resolved to ask him home to his house for the night. The church

clock struck again, and just then the moon emerged
from the cloud, and Allerton sprang up and exclaimed, " Come here, and let us look at the danger
we have passed." He took him by the arm and
brought him to the brink of the cliff, holding him
while he suffered him to look over. Still the stranger
said nothing, but looked down—down into the
seething water, shuddered, and pressed his hand.
Allerton, who was moved himself, spoke to him of
the goodness of God in having preserved their lives ;
and reminded him of the fact, that in imminent
danger there is no possible rest for the human mind
but in calling upon God. Even in that doubtful
light, Dreux wondered that he did not recognise
him ; but being touched by his goodness, and by the
danger they had passed through, he remained silent,
and shrunk from making himself known. Allerton
then went on to speak of the happiness of those
whose hearts are in a state of preparation for death,
and added a few words on the way of salvation and
acceptance with God. Allerton thought he listened
attentively, but the moon just then coming out more
fully, he was obliged to turn his thoughts in another
direction. " Now, then," he exclaimed, with his
natural quickness, " I am going to take you down
by a still steeper way than you came up, but there
are flights of steps. You must follow me, and that
quickly, for I don't know the place very well, and
want to get down while there is light."

They ran down quickly, and, this way being

much shorter, they were soon by the vestry-door; it was opened by a man to whom Allerton stopped to speak, while Dreux looked on. "This is the gentleman," he heard him say; "he is quite safe." The man muttered something about people not liking to be flung down by those they meant to serve. Allerton laughed; the man spoke in the country dialect, and Dreux did not then remember that more than one man had tried to stop him.

"Come to me to-morrow," continued Allerton, dismissing the man. "And, as for you, young gentleman, take my advice, and never climb a strange cliff in the dark again; and never forget this night. Look there." He pointed to a deep ravine, not far from the pathway.

"I see it," replied Dreux, now speaking for the first time aloud; "and I never shall forget. I am deeply grateful to God, and to you. Look here." He drew back a pace or two as he spoke and threw back his disordered hair from his forehead, then he turned so that the full broad moonlight shone upon his features.

Allerton, who was standing on the threshold, had heard his voice at first with a start of incredulous amazement, but the truth no sooner flashed upon him than he uttered an exclamation of horror and almost of affright.

"Allerton! Allerton!" exclaimed Dreux, advancing upon him as he receded into the vestry, "Is it really come to this?—have you thought so hardly of me?—do you hate me so entirely, that, though you have perilled your life to save mine,—though you have prayed for me, when you thought me a stranger, you no sooner know me than you fling my gratitude back, and shrink from the very touch of my hand when I hold it to you?"

Allerton's face was white and rigid, but he drew still further back, and muttered, "You take a mistaken view of the case. You are wrong altogether."

"I do not. I have seen you shrink from me; and you wish to force me from your presence without the common expression of my civility, though you know that I owe you my life—though you know that I *struck* you, and that I never can forgive myself for that act unless I can part with you in amity. You need not turn away,—I see the marks of my hand on your forehead. If I had been a murderer you could not have treated me more "—

"Dreux, Dreux, you don't know what you are talking about. You are killing me."

"I do know, and I will say it;—if I had struck those blows with intent to murder you, and knowing that it was you, you could not have treated me more cruelly."

"You can scarcely stand,—you are excited and oppressed."

"I am sick with the recollection of that yawning gulf, and my feelings have been outraged, but I will not sit down, and I will not go. You shall believe that I am grateful; and you shall shake hands with me."

"I will," said Allerton, coming up to him, with a sigh. "Sit down, or you will faint. Let me open the window; there,—now drink this wine. You are excited, and don't understand—how should you? If you did, you would not grudge me these two or three bruises."

Dreux drank the wine, and made an effort to rise.

"No, no; be quiet for a moment," said Allerton, speaking almost with the tenderness of a woman. "Turn your face to the air. You came upon me so suddenly that I had no time for consideration,—I could not overcome my—my consternation. Oh, how many thousand times your face, with that self-same look, has advanced upon me in my dreams. Oh, my accusing conscience!"

"I have nothing to accuse you of—nothing," said Dreux, faintly.

"Not that you know of. What, you must shake hands? Well.—I don't hate you, Dreux; I love you."

"If you do "—

"If I do I have taken a strange way of showing it. I was beside myself, and your random accusation struck me to the heart."

"I beg your pardon,—I am sorry; but I do not know to what you allude."

"Dreux, you rise,—what do you want to do?"

"It is past midnight; I wish to go back."

"Where?"

"To the inn.   I will see you to-morrow."

"You will not go there, Dreux.   My house is near at hand; you will come with me."

"We cannot understand each other,—we are much better apart."

"How wearily you speak.   For your own sake we can never be friends again; but that, or something else, troubles you more—far more than I could have supposed possible."

"I know we cannot be friends, for I heard you preach to-night, and if your change of principles is not to bring us together, nothing can; but I *should* have liked to know the reason."

"Prospects have changed with you, Dreux; and you have, I know, come through many anxieties. Have you felt them much?"

"Very much.   I had no friend to stand by me."

"Well," said Allerton, bitterly, "it is some comfort to know that you would have been none the better for *my* standing by you.   But it grows late, and you will come with me."

Dreux made no further objection; he was thoroughly dispirited.   As they went through the dark silent street, Allerton suddenly said, "Did you come straight from Westport?   Did you come here on purpose to find me?"

"No; I came to speak to-morrow at your local Meeting. I did not know you were here till I saw you in the desk."

"I have been out for two days, and had not heard who was the deputation."

"If you had known, perhaps you would have kept out of my way"—

"This is my house, Dreux," interrupted Allerton. It stood close to the church; Allerton was admitted by an old housekeeper, a slight repast was set on the table, and a room was soon prepared for the guest. Allerton seemed ill at his ease, restless, and agitated; it was quite a relief to both when the room was declared to be ready; and whatever doubts, speculations, fears, or perplexities, might trouble the mind of either, no explanation was asked or offered, and each was heartily thankful to find himself alone.

They met the next morning to a late breakfast, and it was apparent that the night's rest, or rather the night's solitude (for neither had slept), had made an alteration on each.

Allerton's face was overclouded with gloom, and his manner painfully restless and changeable; he seemed struggling against varied feelings. Now he tried to look calm and cold,—now a sudden gleam of his old affectionate hilarity would shine for an instant in his eyes, and be checked almost as soon as it appeared.

Dreux, on the contrary, was now self-possessed,

and far more cordial than before; his old manner had returned, but he asked not a single question and betrayed no curiosity. His expression and every action seemed to say,—" I will have you back as a friend, if it be possible; and if you will give no explanation, I will do without one."

The Meeting, which was to be at four in the afternoon, supplied them with conversation during breakfast. Afterwards Allerton sat, looking pale and restless, till, suddenly, Dreux opened the glass-door of his study and proposed a walk in the garden; he came out mechanically. The garden was close upon the sea-shore, which, at that point, was nearly flat; they stood, looking about them,— then sauntered back. Allerton became conscious that Dreux was systematically breaking down the barrier of distance which he had erected between them; he talked of their familiar acquaintance; then he took hold of his arm; then he began to talk of his own affairs. Allerton struggled hard against this, but it would not do, his guest approached nearer and nearer; he was now perfectly at his ease, and nothing could make him otherwise. Insensibly Allerton was beguiled into conversation; he forgot himself, and asked a few questions. Dreux answered so frankly, and with such perfect good faith, that he found himself the repository of his most private affairs. He had got a terrible heart-ache; it did it no good to hear Dreux talk as he had been used to do to him, and to him only,—

telling him candidly all his feelings and fancies, as reserved people will to those whom they wholly trust. Allerton felt that he had never so talked since they parted, and that now he was doing battle manfully for the continuance of the privilege. He would not give it up, and he was now working so hard at the barrier that it must have inevitably given way, if a servant had not come up to them and reminded Allerton of some piece of clerical duty.

" I will be back shortly," he said, in a distraught, restless manner.

He returned in half an hour. Behold, the beloved unbidden guest had fallen asleep on his study sofa ! he had been awake the whole night,—that Allerton knew, for he had listened for hours to footsteps pacing overhead. He softly drew near, and contemplated him with a peculiar and most painful sensation.

Tall, somewhat slender, and youthful-looking, he possessed in his waking hours a gravity and weight which added several years to his appearance. Now this gravity had given way to an easy expression of confiding tranquillity. A listless smile parted his lips, and reminded the looker-on of his sister. He was asleep, down to his very finger-ends.

It was a chilly morning, and Allerton passed into the hall and brought a shepherd's plaid to lay over him. As he folded it across him he opened his eyes, and, without any expression of surprise at finding himself so tended, turned and fell asleep again, with Allerton still bending over him.

No need for apology,—he was entirely at home. He had been tired, now he was resting, and nothing could make him think that this was not the best place possible to take it in. He floated out into the land of dreams. Most of them were pleasant ones; perhaps the more so because, being a very light sleeper, he was conscious, after a long time, of a warm hand upon his forehead, moving back his hair.

Light sleepers can reason, after a fashion, even in their dreams: he followed out a long train of misty, entangled reasonings in his. He thought it odd that Allerton should so recoil from him when awake, and now should keep his hand upon his forehead, and touch the little mark of the wound with such a brotherly kiss.

He was conscious of a home feeling, and a sense of security, even in sleep; but when he at length awoke, and looked at Allerton, he found him moody and miserable as ever.

He had built up the barrier between them again, and, with his arms upon his study-table, sat regarding him with a pained, uneasy air.

Dreux set to work to throw his barrier down. " Allerton, I'm very hungry,—I want some lunch."

Allerton smiled at this appeal, and rang the bell, but he kept such stern guard over himself that he preserved as distant a manner as ever.

The lunch speedily appeared. Allerton assisted his guest, but he sat with his untouched plate before him, gazing out of the window. He was beginning to distrust his powers; he should never be able to break down this wall of rock ; he had been mistaken,—there had come no change over Allerton, which made his own conduct appear right and inevitable ; he did not want him, and was restless and anxious for him to be gone.

While he slept his face had looked so youthful and easy that Allerton had felt as if a few months of bitter remorse had made *him* many years the senior; when he awoke, his features had been lighted up with the old cordial smile. But now a cloud of gloom, pain, and wounded feeling had gathered over his brow. He did not touch the offered meal, and sat silent a long time. He had lost confidence ; his old reserve had again crept over him. He had been repulsed, and could not recover.

His host endured this with difficulty. " I thought," he said, " you told me you were hungry ?"

No answer. His late friend poured out a glass of water and drank it hastily ; then he rose slowly, left the room, and, with equal deliberation, walked up stairs. At the top he paused to consider which way he should turn.

Allerton hastily crossed the hall, ran up, and asked what he wanted.

" I want to find my room, and get my carpet-bag."

Allerton would not hear of it;—was urgent, impetuous.   He made him come down again, shut the door of his study, and turning the key, exclaimed, in a low, hurried voice, " Dreux ! are you determined,—are you quite bent upon our still being friends ?"

" No, I do not wish to force myself upon you; I wish to go."

" You shall not go till you have eaten something."

" I cannot eat;—you will not give me what I want."

" Sit down."

" No, I will not sit down again ;—I must go."

" What have I done within the last few minutes to give you this sudden resolution ?"

" Nothing new,—nothing more.   But you have not yet forgiven me, and I cannot, and I will not, remain where I am not wanted."

" Forgiven you !—forgiven you !"

" Yes, forgiven me.   I thought it probable at first that you would have forgiven me, but I find " ——

" Will you look at me ?"

" Well !"

" What do you see ?"

" I see a man who was once my friend,—for whom I cared far more than he ever thought,—

who has no true reason *now* for resentment against me,—and who has no power even now to alienate my regard, for I choose to retain it."

" Dreux !"

" It is useless your trying to make me believe that all your old affection for me is past and over. Why you try, is a mystery that I cannot solve. Why you torment yourself and me by feigning this utter want of interest I cannot fathom. You *have* some kindness left for me still. What does it matter *else* to you that I carry a mark on my forehead? Why must you needs investigate it?—it's nothing to you. Allerton! Allerton! what have I done now?"

He asked the question almost vehemently, for Allerton had started as if he had been struck a blow. He made a gesture of entreaty, and staggered with difficulty to his chair; the veins of his temples were swelled almost to bursting, and he pointed to the window, as if he wanted air.

It was thrown open hastily, and a glass of water held to his lips.

" Dreux," he said, as his late friend, again overstepping the barrier, laid a hand upon his shoulder, and looked anxiously in his face, " you are very kind ;—do you know who you are speaking to ?"

" To a man who saved my life last night."

" There are no other words in the world that it would have done me so much good to hear, and that it would have been so like yourself to say, even if you had known the truth. Well, but do you see no change in me?"

"Yes, I see that you have suffered; I hear it in the sound of your voice. I also see " ——

"What, Dreux? Well, I have suffered;—the curse of Cain I sometimes feel upon me."

"There is no sin that the blood of Christ cannot wash away."

"*No sin.* I have repeated those words many thousand times. It washes away, but it does not save us from the consequences of sin in this world. We may hope to live at peace in heaven with those against whom we have sinned too deeply to deserve any intercourse on earth. What! I have startled you at last! I feel your hand tremble."

"Not with distrust,—only with suspense. It is your manner, far more than your words " ——

"Well, take your hand from my shoulder, for I should not wish to feel it suddenly withdrawn when I tell you the truth. There,—now look me in the face. I am a murderer, Dreux, in will, and almost in deed."

"A murderer in will!"

"Yes, I tell you; and, having begun, I will tell you the rest. I have kept away from you as a duty, but you have found me out at last. And now I must tell you what I would fain have had known only to me and my Maker; least of all I would have had you know it. I would not blacken myself where I would fain have stood well. But you must know, for you want to make a friend of me again."

"I desire no confidence, Allerton. I would be your friend without it if you would let me."

"You would; but I am not quite base enough to permit that. I will tell you all, and you shall do as you please."

"You are excited now; I will not hear anything till you are calm; and even then, I had rather the matter was left, as you have said, between you and your Maker."

"Dreux, your presence while you are ignorant of it, and your friendly confidence, are daggers in my heart. To have you with me, and to hear you say such things as you have said *twice* during these few hours, would be far more than my fortitude could sustain. I told you that I was a murderer. Don't look so much aghast; it was you that I injured,—*you*. Do you hear me? You will not wake from this and find it a dream. Go and sit down, a long way from me. I have begun now, and I will go on to the end. Why do you put your hand to your head?—does it ache?"

Dreux took away his hand, and looked earnestly at Allerton. His remarks had several times appeared irrelevant; now he was excited and agitated.

"My dear Allerton," Dreux began, "you cannot be surprised if I feel a little bewildered; and if I show it"——

"Was that all? I thought you put your hand to your forehead as if you were in pain."

"O these strange suspicions!" thought Dreux; "what do they portend?—I have a slight headache," he explained, with a sigh of irrepressible anxiety, "and I have got a habit of putting up my hand since my accident. Of course one cannot expect such a thing to pass over, leaving no bad effects whatever."

Allerton rose and went to the window, as if he felt half suffocated. "You were in the church last night," he presently said; "why did you not come to me in the vestry?"

Dreux explained to him how he had returned to the church, and how he had failed to overtake him, as he left it hastily with the wine.

"I understand it all now," replied Allerton. "Among the trees you passed a cottage."

"I did not remark one."

"You did, however. After service the man who lives there came and asked me to pray with his wife, who is in a decline. I went, and stayed with her a long while; but just as I was about to leave her, she became so faint, that I ran back to the vestry to get some wine; the woman revived after she had taken it; and as I sat by her she said she saw some one going quickly up among the trees. I could scarcely believe her; for no one can get in there at night after the church-gates are locked, unless by climbing them. I declared she was mistaken;

but she persisted, and said it was a gentleman ; then
I was alarmed, for I knew it must be a stranger.
We left her with her daughter, and I and the
husband ran out after the stranger to warn him
of his danger. You seemed to be bent on rushing
up straight to your destruction. I suppose you
took us for thieves or murderers,—no unlikely
supposition : an unfortunate man was murdered
there last year for the sake of his watch, and his
body thrown over the cliffs. I got so out of breath
with my desperate race, that I could not shout
to you. My heart was in my throat, for I perceived
that my very eagerness in running on made you
rush more blindly up, heedless of the booming
of the water, which otherwise you might have
heard. When I had seized you, I was not prepared
for the strength with which you grappled with me,
resolutely dragging me still further and further
to the edge."

" If the moon had only come out then !"

" If the moon had come out then, you would not
have struck me ; was that what you would say ? But
then I should not have saved your life ; for the light
would have warned you of your danger. But you
are too generous to wish you had not lifted your
hand against me ; at least if you could know all that
I have suffered since we parted you would be glad.
Dreux, you are amazed, you look at me with
wonder. Well, I will tell you why ; but just now
I must rest. It comes upon me with such a sudden,

irresistible happiness, the thought that I should have saved your life—yours—I must think on it a while. No, say nothing, sit where you are, let me think my thoughts out, the bitter will come presently."

He turned from the window, and, as was usual with him when excited, began slowly to pace the room.

" Dreux, you are very patient with me, you always were; well—I will not try you any longer—the bitter returns in greater force than ever—I will sit down and lay it all before you."

He sat silent a few minutes, till Dreux made a movement of irrepressible agitation; the suspense was getting too much for him.

" When I left you that morning," Allerton began at length, speaking with suppressed emotion, "I felt more like a fiend than a human being. In the blindness of my passion I repeated that I hated and despised you—yes, and your sister also; yet in the depth of my heart, I knew you had acted consistently, and I hated your principles even more than yourself."

He looked intently out of the window, and continued in a lower tone: " I went home. I madly vowed that I would never speak to you again; I acknowledged to myself that I had known how it would be from the beginning; and so I had; but I had so resolutely smothered the knowledge, that it came upon me like a thunder-clap. Dreux,

I entered my house—my hand was on the latch of the study-door, when my groom met me and inquired what time my horse was wanted for you. It enraged me just then to hear him mention your name. I told him to hold his tongue, and went in. I don't know what induced the man to follow me, for he must have seen that I was in a passion. Perhaps it was that my condemnation might be the more complete. He asked me the question again, and said, 'Shall I go round and inquire, sir?' It only inflamed me to hear him say it and persist in it, as if he supposed I had not heard him. I told him the horse was not wanted; he said, rather sulkily, that if you rode your own horse, he knew you would be thrown. I cursed you in my heart, if not with my lips. I muttered, as I flung the door to, that nothing would please me better."

"Don't say any more, Allerton," cried his auditor, in a tone of the deepest agitation; "what is this to me? why bring it up again? I cannot bear to hear it; pray spare me; remember last night. If you are not satisfied with what you did for me then"—

"If I am not satisfied," repeated Allerton in the same suppressed tone. "Oh yes, and I am deeply thankful; it shows the goodness of God, in not only forgiving that murderous sin, but sparing me to be serviceable to the man whom I had injured. I told you that I believed I hated you. I fortified myself in this feeling. Dreux, strange to say, my man came again, and knocked at my door. I felt a momentary qualm of conscience. I thought it so odd; but I flung open the door and demanded how he dared interrupt me. He muttered some apology, and seemed aghast to see me in such a rage; and yet he muttered again, was I sure Mr. Dreux did not want the horse? I don't know what I said. I was beside myself; but I denied that it was wanted, and told him to come again at his peril! Oh, Dreux, it sickens me to reflect on that day; my rage grew as I thought on what you had done. I drank a good deal of wine after dinner, for my passion had exhausted me; after that I believe I fell asleep on my study sofa. Dreux, you must hear me to the end."

" No more," urged his auditor; " God has spared me, why need I know all this?"

" Why need you? Because I cannot bear the sight of that smile of yours, while you are in ignorance. I would rather see you look shocked and horrified, as you do now, than see you determined to confide in me, and hear you lament that you lifted your hand against me."

" I will never lament it again, if you will only spare me now."

" Spare you a *little*, just the little remains of your ideal, and not tear it down and soil it in the dust, and despoil it of every vestige of its beauty. Dreux, I know you thought well of me."

" I did, and do."

" Well, Dreux, it was dusk when I awoke, and started upright at a peculiar noise of sobbing. I saw my servants crying in the doorway and wringing their hands, my old man-servant crying as much as any of them.

" They came in, but seemed afraid to speak ; for they knew my affection for you, but not our quarrel. I asked what was the matter ; they told me the most horrible story that ever my ears had listened to : that you had been thrown and dragged a great distance by your horse ; that you were still alive, but there was no hope ; and your horse—that was the most horrible thing of all at the moment—your horse had run back like a mad creature, and rushed, covered with foam and dust, into the open door of my stables."

" Why need that have shocked you ?" urged Dreux, scarcely knowing what he said. " Had he not been put up there times out of number ?"

" I tell you he rushed into my stables covered with blood and foam ; he had injured himself, and died in the night. I had thought that I hated you ; the passing away of that delusion brought with it misery beyond what I had supposed it possible our nature could endure. My people had expected to see me overpowered ; I was more, I was frantic. I tore my hair, I called upon God to revenge you upon me. They talked of what a pleasure it must be to me now to think what good friends we had

always been; every word they said was a dagger in
my heart; they could do nothing with me, and at
last they sent for a physician; and I remember
very little more of that miserable night, or of the
next day."

"And now I have heard it, Allerton; and you
must say no more till you have heard me."

"What would you say, Dreux?"

"That I entreat you—that I *expect* you to forget
this as completely as I will do. No, not to forget
it, then; but to think no more of it as a thing that
need keep us asunder—never to think of it at all
without remembering last night also."

Allerton remained silent; he seemed in a great
measure relieved of the load which had oppressed
him, but did not take the offered hand without
a gesture of pain. He put it aside again, and
motioned to Dreux to go back to his seat, going on
with his narrative, as if he desired at once to say all
that was on his mind.

"Dreux, those were wretched days. I got up
from my bed and walked about, and I saw that
every human being I met pitied me; it was written
on their faces; I saw it, and almost wished they
could have known the truth. You were in great
danger; pains were taken to conceal the fact from
me; but I possessed myself not only of the facts
of the case, but of all the fears of the attendants.

"All your friends and all my own came to me to
comfort me. They were amazed and alarmed at my

state of mind. They all said the same thing. They all pitied me. Their reproaches would have been easy to bear in comparison. But I was dumb. I sat in my study, and neither could answer them, nor exert myself to send them away. But everything that could torture me they said, for there was no kind of praise that ever was bestowed on human sympathy and friendship that they did not lavish upon mine. This went on for three or four days; then I became restless, and wandered about almost ceaselessly night and day.

"I went and called on the Patons, for there I thought I should hear some particulars. I was a good deal altered by remorse, but a sort of dead calm had come over me, which I thought nothing could move. I began to talk; the ladies tried to answer me, but one by one they left the room. The mother, who alone remained, could scarcely speak for tears. This put the climax to my sufferings. I would have told her everything but for the utter weariness that had come upon me. I went away, but I was determined to see you, and I did. Dreux, you are worse than any of them. Don't you remember what you suffered? Don't you know the peril which threatened not only life but reason? and you are speechless with pity! I have seen you often this morning put your hand to your head. Such a blow could scarcely pass, you told me, and leave no bad effects, and yet you look as if there was nothing you would not do to lighten its effects on me. Well, I saw you by night. You were half delirious. I saw your sister sleeping at the foot of your miserable bed, and I repented. I had been stunned before; now my awakened feelings of tenderness added keenness to remorse. I dragged on another week, and then it was given out that your danger was over. I could not believe it; but the next day the report was confirmed. Then a new feeling came over me—I knew that I never could look you in the face again. I left the town, resolved not to return. I wanted exertion—my mind preyed upon my health. I thought change would do me good. I travelled. I walked. I toiled among the mountains. Every day I walked till I was worn out with fatigue, but my sleep was not sweet.

" When I had been absent a month, I went to the Bishop. My altered appearance showed my state of health, and he soon saw that something more than I spoke of was the matter with me. I easily got a six months' leave of absence. I went into Wales. I exerted my bodily strength to the utmost, but the same terrible fears haunted me. If you had died who would have been your murderer? As it was, you might never be restored to health, and then what would become of *me?*

" I had no friend, no person to speak to. I felt as if the lot of Cain had come upon me—to wander —the murderer of my brother, with one more curse in addition to his, one more ingredient in my bitter cup than ever poisoned his,—that I loved *my* brother,

I constantly thought with remorse of what I had done —that in the distance and apart, brooding over my everlasting heart-ache, he seemed to me far better and more to be desired as a friend and companion than ever he had done before. The heart has no bounds for its capacity for suffering, nor for loving. One pain brings another. All my forgotten sins rose up before me with this crowning one at their head.

" In the silence of my life I thought of you both incessantly. If the eye is not satisfied with seeing, how much less is the heart satisfied with loving ! I still worshipped my idols of clay, but in the blindness of my misery I reproached my Maker, ' Thou hast taken away my GODS, and what have I more ? '

" I got a letter one day from Hewly. He said you were much better. You had read prayers and were to preach the next Sunday. I was extremely thankful, but it did not seem to make my crime the less. At first my resolution never to see you again, never to seek any further intercourse with you, or bring you any more within the influence of a temper so violent, had seemed so great a sacrifice that I thought it half atoned ; now that foolish fancy was gone, and the weight of my sins had become almost intolerable. I thought there was nothing I would not do to be released from it—nothing.

" I had done many things, and it grew heavier and harder to bear. On the Sunday when I knew you were to preach, I went out and wandered up the barren mountain which faced the farm-house where I lodged. I came to a cleft in the rock, where a quantity of broom hung out and made a shelter.

" I sat down and took out a Bible, but I did not read. I thought of you and of your sister, and your voice seemed to come back to me, saying such things as you often had done in our arguments and discussions. My mind was empty of comfort—I could not think very connectedly. I unclasped the Bible, and a letter of yours fell out. You had written it while you were away with Elinor; within it were the notes of a sermon on this text,—' There is a friend that sticketh closer than a brother.'"

Allerton paused when he came to this place, but Dreux made no effort to speak; he sat with his eyes intently fixed upon him. He presently went on :—

" I was pleased at the sight of your writing. I read over the letter, and it beguiled me for a few minutes from the weariness of my own thoughts. When I had finished it I picked up the notes of your sermon and began to read *them*. It was for the first time, Dreux. They began with some remarks upon the unsatisfying nature of all earthly affection—they asserted that love was originally the best gift of God to man,—that all his happiness flowed from it,—that now, from this greatest blessing sprung our keenest misfortunes and sorrows. It went on to describe the wretchedness of a man who, having fixed his affections on the earthly, has not the heavenly to turn to when they are taken away.

"I thought it strange you should have chosen to send me such a subject,—I, who was then so well content with the earthly, so wrapt round with the love and the brotherhood that I had chosen.

"But I read on. There *is* a Friend. It described the sympathy of Christ with all human suffering; among others, with that restless worm, *remorse*. It described the bitterness of heart under which I was then suffering, and offered the tenderness of that Friend as a precious substitute for the loss of all others.

"Dreux, you must not interrupt me now. I know what you mean. I see plainly that you will still be my friend. Since it is so I will not gainsay you. It was only for your own sake that I wanted to have it otherwise. Well, I had often said to myself that there was nothing I would not do to relieve myself from the intolerable restlessness that oppressed me; but I had never thought of the religion which you had taken care I should (theoretically) be well acquainted with. I went on reading, and the notes unfolded the scheme of salvation, as you had so often done before. It was familiar, and yet I could scarcely believe that it was truly the same. If these things really were so, how happy, I thought, for me.

"I rested my forehead upon my hands, and through the hours of that long, sunny morning I began to think that though I had despised these things when I was well with my own heart, yet now that I had become vile and hateful in my own eyes, and now that all peace and happiness were over and I was utterly alone, perhaps they might prove a solace to me,—the more so, I thought, because they were yours.

"The longer I sat there the more these thoughts pressed upon me. I was wretched. Here seemed an offer of peace. If, without any merit or fitness of my own, I could be forgiven, I thought it would be a blessed thing, and every sound that reached me in that lonely place seemed to be burdened with the words, 'There is a Friend.' In my own esteem I was far less worthy to apply to this Friend than I had been in the days of my prosperity. I was no murderer then.

"I thought of this a while longer. 'But no,' I said, 'there is no other way. I will try this. I will set my foot on board this ark of refuge. If I remain thus I must perish, and if I go forward I can but die.'

"My soul assented to the certainty of that truth of which you had so often reminded me, that no amendment of life could atone for committed sin, and make a man the more fit to ask forgiveness. I thought the only hope was to throw myself on the pity of God for the past and the future, through that Friend whom I now perceived to be more desirable, more excellent than the sons of men.

"I do not remember that I uttered any distinct petition beyond those verses of Scripture which presented themselves to me.

"I read the rest of your notes; they set forth the goodness of that heavenly Friend. I perceived (and not without something like surprise, Dreux) that my sins had been against *Him*, and in the silence of the place, I prayed for mercy and forgiveness. To my bitter remorse for past sins was added a new, overpowering sorrow,—a scarcely understood affection for that heavenly Friend began to dawn in my heart. I remembered that passage of Scripture, and assented to it in the depths of my soul, ' They shall look upon Him whom they have pierced, and mourn.' "

After a short silence, he went on again,—

"Why need this distress you? I am telling you of the most blessed period of my life. I went down to the farm-house, where I lodged. My sorrow was mingled with astonishment that I should never have seen these things before. I remembered continually more and more of the conversations we had had together. Your words seemed now to have a new application. I wondered how it was, not knowing that the natural man *cannot* discern the things of the Spirit of God, because they are spiritually discerned.

"I felt that night very unwell, though not so restless as usual. The next day one of the children of the house was taken extremely ill with fever, and in the evening the mother sickened. I would have left the house, but the illness I had felt the day before increased upon me. I did not know what was the matter, but as far as I was capable of it in my then condition, I enjoyed a kind of peace. In the middle of the night, both I and the mistress of the house were raving with delirium; it proved to be small-pox. The country Doctor was sent for; the cases were dangerous. I was neglected, and left much to myself,—nearer interests pressed upon the poor people. I was often delirious, but my distracted fancy was always constant to one theme. I had no hope but in Christ. I had put off the burden upon Him, and had said, 'Undertake for me.' The woman of the house died, and a child; the other child and I slowly recovered. I could scarcely speak a word of Welsh, and they knew no English. The accommodation was most wretched, but God's mercy spared me to live and praise Him, and even to preach His Gospel to others. During the tedious weeks of my recovery I thought much and earnestly. The Holy Scriptures were my constant solace. The offer of free salvation became a certain, most undoubted fact to me. I closed with it, and received peace.

" The surgeon who had attended me wished me to go south; therefore I came into Cornwall, and finding the vicar of this place willing to be friendly with me, I helped him a little during the winter, and now he is ill, I take all the duty for him."

Having brought his narrative to this point, he got

up and walked about the room, almost surprised to see how powerfully it had moved his friend. It was so familiar to himself that he had uttered it with calmness, and the former events especially had been so long present to his mind that to put them into words was a relief instead of a pain to him.

CHAPTER XXIV.

THE MINIATURE.

The meeting was over, and in the dusk of evening they walked home together towards Allerton's house.

Allerton, who seemed inexpressibly relieved now that he had unburthened his mind, talked with something of his old cheerfulness; but there was one subject on which he did not touch, though several good opportunities had been given him. Dreux felt that it was not for him to be the first to mention his sister; and as his next greatest wish with regard to Allerton was to have him back at Westport, he introduced that subject, and began earnestly to urge his return.

Allerton, who seemed to take pleasure in being entreated, allowed him to go on for a long while. At length he appeared convinced, and said, certainly it did seem a duty to come and preach against those errors which he had formerly approved.

"And I want a curacy," said Dreux, laughing.

"What! you do? But you told me that you would not go back to Westport,"—for Dreux had related much of the quarrel between Hewly and himself in the morning. "Dreux, you could not be *my* curate,—*you*, so much my superior in standing, in experience, in everything. I could not consent to that."

"You had rather see me some other man's curate? You seriously think I should be better off as curate in some place where I am unknown, and under some other man?"

Allerton reflected a while, and decided to close with the offer. He could then see that he did not overwork himself; it would give him an opportunity to live down the calumnies which had been raised against him ; and as he himself felt all the awkwardness of changing his side in a place where he was so well known, he perceived the advantage of a friend like Dreux to back him. It pained him to think of standing in such a position towards him: but he reflected on his altered prospects. With whom, he thought, would he feel them so little as with himself? Who, from feelings of either affection or duty, would naturally and inevitably care for him so unceasingly? His health might now be very different to what it had been ; who would be so quick to observe it—who would have so much hold over him? "For," Allerton thought, "for my sake he will try to keep well; he will have the pleasure of companionship which he values,—for this, which I must feel, and bitterly, to the end of my days, seems not at all to have struck him as I should have thought;

he has as much confidence in me as ever. Well, I will accept his offer, and all the advantages it brings with it."

" Dreux, if nothing better presents itself for you, I shall be heartily glad to accede to your proposal."

" You were so long considering that I was about to withdraw it."

" I had much rather be *your* curate. You shall do just as you please, Dreux."

" Shall I ? But mind you don't let me domineer over you, Allerton. Your curates have an easy life of it. I often thought at Westport, that to be your curate, and let you do the work, was as gentlemanly an opening for the ambition of a lazy young M.A. as could be desired."

" Well, it gives me pleasure to hear you laugh, even at my own expense. I hope your sister is well ?"

Both parties had been thinking of her for some time ; nevertheless, Dreux started on hearing her name.

" She has been ill," he replied, with rather a constrained manner, for he did not know how Allerton now might feel towards her.

" Not very ill ? "

" Yes, in great danger ; but she is much better."

" If I had known that, I believe I *must* have written."

" I still cannot understand why you did not write to me months ago."

"Not even now, Dreux, when we have got upon this subject?"

"I would have written, if I had been you."

"If I had written, what could I have told you?"

"Part of what you told me this morning; no one could so much rejoice to hear it. Did you give me credit for no anxiety about you?"

"And if I had written so much, what would you have expected my next step to be?"

"Perhaps to return."

"Dreux, you answer with as much hesitation as if you thought it possible for a man who had heartily loved a woman to forget her in six months. If I could have done that, I could and would have written to you; even as it was, I thought of doing so continually. I had constant arguments with myself; but the new religion was precious, for it had raised me out of the very mire of despair. How, then, could I make it a stepping-stone whereby to obtain what I could not hope to have without it? Dreux, if I could so far have departed from uprightness of mind as to do that, I should have begun next to question the very reality of the change which had passed upon me. Even if you had received my tale with the most unquestioning faith, it would have availed me nothing. I must have endured the life-long doubts and dreads of an at least *supposed* self-deceiver."

"My dear Allerton," Dreux answered, "you acted

for the best. My remarks implied no reproach, only regret."

And having now got a most explicit declaration from Allerton respecting his feelings, he did not care to pursue the subject further, and began to talk of indifferent matters, but Allerton was absent and uneasy. He would not mention Elinor again, but could not command his attention for thinking of her state of health.

Dreux was not at all displeased to see this. "I shall go to see Elinor shortly," he said. "She is at Shanklin, and writes me word that she is getting quite well."

Allerton seemed lost in painful thought. "Dreux," he said, after a long pause, "you do not know, as I do, what a painful thing it is to be despised. It has not been the lightest part of my trial to feel how low I must sink in her esteem—and your accident—and our quarrel"—

"Our quarrel,—what should she know of that?"

"What, have you never told her?"

"Why should I tell her? Certainly I did not. Supposing she had loved my friend, it could but give her pain; supposing she did not, I would not let her know anything to his disadvantage."

They had reached Allerton's house, and, as both parties wished to drop the subject of Elinor, they launched into a long discussion about things at Westport. There was a great deal to be said about

Hewly,—his plans, his intended marriage, Mr. Brown's missionary project, the almshouse business, &c.; but everything was made by Dreux to bear, as it were, one moral. Whatever the story he was telling, it terminated by showing the desirableness, propriety, and necessity, of Allerton's returning to Westport immediately.

They supped together, and then went to the coach-office, for Dreux was going east again, and was obliged to leave the place that night. "I have been thinking," he said, "as it is impossible for us to meet till after Sunday, that I had much rather you would come to me, instead of my returning here."

"To be sure," added Allerton; "where shall you be?"

"I think of giving myself Monday and Tuesday as holidays; if we could spend them together we might arrange many things."

"So we might. Give me your address, and I will join you."

"I will give you the address, and if, on consideration, you find you had rather I came to you, write, and I will do so. The address is simply— Shanklin, Isle of Wight."

The start with which Allerton heard this was not lost upon Dreux, but, the coach appearing in sight, they had not much time for last words.

"One moment, Dreux," said Allerton, detaining him. "If I come to Shanklin, you must promise me, beforehand, that all I have told you shall be duly detailed; and if, after that, you think I have any chance—I mean you to tell her of the horse—of our quarrel"—

"And how you saved my life. Well, if you *desire* it, I will. You shall find a letter waiting for you at Portsmouth."

Early on Monday morning he reached South-ampton, and, after arranging to speak at a Meeting there on Wednesday, crossed over to the Isle of Wight and went on to Shanklin. Elinor was quite blooming, and in easy spirits. It was some time since they had met, and there was much to be said; but there was an early dinner ordered, for their aunt retained the old-fashioned notion that no one could "come off a journey" without being quite famished. As much as possible, therefore, of this dinner had to be consumed, and a great many ques-tions of Miss Theresa's answered, before they could think of going out; but at length they effected a move, and, leaving the old lady to doze in her chair, walked forth to explore the Chine.

There, as they sat under the trees, talking about his travels, he quietly introduced Allerton's name, described their meeting, and his own sensations on hearing him preach.

Elinor listened with intense interest.

"I thought it singular," he added, "that Allerton should have made no effort to renew our friend-ship."

"If I had been you," said Elinor, "I should have

felt very much hurt." And not all her joy at seeing her brother could make her feel at ease.

He then went on to describe, as well as his agitation would permit, the after-events of the evening: how Allerton had saved his life, at the peril of his own. He next repeated their morning's conversation; and, as he had been desired, gave Allerton's self-accusations, as well as the facts of the quarrel; but told by him, and touched with his feelings towards the actor, they certainly were softened.

Elinor was tolerably self-possessed; she said nothing, and kept hoping there would be some slight reference to herself, but her brother neither mentioned Allerton's intended visit, nor his acknowledgment of continued attachment. While she sat reflecting, he told her how he had persuaded Allerton to return to Westport, and that he intended to be his curate.

Thereupon followed a long silence.

"How does Mr. Allerton look?" said Elinor, breaking it at length.

"Perfectly well, but not precisely the same. When I saw him in the pulpit, I perceived that he had become calmer. You know he has naturally high spirits and a cheerful disposition,—doubtless he has still; but, when he was not agitated by the things he had to tell, he looked exactly like that little portrait which, no-doubt, you remember."

He took the little picture from his pocket and

gave it to Elinor, who held it in her hand as he proceeded:—

"Independently of the softening influence of Divine grace, I should say that the sufferings he describes have had their natural effect; there was something to me quite touching in the change. Allerton is quite free from morbid feeling; his spirits are always buoyant, unless anything is that moment pressing upon them; but, when he smiles, I can see something now beyond his old affectionate hilarity."

"Don't talk of him any more," said Elinor, covering her face to hide her tears. "Why should you make me unhappy?"

"I did not mean to do so, my sweet Elinor."

"He has saved your life,—I am deeply grateful; but I don't wish to think of him too much. I wonder, Arthur, that you have not more consideration."

Her brother did not seem so penitent as might have been expected; on the contrary, he did not see her emotion without pleasure.

However, by way of peace-offering, he said,— "Elinor, forgive me this once, and I will give you this little picture."

Elinor was surprised; she considered the miniature, as if she expected the calm features to help her decision.

"I value it very much," he continued; "I only offer it to you in the hope that you will take care

of it. You can have it set into a brooch and wear
it, if you like."

" How excessively absurd you are, Arthur," said
Elinor, drying her tears, and laughing in spite of
herself.

" Absurd,—why absurd ?" returned her brother,
with amiable unconsciousness. " Do you think it
too large ? Mrs. Fred Bishop has one quite as
large ; I saw her wearing it the other day."

" Nonsense, Arthur ; I wonder what pleasure
you can find in teazing me. Don't you see the
excessive impropriety of my wearing the portrait
of a gentleman ? It would be most preposterous."

" Oh," said her brother, " then you had better
give it me back."

Elinor gave it with regret. As they went back
to the house she tried to make him talk again, but
he was revelling in the unwonted pleasure of a
holiday, and would keep turning this way and that
way to look about him. Part of the way home he
chose to sing " By the deep, nine ;" he then began
to throw stones into the sea in that dextrous
manner which is called ducks and drakes, for even
clergymen are supposed, at rare intervals, to have
pleasant reminiscences of their boyhood.

Elinor felt inclined to be very angry, both with
him and his high spirits, but after a time she
changed her mind and let him go on as he liked.

When they reached the house, she followed him

into the dining-room, shut the door, and asked him to give her the picture, which he did at once, without smiling or appearing to see anything odd in her request. He then went up stairs to talk to his aunt, leaving her to her own reflections.

She stood some time below, scarcely thinking of anything connectedly, but pleased to look at the little picture. At length, having secured it in a safe place, she walked slowly upstairs and opened the door of the drawing-room; her entrance, she observed, put a stop to a conversation which had been going on between her brother and her aunt, but, as the latter was extremely fond of cooking up little insignificant mysteries and having private conferences, she thought nothing of it.

"And what sort of a looking man is he, Arthur?" she heard her aunt say. "Is he handsome?"

"Handsome—well, no; I don't think he is—not exactly."

"But can't you give me the least notion?—he's not a *pokey*-looking, little knock-kneed fellow, I hope? and I hope he's not a—what I call sanctified—black hair, parted down the middle, and turn-up-eyed man, Arthur?"

"No; he's a fine, well-grown man, with an erect figure."

"Dear me, have you no better talent for description than that, Arthur? Has he a good voice?—has he insinuating manners?"

"Insinuating manners, aunt!" exclaimed Elinor, laughing, "what an idea! Have you hired him, Arthur?"

"Hired him!" repeated the said Arthur, turning round with a look of genuine bewilderment.

"You are talking of the new footman, are you not?"

"Do you think my aunt would take so much interest in a footman?"

Elinor nodded and smiled, for she had heard little for the last week but conjectures as to what this redoubtable footman would be like, he having been recommended by her brother, and not yet inspected by his proposed mistress.

As Elinor stood winding a skein of silk upon the backs of two chairs, Dreux came up to her, lifted her face, and kissed her with a smile.

"My dear, I'm afraid you are a little blunderheaded thing," he said. "At any rate you have a curious habit of jumping at conclusions, like the rest of your sex."

"Then he *is* a good-looking man, Arthur?" continued Mrs. Theresa. "I hope you wouldn't deceive me in that respect?"

"Aunt, you'll be charmed with him."

"And that's really all you have to say about him?"

"Unless it would interest you to know that he weighs about a stone more than I do?"

"Ah, you men are all alike. You delight to teaze."

"Dear aunt," said Elinor, still thinking of the footman, "if he is honest and does his work well, what does it matter how he looks in livery? I hope he will clean the plate better than Simpson does."

The entrance of the said Simpson with the tea-things made a diversion in the conversation. They had a very silent meal, the aunt for once being deep in thought,—so deep, that she actually never observed that Elinor, in a fit of abstraction, had let the urn overflow the teapot.

It was still quite early, and Dreux took his sister out again for a walk on the beach. She wished to prolong it, but he was in a fidget, and kept consulting his watch that they might not be out later than half-past eight. However, they went on the water for half an hour, and it was beginning to get both chilly and dusk when they reached the house. As they entered the door, he said, suddenly, "Oh, Elinor, I expect a friend this evening. I suppose he can get a bed somewhere in the village?"

"Undoubtedly!" she answered. "Who is it?"

"Who is it?" he replied, with a lurking smile in his eyes. "Oh, it's a clerical friend of mine." Having given this information, he began to hum a tune, and Elinor did not say another word.

They found Mrs. Theresa in a very impatient state. "She really had supposed Arthur had more sense than to stay out so late. In fact, the many frights he had given her about his sister when he was a boy were enough to make any watchful aunt afraid to trust him. Such pranks, indeed! Since the day when she had come home without her shoe "—

"But I'm not a boy now, aunt, and you need not fear, I think."

" Ah, it's very well to talk; but it gave me quite a turn, quite a palpitation when you were so late in. Shall I ever forget the day, Elinor, when he singed your hair with the curling-irons? ' What a wonderful smell of hair there is, ma'am,' Morris said to me. (Morris is a careful creature.) Up we both go to the very top of the house; she enters the nursery door first and gives a great scream.

" 'Oh, ma'am, Master Arthur!'

" And there he was in all his glory, as grave as a judge, and, the pretty lamb! all the curls singed off her dear head. Bless her heart! how angry I was!

" 'I'll tell you what, Molyneux,' I said to his father, 'if that boy doesn't disgrace the name of Dreux before he's done—' but he only laughed, poor man. That was in 18—. I really forget the date, but I remember it was only a few months before his death. ' Ah,' I said to him when his papa died, ' no wonder poor papa's gone to heaven, such a naughty boy as you are. It's all your fault.' And I shall never forget how he cried, and screamed, and tried to get into the room."

Having brought these lively recollections to a close, the old lady got up, and remarking that it was past the half-hour, proceeded:—

"I think I shall ask for your arm now, Arthur, and go up stairs, that I may be out of the way."

"Oh, then, my aunt knows that some one is coming," thought Elinor, getting really agitated. "Is it possible that it can be Mr. Allerton?"

When her brother came in, he stood looking out of the window, and she sat upon a couch, unable to enter into conversation.

"What time do you expect your friend?" she said at length, in what was meant to be a careless tone.

"Just at nine o'clock," he replied, and Elinor's heart began to beat quick, for it wanted but ten minutes to the time.

"Here he is, Elinor," said her brother, turning from the window, and at the same instant there was a loud knock at the street-door.

"Oh, don't let him come in yet," cried Elinor, and scarcely knowing what she said, she hastily rose and ran across the room to her brother, threw her arms round him, as if to prevent his leaving the room, and burst into tears, her face quite pale from the rapid beating of her heart.

Elinor heard the door open,—her brother held her to him with one arm, and held out his other hand to some one who was advancing into the room. The new comer said not a word. Elinor

did not attempt to raise her face, and wept more
than ever.

"Do try to be more calm, my dearest," said her
brother, as the guest stood a little withdrawn.

Elinor made an attempt to recover herself, but did
not raise her face, and remained still clinging to him,
as if she had been threatened with every danger
that ever was heard of.

"I have something to say to you, Elinor. I have
a favour to ask of you. You will not refuse me?
Lift up your face, and listen."

Elinor raised her face.

"I have a favour to ask of you," he continued,
"shall I tell you what it is?"

She managed to answer "Yes," and he went on.

"I have a friend, who is extremely dear to me,—
I could scarcely tell you how dear, unless I could
explain every reason why he should be. It would
make me very happy to give him some token of my
affection. I possess only one thing which seems to
me of sufficient value to mark the strength of my
regard. If I thought you would permit me to give
this one thing to him"—

Elinor, surprised, lifted her face again, and, dusk
as it was, she saw enough to know who the person
standing by her must be.

Her brother drew away the hand by which she
still held him, and said, "Let me tell you what it is
that I wish to give him. Look, it is this."

Elinor looked earnestly in his face. The surprise made her calm.

"Does silence give consent?" he asked, after waiting for an answer.

Elinor now did not choose to speak, but released her hold of her brother, permitting him to put her hand into that of the stranger, who, thereupon, found his voice, and as she seemed inclined to listen to him, her brother left them to finish the interview by themselves.

He walked on the beach till eleven. When he returned he was not sorry to find that Elinor had retired. Allerton met him on the lawn before the house. He was about to return to the inn for the night. Dreux was glad to find him in a silent mood, and they parted with a mutual smile of intelligence.

The next morning he rose very early, for he intended to walk to Ryde, and pass over to Gosport, where he had to speak that morning. It was about five o'clock in the afternoon when he returned to Shanklin by the stage, and found his sister and Allerton waiting for him at the rural inn.

Elinor and her aunt were seated in a little pony-chaise. The latter was very anxious to proceed with her airing, and Elinor had no sooner seen her brother and shaken him by the hand, than she was obliged to leave him with Allerton and accompany her aunt. Allerton's face showed that all was going on to his satisfaction. He turned round so often to watch the pony-carriage, that their progress towards the house was slow. At length, when it was quite out of sight, Dreux said to him, " Well, I suppose everything goes on favourably, Allerton."

" Reasonably so, my dear fellow. But, Dreux, you look uncommonly well to-day ! "

" I have nothing on my mind now. I have not felt so well for months. But how you turn from the subject, Allerton ! "

" Have you had the head-ache since we parted ? "

" Not once. I have thought with regret of what I said concerning my health. I now believe it was nothing but anxiety about you and Elinor which prevented my feeling as well as I ever did in my life."

Allerton looked gratefully at him.

" And after this bulletin I suppose I may inquire whether anything is decided ! "

" Yes, we have decided that you shall perform the ceremony."

" The ceremony ! " cried the brother-in-law elect; " well, that is getting on very fast indeed."

To which Allerton replied with this remarkable piece of advice: " Whenever you have a favour to ask of a lady, my dear fellow, take my advice,— don't be humble. I began with that feeling, and I found it a bad one.

" She remarked, that six months was the shortest engagement she could think of. I was dejected, but I gave in. Then she thought the arrangements could not be made in less than a year. At last, when this had gone on some time, I suddenly thought rebellion might have a good effect. 'And pray, Mr. Allerton,' she said, 'how long a time do you propose?' 'Since you ask me, Miss Dreux,' I answered, 'I think six weeks would be a reasonable time.' She was astonished at my presumption, but I persisted. Then I proposed a compromise;—we were to meet each other half-way, and say three months. In fact, instead of giving way, I declared I would not wait any longer, and she instantly succumbed. After which she remarked that she particularly liked your old house at Westport, so I am going to try if I can get it, and shall have it furnished as fast as I can."

"You succumb, in that respect, to her wishes, then."

"Of course. She wishes the library-curtains to be green, Dreux, as they used to be,—green damask. The dining-room is to have a Turkey carpet."

"I am afraid your first rebellion will be your last. Really, you bid fair to be a very reasonable—that is, a very compliant husband."

"In all little things, of course, I shall give way."

"Of course, such little things as houses, furniture, servants, society, et cetera."

Allerton laughed. "I have fought for my own way once," he observed, "and got it. I have made

Elinor agree, that whenever the house is ready, she will be ready to occupy it. She thinks that will be three months; I know it will not be quite two. Having begun with firmness, I now feel that I may venture on indulgence."

" *You* begin with firmness! If ever you show firmness enough to insist upon Elinor's doing any one thing that she doesn't like, may I be there to see!"

It was not long before Mrs. Theresa returned to the house with her niece, and Dreux spent the rest of the evening in admiring Allerton's admirable tactics with the old lady.

He had already managed to win her over to his side, and to the astonishment of Elinor, and the amusement of Dreux, he contrived to get her assent and consent to every thing he proposed. He was not at all what is popularly called a man to "let the grass grow under his feet;" and when he turned from the aunt to indulge in a little talk with the niece, Mrs. Theresa expressed, by many nods and knowing looks to her nephew, how much she was pleased with his friend.

" And a thorough gentleman he looks," she whispered, "though he tells me his great-grandfather was a cheesemonger!"

" Did you ask him the question, aunt?"

" No; but I was just letting him know something about our family, you know, Arthur, my dear;—about the Holy Wars, and William the Conqueror, and all that."

" Oh, indeed."

" Yes; no use letting him think we're a plebeian race. And so he laughed, and told me that of his own accord."

" Indeed."

" Yes, and his grandfather was knighted. He was an Alderman of London, very rich. I forget what his father was."

" A clergyman, aunt."

" Humph! he seems very fond of Elinor. I wish he would come away from the piano,—I want to ask him a few more questions; and really, Arthur, you are quite stupid to-night. And so you are going to remain at Westport, after all?"

" Yes, I am going there with Allerton the day after to-morrow."

Accordingly, the day after to-morrow, about six of the clock p.m., to the unbounded astonishment of Westport, Dreux and Allerton were seen sauntering up and down the square of grass before the almshouses, "just for all the world" (as the first old woman who spied them felicitously expressed it) " as if nothing had happened."

There they were, in the body, and presently the heads of some two or three hundred old men and women were to be seen behind their bright casements, peering at them. They were both great

favourites;—Allerton, because, they said, he had
such a free way with him; Dreux, because, since
he was gone, as they thought, for ever, they had
discovered his good qualities, real and imaginary.

They walked nearly an hour in the evening sunshine, and no one interrupted them; then, exactly
as the church clock struck seven, they turned into
the back lane which ran behind the garden of
Allerton's house, and went away together.

The news soon flew all over the town, and everybody called on Allerton, partly, perhaps, hoping to
hear what had detained him so long. But how
common is disappointment in this world! Allerton
and Dreux were always found together; consequently, neither could be asked any question about
the other, and the callers departed as wise as they
came, saving that they saw no symptoms of their
having quarrelled, and shrewdly suspected that they
had been wrong in their former conjectures on that
head; they also were conscious of a certain change
in Allerton's manner,—he was less impetuous, more
calm and guarded. Sunday, they thought, would
separate this David and Jonathan, and then, perhaps, something might be made out of them to
satisfy curiosity.

Sunday, however, came, and brought fresh surprise. Allerton read prayers in his own church,
and Dreux preached for him. Astonishing! he
sat as still as a stone, as immovable as one of the

pillars, in his desk, while Dreux was making every arch and aisle echo with his eloquence overhead.

And yet it was obvious to the more acute that Allerton's calmness was constrained, and that he was ill at ease. There was a certain restless excitement in the flash of his eyes if he chanced to raise them for an instant, and a certain steadiness of expression, which made him look like a man who had nerved himself up to the performance of some difficult duty, and who could not breathe freely till it was over.

So the gossips thought, and they were right. Who does not know the shame of avowing an utter change of principles, of contradicting former assertions, and avowing former mistakes,—a shame felt quite as strongly by those who turn round from pure motives as those who change from interested ones. In politics, it requires courage in the man who changes sides to get up and avow it before his late constituents; how much more in religion, where any change is so much more important, it requires courage to avow former error, and disenchant those listeners who were well enough satisfied with the teaching of the past?

As the people had expected, in the evening Dreux read prayers. The church was densely crowded by puzzled foes and alarmed friends. Allerton did not keep them long in suspense. At Dreux's request, he had chosen a text which, in the

excited, attentive state of all present, could not fail
to tell them the truth concerning this matter the
moment he uttered it. His evident sensation of
agitation at first interfered with the clearness of his
utterance, but in a few minutes he recovered his
self-possession, and preached a sermon which fully
confirmed the worst fears of his late friends.

There was nothing remarkable in it, excepting
the state of feeling with which it was uttered and
listened to. He never alluded to himself, or to his
change of views. He was not at all an eloquent
man, and heard from the lips of another, and on an
ordinary occasion, his sermon might have passed
without exciting any interest or observation, and
have faded away from the memory of its hearers
with the thousand other appeals which are lost
and forgotten. But heard on such an occasion,
when the nerves of both speaker and listeners were
strained, it could not fail to possess an interest far
greater than either eloquence or power could have
given it: it was the painful parting from old friends,
the anxious holding out of the hand to new ones.
But Allerton was destined to find, as some others
have done, that though his own party were forward
at once to cast him off, the opposite one was shy of
receiving him.

Dreux also was destined to prove that no man,
however popular he has been, or however necessary
he has seemed in a place, can leave it even for a
short time, and returning, take up his old position.

His friends had been excited about him when he left them, and in their expressions of regret and esteem on that occasion, they had exhausted all they felt for him. He now returned to find that they were already accustomed to do without him, and that his place, however inadequately, was filled.

Allerton's natural cheerfulness returned when once he had honestly given utterance to his new feelings. And Dreux was too well pleased with him, with Elinor's prospects, and the hope of remaining at Westport,—which, for many reasons, he wished to do for the present,—to think much about what degree of popularity he was likely to possess. Besides, he had not finished half his work for the Society before mentioned, and, before he had seen another Sunday at Westport, he was obliged to leave Allerton and proceed to Yorkshire.

During the next six weeks he twice made a flying visit to the Isle of Wight, to see how his brother-in-law elect proceeded with his wooing. Mrs. Dorothy Silverstone had been invited to spend a few weeks with Mrs. Theresa, and while Allerton wooed the young lady, the two old ones wooed him. Never was man made so much of. His voice, his hair, his walk, his house, his pedigree, were subjects of never-ceasing discussion and interest; they almost rivalled Elinor's wedding dresses, some of which, by the bye, they made him choose;

and he was discovered one morning by Dreux, with
a milliner's book full of patterns of silk in his hand,
and a very puzzled expression on his face, while he
tried to decide between the merits of brocade, glacé,
shot and striped silk, and betrayed, by his deliberate choice, the most horrid taste, selecting the
largest patterns and the most gaudy colours he
could find.

It has lately been discovered by the learned that
weddings are pretty nearly all alike. The ceremony does not admit of much variety; it must
either be read or chanted; and though (entirely for
the sake of variety) we have heard of one or two
marriages lately which have been conducted by
three or four clergymen, we do not think even one
of these would be worth describing.

If weddings are alike, so must descriptions of
them partake of a certain sameness. When you
have heard whether the bride behaved well, and
whether any good speeches were made at the breakfast, you have heard all that is worth hearing.

On the occasion of Elinor's wedding she behaved
extremely ill, that is to say, she wept in the church
and at the breakfast, though she had no one to take
leave of but her aunt, who certainly betrayed no
answering emotion. As for Allerton, it is a well-
known fact, that on the occasion of his marriage, a
retiring, silent, and even a gloomy man will pluck
up courage, and often make a speech that will
astonish everybody. But nobody ever heard either

a hilarious man, a rattle, or an affectionate, merry-hearted fellow, open his lips on that day without breaking down, stammering, contradicting himself, or betraying great alarm.　Allerton did all this, and yet he sat down with the applause of the company!

But the company, notwithstanding, were glad when that tedious morning was over, and the bride and bridegroom fairly off; for in spite of Elinor's involuntary weeping, and Allerton's nervousness, they were not in any fear for their happiness, for they perceived that the latter had no sooner handed his bride into the carriage than he became himself again, and as for the former, when once the dreaded publicity was over, her face recovered its smiling expression.

CHAPTER XXV.

MARION WAITS AT TABLE.

THE time during which Dreux had agreed to travel
for the Society before mentioned wanted still a
fortnight of its completion, and having seen Allerton and his sister set out on their short wedding
tour, he once more plunged into the exciting business of sermons and meetings. The time passed
rapidly, for he was fond of travelling, and had
now a pleasant future to look forward to. He had
reached his greatest distance from Westport, and
was already turning homeward, when, finding himself within ten miles of his uncle, Colonel Norland,
he thought it only his duty to call upon him. He
had previously received a communication from Mr.
Raeburn, requesting that he would come round
by Swanstead, and hold a local meeting near
there.

It was about one o'clock on a sultry day that
he arrived at the Colonel's house, and was shown
into a small room to wait for him. He had sent in
his card, and, while expecting his uncle's entrance

he stood looking out towards the redoubtable pond which had so completely altered his prospects in life.

Now Colonel Norland, during the last fourteen years, had met with very little to vary his existence. He had got heavier, and had taken to riding a quieter horse, that was all. It was natural, therefore, that he should forget how much the young had changed during the same period. When he was told that his nephew, Mr. Dreux, had called upon him, he thought of him, despite his knowledge that he was in orders, as still the break-neck, mischievous, high-spirited boy who had ridden to cover on one of his best horses, and ruined him by his reckless riding. Such being the case, he was rather astonished when he came into the room to be greeted by a young man of decidedly commanding presence and a full head taller than himself.

" Well, Sir," said the Colonel, after a good stare, " and to what may I be indebted for the honour of this visit ? "

His nephew explained that, being in the neighbourhood, he thought it his duty to call.

" Oh ! " said the old Colonel, and sitting down by the table he commenced an earnest scrutiny of his nephew's person, which that gentleman having some difficulty in sustaining with gravity, turned his face towards the window.

" No, no, Arthur," cried the old man, "—needn't look that way ; that's all forgotten. I bear no

malice—Ahem.   You think your visit particularly
well timed, Sir, don't you?"

This was said with an air of banter which his
nephew could not at all understand.

"It would appear that if I did think so I was
mistaken," he replied.   "But to tell the truth, I
really know no reason why it should be."

"Oh, you don't, don't you," replied the Colonel,
who with a very red face and very white whiskers
sat staring at him as if he did not exactly know
whether to quarrel with him or make him welcome.
"You don't know the disgrace that the family has
sustained lately, don't you?   Joseph Norland, Sir,
your cousin, my heir, he's a—he's a humbug, Sir;
he's been plucked, Sir,—plucked in his little go."

Dreux's look of obvious mortification and annoyance pleased the irrascible old man.

"I wrote to him, Sir," he proceeded, "and I told
him he was the greatest fool that ever disgraced
the name of Norland.   I told him he was a fool, and
so he is.   I told him he should never touch a sixpence that I could keep from him.   The Norland
estate he must have, but he shan't lay his finger on
an inch of my property that's unentailed; no, that
he shan't—no, nor on that estate in the vale of
Swanstead, or the house that Raeburn has a lease
of.   He shall never touch a brick of it, so help
me—.   No, I forgot you were a parson—but he
shan't, Sir, for all that."

There was nothing to be said in reply, so his nephew tried to turn the conversation.

"Joseph, Sir," cried the Colonel, not deigning to notice the interruption, "Joseph is a born fool. He scents himself, Sir. I've told him over and over again that no man but a fool would cover himself with studs and jewels. It's no use. He turn off my water-springs and kill my hunters! No, trust him. And then to go and get plucked. Ugh! If ever he brings his—his odious little pug nose into my presence again "—

Here his nephew burst into an irresistible fit of laughter.

"Sir," cried the Colonel, in a momentary passion, "you play your cards remarkably ill; but you always did,—it's in the family. Your father, Sir, lost his first love by making game of her mother. You'd better mind what you're about. Ring the bell, will you?—I want lunch," he shouted, when the footman appeared. "Sit down, Arthur; you're not going yet. Sit down, I say."

His nephew sat down.

"Well, Sir," proceeded the Colonel, "and so you've lost your property. But if you came to borrow anything of me "—

"I did not," replied his nephew, looking at him steadily; "I can live on my curacy. I did not suppose you would have inquired about my affairs; but you might have been sure I should not have come here unless I could have answered your questions satisfactorily."

" Then how do you live ? " asked the Colonel.

" I live in lodgings on 140*l.* a-year, and I have a pupil. I was in difficulties when first the house failed, but I have paid my debts, and owe nothing to any one."

The old man considered his face attentively. " Then you want nothing of me," he repeated. " Well, I confess I thought you did. You need not look alarmed ; I don't want to force my favours upon you, I am sure."

" Thank you, uncle," replied the nephew, now for the first time giving him his title.

" Ah, ' thank you, uncle,' " repeated the old gentleman, in a musing tone. " If it had not been for your own preposterous conduct, Arthur Dreux, you might still have possessed a handsome income, instead of being a poor parson, with nothing to depend upon but—excuse me—your beggarly pay."

" Sir," said his nephew, " I do not wish to annoy you ; but since it was the circumstance of your renouncing me which put it afterwards in my power to take orders, I must say "—

" Not that you don't regret it. You won't say that."

" My being in orders is my greatest happiness. I wish to devote my life to what I have undertaken. If I had remained your heir, you would not have suffered me to go into the Church."

" No, that I wouldn't,—catch me! You should have been in Parliament before now."

" Then you cannot expect me to regret what has made me my own master."

" You dare to repeat that, Sir! You dare to tell me you are glad of it! Say it again, Sir!"

" Say I am glad I went into the Church?" answered Dreux, calmly and with a smile. " I cannot say otherwise; I am glad."

" Very well, Arthur; you're like your father. You're glad you went into the Church, are you? Oh, very well! If you're glad, so am I."

" Sir," said his nephew, taking out his watch, " I believe I must take my leave of you; I am very happy to have seen you in such good health."

" You are not going yet, young man," was the reply; " sit down, I say. Since that enormous ass, Joseph, showed himself in his true colours, I have scarcely seen any one; I feel quite lonely."

" It was undoubtedly a very mortifying thing for you," replied his nephew. " But, after all, he may make a respectable country gentleman, though it is not in his power to distinguish himself at college."

" May be, Sir; who told *you* that? I should like to know where you got your information. Joseph is every inch a fool. I allow him 500*l.* a-year at college; and he dusts his boots with his silk hand-kerchief, dresses and scents himself, and does no other earthly thing. He's just like his mother. If an old fellow like my poor brother chose to go and

marry a young girl, what could he expect? Of
course, no girl of sense would have him. I should
rather think not; and the consequence is, Sir, that
Joseph is the softest mortal that ever was dandled
and kissed by a doting old father and silly young
mother. Why, I always intended, if possible, to
bring about a match between him and Raeburn's
pretty ward; she is sure to inherit a good slice of
his property. Well, I took Joseph there to dinner
a while ago, and if you had seen how he went on you
would have wondered how any girl of sense could
have endured him."

At this point in the discourse his nephew began
to feel a keen interest, and to be conscious of a
peculiar fluttering of the heart.

"I often joke Miss Greyson about my nephew,
and she blushes so deeply that I really thought the
thing was nearly done to my hands.

"'Well, Joseph, my fine fellow,' I said, as we
went there, 'hold up your head, there's money bid
for you.' 'Au—er,' he says (little fool), 'do you
think Miss Greyson really now—really—er—likes
me?'

"'There's no accounting for taste,' I said, 'and I
can only suppose she does.'

"Well, in we went, and he began to talk. I wonder I didn't bite his head off. Miss Paton, from your
part of the country, was staying there. 'Did he
read the "Quarterly?"' I heard one of the ladies saying, before we were called to dinner, 'or perhaps he

preferred some of the other leading Reviews.' Well, he couldn't give a rational answer, though I looked liked thunder at him.

" ' I suppose you mean to go in for honours, Mr. Norland,' says Miss Paton.

" ' Au—er—I don't think I shall,' says Joseph. ' Au—honours are very well when a man has no property.'

" ' Oh, but,' says Miss Paton, ' honours distinguish a man so much for life, especially among ladies.'

" ' Au—I dare say I could get 'em as well as other people,' says Joseph, simpering, ' if I tried; au—perhaps I shall—can't say.' "

Dreux could not forbear a smile.

" ' For my part,' says Miss Paton, casting up her eyes, ' I never meet a Senior Op. without a thrill of respect; it is something only to sit next him.'

" ' Very true,' says that wicked little puss, Miss Greyson, ' and as for wranglers, they are quite ir-re-sistible !' "

" I have not found it so," thought Dreux. With a sigh of relief to think that at least Marion was not likely to be captivated by the fascinations of his cousin, Joseph Norland, he rose from the lunch table.

" What ! you must go, must you, Arthur ? Well then, I'll tell you what I can do,—I can drive you down as far as Raeburn's gates. So you see there is no chance for Joseph in that quarter."

Dreux was about to answer, " I am very glad of

it," but checked himself just in time, and only said, "Indeed."

"Well, Sir," resumed the Colonel, when they were seated in the carriage, " I suppose you will be looking out now for a lady with money ; that's the only thing for you that I can see. As the old Quaker said, ' Never thee marry for money, but never thee fall in love where there's none.' "

" I hope I have rather a higher sense of honour than to patch up my broken fortune with a rich wife," replied Dreux, colouring. " I should think that the worst kind of dependence. No, Sir, there is no marrying for me. I could not afford to maintain a poor wife, and I would not let a rich one maintain me."

" The worst kind of dependence, hey ?—worse than being dependent on a crabstick of an uncle."

Dreux hesitated. He did not wish to offend and hurt the old man, though he had cast him off. " Dependence is a thing never to be submitted to in any shape," he at length said, " if it can be avoided."

" It can always be avoided, if the young man chooses to work upon the roads."

" *The* young man, Sir! I was only speaking generally."

" But I was not."

" Then," said Dreux, with most perfect temper, and calm, "let the young man whom you have in your mind avoid it, by ' working on the roads ;' let him take his share of toil on the highways or in the byways of life. He cannot do better."

"If it's not an impertinent question, Mr. Dreux, I should be glad to know why you called on me to-day."

"Simply to see you, Colonel."

"Which you have not done for fifteen years."

"Precisely fifteen years."

"At which time I renounced you, and consequently you can have no claim upon me."

"None whatever."

"But I wrote to you at College, Sir, and expressed regret, and—and—congratulated you upon your honours."

"And I replied in some such sort as this, that I hoped if ever we should chance to meet, it would be as friends."

"And in that letter, Sir, you never apologized for the trouble you had given to a crusty old bachelor."

"When I was a boy of fourteen. No; if I had thought much about it, perhaps it would have been thus: Colonel Norland voluntarily undertook the care of a high-spirited, troublesome boy, a spoilt child, and an orphan. He intended to bring him up as his son, and leave him a portion of his property. Finding the responsibility far greater than he had expected, and the experiment not worth trying, he voluntarily gave it up, renounced the boy, surrendered all authority over him, and

denied that he had any claim upon him. It was
his own will and pleasure to try the experiment;
his young kinsman had no hand in it; and had no
right to feel himself aggrieved if, the experiment not
answering, it was given up again."

"Why had you no right to feel aggrieved, Sir?"

"Do you really wish me to tell you, Colonel?"

"Yes, I do."

"Because as soon as I came to years of discretion, I easily perceived that I had not been adopted
for my own good or benefit, but for yours. Of
course, if regard for my father, or if love to my
mother, had been the cause, I should not have been
thrown loose upon the world again, to do almost
as I liked with two weak, flattering guardians,
a perilous command of money, and a wild, high
spirit into the bargain."

"Humph! Well, Sir, according to your theory
anything's better than dependence. How would
you have liked dependence on your father if he had
lived?"

"That would not have been dependence. My
father, if my recollections say true, was more than
commonly attached to me. If he had lived, and
I had loved him as I must have done, to depend
on him would have been far better than liberty.
I should have had such a natural and inevitable
claim, that I should not have lived in constant fear
that one reckless act of folly might some day break the
tie between us; neither would he have been afraid

of snapping it asunder by any exercise of discipline
or authority."

" Should you have become attached to me, if
I had supplied the place of a father?"

" I should have proved ungrateful if I had not."

" You have told me in broad terms that I failed
to fulfil my part; that I flung you out and acted
basely to you when you were young, almost a child.
Now, Sir, since our quarrel, or whatever you like
to call it, was made up by my writing to you at
College—and you say you did not call upon me to
borrow money—I should be glad to know whether
you called to insult me by telling me all that."

" I called simply to see you, Colonel."

" And you expected we should part friends?"

" Undoubtedly; for I felt no bitterness against
you, Colonel; and I have before said that what
you did has turned out to my true advantage."

" You had the audacity to say it, Arthur Dreux,
and I swallowed my indignation. Well, Joseph's
a fool, and I can do nothing with him; and you are
as stiffnecked as ever were the Israelites of old, so
I can do nothing with you. There are always
hospitals and almshouses. Good afternoon, Sir,
these are Raeburn's gates. If you call on me
to-morrow morning before twelve, you may perhaps
find me at home."

With this enigmatical speech the old Colonel
put down his nephew at the gates, and inclined
his head slightly as the young clergyman took off

his hat and bowed at parting. Colonel Norland then drove off, and employed himself in mentally concocting the plan for a huge hospital for decayed tradesmen, to be built in the vale of Swanstead, and decorated with the Norland arms; it should be built of stone, he decided, and have two long rows of almshouses stretching away from it by way of wings. "But he's a fine young fellow," he mused, thinking of his elder nephew; "and as for that little fool Joseph, he cried like a child when I was thought to be dying last autumn. Well, the more fool he. Ah! I'll have it built just there. Rennie shall build it. No, he shan't, Barry shall. I all but promised Dreux I would adopt his boy. So I did. I remember him now, a little curly-headed chap, sitting on his father's bed. Well, I've done my best, I'm not going to humble down at this time of day. Pshaw! I adopted him for my own pleasure, did I? (He was a brave little chap.) I was rather proud of him, to be sure, when he rode to cover at ten years old, and was in at the death. And so he's willing to work on the roads, is he? Anything's better than my yoke. I dare say he remembers me a regular tyrant. I say the hospital shall be a handsome one; he has no claim. Why, he told me so himself. I'll have it built of free-stone. No, I won't. Yes, I think I will. Shall I? Yes, I will; *done*."

In the meantime, while the tall iron gates of the rectory-garden swung behind Dreux, Mr. Raeburn,

who had just returned from a Board of Poor-law
Guardians, which he attended once a week, was
seated at his dinner, for it was now five o'clock, and
old Mrs. Raeburn, his mother, having a great
objection to what she called a late dinner, on these
occasions always dined early with Marion, and left
the Rector to take his meal alone, Marion, according
to ancient custom, waiting upon him. The manner
of the dinner was this: the old footman, who was
so fat that he could scarcely perform the light duties
which ordinarily devolved upon him, set the dishes
on the table and put a chair for his master, after
which he retired to the sideboard, where he stood, lost
in fat, stupidity, and self-importance; while Marion
proceeded to lift up the covers of the vegetable
dishes, help the Rector to gravy, and pour out his
home-brewed beer.

The old footman, who was very deaf, felt in his
heart a fatherly kindness for Marion, and took
a fat, patronizing kind of pleasure in seeing her
hovering about his master, telling him the news
of the day, selecting the very best young kidney
potatoes, and putting them on his plate, then paring
and slicing the cucumber and sprinkling it with
pepper and vinegar to his taste. The dining-room
door was wide open to admit the air, the hall-door
was also open, and they were opposite to each other.
Mr. Raeburn had a full view of the garden, that
is to say, such a view as short-sighted people can
get, which must be a very poor one.

"Somebody at the door, Porson," shouted Mr. Raeburn to his lethargic attendant. The old man moved slowly off, while Mr. Raeburn went on with his dinner, Marion just then laying her hand on his shoulder, and asking if he had been to see a poor market-gardener who was ill. "Don't you remember him, uncle? I wonder at that; he is the very man of whom I bought that black polianthus in the spring; and don't you remember my telling you that it was pin-eyed?"

The somebody at the door had plenty of time to observe her as the servant came slowly towards him. He gave in his card, and was about to be shown into the drawing-room, when Mr. Raeburn, who had mistaken him for a neighbouring clergyman, called out, "Porson, show Mr. Cottle in here."

The supposed Mr. Cottle, on entering, proved to be no other than Mr. Dreux; and Marion, taken quite by surprise, coloured deeply as she advanced and offered her hand, the other being occupied with a sauceboat of melted butter.

Mr. Raeburn ordered another chair to be placed, and pressed his guest to dine. The old servant speedily set another plate and knife and fork; he then retired to the sideboard, evidently having no notion of waiting at table; on that particular day he couldn't think of it.

Neither could Mr. Raeburn think of shouting for everything that was wanted, and knocking his

fork handle on the table to rouse Porson; he therefore said, composedly, "My dear Marion, oblige me
by extending your attentions to our guest."

Marion did as she was requested, excessively
to the discomfort of Dreux. "This is a fancy
of my niece's," proceeded Mr. Raeburn, putting the
wing of a fowl on to the plate which Marion held.
"She has done it occasionally from a child. I assure
you she is an accomplished waitress; but though
there is little precedent for it in this country,
I believe in the North, especially in Sweden and
Norway, the custom of ladies waiting at table still
prevails."

The guest would have been indifferent as to
where it had prevailed, if it had not prevailed there;
and Mr. Raeburn beginning to converse, and Marion
handing him all sorts of things, he got so confused,
that he scarcely knew what he said.

Marion, on the contrary, after her first blush,
which had tinged even the very back of her neck,
recovered herself completely; for she had perceived,
by the sudden, earnest look he directed towards her
at his entrance, that she still retained her empire
over him.

The footman looked on with a pompous kind
of encouragement; the host was very pressing, and
the waitress very attentive, but the guest scarcely
touched a mouthful; he was truly glad when the
dinner was over, and during the rest of the evening
he could not but perceive that Marion treated him

with marked politeness and attention, a solicitude
to please far different to the *insouciance* with which
she had passed over his first advances. She played
and sang for him, she showed him her most beautiful plants, and took infinite pains to explain why
one particular geranium was better than another.

But all she said failed to raise the spirits of their
guest; on the contrary, it made him feel his present
position and his "beggarly pay" the more; his visit
also showed him, what he had not previously known,
that Mr. Raeburn was rich, and Marion, even in the
days of his prosperity, would have been a decidedly
good match for him, if, as the old Colonel had said,
she was to inherit a "good slice of old Raeburn's
property."

The fancy dawned upon him (for he treated
it only as an idle fancy) that, if he now could offer
such a home as he had formerly possessed, and if he
could have time given him to make an impression,
he might possibly get a different answer; but he
put it aside, for the thing was altogether out of the
question, and the less he thought on it the better
for his own peace.

Mr. Raeburn had insisted on his staying the
night, for the next morning they were to go
together to a place about five miles off, to hold
a meeting.

The next day, at breakfast, he felt very much
agitated; poverty had never seemed half so bitter
to him as now,—this was one of its real evils; and,

as he now and then glanced at Marion, he fancied that she, too, looked ill at ease.

How he got over the time till ten o'clock he scarcely knew, though he afterwards remembered that hour as one of the most uncomfortable of his life. His features were pale from agitation; and, in his pre-occupied state of mind, it was with the greatest difficulty that he dragged on a conversation with Mr. Raeburn. Marion did not help, for she scarcely opened her lips, and seemed quite relieved when the phaeton drove to the door.

"Well, good by, my dear, for the present," said Mr. Raeburn. "I shall see our friend into the railway-office before I return, and I shall hope to be at home by dinner-time."

Marion then held out her cold hand to Dreux, but neither looked up nor said a word.

They had not been gone ten minutes when Colonel Norland called, and Marion was obliged to go into the drawing-room to see him.

"So I understand my nephew's gone, my dear," cried the old gentleman; "actually gone without even coming to see me again, though I fully expected him."

"Did he say that he should call again, Colonel?" asked Marion, gently.

"No, my dear; he said he thought he shouldn't have time, but I supposed he knew better than not to find time. My nephew, Miss Greyson, is a fool."

"Which nephew did you mean, Colonel?" asked Marion, in her most gentle tone.

"Why—why, I meant Arthur, my dear."

"Oh," said Marion, irresistibly impelled to take his part, "I should not have thought the appellation was appropriate to Mr. Dreux."

She spoke so calmly, but she blushed so deeply, that the old gentleman looked at her with surprise; then he drew a long breath and nodded, as if congratulating himself on having solved a problem which had long puzzled him, after which he burst into a chuckling laugh, and exclaimed,—"Excuse me, my dear; I forgot that wranglers were irresistible."

Marion instantly remembered when she had said this, and who she had been thinking of at the time.

"Joseph will never be a wrangler," said the old gentleman, pitying her confusion.

"I am sorry I should have intimated as much to him," said Marion, gladly catching at this straw as a diversion; "he has a very kind heart."

"I'm glad to hear you say so, my dear; it shows your penetration. Joseph, Miss Greyson, is a born fool. Don't tell me,—I say he is; and he'll never be any honour to the family—never. I never," continued the old gentleman, striking his stick violently on the ground,—"I never knew a pug-nosed fellow get either military or academical honours. Don't tell me,—they can't do it; it's

not in 'em.   Joseph, like all regularly pug-nosed
fellows, is a little fool."

Having uttered these remarkable sentiments, the
old gentleman kissed his hand to Marion and took
leave.   She was extremely glad to see him drive
away, though her cheeks glowed again when she
remembered how she had blushed.   She returned
to the long drawing-room, and wandered about in a
state of unusual agitation and excitement; her face
was suffused with a soft carnation and her hands
trembled.   She argued with herself, and vainly tried
to think that the departure of that morning was
nothing to her, but it would not do; her usually
serene spirits could not so far suffer her to deceive
herself.   She had continued her effort to be tranquil
perhaps for half an hour, when the housemaid
entered.

" If you please, ma'am, the gentleman who slept
here last night —"

" Mr. Dreux ?" exclaimed Marion, starting, as if
the maid had frightened her.

" Yes, ma'am.   I went just now into his dressing-room, and found this ring upon the washhand-
stand."

Marion received the ring in the palm of her
hand; it was her own,—the one she had permitted
him to take from her after his accident.

" And on the table, ma'am," proceeded the maid,
" the gentleman had left this bunch of keys."

"Oh, how unfortunate!" said Marion. "Give them to me, Sarah; they must be sent after Mr. Dreux, he will perhaps want them."

"Yes, ma'am. Perhaps the carrier could take them. If you remember, one holidays Master Wilfred left his keys behind him, and master sent them after him by the carrier."

"Let the carrier be stopped at the gate, then, Sarah," said Marion, "and he shall take them."

The maid left the room, and Marion ran up-stairs into her own apartment with the ring and the keys, bolted the door, and burst into tears. She was frightened, and ashamed to find how bitter a thing it was to her, that her ring should have been forgotten and left behind; for a moment she thought it must have been done on purpose, to show that no value was felt for it, and yet she could not but remember that her late lover's eyes had sometimes, during his visit, rested on her face with a tenderness which could scarcely be due to gratitude alone.

"But he does not—he cannot love me now," she argued, "or surely he might have said so. He must have seen, by my friendly manner, that at least I like him."

Marion put the ring on her finger, and, the more she thought, the more she instinctively felt that he no longer loved her. And how should she return it to him?—should she not rather, since he no longer needed a remembrance of her, keep it as a remembrance of him? She thought she would. It

was a very sultry morning, and she threw her casement windows open to admit the air. The carrier
was to pass in half an hour; she heard the iron
gates creak, and looked out, but how much was her
agitation increased when, instead of the carrier, she
saw the phaeton, with the two gentlemen in it.

They drove quickly in, and Marion never doubted
that the loss had been discovered, and they were
come back in consequence. She remembered that
they had intended to pay a call on their way, but
that, by giving up this call, they would still be in
time for the Meeting.

And now should she go down and see him
again? She looked at her face, and could not
flatter herself that the traces of tears had entirely
disappeared. But the servants would come to her
for the missing articles, she was sure, or her uncle
might send for them; so she hastily threw a light
scarf over her shoulders and put on her bonnet, the
gauze veil of which she dropped over her face.
Courage, she knew, would not come for waiting for,
so she opened her door, and came down stairs with
a beating heart.

She heard a considerable noise below, moving of
chairs, pulling open of drawers, and slamming of
doors.

" Where's Miss Greyson ?" she heard the Rector
say, in a hurried voice, " perhaps she knows."

Marion entered the study.

" My dear, my dear," cried Mr. Raeburn, in a

great flurry, " what's become of the Local Report and the Subscription List ? "

Marion saw at a glance that Mr. Dreux was perfectly unconscious of his loss ; it was the Rector on whose account they had returned.

As soon as she entered he bowed gravely, and, perhaps, not wishing to appear a spectator of the confusion which his worthy host had excited in his study, walked leisurely out of the room, across the hall, and into the morning-room, the door of which stood open.

Marion set to work to search in all likely drawers and folios for the missing papers, casting now and then a furtive glance towards their guest, who, leaning with his hands upon the back of a chair, stood, with a very serious expression of countenance, looking out of the window.

At last, Mr. Raeburn having turned out every closet he possessed below stairs, ran up-stairs into his dressing-room as a forlorn hope, followed by the two housemaids and Mrs. Mathews.

" And now," thought Marion, " if I mean to give these keys myself it must be done at once."

She crossed the hall with uncertain steps, but her light footfall did not reach Dreux's ears. He still gazed earnestly out of the window, and she actually felt afraid of intruding upon him.

She might have stood there longer if a servant's step on the stairs had not compelled her to advance, unless she wished to be seen.

She had advanced far into the room before he turned. When he did, it was with a sudden start to find her so near to him. His face looked extremely grave—almost stern, she thought; and though she was at home she felt ashamed lest he might think she had needlessly sought his presence. The consciousness of her own strength of feeling for him made her so exquisitely uncomfortable that her face and forehead became suffused with blushes, and she held out the bunch of keys to him, and said, in a slightly unsteady voice, " I believe, Mr. Dreux, these keys are yours ; the housemaid tells me she found them in your dressing-room."

The guest bowed, and took them, thanking her, but without any tendency towards a smile. She fancied his manner expressed surprise, and was afraid he might have observed her confusion, whereas the truth was, he had merely stooped to catch a glimpse of her face, which was half hidden by the white veil.

He evidently had not the slightest idea that he had left anything else behind him, and Marion, who wore the ring upon her gloved hand, could not summon courage to allude to it. He was twirling a little piece of geranium in his hand, and looked troubled and restless ; Marion thought he was afraid of being late. He observed that she was standing, and brought her a chair, then he partially drew down the blind to shield her from the sun. His excitement would not allow him to be still.

" Oh, how he longs to be away," thought Marion, and she wished Mr. Raeburn would come, for she felt an almost childish dislike to the idea of his leaving her and the place where she lived, with unpleasing recollections.

At last Mr. Raeburn came clattering down stairs. Marion's heart sank, for she should have to go through the parting a second time.

" Well, Mr. Dreux, I've found 'em at last. I'm sorry indeed to have kept you waiting."

There was no mistaking the short, quick sigh of relief with which their guest arose, took up his hat, and bowed to Marion. In another moment he was gone. She sat listening to the sound of his voice.

" It was a pity we could not find time to see the Colonel this morning," she heard Mr. Raeburn say as they got into the phaeton.

" Yes, indeed," he answered, in a tone of some regret, " for it may be years before I visit this place again."

" Years ! " thought Marion ; " is that possible ? " and she sat listening to the retiring wheels as long as they were audible, almost frightened to feel how flat and tame everything seemed now that one person was withdrawn. " But I must get something to do," she exclaimed, starting up. " Oh, I must drive these thoughts away ; I must do my German exercises, and put my uncle's papers in order again."

She went into the study and commenced her

task, but it was too easy—she could do it mechanically, and her thoughts followed the phaeton. Now they would have reached the turnpike road— now they were going through the wood. What a strange, intense desire she felt to see him again, to know how he looked just then, and whether he was thinking of her!

As her fancy pictured, he was then going through the wood; the lights and shadows were dancing on his forehead, for the day was sultry, and he had taken off his hat.

Mr. Raeburn after his bustle was very silent. Dreux's face was thoughtful. He was revolving in his mind all the circumstances of his two visits: the Colonel's composed way of falling into discourse without any preamble or explanation—his vehement disgust at Joseph's silliness—his rudeness to himself. Then he thought of Marion—her friendly gentle smile, her confiding manner. "She has forgotten," he thought, "or she would have me forget, that I ever stood before her in the character of a lover, but she looks at me with an interest which she cannot conceal, perhaps because she watched me during those dangerous hours. She is evidently anxious I should not do or say anything to betray a continuance of the old love. Well, it is something to have left her and not to have committed myself. She would not like all intercourse to cease between us, and she looked as conscious and uncomfortable when she brought me those keys as if she had known how near I inevitably was to another declaration. But there is a greater bar to that than her prohibition: all my circumstances forbid so mean an attempt as that to obtain her hand; for my uncle not only repeated all he has ever said about renouncing me, but he never even mentioned that living of Wickley which he promised my father I should have if this good Rector of Swanstead survived him. If I could have known the pain this visit would have given me, I would not have come here—no earthly inducement should have tempted me."

And now, to conclude these soliloquies, let us give that of Colonel Norland, who, having returned from Swanstead, was pacing his library in a very great passion, and tearing a certain letter to pieces with vehement industry. The letter before it was destroyed would have read as follows :—

"DEAR NEPHEW ARTHUR,—This is to inform you that I never exactly *promised* your father I would adopt you, though I let him understand as much, so after all, it is certain you have no claim upon me ; but as I have been considering that when you came to live with me you were but a boy (and, on the whole, I don't know but that I like a boy to show some spirit), I have decided to forgive you this once ; and that precious fool, Joe, having written to me this morning declining to have anything more to do with the University, and taken himself off to

Baden Baden without my leave or advice—I have
decided over again that, as I can't help it, he shall
inherit the Norland estates, and I shall leave you
that estate in the vale of Swanstead, and the house
that Raeburn has a lease of, which was to have been
your mother's fortune if my father had not died
without a will; but I never will admit to my dying
day that either you or Elinor has any claim upon
me, for the old gentleman might have known that
his will was no use at all so long as he kept it by
him unsigned. I shall give Elinor's husband the
living of Wickley when it falls due, which I hope
will not be for a long while, for White plays the
best game of chess of any man within ten miles, and
has the decency to come and play with me whenever I'm laid up with the gout.

"I am writing this overnight, for I had decided
upon it before I left you at Raeburn's gate. No, I
hadn't, for I altered my mind afterwards, being in a
passion with you and your independence. However,
as you are a high-spirited young fellow, I suppose
you thought a contrary conduct would look like
toadyism. But though I have decided upon this, I
don't mean to see you to-morrow morning when you
call, but I have told Mansfield to give you this,
which, you perceive, incloses a cheque for five
hundred pounds, and I expect you forthwith to
wind up your affairs at Westport, and come and
live with me; and I expect you to buy yourself a
capital riding horse, and in the name of patience let

mine alone, lest it should breed another quarrel
between us; and if that's not doing my duty by
you I should like to know what would be.   Mind,
you've no claim !

      " Believe me, young man, yours truly,
                    " P. GRICE NORLAND."

The rage of the old Colonel knew no bounds
when he found that his nephew not only had
omitted to call upon him, but had left Swanstead
before he could get a sight of him.   He not only
tore the needless letter to pieces, and anathematized
pride as being worse than folly and more detestable
than pug-nosedness; but he dismissed the lawyer
who was come to make his will with unmerited
insolence, and sent for three architects, upon whom
he laid his commands to bring him within a month
the handsomest plans for hospitals that they could
possibly devise.

In the meantime, a fit of the gout gave him time
to cool and think matters over, while the unconscious object of his rage finished his travels and
went back to be Allerton's curate; while Joseph
spent a great deal of his money at Baden, and
while Elinor and her husband got settled in their
new house, which was Dreux's old one; while
Athanasius and his mother prepared for their
travels to Smyrna, or some port in the Levant,
and while Marion did quantities of German exercises, all to keep Mr. Dreux out of her head.

CHAPTER XXVI.

MR. AND MRS. FRANCIS ALLERTON.

DREUX returned, and found Allerton and his sister settled in his old house. They were sauntering in the verandah when he entered, and Elinor's busy fingers were twining the branches of the passion-flower, which had been trained the previous autumn according to her wishes.

"How natural it seems to be walking here, Arthur, with you," she said, after the first greetings.

Allerton laughed. "So natural that I feel myself quite an interloper! I sometimes walk about the library, saying, ' This cannot be my house,—I must be come here to dinner. Elinor cannot be my wife,—she's Dreux's sister. I shall see her come in presently, and she will hold out her hand to shake hands with me.' I go down stairs, and forget to sit at the head of the table. The gardener asks for orders: I am about to say, ' Go to your master,' when I see *Miss Dreux* knocking down a peach with her parasol, and the old fellow

says, ' *Missis* told me you would say how it was
to be, Sir.' How I hate to hear them call her
Missis !"

" Mrs. Francis Allerton," said Dreux,—" not a
bad name. And how goes on the parish, Allerton ?"

" I don't know what to make of affairs,—I have
wanted you deplorably. We shall soon be all at
loggerheads, though I have taken incredible pains
to conciliate."

" Indeed ! What is the feud about ?"

" That is the mystery. But I find myself so
much disliked, that really I am afraid· you will
share in my unpopularity, merely for having brought
me back again."

" You bear the matter with tolerable philosophy."

" Dreux, I am only just emerging from my
honeymoon, but I try to be concerned about it ;—
duly concerned, because I ought. But as for *mere*
popularity !—Mrs. Francis Allerton, being only six
weeks old, naturally requires a great deal of super-
vision,—of discipline, you know,—that she may
learn to submit to my will at her present early age ;
and so my time is too much occupied to think very
much about their feuds."

" Oh, the feuds will all come right, dear," said
Mrs. Francis. " And now let us come in ; and I
wish you would draw down the blinds, for the sun
makes these rooms very hot."

Allerton complied with unconscious alacrity, and neither he nor his bride observed the meaning smile with which Dreux watched their movements; how Elinor, without the slightest art, indicated her wishes in a pretty, petted way, and how Allerton waited on her, almost without being aware of it.

"I hope Elinor is a good, obedient little wife," he said, laughing.

"Oh yes, we have no disputes; she is a compliant little creature;—are you not, Elinor?"

"Yes, dear. I wish I had a footstool."

Allerton brought her one.

"I say, Allerton," said Dreux, "you are gradually bringing Elinor round to usefulness and obedience, &c., but I hope you won't be quite a domestic tyrant."

"What is the use of laughing, Dreux?—you don't understand."

"Yes, I do; I understand perfectly."

"A woman is useful, is she not, to her husband, if she performs the part he wants her for, and obedient, if she"—

"If she orders him to bring her footstool."

"You are quite right. My will is, that my wife should be a dear little pretty thing for me to wait on and pet. I am a great, strong, rough fellow; I want a plaything. I want no housekeeper, no strong-minded woman. I don't want my servants to be scolded, and myself made much of. I want no care and protection,—I want to exercise them."

" Oh, then, you and Elinor are exactly suited to each other."

" And you have just discovered that fact ?"

" I discovered some time ago that you were Elinor's humble servant; but as, when I am married, I should like my wife to make much of me, I did not see the peculiar beauty of this arrangement."

" Oh, he would like his wife to pet him and make much of him. Oh, Arthur, how droll of you to say it, too !"

" And to mean it, my dear, for I'm sure he does mean it. Come, Dreux, what sort of petting would you prefer ?"

" If I am to be made game of the moment I come here by both of you, I shall go to my lodgings."

" You shall do no such thing. But, Dreux, how would you have her make much of you ? "

" Oh, nonsense. I only meant I should like her to take an interest in me."

" Interest ! Do I take no interest in Francis ? "

" Of course you do, my dear. Now don't set upon me, both of you in this inhuman manner."

" But I want to know how your wife is to make much of you ?"

" I should like her to behave in her natural manner; but I should like it to be her nature to— Oh, you know what I mean."

"No, we don't. Now, Francis, let him alone. Well, Arthur?"

"Well, if ever I have a wife I have no doubt I shall be very fond of her."

"To be sure you will; and, as far as that goes, you'll so blindly believe in her, you'll think her such perfection, that you will be under her dominion whether you know it or not. But that's not the point."

"Well, if I must speak, I think my meaning was that I should like her to be fond enough of me to take an interest even in little things, and to question me about them, so that I should get over my reserve with her, and not mind talking about myself."

"Which you can't do now excepting to me, Dreux. Why, even Elinor does not know half so much about you as I do. You mean that you would like your wife thoroughly to understand you, to be intimate with your mind, and also to be indulgent, and to be pleased with what you had done, not merely because it was right, but because you had done it. You would like a caressing person, easy, and fit to be confided in,—that's what you would like, you know."

Dreux smiled.

"Now that's not what I require. The moment I saw Elinor I thought she would make me happy—or, rather, she would not break that pretty sort of *insouciance* to run about her house and torment herself about me or anything else, but leave the action of both our lives to me, and let me make her happy."

"Yes; but, Francis, you are always to repeat Arthur's confidences to me when we are alone, for I like to know all about him; and, do you know, I never could get him to tell me anything."

"How are the Patons, Elinor?"

"Ah, he turns the conversation—he doesn't like to be talked about before his face. The Patons? Oh, they are well; but your friend, Wil Greyson, is gone to Swanstead—he was sent for yesterday."

"Indeed! What for?"

"You have heard of that poor lady, Mr. Raeburn's wife?"

"Yes, certainly."

"She is dead. She died very suddenly a few days ago, and he was sent for to go to the funeral."

"I saw Mr. Raeburn ten days since, and my uncle."

"Indeed! Why, did you go of your own accord and call upon him? and was he friendly, Arthur? and did you see Joseph, the heir?"

"How many questions you ask, my dear! Yes, I called of my own accord. The old Colonel is not the least like my recollection of him—not nearly so formidable. He was tolerably friendly—not very. Joseph has been plucked."

"Yes, we knew of that. Francis, do you want me to go?"

"No, my dear; I always want you to stay."

" But I thought you wanted perhaps to talk to
Arthur about your feuds and sermons and things;
besides, I think I must go, for it is time to dress for
dinner."

Allerton opened the door for her and let her
depart, whereupon the brothers-in-law fell into discourse at once about their " sermons and things,"
and Dreux was quite astonished at the degree of ill
feeling which had been manifested against Allerton.

" It appears then that you have no chance of
being useful here," he said, when the narration had
been brought to a close, " because these foolish
disputes, jealousies, and heartburnings are more
respecting you than with you ; and, as they are
quite unreasonable, I do not see how you are to
combat them, or even how you can take notice
of them ; and yet I would not take any steps
towards leaving the town at present."

" No, but we have neither of us any particular
tie to this place, Dreux."

" Certainly not."   And being alone now with his
brother-in-law, Dreux told him without difficulty
his own position with relation to his uncle, taking
particular care that he should not imagine he was
ever likely to inherit anything from him.

Having done this, and relieved his mind of all he
had wished to say, he dined with Allerton and his
sister—attended a stormy vestry meeting—came
back to tea, and went to his lodgings very late,
where, to his surprise, he found a letter bearing the

Norland arms awaiting him. He turned it over
and examined it minntely before opening it, as
people often will do when they expect to find something of importance inside ; then he broke the seal
and sat down by the table to read. Now the old
Colonel during his fit of the gout had forgiven
Dreux, and was even reduced to such a state of
ennui and dependence that he had detected himself
wishing for the plucked and pug-nosed Joseph, who,
to do him justice, was decidedly fond of his crusty
uncle. But then to ask either of them to come to
him when the architects were busy on his hospital
plans appeared, he thought, a meanness. How
could he condescend to be amused by young men
whom he intended to disinherit ? On the other
hand how could he bear to dismiss the said architects, whose high praise of his liberality was always
ringing in his ears, without making himself an
object of ridicule as a doting old fellow, who did not
know his own mind ? He decided to take a middle
course. He put off the architects, as he said, *till the
spring*, and wrote a letter on the sly to Joseph,
peremptorily desiring him to come home and be
forgiven. He then took Dreux into consideration,
and resolved to leave him what he knew was justly
his due, but not to make him any promises. He
accordingly wrote a letter in the imperative mood,
commanding, entreating, exhorting, and permitting
him to come and spend a month at Norland Court,
abusing him for not having called again, and

launching into a digression respecting the conduct of
the late Mr. Dreux when he was in Parliament—at
which time the brothers-in-law had quarrelled—and
concluding with the assurance that no living nephew
had any claim upon him, and that his nephew had
better come or he would rue it. Having thus descended
to threats, he signed himself, " Yours, young man,
according to your behaviour, P. Grice Norland." But
after that followed a postscript in which the poor old
Colonel, probably having slept over the former part
of his letter, could not bear to leave any stone
unturned which he could turn without committing
himself. " His nephew should do pretty much as he
liked—might have the servants in to prayers—
he himself had no objection to hear the lessons for
the day, for as he should leave him nothing he
was willing to make his visit comfortable, and he
supposed, as he was one of Raeburn's sort, he
would want to make his house into a church—so let
him stay away if he dared ! "

Dreux read the letter, and decided to decline his
uncle's invitation, for, indeed, he had scarcely
entered upon his duties as Allerton's curate, and to
leave him now that he was embroiled with his
parishioners, and now that he really wanted advice
and assistance in carrying out the various new
plans he had begun was not to be thought of for a
moment. He put it in his pocket, and the next
morning, when he went to Allerton's house, he showed
it to Elinor, thinking it would amuse her.

"You will go, of course, Arthur?" she remarked when she had read it.

"Go, my dear; no, most certainly I will not go."

"Not go, Arthur! You astonish me—you amaze me beyond measure."

"Why, even supposing I wished to go, my dear, how could I do it consistently with my first duties?"

"Your first duties, Arthur! surely this is one of them."

Dreux smiled, and seemed inclined to put the question by, but she would not hear of it. "I am sure you would agree with me, dearest," she continued, addressing her husband; "read this, and say whether Arthur ought not to go."

"Yes, read it, Allerton, by all means, but mind you give it against her; however, whether you do or not, I shall not accept you as umpire. I shall not go."

Allerton did read the letter, and his opinion so decidedly coincided with that of his wife, he seemed to think it of so much importance that Dreux should go immediately, that, though the latter was fretted and secretly annoyed almost beyond measure, he at last suffered himself to be argued, entreated, and coaxed into it; yet so obvious was his chagrin, that when he had written a letter of acceptance and suffered it to be despatched, his brother and sister almost wished they had let him alone.

During the day, while he was fully occupied, he contrived to forget his mortification; but when the trio again dined together, and the subject was discussed, he could not altogether conceal it.

Allerton, true to his impulsive nature, began to blame himself openly for the part he had taken. Elinor was silent, but she doubted whether she had acted wisely.

"I wish I had sense enough to let other people's affairs alone," said Allerton moodily. "I know nothing about this old uncle, and I have persuaded Dreux to go to him at a time when he particularly wished to stay with us, and we particularly wanted to have him."

"It is only for a month, dear," said Elinor, "and then we shall have him back again."

"The fact was, I urged it the more because I thought he was deterred by the idea of leaving me with too much on my hands."

"Never mind, Allerton," returned his brother-in-law, sighing uneasily, and thinking, that as the thing must be done, he would try to do it graciously; "I dare say you are right, and that it is a duty to go. At any rate, I know that neither you nor Elinor would have urged it, unless you had believed it was for my profit or happiness, and I shall try not to be uneasy about the parish — mere clerical help you can easily get."

"And for the rest we must correspond. I have been so wishing for your cool temper and your clear head, thinking everything would come right when I had them to back me; and now the idea of my having flung them from me against your will!"—

"Do not let us discuss the matter any further. I must start to-morrow; let me enjoy myself here with you while I can."

"But after all," said Elinor, "why so very averse to go?"

"You and Allerton are all I have in the world. Do you think it gives me no pleasure to see you happy? and is it not natural that I should like to be with you after such long separation?"

Elinor fixed her penetrating eyes upon him, and came and sat by him on the sofa; she felt vexed, and uncertain whether what she had done was for his happiness; and now she began to administer some of that sweet innocent flattery of the affections, which has commonly such a soothing effect upon its object. Allerton seconded her; and as it grew dusk, her sweet voice and the tranquillizing effect of evening dissipated Dreux's painful feelings, and he began to look upon the proposed visit more favourably; he could scarcely tell why.

His strong desire to be loved almost amounted to a passion. Elinor consciously, and Allerton unconsciously, flattered this passion to the utmost that night: the one made him see, and the other let him see, of how very much consequence he was to them.

Nevertheless, when he had taken leave of them, his mind shrunk from the idea of the comparative inaction he should have to endure at Norland Court, and especially inaction in the neighbourhood of Marion, from whom he felt that he could not too carefully absent himself, unless he was prepared to lose his peace of mind altogether.

Allerton was with him early the next morning, and he and Elinor carried on the tactics of the previous evening to such perfection that he soon got into good spirits again. He must promise not to ride strange horses; they should be miserable if he did not take care of himself. He was by no means to trouble himself about the duty, or the schools, or anything else. Allerton was rather glad, on second thoughts, that he was not to be mixed up and involved in the petty broils going on in the parish, but they hoped he would not stay if he found it dull; he was to write often, and they would tell him everything of the slightest interest,—they should miss him more than they could tell. In short, they showed such solicitude that the idea flashed upon his mind that Elinor must have guessed the real reason of his dislike to the visit, and have told it to her husband, which was the fact.

He parted from them at last, and on his journey had plenty of time for reflection as to how he should spend the month before him; plenty of clerical employment he knew he could easily get, but he resolved to keep at a respectful distance from Swanstead, and to decline visiting, lest he should meet Marion. He knew Allerton and his sister thought he was sure to regain his lost place in the old Colonel's affections; if so, his worldly prospects would be greatly altered; but he himself knew the old man better than they did, and as they disagreed upon religion, politics, and nearly every other subject that can be mentioned, his highest hope was that the month might pass over without any serious outbreaks between them, and that, if possible, he might be able to draw the old Colonel's mind to the consideration of religious duties.

The second visit, to his surprise, began with an unfeignedly warm welcome. The Colonel was ill, and dispirited. He evidently thought he should have to conciliate, and as his nephew was inclined to be compliant, the first two days passed over extremely well.

Their first storm arose from the old gentleman's presenting the young one with a horse, which he caused to be led up to the window, that they might inspect it together. The nephew admired, would be most happy to use it while he stayed, but remarked, with careless good humour, that a horse was far too expensive a luxury for him to indulge in. Upon which the Colonel demanded, with great heat, whether his nephew thought him such an old niggard as to offer him a horse without providing him with means to keep it. Dreux involuntarily elevated his eyebrows, for the protestations that he never would *leave* him a shilling seemed rather at variance with this offer.

" It does my eyes good to see a man ride well," proceeded the Colonel; "if I taught him myself it does not diminish the pleasure."

There was something so like affection in the way this was said, that Dreux coloured, and tried to make amends by declaring that it would be quite a pleasure to him to ride a good horse while he stayed.

" Keep him, then, Arthur," cried the Colonel, " and I'll pay all expenses connected with him."

A momentary vision of a groom leading this splendid horse up and down before his little lodgings in Westport flashed across Dreux's mind. He thanked the Colonel again, and declined the present. He evidently meant what he said, and during .the outbreak of passionate abuse that followed, which began with invectives against pride, and took in independence, religion in general, parsons, the late Mrs. Dreux, her husband, and Joseph Norland, " that born fool," he stood before him with the most perfect command of temper. At last, when the old man had finished, he began his defence. He described his lodgings, his manner of life, his many occupations, his determination to follow his own persuasions of what was right, and put it to the Colonel whether for him a riding-horse was not both useless and ridiculous ?

"·I suppose you mean to insinuate, Sir," cried the Colonel, "that to keep a fine horse is inconsistent with your beggarly pay,—something like a pearl necklace round a beggar's neck! Well, Sir, what do you think I asked you here for, and what did you come for,—Eh?"

"What did you ask me here for?" retorted his nephew, with a smile in his dark eyes. "Why, Sir, you expressly gave me to understand that it was for the pleasure of my society."

"Your society! Bah,—talk of Joseph! The long and the short of it is, I suppose, that you're determined to have your own way, and you are afraid my yoke would come with my money?"

He paused for a moment. His nephew could not contradict him, nor repress a laugh.

"Well, go along with you," he continued; "take a good hard gallop, and come back in a more tractable temper."

"First, I shall read you the leaders," said Dreux, taking up the unopened "Times."

"Ah, well, Arthur, well, I don't mind if you do. My eyes get worse and worse."

The leaders were read, but the Colonel scarcely heard a sentence, so intent was he on watching the features of his nephew. "He thinks he's got the mastery of me, and is satisfied. Ah, well, we shall see."

"And now, Colonel, suppose we have a game of chess?"

This was touching the old man on his weak point.
He had been a celebrated chess-player in his youth,
and still retained a passionate fondness for the game.
In less than seven minutes he had beaten his nephew
in the most merciless style, though he was a very
tolerable hand.

"Come, Arthur, try again." He moved the pieces
with his left hand, the right being lame with gout.
They did try again, and with the same result. The
third time there seemed a trifling chance for the
weaker party, who played with all his might. But
he was soon discomfited, driven back to his hold,
cooped up, blocked into an unprofitable corner, and
his pieces picked off the board with his adversary's
pawns. "That's how I used to beat your father,"
observed the conqueror. "He called it smothering
him; he always hated a block game."

Dreux murmured something about an oversight.

"Could easily have smashed you before that,
Arthur, but thought I would let you have a squeak
for your life."

He was now in high good humour, and ordered
his nephew to set out for a ride, and bring his horse
up to the window, "for he loved to see his own flesh
and blood well mounted."

Nearly the same scenes were repeated every day,
but the old Colonel, though he tried hard to conceal
it, got extremely fond of his nephew; the less yield-
ing points in his character attracted him far more
than the pains he took to amuse him during his

helpless confinement to his chair; and angry as he
pretended to be when the subject of religion was
introduced, he secretly listened with interest.

At nine o'clock every evening he was wheeled
away to his bedroom, and his nephew had the rest
of his time to himself. He spent it in a way which
would have made every friend he had in the world
lift up hands and eyes in amazement. He could
scarcely believe it himself, but the impulse became
such a tyrant that he could no more resist it than he
could fly. The first evening, upon finding himself
alone, he opened the window to let in the delightful
air. The day had been very hot, and now the moon
was beginning to shine; by degrees she seemed to
separate the twilight into two parts,—clear the
lights, and deepen the shadows.

He stepped out on to the gravel to listen to the
bells of Swanstead striking nine. He turned in
that direction. At the bottom of a hollow, which
bounded the garden, he could just catch a glimpse
of the church and the rectory. Before he knew
what he was about he had leapt the stream and was
in the field. Then he was done for! He began to
walk quickly and steadily towards Swanstead. It
was only a mile and a half, he argued, and a moonlight walk was a very good thing. But why in
that direction? He reproached himself for his folly,
but the tyrant wish had got hold of him. He leapt
the ditches, climbed the gates, hurried across the
meadows, all in a straight line for Swanstead. As

fast as one set of feelings drew him back, the other
goade̓d him on. At last he stopped in the church-
yard, with his hand on the slight gate which led
into the garden. Before his good genius could
make him stop, his evil genius had forced him to
open this gate, and strike into a little path thick
with unpruned laurels. It wound about, till suddenly it brought him nearly in front of the
windows of the ordinary sitting-room. The linen
blinds were drawn down, but the windows were
open. A shadow flitted across,—not a very graceful one,—but his heart beat at the sight of it.
There were strange sounds, like knocking and
rubbing, with moving of chairs and tables.

"Lucky enough, Master and Miss is out," ex-
claimed a coarse voice. "Reach me the bee's-wax,
Sally. We shall get this room very *forrard* to-night.
When does Miss mean to have the study done?"

Well, it was a pity he should have walked so far.
In a few minutes the blind was drawn up by the
footman, and he saw the housemaid on her knees,
scrubbing the oak floor. The house was evidently
undergoing the annual cleaning, and Master and
Miss were gone out to dinner.

He was deeply disgusted with himself, and turning
hastily, made the best of his way home again, scold-
ing himself vehemently, and upbraiding himself in
the most cruel and taunting manner for his romantic
folly. But did he take warning by that night's
experience? No; he made good resolutions all

day, but no sooner was the Colonel gone to bed than he opened the window, and darted off again in the same direction.

He got into the laurel thicket, but did not advance nearly so close to the window, for he was far from wishing to be an eavesdropper; he only wished (he supposed) to see Marion, or her shadow. He again walked backward, for he heard the tones of the piano, and Marion's sweet voice floated towards him, singing, "Waft her, angels!" It sent a thrill to his heart that astonished him: he found himself a romantic lover! (And what business had he to suppose that he should escape the common lot?) When she ceased he walked along the lane towards home, and came in tired and thoroughly dispirited.

Notwithstanding which, he went the next night, and the next, and the next: sometimes he saw nothing, sometimes a shadow crossed the window. Once he thought he heard her laugh; once, the blind being partially drawn up, he saw her bring a cup of tea to Mr. Raeburn, shake up a sofa cushion, and put it at the back of his chair, then stoop to kiss his forehead, of which mark of affection he (insensible man!) took no notice whatever.

By degrees he became very familiar with the garden, and all its little shady walks and alleys were accustomed to the tread of his restless foot: he liked to see the house in different aspects. And now what he had dreaded was fully come upon him, his peace of mind was gone, and, what was worse, he had no power, and scarcely any wish, to escape the charm that bound him. But he still took care not to come into contact with Marion, lest his voice or the perturbation of his manner should betray him.

This had gone on for ten days, when, one evening before the moon rose, he found himself in his usual place. It was very dark under the trees, and as there were no lights in the morning room, he wandered down a certain shady walk under the high garden wall, feeling quite safe, for he believed the family must be out.

The trees and shrubs were very thick on each side of him. He put the branches aside and went heedlessly on, when to his consternation he heard voices behind him. He walked forward : there was no outlet, and he found himself cooped into a corner. He could not turn without meeting the speakers, and he could not go forward. Here was a horrid predicament ! Perhaps he should be obliged to hear their conversation. They came on, and emerged for a moment into the moonlight. There were two persons,—one of them was Marion. She was dressed in white, and had thrown her lace scarf over her golden ringlets. He thought he had never seen her look so lovely, as with one hand she gathered its folds under her chin, and put aside the lilac twigs with the other.

He pressed himself a little backwards into the laurel thicket, and bit his lips with vexation.

They stepped into an arbour quite close to him, and Marion sat so that he could see every change in her usually serene countenance.

Her companion was a very tall young man. He had often seen him before. He looked up to the wall, and forward into the thicket—there was no chance of escape. He was an intruder and an eavesdropper! Wounded pride nearly suffocated him, and his heart beat so painfully that he lost the first few sentences of the speakers, though he never took his eyes off Marion's face.

"You will, then, Marion," said the pleasant voice of the young giant, who was no other than Frank Maidley.

"Yes," answered Marion; she did not look very cordial, though.

"I am glad you like them. I got them at Cambridge. They are rare, they tell me."

"Oh," said Marion. She was holding up the corner of her scarf, apparently examining the pattern.

Her companion seemed aware that he did not stand very high in her good graces, and fidgetted a good deal.

"So you are going to spend the autumn here," she said, suddenly looking up; "I thought"—

"Thought what, Marion?"

Oh, nothing; only I thought you generally went down to Westport, to see"—

"I have no tie there now," said Frank, observing

her hesitation.   "You are perhaps going there,
Marion?"

Marion shook her head.

"You often hear from thence," he proceeded, in
rather a beseeching tone, and when she made no
answer, he said earnestly, "I *should* like if I could,
to know how Dora is."

Marion immediately turned her face towards him
full of sudden interest, but said, in rather an indignant tone, "What, Mr. Maidley?"

"You are very unjust," replied Frank, in the
voice of one who feels himself injured.   "Surely,
if I give her up I do enough; it is rather too much
to expect me to forget her."

Marion replied, with deliberation, "I consider
you the most extraordinary person I ever met with,
Mr. Maidley."

Frank muttered something to the effect that it
was very hard to be so misunderstood, and to be
looked upon so coldly.

Marion gathered her scarf round her, and half
arose.   He stopped her, and begged urgently that
she would remain, and tell him what it was that she
thought so extraordinary.

"I think the explanation quite superfluous," said
Marion, resuming her seat; "you are, I should
suppose, quite aware of what I mean."

"I don't think I have done anything extraordinary," said Frank, very much crestfallen,—"I

have only done what I thought right and generous."

"Right and generous!" exclaimed Marion, her
eyes dilating, and her cheeks flushing; "do you
call it right and generous, then, always to be sitting
next and looking at one particular lady, to read
with her, sing with her, walk with her,—to love her,
and let her see that you do, to try to win her affections, and, for anything you can tell, to succeed,
and then to go away, as if for a few days, and
never return any more?"

"Oh! Marion, don't stand denouncing me,"
pleaded Frank; "don't look at me like an offended
duchess.   I should have expected to find you pleased
with my conduct in that respect; I thought it must
be something else that had offended you.   Oh,
Marion, remember what old friends we are."

Marion was at first inexorable.   However, she
suffered herself to be persuaded to stay, and let him
lead her back to her seat.

Dreux's hopes, which had been high, sunk again
below zero.   It was plain he should have to hear a
great deal more.

"What could I do?" said Frank.   "Only consider, and tell me candidly, Marion."

"Do!" repeated Marion, with a little movement
of impatience.

"I am sure you never can have heard the particulars, or you would not blame me."

"I have never heard any particulars from Dora,"

said Marion, with decision. (Oh! woman, how anxious she is to keep up the dignity of her sex!) " She has never once mentioned the subject in my hearing. I was not even aware that there had been ' *any particulars*' beyond those I mentioned."

" Namely, that I loved her, and then went away without attempting to make her mine ?"

" Exactly so," said Marion. " Was there anything else besides ?"

She asked the question in the gentlest tone of inquiry. It brought a flush of pleasure to Frank's face. He fidgetted a while, and then answered,—

" Perhaps that she liked me ? Yes, I think she did ; I have no doubt of it. But, Marion, I am a beggar !"

" Indeed! More so than when you tried to please Dora ?"

" Most assuredly. Have you never heard,— don't you know that my old aunt had always given out, and promised, that she would leave her property to me ?"

" Well ?" said Marion, gently.

" Well, I was summoned to her death-bed, I attended her funeral, and, when her will was opened, she had not left me one shilling."

" Well," said Marion again ; " and so, with the loss of that ten thousand pounds, you ceased to love Dora ?"

" How you talk, Marion ! How could you say such an unkind thing in such a gentle voice ? No,

I loved her far more than ever, because before, like
a careless puppy as I was, I felt quite secure of my
conquest; afterwards, I knew I should be a scamp
if I could make use of it to drag Dora down into
comparative poverty."

"Your own exertions, then, count for nothing in
the calculation?"

"Nothing certain, at present,—nothing absolutely
certain."

"And Dora's fortune would be comparative
poverty?"

"There's the bitterness of it: I thought Mr.
Paton would think it so mean to ask him for his
daughter in my altered circumstances."

"I do not think he would have encouraged your
addresses if they had *begun* under those altered
circumstances."

"If it had been one of the other daughters," said
Frank, not heeding her, "I would have ventured,
for I really have a good prospect of getting on."

"And if it had been Dora whose fortune had
been lost, should you have expected her to give
you up, lest she should be a burden to you?"

"How can you ask such absurd questions?" said
Frank, laughing. "I beg your pardon, Marion, but
you seem determined to misunderstand."

"So you preferred to sacrifice your happiness,
and perhaps Dora's, to letting her bestow a benefit.
Well, I would not have believed it unless you had

told me yourself. I did not think any one was so proud as that."

" Proud!" repeated Frank.

" Yes," said Marion, as gently as if she had been uttering the most pleasant words, and yet with the decision of one who feels not the slightest doubt. " Oh! Frank, how could you be so proud, so falsely generous, and so romantic, when all Westport knew how attached you were to Dora! When my uncle encouraged your suit, and you knew very well what Dora felt! How could you let your pride get so far the mastery over your better feelings! You really behave like a character in a novel."

Her companion seemed astonished, but he was a little ashamed too, and fidgetted on his seat with an air the most crest-fallen and forlorn.

" And this, too, was not the pride of independence," proceeded Marion, " which makes people labour and deny themselves."

" I have denied myself."

" Yes, denied yourself a great blessing, to save yourself an annoyance which ought not to be worth mentioning,—the annoyance of knowing that idle people would say what a fortunate young man you were, what a good thing it was that you had won the lady before your prospects altered, and that her father had so openly approved, that in honour he could scarcely draw back. But the consequences of what you have done are of small importance to *yourself*,—it is not you who will chiefly suffer. I did not think you considered money of such very great importance."

" *I* do not, but others do."

" You treat those 'others' with extreme deference, considering that none of the parties concerned are of their number. Does their opinion give them any power to make Dora forget those days which you took so much pains to have her remember?"

" Well," said Frank, with a mighty sigh, " it is too late, now at least. If Dora thinks as you do, she would never, never forgive me. Besides, though she always seemed pleased at my presence, she might never have accepted my hand."

" Perhaps not then. But oh ! Frank, how wilfully you misunderstand ! When a man is rich, and it is an easy matter for him to obtain a wife, and he shows no great solicitude about it, then, out of mere carelessness, he may be refused. But if he should afterwards become poor, and most other faces should change to him, in how much higher a position he stands towards a woman who esteems him, and whom he has loved. To marry him before, the world might have said, was to do herself an honour, and if he appears to think so too, it is an easy thing to put that honour aside."

Marion paused ; the earnestness with which she had spoken seemed to surprise her auditor, for he

bent his face to look into hers, quite unconscious
that there was another auditor on whom her words
had made a still deeper impression.

"You think I did wrong, then?" he said, after
a thoughtful silence.

"Very wrong, and very unwisely. It is so easy
to be generous in the common meaning of the word.
To be generous enough to give is easy; but to be
generous enough to permit another to give, when
the gift is one that all the world knows the value
of,—to be generous enough to feel and acknowledge that the giver is fully repaid by receiving
that affection which the world cannot so readily
count over and tell the value of,—to know that we
ourselves would have given, under like circumstances, and to feel no more painful sense of obligation than we should have wished them to feel,—is a
harder and a rarer thing."

"Marion," interrupted Maidley, "how kind you
are; you put my own thoughts into words, but I
have always tried to repress them, because this
seemed such a selfish, romantic view. Oh, Marion,
if you would but write to Dora"—

"*I* write to her?"

"Yes, O do, Marion, and smooth the way for
me a little; for I don't know how it is,—when I
was at Westport I felt so very much at my ease.
I thought, you know, that there was no doubt of
my being accepted. I thought we should be mar-

ried in the ordinary way. I was very fond of Dora,
but "—

"Well?" said Marion, smiling.

"I think I must have been rather a conceited
young fellow. I think losing one's money makes
one romantic; and, certainly, to see that 'the
grapes are sour,' makes one somehow think them
more sweet."

Marion laughed gently.

"That or something else must have altered me
very much. Dora now seems to stand so far above
me, and so far off, I declare I havn't courage to
address her again, and explain all this to her as I
have done to you."

Marion hesitated and made objections; she did
not know whether her uncle, after such long delay,
would accept him for a son-in-law. She could not
be sure that Dora would forgive the past.

Frank got agitated and more urgent; he seemed
quite to believe that his happiness was in Marion's
hands, and, in his old boyish fashion, he began to
beg and entreat. Marion at length appeared to
soften; indeed, her hesitation had been merely
pretence.

"If I thought you deserved it, Frank," she said,
playfully, "I would ask Dora to come again and
stay with me; for, since Mrs. Raeburn's death, my
uncle likes to have visitors in the house, it helps to
make it more cheerful."

But, as if the mention of Mr. Raeburn's name

had brought the speaker into his mind, the voice of the Rector was heard at no great distance, in its loudest tone, calling Marion to come in.

Marion started: "I am coming, dear uncle; I am coming directly. It is not in the least chilly. I have enjoyed the moonlight."

"It's perfectly hot, Sir," said Frank; "a most sultry night."

"Humph!" said the Rector, rather ungraciously. "It clouds over fast,—I expect we shall have a storm."

Something of his old jealousy respecting Frank seemed to have come over him, for, as he tucked Marion's arm under his, he muttered something about thoughtlessness in keeping her out so long, which their guest thought rather unreasonable, for young ladies cannot very well be kept out in a garden against their will.

Their voices grew distant, and at length the prisoner in the thicket ventured to force his way out. It was very dark, and he groped his way slowly towards the little garden-gate. He had never so much in his life suffered from the sensation of shame, as during this conversation; its perfectly confidential nature, its subject, Marion's closeness to him, which enabled him to see every feature and every change of expression, the unqualified way in which she had attacked some of his own weak points and condemned some of his own foibles, made him feel that, if they had chosen their subject, knowing him to be an unbidden listener, they could not have wounded and punished him more effectually.

But perhaps he might have made a different meaning, or, at least, a nearer application, out of some of Marion's sentences, if it had not been for one little circumstance which distracted his attention and filled him with anxiety and chagrin. As Marion talked, she continually put out her hand and twined the honeysuckle tendrils in and out of the broad trellis work; her fingers were often within a foot of his face; on one of them was a ring,—his own lost ring, he was certain; the moonlight shone on it so distinctly that he could not be mistaken. He had left it behind him at Swanstead and forgotten it. The loss never struck him till after he had been back again and was making a speech in the evening at a place about thirty miles off. The sudden observation of its absence spoilt a very eloquent sentence. He never doubted that it was among his luggage, and spent a fruitless hour in searching for it. He then tried to remember where he had seen it last, and traced it on, from day to day, till he got to Swanstead, where he remembered, perfectly, having it on, for he had put on a new glove, and the ring-finger being too tight he had made a small slit in it with his penknife; so, of all places in the world, he must have left it at Swanstead, and only hoped it never might come into Marion's possession.

Now he walked home slowly in the dark, thoroughly oppressed; his lips parted and quivering with the rapid beating of his heart, and his nerves so completely awakened, that all Marion's words rung in his ears with distinct and painful vibrations.

After a restless night he rose early, seeking in violent exercise and action for the means of quieting his excitement.

The next few days passed. He was cured of his evening walks, and used to pace the long library instead. He had promised to stay the month; only three weeks were completed, and he counted the days as a slave might count the time which should give him liberty.

The sensitive shrinking of his mind from the remembrance of his eavesdropping had a greater effect upon his spirits than even his concealed attachment; he could not think of it without a shudder; but it had been done, and he thought it would injure his self-respect for ever.

A few days after this adventure the old Colonel announced that that " born fool, Joseph," had written to say that he was coming home. He felt a curiosity to see him, but rather disliked the idea of the constant contests he supposed he should have to witness. On returning in the afternoon from some clerical duty in the next parish, he found his cousin had already returned.

The old uncle, in his invalid chair, gruffly introduced them to each other, and never was there a

greater contrast in this world than they presented.
Joseph was a small, fair young man, with rosy
cheeks and hair of a sandy tinge; his face might
have been called pretty, but for his little pug-nose;
and he had an incessant simper, two deep dimples,
and the most delicate hands and feet imaginable.

On this occasion he was arrayed in lilac boots,
with little glossy toes, wore a superb set of turquoise
studs, a thick gold chain, and an outrageous silk
neck-tie, the ends of which, deeply fringed, extended far beyond his face like two little cherub's
wings.   He was scented like a whole bed of helio-
tropes.   In contrast to his fair little features and
gay colours, the height, olive complexion, and
clerical black and white of his cousin looked something towering and majestic.   He seemed instinctively conscious of his own inferiority in point
of intellect and manliness, and with simple docility
"knocked under," for it was only with ladies that
he exhibited his self-conceit.

The old Colonel, so vehement against him in his
absence, was perfectly tolerant of his presence. He
did him the justice to know that he could not help
being a soft little fellow.

They had not finished dinner when, to Dreux's
horror, the Colonel said, " Raeburn has been calling
here this morning.   He said he never heard till
yesterday that you were here.   He asked if you
would dine with him to-morrow ?   I said I could

not tell what your engagements might be, and he left a note for you.   Here, Arthur."

Dreux read the twisted missive.   It contained, beside a polite invitation, the request that, if not inconvenient, he would take a funeral for him at three o'clock, as he had another engagement.

He spent half an hour in thinking whether he could not get off.   The very idea of that garden brought a sensitive flush to his face.   But no ; there was not a single loophole for him, so he wrote an answer consenting to take the funeral, but declining the dinner invitation.

The next day was rather a gay one at Swanstead. One of the daughters of a rich miller was to be led to the altar of Hymen by a wealthy young farmer. Mr. Raeburn had been asked by the bride's mother to allow Miss Greyson to officiate as bridesmaid ; so Marion, in an azure silk dress and white crape bonnet, like those worn by the miller's daughters, went to grace the festive occasion.

The company was in gorgeous apparel—the viands were plentiful and of the very best.   Mr. Raeburn stayed to hand the bride into her post-chaise.   Her bridal tour was to be to London.   He and Marion then walked home across two or three fields, and entered the church-yard just as Dreux was retiring after the funeral, followed by his cousin, Joseph Norland.

They all sauntered together up to the house door,

when the two gentlemen showed signs of intending to take leave; but this by no means suited the ideas of the hospitable Rector. They must absolutely stay to dinner; his niece had a splendid bed of dahlias, and it was the pride of her heart to show them.

Mr. Dreux was sure he saw Marion give the Rector a family signal, but the old gentleman did not see it. To stay at all was greatly against his wishes, but to stay against her inclination was wormwood. But Mr. Raeburn was so urgent that he was compelled to give in, and he and Joseph followed Marion into the morning-room, she looking fairer than ever, he thought, in her bridal decorations. She had a bouquet of white flowers in her hand, and as she sat by the table in the window she began to untie them and put them into water.

At last she looked up and said, when there was a pause in little Joseph's small talk, " You remember, dear uncle, that you have promised to go to Wickley school feast this afternoon ? "

The Rector looked unutterable things.

" Your two guests will be quite an acquisition," she hastily added. "Mr. White will be very grateful to you for bringing them, and if they will excuse a cold dinner out in a hayfield, we can take them in the barouche."

" Oh, yes, my dear, to be sure we can," said the Rector, gladly catching at her proposal; for having

made it a great point that they should stay, he was
aghast at the idea of having no dinner for them.

Little Joseph had a great many pretty things to
say, and Marion could not forbear a smile, though
feeling extremely uncomfortable.   Dreux sat in
almost perfect silence, heartily wishing himself
away, and involuntarily occupied with the laurel
thicket which he could see from the window.   At
last the old-fashioned carriage drove up to the door,
and they all set off for Wickley.

CHAPTER XXVII.

ALLERTON PROPOUNDS VARIOUS THEORIES.

THERE was a large party at Wickley, gentle and simple—the latter congregated at one end of a great hay-field, eating cake and drinking beer and tea; the former seated and lounging upon hay under a hedge at the other end, eating something like a *dejeuner à la fourchette*, only it was taking place at six o'clock in the afternoon. Little Joseph was seated by Marion, complimenting and simpering to his heart's content. At her other hand sat the Rector. These three were at the edge of the heap of hay with their feet upon the grass; behind them, altogether perched upon it, was a large detachment of Maidleys, ranging from six years old to four and twenty, with the paternal and maternal Maidley at their head, and behold, at the feet of a young lady, who seemed to be under the special guardianship of Mrs. Maidley, was extended the gallant Frank with his spectacles on. Dreux looked attentively at the said young lady and recognised Miss Paton, to whom he instinctively lifted his hat, and felt excessively foolish—quite as foolish as she did—when she returned his bow.

He was hesitating where to place himself, when a familiar voice from among the mass of Maidleys called out to him, and a hand flourishing a bun was waved in the air.

" Is that you, Greyson?" he exclaimed.

" Yes; do come up here, Mr. Dreux. I'm so glad to see you. I only came yesterday as an escort to my cousin, or I should have called at Norland Court to see you."

As there was no escape, he went and sat down close to Dora, and nearly behind Marion, who turned continually to talk to her cousin and to Frank Maidley.

There were many other groups of visitors, but their own was rather isolated.

" What a pleasant nook this is!" observed Marion. " I like these larch-trees very much, and their delicate shadows."

" They are very well," replied Frank, "but I prefer a thicker shade. I like laurels better. Those laurels in Mr. Raeburn's garden are far more beautiful."

Marion laughed.

" And this hay," she proceeded playfully, " what a pleasant seat it makes!"

" Not half such a capital seat as an arbour," exclaimed Frank; and then remembering what an ungallant speech he was making, he turned and continued to Dora, "but that depends on who one shares it with."

"Of course," returned Marion, again half turning and addressing him with gentle archness: "though you so greatly prefer the arbour in itself, yet sharing the hay with—with *me*, let us say, makes it superior."

Frank laughed, and observing that these remarks seemed to excite a puzzled look among his companions, he abruptly turned to Dreux, and asked if he did not agree with him?

Marion, half resting on her elbow, could not resist a glance at Dreux's face, and was quite surprised at his conscious start and confusion.

His eyes met Marion's, and he felt more than ever like a culprit. He did not attempt any sort of answer, but turned his head slowly towards Frank and inquired what he had said.

"I wanted your opinion as to which made the pleasantest seat, an arbour or a haycock?"

Marion did not hear his answer, for their hostess just then touching her elbow, she stooped to hear the whispered question, "Who is that handsome statue? Does he sit there merely to show his fine dark eyelashes?"

"That is Mr. Dreux, Colonel Norland's nephew," said Marion, vexed to feel that she was blushing. But the handsome statue just then made a diversion for her, by suddenly starting up, and going quickly to meet a gentleman who was advancing along the field toward them, apparently half afraid of intruding.

"Allerton, my dear fellow !" he exclaimed, with genuine joy, "what fortunate winds have blown you here?"

"No wind," was the reply, "but your uncle's letter."

"My uncle's letter?"

"Yes, did you not know he had written? and, Dreux, what's all this about?"

"It's a Sunday-school feast, but I dare say you may make one of the party."

"I will then, as long as you stay, if you will introduce me."

"But what of the letter?"

"Oh, nothing of the least consequence. The old fellow began to storm at me the moment he saw me."

The school children were already marshalling in front of the visitors when they came up, and before Allerton could be introduced they had to listen to a long prosy speech of Mr. White's, partly addressed to the children and partly to the parents, who were listening in the background. Then began a general shout, and a rush towards two female servants, who were drawing near, bearing a clothes-basket, full of rewards.

The ladies sat quietly on their hay ; some of the gentlemen began to assist in distributing the prizes ; neither Allerton nor Dreux were of their number. Dreux relapsed again into silence. Allerton, finding himself sitting next Marion, whom he called "the fair Inexorable," was quite determined to make use of his time, and not let the evening pass without finding out whether there was anything going on between them.

"Dreux," he said, suddenly turning, "how have you liked your visit?"

Dreux was twisting some grasses. He threw them away, and looking calmly at him, answered, "I have liked it as well as a warm welcome and fine weather could make me." He then got up, and walked slowly away towards the school children.

The merciless Allerton then turned towards Marion. "Miss Greyson, you knew something of my brother-in-law before his accident?"

"Oh yes," said Marion.

"Do you think him changed by it? Do you think he bears any appearance of want of health or strength?"

Marion was obliged to answer; in so doing, she lifted up her face, tinged with a soft carnation. "I have not observed any alteration."

"I am glad of that, but I cannot say I think him looking the better for this change of air."

He fixed his eyes on Marion so inquiringly, that she again felt compelled to answer, "I cannot say; I have not seen Mr. Dreux before, since his arrival at Norland Court."

"Miss Greyson," cried one of the little Maidleys, running up, "will you make me a daisy necklace?"

" Tiresome little thing," thought Allerton.

" Sweet little thing," thought Marion, and she began to thread the daisies with the greatest alacrity.

" It's to be a very long one," said the child.

" My wife requested, if I had the pleasure of seeing you, Miss Greyson, that I would give her love to you."

Marion looked up, and murmured her thanks, but could not feel at ease, nor divest her mind of the idea that Allerton had been trying to find out the state of her feelings, and had succeeded.

So much was she disturbed with this thought that she did not observe the dispersion of the children, and was only aroused by the return of Mrs. White, with Frank Maidley, Joseph Norland, and Mr. Dreux, with Greyson and Dora.

" Marion, my dear," said Mrs. White, " we are come to torment you; we want to know all about this wedding at Swanstead."

Marion looked up from her daisy necklace, and began to describe it.

" Oh, no; we know all about wedding-breakfasts and wedding-favours; we want to know whether these ridiculous reports about the bridegroom are true?"

" Indeed ! I cannot tell unless I hear the reports."

" You must have heard them.   Why, it is reported

that he made the bride nine offers before she would accept him."

" I believe that is true," replied Marion, " and may be repeated, as she told it me herself."

" And a very sensible fellow, too," said Allerton ; " let him go down on his knee every day for a month, if he gets his wife at the end of it."

" Sensible fellow ! " repeated Frank, with scorn. " I really wonder at you, Mr. Allerton,—a married man as you are,—to put such thoughts into the heads of the ladies."

" Nonsense ! " persisted Allerton ; " had not a man better make nine offers to one woman, than one to nine different ones? Dreux, what do you think ? "

" I quite agree with you. It seems he knew his own mind, and thinking the lady did NOT know hers"—

" Exactly so ; and what woman does know her own mind? Well, I have got *one*, at least, on my side. Miss Paton, I am sure you agree with me also ? "

Dora laughed, and shook her head.

" You do *not?* I would not have believed it. Gentlemen, and all whom it may concern, Miss Paton had rather marry a man who has attacked nine other ladies, and been refused, than "—

" Indeed, Mr. Allerton, I never hinted at such a thing ; but which way of making offers do you *seriously* advise ? Perhaps you have tried both."

"I declare, upon my honour, I never made but one," exclaimed Allerton, joining in the laugh against himself.

"Oh, I do wish they would talk about something else," thought Marion, as she sat threading her daisies, of which her little friend kept bringing her more, and throwing them into her lap.

"Let Allerton talk of anything in the world but offers," thought Dreux; but they were all grouped together on the hay, and to rise and leave them would have excited observation.

It was very far from Allerton's intention to let the conversation drop; he meant to carry it on, lead it to a topic which he thought wanted illustrating, and, if possible, throw a little light on the said topic.

"For my part," said little Joseph, "I shall certainly never, au—make an offer—unless I'm quite sure, you know, of being accepted beforehand, au— I think that's much the best way to prevent disappointment."

"You do?" said Allerton, in a tone of solemn admonition. "I wouldn't advise you to build too much on appearances beforehand; besides, if you let the lady see beforehand—of course, I don't allude to any lady in particular (Joseph was looking very hard at Marion)—but if you let any lady see that you are sure beforehand, very likely she may say *No*, on purpose to show you that you are mistaken."

Little Joseph seemed awed by Allerton's way of

saying this, and looked as if he meant to take warning by it.

" And Mr. Norland," asked Dora, " how did you mean to find out beforehand ?—how did you propose to know before you asked ?"

Joseph pulled up his collar and played with his cane, but a reply was not forthcoming.

" And which side do you take, Miss Greyson," asked Allerton, turning his clear merry eyes upon her.

" I think the bridegroom paid a very high compliment," said Marion, hesitating.

" You take my side, then ?"

" I think not; for a lady who could so capriciously refuse so many times"—

" Was not worth having ? Oh, Miss Greyson, you were not, surely, going to finish your sentence so unworthily ? It is always said to be the privilege of your sex to change their minds."

" Then, if I must take one side, it shall certainly be that of the bridegroom ; for, at least, his constancy is to be admired !"

" Ah, constancy is indeed a delightful quality in a lover, worth all other good qualities put together. Don't you think so, Miss Greyson ?"

" If I take your side, I suppose I must think as you do."

" Nobly answered ! Miss Greyson is quite my champion. I say constancy is quite irresistible."

At the mention of this well-remembered word

Marion felt the blushes in her cheeks mount nearly to her temples; but fortunately she could still seem occupied with her daisies, and, stooping over them, allowed her long hair to droop forward and help to conceal her face.

"Don't you think it is, Miss Paton?" inquired Allerton.

"O, of course," answered Dora, playfully.

"And you, Miss Greyson?"

"Nearly," replied Marion.

"Not quite? Oh, do believe it quite irresistible. Mrs. White, Maidley, Dreux,—do plead with my champion, she is going back; she won't agree with me after all. Really it is very hard."

"How can I tell whether it is irresistible?" said Marion, rallying, and looking up. "I never put it to the proof. I do not speak from experience, only from hearsay."

"Oh, indeed; she only speaks from hearsay."

"I am sure," said little Joseph, "nobody would ever think—er—of—au—being inconstant to Miss Greyson."

"Why not?" asked Allerton, turning suddenly upon him.

"O—why, because Miss Greyson, you know, is —au—you know she is—au—so very charming."

"Indeed!" said Allerton, with humorous gravity; "being a married man, I, of course, know nothing about *that*,—at least, only by hearsay."

"Will you let my cousin alone, Mr. Allerton?"

said Dora. " I really think you treat your champion very ill."

" Very ill?—how can you say so, Miss Paton? But I quite agree with Mr. Norland, that no one will ever be inconstant to Miss Greyson."

" How do you know anything about that?" asked Wilfred, rather testily.

" My opinion is founded upon a theory which I have, and on my own experience. I believe there is no such thing as inconstancy."

" A very convenient theory, and quite new."

" Newly invented, I assure you. I argue thus: If any man leaves off what he called *loving* while it lasted, that's a proof that he never did truly *love*; for I put it in my creed, that ' love is love for evermore.' "

" You say so seriously, Mr. Allerton!" exclaimed Mrs. White. " Well, you are the most romantic person I ever met with."

" Romantic! Not at all. I said, if a man *truly* loved."

" Oh, but that comes to nothing; for, if we ask you what *truly* means, you will say it means as long as he lives."

" I will have nothing more to do with the question; you all make game of my principles, and refuse to hear my explanations."

" If you had said, ' what a man has *truly* loved he cannot *easily* forget ' "—

" But I did not. I said, what a man has truly

loved,—be it man, woman, or child,—he cannot possibly forget. Of course I can only speak from my own experience; I care nothing about hearsay in these matters."

" Oh, we do not deny that it is true in your own individual case."

" Will any of you admit that it is *not* true in his or her individual case?"

" Of course not; but that proves nothing."

" Dreux, you really might back me when you see me so beset. Consider, you are the first person that I heard propound this theory, and I at once became a convert."

" My dear Allerton, if you are in the right, you want no backing."

" But am I in the right?"

" Of course you are."

" Gentlemen and ladies, behold my champion. I will have nothing more to do with Miss Greyson; she won't go far enough for me. I'm proud of you, Dreux."

" Oh, Mr. Allerton!—what, be inconstant to Miss Greyson, in the face of your theory?"

" The very best of men, Miss Paton, have their inconsistencies."

" I don't know about forgetting," said little Joseph, looking very sage; "when Lion, my dog, died, I was very sorry at first—very sorry,—he had such a beautiful mane; but when I got Quiz instead, I forgot him—au—at least, in a measure."

This would have been a capital opening for Allerton if he had wanted one, but he was satisfied with the point to which he had brought the conversation, and did not care to pursue it farther; and at that moment Mrs. White, observing that several forlorn-looking acquaintances of hers were hovering about near the hay, not liking to sit down for fear of intruding, and not quite well-bred enough to feel at ease, advanced towards them and began to talk. Dora and Marion presently seconded her; the latter was delighted at the breaking up of the conference, and found the greatest relief in amusing a countrified young lady,—a farmer's daughter, and her brother, a very awkward, bashful lad.

Dreux, scarcely knowing whether he was pleased or teazed at the way Allerton had drawn him out, wandered away with Dora, Greyson, and Maidley into the long vicarage garden, Frank Maidley of course occupying the attention of Dora; it was getting rather dusk, and he contrived after a while to withdraw her from the others, and induce her to walk apart with him.

Dreux and Greyson, both lost in thought, sauntered side by side along the walks in silent companionship. At length Greyson fell back, and betook himself to the house, which by this time was lighted up.

Dreux had been leaning some time against an arbour, revolving various matters in his mind, when, looking up, he saw Allerton advancing towards him.

" My dear fellow," said Allerton, " Mrs. White sent me to call you to supper. (I abominate country suppers.) Don't you know, Dreux, that you can be distinctly seen from the house? What are you doing, mooning among these gooseberry-bushes?"

" Doing? oh, nothing particular."

" What are you thinking of, then? Do you expect to stand gazing at a cucumber-frame and some old broken handglasses without exciting observation? That sarcastic little Mrs. White has been proposing to have you whitewashed, and stuck up by the fountain as a statue of Apollo."

" She is very obliging. So you offered to come and tell me?"

" The very first time that I have known you give me a testy answer. No, I whispered mysteriously that you were wrangler in 18—. 'Ah, that accounts for his absence,' she answered gravely; 'he is lost in mathematics at this moment, no doubt!' Come in, Dreux, there are whole piles of tarts and cheesecakes, and quantities of orange wine and gooseberry fool."

" I have no objection to come. How is Elinor?"

" This is the first time you have mentioned her; Oh, Dreux, Dreux, I am afraid you are very far gone; Elinor sent her love, and I brought mine with me, and my eyes also."

" Indeed!"

" Yes, I have discovered that you are desperately in love ;—poor fellow !"

" I wish you would not banter me so."

" You wish no such thing; you are extremely glad I found it out, for you would have wanted to tell me, you know; and you would have undergone agonies of blushing (if your complexion had been capable of it), before you could have managed it. Dreux, will you take your back from that arbour ?"

" There, it is done."

" Be a little more brisk, then, and don't sigh. You will understand that it is a most disinterested thing on my part to bring you in, for I was very pleasantly engaged in conversation with Miss Greyson. I always had a weakness in favour of those very lady-like beings ; and now I am married, of course I may talk to whomsoever I will."

" What have you been talking about ?"

" Why, my dear fellow, how can that possibly concern *you?*"

" It does concern me very much; I am afraid you don't know, Allerton, that Miss Greyson some time ago"—

" I know it all, Dreux ; but that was a long time ago, and I have made her confess, as you heard, that constancy is NEARLY irresistible."

" So it may be in the abstract."

" Abstract ! You are overrun, and almost choked, with the weed of ' a most pernicious modesty.' Oh that I should live to hear abstractions applied to a love affair! Look at the matter hopefully (and don't tread upon Mrs. White's lavender); never was there such a fortunate man as you are, if you choose to think so. That old gentleman, Mr. Raeburn, carefully shuts one eye on your proceedings, and won't see anything with the other, a certain proof that he approves."

" He knows nothing about it."

" Then your uncle sent for you here on purpose that you might prosecute it, for anything you know to the contrary."

" *He* knows nothing about it either."

" And these two things being fully proved, my dear fellow, I congratulate you heartily. If I were you, I should think myself the happiest of men."

" Really, Allerton!"

" Really, Allerton! Why, Dreux, if I were you, if no one had objected, and if I loved a lady, *and she loved me*"—

" And she loved *me*."

" If you speak so loud, they will assuredly hear you inside—we are close to the window. Come in this moment. I won't be pulled away; come in, I say, they can see us distinctly: eat a good supper, and every time you see my eye upon you, take wine with somebody; and mind you hand Miss Greyson into her carriage, and talk nonsense to her all the way home. Do you hear, Dreux?"

" Yes."

"You look quite dazed. Have you two humps on your back, and a double squint in each eye, besides a perfectly empty pate, that you cannot possibly believe any one can fancy you? Come in this instant. Here's Mrs. White coming out to hear you talk unintelligible mathematics!"

CHAPTER XXVIII.

MARION AND DREUX.

It was midnight, and Allerton, left quite alone, was pacing the library at Norland Court. He was deep in cogitation, and that of the most earnest kind. He had again interfered in Dreux's affairs,— had perceived the state of his feelings,—from a few blushes, had jumped at the conclusion that Marion was not indifferent to him,—and had suffered his desire to forward Dreux's cause so completely to get the better of his often-expressed determination never to meddle again, that he had urged him on to offer his hand once more, had put all sorts of hopes into his mind, which might turn out to be mere chimeras, and had made light of the Colonel's interference, which might, after all, prevent any good ensuing, even if all other things went smoothly.

He had ridden to Swanstead on Dreux's horse, which had been lent him by the Colonel. A groom accompanied him to show the way, but, by a dexterous artifice, he got little Joseph to mount Dreux's horse on their return, rode the other himself, leaving

the man to cross the fields on foot, and apologized
to Dreux for leaving him behind at the Rectory-
door, to make his way home when he chose. He
heard Mr. Raeburn ask him to come in; he saw
the Rectory-door shut upon him; and it was not
till left alone at Norland that he began to reflect
what might be the consequences of what he had
done.

Before midnight Joseph retired, and Allerton
having said that he chose to sit up and let Dreux
in, the household retired to bed, and the house was
presently quite still.

He wondered what could make Dreux so late.
It was scarcely ten when they parted at Swanstead; he could not surely have stayed there long.

Allerton pushed down the window-sash, and listened. Swanstead Church struck half-past twelve.
It was a very sultry night, not a breath was
stirring, but the broad moonlight made the birds
restless. He withdrew his head from the window,
and paced backward and forward in the lamplight
within. His imagination was excited; he pictured
to himself Dreux coming home sick at heart from
the sudden throwing down of the high hopes that
he himself had given him.

Another quarter struck. The servants, before
they retired, had brought in a light repast and set
it on the table. Allerton, restless and uneasy,
busied himself in trimming the lamp, setting a
chair, and looking out for the expected occupant.

He thought he heard a slight noise,—a footstep in one of the distant walks. Again,—and presently Dreux emerged into the moonlight, and Allerton strained his attention to discover whether anything decisive had happened, either for good or evil.

He was sauntering so slowly, that while still at a distance, there was ample time for watching him. Now he stopped, as if deep in thought; then he half turned again towards Swanstead; then he came up to a clump of white rose-trees, and gave them an idle push with his foot, apparently to see how many of their thick white petals would fall. He drew nearer: there was no mistaking the musing smile, nor the look of complete abstraction. Certainly nothing had happened to dash his hopes; but whether he had any good reason for them, or whether he was merely pleasing himself with the dreams that Allerton had steeped him in, was another matter.

He set his foot upon the threshold, and Allerton opened the window: neither spoke. Dreux had not half recovered from his musing fit: seeing the chair, he went forward, took off his hat, and sat down mechanically. Allerton put some grapes on his plate and some biscuits, gave him a fruit-knife and a glass of wine. His abstraction was so complete that he never observed Allerton's watchful scrutiny, but ate and drank till his plate was empty.

Allerton shut the window. Swanstead Church struck one. He did not choose to ask any questions, nor even to remind Dreux how late it was. He thought he would let him dream out his reverie of happiness, whether it was reasonable or unreasonable.

At length he roused himself, and went and stretched himself full-length on a couch, his favourite attitude for a colloquy. Allerton, as usual, paced the room. Dreux at length said to him,—

" Why don't you question me ? If you think I can tell you anything without that, you are mistaken."

" Well, my first question shall be, Have you anything to tell,—anything decisive ?"

" Yes ; but, Allerton, something has just occurred to me that your strange revelations put till now out of my head,—Can a man marry with twenty pounds or so in his pocket, and a hundred a-year in prospect ?"

" My dear fellow, I am afraid we ought both to have thought of that before."

" You seem quite out of spirits ?"

" I am vexed with myself for having led you on so far."

" Never repent of a good action, Allerton. I shall not let pride stand in my way. Poor as I am, I shall certainly go and ask Mr. Raeburn for his ward."

" And if he should refuse you ?"

" Why, then I shall still be ten times better off than before."

" How so, Dreux ?   Have you secured the lady's consent ?"

" Yes ; and therefore I shall always have hope, that if there is any change in my prospects, I may yet claim her hand."

" And Colonel Norland ?"

" No chance of anything from him,—he tells me so daily.   Oh, that reminds me ;—why did he send for you ?"

" He only knows.   I would not have come if I had not wanted to get you back with me, for Elinor thought you wrote as if you were in low spirits."

" I am heartily glad you came ;—you are my good genius."

" Dreux, you continually forget.   You say things which cut me to the heart.   Your good genius !"

" Are you never to be thanked for any kindness, because I must for ever be brooding over that one unkindness ?"

" Well, as I said before, I don't know what the Colonel wanted with me unless to inform me that I need not suppose my wife would inherit anything from him.   I told him I did not expect it.   ' Not when you married her ?' he inquired.   I thought it was no good mincing the matter, so I told him roundly, that when I married her I was not aware of his existence !

" He did not disbelieve me, but was evidently so astonished that I asked whether he thought it likely that lovers in general talked about their old uncles. He said he had no doubt it was, when they expected anything from them. ' Then,' I said, ' you may take the silence of Dreux and Elinor as a sign that they do not, or did not expect anything from you.' He seemed quite amazed at my cool assurance, and declared that I was worse than you. ' Why, as to that, Colonel,' I said, ' no amount of cringing would make you leave any part of your property to Dreux and Elinor if you did not wish to do so, or consider it a duty ; and if you do, my plain-speaking will not prevent it, so you need not suppose that I think I am doing myself any harm,—on the contrary, nothing would make you suspect me so much as my setting to work to flatter you, so I hope that point's settled.'

" The old fellow laughed excessively at this, with a sort of chuckling pleasure. ' And now,' I said, ' I should like to know, Colonel, what you sent for me for ?'

" ' What does that matter to you, Sir ? Perhaps I sent for you to keep company with Arthur, for that fool Joseph nearly mopes him to death ; he is much thinner than when he came. Would you like a living in this neighbourhood ?'

" ' Would I ?' I exclaimed, quite surprised ; 'that depends on circumstances.'

" ' Because,' he continued, ' White has had a better living offered him in Yorkshire, and has written to me to say so. It's to be kept secret for a few days.'"

"You surprise me, Allerton; I wonder he did not mention it to me."

"So I said to him. 'I've got a living,' I said, 'and though I wish to leave it as soon as I can, because my parishioners dislike me, you are not the man that should offer me another in preference to your own nephew.'"

"Take it, Allerton; Elinor is as near to him as I am. It is a large parish,—plenty of opportunity for usefulness."

"I shall see, first, if he will not offer it to you, upon proper persuasion. Why, Dreux, it would enable you to marry at once."

"He will never alter his mind. He has had time enough to consider whether I should have it, and has decided against it. Take it, then, and I will be your curate."

"That you may be near Miss Greyson. Well, we will discuss that to-morrow."

"What else did he say?"

"That you were gone to Swanstead, and that, if I liked to take your horse, I could follow you. When I got to Swanstead, I found you had gone on to Wickley, the very place he had spoken of. Do you think Elinor would like the change?"

"Very much indeed."

"Well, you know the rest, and positively I will not say another word till to-morrow."

"I would not have, you build too much on this living; very likely he will alter his mind."

"I thought it was more like banter than anything else when he offered it me."

So saying, they separated for the night, and a very sultry night it was, so much so that the Colonel could not sleep, but, being very much better of his gout, lay at tolerable ease, thinking what he should decide to do for each of his nephews and his niece's husband, and quite convinced that he held the fate, fortune, and happiness of all in his own power.

The morning came. Joseph woke, and began to think about Marion in her blue silk dress and white bonnet. He felt himself always much more attracted by womankind when it appeared in holiday garb. Allerton woke, wished he had let Dreux's affairs alone, and wished he had brought Elinor with him. Dreux awoke, and remembered that Mr. Raeburn had invited him to come over and breakfast at Swanstead. "Invited" is not the proper word. He had said no more than "I shall be happy to see you here to breakfast, Sir," but the tone and his gravity seemed to add, "and I desire that you will not fail to come." He thought the old gentleman seemed out of spirits, and perhaps a little testy, but his manner was as fond as usual when he turned to Marion, drew her arm under his, and led her away into the house.

To Swanstead, therefore, Dreux walked. It was already very hot, though the clock had not struck

eight; and as he went through a shady lane leading
to Mr. Raeburn's house, he took off his hat and
gloves, and lingered, for he was afraid of being too
early.   Hope and joy had altered him so much
already that he had never looked better.   So Mr.
Raeburn thought when at a sudden turn he met
him.   But few fathers and guardians were ever
induced to favour a suitor for his good looks, and
few men care for the impression their appearance
may produce on one another.   If Dreux had been
told to guess what the taciturn old Rector was
thinking of, his own eyes and complexion would
have been the last things he would have hit upon as
likely to occupy his attention.   Yet so it was; the
old man was tracing a likeness, real or imaginary,
between him and the lost Euphemia, and wondering,
if his son had lived, whether he would have been
anything like this.   They walked together to the
house.   Marion met them on the steps.   Nothing
could well be more quiet than the breakfast; the
viands and the weather supplied all the little conversation.   Dreux felt very anxious; there was a
calm depression about the Rector, from which he
augured no good.   Having finished his breakfast,
he rang for family prayers, and when they were
over, withdrew to his study and shut the door.

" And now," thought Dreux, "has he really observed anything, and if so, does he mean to summon
me to an interview, or must I go to seek him?"

He stood irresolute.   Marion had watched her

opportunity, and had glided out of the room; the fat old footman continued to clear away the breakfast things. Dreux watched him, for want of something better to do. When he had smoothed the cloth, he brought Marion's work-basket and set it thereupon, as coolly as if it had been a common piece of wicker-work; and that done, he brought her pretty little desk, her key-basket, and her white bouquet, still blooming, in water, and deposited them beside it, like common, vulgar things !

Marion did not return. She had told him the night before that he must speak to her uncle, so after waiting some time for a summons, he at length crossed the hall, and knocked at the study door.

Mr. Raeburn opened it himself; he seemed neither surprised nor expectant; he had a newspaper in his hand, he gave another to Dreux, and they both sat down.

Mr. Raeburn hated regular discussion and scenes of all sorts; he knew perfectly well what his guest had come about, but it was not his business to help him with it, so he continued looking down the advertisements in the paper, with the slightest possible smile lurking about his mouth. He was rather pleased than otherwise to observe the desperate state of fidget into which Dreux had worked himself; it was, at least, a proof that his consent was considered necessary.

"Well, Sir?" he said, looking up pleasantly from his paper.

Dreux had folded his arms for the encounter; he evidently expected something formidable, some surprise at his communication, perhaps a hint at presumption. Positively he had nerved himself for war, and his face was grave, almost to sternness, as he said,—

"I believe, Mr. Raeburn, you are aware that I have lost my property?"

Mr. Raeburn was quite aware of the fact, but his look of surprise was genuine; this was evidently not exactly how he had expected the conversation to begin.

"But perhaps you are not aware that I have nothing to expect from my uncle, Colonel Norland. I have, however, always taken pains to make it known that I am not likely to inherit any part of his property; my uncle has also proclaimed it constantly."

"He has, Sir,—something about a fish-pond, wasn't it? I've heard that story till I'm sick of it."

The young man heaved a mighty sigh; the old one looked out of the window. There was Marion, sauntering slowly down the garden; she was dressed in a transparent muslin gown, and had thrown a white shawl about her.

"That young lady, Mr. Dreux, is my adopted child,—my daughter; her dutiful affection constitutes about all the happiness of my life. I think it would break my heart to have to part from her."

This was absolutely the first word that was said about Marion, the whole thing was taken for granted. Instead of an elaborate explanation, a formal request, he was shown at once that the object of his visit was known.

"Do you think, then," answered Dreux, "that the ties formed by choice are less enduring and less binding than those of nature? Is your daughter more likely to forget than another man's child?"

"I cannot tell, Mr. Dreux; the bond that held my own children to me was snapped by death in such a very little while; but this, my adopted child, makes up to me for the loss of one.

"And would scarcely care, I think, to hear of any proposal which should involve her leaving you."

Mr. Raeburn had taken up a small brown parasol; his countenance cleared as he listened.

Dreux continued: "And, if I were pleading the cause of some other man, I might urge, though now I can but remind you, that to marry a daughter is not always to lose her; sometimes it is to gain a son."

Mr. Raeburn opened the window: "I see Marion has nearly got to the meadow," he said; "very careless of her to go out without this parasol. Here, Sir, you may take it after her."

His auditor started up, but checked himself almost instantly. It was impossible he could have been understood,—impossible that this could be all; it was as good as a consent to his proceedings. With his hand still extended for the parasol, he looked intently at the arbiter of his fate.

"Did you wish to shake hands first?" said the Rector, with an easy smile. "Well, I have no objection."

"Bless the boy, what a gripe" (every man under thirty was a boy in the Rector's opinion.) "Ah! dashing across the lawn, clearing the flower-beds; good thing Marion did not see him spring over those new fuschias of hers. Ah! (gives her the parasol)—well, he's a fine young fellow. I'll make 'em live with me; I want a curate. What, you want her to go into the meadows, do you?—and sit upon that hay under the hedge, I'll be bound. Ah! your hand on the gate-latch. What next—a book? I think it's a book. You are not going to read to her,—don't tell me! You can talk without a book, or you would never have talked that ring on to your finger. Will she go in?—makes a little difficulty about it—Yes. Then I look upon the matter as settled."

Marion was seated on a kind of flat hay *dais*. Dreux, in a convenient position for looking at her, proposed to read, and occupied a long time in finding a poem to his mind; he did at last, and read a few verses, then broke off.

"Marion—may I call you Marion?"

" I shall certainly not give you leave, Mr. Dreux."

" I think I must venture. Marion, don't you think this is a very uninteresting poem ? "

Marion laughed softly. " Perhaps, if it had been better read, Mr. Dreux "—

" But I cannot read and look at you at the same time."

" Were you obliged to look at me ? "

" Yes ; I wanted to see what kind of work this was that you were doing."

" This ? It is called crochet."

" Oh, I see ; it goes over and over, first a twirl and then a twitch, till, by degrees, it comes into a piece of lace,—how very uninteresting this book is."

" I did not propose to you to read, Mr. Dreux."

" No ; but I have heard you say, that you have no conversational powers, and, as I have none either "—

" You have none either ? "

" None at all. Do answer me one question, my sweet Marion."

" I must hear what it is before I promise ; besides, I want to go on with my work. I cannot talk at all unless I have something to do."

" Cannot you crochet with one hand ?—why did you laugh ? "

" You are so absurd, Mr. Dreux ; and you looked at me so very, very earnestly."

" Because I am so afraid you will get tired of me, —I am certain of it. You only pity me ; you begin to think it must give great pain to love as I have done for so long; so, in the gentleness of your nature, you——Marion, let me hold your hand a little longer. You do not know how many thousand times, between sleeping and waking, I have fancied I felt it again touching my hair and moving it back from my forehead. Will you answer my question?"

"Perhaps."

" On that day when you were sealing those notes (I hated the smell of sealing-wax ever after), was it the stupid way in which I made my offer which induced you to reject it? I know, of course, that I had made no impression; but, if I had managed matters better, would you have wished me to continue to visit you?"

Marion was silent.

" I dare say you thought me an excessively proud, conceited, confident fellow?"

"You exaggerate so very much what I thought, that I can deny it. I did not think so; but whatever I thought must no doubt have been a mistake, since I have changed my mind."

" I know many people think so, for no better reason than that I have a grave face and walk upright."

He spoke with such bitter regret, that Marion saw it was still a sore subject, and answered with sweet gentleness, "We need not mind what they think, as we are not of their opinion."

"But you thought me proud, proud even to you; and there was nothing I would not have given to have been freed from that torturing sensation of reserve and shyness, which binds me round like an iron chain, stiffens all my movements, both of mind and body, and makes my very voice cold enough to chill any one."

Marion looked at him quite surprised. He was thinking only how to explain himself. She was studying the character of her future husband, and unconsciously learning how to establish her empire over him.

"But if you had been very eloquent just then, Mr. Dreux"—

"You would not have consented; but if that unconquerable reserve would have left me for a moment, that I might have explained my feelings, I might have made a pleasanter impression; but the idea that you thought I considered myself sure of success, and despised me"—

"I never despised you, Mr. Dreux; how much you mistake!"

"I despised myself, as I then appeared. I constantly do; but I had an unreasonable fancy that you could understand me, in spite of the heavy cloak of involuntary concealment and reserve in which I was shrouded. You looked at me once or twice so differently to the looks of other people. I get plenty of respect, a great deal more than I like, and people talk gravely and sensibly with me because I am grave; but no warmth for years came near me, my distant manner flung off all familiarity."

"I did not think you cold when once I had seen you smile. I thought that you had the power to feel deep affection. I thought I saw something else, which I now am sure of."

"May I know what it was?"

"That you were very sensitive; but I kept my discovery to myself. Scarcely any one would have believed that you possessed what you were at so much pains to conceal."

"I cannot help taking those pains; it is a part of my nature to hide all those qualities which I yet feel hurt, when I find that people give me credit for being destitute of. I know my manner is icy; and yet all my life I have been tormented with a more than ordinary desire to be loved. I have coveted affection with constant pertinacity, and yet I am absolutely without the power to attract it. My sister has always been fond of me, but even to her I have the greatest difficulty in speaking confidentially. There is but one man living who has cared for me well enough to break down my reserve and become my friend. How grateful I am to him I cannot describe, nor what degree of affection I feel for him. With him I enjoyed the luxury of free communication, literally for the first time."

"Is not this a confidential communication, Mr. Dreux?"

" Yes; and on reflection I find it is all about myself."

" I wish you would continue it. Do you know I perceive that you are very different from what I thought; not so much from what you have said, as because you have looked so different while you said it. You are not so independent as I thought."

" Independent!"

" Yes. I thought after you were gone last night (I did not repent, but still I thought it), that you would often be lofty and unapproachable; that I should sometimes be in your way with my sympathies, and my petting, and my observation of all your moods and changes; for I cannot help watching everything that I consider my own."

" Did you really think so of me? How very strange!"

" You will please to understand, that unless I had been sagacious, I should have thought so still. I thought even with people whom you most loved, you would prove unbending, not looking for, or needing, or liking any affectionate nonsense, any caressing, or petting. In fact, I had quite made up my mind that I must alter my natural manner a good deal; but I little thought that this very day I should tell you so."

" But tell me the rest; tell me what you do think."

" Oh, you will be very covetous of my attention, very exacting—a very tiresome man indeed!"

"No, indeed, I shall be a pattern—the most attentive, the most devoted."

"If you talk and protest like a man in a book, I shall know you are only inventing it, particularly if you laugh. You ought to be grave, and vow in good earnest."

"Who would have thought of my being reproved for not being grave enough? But I thought you were going to draw my character. You have told me what I am not. I want to know what I am."

"Oh, I have discovered that you are the reverse of everything that I have described. You are just as dependent as other people. And, as you have laid open your inmost feelings to me, partly of your own accord, and partly because I have found them out, your reserve cannot be quite unconquerable, Mr. Dreux."

"Not with you. Marion, it is almost impossible for me to believe that you really take an interest in me. I have been so signally unsuccessful hitherto in getting any one to care for me, that the idea of *your* caring, you—it really is past belief—taking the trouble, too, to find out my character and understand me"—

"And pity you, as you said before; yes, and rally you. Does Mr. Allerton ever do that?"

"Very often."

"I am very much afraid of him; he seemed yesterday to be reading my inmost thoughts."

" I shall tell him not to alarm you in future with his penetration.".

" You can tell him, too, that he was entirely mistaken in some of his conjectures, some of his thoughts which he did not mention, but which I know he did think."

" What were they ?"

" Ah, that is another question ; but I should not be at all surprised if he communicated some of them to you. What did he say to you, Mr. Dreux, when Mrs. White made him fetch you in to supper ?"

" Marion, do you really care for me ?"

" Instead of answering my question, you ask me another. I think you had better go on with the reading."

" But I want to know whether you care for me."

" Havn't I taken the trouble to understand you ? and havn't I let you interrupt my work a great many times ? Look what a little piece I have done ; but, Mr. Dreux, what a very little time you were with my uncle !"

" Yes, he cut me short just as I was beginning what I had to say."

" Indeed ! But I said "—

" That his consent was quite indispensable."

" Then, Mr. Dreux, you must leave me, and go to him and explain more particularly."

" Don't be displeased ; it is a very unaccountable thing ; but he did virtually give his consent. He

pointed you out to me in the garden, and sent me
to you himself; and he shook hands with me. He
hinted that it would be a great pain to him to have
to part with you."

Marion's eyes filled with tears.

" My hopes had been too sudden and overwhelming to be very defined, but I intimated that I
should never dream of such a thing as trying to persuade you to leave him, and involuntarily I sprung
at once to my hoped-for conclusion. My own
Marion, you thought me proud when I really was
diffident and humble, now you think me less so
when I have proved myself the most presumptuous
fellow possible! How I could have the face to do
it I cannot think: and he actually never asked me
one single question."

" Then you will never ask me to leave this
place?"

" O no, never. I mean to ask him to-night if he
will have me for a curate. At least if you think
that my having the opportunity to see you so often
would not weary you of me."

" You seem still to suppose that I do not know
my own mind."

" No, indeed; but at least it was a sudden change
in my favour. It *may* have been founded on some
momentary thing that I said or did, which, when
you know me better, you may find is not habitual
with me. It might even have been, perhaps, that
yesterday the wind blew the hair back from that

little mark on my forehead, and when you remembered the kindness and thought you had bestowed upon me when I lay between life and death, you could not bear to see my mental suffering on your account."

" You are a most incredulous man, and certainly not conceited, therefore I will tell you that this change of mine was not a sudden change."

" If you would tell me what cause it had for beginning, and when it began."

" It began some time ago."

" The last time I came here ? "

" No."

" When you first gave me this ring ? "

" No."

" You will not refuse to tell me ? "

" Certainly not ; but unless you had been exactly the kind of man that you are, I would have taken pains to conceal it, lest it should make you what you just now called yourself."

" What was that, Marion ? "

" Presumptuous."

" Is it something, then, that I shall be so very much delighted to hear ? "

" I suppose so, since you wish so much to be loved."

" Tell it me, then ; I will not be presumptuous— not more presumptuous than I am at present."

" And you will not tell Mr. Allerton ? "

" No, certainly not. How much he would be

amused at your fear of him! Tell me, Marion; I should like to have a secret confided to me—something known only to you and to myself."

"When you came and offered me your hand I certainly felt flattered, though when I looked up I saw a man who had not taken much pains to please me, whom I had been taught to think somewhat, however little, spoiled by the—I must call it—*absurd* flattery which had been heaped upon him in his clerical character. I saw, as I thought, a man to whom my refusal could be of but little moment, who wanted nothing, not even affection, to lean upon, and lean towards, and who could stand best alone.

"But the next day I saw him helpless and nearly insensible on a couch, left quite without any supporter or comforter: the lines of the face were so changed, the voice was so different, I began to think that I *might* have been something even to him—that no one was so able to be alone, and to stand alone, as he had seemed to be. When I lifted up his hand and moved it away from his forehead, it pained me to think that I gave him involuntary uneasiness, and that I might never hear him speak again. But he did speak,—he uttered *my* name. Then, as I bent over him, half unconscious as he was, I began to feel affection for him. Never since has he appeared to me the same man whom I knew so imperfectly before.

"I watched and watched. His face was never

the same three minutes at a time. I saw all the
helplessness, forlornness, dependence—for an instant I saw all the tenderness that a human face is
capable of expressing. Are you satisfied now, Mr.
Dreux ? "

This was asked in the sweetest of modest femi-
nine tones, and seemed to say that the speaker was
quite above trifling for a moment with the feelings
of any man, least of all with the one before her.
The reply was given with heartfelt earnestness, and
a smile most suddenly sweet—" Quite, far more
than satisfied ; and all this, but for Allerton's
upbraidings of my faint heart, I never should have
known."

" Most assuredly not. But, Mr. Dreux, let me
go on with my work ; it must be nearly lunch time,
and I have done only half an inch of pattern."

" Is this the table of directions in this little open
book ? Ah ! I see. For collar, for child's jacket,
for lace, crown-pattern ; do., rose-pattern. What
strange jargon it is ; I cannot make sense of it."

" But I can make lace of it ; and if you wish to
read I should prefer the other book."

" I don't wish to do anything but sit here. This
is the most delightful day I have ever been out in—
the most delightful sky I ever sat under. I am
certain I never saw such a hawthorn hedge before,
and I never saw such a smile before,—it must have
been meant for me."

And so, in spite of reserve and the want of conversational powers, they continued to talk for more than an hour, during which time they said nearly as much as would have filled a volume.

"To marry a daughter is not always to lose her; sometimes it is to gain a son."

Dreux had spent a long day at Swanstead, and was walking home in the moonlight, when these words, which he had said in a moment of excitement, returned to his recollection, and considerably tempered his happiness.

A man, of whom he knew but little, had, in consequence of these few words,—said with no knowledge of how important they would prove,—implied in the morning, and promised at night, that he would give him his adopted child—no light gift in the eyes of either giver or receiver. Worldly advantages, as it so chanced, were to come with her; and for all this the vague and unsubstantial equivalent that he had held out was that he would be a son to him.

He began to be alarmed. How could he be a son to this old gentleman! He thought him agreeable, and his peculiarities were just such as to make him feel particularly at ease in his company. He was just the man he could have fixed on for his Rector or his father-in-law; but something different had been meant and understood by that speech of the morning. He saw that it had won him his wife, and made him an object of inexpressible interest to her singular guardian; and he began to feel that if he had been bidden, like Naaman the Syrian, to do "some great thing," it would not have oppressed him half so much as the thought of failing in this sonship, for it was a peculiar relation, and he scarcely thought he could take it upon him with much credit or success. At midnight he reached the library window, and, as before, it was opened by Allerton.

"Well," said this fast friend, "all goes on well, I see. Joseph is gone to bed in a fit of the sulks. Miss Greyson has much to answer for,—that blue gown of hers has half distracted him!"

"What have you been doing with yourself all day?" said Dreux, with a smile.

"Doing? Why, I have been back by express to Westport, and it is not an hour since I returned."

"To Westport! What for?"

Allerton laughed, and, pointing upward to the ceiling, said, "Listen."

A very light footstep was passing softly about in the room overhead. "Why, you don't mean to say you have fetched Elinor," exclaimed Dreux, incredulously.

"Even so. She is tired, so she went up stairs, and left her love to you. I thought I should like her to see Wickley, for your uncle renewed his offer this morning, and I closed with it, on condition that she liked the place."

"I am glad you brought her. Is there any Westport news?"

"Yes; Mrs. Fred Bishop has a son and heir. Her father is nearly out of his wits with joy,—sons are so scarce in his family. And your old flame, Mrs. Dorothy Silverstone, is going to be married."

"Nonsense!"

"There's what I get for telling you unwelcome news! I tell you it is not nonsense; I heard it from two or three people. Why, Dreux, do you want two strings to your bow? It is much more for the happiness of your intended that she should be without a rival."

"Mrs. Dorothy Silverstone! Pooh!—it is a mistake."

"It is either she or some other old woman; ask Elinor. But no, I am certain I am right. And now open your eyes wide. Who do you think is to be the happy bridegroom?"

"Why, if one thing would be more ridiculous than another, it would be her marrying Athanasius."

"Your prescience must have aided you in linking their names; he is the very man."

"Allerton, I am sure you're making game of me."

"No such thing. I tell you she is going to marry Athanasius, and go out with him as a missionary. Don't look at me in that way. Can I help it if people will make fools of themselves?"

"Why, she is old enough to be his mother."

"To be sure she is. I wonder whether she or his true mother will be called old Mrs. Brown. Come in, Dreux; let us eat some grapes, and talk it over."

" Has my uncle seen Elinor ? "

" Yes, he sat up till she arrived, and gave her a warm welcome. Afterwards he rather seemed to take it ill that she was not so handsome as he had expected. I understand he was in a towering rage this morning."

"Indeed; but he is nearly every day."

" So I suppose. You were the subject of his passion, for during the morning Mr. Raeburn called on him, and told him you had proposed for his ward, and he had authorized you to prosecute your suit. Joseph told me all this, and very cross he is about it, poor little fellow ! I understand the Colonel told Mr. Raeburn he wondered he should want to secure a penniless man for his ward. Raeburn answered that he cared for position, family, and character much, and for fortune not at all, as he would take care about that,—it should come on the lady's side. And he distinctly declared that he was mainly induced by the fact that you were disinherited to favour your suit, because a man with an estate would take his wife away to live upon it, but you, having none, would be willing to live with him. ' And do you mean to say,' cried the old fellow, in such a passion that he stuttered and almost screamed,—'do you presume to say that I am obliged to disinherit my nephew just because *you* desire it? Am I to lay myself under an obligation to *you*, and let YOU enrich my family?' ' I understand,' Mr. Raeburn replied; 'your changing your mind in that matter,

Colonel, is of course within your power; it will not at all affect my interests, as I have a distinct understanding that Mr. Dreux is to live with me; therefore, as he will be so near, you can easily settle any business matters with him; I have nothing to do with them.'   Cool, wasn't it?"

"Very; and no doubt the whole object of the call was to let my uncle know that, heir or no heir, he need not expect to have any claim upon me, since he had clearly disavowed it.   Well, it is something new and strange to have people contending about one in this way,—rather flattering, too."

"Yes, and the old gentleman spoke very handsomely of you to the Colonel.   What a strange man he seems to be!   His wife has been dead a very short time, and they say he has been in better spirits since than for years."

"I do not think that singular, as she had been deranged from her youth.   Miss Greyson tells me he would not allow her to put on mourning for the poor lady.   Miss Greyson, Allerton, has a great idea of your penetration."

"I have given her cause."

"What cause?"

"If she likes to tell you, I have no objection; but I could not think of betraying a lady's confidence."

"Why not?—you continually betray mine! Whenever I tell you any secret, I shortly afterwards find Elinor in possession of it.   Come, will you tell me what cause you have given Miss Greyson?"

" Will you have another bunch of grapes, Dreux? I'll tell you nothing more. Things are come to a pretty pass if I am to be cross-questioned by you! Mrs. Dorothy Silverstone is attached to Athanasius Brown;—I told you that, didn't I? Quite enough news for one night. If you want to know who Miss Greyson is attached to, ask her yourself."

Whether he did ask her has not transpired, but Mr. Brown soon settled the other point, by marrying a Miss Dorothy Silverstone certainly,—not the old lady, but her niece. And this he did to the great contentment of his mother, who, not knowing much about the Levant, had privately dreaded lest her son should marry " one of the Blacks who inhabit those parts."

CHAPTER XXIX.

THE IVYED CASEMENT.

"Welcome the coming, speed the parting guest,"
is the saying of old Homer. The same thing may
be said of a book,—the glimpses it affords of human
life and feeling are often welcome; but its actors
must not be suffered to linger too long when
they are ready to depart. Take, however, one
or two more glances at them, reader, if you
will, ere they retire to the place from whence
they came.

Marion has returned from her bridal tour. She
has been anxious as to how her husband will fulfil
the duties evidently expected of him; now she is
quite át her ease, and as she sits by the window
in the morning-room, smiles to think, that though
she keeps her old place in her guardian's heart,
some one else has unconsciously stepped into a
higher one. "How well they get on together,"
she thinks. "How fond my uncle is of Arthur,
and yet what contrary beings they are! There
must be some curious affinities between them which

make it impossible for them ever to be in one another's way."

Marion knew that when she was in a mood to sing, the Rector would partially open his door, that he might listen as he sat reading and writing. If she and Elinor were laughing and talking together, he would furtively stop his walk about the hall to catch the sound of their voices, and participate privately in their amusement. She soon found that her husband's step, his voice, and the life and spirit he had brought into the house, gave even more pleasure. When he ran up stairs, or walked about the house, he did it like a man who by no means feared the sound of his own footsteps, and when he rang his bell, he pulled it with a will. He had another habit, which won him golden opinions,— he loved to read aloud. Every interesting book that he could get hold of he read aloud to his wife, principally in the evening.

The old gentleman had long been dependent on Marion for his evening's amusement, as his eye-sight was very indifferent. It sometimes strained her voice to read to him for long together. What a treasure was a man whose voice at its natural pitch was perfectly audible, and who was obliged to any one who would listen to him! He, in fact, often declared, that he could not thoroughly enjoy any book unless he read it aloud; therefore, when-ever he was seen, about eight of the clock, to stretch himself on a sofa, and seize some newly-

received volume, while Marion made the tea, old
Mr. Raeburn used eagerly to draw his easy chair
close to him, and prepare for a treat with all the
self-complacency meanwhile of a man who was conferring a charity.

Then, again, he had very few notions about
music, and though excessively proud of his wife's
singing, never presumed to interfere with Mr.
Raeburn's prerogative of instructing, approving,
blaming, &c. Complete and indiscriminate admiration was all he ever ventured upon, and this, though
a proof of ignorance, was thought to exhibit his
devoted affection for his wife, which he certainly
showed in many other less equivocal ways.

And moreover he loved, as hath before been
said, to be questioned,—it saved all the trouble of
concocting and relating his own story.

How few young men like to be questioned, especially by an old one! Some young men are wont
to declare that it nearly drives them wild to have to
answer such daily questionings as, " Well, and who
did you meet?" " Where did you go?" " Did you
see Mr. So-and-so?" " Ah! indeed, and what did
he say?" " And how was Widow Green?" " Did
you come home by the fields, Arthur?" " You
did, eh?" " Well, and how do Tom Hurder's turnips look?"

To all and every such question Dreux answered
pleasantly. He seldom volunteered any information, but any species of news about himself, the

parish, or the neighbourhood, any opinion he wanted to get from him, the Rector might always have for the asking.

With his wife, her guardian and his friend, he had no intentional reservation; but true to his character, even where he most deeply loved, he could only draw near when invited; he could not expand, and, as it were, unfold himself, without encouragement.

Take another glance.

Marion, as before, is seated near the window, with an infant on her lap; Dreux is standing beside her, with a little note-book in his hand.

" And don't forget to go to Mrs. Mills," she says, " and tell her I wish a hat for baby just like the one Elinor got for her child."

Dreux writes, and inquires whether Mrs. Mills will know how large it is to be. " You had better have given this commission to Allerton, my love."

" Ah! Dreux, Dreux," answers the said Allerton, " I am afraid the instincts of humanity are beginning to fail. Whenever I see a man afraid of a baby I think the world must be coming to an end. Do you think Adam did not know how, instinctively, to handle an infant and carry it about without making it scream?"

" No matter whether he did or not; there were no nursemaids in his time; so let us hope he did. I don't know that I should have any particular objection to carrying that little fellow up stairs if Marion would trust me with him."

"You know better than to think she would. Didn't I put our baby into your arms the other day, and didn't you testify unmanly fear, and quake, and declare you should drop it if it would wriggle so? Do you think Adam knew no better than that, when Eve gave him the baby to hold while she pacified the other children?"

"If Adam had any sense he let Eve keep the baby, and pacified the other children himself."

"Ah, you are never tired of petting that little Euphemia of yours. She will be spoilt ;—mark my words."

"And as for you, I wonder, since you have a genius that way, that Elinor does not leave the infant to you altogether. I shall expect to see you take it up into the pulpit some day."

"He is not so wise as he thinks," said Elinor, calmly ; "I am very glad we are not Adam and Eve."

"Here comes the phaeton. Lift up the boy, dearest, and I'll kiss him. Good by till to-morrow. Allerton, take care of my wife and CHILDREN."

Mr. Raeburn drives up in the phaeton.

"It is just about time to be off," he observes ; "but I suppose there are some last words to detain us, as usual."

He has no wish to prevent these last words, for Dreux and Marion always amuse and interest him by their more than common attachment for each other, yet he pretends to be in a hurry, and makes as if he could not possibly wait.

There are a good many last words, for Marion has sent away her baby, and bethought herself of some more commissions.

"Mind you remember those French marigold seeds, my love, and—oh, I knew there was something else—an Indian rubber ball for Effie."

"Ahem !" says the Rector, "if we're late I suppose it is of no great consequence."

"There are five minutes good, uncle. Dearest, I just wanted to say "—

"Then say it to-morrow, my pretty—Pshaw ! one would think he was to be away for a month, instead of a night. Arthur, do you mean to come at all ? "

"This minute—directly. Good by, my love ! " and so saying he jumped into the phaeton, which had not proceeded ten yards before there was another delay.

Two little fat hands were tapping at the glass of an upper window : the phaeton was stopped, and the two gentlemen looked up to the ivyed casement of the nursery.

A nurse opened it, and a little face peeped out— a little dark-eyed Euphemia. She laughed and nodded to them, and then she kissed her hands, and pushing back her waving hair from her forehead, cried out, "Baby's asleep, so he can't come to look at you. Good by, dear papa; good by, dear grandpapa."

The young father kissed his hand, and turned away with a smile. The old man, who was called by a name that was not his, laughed with heartfelt satisfaction. The adopted daughter and the adopted son were as much to him as his own could ever have been; they were making him rich in his old age,—setting children on his knees who would grow up to love and honour him.

Happy for him that he had not shut up his solitary heart to brood over the bereavements of his prime,—for now this son and this daughter were his, and their children were his, and those who slept beneath the cedar-trees were still his, for they were neither lamented with repinings, nor unloved, nor forgotten.

THE END.

Macintosh, Printer, Great New-street, London.